# THE DA[RK] KI[NG]

A snicker of stone against stone made him look up.

They'd been waiting.

Thakhati fell from the building like spiders descending on a kill.

*"Gaoth!"* Aranok instinctively used a burst of air to throw them back up and away. There were too many. Ten, twelve... more. Like rain.

"Run!"

They landed everywhere. One to Aranok's right and he pushed it away with *gluais*. Another running toward them from the wall. Where had that come from? Aranok grabbed hold of it and Allandria speared its mouth, withdrawing her blade and turning to fend off another from behind her. Aranok grabbed that one too, and Allandria dispatched it.

Wait. Where was Keft?

*Fuck!*

# PRAISE FOR
# JUSTIN LEE ANDERSON AND THE EIDYN SAGA

"An eclectic cast of characters traverse a war-ravaged kingdom as Anderson's cleverly constructed plot winds its way toward a truly unexpected denouement. Rich in action and intrigue, this fantasy adventure with a Scottish flavor is sure to please fans of David Gemmell"

Anthony Ryan, *New York Times* bestselling author, on *The Lost War*

"Excellent—full of great characters, tense action scenes, and truly surprising twists. A highly recommended read"

James Islington, author of *The Shadow of What Was Lost*, on *The Lost War*

"Justin's book reads like you've been dropped in the middle of a classic fantasy adventure, full of familiar elements twisted to be terrifying again—and then ramps up the tension to distract you from the sucker punch he's been planning all along. Exquisite"

Gareth Hanrahan, author of *The Sword Defiant*, on *The Lost War*

"A fantastic read. A twist that is just magnificent. It's an exceptional book, and I can't recommend it enough"

Steve McHugh, author of *The Last Raven*, on *The Lost War*

"Strikingly intense... Immersive and thoroughly compelling"

*SFX* on *The Lost War*

"Another page-turning adventure propelled by an inventive plot and three-dimensional characters. Readers will once again be left clamoring for a sequel"

*Publishers Weekly* on *The Bitter Crown*
(starred review)

"Propulsive and fast-paced, you'll be impressed at both Anderson's nerve and his confident way of rising to his own challenge"

*Paste* magazine on *The Bitter Crown*

By Justin Lee Anderson

*The Eidyn Saga*

The Lost War
The Bitter Crown
The Damned King

# THE DAMNED KING

## The Eidyn Saga: Book Three

## JUSTIN LEE ANDERSON

orbit-books.co.uk

ORBIT

First published in Great Britain in 2025 by Orbit

13 5 7 9 10 8 6 4 2

Copyright © 2025 by King Lot Publishing Ltd.

Map by Tim Paul

Excerpt from *Between Dragons and Their Wrath* by Devin Madson
Copyright © 2024 by Devin Madson

The moral right of the author has been asserted.

*All characters and events in this publication, other than those
clearly in the public domain, are fictitious and any resemblance
to real persons, living or dead, is purely coincidental.*

All rights reserved.
No part of this publication may be reproduced, stored in a
retrieval system, or transmitted, in any form or by any means, without
the prior permission in writing of the publisher, nor be otherwise circulated
in any form of binding or cover other than that in which it is published
and without a similar condition including this condition being
imposed on the subsequent purchaser.

A CIP catalogue record for this book
is available from the British Library.

ISBN 978-0-356-51957-9

Printed and bound in Great Britain by Clays Ltd, Elcograf, S.p.A.

Papers used by Orbit are from well-managed forests
and other responsible sources.

| Orbit | The authorised representative |
| An imprint of | in the EEA is |
| Little, Brown Book Group | Hachette Ireland |
| Carmelite House | 8 Castlecourt Centre |
| 50 Victoria Embankment | Dublin 15, D15 XTP3, Ireland |
| London, EC4Y 0DZ | (email: info@hbgi.ie) |

An Hachette UK Company
www.hachette.co.uk

orbit-books.co.uk

*Never give up hope. When we lose hope, they win.*

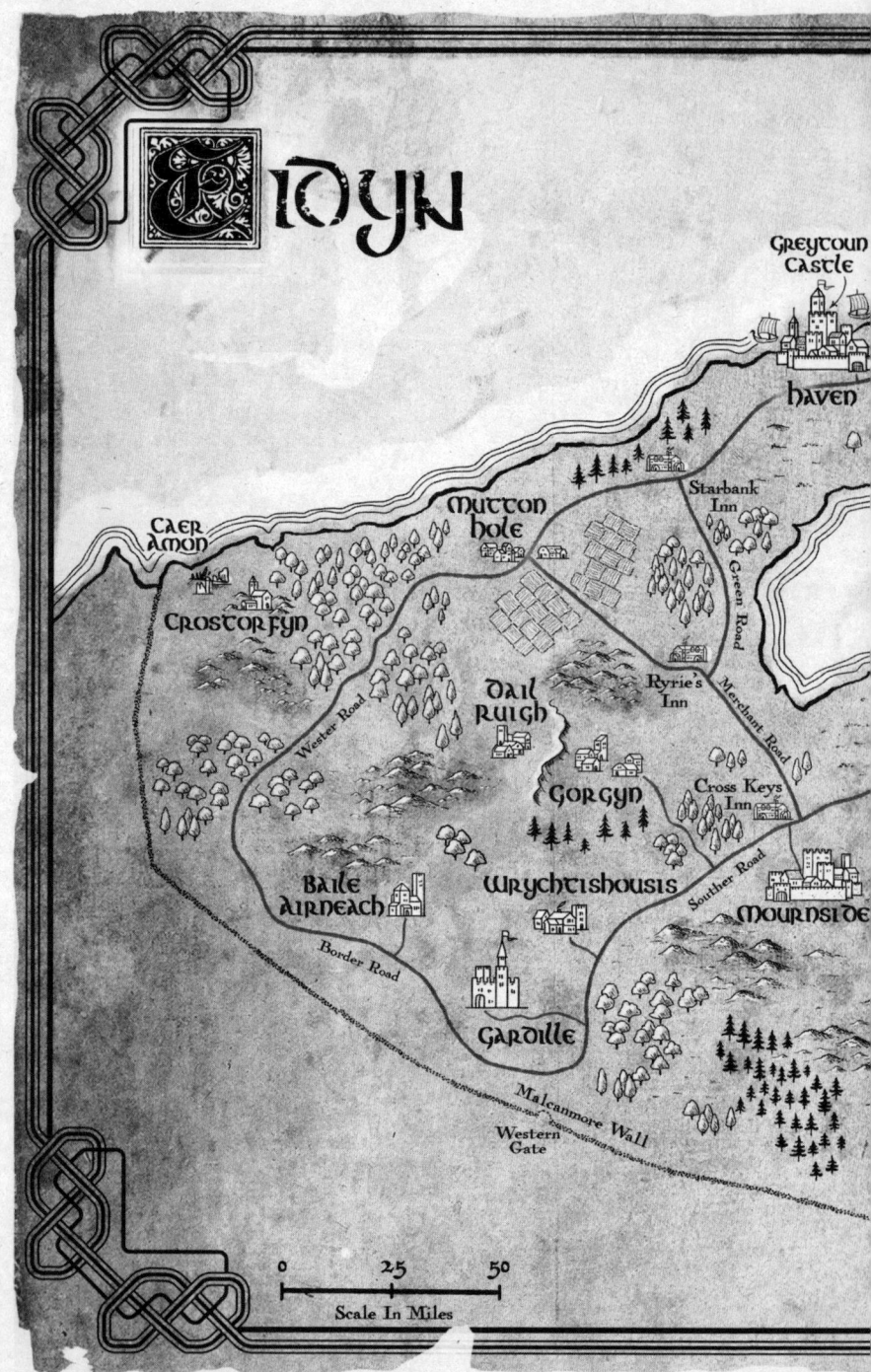

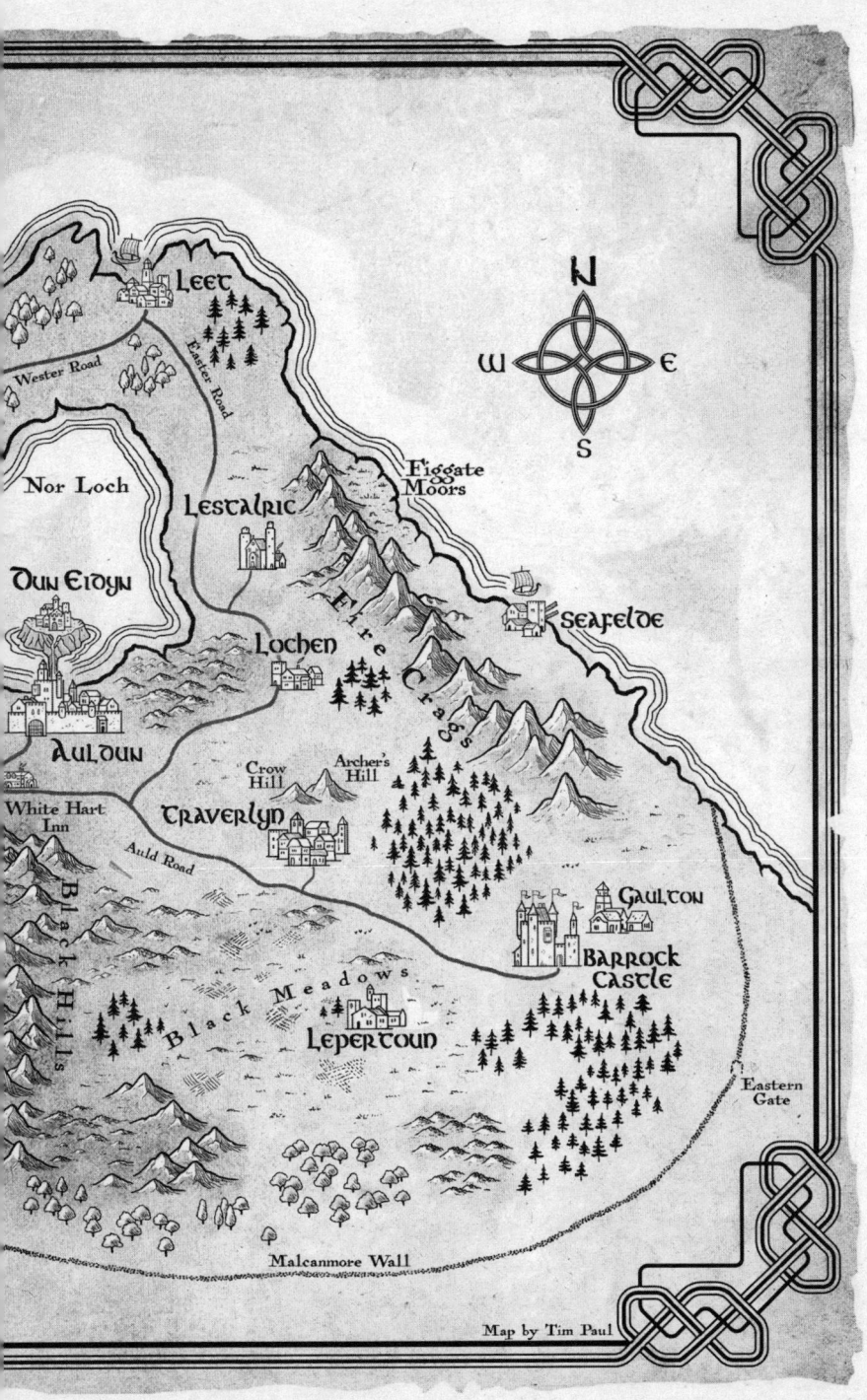

# A STORY OF A BITTER CROWN...

I sit back down and place the old boy's mug in front of him, a dribble of foam sliding down the side. His eyes glint with a mix of excitement and intoxication. He's less careful now. Less fearful. The beer has bolstered him. He's forgotten that he should be scared.

"*Slàinte mhath.*" He raises the drink and knocks it gently against my own before dousing his dirty moustache in foam.

He's yet to tell me his name, I realise. And it's too late to ask. We've been chatting for too long. Asking would be awkward. Forced. Suspicious. So I leave it. He'll tell me or he won't. It doesn't matter.

Having knocked back at least half the mug in one drawn-out swallow, he clunks the mug back down and smiles gratefully. "So, where were we?" His eyes go to the dark ceiling as if looking for a record of all he's told me so far. "Aranok, Allandria, Samily and Mynygogg had to get out of Dun Eidyn, right? But Auldun was still full of Dead and Aranok had made a mess of the Crosscauseway to hold them off when they were fighting the big lizard demon the night before.

"So Aranok—'cause he's got his memory back proper now—he uses his magic to pull a whole new bridge out the water! Just grows it right from the mud at the bottom of the Nor Loch! Can you imagine?" He raises his arms reverentially, eyes wide, as if seeing the thing happen in my place. "Something, right?"

"Something," I agree, and lift my drink.

"So they get to Auldun, but the Crosscauseway gets wrecked in the process, 'cause the new bridge unsettled the ground, like. That's why it collapsed. Nowt to do wi' age, like *they* say." He says the last sentence in a dramatic hush, as though revealing a great secret. But I've seen Auldun. Seen the destruction, and what's been made of it. I've heard more stories about what happened there than I can count, including variations on this one. When I don't offer him the wonder he's hoping for, he seems to take it as a challenge.

"Now, they're in a hurry to get back to Traverlyn, since Rasa was going there before going to Janaeus, and if she does that, he'll ken they've been snooping into things and..." He opens his hands, as if the threat is clear.

"So they make it out of Auldun, find their horses back at the White Hart and ride. Hard. Barely sleeping; chased by demons. They make it in a few days. But too late.

"Rasa and Meristan—who's no a monk, by the way, but a White Thorn; *the* White Thorn, only he doesnae ken it—have ridden off for Haven that morning. So they sort out a few folk's memories—mainly Nirea's, who it turns out is no just an old pirate, but *the queen*."

A long pause and he takes another drink. He wants to see my astonishment. I raise an eyebrow, frown and nod slowly. The couple to our right are deep in conversation about the price of meat. Complaining. The man lowers his voice when he realises we've stopped speaking. Glances at us uncomfortably. The old boy's oblivious. Licks his teeth, preparing for what's coming.

"They also get one of Aranok's old masters: Balaban, who helped them before, aye? And he works out who must've killed Conifax, because there's a master called Rotan, who isnae a master at all! So they chuck him in the gaol." He leans in and says the next bit under his breath. "Though Aranok would have killed him, given the chance. Right?"

"I can see that," I agree. He smiles. Leans back. Eyes now roam the room, but not in a suspicious way. Like he's just...sizing up the place. As if it belongs to him, and all these folk are his guests.

"Anyway, they're in a hurry to get after the others, but they're knackered, so they also get the principal of the university, Keft, who's an energy *draoidh*. He gives Aranok and Samily the energy to keep on.

"Now, up ahead, Meristan and Rasa arrive at Lestalric, because, see, before they left, your boy Rotan had slipped them a letter—said it was from Keft—to deliver to the Baroness de Lestalric on their way to the Nor Loch ferry. Course, it wasnae that at all.

"Truth was, the baroness was Shayella, the necromancer from the Hellfire Club, who'd been fighting the war with Janaeus and Anhel Weyr. Meristan wakes up in the night and finds Rasa's missing, and when he goes searching for her, he finds Shayella in the basement, wi' her daughter—who's Dead. Like, no *dead dead*, y'know: Dead. Not dead. And they've got the old messenger, Darginn Argyll, strapped to a board wi' his legs cut off."

His face turns serious. Grave. As if he's not sure he can say what's coming next. But the hesitation passes quickly. "She'd been *feeding* him to the girl. Keep her from rotting. Did you know that was a thing they could do?"

"I didn't," I answer. And I feel a moment of repulsion. It's not just blasphemous, but...inhuman. If it's true.

"Aye. But thankfully, Aranok and Samily had a warning about all this, from a wee stable boy back in Traverlyn. So him and Samily show up and between the three of them—after Aranok gives Meristan his memory back—they kill a load of Dead and take Shayella and her daughter. They find Rasa inside one o' them Thakhati cocoons, and Samily turns her body back to normal, but she doesnae wake up. Oh, and Samily also heals the messenger! But...the boy's a mess up here." He taps his head. Nods knowingly.

"Next day, they all head back to Traverlyn, and on the way, Aranok gets a story out of Shayella. Turns out she went bad after some local bairns drowned her daughter for being a 'witch,' which she wasnae. Her ma was *draoidh*, but no her. Drowned her. And nothing came of it. I mean, what could they do? Gaol a bunch of kids? Or their parents? But that drove her mad, see. Losing her wee girl like that. Which is why she brought her back. And for a' that, she started the Blackening. Used to live in Lepertoun, see? Started it there.

"So all that means that suddenly Aranok's protecting her, right? 'Cause he feels guilty about her daughter dying, and him and Mynygogg not having done enough to change things for *draoidhs*. Which means, when they get back to Traverlyn..." A dramatic pause, as if he wants me to finish his sentence. "Massive fight. Aranok, Allandria, Mynygogg and Nirea all get into it, 'cause Aranok says he won't let them kill her, and Mynygogg says they should do, just for what she's done, but also because it might cure the Blackening—though they're no sure about that.

"In the end, Allandria takes Aranok's side despite the fact Nirea's asked her to be the new queen's envoy. It's a mess. But they work it out. Aranok insists he can get the heart of devastation off Janaeus if he pretends to still be under the spell, and Mynygogg sends Nirea with him. They also take a master called Dialla, who's another energy *draoidh*, and Darginn Argyll, who's from Haven.

"At the same time, Mynygogg and Allandria head for the Reiver Lands, 'cause the king reckons they need peace with the Reiver council to stop that becoming another war. Meristan travels with them, 'cause he's going to Baile Airneach to get the White Thorns onside. And Samily's remembered that a landlord in Dail Ruigh said something about a memory *draoidh*, so she and Rasa, who they sorted out with the help of another master, go to look for them."

He stops for another large drink and takes a deep breath as if steeling himself before diving in again. As he does, I realise the couple at the next table haven't spoken a word to each other in a while. She gives him a surreptitious look. They've been listening. Do I need to worry about that? If they suddenly get up to leave, maybe we need to do something. For the moment, I let the old boy carry on.

"So, I'll take them one at a time, right?"

I nod. "Sensible."

"Aranok and his lot get to Greytoun in the middle of a big party for the lairds, and on the way in, he manages to clear the memory of the head of the kingsguard, boy called Leondar, who's out guarding the gate for some reason. Aranok, Nirea and Dialla go into the party, and Aranok gets Janaeus alone. He's all for pretending he's under the spell still, but Janaeus already knows he's not. He's figured it out. But turns out, he was actually trying to be helpful by stopping the war, and somehow Aranok convinces him to help put everything back. Because the big news is... the relic's gone. After using it, Janaeus says he destroyed it—chucked it in the sea. So they can't use that to clear everyone's memories. But still, Aranok's got Janaeus on their side.

"Except, when he goes back out, Nirea doesnae believe him. Or at least, she doesnae believe Janaeus. And she and Mynygogg had their own plan. She orders Dialla to kill Janaeus. Which she does, right there in the room. And, well...that goes straight to Hell. Absolute shitstorm. Massive fight. Couple of *draoidhs*, loads of demon guards, because Anhel Weyr's in the castle too. Several folk killed, but the three of them get away with help from Leondar. They run back to Darginn Argyll's house—where Aranok lays into Nirea for killing Janaeus. She says Janaeus was probably lying, and he's already sent them into a trap that killed Glorbad. They're properly at each other's throats.

"But before they run from Haven, 'cause every guard in the town's after them now, Aranok reckons they have to try to get the head messenger onside. So three of them—Aranok, Nirea and Darginn—go to see Madu at Havenport. And they tell her everything. But..."

Another raised finger. A new reveal is coming.

"That's a mistake. Because she's been working with Janaeus! And she tricks them into giving up their only memory charm, which she chucks in the sea. Then she tells them that if she dies, she's got contracts with assassins that'll kill folk they love!" He opens his hands, eyes wide. "What do they do?

"Turns out, they don't get a choice, because when Darginn realises she sent him to Shayella, knowing what would happen to him, he goes mental and all but cuts off her head.

"So they run from Haven, along with Darginn's whole family. Nirea agrees to take them all back to Traverlyn, except Aranok insists he's going to Mournside to warn his family. Now they're properly in the shite, right? Because they've not got the relic *or* a memory charm. So on the way home, Aranok literally digs up his old friend Korvin to get the charm he was buried with." Another deep breath, and he lets it out slowly to demonstrate how dramatic I should find that. In fairness, it sounds bloody awful.

"Anyway, that means when he gets back to his folks, he can not only warn them about these assassins, but clear their memories too. And his mum's fine, but his dad—doesnae go well. Refuses to believe Aranok.

Reckons *he's* the one under a spell, right? And when Aranok just forces the charm on him, he goes mental. Chucks Aranok out the house, the whole lot.

"As it happens, there's a messenger setting up in Mourning Square. He announces that Anhel Weyr has taken the throne and blamed Aranok for killing Janaeus, along with every laird at that party—who *somehow* ended up burned to death."

He's implying King Anhel Weyr murdered the Lairds' Council. I glance right. The couple still aren't talking.

"So Aranok realises things are even worse than he thought, and heads back for Traverlyn. So that's that story. The others are shorter."

*I sincerely hope so.*

"First of all, Mynygogg, Allandria and Meristan run into a fight between soldiers and some Reiver spies on the way south. They try to intervene, but it goes to Hell anyway, and folk die on both sides. But Meristan has stood with the Reivers, along with another Thorn that was originally with the soldiers, and that's a problem. So the two of them ride off for Baile Airneach in a hurry. And 'cause they helped them, the Reivers agree to take Allandria and Mynygogg to Calcheugh, to see the Reiver council. When they get there, though, it's no a meeting that's waiting for them, but a trial! Mynygogg's to be tried for breaking their peace treaty. In the end, the council votes three to three, meaning trial by combat. But when Mynygogg offers to sacrifice himself to prevent any more killing, the council chief changes his mind and agrees to give Mynygogg a chance to take back Eidyn.

"Meanwhile, Meristan gets back to Baile Airneach and manages to somehow convince them he's not just a monk, but while he's there, a load of soldiers show up from Gardille, intent on arresting them. Meristan tells them that he's on a secret mission from the king—though he doesnae say *which* king." The old boy gives a sly wink. "So the general leaves, saying he'll be back if that's no true. Meristan sends folk out to gather other Thorns, so he can take as many as he can back to Traverlyn before the general finds out he's no exactly telling the truth and comes back!

"And finally...Samily and Rasa. They manage to track down the memory *draoidh* in Dail Ruigh eventually—a woman called Quellaria.

She doesnae want to help, but they basically tie her up and force her to come with them."

He sits back and stretches, as if he's been wrestling this mad tale from his chest, and his shoulders have taken the strain. I've all but lost track of half of it, and I'm more concerned with the couple next to us. I'm going to have to deal with them. Just need to decide how. And when. After the old boy lets out a creak like a rusty well handle, he settles in and slugs back another big gulp of beer. A raised eyebrow tells me it's almost time for another. But first, he launches back into the story.

"So everyone's headed back for Traverlyn. Nirea gets there first, followed by Aranok. When he arrives...massive fight. He's still angry; she's not budging. Then Mynygogg and Allandria get back and there's more arguing about what to do with Shayella. Aranok's adamant they can't kill her. Then Samily and Rasa get back and...it gets proper messy. Because they've discovered that the Thakhati outside Traverlyn have been turning the Blackened into more Thakhati. And Samily is *not happy* they let that happen. So she goes to kill Shayella herself, but Aranok arrives just as she does it, and *he* attacks *her*! Samily beats him using her time skill but cuts off his hands in the process. Then Allandria shows up, makes her restore Aranok's hands and takes him off. He's an absolute mess.

"Good news, though: Killing Shayella has ended the Blackening! That's how it *really* went away.

"But Samily's been reminded of all the Blackened on the Auld Road that now need help, and of course, there's Vastin, who's been in the hospital all along! Thanks to a neat trick Master Balaban cooks up, they manage to transfer the curse from Morienne—the woman from Lepertoun—to Samily, making *her* immune to the Blackening, so she can heal Vastin and all the other Blackened. So she heads off to do that with Morienne and Dialla.

"But then, another twist." The last drops of beer are drained, and the hollow thunk of the empty mug back on the table is a little louder than before. He licks his lips clean, wipes his beard with the back of his hand. "While Aranok's laid up, guards report that Rotan, the boy who killed Conifax, has been murdered—by Aranok! Allandria and

Mynygogg talk to him, and Aranok realises what must have happened: Anhel Weyr's got an illusionist assassin in Traverlyn!

"Now, here's the important thing. The only reason Traverlyn's been safe from the Thakhati—'cause they die in sunlight, right?—is this giant sphere on top of Traverlyn Kirk that Conifax had set up to store sun all day and let it out at night. Sunspire, they called it. Since Conifax died and Aranok was away, a wee student had been keeping it going, and, well, guess who else had been killed by the assassin?

"And it's getting dark."

He slaps his hands down on the table, and seems to surprise himself with the bang. The woman beside us chokes on a giggle and the man urgently picks up his drink to hide a smile.

It *is* a problem.

The old boy looks about and hunches forward, leaning on crossed arms. He probably thinks he's whispering when he says:

"You surely want to hear the rest now, right?"

# CHAPTER 1

It began in silence.
The whisper of a crackling fire. The hush of the twilight breeze. The hammer of Aranok's heart.

They waited in the vast, heavy quiet of inevitability.

No words of camaraderie. No encouraging smiles.

Just the coming dark.

Traverlyn was not made for a siege. Its people were academics, medics, artists and musicians. Many were elderly, or young. The bulk of the population were still hurriedly evacuating to inns, the hospital or the university. Anywhere they could huddle together against the horror.

But what they had were *draoidhs*.

Aranok, Keft, Opiassa, Macwin and a few other masters, as well as some senior students. Three more physic *draoidhs*. Six more nature.

Aranok's skin itched with the energy boost Keft had given him to burn the opium out of his system. He clenched and unclenched fists, shuffled from foot to foot. Allandria put a calming hand on his arm. With an illusionist assassin in Traverlyn, he wasn't letting her out of his sight.

But there was no conversation. No easy banter. Nothing to say.

Hells, how they could have done with Dialla, Samily and Rasa. But there was every chance that was why Anhel's assassin had struck. Because they were gone. Because Aranok was crippled.

They'd discussed, in the bare twilight hours, mounting a major defence here at the southern road into town—of summoning the Guard, digging a pit, setting shield walls. None of it would have worked. The Thakhati would not fight like an army. They were a swarm. They would come from every angle. Hunt like wolves. They could handle a few. Small numbers. But if what Rasa had told Mynygogg was right, that there were hundreds, maybe thousands, waiting in the trees…

They'd harvested the Blackened. He didn't have time to think on that now. How all those people he'd thought waiting to be saved were gone. How Shay's death had meant nothing for them. They were already lost.

The nature *draoidhs* could try to keep them out, using the natural wall that surrounded the town to hold and entrap them, but there weren't enough of them to defend the whole perimeter. That too was a doomed strategy.

Instead, the Guard were sent to organise the evacuation. Get everyone off the streets. Lamplighters were roused for the first time in weeks, asked to set not only torches, but bonfires anywhere they could be made. They needed as much light, as much flame as the town could muster. As much energy.

Their only hope was not to win, but to survive. Come morning, come sunrise, the Thakhati would be forced back into cocoons. But standing there, watching the last of the purple sky fade to black, morning felt like another country.

When the last light dipped below the horizon, the chattering began. Like stone screaming in hunger. Like death.

"Are we really doing this?" Allandria whispered.

"We are." Aranok tried to sound reassuring. The truth was, some of the fourteen gathered on that little hillock would be dead by sunup. But this tactic, mad as it had sounded when he'd come up with it, was going to give them their best chance. "Everybody ready?"

Keft's face was ashen, but he nodded silently, staring across the open field.

"As I'll ever be," said Macwin, with a smile that seemed a little too genuine. Others made noises of agreement. Opiassa slapped one of her giant pauldrons. The physic *draoidhs* stood at least seven foot tall and about as wide, each carrying a war hammer too large for any normal human to bear. They, at least, were prepared for battle. Opiassa took her role as head of security seriously. Apparently, she'd had the outsize armour and weapons forged during the Hellfire War. It glinted in the firelight like virgin snow.

They were ready. They had to be.

Aranok turned to Macwin. "All right. Let them in."

The nature *draoidh* raised his arms, and the enormous wall of trees, bushes and vines parted like a theatrical curtain, exposing a pitch-black void. For a moment, the chattering slowed—curious. Wary.

Then it burst to a crescendo as a wave of grey claws came shrieking through the gap.

*My God.*

"Draw them in, but keep them back!" Aranok already needed to shout over the havoc.

Allandria nocked an arrow. "That makes no sense."

"I know."

Two new walls of trees grew toward them on either side of the Thakhati horde, funnelling them toward the *draoidhs*. It only served to heighten their frenzy. Aranok felt his guts twist in horror as they came roaring across the grass. Nobody could stand in the face of that carnage and not feel their certainty shudder beneath them. They had to slow but not stop the flood.

"*Sgàineadh!*" Aranok raised his arms wide as a trench opened before them and Thakhati poured in.

Screeching, furious, they rolled into the pit, clambering over each other to reach their prey. One crawled up over the edge and was met with a blow from a war hammer that all but took its head off. It sunk back into the morass, which only increased in frenzy as they ripped the wounded demon apart. Another breached the lip and got the same. Several were trying to climb the tree walls now, but vines twisted and contorted to hold them down. Still they poured through the gate. Easily hundreds. Could already be a thousand. Rasa hadn't exaggerated.

The pit was filling. In moments, they'd start pouring out and into the town.

"Keft! Now!" Aranok called.

A burst of energy from the principal punched the Thakhati back, shattering them into each other. They tussled amongst themselves briefly, paused and came again.

"*Balla na talamh!*" The near edge of the pit rose from the earth, trapping those trying to climb out. For now.

"Opiassa!" Aranok pointed to each side. The four physic *draoidhs* split, each pair taking a side to patrol against Thakhati making it out of the pit.

Allandria pointed to the gate in the natural wall. "Fucking Hell, they're still coming."

They were. And they needed all of them. But God in Hell, they weren't slowing.

The morass closed in again, pushed by the sheer pressure of numbers. They were in less of a hurry, but still they came, grating, snarling.

A cry, from somewhere in the middle. High-pitched. Painful enough it made Aranok lift his hands to his ears. And they all stopped. No more frenzy. Barely a sound at all beyond the scrape of their skin against itself. They crouched, all down on their six limbs, except one.

One stood proud of the simmering fury, upper arms raised. A leader? They'd seen behaviour like this before, but not on this scale.

"Does that look like...?" Allandria left the question hanging.

"A general," Aranok finished. "*Creag.*" He tore a chunk of rock from the wall and hurled it at the leader. The monster screamed again and a wave of Thakhati raised before him, taking the hit—crushed under it.

*Fuck.*

The general lifted its arms wide. Another screech—and the horde parted like liquid. They made en masse for the side trees, clambering up the new walls that penned them in.

"Envoy!" Macwin called. "We can't hold them all!"

He was right. They were beginning to break over the pit wall too. Opiassa's physics were in danger of being overrun. It had to be now.

"Right. Stand close." The others pulled in tight around him. "*Colbh talmhainn.*" A pillar of earth rose beneath them, lifting them up just as a pair of Thakhati were scrambling close. Keft punched them back with a burst of energy. The pillar took them up twenty feet. Well above the reach of the Thakhati. But they would just go on past, into the town. They were still pouring through the gap. It wasn't all of them. But Aranok had waited as long as he could.

He lifted his hand high. "Cover your eyes!

"*Spreadhadh!*"

The sunstone exploded in light. Thakhati screamed.

"God almighty!" Allandria yelled over the noise of the dying things. It was the awful sound of rage and death, of creatures cursing their gods, whatever twisted nightmares they might be.

In a moment, it was done. The field before them was a smoking mass of singed stone. But still—there was movement. Here and there, a wriggle, a shudder of limbs. Some had survived, shielded by the bodies of others. And in the distance, in the dark: chattering.

"Macwin, close it!" Aranok ordered.

The *draoidh* gestured and the gate he'd opened in the tree wall stitched itself together, shutting what was left of the monsters outside. For now.

He pointed to the field of corpses. "Opiassa! Finish them!" The physic master gave a gesture of salute. Aranok dropped the earth wall back into the pit, crushing anything left alive inside, he hoped. It didn't quite give the physic *draoidhs* a solid footing to cross, but they didn't need it. Each of them made the leap across with what seemed relative ease, and stalked the field, hammering the life out of anything that moved.

Aranok lowered the pillar back down. "That was it. That was our one shot." He held out the dead sunstone. "Now it's a street fight."

---

"Who the fuck are you!?"

Nirea pinned the woman to the red brick wall, forearm across her neck, wary of her hands.

"For God's sake, put Brode down!" Egretta tugged at her arm. "She can't answer if you're choking her!"

Brode? The name wasn't familiar. The woman had smiled at her. Said "Hello again, Majesty" and reached into her apron.

It was the *again* that did it. A pretence at familiarity. She did not know this woman.

Mynygogg had burst into their chamber what seemed like minutes ago but must have been an hour. Maybe two. Raving. Manic. He couldn't explain himself until, in what seemed more like desperation than love, he'd kissed her passionately. She'd thought his mind lost until he explained what Aranok had claimed—that Rotan's murderer was an illusionist assassin. Mynygogg had to be sure she was herself, and safe, which was sweet. His first thought had been to find her. Even as king, his instincts were for Nirea.

That had been minor succour when they realised the sunspire had not begun to shine as the light faded over Traverlyn. At first, it had seemed so normal. The sun sinking into the trees as dusk settled like a blanket of peace. It was when she reached for a candle, she'd realised.

*It should not be dark.*

Fretting over the assassin was lost to absolute panic over the Thakhati outside town. Aranok had sent a runner with news that the student maintaining the sunspire had also been murdered—and she had no reason to suspect him of that. They were formulating a plan to defend the hospital when this woman had approached her.

Anyone could be an assassin now. *Anyone.*

But that didn't mean everyone. Egretta was insistent that the woman was innocent. Nirea relaxed her arm, allowing the medic to take a breath. "Please, Majesty," she panted, "I only brought this." A tear trickled down her nose. "I thought you may need more."

From the apron, Brode produced a small tub, and Nirea remembered. This was the woman who'd brought lotion for Quellaria's wrists. She'd been so distracted, so focused on Quell that she'd barely looked the woman in the eye. Gods, she'd handled this badly. She was jumpy. Paranoid.

*Fuck!*

"I'm sorry, I…" What could she say? They couldn't go around announcing that they knew about an illusionist assassin to every medic in the building—one of them could be the very person they were worried about. And then the assassin would be warned. More careful. "There is a lot happening." That would have to do. For now, they needed to secure the hospital. She released Brode completely, stroking her shoulder in passing, as if that would make a difference. The assassin was only looking for them, probably. They'd killed Rotan and the *draoidh* girl. She couldn't think who else would be a target now. Just her, Gogg, Aranok and Allandria, likely. They might be after the book too. The thing that would help prove the truth. Maybe.

She'd told Egretta, though. The senior medic needed to know there could be an assassin in her hospital. She knew her staff. Would know if one of them behaved oddly. She'd just had to make sure that the old matron was herself, first. A brief conversation, quizzing her over their arrival and the events she'd been witness to since was enough. The two of them were working together to organise the staff and patients, while Gogg went with Leondar to help people get inside. It was a large building, but solid. It could, perhaps, keep out the Thakhati. More so than many of the houses in Traverlyn.

They had so little time.

Brode wiped her eye, bowed and backed away. Nirea had done nothing for her reputation as a benevolent queen. In fact, it was the second time she'd treated Brode badly, and the woman had deserved neither. A problem for later. The more immediate problem was Egretta's fucking stupid plan.

"We can't put all the patients in the lecture hall."

Egretta frowned. "Not all, obviously. Some cannot be moved and—"

"No," Nirea cut her off. "They stay where they are. We lock their rooms."

The medic's eyes opened in a mix of ire and surprise. "I can't take care of them all if we can't move around the building!"

The central lecture hall was where much of the hospital's teaching occurred. It was the biggest single room in the building, built with decorative arches and intricate carvings to be the centrepiece of an inspiring building. They would fit many of the patients in there, given need.

"If we put them all in one place, behind one set of doors, when those doors give—and they will, eventually—we're serving them up as a banquet. If the Thakhati get in here, the best hope we have is to fight them in small numbers. Let them spread out around the building. If they get through one door, they take one prize only. We have to make this difficult for them."

Egretta's face hardened. "Those people are sick. Injured. *Children*. They'll be alone and defenceless. Some will die without care!"

"Then leave a medic with them."

Egretta's hand went to her head.

"You would leave them to die too?"

"I'm trying to save as many of them as I can, and I don't have time to argue. We lock them in their rooms, Egretta. It's the best chance for the most people."

The medic's mouth crumpled into a sceptical pout, defiance dancing at her lips, but she didn't argue further. "Fine."

Egretta had called her a stupid child not long ago, but now Nirea was queen again.

And the queen's word still had weight.

"Excellent. Let's get it done. We're running out of time."

# CHAPTER 2

*I shouldn't be here. Oh God, I shouldn't be here.*

Vastin listened at the door of the forge, fingers trembling against the wood. Distant screaming. Metal clashing with stone. Inhuman growls. And fire. The crackle of flame seemed to be everywhere.

When the alarm had gone up that the Thakhati were coming, his first thought had been to get his armour. He'd been to the forge that afternoon. Rorach, the blacksmith, had been happy to offer his grindstone for Vastin to sharpen the edge of Demon's Blood. Curk, his wee boy, excitedly listened to the story of how the axe got its name. It had pained Vastin to tell it, but he also took pride in sharing the story of Glorbad's sacrifice. He should be remembered. He was worthy of a song. If Vastin ever met a decent bard, he might try to convince them of the idea.

He had left his armour, planning to come back tomorrow and give it a proper polish. It had been nice to spend time at a forge again. Felt like home.

And now he was fucked. He'd come too late. Taken too long to get the armour on. He'd planned to get back to the hospital. Help defend it from the Thakhati. Instead, he was stuck inside, alone, with monsters roaming the streets.

*Stupid twat!*

Imagining himself a hero. All he'd done was likely get himself killed. Maybe if he was very quiet, if he found a dark space to sit in, he could just survive the night.

Another scream. Closer.

No.

He wasn't a child. Nirea had called them companions. He'd ridden with Eidyn's rulers. His axe had killed bigger than these things. He wasn't going to die here, in hiding. A coward.

He could make it back to the hospital. There were others out there fighting. Laird Aranok. The *draoidhs*. The Guard. The sound of battle rang across the night. Demon's Blood had a sharp edge. He could make it.

*He could make it.*

"Nooooo!"

Vastin's courage bled from him. That was close. *Really* close. Oh God, oh Hells, what was he going to do?

He had to help. Whoever that was, they wouldn't have his armour, his experience, his weapon. He had to help.

Glorbad would help.

Before the fear could grip him again, Vastin slid the bolt and opened the door. In the street before him, barely ten feet away, it turned to look directly at him.

---

"Shh, shhh, please, girl." Tobin stroked Dancer's nose as reassuringly as he could. But he heard it too. Scuttling, scraping, on the roof of the stable.

He wasn't meant to be here. Been told to go to an inn. Or the hospital. But truth was, the stable was home. The horses were his family. He couldn't stand the thought of them being left alone. And nobody had latched the windows that evening. No reason to, so they thought.

He had to come here. To make it safe. As safe as it could be.

He'd heard stories about demons. Everyone in Traverlyn had. The medics heard them from their patients and they told them in the inns, and... everyone knew them. Claws and teeth and eyes—impossible nightmares, they said.

He'd hoped, for some reason, that he'd be safer here too. He always *felt* safer here. With it just being a stable full of horses, maybe the demons wouldn't come here. But maybe demons didn't know that. Maybe they destroyed everything. Killed everything.

Much of the stable was stone, but the door, the gates at either end and the windows were all wood. Wood wouldn't stand up long to a demon, he suspected.

If he could stay quiet—keep the animals quiet…

But Dancer was jumpy. She was always jumpy. And that had startled Lavender, who'd whinnied back at her. That had made Bear squeal.

The scrabbling stopped. It was listening. It heard.

Then a roar, and scratching, tearing, screeching.

Oh God, it was tearing through the thatch.

It was coming.

---

Tia clamped her hands across her mouth, desperately trying to stuff back in the word that had squeaked from her.

"Daddy."

She was shaking so hard tears poured onto her arms. They'd come here, to this inn, because Daddy said it would be safe. That the monsters wouldn't get them here.

But they got in. Daddy lay on the floor, his face turned toward her. The last thing he'd tried to do was reach her. He tried to say something. But it was too quiet. Now his eyes had gone dark and glassy and Tia was sure he was dead but he couldn't be dead, it couldn't be real. The monster was still there, somewhere. She stood halfway up the stairs, where Daddy had told her to run. But she couldn't leave him. She couldn't—and he'd tried to stop the monster. Him and some other nice people from the inn. And now they were all dead and bloody and there were *eating* noises and Tia wanted to be gone. To be tiny or invisible or not be here or *wake up*!

But none of that.

Not now.

Daddy was dead. And she had to go. Or the monsters would get her.

She turned and ran up the steps as quick as she could. She found an open door and slipped inside. As she slowly closed it, something changed. Nothing new. But different. What was it?

Oh.

Too quiet.

The eating noise had stopped.

---

Vastin's first instinct was to slam the door shut, but his arm wouldn't move, just for a moment—a moment too long.

The Thakhati lunged and instinct moved him. He stepped to the left, using his shield to deflect the monster past him. But now it was inside.

He could run. Slam the door behind him and hope the thing would fumble with the door. But then it would be inside. Waiting for Rorach and Curk.

He could come back. He could warn them.

If he survived.

If he didn't…

He had to fight.

Before the thing could turn, Vastin did the one thing that had worked before. He set his shoulder, braced his shield before him and charged. He half caught the Thakhati in the side, stumbling past a worktable and forcing them both into a corner.

Now what? What had Glorbad shown him?

He dropped the top of the shield and brought his axe over. It clattered off the Thakhati's shoulder, rattling Vastin's wrist.

*No, no, no.*

*Thakhati.*

You have to cut *up*.

Vastin went to step back, but his shield didn't come with him. Instinctively, he jerked at it, but a pair of Thakhati claws gripped it tight, pulling him back. Vastin shifted his weight and hurled himself at the beast again, battering it against the wall, then slipped his arm from the straps and danced back.

He was more vulnerable now, but he had two hands to wield Demon's Blood.

The workbench was in the way, though. He couldn't lower the axe enough to get an upwards swing. Not with the blade at the right angle. This might be the worst place he could be trying to fight this thing!

He stepped back farther as the Thakhati cast his shield aside and roared again. Was it a threat? Or a call? Fuck, he'd left the door open! What if more were coming now? What if…

The Thakhati lunged forward.

---

Tia clicked the door closed. But it was too loud. The monster had heard, she was sure.

Where could she hide?

There was nowhere. The bed was too low to squeeze under. She couldn't go out the window—there were more monsters outside. She didn't have the key to lock the door. But there was a bolt. She could bolt it…

Footsteps. Monster footsteps. It was too late.

Tia jumped onto the bed and burrowed under the blanket. She pulled a pillow down in front of her. Maybe the monster would think she was a pillow, if she lay very, very still. If she didn't move. If she didn't breathe.

The footsteps came closer. Closer. And stopped.

Tia's heart raced so fast it was scary. She wanted to run and scream and cry, but she had to be quiet. Daddy had said. If you have to hide, you have to be *quiet*. So she bit down on her lips, cuddled the pillow and prayed.

The door. The door creaked open.

Oh no. Oh no. Oh no!

She had to stay still. Like a statue. Maybe she could pretend to be dead.

Like Daddy.

Her breathing wouldn't slow down. She needed it to be quiet. Take small breaths. But it was so loud in her ears! Why was her breathing so loud?

Still.
Silent.
A scream from outside and she jumped.
*Oh no.*

---

Thresh rained from the rafters, aggravating the horses even more. Their squeals and high-pitched whinnies seemed to make the demon more agitated, and it dug even harder.

Tobin cast about, as if an answer might present itself. What was he going to do?

The hay fork, sitting against the wall. It was the closest thing he might find to a weapon. As he reached for it, the demon screeched, and it was like nothing Tobin had heard before. Like a sheet of metal dragged over stone. He flinched, and the fork banged back against the wood.

*Oh God, oh God.*

Tobin looked up. The demon's face scowled down at him. It wouldn't be long now. It would be through soon. It would...

He had to let the horses out. They would die if he kept them here. That was the answer. That was the only answer.

Tobin abandoned the fork and began releasing the horses' ropes. He could free them all and then, once they were out, open a gate. Let them go. They could run—outrun the demons. Better that than here, tied up waiting to be sacrificed.

It would have to be quick, but he could be quick. The knots fell apart in his hands, used to tying and untying them without thought.

More thresh poured down, and the demon screeched again.

Bear squealed a response, stamping his front hooves as if in challenge. He was scared. They all were. Six done. Two more and they'd all be loose—free to run. But the digging had stopped.

Tobin looked up—the night sky peered back at him through a gaping hole in the thatched roof.

It was inside.

---

Vastin brought the axe up and connected with the Thakhati's chin, lifting its head as it barrelled into him. They fell together, Vastin landing on his back. Arms everywhere, and a howl of pain. The demon bounced up and away, four limbs landing on the worktop—one grasping at its chin, where blood dripped through its claws.

To his left, on the floor, a pair of stone scales. Demon's Blood had taken them off its face, and now it was wary. Wary enough to give Vastin time to regain his feet.

"Come on, then!" Rage and blood fuelled his belief. He could win. "Come on!"

He was wrong. It wasn't wary; it was angry.

The Thakhati leapt high this time, just avoiding the rafters, coming down at him from above. Instinctively, Vastin crouched, praying his armour would protect him. The weight hit him like a boulder, kicking him sideways with a resonant crack.

The Thakhati scrabbled at him, but it was half-hearted. Vastin rolled away, waiting for the pain to tell him what was broken. A shoulder? *God, not a leg. Please not a leg.* But he stumbled back to his feet, panting, still waiting for the stab of agony.

It wasn't him.

Demon's Blood had wedged beneath the demon as it landed, snapping the handle in the middle. The blade was somewhere beneath the Thakhati. And it wasn't moving in a hurry.

What now? Vastin cast about, looking for another weapon.

A screech, from the door.

*God, no, another one.* It sniffed at the air like a wolf, barely seemed to notice Vastin. If it came at him, he had nothing. No axe, no shield.

Wait—on the worktable. A hammer. That was...something. If he could reach it...But that might just take the thing's attention. What to do?

The time it took him to think answered for him. The new Thakhati skittered across the table and landed on the other, claws tearing into its back, throwing off scales, blood and flesh like water.

But Vastin still had no weapon. He crept slowly to the table, eyes fixed on the almost fascinating fountain of gore. He slipped his fingers around the hammer and carefully raised it.

A thunk as the head slipped back against the table.
The Thakhati turned, a frenzied lust in its eyes.
Vastin screamed and swung the hammer with everything he had.

---

Tobin slipped the last knot and ran for the gate. He'd left the fork at the other end of the stable. The horses were in chaos now. They sensed the danger, same as him. He had to let them free.

A scream. From one of the horses. Up the back.

*Oh God, no, please no.*

He lifted the latch, threw open the gate and slapped Dandelion on the rump. The horse bolted into the night and the rest followed. Tobin couldn't run. He had to help them all.

He clambered over one of the stalls and peered back into the building. A splash of blood against the wall.

One of the horses was hurt. Bad.

Bear reared up, squealing like Tobin had never heard before. And the demon screeched back. Could he get to the hay fork without being seen? He clambered past the next stall, and the next. The noise of the fight between Bear and the demon was hiding him—or at least distracting the demon. He made it to the end. Found the fork. Trembling, shaking, he grabbed it with both hands and stepped out.

He was behind the demon, and now he could see what was happening. One horse lay on the floor, covered in blood. So much blood. Tobin couldn't even tell which one it was. Too small for one of the Calladells, he reckoned. But otherwise—God, could it survive losing that much blood?

Bear reared repeatedly, forehooves flailing at the demon. The thing had six limbs and looked to be covered in armour. God, how could he hurt something like that? It screeched and swiped, wary of the great horse. It knew well enough to avoid a hit from those hooves. But Bear couldn't turn, couldn't run. And he'd tire eventually.

Tobin had to help. He lunged, screaming, at the demon, stabbing at it with the fork.

It half turned and took the blow between its upper- and lower-left arms. As it tumbled back against the felled horse, Tobin felt the fork bite. So there was flesh under there.

The demon screeched in rage, thrashing its claws, throwing up a spray of blood from the horse beneath it. Tobin winced—the horse didn't move. It was already dead.

Bear reared up again and stamped down, just missing the demon's head as it rolled back toward Tobin. Likely saw him as an easier target than the big Calladell. But he wouldn't be easy.

"Come on, then!" he screamed, brandishing his hay fork, its teeth tipped with the demon's blood. "Run, Bear!" he ordered the animal. "Now!"

The demon lunged at him with its good right arms. Tobin stabbed, but timed it wrong, and the fork was battered out of his hands. He glanced down to it on the floor, lying amidst the hay and scattered thresh.

*Oh shit.*

He had no defence now. This was it.

But at least the horses had got away. Most of them, anyway.

Tobin stumbled backwards and fell onto his arse. He scrambled away as the demon stalked toward him. It was slow, for some reason. It cocked a head at him, as if curious. What was it doing?

Tobin dropped to his back just as the demon flew over him and battered against the stable wall with a wet screech.

*Bear!*

The giant Calladell had kicked the thing with his hind legs. And it wasn't getting up.

Tobin scrambled to his feet, grabbed the fork and clambered onto Bear's back.

"Right, big yin, go..." The words died in his throat.

At the gate, two more demons.

---

The blanket flew off and the monster roared. Tia screamed.

She pushed herself back, back, back into the corner, feet kicking wildly against the bed, trying to push herself into the wall and away from the teeth and the claws and the eyes.

Oh no, oh no, she was going to die.

More footsteps.

"Hey!"

The monster turned.

*"Dearmad."*

Tia could barely breathe, sobs catching in her throat. What was happening? Why? Who? Her feet were still moving, still trying to shove her back, and away, away, away...

But the monster had stopped. It just stood there, still.

Like a statue.

What happened?

And then a lady. A nice lady in a pretty dress. She tiptoed past the monster in bare feet, watching it. Her dress was so nice. She looked like a queen.

"You all right, honey?" she whispered.

Tia tried to nod, but she was shaking so hard she wasn't sure.

"What's...what's..." The words wouldn't come, so she pointed at the monster.

The lady sat on the edge of the bed, smiled and took her hand.

"It's all right. He's not going to hurt us."

"Wh-why?"

The lady put her arm around Tia's shoulder, pulled her in and whispered. "Because I did a little magic on him. And now he doesn't want to hurt us anymore."

*Oh.*

She was a magic lady. But if her magic controlled the monsters, was she...?

Tia shied away, trying to pull herself from the lady's arms. "Are...? Did you...?" Again, she looked at the monster.

The lady seemed confused at first, but then smiled again. "Oh, no, no, honey, that wasn't...I can't control them. I just...made him forget. What he is."

"Forget?"

"Yeah. But it took a lot of energy and I'm pretty tired now. Do you mind if we just sit here for a minute while I catch my breath?"

Tia scooched back toward the lady and leaned in. Her dress was silky. It felt nice under her fingers. She scrunched a little handful and leaned her head against the lady's side. "Are you a queen?"

She laughed. It was a nice laugh. "Not me, sweetheart."

Tia didn't know why that was funny, but the laugh was nice. She was still shaking, though.

"What's your name, honey?"

"Tia," she whispered.

"Tia. That's a nice name. I like it. That's a name for a princess, that is."

Tia smiled. But it felt wrong. The monster was still *right there*. And Daddy was dead.

"What's *your* name?"

"Well, my friends call me Quell. I think we're friends, right?"

Tia nodded. She needed a friend.

"All right, Tia, how about we look after each other?"

She nodded again. Words were scary. But she was uncomfortable.

"Quell?"

"Yes, honey?"

"I think I peed myself."

Quell smiled down at her.

"Oh, me too, honey. Me too."

---

Vastin crept to the gate. This was where the scream had come from, he was sure. Though he'd passed several bodies on the way here. Long past help.

Something was moving inside. He hadn't seen any Thakhati on the streets, thank God. But he could hear them. He could hear the screams. They were everywhere. Fires burned across the town. Some of them bonfires, but some of them— Buildings had gone up, he reckoned. How much of Traverlyn would be left by morning?

Carefully, slowly, Vastin leaned his head into the open gateway. Nothing obvious but a body on the floor.

A horse. Hells, it was barely recognisable. But he could make out the head.

And still, something was moving.

Vastin walked as slowly and as quietly as he could. His armour was lighter than most, but it was no White. He couldn't be completely silent. Just had to hope the noises of battle would hide him.

No luck. A Thakhati head appeared from a stall, its jaw dripping blood.

All right, then.

The monster raced toward him, galloping on four limbs, the other two grasping for him.

But Vastin wasn't afraid. Not anymore. Because he'd learned that while these things were tough, they weren't immortal. Their "armour" was just as limited as any. And it didn't take well to blunt force.

Vastin swung the sledgehammer wide and crashed it into the demon, knocking it flying into another stall. Before it could recover its footing, he followed, bringing the hammer down again, shattering the thing's back. It screamed in agony, thrashing its arms, and Vastin felt his courage grow. Again he lifted the hammer and, taking a moment to be sure of his aim this time, brought it down on the thing's head. It burst like a winter melon, throwing gore up the back of the stall. And then it was still.

"Fuck you," Vastin whispered. "Fuck you and your master."

He heard the scrape just a moment too late. The hit knocked him sideways, against the stall. His left shoulder screamed and went numb for a moment.

*Stupid.*

He should have checked there weren't more. Now he was in trouble.

Claws scrabbled at his helm—thank God he'd kept it on. Though it might have contributed to this Thakhati sneaking up on him. He reached down to grasp the sledgehammer and made to swing it up, but there was no room. He needed to make room. So he did something even more stupid.

Vastin turned to face the Thakhati, back against the wall. Its frenzied screeching matched the manic swings of its claws, battering his armour again and again. Vastin waited, picked his moment, raised a leg and kicked the thing backwards. He almost stumbled after it but kept his footing enough to bring up the hammer.

The Thakhati came at him again and he swung from the left this time, battering it back out into the main stable. As it landed, another scream, or a squeal?

A clattering of hooves and a great black shape trampled across the Thakhati, bouncing it off the ground like a rain of stone.

The monster whimpered, but it had at least one massive hole in its chest. Hoof must have gone straight through.

The way it squealed, the way it tried to crawl away... It was smaller than the other. Maybe it had been a child, before. Vastin almost felt pity for it. But he saw the horse's body, and the pity washed away. It wasn't a child anymore. It was a demon. And it needed to die.

Vastin brought the hammer down again, ending its struggle.

This time, he wouldn't be stupid. He turned, alert, hammer raised. If there were more here, he couldn't be caught off guard again. He checked each stall, making sure there was nothing in them. Each was empty, most with no sign of violence. Whatever had happened to the horses, they hadn't died here.

Down at the other end of the stable, the horse that had appeared from nowhere stood nuzzling a bloody mess on the floor. He had three large gashes on his flank, where he must have taken a battering from one of the Thakhati.

At first, the bloody heap looked like part of the same horse that lay carved up before him, but with a closer look, Vastin realised—it was human. A boy by the look of what was left of him. Maybe one of the stable boys. Poor bastard. The big horse nudged the body, whinnying sadly.

"I know," said Vastin. "I know. I'm sorry."

The boy was a long way beyond help.

Vastin took the horse's lead. Biggest bloody beast he'd ever seen. He stroked it gently.

"Come on. Let's find us both somewhere safer, eh?"

# CHAPTER 3

"*Gluais!*" Aranok launched the Thakhati into the sky. Hopefully the landing would be enough to cripple it. At least it would land far enough away to give them a breather.

"Keft!" He stumbled toward the bonfire in the middle of the square, where the principal stood sentry, battering any of the demons that got near him with bursts of energy.

Keft nodded and grasped his hand. The fire dipped briefly as energy flowed into Aranok, filling him like water. He was reminded of his story, explaining the use of energy to Samily, of emptying the watering can with every use. This was different. Even with controlling his energy levels, he was burning through it and needing refilled often. The monsters just kept coming. God, how long had it been? Not long enough. Morning was still far away.

"Aranok!" Allandria's call sounded more warning than panic, but his first thought was still to spin toward her. Good thing, because there were two she hadn't seen on the roof above her. Her shout had given away her position.

"Above you!" he called, as something hit him in the back. He was punched forward, but more from the force of his armour's charge throwing the Thakhati back than from the hit itself. Aranok landed face down, but the armour took the brunt of that too. He heard Keft throw a burst of energy and assumed he'd dealt with that one. Good, because Aranok needed to get to the other two.

Allandria held one at bay with her sword, but she was trapped against the wall, and the second was going to flank her.

He raised his hand and began to speak the word, when he was battered back to the ground.

*Fuck!*

---

"Just try to sleep, sweetheart." Jena stroked wee Liana's head, which was resting on her lap. The girl was scared and confused, bless her. They all were. Yavick sat facing the door of their room, the axe he'd lifted from the back of the inn across his knees. He was a big man, but he was a stonemason, not a fighter. Still, Darginn knew he'd give everything to protect his wife and daughter if one of those things came through the door. It was mild consolation. Darginn had got used to feeling safe around much more formidable company of late, but his son-in-law was at least a torch in a thunderstorm.

When the Guard had come round, ordering everyone inside, Darginn's first thought was that Ismar was out again. His son still hadn't explained where he was spending his days, and neither Darginn nor Isadona had wanted to invade his privacy—but having no idea where the Hell he was, there was no way Darginn could go looking for him. The boy could literally be anywhere in town. They just had to pray he had the sense to take cover wherever he was.

"Dad? Why don't you tell us a story?" Jena's smile was forced, but welcome all the same. She looked down at her daughter. "That would be nice, wouldn't it?"

Liana's fragile eyes peered up from her mother's lap. Darginn easily found a smile—he always could for her. She nodded gently, sat up and wiped the hair away from her face.

But in that moment, every story Darginn had ever heard disappeared from his mind. All except the ones he couldn't share with his family. The ones that would have them terrified every time he left for work. Only one came to him, from that afternoon.

"Right, well, I met a man in the bar earlier—"

Isadona put a hand on his shoulder. "Darginn, is this an appropriate story for our granddaughter?" It was said in jest, but there was a wee corner of nerves in her voice. Probably concern for Ismar. Hard not to be thinking about him. Darginn waved his wife away, nodding reassuringly.

"And we had a really interesting conversation. You know the phrase *doggies' years*?" Nods from everyone but Yavick, who was still watching the door. "Well, it's an odd phrase, isn't it? Because it means ages, like a long time, but dogs don't live as long as us, do they?"

Liana shook her head, her wide eyes showing her interest. It didn't take much of a story to fascinate her. Maybe it was in the telling.

"Oh." Jena's face scrunched up. "I've never thought about that, right enough. That is odd."

"Well, apparently, according to this man, that's because the phrase was originally *donkeys' years*. Which makes more sense, right, because donkeys live a lot longer than dogs. I've heard of them lasting forty-five, fifty years."

"That's still not old," said Isadona, smiling.

"It is not," Darginn answered. "Anyway, he reckoned that what happened is, at some point, when some monk or master was writing it down, he must have misheard it. Maybe was a wee bit deaf or just no listening very well. For whatever reason, it got written down wrong, and then people started saying *doggies' years*, even though it didnae really make sense. Isn't that funny?"

"So we should be saying donkeys' years instead of doggies' years?" Jena tousled Liana's hair. "D'you think we can do that? Change it back to donkeys?"

Liana pouted in thought for a bit before answering. "Won't the doggies be sad?"

Laughs from everyone then. Except Yavick. Darginn hoped they were loud enough that Liana didn't hear the screech from outside.

Or the scream that followed it.

---

Aranok felt the claws scrabbling at his armour. He had seconds before it tried for the head, and his hood was a lot less protective. He hadn't had a chance to recharge his armour, so that wasn't going to help. Best he could do was get them both off the ground.

"*Gaoth.*" A burst of wind threw them both into the air. The Thakhati instinctively let go, grasping frantically for something to hold on to. Good. It fell before Aranok reached his peak. He heard the sickening crunch of it landing back on the cobbles as he cushioned his own landing.

"Aranok!"

This call was panic. God, she was in trouble.

He couldn't see Allandria. Just the back of a Thakhati. He didn't have time to think.

Just act.

The demon stopped, only a moment, then burst in two as Aranok's magic ripped it apart.

He ran to her. "You all right?"

Allandria's wide eyes peered over the shoulder of the dead Thakhati she was trapped beneath. She must have taken that one but got herself stuck under its corpse as the second closed in.

"What the fuck was that?" she asked.

Hell, good question. He'd never done that before. And fuck, he'd spent most of his energy on it. "New trick." He wasn't even sure what he'd done—it was pure instinct. Something to figure out later. He dragged the demon off Allandria and pulled her to her feet.

"Keft!" he called. "Again!"

---

A thumping from downstairs. An insistent hammering. Isadona gripped Darginn's arm. They were thinking the same thing.

*It might be Ismar.*

Hope leapt in his chest. But the banging continued. Insistent. Urgent.

Unanswered.

People were staying in their rooms. Innkeeper might not be willing to open the door—risk one of them demons getting in. But it could be his son out there.

"Darginn..." His wife's trembling eyes asked the same question: *What if?*

"Yavick, come on." Darginn put a hand on his son-in-law's shoulder.

"Mm?" the big man grunted.

"Dad, what are you doing?" Jena sounded confused. She hadn't thought. Maybe assumed Ismar was safe somewhere. Convinced herself it couldn't be him desperate to get in. He was smarter than that. Wiser than that. Maybe she had to believe that. But God alone knew what might have happened out there. What *was* happening.

Darginn couldn't imagine having to live with the knowledge his youngest child had been murdered in the street while he cowered inside. "Could be your brother."

Jena's eyes widened. She might have leapt up herself, but for Liana, who was out cold across her legs. Instead, she just nodded.

"Aye. All right," said Yavick.

They took the stairs carefully in the dark, Yavick leading the way down. No candles left lit, no fire. Nothing to attract the monsters. The banging was louder out here. And there was a voice, but it was faint. Weak. That probably wasn't good. Maybe he was trying not to draw attention to himself.

"What you doing?" An urgent whisper in the dark.

"Letting them in," Darginn answered.

When he was close enough, Darginn's eyes focused on the face. Just enough light filtering round the edges of the shutters. Must be fires everywhere outside. Wedick—the innkeeper. Been standing behind the bar, in the dark, it seemed. Maybe thinking about opening that door. Maybe weighing his chances of helping someone versus getting himself killed. Maybe all his loved ones were already inside, so he wasn't likely to risk it. But how could anyone hear that thumping, that abject desperation, and do nothing? Even if it wasn't Ismar, they had to let them in.

"Like Hell you will."

---

Aranok leaned on his knees, lungs heaving. His head was spinning.

"It's the energy," said Keft. "It's confusing your body. You're not meant to keep going up and down like this. Maybe we should—"

"No," Aranok cut him off. "We rest in the morning. We rest in sunlight."

Keft nodded grimly. He understood. However hard they pushed themselves tonight, it just had to be. There might not be a tomorrow. For some, it was already gone.

A screech from Aranok's right. Keft blasted another Thakhati against a wall. Aranok held it there with *gluais* and Allandria drove her sword through its throat. The three of them had been effective as a team, learning how best to use their complementary abilities on the hoof.

"Envoy! Principal!" A hulking metal giant came barrelling toward them at an impossible speed, grinding to a halt in the dirt. One of the physic *draoidhs*. "Master Opiassa sent me. The library is burning!"

Keft's face turned ashen. "God in Heaven." He looked to Aranok. There was no need to speak. The loss of that knowledge, the loss of the experience in those books...Eidyn could be crippled for generations. That was without considering how many of the country's greatest minds may not survive the night.

And Anhel would want the library burned—rid of any evidence of Mynygogg, memory magic—all of it.

They ran.

---

"Move," Yavick growled. He still held the axe across his stomach. The innkeeper looked down at it, and back up at Yavick's face, likely deciding if the big lad was really prepared to use it on him.

"You cannae. It's locked," he answered.

*Thump thump thump.*

"Then give us the key." Darginn thrust his hand toward the man.

He stepped back. "You know what's out there?"

"Somebody needs help. Might be my son."

The innkeeper took another step back, edging toward the bar. Did he have a weapon back there? Was he really going to fight Yavick?

*Thump thump.*

Yavick stepped forward and grabbed the man by the shirt. "Just give us the key."

The innkeeper looked over his shoulder, back where Darginn reckoned his living quarters must be. "I can't, my—"

Yavick head-butted the man in the face and blood burst from his nose. "Now."

"Fuck!" The innkeeper spat blood on the floor. "I can't!"

Yavick held the axe out to Darginn. "Hold this."

Darginn took it while his son-in-law rifled the man's pockets, finally pulling a key from his waistcoat.

"You're going to get us killed!" the innkeeper protested from the ground. But Yavick was already unlocking the door. He lifted the bar and paused.

"You better give me that." He put his hand out for the axe. Darginn realised he had felt a little safer holding it. But Yavick would be the one to use it if it came to it. So he gave it back to him and moved to the door himself.

*Thump thump thump.*

It rattled against Darginn's hand. He nodded to Yavick. If it wasn't safe, he might have to shove this door closed again quick smart.

He pulled it open and a body all but fell in on top of him. Darginn let go of the door to catch the man. He was wet. "Bloody Hell!" Darginn didn't even get a look outside. Yavick slammed the door closed and put the bar back down.

Darginn fumbled with the man in the half-light. There was something wrong. "Light! I need light!"

The innkeeper sparked a lantern and brought it near as Darginn lowered the man onto the floor. It wasn't Ismar. But he could see the source of the wetness now.

Half his arm was missing.

Darginn staggered backwards, a wave of dizziness, confusion and terror all flooding him at once.

*What the Hell?*

He needed to steady his head.

"Belt!" he heard Yavick say, and they burst into action. But Darginn's head was swimming. He stumbled to the bar and found a bottle of whisky on the counter. A swig and the peaty burn on the roof of his mouth; the heat as it travelled down his throat brought him back. His eyes began to clear again. Why had he reacted so badly to that? He'd seen wounds before, for goodness' sake.

But it wasn't Ismar. Maybe that was why. Because a huge part of him had been praying it was his son out there, and that he was home safe.

"Looks like a guard," said the innkeeper. Now that Darginn could stand again, he moved back to the door. Aye. It was a guard uniform. Boy must've got hurt in the fighting, somehow got away. Every chance some others died. Every chance a lot of people were going to die.

Another scream from outside.

*God almighty.*

"Lock it. Lock it!" Darginn barked at the innkeeper. Daft, really. That wee lock would make little difference if they came.

The guard's arm was missing just below the elbow. Yavick had tied it off with a belt, slowing the bleeding. It wouldn't be enough. Darginn had enough field medicine experience to know that. He'd bleed to death by morning.

The lock clicked shut again. It was soothing. Just for a moment.

"We need a fire," said Darginn.

"What...? We can't." The innkeeper looked nervously to the door.

"We need a fire. This boy's going to die if we do nothing. *Get it lit.*"

---

"They're everywhere!" Allandria ducked and rolled away, avoiding the Thakhati's diving lunge. Rasa had said there were thousands. They'd killed hundreds at nightfall and it seemed they'd hardly made a dent. The run to the library had been slowed at every turn. How long had it been? Hours? She'd lost all track of time. Just fighting. Killing. Resting when they could. She felt hopelessly out of her depth out here, surrounded by *draoidhs*, but she wasn't leaving Aranok. He'd barely had a minute to recover from the trauma, from the drugged haze she'd put him into. God knew how he was still going. It was as if something had tripped inside him and...he was back.

But he couldn't be. Not this quickly. Not this easily. There was going to be a price to pay. But at least he had rested. Better than Allandria could say. Any time her life wasn't in immediate danger, she felt her muscles aching to stop. There was an insistent, almost constant tremble in her hands now. But imminent death will focus you.

Aranok grabbed the Thakhati and pinned it to the ground. Allandria slipped her sword between its armour, to where the heart should be—assuming they kept their previous human biology on the inside. It gave a "*hurk*" and was still.

They had to keep moving.

Another corner, another pair of Thakhati. Keft blasted one so hard she heard it crunch like a snapped branch when it smacked against the wall of a house. It tried to move but its back was broken. Aranok launched the other into the sky. They couldn't waste too much time on killing them.

Finally, round a last bend and there it was—the beautiful university library building, its roof screaming fire into the night sky.

Keft stopped so quickly he almost fell over his own feet. "My God. Aranok."

"I know." Aranok began making a gesture, but Keft grasped his hand, interrupting him.

"What are you doing?" the principal asked.

"Water," he answered, as if it were obvious. It did seem obvious.

"No, no, no!" Keft waved his hands as if to dampen Aranok himself. "Water will damage the books too. You need to get me up there!" Keft pointed to the burning roof.

Aranok looked at the fire and back at the principal. They'd seen him do incredible things. Allandria had a whole new appreciation for the power of an energy *draoidh* now. But could he put out a blaze of that size? It took Aranok a few seconds to decide.

"Over there." He pointed to the corner of the building. When Keft was in position, Aranok lifted another pillar from the earth, raising the energy *draoidh* up level with the blaze.

"Will he be able to...?" Allandria asked.

"We'll see." Aranok's eyes were fixed on the master. Allandria had to be on guard. She turned and scanned the area. Spots of fire all over the town. Light and dark clashing like swords; dancing like lovers. The constant rumble of conflict. A town on fire, infested with demons.

Hell.

Keft shouted something into the night, and the flames on the library dimmed as fire erupted from his left hand, shooting into the night sky, making it brighter than day.

"Holy shit," Aranok whispered. She wasn't the only one who was impressed, then.

"Have you seen that before?"

He shook his head. "I saw Dialla do something but... not like that. Not that size."

It took a minute, maybe less, and the fire seemed to be out. The massive plume of flame that had run through Keft died too, and without either fire, the road suddenly felt awfully dark.

Then the screaming started. Chattering. Scampering. Across rooftops and over cobbles. Allandria's eyes met Aranok's and they both knew.

That flame had been a beacon. They were coming.

"Keft! Jump!" Aranok called up to him.

"What?" the older man shouted back.

"You have to jump! Now!"

No response, but suddenly a mess of robes plummeted toward them.

*"Gluais!"* Aranok caught him about ten feet off the ground and lowered him to his feet.

"We have to go!" Allandria turned.

It was too late.

There was nowhere to run.

# CHAPTER 4

"We should be out there." Gogg was pacing like a trapped wolf. "We have no idea what's happening."

Nirea understood his instincts. She felt the same. Cowering here, inside the hospital, felt like abandoning their responsibilities. But there were good reasons. The people inside the hospital needed protection if Thakhati got in. The huge oak doors that usually seemed imposing felt flimsy, knowing what was outside. She'd tried whittling earlier, to distract herself. Fruitless. Nothing was taking her mind off what they were living through tonight. And that was the key. They had to live through it.

Tomorrow, in a matter of hours, when the sun came up, they could start again. Aranok could set the sunspire and Traverlyn could be safe.

Assuming Aranok survived the night.

Both of their envoys were outside, fighting. Nirea longed to join them. But they'd discussed it. Leondar had absolutely insisted that they were too important to die here. It still seemed wrong.

They'd ended up with the lecture hall full anyway, even after her argument with Egretta. Just with the public instead of patients. Everyone who came running for shelter when the word got out. But any one of them could also be the assassin, so Nirea and Mynygogg had to stay out of the crowd, or risk an opportunistic dagger in the back.

So here they stood, inside the hospital's main entrance. Pacing. Waiting.

Going mad.

"Sire, it's vital that you stay here. Please." Leondar's voice was both respectful and forceful. He took his role seriously. But he'd never been afraid to disagree with either of them. It was one of the reasons Gogg had made him captain. An excellent tactician and fighter during the rebellion, and now a loyal ally and guard. He'd turned against Hofnag quickly, given the opportunity. Never liked serving under such a prick. Mynygogg's vision had swayed him, like so many. A poor boy who'd joined the army and risen through the ranks with natural talent—but too thoughtful to be mindlessly loyal to an arsehole king. His loyalty had to be earned by someone who deserved it.

"I know, I know, Leondar." Gogg waved him away. "I agree, I just..."

He turned to Nirea and his eyes mirrored everything she was feeling. Frustration. Impatience. Impotence. Guilt.

Fear.

Nirea closed her eyes and nodded gently. She knew. They both did.

If they died, Anhel won.

And that simply could not be.

---

Brontid held his hand against his chest, willing his heart to slow. It felt like it was going to burst. His lungs heaved, trying to suck in enough air, legs trembling beneath him.

He hadn't joined the Guard for this. Being a guard in Traverlyn was meant to be simple. Barely any crime. He'd watched six of his fellows ripped apart tonight. They couldn't fight these things. Not in these numbers. Not alone.

He could have been a farmer. God, how he wished he was a farmer in that moment. His brother had taken that road. But Brontid wasn't interested in that kind of labour. Didn't want to live in the arsehole of nowhere, tending sheep and tilling fields. He hadn't had the intellect to get him into the university, but they'd taken him into guard training.

Traverlyn had always been his hope. He'd visited with his folks when they were younger. His aunt and uncle had lived here, in a mad blue house that looked like a melted teapot on its end—though the spout was just a chimney. And he'd loved it. The town was so much more than anywhere else he'd ever seen. Life and colours and just...kindness. Nothing like he'd experienced growing up near Gorgyn, where everything was work and keep your head down. Here they had music. And maybe he could learn to play an instrument.

His sword had snapped off in the first demon he'd managed to stab. Bloody things were like stone!

Had to plunder a new one from another guard, who didn't have enough face left for Brontid to know him. They weren't much use. Had to get the angle just right.

Killed two more before he lost another sword. Only thing to do then was run. And he ran. Ran his arse off. Hammered on a few doors, hoping to get in. No answers. Either too scared or already gone.

So he ducked into an alley for a moment. Catch his breath. Get his head back on. He needed to get inside. Now.

The hospital wasn't too far. They'd let him in, right? Surely.

*Surely.*

All right. He had control of his lungs again. His heart had stopped thumping in his ears. He could go again. Just needed to head east.

He stepped out from the alleyway. And froze.

On the roof of the tanner opposite, two demons fought over a limp body like starving dogs.

Brontid could barely move. He had nothing to protect himself. If they saw him...

With a wet sound that shivered through him, the body ripped in half, spattering the monsters with gore. They made an odd noise then. Like a rhythmic grunting. Were they...laughing?

Brontid backed slowly toward the alley. He just had to get out of sight before...

One of them looked directly at him.

He turned and ran.

Aranok scanned desperately for a way out. Every direction was cut off. They had seconds to retreat, or they were going to have to fight.

"Inside!" Keft bellowed, charging up the stairs toward the doors of the library. Allandria followed and Aranok backed his way up, keeping an eye on the swarm coming toward them. He heard a door open, turned and sprinted up the last steps.

Allandria slammed the door shut behind him. "There's too many!"

Yes, there were. Aranok grabbed one of the heavy old bookcases with *gluais* and dropped it behind the doors. The place stank like a bonfire, but Keft had taken every ounce of the fire. There was a light residual heat, but the fire seemed to have mainly stayed on the top floor. And the roof was still partially intact, though from the ground it looked like it might break in a stiff breeze.

"They'll come through the roof," Aranok said. "We don't have long." Keft was twitching, much like Dialla had been at Greytoun after killing Janaeus. He was overloaded with energy from the fire. "D'you want to give us some of that?"

Keft looked down at his hand as if surprised it was there. "What? Oh, yes. Of course."

The principal quickly transferred energy to the two of them. Good. They needed their wits.

Battering at the door reminded them of what waited outside.

"Now what?" Allandria asked. "Is there another way out?"

"Not that I know of." Aranok looked to Keft.

"There is a basement, used for storage. But otherwise, no."

"So what do we do with no exit?" said Allandria.

Aranok looked into the gloom, toward the back of the library. "We make one."

---

Brontid barrelled around the corner and into the next street. God, where was he going? He wasn't even sure where he was at this point—just had to keep running! Was there anyone even in these houses? At least one of the demons was following. He could hear its stony claws clattering behind him.

*Shit!*

He stumbled over something, landing hard on his hip, arms sprawling.

He had to get up. Had to move. Scrambling to get back to his feet, he caught sight of it. The thing he'd stumbled over.

A leg. A human leg.

*Move!*

He hurtled forward so quickly he almost toppled over again. There were barrels stacked beside the building ahead. What was it? Didn't matter. Not an inn. Maybe a warehouse? Could he hide there? Behind them? In one?

He reached them to find there was neither space nor an easy way to open one.

*Run!*

God, he could barely feel his legs anymore. The screaming exhaustion, the pain, the terror…

Noises. Chasing him. Right behind him.

He couldn't look back. Had to keep running.

Something battered him across the back and again he was falling, splayed out across the cobbles like a butcher's pig. The dull pain in his back turned sharp and he realised he was cut.

*God, no.*

This was it. He was going to die.

His mother's face flashed before him. Kind. Loving.

Instinctively, he rolled onto his back, raising his arms as protection.

Two Thakhati crept toward him.

More clattering of claws coming from somewhere too.

Wait. Was that claws or…?

The right-hand demon's head came off with a battering of iron. The second tried to move, but it was too slow and was sent careering away by a giant horse's hooves. The animal turned and a soldier in full armour sat mounted on it, wielding what looked like a hammer.

Oh God, was he saved? The remaining Thakhati screeched a warning. The soldier sat proud in the saddle, waving the demon toward him. It leapt and the man brought the hammer down again, catching it on the shoulder and arresting its leap. It crumpled to its knees, almost whimpering, but there was a guttural nature to it. It was still angry. Still dangerous.

Until the soldier smashed its skull in.

Brontid collapsed forward.

God, his back was screaming in pain. But he was alive. Thank God.

The soldier approached and offered him a hand.

"Come on. I'm going to the hospital."

---

*"Gluais."* Aranok pushed against the section of stones he'd carefully cracked around. They slid out slowly until free of the rest of the wall, tipped and thumped onto the grass. Aranok stuck his head out. No sign of Thakhati. But he could hear them clattering around on the roof. They'd get in before long.

"Come on," he whispered.

Allandria and Keft followed him out.

Now where? There was little or no cover out here. The library was surrounded by grass on three sides, with trees dotted about. Fifty yards away, a path ran perpendicular to them, leading to the student lodgings one way and the main university quadrangle the other. But on the other side of the path, a stone wall, bordering the university's botanical garden. Aranok pointed and the others nodded their understanding. If they could get over that wall, they could make some space for themselves.

Their purpose in being outside was to kill Thakhati, but not that many at once. And they needed to find their way to another bonfire.

A snicker of stone against stone made him look up.

They'd been waiting.

Thakhati fell from the building like spiders descending on a kill.

*"Gaoth!"* Aranok instinctively used a burst of air to throw them back up and away. There were too many. Ten, twelve... more. Like rain.

"Run!"

They landed everywhere. One to Aranok's right and he pushed it away with *gluais*. Another running toward them from the wall. Where had that come from? Aranok grabbed hold of it and Allandria speared its mouth, withdrawing her blade and turning to fend off another from behind her. Aranok grabbed that one too, and Allandria dispatched it.

Wait. Where was Keft?

*Fuck!*

"Keft!"

A blast of energy and two Thakhati burst into the sky. He was back by the building. Why hadn't he run?

They had to go back for him. Four Thakhati now, creeping toward them. Aranok and Allandria couldn't do their usual trick. He couldn't hold four at once. So he opted for something different.

*"Uisge."* Water burst from each of his hands, punching the left two back. The other two ran at Allandria. He swapped the water to the nearest one, leaving her only one to deal with. She could handle that. And she did. Parrying its lunge and swiftly getting her blade under its armpit. It screeched in pain and she rammed a dagger in its mouth.

Still he couldn't see Keft clearly in the murk. "Keft! You all right?"

No answer. But another Thakhati went flying past them to crunch viciously into the garden wall. Keft was fine.

Another came at them and Aranok threw it into the sky. They ran back toward the library.

The two to Aranok's left came bounding back. *Gaoth* blew them away.

He was acting on instinct now. There—he saw Keft, still beside the building. He was surrounded on three sides, his back to the library.

A turn of the energy *draoidh*'s hands and all three went flying. But he'd missed one. It dropped on the principal from above.

"Keft!"

Aranok went to use *gluais* but was clattered from behind.

*Fuck!*

He tucked his shoulder and rolled with the thing's lower arms scrabbling at his waist. His armour held. But he was belly up. Literally. And he couldn't make gestures because he was using his hands to protect his face.

One claw and then another, battering at him, searching for soft flesh to tear.

A screech of agony and it reared up, giving him a moment. He grabbed it with *gluais* and Allandria drew her sword from its back to stab it in the neck. Aranok tossed its corpse sideways.

He rolled over his hip and onto his knees. A stab of pain told him he'd hurt something. It would have to wait.

There was no movement. From the Thakhati or Keft.

Aranok grabbed the demon and tossed it away—it went like a limp rag, already dead.

"Keft!"

"I'm fine." The principal pulled himself up to sitting. "Just needed a moment. I..." His eyes widened and his hand grasped his chest. He was shaking like a leaf.

"What's wrong?" Allandria asked.

Aranok threw another Thakhati into the sky.

*A moment, just a moment to catch my breath. Please.*

Allandria fussed over Keft as Aranok fended off another two.

*Come on. Just a moment!*

Finally, finally, that seemed to be it. No more came at them. Aranok turned and knelt beside the others.

Keft's vacant eyes stared into the dark sky.

*Fuck.*

Allandria's eyes were panicked and apologetic. "I don't know what happened! He just...expired!"

Aranok knew what had happened. That last Thakhati. With it right on top of him, Keft must have drained it to kill it. And that had been the final straw. The danger for all energy *draoidhs* was overtaxing their hearts with too much energy. That Thakhati's full energy plus his own had been too much. "I think his heart burst."

"Oh God. Oh God." Tears broke from Allandria. "What do we do?"

A spat of rain on Aranok's hand. He looked up at the dark clouds looming overhead. If it rained, their fires would go out. Not that it mattered.

Their only energy *draoidh* was dead.

And so were they.

# CHAPTER 5

Zizou was a *god*. She'd always wondered if she'd have the stomach for battle. Feared she'd turn and run at the sight of blood. But she relished it. Her heart raced, buzzing along with her mind.

She'd been a precocious talent from the day her nature skill developed. It just always felt *natural*. When she'd come to the university, almost every master commented on how she must have had some training. *"Who have you worked with?"*

She'd mastered flora by fourteen. Moved into advanced fauna by sixteen. And now, at seventeen, she was already using telepathy with small animals. Beyond what most nature *draoidhs* ever managed.

Before the battle, when the Laird Envoy had stood on that hill, waiting—waiting for the dark—she'd been scared. Terrified. Not of what was coming. Not really. Of herself. Would she perform? Would she make her masters, her family, proud? Would she prove she was as good as she wanted, needed to believe?

But oh Gods, she had been revealed when it began. The trees, the vines had moved like her limbs, grasping, holding, crushing the Thakhati. Spikes drove between their plates, into their eyes, their throats—finding the soft places and piercing. Killing. Ending.

They died like all animals. Nothing was unkillable.

But in that moment, Zizou felt immortal. Untouchable. Legendary.

Lifted above the huge oak in the centre of the square, wrapped in vine armour; the oak crushing, grabbing, throwing Thakhati back like fleas. Like dust.

Her body ran with lightning, skin quivering, hairs on edge.

There was no fear. Only wrath. Only death.

She held three Thakhati in her branches, glowering down at them. These pathetic monsters, thrashing and screaming, as if that might scare her. As if she might show them mercy. These twisted, unnatural things. How dare they approach her?

Zizou clenched her fists and all three Thakhati screamed, then were silenced. She dropped their corpses to the earth, amongst their brethren.

She closed her eyes, breathed in the smoke and the blood and the death. And she screamed.

"Come on!"

Here, at the peak of her powers, she was glorious, and a grin spread wide across her face when she saw the crowd she'd summoned to her.

They came in numbers this time. Eight, maybe. Ten, perhaps.

She would slow them, first.

"Scatter them," she commanded her army. The night sky cried in response. It broke, and a cloud of wings descended on the monsters. The Thakhati stopped, thrashing, waving at the bats. Their squeals seemed to disorientate the Thakhati, and their teeth threatened their eyes.

Finally, the first few broke toward her, recognising, maybe, that the bats were her doing. They came as if she would be terrified. As if she were vulnerable.

Stupid creatures. The oak's branches tore them in two. She held their sundered corpses in the air, black blood dripping onto stone. An offering to the others. *This is what's coming for you.*

Zizou's heart skipped. What was that? A shard of doubt. She'd missed something. A flash of movement to her left. Her head snapped round to see four Thakhati clambering across the roof of the prison, maybe twenty yards away. *Oh God.*

*They'd* been distracting *her.*

She threw out branches like a shield as they rained from the dark. One was caught. Two were deflected and fell to the earth. One got through. The smallest. Hell, it was quick! Zizou tried to open the tree's branches, give it nothing to cling to, but it leapt like a frog from one branch to another until...a vine came up and snared its leg. She pulled it up and away, hanging upside down like a fish on a hook.

But it was not scared. It did not thrash or scream. It simply cocked its head and looked at her. Looked *past* her.

A shudder from behind and Zizou's eyes exploded in red.

She instinctively pulled the tree around her, built a shell of wood and vine, and screamed for help from any animals, anything that could hear her. She quickly heard the beating of bats' wings, their shrill cries, and the Thakhati's shrieks in return. But she couldn't see.

The Thakhati that had snuck up from behind had hit her hard. Her ears squealed, her eyes still black, dotted with rainbow stars. She couldn't attack if she couldn't *see*.

A shudder that shook the earth. No. Just the tree. They were attacking the trunk. If they felled it...

Zizou threw branches down blindly, swinging wildly, looking for the Thakhati attacking. But they were getting close to her too. They were going to overrun her. A piercing light, a pinhole, and her sight was coming back. The tree was no longer shuddering, the monsters below forced back, but they were still coming for her—digging their way through the branches faster than she could grow them. The effort was tiring. She hadn't had to work this hard, this fast, all night. And suddenly, she was aware of her fatigue. She'd had a few boosts from Principal Keft earlier in the evening, but it had been hours since she'd seen him and...she was in trouble.

*No.*

*I am a god.*

Her sight fully returned, Zizou burst from the tree on a pillar of branches, raising her, worshipping her.

Three on top of the tree. She swept them away, clearing the canopy. Then she forced the branches down, down, down the trunk, clearing anything beneath her. Forcing them out where she could see them. Where she could kill them.

The tree creaked horribly. Had it taken too much damage? She felt it tip and threw out stabilising branches. But they snapped. Torn. Cut by the Thakhati. They were working together. Coordinating.

*Oh God, I'm going to die.*

Escape. Escape was her only way out now. She wrapped herself in a cocoon of vines, snapped them from the oak. Branches swayed together, springing back and launching her into the air—over rooftops. For a moment, she was flying, lighter than air. And then her stomach lurched, her back went numb and she was falling.

---

Nirea nearly jumped out of her skin when there was a hammering at the hospital doors. Her first reaction was that the Thakhati had finally found their way to them. That they were going to have to weather a siege. But then a voice. Familiar. Urgent.

"Please..." was all she could make out. A second of glancing between Gogg and Leondar, and the kingsguard was lifting the bar off the back of the doors. He and Nirea stood ready as her husband threw open the left-hand door. Two men. One a soldier in full armour, the other a guard by the look of him. And... a horse?

The guard was injured, his left arm slung over the soldier's neck. He was pale.

"Get in!" Gogg ordered, opening the other door to allow room for the horse. It was bloody massive.

As they hobbled inside, Nirea stepped out to take in the town.

Gods, it was a mess. Fires everywhere. Only some of them their own. Buildings were burning. But there were smatterings of rain. If it got worse, those fires would at least go out.

It was eerily quiet, though. A distant clash of metal and stone.

"Is this... Bear?" Mynygogg asked behind her.

Nirea turned to see the soldier remove his helm. "Dunno," said Vastin, hair plastered down with sweat.

"Oh!" Nirea grabbed the boy into a hug so quickly she nearly knocked him over. "What the Hell were you doing out there?"

He grinned sheepishly. "Long story. I..." His eyes strayed over her shoulder and his face fell.

"Dear God," said Leondar. A swarm of Thakhati were forming down the road. A distant storm rumbling toward them.

"Close it!" Gogg moved to swing the left door shut.

"Wait!" Vastin grabbed the edge of the door. "There's someone out there!"

He was right. The Thakhati weren't just coming toward the hospital. They were stalking something. Someone.

Nirea stepped forward. "Leondar, with me. Gogg, shut this behind us and *stay inside* until I tell you to open it again."

He didn't argue. It was the right decision. One of them had to survive, and she was the more experienced fighter. Leondar stepped out with her, sword drawn.

"Wait!" A hand in the door, as it was all but closed. It swung back and Vastin stepped through, helm back in place, carrying a huge, long-handled hammer. Her face must have betrayed her curiosity.

"More effective than the axe," he explained.

A glance back and she caught Gogg's eye as the door shut. He was terrified—for her. No time to dwell on that…

A massive blast of air sent Thakhati scattering and suddenly she could see who they were about to defend.

"It's Aranok! And Allandria!" Vastin was halfway down the steps already.

"Wait." Leondar grabbed the boy's shoulder. "Laird Aranok can handle himself. No point us getting stuck out there with him. We wait here and defend the door to let them in."

Sound tactic. But it didn't look like they were handling themselves all that well. At least seven Thakhati were coming at them from different angles, and they were getting awfully close before Aranok blasted them away. No. They were struggling.

They wouldn't make it.

Nirea bounded down the steps. "They need us!"

She heard the men's footsteps clattering behind her, but she was easily the quickest. She felt the blood coursing within her, the thrill of the fight. This was what she'd been itching for all night.

She reached the first Thakhati and smashed a scimitar off its neck, dancing back as it swung a pair of arms round at her. Another two turned at the sound.

Good. Now they weren't all focused on Aranok and Allandria. "You all right?"

"Fuck no!" Allandria called back.

Leondar arrived to batter into another Thakhati. He hit it so hard it staggered backwards and stumbled halfway onto its arse, only catching itself with its extra arms.

Nirea's lunged with its right arms and she parried them with both swords, spinning away to her right. There were still too many between them. One flew up into the air and disappeared into the night.

The Thakhati tried to catch her off guard, lunging in, but she ducked and slipped a blade up into its crotch. The scream was satisfying. She brought her other blade over and into the bastard's mouth. As she stood and retrieved both scimitars, the Thakhati collapsed at her feet.

A resonant thud behind her. She turned to see Vastin shatter the abdomen of another, then bring up the hammer and snap its head backward, so hard it nearly came off. Another was behind him, but he turned and brought the hammer round, smashing it sideways into Leondar. The big man kicked it back and Vastin hit it again, caving in its face.

"Fucking Hell," she muttered. The kid wasn't wrong about the hammer. He just wasn't the one to wield it right now. "Vastin! Give that thing to Leondar!"

He paused, looking at them a moment, as if confused, but quickly handed the weapon to the much larger man.

She did not need to tell him what to do.

Leondar dropped his sword and swung the hammer like a child's toy, battering the Thakhati back, up, down, shattering limbs, breaking skulls. She just about stopped to watch. It was majestic.

A few minutes and they were clear. Aranok and Allandria limped toward them, holding each other up.

"Come on!" She gestured to Vastin. The boy lifted Leondar's sword as he passed, and they each took the weight of one of the envoys.

"I'm glad you're alive," she told Allandria as she half dragged her toward the hospital. Her envoy said something back, but it was so faint as to be inaudible. Another Thakhati dropped from a roof, and Leondar smashed it away. Several of them were still alive, but far too broken to be able to move.

Finally, maybe fifty feet from the hospital, they stopped coming. As if they had learned. They weren't going to get through the kingsguard. Or maybe they'd got them all.

Wishful thinking. Now that she was outside, she could hear the distant sounds of battle more clearly. They needed to get back in. Now.

When they reached the top of the steps, Nirea hammered on the door. "Gogg! It's us!" She'd barely finished speaking when it swung open. The five of them fell into the hallway, lungs heaving. The echo of the door slamming shut behind them was the best sound she'd ever heard.

Now they could get a look at the two of them.

Allandria's leathers were ripped in multiple places, and her left arm was covered in blood. Aranok had taken a hit to the head, judging by the red mat of hair.

"I'll get Egretta!" Gogg ran.

"Leondar—with him!" Nirea ordered. She'd not forgotten about the assassin, regardless of all else. The big man nodded and ran after his king.

Now that she had time to notice, the pair of them stank of smoke. "What happened?"

Aranok slumped down against the wall.

"Keft's dead."

---

"Hey. Hey. Are you alive? You're breathing, right?"

Zizou's eyes blinked open. Nothing solid. Just a blur of light. A face? Where was she?

She tried to open her mouth, but her right ear exploded in pain. She lifted a hand to it.

"Easy. You're a mess. I think you fell. From *high*. Looks like the vines protected you a little. At least. Can...can you understand me?"

Zizou nodded, and her head swam. A guttural retching sound from her chest. God, her legs, she couldn't feel them. Had she...?

Her vision began to return. A face. A woman's face?

"Whurr..." She tried to speak again, but her jaw wouldn't move. It was...Was it broken? She couldn't really tell. It felt *wrong*.

Where was she?

"Listen, I'm going to get you to the hospital, all right? But first... first I need you to come to the gate with me. All right?" A nice voice. Gentle. She should go to the hospital, yes. Something was wrong.

"I'm going to turn into a horse, all right? Do you think you can hold on? Can you ride? I'll be careful. I just... We have to get to the gate."

Could Zizou ride? Her arms seemed to work. She could hold... Wait. Did she say she would *turn into* a horse? A metamorph? But why the gate? They were long past keeping the Thakhati out.

Oh! The Thakhati. That's where she—the tree. Yes, she remembered.

God, if they were outside. They couldn't be safe. But if this woman was a metamorph—maybe she *could* get them to the hospital.

Zizou nodded. She would ride. She had to.

---

Tia ran as fast as her legs would go to keep up with Quell. Her shoulder sort of hurt from Quell pulling her arm, but she was too scared to complain.

She could hear the noises.

Quell had said they shouldn't stay in the inn with the monsters, just in case. And she'd carried Tia down the steps, because she said Tia had to keep her eyes closed.

The downstairs bar had smelled funny. Like a coin pouch, but worse. She tried not to remember Daddy's face when—

Quell suddenly stopped and Tia ran face first into her leg. "Oh!"

"Shh." Quell put a finger to her mouth. Where were they? Quell had said they needed to find somewhere safer, but she hadn't said where. Tia was afraid to go outside, but she felt safer with Quell than being left alone. Outside was really scary. She kept thinking she could see monsters in shadows and on roofs. Everywhere.

But Quell was magic. She would protect her.

They'd stopped in front of a big building with some barrels outside under an overhanging roof. Some were stacked on top of others with a sign that Tia couldn't read. Quell pulled her behind them and crouched down. Her eyes widened and she put a finger to her lips. Tia nodded that she understood and pressed her lips tight.

Footsteps on the road. But sharp and... strange.

Tia's breathing got very heavy and she tried to keep it quiet, but she was shaking a lot and that made it really hard, so she just took a breath and held it deep instead. The steps got louder, until they were right on the other side of the barrels. Tia could feel tears coming, but Quell squeezed her hand very tight and she bit down on her lips so hard...

The footsteps walked away.

When she couldn't hear them at all anymore, Tia finally let out her breath and then she was breathing so quickly it felt hard to stop. But Quell grabbed her and hugged her tight, and that helped. When Tia had finally got her breathing back to normal, Quell put her finger to her lips again and then waved her hand for Tia to move back a bit, against the wall. She pointed to herself, and then to the edge of the barrels.

Tia tucked herself back against the wall and Quell squeezed past. Tia took a handful of Quell's dress as she did, rubbing it between her fingers. It felt nice. Soothing.

Quell got to the last barrels, looked back at Tia and slowly stuck her head out.

She didn't move for what seemed like a very long time before whispering, "Shit." She turned her head back to Tia. "Stay here."

And then the dress Tia had been rubbing was whipped out of her hand as Quell burst into a run. Tia almost screamed, but she absolutely knew the most important thing was that she had to be quiet, so all that came out was a sharp breath. She bit down on her lip again as she watched Quell's dress disappear into the distance. Then she saw why.

Another monster, galloping after her like a lopsided horse, "hooves" clattering against cobbles.

*Oh no.*

Quell was magic. Quell would be all right. She would just magic it again. Like the first one. She'd be safe.

But Tia was alone again. And she could still hear the noises. The scratch-scratch of claws. The hollow roars. The awful screams. And everywhere, the burning, still, despite the pitter-pat of rain.

Tia was on her own. And now the tears really came.

# CHAPTER 6

Zizou shook awake. Her head was heavy, her neck sore. Where... where was she? A lurch as gravity pulled her sideways. Her hands scrabbled for a grip, anything to hold on to. Her right hand found a mane of hair and caught it tight, arresting her slide.

Horse.

She was on a horse.

It was... Where were they going?

The hospital. She needed a hospital. There was something wet on her hand. Sticky and warm. Her arm felt strange. Sort of hot and numb. The horse slowed. They were in a field. Somewhere.

This wasn't the hospital. God, it was hard to think. Was she supposed to be here?

The horse knelt and ducked its head, offering Zizou an easy slide off. Her left leg crumpled beneath her, though, and she hit the ground hard.

*Ouch.*

Everything swam. She had grass in her face. Zizou smacked her lips, trying to clear her mouth with her tongue. She felt like a cow chewing cud. That was weird.

She was tired. Maybe she could just sleep here a bit. That would be nice. Her eyes felt like stone sacks, and the deep black was pulling her down.

"Hey. Hey! Don't pass out. Come on!" A hand slapped her cheek, and her jaw exploded in pain again. Zizou's eyes popped open in anger. A woman. A naked woman? What did she...? Who was she?

"Come on, come on." The woman got an arm under each of Zizou's, pulling her up. It was no use, her legs wouldn't take her weight. They felt wrong. Like, tingly. Not really there. Someone else's legs.

Zizou lifted her head. They were at the tree wall. She'd started the evening not a hundred yards from here. Helped create the walls that funnelled the Thakhati toward the Laird Envoy. When was that? Was that today?

God, she was going to be sick.

A moment, and the nausea passed. Her head still spun.

Was she being dragged? "Wu..." *Damn*. She'd forgotten she couldn't speak. Her mouth wouldn't work. And it bloody hurt.

...

Zizou's eyes opened. Oh. Had she slept? Everything was still blurry and her right ear was ringing.

"Come on. This is it." A hand pulled her arm up, placing her hand against... a tree. Zizou instantly felt the connection to the great ash, its roots twisting deep into the cool earth and, through it, the other trees and plants that wrapped together to protect Traverlyn. Why had they come here?

"Whu wan?" It was the best Zizou could manage without moving her jaw. Would the woman understand? What did she want?

"Quickly, please, please. You have to open it. Open the gate."

*Open the gate?*

The Thakhati were outside! Why would she open the gate? Oh God, this woman, she must be working with them. She was... she was a metamorph! She was the horse. She brought Zizou here. Said she was taking her to the hospital. *Liar!*

She couldn't open the gate. But she couldn't move either. And she would really like to just sleep now. Her chin dipped against her head, as words faded into the distance.

*"Please, open it... Please!"*

It was cold. Tia hadn't really felt it until she had to stay still. Now she was shivering. She hadn't had time to find her overcoat before she and Quell had run from the inn. And now she was alone, and scared, and really, really cold.

A while after Quell left, she'd noticed the window along the wall from her was open a crack. Enough to get her fingers in and prise it open. She'd stood on a barrel to climb through and get inside. It felt safer inside. But it wasn't warmer.

The huge warehouse was just full of more barrels. Rows and rows of them. And it smelled weird. Like an odd mix of fresh-cut wood with a sour edge that crinkled Tia's nose. It sort of smelled like a bar in the morning. Sickly but sweet.

Tia found a dark space between two rows and huddled there. At least she was out of the wind. And the monsters shouldn't come in here. They had no reason to. People shouldn't be in here. She was tired too. But it was so cold. Rain was beginning to drum on the roof, which helped to drown out the other sounds.

Maybe if she just closed her eyes, maybe she'd fall asleep, and maybe she could wake up back in bed, in the inn, with Daddy snoring beside her and...

*Daddy.*

Tears came again. Tears, and finally, a slow, dark slip into quiet.

...

Tia's eyes snapped open. Something had woken her. A sound. Something that shouldn't be there.

Scraping on wood.

*Oh no.*

Footsteps.

There was someone in the warehouse. Some*thing*.

Tia sat up as quietly as she could and pulled her knees tight against her chest. She had to be quiet now. Extra-special quiet, Daddy had said. So the monsters couldn't hear her. So nobody could hear her.

But she could hear. It was coming closer. Breathing heavy. Sniffing? Oh no, could it smell her? Like the giant from the story Daddy told. It smelled little children from miles away.

She might have to run. But where to?

She'd seen a door when she climbed in. It wasn't far, was it?

Sniffing again. Steps getting closer.

As quiet as she could, Tia crawled to the end of the row—away from the sounds. She didn't want to look, didn't want to see.

There. The door. It had a bolt, but it didn't look too high. She could reach it. But as soon as she stood up, the monster would see her.

Hide-and-seek. When she played with her cousin Stilk, he had tricked her that time. Made her look in the wrong place. Tia scanned the floor with her hands, feeling for anything she could use. She found a small, spongy, wooden thing. Sort of round, but also long. And light. It would do.

Tia carefully turned and threw it as far as she could toward the other end of the warehouse. She was a good thrower. It landed and bounced. The monster snorted, turned and clumped away from her.

*Now.*

Tia walked as quickly and quietly as she could. If she could just get to the door without it noticing, she could get outside. She dared not look back.

She reached for the bolt and the metal screeched as she slid it back.

Tia froze.

A moment of silence, and then a storm of noise. Tia threw open the door and raced out into the night rain. Her feet splashed in puddles on wet cobbles. Where could she go? Where? Where?

A bush. There was a hedge. She could hide under it. Behind it.

Tia dived onto her knees and crawled under the low leaves, burrowing, digging for safety, for...

Her foot snagged.

It had her.

Tia screamed, digging her fingers into the earth. Desperately trying to hold on, to grab something, anything.

She wasn't strong enough. A branch scratched her face as she was dragged back and lifted.

She saw the monster's arm first, all rocky and hard. Then she looked up.

She couldn't move. It was all teeth and red eyes, looking over her in the rain.

*Oh no, oh no, oh no.*

The monster grabbed her by the throat and lifted her up to face it. So many arms! Why did it have so many arms? Tia closed her eyes. She was going to die.

*Oh please, please, Daddy, somebody, please help me!*

A metallic swipe, a momentary scream, and Tia fell to the ground with a wet thud.

...

It took her a moment to open her eyes. To dare to see what had happened. Her knees hurt from landing on them. The monster had let her go, but she could still feel it. But what she saw was... wrong. The monster lay on the ground in front of her, but its head was away from its neck.

*What... what happened?*

Movement. Beside her. Tia flinched away until she heard the voice.

"It's all right, child." It was a nice voice. Dark and warm. Tia looked up to see the armoured man reaching a hand down. She took it and let him pull her back to her feet. She was soaking now, but the man's kind smile made it all right. He had dark skin and no hair, but a fuzzy beard.

"What's your name?" he asked, crouching down to face her.

"Tia," she whispered.

He smiled. It was a nice smile. Kind. Brave.

"Tia, my name's Meristan. You're safe now."

---

Vastin turned the sword over in his hand. What a strange situation. He stood beside the king of Eidyn, bearing a kingsguard's sword, defending a hospital from demons. The silence was bitter and awkward. Mynygogg had said almost nothing since Queen Nirea and Leondar had left. Laird Aranok and Lady Allandria had been all but carried into the big hall to be treated by medics. There had been gasps from the people of Traverlyn when they saw them.

He understood. Vastin had been just as shaken at first sight of their wounds, but not for the same reasons. For the others, Aranok was a symbol of hope for their own survival. He and the other *draoidhs* were their shield. Seeing him defeated and broken must have been terrifying. But for Vastin, his first concern had been for his friends. A bizarre thought, but there it was.

He'd feel a lot better if he still had that hammer, though. Made a big difference to his confidence that he'd survive the rest of the night. He'd sort of lost all notion of time. Had a few hours passed? Four? More? He just had to keep going. He'd had plenty of rest while he was Blackened.

A hammering at the door shook him from his thoughts and brought the sword up before him. Vastin looked to Mynygogg.

"Who's there?" the king shouted.

"Rasa! Please, we need help!"

Rasa? He'd heard the name, but... Obviously it was someone Mynygogg trusted, as he lurched forward to open the door. Rain burst in through the gap, followed by two women—one of whom was naked. Under other circumstances, that would have been awkward, but the other woman looked like she'd had her face smashed with a hammer herself. Vastin dropped the blade and moved to help them both inside.

"Rasa, thank God you're safe," said Mynygogg. "What news? What have you seen?"

She all but collapsed against the king, and only then did Vastin see a nasty wound running down across her hip and thigh. They needed medics. He carefully sat the other woman against the wall and burst into the main hall, grabbed the first two medics he could see and pulled them with him.

When they arrived back at the door, Rasa sat on the floor, leaning away from her wound, with the other woman sprawled beside her.

The medics dropped to tending them. The second woman hadn't said much. She'd barely moved since he'd laid her down, in fact. God, how many people were going to die tonight?

"Right, let's get you inside," the older medic said. "You both need a bed."

"Wait..." Rasa raised a hand and gestured for Mynygogg to come near. When he did, she pointed to the other woman. "You have to save her. She opened the gate. To let them in."

"Let who in?" Mynygogg asked.

Rasa took his hand and smiled. "The White Thorns."

Vastin's skin flushed with excitement. *Samily!*

Mynygogg's face reflected Vastin's heart. His eyes lit with hope. "Meristan? Is Meristan here?"

She nodded. "And more."

"How many? Rasa, how many Thorns are here?"

She gave a shrug.

"All of them."

# CHAPTER 7

Nirea raced up the steps. Of all the hospital's weaknesses—wooden doors, windows—she hadn't thought about the major one. The one vast part of the structure that wasn't made from stone. The roof.

As soon as they'd heard the crash, she'd realised. Leondar came trailing behind her. They'd left Mynygogg and Vastin guarding the front door. Aranok could barely stand and Allandria struggled to use her left arm at all. Medics were seeing to them both. They'd be no more use tonight.

It was down to them. Nirea, Leondar and that big fucking hammer.

Actually, that was a bloody good point. She should slow down and let the kingsguard get ahead of her. He was a lot more effective than she was against the Thakhati's hide. She slowed her run, letting Leondar catch up. He gave a half nod as he passed, and she followed him up to the top floor.

The first thing Nirea noticed was the rain. No longer just spattering on the windows, she could hear it clearly bouncing off the corridor floor. The incongruence of the wet, earthy smell, the light breeze, on the top floor of a hospital that usually smelled of sickness and the sweet, perfumed cleaning waters they used to disguise the rot. There was no sound of violence. No screams. Nothing to tell them which way to turn—except that rain, pouring through the massive hole in the roof.

Had something else caused this...?

No. A Thakhati was inside. Somewhere. At least one.

Nirea considered a stealthy approach, but they had no time for that. Truth was, they wanted it to know they were here. Come to them, instead of savaging some defenceless patient.

Her scimitar clanged off the stone wall. "Hey! Here! We're right here!"

Leondar joined her, thumping his fist on his armoured chest. "Helloooooo! Come at us!"

A rumble then, in response. A loud rumble. Too much.

There was more than one.

She turned to Leondar. "You take point with that thing; I'll step in for anything that causes you trouble."

He nodded sharply and stepped forward.

The cacophony finally turned the corner before them and Nirea's heart stuttered.

A storm of teeth and claws rolled toward them like a wave.

There were too many. Far too many for this small space.

At least six, she reckoned, before she had to stop trying to count them and act. Leondar would be overrun.

She stepped forward, beside him, but the kingsguard threw out a giant arm and tossed her back like a sack of flour. She stumbled, catching herself on the banister. Just in time to see the wall of Thakhati crash against Leondar's hammer. One went straight down, but the others came on, smothering the big man and knocking him to his back.

Nirea screamed as claws hammered at his armour, his head. Leondar bounced off the ground like a broken toy. She lurched forward, smacking one in the neck with her sword, but the angle was wrong and it just bounced off. They were like insects, swarming, frenzied and murderous.

"Get off him!" she bellowed, this time finding a slat near a shoulder with her blade. The Thakhati screeched, looked up at her venomously and leapt at her. Nirea raised an arm in defence, but the demon never landed.

It hung before her in the air, held fast by some sort of vines. Nirea didn't wait for an explanation; she rammed her sword in its neck.

Behind it, the rest were thrashing and struggling with vines coming from down the corridor. Nirea hadn't realised they'd brought a nature *draoidh* in, but she was suddenly bloody glad of it. She picked them off, one by one, finding soft spots as the vines held the monsters tight.

When they were all dead, she fell at Leondar's side.

*God in Hell.*

It was bad. His armour had mostly held, but his helm had come up. Half the man's face was missing. His jaw resembled a roast chicken carcass, all but picked clean. But he was still breathing. He wasn't dead yet.

"Medic!" she screamed. "Medic!"

"Here, I'm coming!" An unfamiliar voice. The vines cleared and Nirea recognised the Reiver, Teyjan, stumbling through the carnage. The man Mynygogg had brought here to be saved.

Behind him, the other two, Jazere and Cuda. Of course. Jazere was the *draoidh*. She'd forgotten they were even here. Cuda seemed to be pushing a potted bush along on a trolley. That explained where the plant had come from.

Teyjan dropped to his knees beside Leondar and turned grey. "Holy Hell."

It was as bad as it looked. At least he was unconscious. He wouldn't know much about it.

"We need to get him into a bed." Teyjan turned to Jazere. "Can you lift him back to our room?"

"Fuck! Here! Here! Look!"

They all turned at Cuda's urgent cry.

More Thakhati crawling in the hole. Three of them. Fuck. They were going to have to close that. Somehow.

Jazere gestured and branches twisted with her, growing toward the demons.

And then, a distant shriek. A cry that grew louder as it was joined by more voices. The three Thakhati on the ceiling stopped, cocked their heads and screamed.

Gods, it was so loud Nirea had to cover her ears to stop it from piercing her brain! What the Hell were they doing? The others had also covered their ears, so Jazere's hands were no longer free to use her skill. Was this an attack? To prevent them from defending themselves? It was like a splinter in her head, even through her hands. Hell, when would it stop?

And then, in an instant, there was silence. The Thakhati turned and scampered back out the roof and into the wet dark. They were gone.

Nirea lifted her hands from her ears. There was still a ringing, as if in the distance.

"What the fuck was that about?" Cuda asked.

"No idea," said Nirea. "But let's not waste the moment. Jazere?"

The nature *draoidh* nodded and her branches wrapped under Leondar, lifting him gently off the ground. Quickly, they moved him to the Reivers' room and settled him on the bed that had been Teyjan's.

"What should we do?" Nirea asked nervously. She had no idea how to help Leondar. She'd never seen such a wound on a living man.

"First, we make sure he can breathe," said Teyjan, poking his fingers into Leondar's throat. "Then I need bandages. Lots of bandages. Cuda?"

"Aye." The elder woman stalked into the hallway.

"Will he be all right?" Nirea asked, and immediately regretted it. She knew the likely answer. She didn't want to hear it.

"His best hope is your miracle girl. Can you get her?" Teyjan asked.

*Samily.*

"No. She's gone."

The Reiver turned to her with a look of surprise and sorrow. "Oh. I'll do what I can to make him comfortable."

*Comfortable.* That wasn't good.

A tap on her shoulder. Nirea turned to see Jazere gesturing at her.

"I'm sorry; I don't understand," Nirea said.

The *draoidh* tapped Teyjan and repeated the gestures. "She's asking where the demons went," he explained.

Good question. She had no idea. But wherever it was, somebody else was in trouble for the moment. "I don't know. Can you use that bush to seal the hole?"

Jazere nodded and followed Cuda out the door.

For now, for whatever reason, they had a moment of respite. *Why*, she'd have to learn later.

"Thorns! On me!" Meristan's raised fist called the knights to formation. "Circle up! We move together. Keep these people surrounded!"

They'd fought their way into the town centre after Rasa had got the gate open for them and collected strays as they worked their way in, picking up people caught out in the street, or maybe forced out, fleeing the Thakhati. The demons had numbers, but they were no match for more than twenty White Thorns fighting together. Green blades cut them down like butter. Thank God they'd been close and Rasa had found their camp. Otherwise they'd have slept the night in the Black Meadows and discovered Traverlyn a ruin in the morning.

These damned monsters. If Meristan had his way, they'd be exterminated tonight. And Anhel Weyr would pay for the lost.

Here they stood, in the street outside the Sheep's Heid, where he'd been drinking with Darginn Argyll a few weeks ago. Not somewhere he'd expected to be in pitched battle with his fellow Thorns. But war makes the familiar strange.

It had been a while since they'd seen the demons. Several had come at them alone, but others became wary when they were cut down with ease. One of them had reared up and shrieked some ungodly call, which had become a hideous chorus before they all disappeared.

Where had they gone? Why had they gone? That was the worry.

"Bruh...Meristan. Where next?" Tull had been finding it difficult to stop calling him Brother since Asha brought him back to Baile Airneach. He'd not been there to see Meristan prove his skill with Brontas and had had to take the word of his friends. Which he'd done, but still. Tonight he'd seen Meristan in full-blooded battle—they all had. Any doubts would be gone now. And everything would be clear once they found Aranok and had their memories restored. But it was a valid question. They had innocents to protect, but they needed to hunt the rest of the Thakhati, lest they kill more people.

The hospital. That was likely the safest place to leave the souls they'd collected. That's where the king and queen would be embedded, he hoped. If they'd been sensible enough to stay inside. Most defensible building in the town, probably, being primarily stone.

"We'll move these people to the hospital. That way." Meristan pointed into the night, but when he looked up, something caught his attention.

Movement, on the edge of his sight. On a roof. A Thakhati, crawling, sneaking? Trying to catch them off guard? Wait. More than one.

Two. More.

"Look up! The roofs!" Every roof in the square was crawling with them. They hadn't run. They hadn't gone.

They had regrouped.

---

Tia screamed. She didn't mean to; it just came out. The monsters were everywhere. Pouring off the roofs on both sides of the street. The noise! The noise was so loud. The nice lady who'd taken her hand pulled her closer and whispered, "Close your eyes."

But she couldn't. It would be worse if Tia couldn't see. Her arms shook and tears streamed down her face. How could they get away now? They were surrounded; the monsters were everywhere.

But the knights weren't scared.

In their shiny white armour, they fought back the monsters. It was like watching moths fly into flames, as the monsters poured forward and the knights cut them down, again and again and again. And suddenly, Tia wasn't scared. Because not one—not one!—of the knights was hurt. If one had too many monsters to fight, another one moved to help. It was like they could all talk to each other with their minds, like Tia had always wished she could do.

And Meristan, the one who had saved her, even with his helmet back on she knew which one was him. He killed the most, she thought, cutting them down over and over. He was like a marble statue that wouldn't be moved, chopping them down like wood. The longer Tia watched, the better she felt.

Because now the monsters were scared.

"Look," she whispered to the lady, who *had* closed her eyes. "Look, it's all right."

She did and Tia watched as her whimpers slowly became a smile, and then laughter. Which felt a bit weird, but then Tia was smiling too, and a giggle came from her chest.

The knights were going to win. They were going to save them. They had come, with their magic swords and their beautiful armour, to kill the monsters. And more people started laughing. The man with the shaved head and the boy with the broken arm. They all laughed, and it was odd, but it felt so good. Like a feeling she never thought she'd have again. Joy.

It seemed like an age, but it also felt like it flew by, because Tia felt truly safe for the first time since dinner. They were surrounded by monsters, but it didn't matter. Because they were safe. The good people had come to save them from the monsters, just like Daddy had said they would.

And then she remembered Daddy, and stopped laughing.

---

Nirea staggered back down the steps, dragging the hammer behind her. Leondar's face. God in Hell. How could a man live through that? If not for Jazere, she'd be lying beside him on the floor of the hall, or inside a Thakhati cocoon. But she wasn't. So she had a job to do.

Jazere had used the potted bush to block the hole in the ceiling. It was nothing like a permanent fix, but she'd agreed to keep an eye on it, allowing Nirea to get back to the main door.

As she descended from the second floor, a roar came from below. Her exhausted legs found new life and she sprinted the rest of the way.

When she finally reached the bottom, a moment of panic. Mynygogg and Vastin were both missing. The doors were unguarded, and then—horror—she saw that the doors to the lecture hall were laid wide.

But wait. The noise. It wasn't fear. Nor battle. It was…celebration? She almost dropped the hammer as she turned to find the hall full of happiness. Of elation and joy.

What the Hell had she missed?

After a moment, she spotted her husband, mingling with the folk of Traverlyn. Hugging strangers and shaking hands, with a reassuring touch on a shoulder.

Vastin came bounding toward her like a puppy, no longer even carrying the sword Leondar had left him.

"What the fuck is happening?" she asked.

The boy grinned like it was his birth day. "The Thorns. The White Thorns are here! In Traverlyn."

Every hair on Nirea's body stood on end as a rush of confusion and relief washed through her. Now it made sense. The smiles, the celebration. Nirea's legs crumpled and she plonked down on the top step that led down into the room.

*My God.*

They were going to live.

Only then did Nirea face the terror that had been pulling at her soul all night. That she wasn't going to see the dawn. That tonight was the last night of her life. And she'd reconciled with that, apparently. The spectre of death was something pirates learned to live with, but it had been some time since she woke up knowing there was a decent chance she'd be dead by dusk. Tonight—tonight, she'd been certain of it, somewhere deep inside. And now she was not. Now, suddenly, that certainty was lifted, and she had a future again.

And she buried her face in her hands and wept huge, grateful tears.

---

"Hey. Wake up."

Aranok blinked his eyes open and immediately lifted a hand to shade them from the light. His head pounded in response, warning him not to move. Where was he?

"You all right?" Allandria's voice. A weird sense of familiarity and wrongness. Why would he...? Oh God. He shouldn't have been asleep! The Thakhati!

Aranok bolted upright, ignoring his throbbing head. "What happened? What's the...?" Allandria put a finger to his lips.

"Shh. Just look." She pointed to the open window. Aranok's mouth dropped open and he stumbled across the room. Outside, the sun rose above distant trees, bathing the rooftops of Traverlyn in light through the fine, lingering rain.

They had made it.

But smoke still billowed from the remnants of buildings gutted by fire. Hell, the library. What had they managed to save? Keft! Fuck, Keft. The principal's body was abandoned out there, in the carnage. How many others had they lost?

He turned back to Allandria. Her left arm was strapped to her chest, her hand tucked just below her throat. She followed his eyes and answered the unspoken question. "It's broken. It'll heal. With time. We were lucky, I suppose, in the end."

*Lucky*. It didn't feel lucky. His head was pounding like the inside of a drum. Aranok sat back on the edge of the bed. "What happened?"

His memory was patchy. He remembered stumbling back to the hospital. His head had been spinning after that Thakhati had dropped from above and all but landed on him. Had they seen Leondar? And Nirea, maybe? Yes, that was familiar. But then... noise, and people and medics and...

"You passed out," Allandria explained. "That hit to your head—Egretta was worried. Said it could be bad. She was worried you might just stop breathing. In your sleep."

"So you stayed to watch me?"

Allandria smiled. Of course she did. He'd have done the same. Aranok put a hand to her face and it tingled against her skin. They were going to live. "Thank you."

But the war wasn't over.

"We need to go—to see what the damage is—I need to start the sunspire again." Thakhati would come again that night, if Traverlyn was dark.

Allandria put a hand on his arm, preventing him from moving. "Meristan brought the Thorns. Most of the Thakhati are dead."

"What? How?" Meristan had left weeks ago. The chances of the Thorns just showing up in the middle of the night, then, when they needed them were... miraculously small.

"Rasa was returning from Mournside. Flew over the Thorn camp on the way—they were only a few miles south. When she got here and saw the Thakhati inside the walls, she flew back. Roused the Thorns and got them back here, found a nature *draoidh* to open the gate and..."

Rasa. Rasa had saved Traverlyn. Aranok had a vague memory the metamorph had said she was going to Mournside, to protect his family.

Had he dreamed that? It was hard to say. It felt real but also not. Hmm. She must have gone but come back. Thank fuck she had, or a lot more people would be dead.

"Incredible." Aranok slumped back on the pillow. Gently. His head still throbbed and now he was conscious of the bandages wrapping it. "Still, I should move. We need the sunspire, even if most of them are dead."

"All right, yes, we'll do that, but first, budge up." Allandria nudged his leg. Aranok sidled over to make some room and she carefully lay beside him, protecting her broken arm. "I thought we might die last night. And I thought you might die on this bed. So can we just lie here for a bit and appreciate not being dead, please?"

She was right. They could take a moment. And now that they had it, there was something else he needed to say. "Al. I heard you. What you said? I heard it."

"All right." Her voice was suddenly tense. He was being awkward. *Fuck, man, just say it.*

"I love you. Too. I mean, just, I love you. Really. I missed you. I need you. You're—"

She leaned in and kissed him delicately, then firmly, as if they'd never done it before. In a way, they hadn't. Before, Jan had chosen for them. This time, they were choosing for themselves. And if he'd learned anything from the last weeks, it was that this was right.

"Ow, fuck!" Allandria rolled away, cradling her left arm. For some reason, that was hilarious and he laughed. A scowl and a raised eyebrow, and then she laughed with him.

And that was perfect.

# CHAPTER 8

Darginn hurried across the wet cobbles, a steadying hand against the edge of the cart Yavick pushed. The earthy smell of the damp town was drowned in ash and blood. Fires had gone out, but smoke still rose over roofs. It was an uncomfortable mix of relief and despair. So many had died, though Darginn's family had lived. But the guard they'd brought in—he was bad. As soon as it was light, he and Yavick had gone looking for a barrow—anything to get the boy to the hospital. Few words had passed between them since they got him on the cart. Mostly just Darginn giving directions. "This way." "Up here."

Because the thing they couldn't discuss, that they couldn't broach, was that Ismar was still missing. And for all they could hope for him to have had the sense to stay wherever he was, they had no earthly idea where to look for him. The boy was an adult. Had he moved on to another town, another country, as he might yet, Darginn wouldn't know for months, maybe years, what he was up to. It was the fact that he was used to him living so close, to seeing him every day, that made it difficult.

Isadona lived with that fear, he supposed. When Darginn was on the road, his wife simply had to trust he would come home. But that was different, he reckoned. Knowing your man has a job that comes with some risk, especially during a war, was a hardship, but not like knowing your child is in danger. Not that hollow nausea in your bowels that pulls you screaming into a dark hole, imagining all that's been done to him, and you not there to help.

Folk aren't meant to lose children. It's not right. It's not the way nature intends, surely. Not the way God intends. How could it be?

For all Darginn had survived, for all he'd endured, to lose his only son...

He should have been closer to the boy. Made more effort. Discovered what he was up to when he disappeared into the evenings. But he was so private. Sullen. If anything, Darginn had been irritated by his constant gloom. Worried about how it might seep into the rest of them—to Liana. She was so much easier to affect. Getting a smile from that girl was a matter of making a daft face or tickling her. Kids were easier at that age. More work, aye, but easier. A wee cuddle would comfort them. Their tragedies were small and passing. But as they got older, the hardships became real and the wounds deeper. And Ismar had never been a talker. Not really. All Darginn's wishing he could get the boy to talk to him, so he could understand, so he could help... He'd wrap the boy in his arms and hold him while he cried if that was what was needed, but it had never been that simple with him—not for a long time.

And now the thought that he could have missed his chance to fix it, to make things right with him—the terror of that was almost crippling. So he focused on what he could. Isadona, Jena, Liana and Yavick were safe. Maybe he could help keep this poor boy alive too.

"There it is," Yavick grunted, nodding ahead. The steps of the great red building rose before them, and they were packed. People coming and going. Medics fussing over folk sitting on the steps—some of them not even managing to sit. So many wounded. More dead, he feared. It was like the war all over again. People with limbs missing, drenched in their own blood—in the blood of others. As they got closer, he could smell it too. The mix of smoke and the coppery tang of blood in the air. Same as always, after a battle.

A barrage of caws from above pulled Darginn's gaze up to the roof. Crows, perching above. Watching. Waiting. More birds circled the town. There was plenty of food for them already.

As they got closer, Darginn spotted a familiar face, and it brought an unexpected smile. There, amongst the medics and the wounded, helping a man to his feet was King Mynygogg. It was good to see him alive, and to see him being the man Darginn thought him.

"What have you got?" A fair-haired young man in a medic's tunic came toward them, eyeing the cart. Yavick stopped pushing and tilted it gently to the ground, and the medic came round to see the guard.

He was a mess. They'd stopped the bleeding, but the boy was pale as virgin snow and still as the grave.

"We did what we could." Darginn gestured to the blackened stump they'd cauterised, feeling a sudden need to apologise. The medic didn't even look at him, just clambered onto the cart and put his fingers to the boy's throat. After a long moment, he breathed in and sighed.

"He's alive. Let's get him inside." He waved a hand and two large men arrived carrying a cot between them. Yavick and Darginn stepped back and gave them room to work.

"Darginn! You're alive."

Darginn turned to see the queen smiling broadly. "I am, Majesty. Thank God."

She clasped his hand and put the other on his shoulder. "I'm glad to see it. Your family?" She looked up at Yavick, smiled and nodded. He nodded back. Mad how the queen of Eidyn knew his entire family now.

"Well, mostly good, aye," he answered. "But..."

"But what?" She seemed genuinely concerned.

"It's just...Ismar hasnae come back yet. He was out last night and..."

"Do you know where he was?"

Darginn shook his head. It was hard to admit. Especially to the queen, for some reason.

Nirea turned to look at the human chaos around her. "All right. I'll keep an eye out for him here. Best thing you can do is go home, Darginn. The Thorns are still patrolling, finishing the Thakhati and hunting cocoons. No point you wandering the streets, putting yourself in danger. He'll come home, or he'll come here, I'm sure. If it's here, I'll send a runner for you."

"Thank you, Majesty." Darginn gave a wee bow of appreciation and respect. It was damn kind of the monarch to be looking out for Ismar.

And he knew she would too. They'd been companions for days on the trek from Haven. Maybe didn't speak that much, but still. Obviously meant something to her, and that meant something to Darginn.

They'd delivered the boy to the hospital. Done what they could to keep him alive. He was someone's son too. Maybe a stranger had done something for *his* son. Kept him safe. Protected him when Darginn couldn't.

He had to hope.

---

Aranok grasped the banister as his head spun.

"Whoa. You all right?" Allandria's hand on his elbow. The steps lurched up at him and he almost keeled over backwards compensating.

"Apparently not, no. Give me a minute." Between them, they lowered him to sitting on the top step. Chaos fluttered around them. Medics running to tend a patient, get supplies, deliver patients to rooms... The hospital had never been this busy. They'd already seen a few people Aranok suspected would do well to survive the day. And them blocking the top of this set of stairs wasn't helping anyone.

"Laird Envoy? You all right? Do you need help?"

Aranok turned to see a medic whose face was familiar. A kindly, dark-skinned young woman with pale eyes and strong cheekbones over her dimples. "I'll be fine. Just dizzy."

"How dizzy?" the woman asked.

"It comes and goes," Allandria answered for him. "Worse when he moves around."

The medic's mouth crumpled. "You should be in bed. Can we get you back to your room? I can look for a wheeled chair..." She was already casting her eyes down the hallway.

"No, thank you. It's already clearing," Aranok lied. His eyes felt like someone was trying to pop them out of his skull, his neck seemed to be permanently seized in a cramp and his head felt stuffed with feathers. But he had a job to do.

"Hmm." The medic looked at him a long minute, making it quite clear his deception was evident. Allandria rolled her eyes, as if to offer some solidarity with her predicament. "All right, at least wait there a moment, please?"

Aranok agreed and she scurried away.

"You *should* be in bed," Allandria teased.

"You've got underlying motives." He grinned and she slapped his leg.

"Not until this is healed, I don't." Allandria nodded to her broken arm. "But after that...yes, I do."

That was a nice thought.

"But listen..." Allandria put a firm hand on his thigh. "There's something I need to say to you, while we're sitting here doing nothing. And I know I've sort of said it before, but..." She sighed. "I need you to hear it from me now and know that I mean it."

Where was this going? Allandria took his left hand in her right and shifted slightly to turn toward him and look him in the eye. He was just about focusing solidly again when she continued.

"You don't have to do this. I know you think you do, but you don't."

"What, the sunspire?" Even if the Thorns had been able to clear the town, there would be more Thakhati. They still needed the sunspire. And he'd at least want to speak to Meristan to find out what their plans were. If they were leaving some Thorns here, that was one thing, but he was pretty sure Mynygogg would have plans for the knights.

"No. Well, yes, but no. All of it. Any of it." A medic bustled past and Allandria lowered her voice. "We can just go. Get out. We stay here until we recover and then...we leave. This doesn't have to be your fight. It's not your responsibility. It never was."

That wasn't what he was expecting. And he didn't really remember her saying that before. But it felt sort of familiar. Either way... "It is, though. I'm the only one who can light the sunspire. If I'd done it before, Girette would still be alive. That *is* my responsibility." He hadn't really dealt with that, and the image of the girl's cold corpse, dumped on the floor of her dorm room like discarded meat, came back to him with a wave of sadness.

"No, that's what I mean." Her voice was firm. "It is *not*. You chose to do this. You and Mynygogg. And I feel like...I don't know, this might not be right, but...I get the impression maybe you're doing this out of obligation...to *him*? Like, you said you would do it and now you're still doing it because you said you would. And I suppose what I'm saying is that...you don't have to. You can choose differently. And it would be fine. Aranok, you have every right to just...walk away. Live your life."

A pounding in his chest and Aranok was reminded of the "panic" he'd had before. He gripped Allandria's hand a little tighter and breathed slowly. She said nothing, waiting for his reply. Another medic came scurrying toward them. As Aranok was about to answer, he realised it was the same one who'd asked him to wait.

"Here, Laird. I can't spare you a wheeled chair, but this should be of use. Help keep you on your feet." She handed him a solid wooden cane with a curved handle.

It was not what he'd been expecting her to come back with, but after a moment of instant rejection, he realised it would probably be a good idea and took it with good grace. "Thank you, that's very kind. Don't let us keep you; we're fine."

The medic looked at Allandria, who smiled and nodded. Seemingly satisfied she'd done what she could, the woman descended the stairs and, without looking back, said, "You really should go back to bed."

Yes, he probably should. But he wasn't going to. He turned back to Allandria and opened his mouth to answer, but nothing came out, so he closed it again. What could he say? Was she right? Could they just leave? Could *he* really leave? It felt like being told he could just *decide* to fly. Utterly ridiculous.

Allandria finally spoke instead. "It's all right; you don't have to say anything. I'm not asking you to do anything. I just need you to know you have a choice. What you do—what we do next. You can choose. It doesn't have to be the same as it's been. And even if you know that, here"—she touched two fingers gently to his head, just below the line of the bandages—"it matters more that you know it *here*." She moved the hand down and placed her open palm over his heart.

Aranok swallowed hard. She would feel his heart pounding. But... that was all right. It was Allandria. He didn't have to hide anything from her. He'd confessed his deepest shame to her, and she was still here. That was both terrifying and glorious. "Thank you" was all he said in the end. They sat in silence there, for a moment, Aranok not knowing how to move on. Thankfully, Allandria did it for him.

"There was another thing I wanted to ask."

"Oh?"

"That Thakhati you killed, the one where... it looked like you sort of... tore it apart. What was...? How did you do that?"

Fuck, he'd forgotten that entirely. But she was right. When she'd been trapped, he'd just... acted. Had he even said *gluais*? Made a gesture? Maybe. God, so much of the night was a blur and his brain was thumping silently against his skull. What *had* he done? After his loss of control with Samily, the thought that he'd done it again, even though it ended well... Instinct whispered to him, telling to make something up. Tell her it was *gluais* and he knew what he was doing, but... no. No, he wasn't doing that with her now. Not anymore. Allandria was his haven, and he was going to treat that with the respect it deserved.

"I don't know. I just needed to protect you. I'm not sure how I did it. It might have been *gluais*, but... I just did it." He shrugged.

Allandria took a deep breath, meeting his eyes. They both knew what that meant. What it might mean. "All right." She put a hand on his knee and gently squeezed.

Aranok looked down the stairs and realised his head had stopped spinning. "We should go. I do want to get this thing started. And then we can go back to bed...?"

Allandria smiled. "Deal."

Two flights of carefully navigated stairs later, they arrived at the hub of the chaos. The front entrance hall was mobbed with injured being helped or carried into the lecture hall. Where last night people had huddled for safety, now the injured who hadn't made it inside were assessed and treated. The chorus of voices, the clatter of medical instruments, the moans of pain: a discordant symphony. There amidst the chaos was Mynygogg, holding an elderly woman's hand as she shuffled toward a seat. Nirea too was there, on the doorstep, squatting in front of a man who sat with an arm wrapped across his gut.

"Aranok! Allandria!" A familiar voice, and it brought an instant smile. Vastin came toward them, grinning widely. It seemed as though he would barrel straight into them, but he checked himself as he got closer, noting Allandria's arm and the cane Aranok was now leaning on. "How are you both? I was worried after..."

"We'll live," said Allandria. "With thanks to you." Aranok didn't understand why that was the case, and it must have registered on his face. "Vastin was the one in the armour, last night. With Nirea and Leondar. They got us in the door."

"Oh?" In honesty, Aranok sort of remembered Nirea, but that was about it. He'd been busy staying upright and using the little energy he could muster to throw the demons out of their path. But Vastin had been out there with them, fighting the Thakhati? "Good lad. I guess we're even now. Thank you." He put his left hand on the boy's shoulder and had to lean hard on the cane in his right. God damn, but *everything* hurt. Maybe they could scavenge some poppy milk when they got back.

"You don't remember?" Vastin asked. Aranok grimaced and pointed to the bandages.

"His brain's broken," said Allandria. "Again." She turned to him. "Happens a lot."

Aranok shrugged. "Occupational hazard."

"Aranok, Allandria, how are you?" Same question, different voice. The king had noticed them and made his way over. Aranok noticed Nirea turn her head too, then go back to the man she was engaged with.

"Been better," Aranok answered. "Been a lot worse." Quite recently too.

"Mmm. Good to see you on your feet," said Gogg. "We have a lot to talk about. But listen: I saw Opiassa earlier. She brought in one of her students."

"Oh? One of the physic *draoidhs*?" Aranok hadn't seen much of them through the night. But they had probably been the most effective against the Thakhati with their massive war hammers.

"Aye. Seems he got overwhelmed at one point. Lucky for him, Opiassa was close. Pulled him out. But...well, he's not good."

Allandria sucked air through her teeth. *Not good*. A lot of people weren't good today. Many were past help. Aranok nodded in understanding.

"Anyway, Aranok," Mynygogg carried on, "what you did last night. The thing with the sunstone—brilliant. Considering everything... You wiped out enough of them to give us a chance. I just wanted to say...thank you."

Aranok noticed Vastin was grinning from ear to ear, and it was hard not to smile with him. "Well, that's what we're on the way to do." He gestured to Allandria. "Set up the sunspire, for tonight."

Mynygogg's face changed. "Are you fit for that?"

"I said the same thing," Allandria added.

Aranok shrugged. "Best of my knowledge, the oldest earth *draoidh* left in the university is about eleven."

"Right." Mynygogg's voice was tired, resigned. "Yes, we can't do that. I understand."

No way he was allowing another child, even younger than Girette, to become a target for the assassin. Assuming they were still in town. It was entirely feasible they'd set this whole thing off and then run for it, making sure they were out of town before the Thakhati came. But he couldn't assume that. They had to stay in pairs until they knew it was safe.

"All right. Just be careful," said the king. "That's a lot of stairs, I hear."

"I'll follow him up, catch him if he falls," Allandria said with a grin.

Mynygogg smiled and nodded. "Good luck with that. But seriously, when you're done, when this"—he gestured to the morass around them—"is done, we need to meet. All of us. To plan." He pointed vaguely at the ceiling. "I think there are people being treated in the meeting room. We'll need somewhere else. Maybe outside. I don't know. But if you see Meristan, or any of the Thorns…"

"We'll tell him," Allandria said.

That was a point. The Thorns would need their memories cleared too. And once that was done, God, what an asset they would have. The best army imaginable. Maybe they had a chance of doing this after all.

"D'you want me to come with you? Just in case, I dunno, I can help?" Vastin looked eagerly up at them.

Aranok instinctively went to say no, then realised it might be nice to have the boy's company. He was a ray of light in the gloom. And for whatever reason, he seemed especially chirpy this morning. But then Aranok remembered the assassin, and his mood soured. Surely it was only a tiny chance, but Allandria was the sole person he was currently absolutely certain was not the illusionist.

"Depends," he began carefully. "Can you remind me why your shields are so strong?"

Vastin crinkled his eyebrows and gave Mynygogg a sideways look. "What?" Assuming it was the boy, it was a mad question to ask in the moment, but it was something he was confident the assassin would have no idea about.

"Answer it," Mynygogg said reassuringly.

The boy looked utterly befuddled. "Well, it's the folding. Dad learned it out East. Lots of folds of very thin metal, then you—"

"That'll do." Aranok stopped him. That was enough information to convince him, and he wasn't all that interested in a lesson in forging. Aranok looked to Mynygogg. "We need some sort of password."

"Agreed. For now, we'll use *Dancer*. We can sort something better this afternoon," said the king.

Vastin watched them as if they spoke Gaullic. Allandria ruffled his hair with her good hand. "Come on. I'll explain while we walk."

# CHAPTER 9

"*Sùgh.*" Aranok's vision took a little spin as the spell began to work, and he was glad to be leaning against the great gold dome atop Traverlyn Kirk. The climb up the steps had been challenging. He was awkward using the cane, exhausted by the steps, and his bloody knee had started aching too—a burn up both sides that bit with every step. His entire body seemed to be in revolt of late, and he very much wanted to go and lie down for the rest of the day.

Sadly, that wasn't on the cards—at least not yet. First up, they had to climb back down, and from experience, that was only going to make his knee complain more.

"All right?" Allandria asked. Trust her to notice his wobble. He wasn't going to get away with hiding infirmities from her. But the thought of her attentiveness brought a genuine smile. It was so much better having her back. And whatever this new thing was between them, wherever it went, it was good.

"I will be. Just need a minute."

She frowned sympathetically. "Then we'll take a minute."

"This view is...wow." Vastin leaned on the iron railing that ringed the walkway around the dome. It was designed to allow for cleaning and repairs, not for sightseeing. But Aranok could easily imagine the priest coming up here on a bright day to look out over the town. Surveying his subjects. Communing with his god. The view was usually less depressing, though. In the university campus, amongst the elegant, tall stone buildings, the library still billowed smoke into the late morning sky. Houses were shattered, with roofs caved in or torn open. The horror these people must have felt, with demons tearing their way into their homes.

Why had Anhel done this? Why now? What purpose did it serve? He'd largely left Traverlyn alone during the war. Aranok had presumed that was because of the *draoidh* population, but maybe there was another reason. He'd been refused by the university, so he had no love for the institution or its masters. Perhaps the only reason Traverlyn had really been spared was...Shayella. He could see her refusing to attack the town for all the reasons Aranok had previously assumed. So it was entirely possible Traverlyn had only been safe while Shayella was alive.

Of course, that meant his spy was keeping an extremely close eye on things. They may also have known Samily had gone—and Dialla. And that Aranok was *indisposed*. Strategically, they were unlikely to get much weaker than last night, and without Shayella to object... Yes, that made sense. Anhel wasn't in this for the *draoidhs*; Anhel was in it for Anhel. He would use whoever he needed to get what he wanted.

Power. Privilege. Wealth. All of it. He'd crowned himself king before Jan's body was cold. Murdered the lairds before they could consider appointing someone else. The more Aranok thought about it, it actually made a great deal of sense. *Fucker.*

The thought that Samily killing Shay, putting him in a bed and leaving with Dialla had all directly led to the Thakhati attack—to Girette's murder, and Keft's, and...His heart began to race, and he thought better of going down that hole. There was nothing but a pit at the bottom, and he didn't have time for wallowing. Things still had to be done. And if anything, he needed to look for positives. Choose to see the sun.

"It's such a beautiful town, isn't it?" Allandria leaned on the rail next to Vastin.

The roof of the kirk was spattered with bird droppings and discarded feathers. But there were no birds. Scared away by the Thakhati, he assumed. Or maybe warned away by the nature *draoidhs*? Some could communicate with them. The most skilled.

How many had died last night? He tried not to look too closely at the streets. Not to see the bodies, or the blood. God, he needed to talk. Get his mind on something else.

"Vastin, what was the name of the girl? From the Chain Pier? Your friend."

"Amollari?" he answered.

"Yes, Amollari."

"What about her?"

"That's our password. Between us three. We need to verify who we are, *Amollari* is the word." It was a solid choice. A name that wouldn't mean much to anyone else, and certainly not something an assassin could just guess.

"Don't we need two?" Allandria asked. "Or even one each?"

"Do we?" said Aranok.

"Well, imagine we come together—we've all been somewhere else. Don't we each need a password to prove it's us? If we only have one, once somebody says it, the others know it."

That was a good point. Each of them needed to prove their identity.

Aranok looked around. "Bird shit."

Allandria's eyebrow went up. "Seriously?"

"Who's going to guess that?" He looked at her as innocently as he could manage without breaking into a grin.

She sighed. "You're ridiculous."

"What's your word, then, master spy?"

Allandria pursed her lips. "Purple."

"Purple?" Vastin asked, smiling.

"Purple," she repeated confidently. "I like purple."

"Right, then. *Amollari, purple, bird shit*," said Aranok, pointing to each of them in turn.

*Laughter.*

A glorious sound. Aranok felt a little lighter for it and his shoulders dropped an inch. Allandria turned and walked toward the stairs.

"Are we going, then?" Aranok asked.

"Not necessarily." Allandria turned back to them as she opened the door to the stairs. "But I should probably make sure nobody was listening to that conversation, eh?"

---

"Carefully. *Carefully.*" Meristan held his blade levelled at the cocoon as Greste carved a gash in the side with her own.

"I know," she answered calmly. More calm than Meristan felt. He was tired. They all were. And this cocoon might contain another Thakhati, or it might be a victim they could save. They wouldn't know until they cut it open.

The house was small. Just a simple living room with a kitchen off it, and stairs leading up to a bedroom. Looked like only one person lived here. An artist, by the work dotted about the walls, floor and on what probably should have been a dining table. Nothing recognisable, more colours and shapes, like reminiscing in dreams. Passion and pain applied directly to canvas. Beautiful. Many of them destroyed now, though. When the Thakhati had got in. Thatched roofs had been a real weakness, it seemed. Perhaps it was time to replace them with something sturdier. Less flammable too.

Greste worked her Green blade along. As it passed halfway, the slit opened with a wet rip and a body slopped out. Meristan dropped his own blade and lurched forward to catch it.

Definitely still human. Clothes mostly intact. She hadn't been in very long.

*Maybe... maybe...*

"Put her down!" Greste ordered. He did, and felt her throat for a heartbeat. Greste threw off her gloves and used two fingers to fish the stinking ooze out of the woman's mouth, then turned her on her side and thumped her on the back. "Come on..."

Again, she hit her. Again. The fourth time, the woman made a hideous retching noise, half coughed and then vomited up more of the slime and convulsed into a coughing fit.

"All right, all right, get it all out," Greste soothed her, supporting the woman's head.

Meristan felt a wave of joy rinse through him. They'd saved another.

Thank God.

He collapsed onto his backside with a grin that felt inappropriate. But every life they saved felt like a victory.

"Fetch some water," said Greste, using a paint-spattered cloth to wipe the woman's face clear.

Meristan pulled himself to his feet and stepped out into the sunlight. The warmth on his head was soothing, surety that the dark was gone, for now. When he had time, he should get up to the hospital. See how his friends were. They would be fine, he was certain. All capable of looking after themselves. Especially Samily. He hadn't seen her, but she may not even have made it back from tracking that memory *draoidh* yet. Half of him hoped she'd been here, to help. Would *be* here, to heal. The other half hoped she'd been far away, after seeing the way the Thakhati had organised to attack the Thorns during the night. If she'd been the only one here...

No. No point fretting.

*Clear your mind, trust in God and... do your job, Meristan!*

He was on his way back from the well with a bucket of fresh water when another Thorn rushed toward him. His heart skipped a moment, thinking it might be Samily, but a proper look showed it clearly was not.

"Meristan!" Tull raised a hand as he trotted toward him.

Meristan stopped and let the boy catch up to him. "What is it? All well?"

"Aye, all well. I have a message."

"For me?"

"I saw Laird Aranok and Lady Allandria. They asked me to find you, to tell you—"

"Aranok and Allandria are well?" The words were out before he intended them.

It took Tull a moment to rethread his thoughts. "Well, yes and no. Injured, but alive. Laird Aranok walks with a cane and Lady Allandria's arm looked broken."

*Well.* Alive was good. The rest could be mended. "And what news?"

"Yes, that's what... They asked me to summon you to a meeting with the king. As soon as you are available." He leaned in close then. "And the queen." A wink.

Ah. So Aranok had taken the time to clear Tull's memory before sending him back. Useful. And helpful of him.

Meristan grinned again. "Welcome back, Tull. It's good to have you with me."

The knight smiled. "I'm still wrapping my head around it, if I'm honest."

Meristan clapped him on the shoulder. "Give it a day. You'll be fine." Presumably the boy would not have had a great deal changed, beyond his memories of Mynygogg and Meristan. He should settle fairly easily. "Did you happen to ask...?"

"Samily is not here. She left the day before yesterday, I'm told."

Left? So she'd been there and gone again? He had missed her by two days. Shame. Well, he'd hear the story of it soon enough. "Where am I to go?"

"Laird Aranok said just to go to the hospital. He seemed unsure where they'd actually meet, but that you would find them there."

Right. So Aranok, Allandria, Mynygogg, Nirea and Samily had all survived the night, thank God. Fine, he would make his way to the hospital. The Thorns were spread through the town, clearing up lingering Thakhati and opening any cocoons they could find inside. They could manage that without him for an hour. Meristan held the bucket out to Tull. "Here, take this to Greste. She's in that house, there. Tell her I've been summoned by the king, and I'll find you again later. Actually, no, scratch that: Tell everyone to make their way to the hospital when they need food and rest. We must be wary in case they come again tonight."

Tull nodded and took the bucket. "Aye, sir." He turned to walk toward the house, got halfway and stopped. "Oh, there was another message. There was a boy with them."

"With Aranok and Allandria?"

"Yes. Said to give you his best, and he looked forward to seeing you again."

A boy?

"What was his name?"

"Vastin, he said."

Meristan's grin widened.

"There's no much we can do for these ones. Just...make them comfortable." Egretta's face was grey and drawn. Her nails were bitten to the quick and the ragged skin around them an angry pink. In an upper hall—a secondary lecture hall that seemed to have been primarily used for storing chairs and other surplus furniture—Egretta had set up a palliative room. For those not expected to survive their wounds. "We've had to triage—focus on those who've a chance of...I'm sorry."

Nirea stood beside Leondar's bed.

She was going to lose another man who'd put himself between her and danger. Another good man.

They'd cauterised his wounded face. God alone knew how the man was still breathing. But he was. He wasn't giving up without a fight.

A medic fussed about a woman who'd moaned relentlessly since Nirea came in. Half her gut was wrapped in blood-soaked bandages and her eyes wandered the room, searching blindly for relief. Nirea had seen that before. Usually in sailors whose wounds were rotting. Not much you could do for them then. This woman couldn't be that far gone already, but between the pain and the poppy she was probably on...And they were having to ration that. Stocks of opium were not prepared for the mass influx they'd had overnight. Not remotely. But this woman...Surely the only thing was to give her enough to knock her out?

There were at least fifty patients in the space. Maybe more. Some on beds, others on makeshift cots and the least fortunate on mattresses placed directly on the floor. And they were all going to die here. Unless she did something.

"We need Samily. We need her back. I...Can you just...keep them alive...until I can get her?" She could do that. She could send Rasa... Shite, no, Rasa was injured. A messenger, then. A soldier. Anyone! Fuck, maybe she should just go herself. If she rode hard, she could catch them by, what, tomorrow? The next day at most. They'd be moving slowly. Helping the Cured. Yes, she could do that. She needed to go to the meeting Mynygogg had called, but after that...Yes. She would go herself. Too many were going to die without Samily.

Egretta looked back at her with a mix of pity and exhaustion. "I'll do my best. Can't promise."

Nirea's head turned at the sound of a faint sob. Six patients over, a wee girl knelt, head bowed so that her hair hid her face. She held the hand of a woman—her mother, Nirea supposed. It looked like she'd been badly burned. Her entire head was wrapped in bandages and angry red welts showed through singed holes in her ravaged dress. Poor child. Not the only orphan after today. She shouldn't be alone here, watching her mother slowly expire. Not like that.

Nirea put a sympathetic hand on Egretta's arm and turned away. She hoped it said all that she intended. When she reached the girl, Nirea squatted down to her level.

"Hi."

The girl turned her head and pink eyes peered from behind her lank hair. She said nothing.

"Your mum?"

Her head shook gently.

"Sister?"

Another no. "She's my friend." Her voice was tiny and broken.

Well, maybe not orphaned, then. "Do you know where your parents are?"

The girl's mouth crumpled and Nirea instantly regretted asking the question. Already an orphan. Probably saw her parents killed.

*Hell.* What to say now?

"What's your name, sweetheart?"

"Tia."

"Tia, are you hurt anywhere? Has a medic looked at you?" Any excuse to get her out of that room.

Another shake of the head.

"No, you're not hurt, or...?"

Tia pointed to the woman. "She saved me. From the monster." Her voice became even smaller then, barely a whisper: "It killed Daddy."

*Fuck.* Just what she'd feared. "Well, then your friend is a hero."

Tia nodded and more tears came. There would be dozens more similar stories. Folk giving their lives to protect loved ones. Every person in that room, doomed to die, might have saved someone else. Or tried to.

She was going to get Samily back. The girl should never have left.

"Tia, my name is Nirea. Can we maybe get you some food?" And some clean clothes. Even amongst the reek of blood and ash, the girl stank of urine. Hardly surprising. But not good for her. There would be spare clothes somewhere, surely. Nirea looked for Egretta at the thought, but the head medic had gone—moved on to another urgent task. Nirea didn't envy her. There was no rest in sight for any of the staff here. Or anyone else.

"Will Lady Quell be all right?"

Nirea was halfway to her feet and nearly fell over, catching herself on the edge of the bed behind her.

"Did you... did you say... *Quell*?"

Tia nodded. "She's magic."

Nirea pointed at the woman. "This? This is Quell?!"

Another nod.

"She *saved* you?"

Furious nodding. "She made the monster forget."

*Dear God...*

"You're *sure* this is her?"

Tia reached down and gently lifted an edge of tattered fabric. "It's her dress."

*Holy fucking Hells!*

Nirea picked up the girl and marched from the room. If Quellaria had stayed in Traverlyn, if she'd actually saved this girl, risked herself...

She had to get Samily.

# CHAPTER 10

Allandria's head was spinning. Partially because of the opium Egretta had given her for the broken arm, but also because of what she'd told her. The break was bad. Her arm could take three months to heal, and even then, it could take years for her to have full strength and use of it again.

Which almost certainly meant no bow.

She hadn't said anything to Aranok. Not that long ago, there would have been no alternative, but now she just needed to see Samily again. They had not parted with the knight on good terms. She may be reluctant to help them. Or to see them at all.

But there was a tiny part of Allandria that felt…relieved. If she couldn't draw a bow, couldn't effectively fight, maybe there was a chance she could actually change things. Maybe being the queen's envoy didn't have to be a life of violence. Or maybe it did. And maybe she didn't want that after all.

A quiet cottage in the forest might be nice. A wee burn, trickling past the window. Birds greeting the sun every morning. That could be a good life.

But how likely was it? Could she realistically get Aranok out of this mess? *Should* she? If this was what he really wanted to do, was passionate about, would he be happy with a quiet life? Could he *allow* himself to be happy?

God alone knew. For now, the choice was out of her hands. Her arm was useless unless Samily was prepared to repair it. And maybe that was fine.

"In here?" Aranok's voice was incredulous. With most of the hospital stuffed with wounded, Mynygogg had found them the only private space left in the building—a storage room in the basement. It stank of mildew and dust; even the candles that provided the only light seemed to reek of festering decay. Shelves were stacked with odds and ends Allandria didn't recognise, including a couple of metal contraptions that looked more useful for torture than healing. Rows of leather-bound books sat on shelves along the back wall, cobwebs hanging from them like Midwinter decorations.

"It'll do," said the king. "I tried to light a fire, but the wood was damp. There's a girl fetching us some burnable stock."

Aranok's cane clicked against the stone floor as he crossed to a simple wooden chair with a rounded back. One of six laid out in a vague circle.

"Who are we expecting?" Allandria asked as she took the seat next to him.

"Nirea should be here shortly," Mynygogg answered. "Meristan, of course, assuming your message reached him. And I've asked Opiassa to represent the university. For now, at least."

Aranok shifted in his seat. "They'll need to elect a new principal. Decent chance it could be her, I suppose."

"Indeed," said Mynygogg. "Either way, I think we need her security perspective."

That made sense. The university wasn't going to be doing a lot of teaching for a while. Security was a much bigger priority.

"Where *is* Nirea? Who's with her?" Aranok asked. "You two shouldn't be apart. You're risking—"

"I know." Mynygogg cut him off. "It's a calculated risk, for now. Yes, I know the hospital is chaos and it could be a perfect opportunity to pick us off, but we both suspect that the assassin likely absented themself after killing the *draoidh* girl—"

"Girette," Aranok added.

"Indeed, Girette." The king gave a half nod of respect. "We suspect they will have gotten themselves out of Traverlyn, knowing what was coming, and so we're likely safe, for a little while, at least."

Aranok frowned. "Risky assumption."

"Do you have a password or a sign for each other?" Allandria asked. The biggest risk might be that they stopped knowing who they could trust.

Mynygogg smiled ambiguously. "We do."

"Knock, knock." Meristan matched the words with actual soft knocks on the open door.

Mynygogg turned with a huge grin. "The Great Bear! My God, I can't tell you how grateful I am to see you." He stepped toward the knight, but Aranok leapt to his feet.

"Hold on, for fuck's sake!"

The two men stopped and turned to look at him.

Aranok's irritable tone continued. "You don't know that's him!"

"I...What?" The big man looked utterly befuddled. Understandably. He didn't know about the illusionist assassin who'd killed Rotan, Girette and others just the day before.

"Meristan," Aranok said. "Where did we meet you on the road? With Samily?"

"You mean at Mutton Hole?" His answer was that of a man who felt he was being asked what colour the sky was today.

"Aye. And what about the farmer we stayed with?"

"Dahev?"

"All right. That's enough." Mynygogg put a hand on the Thorn's shoulder and ushered him toward a seat.

"Have I missed something?" Meristan asked once he was sitting.

"Where's Glorbad?" Aranok asked, as if neither man had spoken. Both of them turned to face him with wide eyes, Meristan's trembling with confusion and hurt.

"What? Why would you...?"

"That's enough," said Allandria. "It's him. It's clearly him." The pain, the horror he'd shown at their dead friend's name—no illusionist could fake that, surely. Allandria leaned over to put a hand on Meristan's leg. "It's really good to see you. Thank you so much for...everything." For bringing the Thorns, for routing the Thakhati, for saving the town. All of it. He knew what she meant.

"Aye," said Aranok. "Thank you. You timed that well."

"I can't claim any credit for that, Laird Envoy," Meristan answered. "God put us in the right place, and Rasa brought us at the right time. How is she, by the way? The *draoidh* girl with her was in a bad way."

Mynygogg stood behind his chair, leaning on the back. "They're both in care. Rasa's wounds weren't serious. They'll heal. The girl's jaw was broken. Dislocated, I believe. Took a nasty hit to the head. Medics can't say much for her yet. Depends how bad the damage is inside, I understand."

"Mmm." Meristan looked down at the floor. "Hope she makes it. We'd still be outside, if not for her."

"We have to get Samily back. Now." Nirea marched in the door like a harsh wind. "I'm going after her. Today."

Mynygogg raised his hands and his eyebrows. "Hang on, let's just—"

"Gogg," Aranok insisted. He opened his hands and gestured to the queen.

"Of course," Mynygogg said. "Nirea, we need to…" He opened his hand toward her. She took a moment, visibly deflated, stepped forward and kissed him deeply, almost violently. It was a little awkward. Allandria found the floor suddenly very interesting.

"All right?" Nirea asked when she'd released her husband.

Mynygogg turned to Aranok. "I am certain this is my wife." Aranok gave a grudging shrug and the king turned back to the queen. "Now sit and tell me about this Samily plan."

Nirea did not sit; she paced like a trapped cat.

"Quell's here. But she's dying. And so is Leondar. And others. We need Samily. To save them."

"Quellaria?" Mynygogg asked.

The memory *draoidh*? That was interesting. If they could bring her back onside, the effort to restore the memories of Eidyn became a damn sight more possible.

"Yes. She's here. So I need to go, yes?" Nirea was half out the door already. Mynygogg caught her arm.

"Wait. My love, she already made it clear she won't help us. I'm not saying 'let her die,' but… don't go charging off to get Samily just because you think she might have changed her mind. We can't assume anything."

Nirea turned and pulled her arm free. "No, you don't understand. She saved a girl. A girl that I don't think she even knew. Saved her from a Thakhati."

Mynygogg's brow crinkled. "So?"

"She cared!" Nirea shouted. "She actually cared! She could have run and saved herself, but she put herself at risk to save a little girl she'd never met!"

That was good, of course, but it seemed to mean more to Nirea. "Most people would do that, though, wouldn't they?" Allandria looked at the men for confirmation of her belief in basic human decency. "I mean, who would let a little girl die if they could help her?"

Nirea pointed at her as if Allandria had made her point for her. "Most people, yes. But not Quell. Not the Quell she wants us to see, anyway. If she was the woman she's playing at, she would have left that girl to her death. But she isn't, see? She isn't!"

Mynygogg frowned. "So you think you might change her mind? Because of that?"

"I think if we heal her now, save her life, after what Weyr put Traverlyn through last night, I think maybe she's on our side."

"Maybe," said Aranok. "Maybe not." He turned his eyes to Mynygogg. "But it's worth the attempt."

Nirea turned to Aranok with what Allandria would have called surprise and confusion. Her face was a mask for a moment, before she gave him a nod of thanks.

"All right, all right." Mynygogg finally took his own seat. "It's worth the effort. But why does it have to be you? It's risky, you going out there alone. Is Rasa fit to travel?"

"I don't know. Probably not," said Nirea. "But I have to go. It's too important, Gogg."

The king sat back and pursed his lips. The room was silent for a moment.

"Where is Samily?" Meristan asked.

Of course. Meristan hadn't been here. He had no idea what had happened. Or what it had caused. Mynygogg looked surreptitiously at Allandria before answering.

"We cured the Blackening. It's a long story, but the short version is that Balaban was able to transfer Morienne's curse to Samily, and now Samily can take the Blackened survivors back to before they were Blackened without being infected. She went to the Auld Road with Morienne and Master Dialla, to aid those cured."

"Hmm." Meristan crossed his arms and cradled his chin in one hand. After a moment, he looked directly at Nirea. "She won't come."

"What? Why not?" The queen's voice broke on the last word.

"Consider the situation here and that on the Auld Road," the Thorn said. "As she will see it, they are vulnerable and in need of help in the wild, while these people here are already in a hospital, under the care of medics. Those here could survive without her. Many will not, on the road. She will weigh that decision, and make it."

The silence returned with a vengeance. Nirea's mouth hung open, tears threatening the rims of her eyes. It clearly hadn't occurred to her that the miracle "healer" might refuse her call. She turned to Mynygogg. "But...Leondar..."

The king closed his eyes and nodded. "I know. But if Meristan says she won't come, then—"

"You could go!" Nirea said. "You could go and order her. She would come for you."

Meristan took a deep breath and paused. "I could. And she probably would. But I won't. I have made the mistake of making choices for her before, and I am loath to do it again."

Nirea stared, open-mouthed. Aranok snorted air through his nose and looked away.

Meristan turned to him with raised eyebrows. "You don't understand, Envoy? After what happened in—"

"I'm not sure leaving a nineteen-year-old girl to make choices about the future of the country is a wise course of action." Aranok's tone was bitter, and the Thorn moved slightly back from it. This was suddenly dangerous ground. Meristan did not know what had happened between Aranok and Samily, and his confusion at Aranok's attitude was palpable.

"You see?" Nirea leapt on the opening. "Aranok agrees. We need to get her back, for the sake of the country!"

Considering where these two had last left things, they were an unlikely alliance. Allandria was suddenly very aware of just how fragile this council was. Like fractured glass. The wrong tone and it would shatter.

Mynygogg put a hand on Nirea's arm, and she immediately shrugged it off. His mouth twisted into consternation. "Nirea, if Meristan doesn't believe Samily will come, and more importantly if he is not comfortable in forcing her to come, then we have to respect that. As I already said, Quellaria made her position clear when she left. As you told her she was free to do. There's no point getting caught up in this. We need to deal with the situation as we find it."

Nirea jerked her head toward him. "We let them die, when we could save them? When we could save *Leondar*?"

"I thought a queen's job was to make the best decisions for the country, not just the people she cares about," Aranok said snidely.

Wide-eyed, Allandria looked at him. What the Hell was he doing?

Nirea's eyes were dark as sin when she turned to him. "I beg your pardon?"

"That's what you said, right? We have to be prepared to sacrifice for the good of the country?"

*Oh shit.* Something had pissed him off and he'd fallen into pure aggravation. He was trying to rile her now, and Nirea was already on her last nerve.

"You were agreeing with me a minute ago," she said, hands on her head.

Mynygogg stepped between them, hands placatingly raised. "Let's just calm down."

Aranok carried on as if the king hadn't spoken. "I *am* on your side. I think we *should* get Samily back here and *order* her to fucking save people. Starting with Quellaria and Leondar. But so do you, don't you?"

Meristan bristled in his chair and might have spoken, but Nirea didn't give him a breath to do it. "Of course I do! What the fuck point are you making?"

Aranok stood to match her, leaning on his cane to help him up. "I'm saying that it makes a difference when it's *your* friend whose life is threatened!"

"He's your friend too!" Nirea shouted.

"And I would still support you saving him if he wasn't! Because he's *your* friend!"

Silence as Nirea took in his meaning. He was still angry about Janaeus and Shayella: angry that Nirea had made Dialla kill him; angry that Samily had executed her. It had all been there, still. Lurking under the surface, waiting to boil. Aranok was not ready for this meeting. Or if he was, his objectives were not... useful.

Allandria stood beside him. "All right, maybe it's time for a break, so everyone can cool down."

Meristan still looked utterly befuddled, and he stood too, almost looming over the rest of them. "My friends, I don't know what I have missed, but surely we are all still allies. We share the same goals. We want the same things. Times are hard and we are sorely tested, but we are all still on the same side, are we not?"

Nirea looked pointedly at Aranok. "You should probably ask Samily about that, considering *he* tried to kill her."

*Oh, fucking Hell.*

Meristan half smiled and raised an eyebrow, as if searching for the humour in a joke he didn't understand. But Aranok looked shamefully at the floor, and the Thorn realised there was no jest. "What did you do?"

He stepped toward Aranok, and Allandria instinctively put herself between them. "No."

Meristan's voice was barely contained rage. Mynygogg stepped beside him, a hand on his arm. "Wait, Meristan." The big man shook him off and glowered over Allandria's shoulder.

"Aranok, explain what she means. *Now.*"

He didn't answer, and that only seemed to infuriate the Thorn further. He put a hand on Allandria's bad shoulder and began to push her aside, but she pivoted and used her good arm to push his arm up and away. "Meristan, there's context you don't understand. It's more complicated than that." Allandria shot Nirea a venomous look.

The queen stared defiantly back at her, then closed her eyes, slumped her shoulders and finally spoke. "All right, fine, it was complicated. I shouldn't have said it like that."

Meristan turned his ire on her. "Then how *should* you have said it?"

Nirea waved a dismissive hand at Aranok. "Samily killed Shayella. That's how the Blackening ended. Aranok was there. They fought."

He turned back to Aranok. "You *fought*? *How* did you fight?"

"I attacked her," Aranok said pathetically.

Oh God, that wasn't enough either. Meristan was only angrier now. Allandria had to do something—something she'd been sure until this moment was a terrible idea. She was going to have to tell the truth.

"He lost control of his powers! It was an accident!"

Every eye in the room turned to her then, each as shocked as the next. Aranok because they'd agreed to keep that to themselves. But circumstances had overtaken them.

The king was the first to break the silence. "Aranok? Is that true?"

He looked sideways at Allandria before answering. "I was angry. I threatened her. But I didn't make the gestures. I never spoke the word."

Meristan softened and seemed to shrink in height. "What happened?"

Allandria took Aranok's hand in hers. "She used her time skill. Cut off his hands." She squeezed his hand as she said it, hoping it would be solace. It took a moment, but he squeezed back. He understood.

Meristan slumped back into his seat. "You're lucky to be alive, Envoy." It wasn't clear if he meant Samily could have killed him or that Meristan might yet. But at least the heat was gone from the room.

Aranok sat back down then, and Allandria did the same. Nirea was staring at him as if he were a puzzle. Her behaviour had been appalling, and Allandria was going to tell her so when they had a moment alone. Regardless of the stress she was under—Hell, they were all long beyond the breaking point.

Mynygogg was, again, the one to speak first. "Aranok, I didn't know that could happen. Has it happened before?"

"No…" Aranok stopped as if something had hit him. His eyes scanned the air for a moment. "Maybe. Once. With Janaeus."

"At Greytoun?" Nirea asked.

Aranok nodded. "I didn't remember saying the word, but…I just assumed I'd done it subconsciously. Maybe I didn't. I don't know."

Mynygogg ran his hands over his stubbled head and locked them behind his neck. "Well, fuck. What do we do with that?"

"You don't have to do anything," Aranok answered. "It's my issue. I'm handling it."

"*Are* you?" said Nirea.

"He *is*." Allandria could feel her own anger rising, and Nirea needed to stop fuelling it. She looked back at Allandria with an ambiguous half smile.

"All right, everyone just sit, please..." Mynygogg waved them all down. "...Let's...just...sit." Nirea was the last to take a seat. "We've been through a lot and we're all tired. There are clearly issues that need to be...addressed. But for now, we need to discuss the rest of the day. Let's just get through today, can we?"

Aranok sat up straight and freed his hand from Allandria's. "First, we need to establish something."

"All right. What?" Mynygogg asked calmly.

Aranok pointed at his friend. "You're not king." He moved the hand toward Nirea. "And she's not queen. You were, but now you're not. We are all going to agree, here and now, that if we are going to keep working together, we are equals. Outside of this group, you want to use your old titles to get people on board, on you go. But between us, no more rank. We work *together*, or we don't."

*Well*. They hadn't discussed that. But Allandria could see where it came from. Mynygogg began as if to speak, but Aranok cut him off, with an emphasised point of his finger. "No more fucking secrets."

He was also still angry that Mynygogg and Nirea had conspired to kill Janaeus if they couldn't get the heart of devastation. Well, if they were going to move forward, they needed to lance these boils.

Mynygogg's face turned dark and he looked back at Aranok a long time. "Fine."

Nirea huffed audibly but didn't say anything. They both recognised Aranok was not going to negotiate the point. Not now, anyway.

Instead, Aranok stood and crossed toward the door. "Good. Meristan, we should clear the Thorns while I still have the energy. Then I'm going to need to rest, since I'm powering the sunspire." He paused and looked down at Nirea. "We also need Dialla back." Nirea's entire demeanour changed. She sat up straighter and her eyes lit with something. What had she taken from Aranok's words that Allandria was missing? "We should reconvene tomorrow." Aranok carried on out of the room and was gone. A flair for the dramatic, he'd always had. After a moment, Meristan stood and followed him without another word. Allandria made to follow them both but stopped when Nirea grabbed her arm.

"Do I need to be worried?" she asked.

"About what?"

"About you. About him." She nodded to the open door. She wanted to know whose side Allandria would take, if pushed. The truth was, she would say what she believed. But was she still the queen's envoy? Or was she Aranok's bodyguard? His lover? Could she be all of those things? For now, she gave the answer she knew in her heart.

"That was a catastrophic failure of leadership. If you want to be queen again, you're going to have to be better."

Nirea dropped her hand, and Allandria followed Aranok upstairs.

# CHAPTER 11

"Is it me, or is this getting harder?" Nirea's head was pounding and her entire body ached. Mynygogg was grey. The meeting was an absolute disaster. Hell, Opiassa hadn't even arrived yet and half the "council" had walked out.

Gogg nodded silently, leaned over and put a hand on hers. "My love, you know I support you, but you did not handle that well."

No, she hadn't. She was desperate and exhausted and Aranok had pressed on every open nerve. The pirate had overtaken the queen and made a bloody mess. "I know. I'll fix it. But Meristan needed to know what happened. If we'd kept it from him…"

Gogg sat back and grimaced. "Yes, but not like that. You threw a lit torch at an oil barrel."

Yes, she did. And she had done it out of anger and spite. Because, loath as she was to admit it, Aranok was right. She wanted to save Leondar and Quell. And part of her had seen Quell not as the asset to saving the kingdom, but as an excuse to get Samily back. A queen's justification for a human desire. She didn't want to lose Leondar. Maybe because it felt too much like losing Glorbad again, and that pain was still raw. So she'd thrown all of it at Aranok for seeing her hypocrisy. *Fuck.*

"All right, yes. You're right. I made an arse of it."

"Don't misunderstand me," said Mynygogg. "So did he. Aranok

was angling for a fight. You both made valid points, but we can't keep allowing our emotions to sabotage us. Last night, when we had to, we worked together. No questions, no arguments, we just did it. We have to remember that. We have to remember we all want the same thing."

Nirea nodded solemnly and felt herself blink very slowly. The sting in her eyes was temporarily salved.

"Um, hello, sorry, Majesties? Am I late?" Opiassa stood at the door, returned to her natural size and without the colossal set of armour she'd worn through the night. She was still imposing, but nothing like the giant she could become. She too looked drained.

"Please, Master Opiassa, come in." Mynygogg crossed to shake her hand and directed her to a chair. "I'm afraid the rest of our companions were needed elsewhere. They've gone to clear the memories of the White Thorns. But I'm glad to see you. What can you tell us?"

The master seemed to shrink even further. "I wish I had better news, sire. The town is devastated. We've lost hundreds, at least. Homes are in ruins. There are still cocoons within buildings, though the Thorns are doing exceptional work rooting them out. I..." Opiassa's voice broke as her lip quivered. "There are..."

Nirea moved to kneel before her and took her hands. "I know. I know."

Mynygogg poured a cup of water and handed it to the master in silence. What could they say? There were no words to heal the trauma of the last night. Not yet.

"Thank you." Opiassa drank tentatively, then wiped her damp eyes on her sleeve. With a deep breath, she composed herself, sat up and began again. "We lost several *draoidhs* too. At least three, that I know of. Two more are in serious condition. The rest have survivable injuries."

The *draoidhs* had been the front line. They'd held back the storm until the Thorns arrived. And they'd paid for it. If nothing else, Nirea doubted any *draoidh* in Traverlyn would side with Weyr after this. But that was a thought for tomorrow. There were more urgent issues.

"Master Opiassa, we cannot thank you enough for what you and your... friends have done for us, and for Traverlyn," said Mynygogg. "I am deeply, deeply sorry for your losses. Is there anything we can do to offer aid?"

There was definitely something Nirea could do, and she was going to do it the minute this meeting was over.

"I don't believe so, sire. If Laird Aranok has reinstated the sunspire, and the Thorns will be here for some time, I'm not sure there is more that we can do, beyond tending the wounded and burning the dead. We'll need to clear the streets as soon as we can, to avoid the spread of disease."

At least they didn't have to worry about the dead getting back up to attack them. Small mercy.

"All right, Master, thank you." Mynygogg stood and offered a hand again, which she rose to take. "Please, carry on. But also, please remember to rest. We can't afford to have people making mistakes out of exhaustion."

Opiassa bowed respectfully. "Yes, Majesty, thank you. I should be fine."

Gogg left unspoken the real horror, that they couldn't afford to be exhausted because they had no idea what Weyr might do next. If he sent demons to finish the Thakhati's effort... at least they had the Thorns. That was a comfort. To everyone.

When the master had returned to duty, Nirea clapped her hands and rubbed them together for warmth. Only then had she noticed how cold the little basement room was.

"Gogg, I'm still going after Samily."

He nodded knowingly. "Take a Thorn with you."

That wasn't what she'd expected. In fact, she'd prepared an entire argument, anticipating her husband's objections and ready to counter them. It was a pleasant surprise she didn't have to. "All right."

"And tread lightly. Please."

Irritation instinctively rose in her, but she snuffed it for the moment. He may have a point. She wasn't thinking particularly clearly and this wasn't the time to start another fight. "I will. And you need company. The assassin." If she wasn't going to be here, someone else needed to pair with him. Someone they could verify and trust. Keft would have been an ideal candidate. Egretta had too much else to do. Opiassa and Meristan, the same.

Mynygogg smiled. "I believe there is a young blacksmith who would be ideal."

"You have to forgive him," Allandria whispered.

Aranok was snoring in the chair he'd been sitting in to clear memories for the Thorns. They'd gotten through eleven more, including Asha—who had been surprisingly delighted to see Allandria again—before the sacks under Aranok's eyes were so dark that she had insisted he take a break. Between the lack of sleep, the weeks he'd pushed himself without decent rest before that, the emotional trauma he'd endured, the head injury, the sunspire and now this... It was a miracle he was still functioning at all. If not for the opium-fuelled rest she'd forced on him... And the guilt she knew he was feeling over Shayella—and Samily—was just another weight dragging him down.

Meristan ran his hand through his beard and across his mouth, and crossed to the bar. They'd taken residence in the Auld Hoose Inn, so named because it was one of the original houses in the area. A wealthy laird named Olifin had settled near the Sheep's Heid and become a major patron to the musicians who played there, helping to attract even more hoping to catch his eye, and his purse. Several generations after his death, having got through what was left of his money, Olifin's descendants had converted the vast home into an inn, honouring his memory by hosting live music, and paying well for it. The current proprietor, Nairne, was apparently more of a poet than a musician, but she still honoured her ancestor's passion.

With great glass windows across the front of the building to entice people in, nobody had been keen to settle there the night before, so the place had been empty when they came across three White Thorns checking it for cocoons. Nairne had been grateful to see them, and to know the building was safe to move back in, so she'd been wholly agreeable when Aranok had asked if they could use the bar. In fact, she'd seemed relieved not to be left alone.

Once they'd explained the threat of the illusionist assassin to Meristan, he'd agreed that he should stay with them and just have the cleared Thorns send the others to the inn.

The bar was warm and open, with glass lanterns hanging from the roof beams and wooden tables carved with intricate art. The walls had a natural tree facade, suggesting they'd grown, rather than been built, and Allandria assumed a nature *draoidh* had been involved in the decoration if not the actual building of the original house.

Meristan lifted a bottle of whisky and poured himself a measure. He sat on a stool and took a long sip—so much so that Allandria began to wonder if he was deliberately taking his time so as to irritate her. But that wasn't Meristan's character. He was thinking. So she let him, waiting in the silence for a response.

"I think, perhaps, with respect, you are asking more from me than you would be able to offer," he finally said quietly.

"In what way?" Allandria looked sideways to ensure Aranok was still sound asleep. She didn't want him overhearing this conversation.

Meristan took another sip, then looked her in the eye. "Imagine I had assaulted your family for something they had done. Or him." He pointed to Aranok. "Or, maybe a better example, his *niece*."

The last word was pointed. And she understood. Samily was his child. Emelina was the closest equal he could find for Allandria, despite the girl's youth. Because that was still who Samily was to Meristan: not the most powerful person in Eidyn; his little girl.

"I take your point—"

"Do you? How quickly do you imagine you would find forgiveness? How long before the terror that you might have lost her, and the anger—the rage in your heart for the person who tried to harm her—how long before that would subside?" Meristan tipped the glass to her and emptied the last of it into his mouth.

That was fair. But she still needed to do what she could. "Meristan, he was already a mess. For...a lot of reasons." She wasn't going to betray Aranok's confidence, but the whole situation was so complex. "Especially after Janaeus's death. He was feeling guilty and angry—particularly at Nirea. As you saw."

Meristan raised his chin in recognition, and perhaps more understanding of the rancour between the two of them earlier.

"And then Samily cut Shayella's head off, right in front of him." Allandria left that a moment to sink in. Something flickered in Meristan's eyes. Surprise? Concern, maybe? "He begged her not to. He stood there and begged her not to kill Shayella. And she did it anyway."

Meristan pursed his lips and looked away. "She'll have believed she was doing the right thing."

Allandria stood and crossed to join him at the bar. She could not risk Aranok catching a word of what she was going to say next. She leaned in close and whispered, "I'm not sure she was wrong. But I know it broke him, and I know he wasn't in control. What he's been through...?" She turned and pointed back at Aranok. "I'm not sure I'd still be here." She probably wouldn't, one way or another. "All I'm asking is... the benefit of the doubt. Please?"

Meristan sighed deeply, frowned and poured another drink. Allandria pulled a second glass up from under the bar and he filled that too. They drank together then in the almost silence, broken only by gentle snoring.

It was scary. Knowing the extent of his powers, the idea that Aranok, as broken and complex as he was, could be out of control. The damage he could do... That wasn't part of why people feared *draoidhs*, as far as Allandria knew, but she was beginning to wonder if it shouldn't be.

An age passed before either of them spoke. Meristan lifted his eyes from the ground and looked her directly in the eye. "I'm going to hear Samily's story."

"Of course."

"Then we'll see."

---

"Holy fuck." Nirea covered her mouth in horror. The mess beneath her—God, she'd almost *stood* in it.

"Majesty?" Greste trotted urgently from the other end of the stable. It had taken Nirea over an hour to find a Thorn who knew who she was and would accept her request for an escort without needing to confirm with Meristan. She'd told the woman that time was of the essence, and that was true, but she would also prefer not having Greste know Meristan's opinion of this mission. Thankfully, the woman was old enough and clever enough to think for herself.

"I think," she said, suppressing a gag, "I think it's the stable boy. Tobin." There wasn't enough left of him to identify properly, but the remains, what there was of them, were about the right size, and what she could see of the hair that wasn't soaked in gore looked right.

"God save him." Greste sat cross-legged for a moment and offered up a gentle prayer. If there was a Heaven, that boy deserved to be in it. Nirea turned and walked away. She couldn't keep looking at it. *Smelling* it. Even with everything else she'd seen, this was hideous. How would they even begin to remove the remains for burning? With a shovel?

*Fuck these monsters. And fuck Anhel Weyr.*

Bear was tied up by the door. She'd brought him from the hospital, but they needed more. Horses had been running free in the town since last night. She'd hoped some might still be stabled here. Maybe that's why Tobin had come. To let them out. Give them a chance. Brave boy.

Stupid boy.

Vastin had said he'd found Bear here last night. Hadn't mentioned the bloody smear the Thakhati had left behind. Maybe it happened after Vastin was there. Or maybe it was nothing anyone would want to recall. They were probably about the same age, the boys. Tobin maybe a bit younger. Gods, what a life. Cut so short.

"We left our horses tied up outside the town." Greste had finished her prayer and come away to join Nirea as far from the remains as they could be within the stable. "Perhaps we could simply pick some of them up?"

They could, but it would slow them down. And it wouldn't solve the main issue. Bear was too damn big to attach to a cart without everything falling out the back. They needed a pair of standard horses. "No. But come on—he'll carry both of us for now. We'll find a couple of horses somewhere. Maybe in the fields at the edge of town."

Greste nodded. "Makes sense. They would want to get as far away from the noise as possible. Space to run from the Thakhati too."

"Right. Yes. Let's do that." Nirea helped the Thorn up onto the Calladell's back and then took her place in front. She was excruciatingly aware that every minute they wasted here was reducing the chances of saving people, but if they went off half-assed now, Samily probably wouldn't come back with them anyway. She needed every bit of this plan if she was going to convince the girl.

They needed that cart. Which meant they needed some damned horses.

# CHAPTER 12

The bonfire crackled, throwing little orange sparks dancing into the night sky. An odd time to notice the art of creation, perhaps, but still Samily found herself recognising the beauty in it. It was everywhere, if one was prepared to see it. Even here.

"Does this bother you?" Morienne asked.

"Why would it bother me?"

"Because, I don't know, it seems sort of disrespectful? Just burning them all in a pile like this?"

There was, perhaps, some lack of dignity in it. "I take your point, but the alternatives are worse. If we stopped to bury every body we found, those along the road may die waiting for us. If we left them to nature, they would rot and attract vermin, spreading disease. And if not, their bodies may be taken by the Thakhati. Have faith. It is not ideal, but God will find them."

Morienne sighed deeply. "I suppose. And a lot of people choose a funeral pyre over burial anyway, don't they?"

"Indeed. It is considered by some a sign of great respect and a celebration of life. How we honour our lost is only a matter for us. The dead have moved on."

Morienne nodded solemnly and turned back to watching the flames.

The fire had also provided an opportunity for Dialla to restore their energy so that they could continue through the night. She had warned that they could not do so indefinitely, but recognised that the first days were the most urgent, and the more progress they could make, the more lives they would save. But they also could not simply leave a bonfire in the middle of the road. It could catch the surrounding flora. Thus they had carefully picked a spot without overhanging trees and with minimal hedging along the roadside. Here the road was mostly mud and stone. It gave them a chance to eat too, and Dialla was tending a brace of hares. Between that and the rations they had brought from Traverlyn, they would be able to feed everyone at least a small meal—enough to keep them going.

They'd been joined by seven Cured so far. Those who had been far away enough to avoid the Thakhati and not so withered as to die when the curse was lifted. They'd actually restored more like twenty-five, Samily reckoned. But most had chosen to head for home, or to look for loved ones.

Twenty-five. Not nearly as many as she'd hoped. The pyre held at least that many. All that they could pile onto the rickety cart they'd collected from an abandoned farm. It slowed them down, but... it was a matter of choices. Complex choices. Nothing was simple anymore.

"Excuse me, Lady." Samily turned to see a young woman with deep green eyes, peering up under a fringe of long blond hair, her head almost entirely bowed. "Master Dialla says food is ready."

"Thank you." Samily nodded gratefully and the woman smiled shyly in return.

The campfire was set back off the road. They'd not come across a single traveller yet. But now that the Blackened were cleared, there could be folk on the move. Soldiers, maybe. Anhel Weyr's soldiers. Samily would happily deal with them, but she would prefer not to enter into a fight with those whose minds were not their own. And others might be hurt in the churn of battle. Better to avoid conflict if they could. Even if they were effectively lighting a beacon each night.

At the fire, Dialla was handing out portions of rabbit meat with bread. Seven bodies huddled round the flame. Seven souls that had been through Hell and would never remember it. Of course, their minds were still not their own. She did not carry one of the envoy's charms and therefore could do nothing for their memories. Just another way in which they had been violated. But the identity of their king mattered little to these wretches, whose lives, perhaps their homes, their families, had been stolen from them. For now, they needed food and protection. The rest would wait.

Dialla stepped toward them and offered out a portion of food. The young woman who'd been sent to fetch them stepped back and demurred. "After you, Lady."

"Oh no, please," said Samily. "Take it."

Another shy smile and she accepted the food, then took a place at the fire next to an older man. They spoke in conspiratorial whispers.

Morienne nudged Samily gently. "You're their hero, you know?"

Dialla offered another portion of food and Samily accepted this one. "Pardon?"

"They revere you," said Morienne. "You saved them."

"I...But..." Samily could not say why, but she was deeply uncomfortable with that idea. It felt wrong. It felt...vain.

Dialla brought another portion for Morienne and one for herself. The three of them stood on the edge of the firelight, able to speak quietly without being heard.

Morienne turned to Dialla. "They do, don't they? They worship her."

Dialla looked to the fire for a moment before answering. "They do consider you a wonder, Samily. By their words, you are akin to an angel."

"What? No," Samily sputtered with a mouthful of rabbit. That was definitely wrong. She had to explain. Had to tell these people that she was merely God's servant. That their thanks, their love, should be directed to God, not to her. What would Meristan think of such blasphemy?

Her intent must have been plain, because as she stepped toward the fire, Dialla moved to block her. "Samily, let them have this. For now. If you feel the need to say something, it will wait. They need hope, and you are comfort. Don't take that from them. Give them time."

Samily bristled. But she should listen. Master Dialla had lost her family, just days ago. When she spoke of comfort, of hope, she spoke also of herself. Even allowing these people's misconceptions to carry on for a short time seemed awful. But if Dialla was right, perhaps it would only be cruel to correct them. More complexity. More grey. But Samily's discomfort was a small matter, in the grand scheme.

"Fine. I will leave it. For now. But truly, Morienne, what we do here is no different from what you did in Lepertoun. Had they known the kindness you did for…" Samily stopped, because Morienne's face had fallen as if she'd been stabbed.

"Oh God. Oh God, Samily. *Lepertoun!*" Even in the firelight, Samily could see the colour drain from the woman's face. "I left them…! They will be… Oh God, no." Morienne's hands trembled over her mouth.

"I don't understand, what's wrong?" Dialla asked.

A lot. With the Auld Road being so urgent, they'd forgotten those poor souls they'd left tied and bound in Lepertoun.

Dialla's eyes widened as Samily explained. "Oh. Oh no. Might they have survived? How advanced were they?"

"Maybe? Some of them?" Morienne looked on the verge of tears. Amaru might… at least… Oh, Samily, I have to go!"

"Of course. Come, we'll separate the rations and fill your pack. You'll need a decent amount for you and the Cured." Without Samily to heal them, they would need whatever could be spared.

"Will you be all right, travelling alone?" Dialla asked.

A bittersweet smile from Morienne. "I'm used to it."

It took them less than half an hour to have her stocked and ready to go.

"Thank you. Both," said Morienne, reaching down from her horse to grasp each of their hands in turn. "Samily, it has been… I don't even know how to say… What you've done. For me…"

"You speak as if we are parting forever," Samily interrupted. "I do not believe that to be so. God travels with us both. We will see each other again."

"Of course. You're right." She smiled. "I'll see you both soon."

With a small wave, Morienne kicked her horse into a canter and disappeared into the dark.

---

"Samily! Here!" Dialla's voice was urgent, and Samily dropped the body she was moving to the cart. On the other side of the road, the master knelt in waist-high wildflowers. "Here! Quick!"

Samily almost stumbled off the edge of the road in her haste. Dialla cradled the head of a skeletal man, his skin as grey as the wispy beard on his chin. But Dialla's fingers were at his throat, her eyes wide.

"His heart still beats!"

"All right, let me take him." Samily pulled off her gloves and gently took the man's head. He was barely alive.

*"Air…"*

A scream like nothing she'd ever heard. Terror and fear and pain.

*"…ais!"*

Samily shuddered and jerked her head up toward the scream. Dialla had also turned to face it. "What was that?"

It was the sound of distress. That was all that mattered.

"Hello?" An unexpected voice from her lap. Samily looked down to see a middle-aged man with ruddy cheeks and a thick black beard.

*Oh!*

When she'd been startled, she must have taken the old man back much further than she intended. She did not have time to explain to him now. "You will be fine. Take your time to get up."

Samily slipped her legs from underneath him, but as she stood, her head spun. S'grace, she must have used too much energy! "Dialla! Please, I need…" She reached out a hand and the master understood.

Dialla took Samily's hand and said, *"Thoir."* Samily felt her mind clear, her muscles loosen and her vision sharpen.

"Thank you." Samily stood and moved to her horse—the only one not attached to the cart. "Follow me when you can."

"Samily, wait…" said Dialla. "You can't go alone. You don't know what that was. We'll all go."

"No. Stay here. Help this man." For all her power, Master Dialla was a teacher. Besides, if this was something awful and Samily could not contain it, the Cured needed protection. They certainly should not be running toward it.

Samily mounted the horse and replaced her helm. "I am a White Thorn. This is what we do."

The screaming did not repeat as Samily rode hard. Fear was at least a sign of life.

She turned a corner in the road and the trees opened to reveal a nightmare—a giant, misshapen baby with skin the colour of a fading bruise and a hugely overgrown forehead. The demon sat in a field, its bloated legs extending onto the road. In its left hand a person hung limp. Idly, the demon lifted the figure toward its huge mouth, eyes blankly staring into the distance.

She was too far away.

"No!" Samily urged the horse to run even faster. "Stop!"

The monster jerked as if disturbed from sleep and slowly turned its head toward her. But still the hand rose.

"No! No! Stop!"

She wasn't going to make it.

The demon looked back at her like a curiosity. Samily drew her blade, but she wasn't going to get there in time. The horse's hooves pounded the earth beneath her, her Green blade sung in her hand, ready to strike. Heaven, no, she could not, would not watch this person devoured.

She had to do *something*!

*No, no, no, no... "Stop!"*

...

Samily was still. She sat atop the horse, blade aloft, frozen in place. The demon stared back at her, still thirty yards away, equally motionless.

*What on earth have I done?*

She'd spoken no *draoidh* word.

It must be some emanation of her time skill, but what?

And how in Heaven's name was she to undo it if she couldn't move?

But then, if she did, the demon might also be released. And the woman—as she now appeared to be—would die an unspeakable death before Samily reached her.

No point panicking. She was going to have to wait.

*Clear your mind, trust in God and stand your ground.*

Samily surrendered to the stillness. There was nothing she could do, should do, should have done. The wind rustled leaves. She could not feel it, covered head to toe in her White armour, but the sound still raised a tingle of joy in her. A bird called in the distance. It was bizarrely serene. She might have closed her eyes and simply basked in nature, were she able.

But she could not take her eyes away from the monster on the verge of devouring a woman. Her head was mere feet from the thing's open maw.

After an age, the clop of hoofbeats and the squeak of cart wheels.

"Samily? Samily!"

Footsteps, pounding in the dirt. Dialla placed a hand on her leg, but Samily felt nothing, only saw it on the edge of her vision. "Samily? What's happening?"

Several other figures surrounded her horse—some of the Cured, fussing over her, touching her, touching the horse. Confused. Scared.

"Everyone, step back, please." Nothing changed, and Dialla's voice became as stern as Samily had ever heard it. *"Please."*

"What the Hell is that?" A male voice. He'd seen the demon. Fear in their voices now, as they backed away, back toward the cart. Good. Out of the way. Only one young woman crept closer, her blond head cocked curiously—the woman who'd fetched Samily to dinner last night. Ayla, her name was.

"Samily, I'm going to assume you can hear me, because, well, if you can't it really makes no difference." Dialla had come to the front of the horse and stood directly under her eyeline. "This must be your skill. I assume you did this to stop that." She pointed at the demon, which Ayla crept still closer to. Samily would rather she kept her distance in case whatever she'd done was suddenly ended.

"When *draoidhs* are children, the first emanations of our skills are often 'wild.' They are out of control and sometimes far too powerful for what we might have intended. I suspect you have tapped into a wild skill you were not aware of. I don't know enough about time magic to be sure, but it looks likely you have frozen yourself, your horse and the demon in time."

She knew Dialla would know what to do. "Wild" magic? What else might she be able to do, when she had it under control?

Dialla put her hand to her mouth and turned. Ayla was almost on the demon now. "Not too close!" the master called.

"It's fine!" she replied. "It's not moving! I'm trying to see…"

"See what?"

"The woman," Ayla called back. "I think she's alive! Hang on."

Ayla bound up her skirt and clambered up the demon's limbs as if it were a malformed tree. When she reached the woman, she turned her head back. "Can't tell for certain, but she might be!"

"All right, please come down." Dialla's voice was tinged with concern. "I don't fully understand what has happened, but it could end at any moment!"

"Hang on, while I'm here, I can just…" Ayla produced something—a knife?—from her pocket and swung her arm down at the demon's eye, but what seemed an invisible wall deflected the blade away and the woman tumbled down its front, landing heavily with a resonant crack.

"Ayla!" Dialla ran toward her, as did a few of the Cured men, including, it seemed, the man she'd accidentally made a lot younger. They both carried makeshift weapons of broken branches. Samily could not see from the distance what had happened, but it looked bad. Dialla and the men fussed over Ayla, and Samily felt the excruciating frustration of not being able to do anything. S'grace, if she was hurt, Samily could mend her in a moment, if only she could *move*!

Finally, Dialla came running back toward her. "I think she has broken her back, Samily. She's unconscious but breathing. I'm afraid to move her for fear of making it worse. Damn it!" She rubbed agitatedly at her forehead. "Fine, fine, all right. We need you back, but we also need to stop that demon. And now we need it urgently, because…" She didn't finish the sentence, but Samily understood. Now there was a clock to race.

"All right, all right, we can do this. Samily, I want you to listen to me carefully, but *do not follow* these instructions yet, understand?" She paused for a moment, as if Samily might answer. "I know that when a metamorph first transforms, they can become stuck in their new form for a time. What they describe when they manage to change back to their own form is largely similar. Firstly, they really *wanted* to change back. It was the most important thing in the world. And secondly, they imagined themselves back in their bodies. In a minute, when I signal you, I need you to want to move again like nothing you've ever wanted before. And then I need you to picture yourself moving. Feel it. Feel every joint, every muscle fluid and moving toward that demon.

"I will protect everyone until you can reach us. Do you understand?"

Samily would have nodded. She tried to blink. She hoped something changed in her eyes that made it clear that, yes, she understood. And she was ready.

"All right," said Dialla. "Wait for my signal." The master turned and ran back to the demon. There was some discussion, and the younger man mimicked Ayla's climb, getting himself to the thing's mouth. He reached back to take the broken branches and jammed them between the demon's jaws, propping them open. Then the man took something else handed up to him, clambered onto the demon's massive forehead and braced, seemingly ready to finish the job Ayla had attempted.

Dialla placed one hand on the demon's gnarled foot, turned and raised the other hand. "Now!"

*Come on, Samily. This must be it.*

She pictured herself racing toward the demon, imagined she could feel it in her every muscle, just as Dialla had said. And, Heaven, she wanted it, she wanted it so badly. To save her friend, to save the others, to kill that damned demon and to be free again!

*Come on!*

Nothing. She was still frozen. Frustration boiled in her, and she fought it down, searching for her centre and calm. *Please, God. Please help me. Help me to move.*

Still nothing.

"Samily?" Panic in Dialla's voice again. Ayla must be in a bad way.

She was going to die while Samily sat and watched.

*Please, God! Please!*

Hang on. If it was "wild" magic... Samily had been emotional when it happened. Desperate. Angry. Perhaps she shouldn't be burying her frustration. Perhaps that was exactly what she needed. And it *was* frustrating. She was stuck watching while people suffered. And actually, it was not serene. It was irritating. *Aggravating.*

Like all the times people had picked stupid fights over her faith. Like when Aranok had attacked her. Like when Allandria and then Rasa had practically said it was *her* fault.

*Come on, Samily!*

People were going to die, and she was sitting here on this stupid horse doing *nothing*!

When it finally broke, a cry of rage and anger and absolute release burst from her chest. The horse raced on into chaos.

The demon, befuddled, attempted to bite down but found its palate crammed with wood. It moved the woman away, lifting its empty hand to clear the blockage. The man on its head rammed the knife down at its eye, but the head had moved, tilting him to the side, and he missed, dropped the weapon and slid down its back.

But Dialla was there. And she was ready. She couldn't just blast the thing, or she risked hurting the others, but she could do what Samily assumed she was doing—drain the life from it.

The demon's head began to loll and its arm dropped to its side. It was a huge thing, though, and surely there was no way Dialla could contain all its energy. But she slowed it, and that was enough.

Samily leapt from the horse's back.

Her first blow took the left hand off halfway up its forearm. It spilled to the ground, releasing its captive.

The pain gave the monster a burst of energy and it swung its right hand toward her. Samily ducked, rolled left, came up and caught the arm in the backswing, severing it just below the wrist. The demon roared and kicked out, throwing Dialla backwards. It leaned forward, attempting to bite Samily with its granite teeth. She danced back from its reach, then lunged, spearing it through its massive forehead.

The demon's jaw went limp, the eyes glazed, and it slumped in half, lifeless head between its own grotesque feet.

The moment she was sure it was dead, Samily turned to find Ayla. She was the shade of old snow and Samily understood Dialla's concern. Again, she threw off her gloves and dropped at her side. *"Air ais."*

Colour rose in her face and Ayla jerked straight as broken bones clicked back into place.

The woman lay still entangled in the severed hand, head hanging at an unnatural angle.

*Please, please let her be alive.*

Samily placed a hand on her head and focused on taking her whole body back, back to before the scream, to before this thing had got its hands on her.

*"Air ais!"*

Again, bones clicked into place, wounds healed and eyes fluttered. "Hello? Hello?" Samily asked urgently.

Her hand twitched and rose. She was weak as water. Of course, she must have been Blackened. Samily needed to take her back again, further. *"Air ais."*

This time she was focused. Followed the path back. Through being Blackened and just before...

With a huge breath in, the woman jerked upright, her eyes wide in fear and wonder.

"It's all right," said Samily. "You're safe."

The woman collapsed against Samily's shoulder and wept great wracking sobs.

And then, a bizarre sound. A sound Samily was utterly unprepared for. It seemed so incongruous as to have to be the product of some fever dream.

*Applause.*

Samily looked around to see the Cured—the men who had helped and the others who'd stayed back. They stood, all of them... *clapping*.

"I don't...I..." Samily sputtered. And then she noticed Dialla was clapping too. And smiling.

Samily had never felt more uncomfortable in her life.

# CHAPTER 13

The demon's corpse had been burning for several hours when night fell. That morning's rain had left the ground damp, but Samily still felt the need to keep an eye on the fire. A man had found his way to them once it went up—a farmer called Torssen. It wasn't the first time a fire had brought a straggler. He was confused; came back from the Blackening alone in the wilds, with no memory of how he got there. He was on the road home to his farm, near Lochen. Didn't know how long he'd been Blackened. Just that he'd been on the road with a cart of produce bound for market when the Blackened overtook him. The cart was nowhere to be found. He couldn't have been gone long, she assumed—he was still fit to walk a long way in the few days since the Blackening was cured. But he was carrying substantially more weight when Samily restored him, and she had to reassess her guess at how long he might have been Blackened. The heft of a well-fed farmer had possibly kept him alive.

Torssen opted to stay with them for a bit, share some rations and rest before heading on. The woman Samily had saved from the demon had not yet spoken, but she sat in the firelight, jealously devouring a portion of bread and cheese. She must have been starving, bless her. Bless them all.

"Ho there!" A call from back down the road. In the darkness. Samily drew her sword and beckoned Dialla to join her. The master was better with words than Samily. That could be useful in avoiding a fight.

The two of them strode toward the voices. "Hello?" Dialla called.

More hoofbeats. More cartwheels. Sounded more like a trader than a patrol of soldiers. Good.

As they entered the edge of the light, a figure stood waving enthusiastically.

"Samily! Dialla! Thank God, we've found you!"

Samily almost said "*Majesty*" out loud but realised that perhaps that information remained best concealed. Dialla called back, "Lady Nirea!" and the surprise in her voice mirrored Samily's own.

Once the cart came to a halt, Samily recognised another face, and this one was a delightful surprise. "Greste!"

The woman climbed down and spread her arms. "Samily. It has been too long, child." Her kind, wise eyes sparkled with the reflected flames. Ah, it was wonderful to see a familiar face! Samily embraced her with joy and felt an unrealised weight lift from her.

"What are you doing here?" she asked.

"I was asked to accompany the queen," Greste said quietly. Her memory had been cleared. Good. "And the benefit of seeing you was impossible to refuse."

Greste had always seemed almost too gentle for a White Thorn. She was a storyteller, and a maternal figure for the younger Thorns in training. She maintained that role even into adulthood and was often the one reminding others to look after themselves, to eat and to rest. She was probably as close as Samily had to a mother, and the wave of emotion that came with her embrace took Samily by surprise. "It's wonderful to see you!" Her voice broke slightly as she spoke it out loud.

Greste held her at arm's length. "I hear incredible things about you, young lady. You're going to have to tell me all about it."

That would be nice, actually. "I would enjoy that," she answered.

"I'm sorry to interrupt, but, Samily, we need to speak urgently." Nirea had come around the front of the cart.

Samily glanced over her shoulder to confirm none of the Cured were close enough to hear. They had stayed by the fire, seemingly happy to allow Samily and Dialla to deal with the new arrivals. "What can I do, Your Majesty?" Another three people appeared from the cart. They seemed by their dress to be medics. "Ah! You have brought help! Thank you, Majesty, this is wonderful. They can perhaps move ahead when we need to stop, and stabilise those they find until we can reach them."

The queen's face remained dark, which seemed incongruous. Had she not come to assist them?

"Samily, we should talk in private. Well"—she looked to Master Dialla—"the three of us should talk."

Greste nodded respectfully and led the medics to the campfire. Once they were all out of earshot, Nirea spoke urgently.

"I have dire news, I'm afraid. Traverlyn was sacked two nights ago. Thakhati."

Dialla gasped.

"How?" Samily asked.

"The sunspire?" said Dialla.

"The spire did not light. The student maintaining it was murdered."

"No! *Girette?* No!" Dialla raised both hands to her mouth, her eyes wide in horror.

"I am sorry to say, yes." Nirea put a reassuring hand on Dialla's arm.

"I am sorry for your loss, Master," said Samily.

"Unfortunately, there is much more," said the queen. "The town was overrun. Hundreds, perhaps thousands, are dead. More are dying." She looked Samily in the eye. "Samily, we need you. Urgently."

*Oh no.*

With everything that had happened—curing the Blackening, taking Morienne's curse—Samily was absolutely sure this was where God wanted her. How could she abandon that task now? She looked over to the campfire. To the nine souls there who could well be dead without her. She thought of the dozens of others she had healed, who were now on their way home. How many would have died had she not been here to kill the demon? How many had already died because she was not here sooner?

"I'm sorry, Majesty, but I am needed here too. I will pray that those wounded in Traverlyn can hold on."

Nirea sighed. "I thought you might say that, Samily, which is why I brought these medics, and the supplies." She gestured to the cart. "We have bandages, medicine and rations. Enough for many people. I raided the stores of whatever I could lay my hands on. These medics will carry on and they should meet up with Lady Ikara soon, right? They can then bring everyone they find back to Traverlyn, to the hospital, where you will be waiting for them." She shook her head solemnly. "Samily, we truly need you. Now."

Samily bit down on her lips. This was no easy choice. It seemed, whatever she did, people were going to die. Before she could respond, Nirea spoke again.

"I have to tell you, there is even more at stake than the lives of those in danger. Quellaria is amongst the severely injured, Samily. She was badly burned, rescuing a young girl. She faced a Thakhati alone to save her. She won't survive without you. You know how much she means to us. To Eidyn."

Samily didn't know how to react to that. Quellaria rescuing a child? Did that seem like the abrasive, selfish, awful woman she'd spent days with? Not at all. But Samily did understand her importance. Still, was she so vital as to make her life worth more than those who had been neglected and left to die by the queen, the king, the envoy? Samily was loath to trade lives. But there was a crucial factor here.

"With respect, I understand your position, Majesty. But there are people out here dying who can only be saved by me. Only I can restore them to before they were Blackened without risking the curse returning. In Traverlyn, at least there is the hospital. Nobody else can do what I do here."

And that was the cut of it. She was one person, and the only one who could save some of these lives. Nirea was silent for a moment, as if considering something. "All right, Samily. I understand. The choice is yours, of course." There was something about the way she said it, though, as if she meant the opposite. It was odd.

Nirea turned to Dialla. "Master Dialla, I am deeply, deeply sorry to have to give you further bad news." She took the master's hands between her own. Dialla's lip trembled and tears already trickled from her eyes. "Principal Keft was lost in the fight with the Thakhati." Dialla's face crumpled and her eyes closed. "And Leondar is amongst the severely wounded. He does not have long."

Dialla's head jerked up, her eyes wide. "What? No. No, no, no, no, no. *Please, no.*"

"I am sorry." Nirea bowed her head. "He was wounded protecting me."

The queen's voice cracked on the last words, and Samily saw that she was carrying as much pain as Dialla. It was awful. She wanted to help them. But…

"Samily, we have to go," Dialla said suddenly. "Please, we have to go. Now. The three of us. We can ride directly back to Traverlyn. With my skill, we can be there in, what, a day and a half?" She looked to Nirea, and the queen nodded her agreement. "You can heal those in need, and we will ride straight back out here. I will not sleep. We can eat as we ride. These medics…"—she gestured toward the campfire—"the Cured, they can surely save most people here until we get back. Please, Samily."

*Oh.* This felt *all* wrong. Completely wrong. Now she was condemning a friend of both Nirea's and, evidently, Dialla's if she did not choose to go back with them. That was unfair. She had been backed into a corner.

"Samily, I'm going either way," said Dialla.

And that was worse. Samily felt a wave of genuine anger rise in her. But it would not be helpful. She needed a moment to think. "Excuse me." Samily turned and walked away. She breathed deep into her belly, letting the air cool her heart and calm her mind.

She was being asked to choose. To choose who lived and who died. That was not her right. She could save lives here, she knew that. But that would cost lives in Traverlyn. Or she could save those lives, and who knows how many would die alone on the Auld Road?

It was not fair.

It should not be her choice.

Samily sat cross-legged in the middle of the Auld Road and prayed.

*Please, God, show me the way. I will do what you guide me to.*

All was silence but the crackling of the fire and the wind in the grass. A bat swooped down before her, looping between trees in the dark. Searching for food.

Whatever she did, people would die. Without Dialla here, she could do less than before. She would need to rest more often. To sleep. Would that time lost be much less than riding to Traverlyn and back? From

Nirea's description, many would definitely die in Traverlyn. She could save them. For certain. Those out here, who knew how many they were?

Alone, desperate, dying.

And she had caused that. She had ended the Blackening too suddenly. If she was honest with herself, was that why she was so insistent on staying out here?

*S'grace!* How could she make this choice?

"Samily?" It was the queen's voice. "May I join you?"

Samily looked at her and back at the ground. She could not bring herself to invite Nirea to sit. She sat anyway.

"Samily, I'm sorry to put you in this position. It's not fair. There is something else you may not have considered, though."

Samily turned her head to look at the queen.

"Quellaria could be key to helping us retake the kingdom. To take it back from Anhel Weyr. To stop him. If you save her, Samily, you have no idea how many lives you could make better—how many lives you might save from his demons."

"Did she agree to help?"

Nirea sighed and looked to the sky. "She hadn't given me a decision. But I have to think... Samily, she saved that girl. That has to mean something."

Perhaps it did. Perhaps it only meant that Quellaria had the basic human instinct to protect a child. Perhaps it meant she was a better person than she seemed. But that was no guarantee.

Something occurred to her then. *Greste.* "Why is Greste with you? Are the Thorns in Traverlyn?"

Nirea smiled. "They are. They arrived in the night. The Thorns are the only reason Traverlyn wasn't levelled, Samily. Anhel Weyr sent the Thakhati to destroy it."

"And Meristan? Did you speak to him?"

"I did."

"What did he say? About me coming back?"

"He said it had to be your choice, and that he would not choose for you."

That made for a confusing mix of emotions. At once, she was glad of the respect her master had shown her, but equally, she would have valued his counsel now. The one time she might have wished for him to make the choice...

Nirea shifted to her feet. "I've said what I came to say. Dialla is keen to go. She's packing one of the horses."

"Now?" Samily jumped up. "I have to choose *now*?" Heavens no, she wasn't ready.

"I am sorry, Samily. I won't force you, but we need to go. Without Keft in Traverlyn, Dialla's skill is also needed. And if Leondar is going to die, Dialla has little time to see him." She lowered her voice. "It could already be too late."

With every fibre of her being, Samily resented being put in this position. But maybe, *maybe* on balance, going back to Traverlyn now was the best option.

And maybe Nirea had to make choices like this all the time.

Was that the weight of being queen? Choosing who lives and who dies? It was more power than anyone should have, and more responsibility than anyone should bear. Perhaps this was an instance when surrendering to a higher authority than herself was wise.

"Fine. I'll come with you. Just give me a moment."

Nirea smiled, and when she spoke, it was with a great sigh, as if a weight lifted from her. "Of course."

First, Samily had to speak to Greste. After what she'd seen today, the Cured needed protection. If Greste would stay with them and the other medics, then Samily would go.

She couldn't imagine Greste refusing.

And then she would go back to Traverlyn and try not to resent how she had been forced into that choice. She could easily find sympathy for Dialla. The poor woman seemed to be losing people like sand through her fingers. And she did not even know if the master had faith to console her.

At least Samily knew that those who were lost because she wouldn't be here to save them would find their way to God. That was something. That was comfort.

And she would hold tight to it.

# CHAPTER 14

Three days. Three days since the attack and, if anything, Aranok was getting worse. They'd woken early that morning to set the sunspire for the day, and Aranok had been so lethargic that Allandria insisted they come back to the room and let him get more sleep.

He'd been trying to keep up with the memory clearances too, since he didn't feel fit for much else, but by early afternoon yesterday he'd been suffering with dizziness and was struggling to remember people's names. It was too much. The blow to his head—whatever it had done—wasn't healing. And Allandria was fairly certain that the drain of the sunspire was part of the reason.

He wasn't fit for this. They needed an alternative.

A gentle knock at the door.

Allandria adjusted Aranok's cover and cracked open the door. As she'd hoped, the king was outside with his now-constant companion, Vastin. She'd asked a medic hours ago to send him this way if possible. She smiled and stepped out into the hall. He too looked exhausted, wearing a medic's apron stained with old blood. He'd been assisting with the wounded and the dying.

"Allandria. How are you both?" the king asked, looking pointedly at her broken arm. Vastin gave her a salutatory smile.

"I'm fine," she answered. "It only really hurts when I move it."

"Mmm." Mynygogg nodded knowingly. "And Aranok?"

That was the issue. "Less so. He's exhausted. He's...getting worse. And you know he won't stop. I can barely slow him down."

Mynygogg crossed his arms, leaned back against the opposite wall and looked at the ceiling. "All right. What can we do?"

Allandria clicked the door completely shut and spoke quietly. "We need someone else to operate that spire. He can't do it. Not like this. It's killing him."

"He told me the oldest earth *draoidh* student here is too young. And I tend to agree. Especially after what happened to..." Mynygogg opened his hands toward her. And he was right, they couldn't risk another child. But there had to be another answer.

"Surely there are other earth *draoidhs*? And surely someone here—a master—would know them? I mean, they'll have studied here...?"

"Oh, yeah," said Vastin. "That makes sense."

"All right. All right," said Mynygogg. "I'll mention it to Opiassa later."

As far as Allandria knew, the king, Meristan and Opiassa were effectively running things for the moment with Nirea away and Aranok and Allandria recovering. But Aranok had made it clear that they were all equals now in his eyes, and that, by extension, meant she was too. Which was strange, since she'd only been promoted to envoy what felt like days ago. But she did have a voice, and it was important to remember that. "How are things? Where are we?"

"Hard," said Mynygogg. "We're doing our best, but...having the sunspire is a huge boon. The Thorns are working with the Guard to help any injured who either couldn't make it here or who chose not to, for whatever reason. The rain put out the fires, but some of the damaged buildings are still in danger of collapsing. We've managed to organise stonemasons and carpenters to attend those in some sort of order. The Thakhati corpses burn in the sunlight, which is helpful, since it stops them poisoning the earth. But we've got a parade of pyres going in the western fields. We're trying to hold the dead as long as we can, though, because people keep coming looking for family and..."

And they didn't want to burn a corpse before their family knew they were dead. God, it was hideous. No wonder he looked exhausted.

"So, *messy*," she said.

"Aye, messy." A wry smile.

"I'll update him when he wakes up." Allandria nodded to the door. "He'll want to know."

"Good, yes." Mynygogg looked down the corridor for a moment. "Allandria, Nirea has gone for Samily."

"I know."

"Yes, but... *if* she brings her back... will this be a problem?" He gestured to the door then. "Can we fix this?"

It was a good question. Could they repair the schism between Aranok and Samily? Each had arguably legitimate grudges against the other. She could explain Aranok's actions to the girl, properly this time. But would he even want her to? Could anything salve his anger at her execution of Shayella? Maybe, once he was thinking more clearly. He was ashamed of what he'd done, that was clear. But she wasn't sure that was enough for Aranok to forgive her.

"I don't know. It's complicated," she said.

"Aye. That it is," Mynygogg answered.

"Is it, though?" Vastin looked up at them with consternation. "Is it really? Because, well, we know they're both good people, right? And what's happened, I mean, weren't they both just trying to help people? Not themselves, but others, right? So, can't we just... help them see that? Help them see each other... better?"

Allandria smiled. Sometimes it took the innocence of youth to see through complexity.

Mynygogg put a hand on the boy's shoulder. "Young man, you are a damn sight wiser than you have any right to be. That is exactly what we need to do. Perhaps I need to put *you* on my council."

Vastin's cheeks reddened as he looked down at his feet. "Just, you know, it's wrong, them being angry at each other."

Allandria wrapped her good arm around the boy and kissed him on the top of the head. He looked up from under his eyebrows with a shy smile.

"Thank you," she said.

"For what?"

"For doing both of my jobs while I can't."

It had been too long. Darginn must have walked every foot of Traverlyn. And still Ismar hadn't come home. Isadona was a wreck. Every time Darginn looked at his wife too long she burst into tears. So he didn't look at her. Living in each other's pockets the way they were... And, God, Darginn had brought them here. Because it was meant to be safe. Safer than Haven. And Ismar hadn't wanted to come...

And all that had led him here, back to the hospital. Not so busy at the front steps as it had been when he and Yavick had come three days ago. Most folk either already inside or already passed on now, he reckoned. A young medic with dark skin and deep, kind brown eyes met him inside the main doors. The double doors leading into a big hall were flung wide, and countless medics bustled amongst beds, tending the wounded.

"Aye, hello. Um, I was wondering, is..." Should he assume everyone knows who she is now? "...the queen...about?"

The medic smiled. She reminded him a wee bit of Lady Allandria, but shorter, and more fresh-faced. Well, he imagined she would be, but for now she looked as knackered as everyone else.

"I believe Her Majesty has left. A few days ago. Can I help?"

*Left?* Darginn's first reaction was shock, then a flare of anger. He'd been relying on her to let him know if Ismar turned up at the hospital. It was the only reason he hadn't been there every day.

But then, *hope*.

If Queen Nirea wasn't there, it was a damn sight more possible that Ismar had been brought in, and just nobody recognised him.

"Oh! Eh, I'm looking for my son. I thought he might be here, somewhere?" Darginn could barely contain the desire to rush inside and call out Ismar's name.

The medic smiled sympathetically. "What does he look like?"

"Oh, um, he's twenty-six, pale, thin, strong nose. And cheeks. Dark hair wi' a wee bit of grey." Ismar's hair had started to pepper when he was barely eighteen. Always made him look older than his years.

The medic seemed to think for a moment, then scrunched up half her face as if bracing herself against her own words. "Brown jacket?"

*Brown...* "Aye! Aye, brown leather jacket!" Darginn's heart danced. He was here! He was...Wait. Was he alive? The medic's face turned sour. Sad. Oh God, was he...?

"Follow me." Her words were gentle, which made them all the worse. The medic turned and led Darginn up several flights of stairs to another room full of beds. This one was a lot quieter than the other. Only a few medics here, and much less busy. The stench was enough to make Darginn blink.

She picked her way through the beds and stopped at the end of one right in the back corner. When she turned back, she looked afraid. "Is this him?"

Darginn paused. What if it was? It couldn't be good news, not with how the medic looked. What if...? *Damn it, man, at least you'll know! Be a father!*

He stepped forward.

It was Ismar. Paler, thinner even than he'd been. Darginn's stoicism crumbled and he dropped to his knees, grasping his son's frail hand in his own. "Ismar. Ismar. Oh God."

He felt the medic's hand on his shoulder. "Let me...let me get someone."

Darginn cupped the boy's cheek in his hand. It was so cold. He shouldn't be so cold. His eyes were set deep in dark pools. What had happened to him? But he was alive, surely. Medics didn't tend the dead. So why had the woman...?

Time passed and Darginn knelt in silence. Here was his boy, his sad, distracted, isolated boy. And Darginn had no idea how to help him.

"Sir?"

Darginn turned to see an older medic—a man with bushy eyebrows and a light beard.

"Yes?"

"Mystolla came for me." He indicated the medic, who stood nervously at a distance. "She's my student. My name is Farich. I understand this may be your son?"

"Aye. It is."

"All right. There's not a lot I can tell you. I believe he was pulled from the ruins of a collapsed house. He was the only survivor. So he's strong. But..."

"But what?"

Farich crouched beside Darginn so their faces were at the same level.

"Truthfully, I don't know why he's still alive. He's taken so much damage, inside, for everything I know; honestly, I'm sorry, but he should already be dead. It's a miracle he's not."

*A miracle?*

"How...? What...what can I do?" Darginn stuttered.

Farich stood and offered Darginn his hand to help him to his feet. He walked a wee bit away from the bed and gestured for Darginn to join him.

"Do you have other family? His mother?"

Darginn nodded.

"Bring her here. Spend time with him. If he goes, you can say goodbye. But if whatever's keeping him alive gives him a chance...I don't know. Maybe having you here..."

"Right...right." Darginn nodded. "Thank you." He took the medic's hand between his and shook it. Turned and smiled to Mystolla too. "Thank you."

When they'd both gone, he went back to Ismar's bed and gently kissed his son on the forehead.

"Don't go anywhere, boy. Mum's coming. Just you wait here, all right? Please?"

With a final stroke of his son's chest, Darginn turned and rushed back down the stairs.

---

Another knock at the door. Allandria had become practised at this. She opened it just a crack, enough to have a conversation, but kept herself behind the door. Now that people were coming and going from Traverlyn again, they had to assume the assassin might have come back—if they had ever left. So every person they encountered was suspect. "Who's there?"

"Teyjan. Lady Allandria?"

Hmm. She hadn't known Teyjan was still there. Why was he still there? He'd been healed a good while ago. Could easily have gone before the attack. Though she hadn't checked either way. "Oh, hello. I thought you were gone."

"Eh, no. Stayed to help, what wi' all the wounded. Seemed like the decent thing to do, y'know?"

Of course, the Reiver was a medic. That did make sense. Still, she had to be sure.

"Teyjan, I need you to answer a question for me."

"Aye?" His tone was confused. Allandria still had not shown herself at all. She would have been confused on his side of the door.

"Back in Pebyl, what's your chieftain's name again?"

A moment of silence. Allandria gripped the dagger in her good hand tighter.

"Sorry, d'you mean Galche?"

Good start. She'd deliberately mistaken his clan. But anyone might have known that from his painted leathers. "Sorry, of course. Galche."

"It's Chief Hombuck."

Of course it was. But again, anyone could know that, theoretically. She needed to be more direct.

"Teyjan, when we met..." Could she really ask this? Was it cruel?

It was. She wasn't going to remind the man of Tecatt's death. Not now. "Sorry, I mean..." What could she ask him that wasn't common knowledge? She suddenly couldn't remember a single damn conversation the two of them had had on the road. Fuck it, the best she could do was something she knew there was only a handful of witnesses to. "Where did we bury Tecatt?"

"What?" Stunned silence. To be honest, even the emotion she could hear in his voice was enough. But she had to be certain.

"Tecatt. Where did we bury him?"

Teyjan cleared his throat. "Jazere grew him a memorial tree."

Allandria opened the door to find the Reiver wearing a medic's apron over a shirt and trousers rather than the brightly painted leathers he usually wore. He scowled at her.

"I'm sorry; I had to be sure it was you. It's a long story."

The scowl turned to a curious frown. "Are you in danger?"

God, when were they not? "Maybe. Well, yes. I suppose we are."

"Anything I can do?" he asked.

"What's happening?" Aranok's groggy voice from behind her. The conversation had woken him.

Allandria turned to him, stepping back to allow Teyjan and Aranok to see each other. "It's just Teyjan. The Reiver. Remember?"

Aranok shaded his eyes. "The one with the beard?"

Teyjan stroked his long black-and-white beard. "Aye, Laird, that's me."

Aranok shuffled to sit up in his bed. He'd not spent a lot of time out of it since yesterday. The dizziness was worse and the fatigue was heavy. He slept about sixteen hours a day at the moment. And she just sat and kept guard, with her one useful arm. She'd gotten accustomed to sleeping on the chair with her sword on her lap. Made it easier to keep her broken arm in a position that the pain didn't keep her awake.

"Come in," Aranok said when he'd settled himself. He looked a right mess with the hair that was free from the bandaging around his head sticking up like dishevelled hay.

Teyjan stepped in and Allandria closed and locked the door behind him. "So, is there...? Can I do anything?"

Aranok waved his question away. "No, thank you, we're fine. Do you need something?"

"Oh, I'm just delivering a message. I've been looking after this lady, Rasa?"

"Rasa? How is she?" Allandria asked. She'd heard the metamorph had been hurt, but nothing much since.

"She'll be all right," Teyjan answered. "Been out o' it for a good few days, like. Nasty gashes down her side." Teyjan ran his hand from just below his ribs on his left side to halfway down his thigh. "Apparently, she was a horse...? Anyway, she canna really move 'cause of her stitches, but when she woke up today she was very keen to speak to you, Laird Aranok. Something about your family, I think."

Aranok whipped off the sheets and was halfway to standing when he put up a hand and sat back down again. Thankfully, he'd fallen asleep in his clothes. But his balance was still off. Allandria grabbed his cane and helped him to his feet.

"That happening a lot?" Teyjan asked.

"Yes," Allandria answered. "And he's exhausted all the time. Could be the fact that he's also powering the sunspire."

"It's fine," said Aranok. "Just take us to Rasa."

"Hang on." Teyjan lifted a candle from the mantelpiece and held it near the side of Aranok's head. "Just look at me, aye?"

Aranok nodded and Teyjan moved the candle slowly toward Aranok's nose, *hmm*ed and did the same on the other side. "You had any other head knocks recently?"

"No, I—" Aranok started, but Allandria cut him off.

"Yes. A few, actually."

"Right. And Lady Samily, is she still around?" Teyjan asked.

"Not that I know of," Aranok said tersely.

"All right, listen. I'm no happy with the state of you," said Teyjan. "Before we go, can I just look at your head?" Aranok opened his mouth to object, but Teyjan didn't let him speak. "It'll only take a minute. And then we'll go."

Aranok sighed. "Fine."

It didn't take long, as Teyjan had promised, and he replaced the bandages with clean ones. Allandria was actually glad to see him get a bit of attention. With all the other injured and dying, medics weren't tending to those not in urgent need, and Aranok wouldn't go looking for one until he was probably too incapacitated to do it.

"Right," Teyjan said to Allandria. "If this doesn't improve in a few days, you come and find me, all right? I'll try to check in when I can."

"It'll be fine." Aranok was back on his feet, leaning on the cane again. "Can we see Rasa?"

"Of course." Teyjan opened the door. "But take your time, please."

---

Aranok slumped down awkwardly onto the chair next to Rasa's bed. The walk to her room had been tiring, and he was glad to get off his feet again.

"Miss Rasa?" Teyjan gently nudged her awake.

Rasa's eyes blinked open and she smiled when she saw Allandria.

"Hello." She looked round and saw Aranok. "Hello, Envoy. You look like I feel."

"Rasa. How are you?" Aranok asked. "I hear Traverlyn owes you."

"I hear the same about you," she answered. Her voice was soft, as if lined with cotton. Quieter than usual. Her eyes were a little glassy. Poppy milk. Aranok had been trying to minimise what he took. His head was already a muddle; it didn't need more dulling.

"Looks like we both paid for it," said Aranok.

"Excuse me, Laird, Ladies, I'll leave you to it." Teyjan moved to the door. "All of you, be gentle with yourselves. None of you's immortal. All right?" With a nod, he was gone. Seemed like a good man. Allandria spoke well of him.

"How are you feeling, Rasa?" Allandria asked.

"Sore. But mostly well, as long as I stay still. I'm told I will be here awhile."

Unless Samily reappeared. But Aranok wasn't in a hurry to see her again. Not yet, anyway. Though they could all do with her "healing."

"Rasa, Teyjan said you needed to speak to me. About my family." Aranok had been desperate to hear what she had to say since the Reiver had mentioned it, but he was sure she would have found a way to him sooner if it were urgent. Or if it were bad. He hoped so, anyway. He'd spent the walk here convincing himself that whatever she had to say couldn't be *too* awful.

"Yes." Rasa moved a weak hand onto his knee. "There was an attempt, on your family." Aranok's world shifted sideways. He'd been wrong. "They are fine. But it's why I stayed an extra day. They... Lady Ikara said to tell you that she convinced your father. He hired guards. For the house. But one of them..." Rasa trailed off and pursed her lips tightly.

"One of them?" Aranok prompted her.

"One of them, I think... Aranok, I think your father may have hired an assassin himself. He's the one who caught the assassin. And killed him. And... nobody knew anything, until the morning. He just caught this man sneaking in, killed him, put the body in the garden and waited for morning."

He should probably be appalled, based on the look on Allandria's face, but Aranok couldn't help but be impressed. Firstly, that the "guard" had been so effective, and secondly, that his father had had the wisdom to hire an assassin to hunt an assassin.

With any luck, Madu's contract on Aranok's family died with him. Bizarrely, this could actually be good news.

"Ari? Say something." Allandria nudged him.

"Sorry, yes, um, they're all right?"

"They are," said Rasa. "Ikara and Sumara were upset. They managed to keep it from Emelina, I think. I spent the day with her. Your father...didn't say much."

Aranok should be overcome with horror. Someone really had tried to kill his family. But the relief that they were safe, and that maybe he could stop worrying about them...

But it also meant Madu's threat was real. Which meant the threat to Allandria's parents was real.

*Shit.*

He turned to Allandria. "I'm sorry; I just realised..."

She nodded solemnly. "They'll be fine. They'll be gone."

"We're going to check. As soon as we can. I promise."

She closed her eyes and nodded again.

"Thank you, Rasa. For everything. We should let you rest." Aranok stood.

"Wait, wait." Rasa waved him back down. "The man. The assassin. I was...I had an instinct about him. He made my flesh crawl. I just...I'm not sure I trust him, Aranok. I think you should go. See for yourself. He was hiding something."

Right. That could be something. Could be nothing. The kind of person who became an assassin—the very nature of their work was mercenary. Secretive. As long as he was being paid by Dorann, he should be fine. But if Rasa was concerned enough to tell him about it...maybe he needed to get home. Without being caught, or just putting his family in more danger.

While also keeping the sunspire going.

Somehow.

*Fuck.*

# CHAPTER 15

"Oh, oh Heavens, is that, is it, oh, thank God, is that...Lady Samily?"

It took Nirea a moment to recognise Isadona, Darginn's wife, rushing toward them. It had been too long since she'd slept and the world was all a bit sharp in the wrong places. Samily turned to her with a kind but bemused smile. She seemed to have no idea who the woman was.

Nirea had tried to bring Samily and Dialla in quietly to get them to this palliative room. The master gasped and rushed to Leondar's bed. Nirea let her go, delighted to assume the kingsguard was still alive.

Isadona reached them and placed both hands on Samily's forearm. "Oh, thank God, you've come to save him! You've come to save our boy!" She was weeping so profoundly that by the end it was difficult to understand her.

"I...Yes..." Samily stuttered. Darginn stepped up behind his wife, and the Thorn's face melted into recognition. "Darginn Argyll!" Now she smiled broadly.

Darginn paused briefly, as if surprised by Samily's warm reaction.

*Oh shit.*

She didn't know his memory had been changed. If she said the wrong thing...Nirea touched Samily's shoulder and tried to steer her toward the bed where she knew Leondar lay. But the knight shook off her hand with a raised eyebrow and turned back to the couple.

"Darginn, it is your son who is injured?"

"Aye, aye, it is," said Darginn. "We'd be so grateful if you could help him, please."

"Show me." Darginn and Isadona turned toward the bed they'd come from. Nirea caught Samily's arm and pulled her back before she could follow them. The knight turned and glowered. "What?"

Nirea leaned in close. "He doesn't remember what happened to him. At Lestalric."

Her forehead crumpled in confusion. "What?"

"I...Quellaria *helped* him. With his nightmares." She raised her eyebrows and hoped Samily understood. "Be careful what you say. Isadona knows."

Samily looked at her a moment as if assessing how she felt about that information but finally nodded and followed the couple. It would do no harm to allow Samily to heal Ismar. Nirea was pleased he'd turned up, though he wouldn't be here if he wasn't at death's door. It must have been a hard time for his parents, waiting, helpless, for him to die. And now he wouldn't. Nirea felt a little bit good about that. She'd done that.

She moved to Quellaria's bed. The one next to it was empty. And the next one. They'd lost people while she was away—grimy sheets stained with dark brown blood the only remnants of their time here. But Quell was alive. Unrecognisable, except to Tia. If not for that wee girl, they'd never have known their memory *draoidh* was right here under their noses. What a bloody tragedy that would have been.

A sudden burst of excitement and joy from the other side of the room told Nirea that Samily had restored Ismar. Even the three medics who tended the room had gathered at his bed, and seemed almost as delighted as the family. "My boy! My boy!" she heard Darginn cry. Ah, it was music.

Two of the medics, both young—maybe students—hurried from the room, leaving only the older, bearded man behind. He seemed to be engaging Samily in some conversation. Probably obsessing about all the lives she could save here. Nirea might have left them to it, but there were other urgent cases. Nirea moved toward Leondar's bed.

"Samily? Could you...?" She pointed and the knight nodded. The medic deferred and stepped back, as Nirea had intended. Most people in the building knew who she was now. Possibly all of them.

Dialla was kneeling at Leondar's side, hand on his chest, tears pouring from her. "His face. His beautiful face." She raised a trembling hand as if she would touch the cheek that was no longer there. Just a gaping hole exposing his teeth and tongue, like some hideous medical drawing.

"Dialla. May I?" Samily asked. The master shuffled aside and gave the Thorn room. *"Air ais."*

Muscle and skin regrew as Leondar's face knit itself back together. It was over so quickly that Nirea almost regretted not watching more closely. *Miraculous* really was a fair description of this girl's skill. The big man's eyes drowsily blinked open. "What... What...?"

Dialla threw herself on his chest, crying huge, exhausted tears. Nirea had been certain of the connection between these two. She had relied on it. When Aranok had reminded her Dialla was with Samily, that had been her way in. She knew if she couldn't get Samily to come back for the right reasons, she could get Dialla to come for Leondar. And that, she had rightly hoped, might tip the scales to get Samily too. Ah! At least this... this had worked out.

She maybe wanted to hug the man almost as much as Dialla did. But it wasn't her time. Whatever means it had taken, however she'd justified it, she'd saved him. Now she'd have a chance to thank him for saving her.

A commotion at the door and a throng of medics bustled in. This was the chaos she'd been hoping to avoid. Samily would be pulled in too many different directions and they needed to prioritise. Nirea held up her hands.

"Everyone! Please! Just... Could I have quiet, please?" The chatter stopped as they each recognised who had asked. "Yes, Lady Samily is here and will be helping as many people as she can. For now, while she tends to the most urgent in this room, could you all please step outside?"

The excitement faded to disappointment as several pairs of eyes looked to the floor, while others stared longingly toward the wondrous time *draoidh*. Samily said nothing. She'd gone even longer than Nirea without sleep.

When the room was quiet again, Samily and Nirea crossed to Quell's bed.

"This is Quellaria?" Samily asked.

Nirea nodded.

"How do you know?"

It was a fair question. "I didn't. Tia, the girl she saved? She said this is her dress. It's how she knew."

Samily frowned. "So... it may not be her?"

*Oh Hell.* Nirea's stomach flipped. That thought hadn't occurred to her. Tia had been so certain. But she was a girl. A traumatised little girl. Was it possible she had brought Samily all the way back here hunting a dead deer? "I...I don't think so." But truthfully, she didn't know. They were about to find out either way.

With a sigh, Samily placed a hand on the woman's chest. *"Air ais."*

This time, it took a little longer, or maybe it just seemed like it, as thick black scabs and angry red wounds softened to peach and hair sprouted from her scalp. Slowly her features returned, as if they were rebuilt, and Nirea recognised the distinct face of the memory *draoidh*.

*Thank God!*

"Hmm." Samily looked at her as if deciding whether she was happy. When the woman's eyes didn't open, she turned back to the only medic left in the room, the man with the beard. "Who is the most in need?"

The medic bustled over. "Well, I suppose they all are. But...."—he rubbed his hand over his head—"perhaps this woman?"

He led Samily across the room, back near the door. Only then did Nirea realise how loud it now was. Or how quiet it had been. Silence had been a shroud here. Now Darginn and Isadona chatted excitedly with Ismar, and Leondar had roused enough that he and Dialla were having a hushed conversation. Life. Life had returned.

"Hey, Red." The voice was groggy. Sluggish.

But Nirea's grin was as wide as her ears. And when she looked down at Quell, she noticed that Samily had not only healed the woman but restored her dress too. She knew how Quell felt about her dresses. That was an unexpected touch of kindness. Maybe she'd been impressed by the memory *draoidh*'s actions after all.

"Quellaria. I hear you've been quite the hero."

"Pfft. Doesn't sound like me."

Nirea pulled over a chair from a few beds away. "Seriously. Did you sacrifice yourself for a little girl?"

"Not really. I sort of... Things got out of hand. She happened to be there, was all."

It was true. She'd more likely claim the credit if it wasn't. Excellent. That was a good sign.

"You got the mad girl to heal me?" Quell asked. "Handy little trick to have on tap, isn't she?"

"Ha!" Nirea blurted. She leaned in closer. "Not only did I have to go and get her back from several days' ride away, I also had to *persuade* her to come."

Quell put a hand to her chest in mock surprise. "She wouldn't come just for me?"

Nirea smiled. Despite all that had passed between the two of them, there was actually some sort of connection there. That spark when you connect with someone on a level of unspoken understanding. Nirea had had to let her guard down completely to try to convince Quellaria to stay before the attack. And, honestly, it had been a relief. Unnerving, but a relief. She could just be herself with this woman. In fact, it was necessary. She saw through masks like windows. But, of course, she'd fucked off the minute Nirea turned her back. And that had hurt, actually. More than Nirea had realised. She'd been angry to lose her, when she was so important, but also... it hurt.

And now, if she was going to convince her to change her mind, to stay and work with them, she was going to have to do it all over again. And maybe force the *draoidh* to do the same.

"Quell, why did you run? Seriously, please. Tell me the truth."

The *draoidh* sighed and tilted her head back to look at the ceiling. "Ah, fuck, I don't know. It was a lot. I'm not... People don't... Fuck, I was rattled, all right? I look after myself. And that's fine. Right? But... I don't know. It's all so... big."

Yes. It was big. It was a lot to ask. And not everyone was up to a rebellion. Most people just wanted a quiet life. To be left alone and allowed to get by however they could. Asking them to see the big problems—to *solve* the big problems—was a lot. Some people just weren't made for it. "All right. So it wasn't because you're against us?"

Quell snapped her head forward to look at Nirea. "After this?" She gestured to the whole room. "Fuck me, Red, after what that prick Weyr did? To me? I want his smarmy bloody face pinned to a wall."

All right. If hatred of Weyr was enough to get her back on their side, that would do. Hate could be as good a motivator as any. "So you're with us?"

Quell flattened her mouth sceptically. "I'll help you. And we'll see."

*Good enough.*

"That wee girl. Tia. She all right?" Quell asked.

"I'll go and get her," said Nirea. "You can see for yourself." She turned for the door, only to see her husband coming toward her.

"My love!" He kissed her, as had quickly become their custom, both to confirm their identities to each other and also, frankly, because it was nice. "You did it." Mynygogg looked to Samily, then down at Quellaria, who looked not a little amused at being witness to their reunion.

The *draoidh* raised a hand. "Don't stop on my account. I've got nothing else to do."

"Quellaria." Mynygogg turned solemn. "I'm delighted you're well. Can I do anything for you?"

"Nothing your wife wouldn't object to, Your Majesty." She grinned lasciviously and raised her eyebrows. It took Gogg a moment to recognise her meaning, and he had no idea how to react. Nirea snorted a laugh and Quell's eyes sparkled with mirth.

"Don't worry," said Nirea. "You don't have to keep being nice to her. She's already agreed to help."

"Oh! Oh." Mynygogg's face melted into delight. "That's wonderful. Quell, thank you. Thank you. This means...I can't even put it into words. Thank you."

Quellaria gave a sort of half-hearted salute. "Your wife still owes me wine."

"Hey." Nirea pointed at her. "I showed up with that. You were gone."

"So you drank it?" she asked.

"I...broke it."

Quell laughed. "Fair."

Mynygogg pulled at Nirea's arm. "Excuse us, Quell, I need the queen for a moment. We'll check in on you later."

"I'll be fine. Gonna have a nap."

That was probably best. She would still have a heavy dose of opium in her, even though they'd been forced to ration their supplies. They all would, and they'd need time to burn it off. The two of them stepped away to a spot in the middle of the room, as far from a bed as it was possible to get.

Mynygogg spoke quietly. "While Samily's here, we need to get everyone together. Even just for an hour."

That sounded dangerous. Samily would not be keen to see Aranok, and frankly neither was she. "Are you sure?"

"Absolutely," he said firmly. "We're going to fix this. Today."

# CHAPTER 16

There was still blood on the cobbles. In the earth between them. Dried and black. Meristan had spent days surrounded by death and pain in these streets. It was draining on even the staunchest of hearts. How did the faithless reconcile themselves to this carnage? How did they begin to come to terms with loss on this scale? In many ways, he pitied his friends who did not or could not believe. If he had no comfort that those lost souls were at peace, he might not be able to bear it.

"Meristan?"

He knew the voice instantly and his heavy heart filled with joy. He turned to see Samily walking toward him and burst into a run, bundling her into his arms. "Samily! You're back."

She was too old now to be lifted off her feet, but joy overtook him. It was a painful mistake, pulling at the new stitches Egretta had put in his chest to replace those he'd burst fighting the Thakhati. Samily might sort that for him later. He released his grasp with a final, gentle squeeze and stepped back. "How are you?"

But now that he could see her, she clearly was not well. Her eyes were rimmed red, her skin pale, as if stretched too thin. Her cheeks drawn. Her head fell forward as she looked at the ground. "I am... I'm... tired." Her voice broke on the last word and she stepped back into Meristan's embrace, sobbing against his chest plate.

"Oh, my girl. What is it? What's happened?"

She shook her head, unable to answer, so they simply stood there, in the middle of the street, Meristan holding his girl, silently stroking her hair while she cried.

After a while, when her breathing returned to normal, Samily pushed herself away from Meristan and wiped her eyes. "I am sorry. I am just—"

"You need never apologise to me, Samily."

She smiled weakly, but there was light in her eyes, at least. "Were you...going to the meeting?"

Mynygogg had sent a message, asking him to a meeting at the Auld Hoose as soon as he could make it there. He'd had no idea Samily would be there.

"I am. When did you get back? What has happened?"

She sighed deeply. "There is a lot. I would have welcomed your advice more than once. It is a relief to see you."

"Do you want to tell me about it?" What he really wanted to ask was what happened between her and Aranok. And preferably before they reached the inn, where he might be waiting. But that may not be her priority. So he would let her lead, and perhaps slow their walk.

"I...have not slept for...some days. Master Dialla has been providing us with energy so that we could heal the Cured, but then Queen Nirea arrived and told us of what had happened here, and..."

"And you chose to come back?" Meristan had not expected that. But he was glad of it, all the same.

"Well, not at first. No. But when the queen told Dialla about Leondar— They have a relationship. She insisted on coming back, so we would have had to sleep anyway, and...I didn't know what was best. So I agreed."

Meristan's jaw tightened. Nirea had used Dialla to manipulate her. That was unfair. And he had helped, unwittingly, by telling Nirea what to expect from Samily. Yet he wasn't sure it was the wrong decision. It was the burden of that decision on Samily that he resented. Maybe he should have gone and ordered her back. Would that have been better for her? For everyone? It didn't matter now. What was done was done. "And were you able to help?" She looked up at him, unsure as to his meaning. "With the wounded? With...Quellaria?"

Samily nodded. "Of course. I mean, we were in time, yes. For her and Leondar. And for Darginn Argyll's son and many others. And I will do more, for those who need it urgently, before Dialla and I return to the Auld Road. We leave tonight."

Without rest. Again. "Samily, how long is it since you slept?"

"I have lost count." She shrugged. "It does not matter. Lives are at stake."

They approached a turning where a right would have them soon at the Auld Hoose. Meristan walked confidently past it. Samily gave no sign of noticing.

"I think it does matter, Samily. You are a wonder, but you are human. Your body, your mind are exhausted, regardless of the energy Master Dialla has provided you. It is not your responsibility to save everyone."

"But I am the only one who can! And..." She trailed off and Meristan wondered if she would continue. He left the silence for her to fill—a lesson from Severianos. The streets were quiet, the only sound their boots crunching on the cobbles. The town was in mourning. Would be for some time. People were staying home. Afraid; grieving; recovering. Their footsteps had fallen into time with each other, Meristan noticed. A gentle pace.

"I *did* this," Samily said after a few minutes. She looked up at him. "Have you heard?"

"I've heard a story," Meristan answered calmly. "I'd like to hear yours."

Samily took a deep breath and spoke. "On the way back to Traverlyn, Rasa and I found that the Blackened were being harvested by the Thakhati. We brought Quellaria to the king and queen, and reported that to them, but they did nothing! They said the envoy was dealing with it. But people were dying! Every day! Every hour! And they seemed so caught up in their, I do not know, politics? Negotiations? They were not going to act. So I acted."

She paused then, as if waiting for a response. Meristan simply nodded encouragingly.

"But I did not go to kill the necromancer. I swear it. I went to convince her to end the Blackening. Without delay. But she...I found her and...she had made a deal. With the envoy. He was to feed the

Dead girl, and she would help." Another pause. Waiting for a response. Meristan was not ready to pass judgement either way, but he had not heard of this deal, and he wondered how on earth Aranok had planned to fulfil his end, given the girl had needed fresh meat.

"Go on," he said.

"We talked. I told her to forget the deal. She had to act. And she attacked me."

"She attacked you?" The shock was clear in his voice. If Samily had been acting in self-defence, then Aranok's complaints were dead in the water.

"Well." Samily appeared to think for a moment. "I... She was feeding her own hand to the girl. It was ungodly! And I drew my sword then, I think..."

S'grace. That was an image he'd been glad not to see. But it fit. That motherly love he'd seen from Shayella, the longing, the fire to save her little girl. Yes, that made sense. She'd have given her life for that child in an instant, though Kiana was already dead. It was not as clear-cut as it might have seemed. "Then what?"

"She conjured some poison mist against me. I could not open my eyes. And she came at me. I was defending myself when I accidentally speared the Dead girl. In the head. I thought it was the necromancer, honestly."

So she'd ended the girl in error. Self-defence. But she'd arguably begun the fight, drawing her blade. Heavens above. Where was fault here? Was there any? He'd been worried about Samily's desire to punish Shayella after what she had done to Darginn. Seen a streak of ire in her he'd never experienced before. And Shayella was mad. That was unquestionable.

"I understand. Then what?"

"Then the envoy arrived. He cleared the mist. And Shayella, well, she collapsed. On the girl. The envoy was angry. He spoke to Shayella. Asked her forgiveness, I think. Ordered me to stand down. But Shayella, in the end, she told me to do it. To execute her."

Because her daughter was gone from her. Finally and completely. And Aranok stood watching her grieve over that girl, who Samily saw only as a mockery of a life, but who to Shayella was everything. And

Samily simply saw a way to save the Blackened. Serving God's children. Exactly as she was raised.

Damn it all, it was complex indeed.

"Then he attacked me," said Samily. "With flame." Her tone was defiant now. As if expecting a challenge.

"I've heard, yes. I'm sorry that happened." How to ask the next bit? How to ascertain whether the envoy had lost his mind or just control? He stopped walking and turned to her. "Samily, this is crucial. I understand it was...messy. But can you remember Aranok saying his magic word? Or making gestures with his hands? To create the fire?"

Samily cocked her head and crinkled her brow. "Well, he must have."

"Do you remember it, Samily? Think."

She looked away and breathed deeply. "I...looked up. He wanted me to use my skill. Turn back time."

And she had refused. Despite the fact that the Blackening was cured already. That was...He didn't know what that was. Mercy? Or punishment? Justice? Only God would know, in truth. "And...?"

"And he had fire around his fists and—"

"Did he say the word? Make any gestures?"

"I don't..."

"Did you see them?"

"I don't think so. I am not sure, but I do not think so. I would honestly not have considered it important had you not asked." Samily's manner was now defensive, which checked Meristan's passion. The frustration, the fear, the anger he'd had no outlet for had all bubbled up at once, and he needed to bring them back under control, especially toward Samily, who deserved none of it.

"I'm sorry. It's...all right. There is more here than you know. Allandria tells me—"

"She told me it was my fault," Samily interrupted.

Meristan bristled again at that. But there would be more to that story too. "Well, this is key for all of us to understand. Allandria told me that Aranok lost control of his power. He did not mean to attack you. Or at least, he did not choose to attack you. Apparently, this is how *draoidh* skills manifest in childhood. It is highly unusual for them to behave so in adulthood, but—"

"Oh!" Samily's entire demeanour changed. "That makes sense. Of course. I understand."

Meristan barely knew what to say. It was that simple? Samily was always a straightforward person, but this was… "You do?"

"I did the same. With a new ability. I stopped a demon. And myself. With no words or anything. We were frozen in time. Master Dialla had to help me out of it."

"Oh!" Meristan almost stepped back in surprise. A whole new ability, and enough for her to understand what had happened to Aranok. So quickly. "So you… you think we should forgive him?"

"Forgive? I am not sure I would say that. A man as powerful as him, losing control of his skills? That is dangerous. But… I suppose, between you, Allandria and Rasa, perhaps I have some… understanding of what happened. But I would be wary of it happening again."

*Rasa?* "What did Rasa say?"

Samily looked around, as if the houses had suddenly appeared from a fog. "Wait. Where are we? This is not the way."

Meristan pretended to be as puzzled as her. "You're right. We've walked too far." They turned back toward the inn. "Tell me what Rasa said."

Samily was almost chirpy now. It was bizarre. Had she wanted a reason to let go of that resentment? Or did knowing it was accidental in itself make her feel better? Meristan found himself, not for the first time, struggling to follow a leap of her emotions.

"Rasa's mother… Oh, I do not know if I should share this. No, I think it is important. I believe she would understand. Rasa's mother had a sickness. Of the mind. A sadness, she called it. She hanged herself when Rasa was young."

"Oh Heavens." What an awful tragedy. Meristan stroked the light symbol on his pauldron. Some believed those who took their own lives never found God in death. He hoped that was wrong.

"She believes Laird Aranok may have that same sickness. And she thought that, perhaps, he attacked me expecting me to kill him."

Meristan blew out air from full cheeks. What on earth to do with that idea? Aranok may wish himself dead? What a godforsaken mess. All these damaged people crashing into each other's lives and… Nothing was simple.

"All right. Thank you, Samily. That was...enlightening. At least I have a better idea of what happened."

Samily stopped walking and was quiet a moment. Clearly, a thought was playing at her. "Was it...Did I do the wrong thing? Was it my fault?"

Meristan took her by the shoulders and looked her in the eye. "Samily, whatever came of it, I know without reservation that you acted in the best interests of the most people. You acted out of kindness and love and responsibility. You took action because people were dying. Whatever the cause of what happened next, I say with absolute certainty that you did not deserve anything that happened to you. The situation was unbearable."

She smiled weakly but with genuine happiness. "Thank you."

That would have to do for the moment, because the Auld Hoose was round the next corner, and they clearly had a lot to discuss. For now, he was simply going to appreciate that his girl was alive and well.

He looked down at her, stoic, beautiful. So like her mother when he'd met her all those years ago.

*Wait.*

*What?*

---

"What?" Samily must have misheard. But her stomach was suddenly full of worms. Had Meristan really said...

"I met your mother! S'grace, Samily, I hadn't remembered—well, I didn't remember because...Oh Heavens, girl, we should sit down." Meristan looked around and then pulled her to a bench in front of a cheesemonger.

Her head was spinning. How could Meristan have met her mother? He'd talked repeatedly about the day he found her on the street in Apardion. How he'd looked for her family and learned she had none. Then brought her home with him to Baile Airneach, to train as a Thorn. That was her history. That was who she was. "I don't understand."

Meristan's eyes darted about and blinked as if watching some invisible insects dance in the air before him. "I...All right, all right. I think I understand. I think I know what has happened. When Aranok restored my memory, so much came back to me. It was a wave, washing over me when I awoke. My memory of who I was, returned to me. It was so big, huge—and then we fought the Dead. And...I just never..." He seemed to be struggling to find words. "Samily, I've only just realised. I'm so sorry. I just hadn't thought on it before." He took her hands gently. "I met your mother. She asked me to take you. Begged me to take you. Samily, your mother was a memory *draoidh*."

"I don't...I don't understand. If she...If you met her. If I was..." She could barely form the words. "Did she not love me?" With all Meristan had told her of the love of a parent, how could her own mother have given her away?

"Oh, oh no. She adored you. You were everything to her. Heavens, I'm almost loath to...The truth of it is tragic." Now he looked directly at her, and his mouth curled sadly. "She was not much older than you. And...her parents had thrown her out. When they discovered she was *draoidh*. Eidyn is sadly not the only place where *draoidhs* are mistreated. There was no university for her. Nowhere to take her in. She asked me to take you. I was reticent. I didn't want to take a child from her mother. You were so young. But she was desperate. She didn't want you to grow up like her. She was the one who told me to keep your skill a secret. To think of you as a healer, not a *draoidh*. She put all of that in my mind—and then erased my memory of her. Replaced it with me finding you on the street. And..." He opened his hands.

And that was the story Samily had grown up with. The lie. Her mother might be alive. She had given Samily up out of...love? So she would have a better life than her mother. "Her life was really so bad? Just for being *draoidh*?"

Meristan nodded. "So she told it. And with what we've seen here? I have no reason to doubt it."

Samily was numb. She had no idea how to feel. Quellaria had mocked her for not growing up *draoidh*. For not having suffered as a *draoidh* child would have. But she had. She had lost her mother. Because they were both *draoidh*. Part of her was furious; part was devastated. But another part was...happy? To know her mother had loved her. Had wanted better for her. How different her life might have been. Goodness!

"She could still be alive?"

Meristan's eyes widened as he sat back. "She could. Absolutely. Somewhere in Apardion, I suppose."

"And she is a memory *draoidh*?"

"I can't believe it took me this long," said Meristan. "I just...I suppose when my memory was restored...I don't know. I'm so sorry, Samily."

That was odd. Why was he sorry? "For what?"

"For...Maybe I shouldn't have told you. Now, anyway. We have this meeting, and you've been through so much. Perhaps I should have—"

"No." She put her hands over his this time. "Please. You have done all that I would ever have wanted from you. You told me the truth. As soon as you could. And you have been kind, as you always are. Thank you." Samily leaned forward and hugged him. "I could not have wished for a better parent."

A redwing watched them from the roof of a house across the road. It cocked its head curiously—or was it wary? Hard to know what a bird was thinking. It had a beautiful vivid green head over a grey chest and the wine-red wings that gave it its name. When they did not move for a while, it carried on picking at the thatched roof. Nesting for winter, she assumed. For its family, maybe.

"How are you?" Meristan asked. "How do you feel? Are you all right?"

Was she? It was hard to think, after all they'd been through on this simple journey. Her entire world had changed. So many things she thought she understood were different. Not least, her own life. But she was still herself. That had not changed. And God. God was constant. She would be fine. "I am," she answered. "I think. For now, we should go to this meeting. And perhaps we can talk more later?"

"Whenever you like," he said.

They walked in silence for a short while, until Samily saw the pub sign ahead. THE AULD HOOSE. Oddly, it had a lute and a drum on the sign, which hung between two huge windows that had somehow survived the Thakhati.

"Cuora," said Meristan.

"Pardon?"

"Your mother's name was Cuora."

# CHAPTER 17

Vastin had often felt out of place, but this was so uncomfortable he could have climbed out of his own skin to hide. He had no idea why he'd been asked to this meeting. King Mynygogg and Queen Nirea leaned against the bar of the Auld Hoose, talking quietly. Laird Aranok and Lady Allandria were sat either side of a small table opposite Vastin. With her good right arm, she held Aranok's hand across the table. They also talked in hushed tones. And Vastin sat quietly contemplating his knees, because it meant he didn't have to look at anyone. The tension was awful.

He jumped when the little bell suspended above the front door rang and was delighted to see Samily and Meristan enter. He gave Samily a welcoming smile and she actually seemed to acknowledge and return it, if half-heartedly. But they looked blackly serious too, and so the room's tone did not improve at all.

Samily paused a moment on seeing the others, gave a polite nod toward the table, then to the bar, before she and Meristan took seats at another table to Vastin's left. And still he felt like a fish stranded on land.

"All right. Good," said the king. He crossed to the door and locked it without another word, returned to the bar and pulled a bunch of glasses up from under the counter. The pop of the cork in the whisky resonated in the insistent silence, and it seemed to take an age for the king to fill all seven glasses.

He put two on each table, then handed one to Vastin with a smile and a glint in his eye that felt completely unwarranted. Vastin wasn't a big whisky drinker. He'd tried a few but mostly found they caught the back of his throat and made him cough. Beer was his drink, and even then, not too much. He considered asking if he could swap, but speaking then would have felt like farting in kirk, so he sat quietly, cradling his unwanted whisky.

"Now." Mynygogg stood in the centre of the room, right in the middle of them all. "We're going to do something that is well overdue." He raised his glass solemnly. "To one of the best men, the best people, I've ever known. A man who was loyal, brave, honourable, and one of the funniest bastards I ever had the pleasure of drinking with. He told a damn good story. But he was also a warrior. And he suffered more than most. Lost more than many could bear. In the end, though he died defending his queen, he only knew he was protecting his friend. That is the man he was. My general. My ally. My friend. We will remember him and we will miss him.

"Glorbad." The king raised his glass higher and turned to face the others in turn. As he did, they each raised theirs back at him and repeated the soldier's name.

And then they drank. Vastin felt the peaty, fiery liquid catch his throat as it always had, but this time he didn't choke. He breathed deep and remembered his friend. And he missed him.

Only then did it occur to Vastin that this was the first time they'd all been together again, without Glorbad. Meristan, Samily, Aranok, Allandria, Nirea and him, surrounding the king of Eidyn—the man they'd come together believing their enemy. But they were not the same group they'd been. They were damaged. There had been tension, of course, at the start, mostly between Glorbad and Aranok. In the end, they'd made peace. Fought together, he'd been told. Stood against the Thakhati. But more than that, they'd been good friends before Janaeus stole their memories. Shared much more than Vastin had ever been aware of. And whatever else the general had been, he'd been his friend. Maybe only for a short time, but he'd shown Vastin kindness with no expectation of reward. And Vastin had, at least once, returned it with spite.

God, it was like another life. He felt so much older now, so far from that inexperienced young boy who'd fawned over Samily like a puppy. It had been, what, a month ago? More. But he'd missed a lot, being Blackened. It could be counted in days, and yet, he was different now. So much had changed. He'd seen things.

Nirea scowled and wiped a tear from her cheek. She had been there, to see Glorbad die. And he really was her friend. Allandria's eyes were red-tinged and Laird Aranok looked at the ceiling in silent contemplation. The Thorns had both closed their eyes and bowed their heads. Prayers, maybe?

"And if he were here now"—the king's voice shattered the silence like a rock—"he'd call us a bunch of silly cunts who need our heads bashed together."

Vastin snorted a nervous laugh. Samily scowled at the king a moment, but Meristan gave a knowing smile and a tilt of his head.

"Aye, he probably would," said the queen.

"Right?" Mynygogg responded. "He would, wouldn't he? So we're going to sort out the shite that—"

"Wait." Laird Aranok stood and leaned on his cane. He walked unsteadily toward the king, who looked both confused and a little irritated. "Before you say anything else: I know that is Allandria and that is Vastin." He pointed to each of them. "We have a code. I trust you know that is Nirea."

The king nodded.

Aranok turned to the White Thorns. "Are you each certain that the other is who they seem to be?"

"What?" Samily asked. "Who else would he be?"

She didn't know.

"There is an illusionist assassin in Traverlyn," Aranok explained. "Or at least there was. They can wear any face. And they could have reason to kill any one of us. So we have to be able to identify each other." He looked to Meristan. "Are you sure that's Samily?"

It certainly looked like her, but Aranok was right. They needed to be sure. Meristan turned to look at her. "I mean...yes, I think...yes, I'm sure."

"You haven't verified it?" Aranok asked.

"Say a word. Any single word," said Samily. "All right?"

Aranok looked confused for a moment, then seemed to understand. "Ready?"

"Now," she answered.

"Behemoth," they both said in unison.

*That was weird.*

"What just happened?" Vastin asked.

"Samily waited for me to say the word, turned back time a few seconds and said it with me," Aranok explained. "Literally nobody else could do that." He turned back to the Thorn. "Smart. Now, can you confirm he is Meristan?"

"I am certain," she answered.

"Based on what?"

"On the conversation we had on the way here. I am absolutely without doubt that this is Meristan. You have my word," said Samily. Aranok didn't look satisfied. "You doubt me, Envoy?"

He shifted, lifting and replacing his cane. "Not…as such, I just… would prefer to know *why* you are certain."

Samily shrugged. "The things he said; the way he said them. His kindness, his wisdom. His voice! That cannot be copied by an illusion based on sight, correct?"

Still Aranok did not seem convinced. "Theoretically, no, you're right. But it's been speculated that an exceptional illusionist could mimic sound. Their skill works on the mind, showing each person what they expect to see from the *draoidh*'s suggestion. That being the case, it's possible they could also affect sound, scent, perhaps even touch. We cannot assume anything. We've underestimated our enemy before."

He said the last sentence to King Mynygogg, who gave a small nod of understanding.

"Aranok, when you found me in Lestalric, I had lost this ear"—Meristan touched his hand to the side of his head—"and Kiana had stabbed me in the thigh. Yes?"

Aranok smiled. "Yes. Thank you." The envoy moved back to his seat.

"Happy?" the king asked.

"Are we definitely alone here?" Aranok looked to the door behind the bar.

"We are," said Nirea. "Gogg and I checked. We asked Nairne to go for a drink elsewhere. The building is empty."

Aranok nodded. "Good. We all need passwords. And we're going to need to stay together—at least two of us at all times. Mine is *bird shit*."

He pointed to Allandria. *"Purple."* She smiled.

And then to Vastin. *"Amollari,"* he said as confidently as he could muster.

"Pick one. Something random," said Aranok.

"Like *behemoth*?" Mynygogg asked with a smirk.

"That'll do." Aranok turned to look at Nirea.

*"Bluebell,"* she said after a moment.

Aranok pointed to Meristan. *"Bear?"* the Thorn suggested.

"No. Too easy," said Aranok. "Something else."

"Oh, um, maybe *bumblebee*?"

"Fine," said Aranok. "Samily?"

*"Cuora,"* she said firmly. Meristan snapped his head toward her, smiled and placed a hand on her arm.

"That's a pretty name," said Vastin.

"Thank you." Samily smiled warmly at him—more so than he felt it deserved. But it was nice.

"Right. Everyone got those?" said Aranok. There was general nodding from everyone. "Good. That's how we know each other now."

"All right," said the king. "Can I...?"

"Carry on." Aranok waved a hand at him.

Mynygogg took a deep breath. "Good. Let's begin." He knocked back the rest of his whisky and plonked the glass on the table beside him. "Anhel Weyr is winning. He's winning because *we are letting him*."

That seemed a little harsh to Vastin, and Aranok's puckered lips appeared to agree.

"We are!" the king continued, waving his arms. "Look at us! Instead of working together to bring him down, we're fighting each other! This is *exactly* what he would want. He doesn't have to beat us if we destroy ourselves."

Meristan shifted in his seat. Allandria gave Nirea a sideways glance. It was awkward again. But the king ploughed ahead.

"Vastin!"

*Oh no.*

"Majesty?" he asked nervously.

The king opened an arm toward him and gestured for Vastin to join him. He stood up, feeling every eye on him, still wondering why on earth he was there. But when he reached Mynygogg, the king put the arm around his shoulders. "When we spoke before, about Aranok and Samily, what did you say?"

Vastin felt even worse then. He looked anxiously between the envoy and the Thorn, suddenly feeling guilty that he'd been speaking about them behind their backs. "Well, I..." The words didn't want to come out.

"Go on, please, it's fine. It's important," said the king.

Vastin took a breath and tried to remember exactly what he had said. It had just been the words that fell from him in the moment. Of frustration and concern. "I think I said that it was wrong they were angry with each other. Because they're both heroes. And...maybe they just can't see each other properly?"

"Yes!" Mynygogg pointed at him forcefully, such that Vastin actually flinched away. "We are not *seeing* each other. Thank you, Vastin." He released his arm and Vastin quickly shuffled back to his chair. He grabbed the glass and necked the last wee bit of whisky, which did make him cough this time.

"We need to *see* each other again. And to do that, we're going to have to be honest with each other." The king turned again to his envoy. "Aranok. You were right. We were too slow with the new *draoidh* laws. What happened to Shayella's daughter was partially my fault. And I should have trusted you to deal with Janaeus. That doesn't mean"—he turned to Nirea—"that I think you did the wrong thing. Based on the situation and what we knew—what we had discussed—you acted for the best. I know that." Back to Aranok. "And so do you. It *might* have been a mistake, and we may never know, but every choice was a gamble at that point. Allowing Janaeus to cast his spell again would have been the end. Nirea addressed the biggest risk. It wasn't a bad decision under the circumstances. If it had been anyone else, you would have done it yourself."

Aranok's face was still fairly dark, but it did seem to soften, at least a little. That was good. Maybe? Allandria still looked anxious, which wasn't helping.

"Samily." Mynygogg turned to her. "You were right about the Blackened. We did leave them too long and it was our fault they were taken by the Thakhati. And, I will add, that makes the siege our fault too. There wouldn't have been so many of them had we acted sooner. We assumed they were safe for the short term and we were *catastrophically* wrong. Had you not come when you did"—he nodded to Meristan—"we might be dead."

Meristan returned the nod. Was this helping? Everyone still seemed very... cautious. But maybe the tension was lifting? A little?

The king crossed his hands and thumped them to his chest. "I take responsibility for those failings. They were mine and—"

"They were *ours*," Nirea interrupted.

Mynygogg smiled and turned back to her. "Thank you. They were ours. And we take responsibility for them."

He left a silence then, as his words seemed to seep into everyone there, into the very wood of the place. Vastin felt the hair on his forearms lift and tingle. The silence had almost become unbearable when Meristan finally broke it.

"Noble words, Majesty. I'm sure we all thank you for them."

The king pointed at the White Thorn. "And that is another thing, thank you, Meristan. Aranok made a valid point. Nirea and I are no longer on the throne. We have no authority. So between this group of us here, there will be no rank. This is no longer a king's council, it is a rebellion. We are its leaders. We make decisions together. It's the only way we're going to get anything done. Agreed?"

That was a little scary. Firstly, of course, the king wasn't including Vastin in that. *Leaders.* He was just here for... Well, it seemed to repeat what he'd said the other day. But beyond that, he had no place here. God, he was just a blacksmith.

But second, Mynygogg not king? Nirea not queen? He'd just about got used to them treating him like... well, like a friend. But the idea of them conceding their thrones, to Anhel Weyr? That raised an empty pit in his guts. Being in league with exiled monarchs was one thing, but somehow being in a rebellion was... worse. Not exciting, as he'd imagined it as a child. He'd seen the reality of it now. There was no glory. Just suffering.

And arguments.

But it seemed that suited Laird Aranok. He actually sat up straighter and gave the king a respectful nod. And Allandria smiled.

"Understood," said Meristan. "But the White Thorns were never with you because of your crown. We are with you because you do God's work."

Mynygogg smiled in response, but Aranok audibly sighed, which brought a scowl and a sideways glance from Meristan.

"Right. Now." Mynygogg clapped his hands together. "This." He pointed vaguely to each table. "This needs sorted. Now. In fact"—he turned back to gesture to Nirea—"all of this. The three of you, Aranok, Samily, Nirea. This needs to end. So get it out. Each of you. Say your piece. Who's going to go first?"

Unexpectedly, it was Meristan who stood. "Actually, if I may?"

Mynygogg retracted his head in obvious surprise but then spread his hands wide and took a chair. "Please."

Meristan turned to Samily, his raised eyebrows appearing to ask her permission. She looked to Aranok, for a moment not seeming to understand what was asked of her. But she gave her master a firm nod, closing her eyes briefly. Whatever permission Meristan sought, she had granted it. The Great Bear stepped into the centre of the room and turned to the envoy. Vastin wasn't aware of conflict between them—except, he supposed, over the fight with Samily. He hoped there was nothing else.

"Aranok. There are things you need to know and there are things I need to say to you. First is this. Samily did not go into that room to kill Shayella. She went to convince her to cure the Blackened. They argued and Shayella attacked her. Samily didn't mean to end the girl when she did. It was self-defence."

Aranok took a deep breath and sat back in his chair. He nodded quietly.

"And," Meristan continued, "we know you didn't intend to use your skill. Samily has confirmed she doesn't remember you saying any *draoidh* words or making gestures. And I have...sympathy for what you have experienced. Seeing your childhood friends die. I will not feather my words, Aranok. Too much has gone between us for iron words veiled in lace.

"I will tolerate this mistake *once*."

Again, Aranok nodded. "I understand." He looked at Samily. "It won't happen again." She nodded back in acknowledgement.

"No," said Meristan. "It will not." After a moment, seemingly satisfied he'd made his point, the big man turned to face the queen. "As for you."

That raised Mynygogg's eyebrows. But he said nothing to interrupt.

"Nirea, you manipulated Samily to get her back here. You used Dialla and you used my honestly given opinion on why she would not choose to come. While you may need such guile in court, it is unbecoming amongst allies. Especially when used on someone who has no use for it herself. I did not appreciate it."

Nirea puckered her mouth, raised her glass and emptied it before answering. "We needed her here. We needed—we *need* Quell. We have her now. She's agreed to work with us. And had I not told Dialla that Leondar was dying, how do you imagine she would have felt when she came back here to find him gone? Along with Keft? Having already lost her family? Do you think she would have forgiven me for not giving her the choice to return? For making that choice for her?"

"But that is not why you did it," said Meristan. "Is it?"

"Actually, it is. In part, at least. Once it occurred to me, which—I also won't mince my words—it didn't, until it was useful. So did I do the right thing for the wrong reason? Or the wrong thing for the right reason? Or, maybe, I did a *difficult* thing with good reason. Because I had the perspective to see it, and Samily did not. I won't apologise for my choices, Meristan. I *am* sorry that you are aggrieved by them. But I would do it again, because it was necessary. And doing what is necessary is how I got here."

That didn't feel like it was resolved. Meristan looked at her for what felt like an age.

"Why was it necessary?" Mynygogg asked, standing again like some travelling showman.

Nirea's brow wrinkled in confusion. "What do you mean?"

"To what end? What purpose did it serve?" he asked.

"Saving Quell," she answered, as if talking to an idiot.

"For what?" the king continued, undaunted.

"So she can clear memories."

"Why?"

Nirea was becoming irritated. "What do you mean, *why*?"

"Tell me why!" Mynygogg waved his arm in a performative manner. "Why should we clear everyone's memories?"

"To...get us...back on the throne." Nirea still seemed confused. And a little irritated. If it had been Vastin asking the questions, he would definitely have stopped now.

Mynygogg did not stop. "Yes! And why? What is the point of us being back on the throne? Why does that matter?"

Suddenly Nirea seemed to understand the question. "The better Eidyn."

"Which means what? To you. In your words." Mynygogg held his hands together, offering them toward his wife as if in supplication.

Nirea stood tall and took a moment of consideration. "Better lives. For everyone. Children growing up"—she looked at Vastin—"with their parents. Fed. Clothed. Loved. Happy." Her voice cracked on the last word.

Mynygogg turned to face Meristan and spread his arms wide. "And you, God's Own Blade? Why are you here?"

Meristan crossed his arms. "I take your point."

"No!" said Mynygogg. "This matters. Why are you here?"

"To make a better world for God's children," he said solemnly.

Mynygogg simply turned up his palms and lifted his shoulders, silently asking Meristan to see the similarity in their answers. But he didn't stop there, as an energy seemed to fill him. "Samily! Why are you here? Why are you with us?"

"To serve God," she said plainly.

"And what is your first priority in doing that?" Mynygogg asked.

"Protecting God's children."

"Yes!" Now the king turned to Aranok. "Why are you here? Why are we doing any of this?"

"All right. Yes. The better Eidyn. For *draoidhs*." Aranok said the last word pointedly.

"Arguably the most ill-treated." Mynygogg was in full flow now. "Allandria? Why are you here?"

The archer looked at Aranok for a moment, considering her answer. It took her a little longer than Vastin expected, and the silence almost became awkward. But finally, she did answer. "Because it's the right thing to do. The better Eidyn."

Vastin should have seen it coming, of course, but he still nearly jumped out his skin when the king turned to him. "And Vastin! Why are you here? Why are you with us?"

Everyone else's answers had been so strong, so purposeful. And Vastin wanted to repeat them, but then he'd just be saying what they said, right? He'd look an idiot. What could he say different? Why *was* he there? Reflecting on his own reasons a moment, there was only one answer he could really put into words.

"I just want to...help."

Mynygogg slapped his hand on the table, making Vastin jump again. "Help! That's what we're all here for. Not for ourselves! Not for glory or riches or any other selfish pursuit. We are all here to *help*! Right? I don't *want* the crown. In fact, anyone who *does* want the crown should be barred from ever wearing it! Properly worn, the crown is a burden! A weight. But it comes with the power to *help*. So that weight is worth carrying. Yes?"

He spread his arms wide again and turned in a circle, stopping to linger on each of them a moment. There were nods. Smiles, even. Like the king had reminded them of who they were. Like, maybe, they were seeing each other again.

Aranok went to stand but seemed to lose his balance and toppled back onto his chair. "Fuck!" He grabbed his cane and threw it across the room. It bounced off a table leg before clattering painfully off Vastin's shin. He sucked in air through his teeth but tried not to make too much of it. "Ach, shite. Sorry, Vastin."

Vastin put up a hand in acknowledgement. There was no real harm done.

Samily stood, then crossed to Aranok and Allandria. The envoy leaned slightly back in his chair, which made the Thorn pause. "May I?" She reached a hand toward his bandaged head. Aranok paused, then nodded warily. Samily put her fingertips on his bandage.

"Wait," said Allandria, catching Samily with her mouth open. "If you... It needs to be further. Egretta said. Before Mutton Hole. Before the demon."

"Really?" Samily asked.

"Really," said Allandria. "He hit his head then. Hard."

Vastin remembered. Aranok had thrown himself at the demon to protect him.

"Of course," Samily said, then, "*Air ais.*" She almost stumbled herself, but Aranok shot out a hand and caught her forearm, then stood to support her.

"You all right?" he asked.

Samily put a hand to her head. "I will be, thank you. I just... have not slept."

"Thank you, Samily," he said. "And... I'm sorry."

Samily put her free hand on his arm. "Aranok, I am weary of crossing swords with you. I only want to help people. I believe you do too. And I have just learned"—she turned to briefly look at Meristan—"that my mother was *draoidh*. A memory *draoidh*."

"What?" Aranok's tone was pure confusion. He looked to Meristan. "I thought..."

"As did I," said Meristan. "Until you cleared my memory. It took me a little while to realise you'd restored more than the memories Janaeus took."

"She hoped to give me a better life," said Samily, "because her own in Apardion was so miserable. And if being a *draoidh* can be so awful that a mother would give away her child rather than see her suffer the same fate... perhaps I have a little better understanding of... your life."

Aranok softened greatly then—all tension seemed to drain from him.

Nirea crossed from the bar to join them, putting her hand gently on Samily's back. "That's big news, Samily. How do you feel about it?"

"Honestly, I don't know," she answered. "It is a lot to take on. My mother may yet be alive. I think I will need some time to think."

"Of course you will," said Allandria. "That's a huge thing to learn at your age."

Samily looked at her and shook her head gently as if waking from a half dream. "Sorry, Allandria, may I heal your arm?"

"No," Allandria said firmly, making the knight pause mid-stride. "You're exhausted. And this'll wait."

"It will only take—"

"No, Samily. I have experience of seeing a *draoidh* push themself too far. When you're rested, I'll happily take your help. But this is minor. And you're human."

"If you are certain." Samily smiled and returned to her seat.

The tension really had melted like butter by the fire. Walls had fallen and arms opened. Suddenly there was warmth amongst them again—a warmth Vastin had not seen since—actually, he'd never seen it. Not in this group. But it was there now and it was so, so welcome.

"All right. All right," said Mynygogg. He pulled a chair to a table beside him and gestured to Nirea to do the same. Now the six of them sat in a relatively close triangle.

Nirea turned and waved Vastin over. "No point being away over there."

Awkwardly, he stood and dragged his chair closer, between Nirea and Samily. He sat again and said nothing. His mother would have told him to keep his mouth shut unless spoken to in this company, and that was exactly what he was going to do.

"So, can I tell you all what I think we should do next?" Mynygogg asked. There was a general murmur of consent. "We have three ways to clear memories now. So we go to three locations. Someone stays here. Someone should go to Mournside—we need to cut off Anhel's taxes. And we choose one other location. Thoughts?"

"Leet," said Nirea. "I'll take Quell to Leet. If we can't get the army back, maybe we can get the navy."

"All right. Good," said Mynygogg. "Aranok? You and Allandria have the charms. What do you think?"

Aranok drummed his fingers on the table. "I need to go to Mournside. But...I can't. The sunstone."

"Why do you need to go to Mournside?" asked Mynygogg. "Every city guard will be looking for you. I assumed you would stay here."

"There was an attempt on my family," Aranok answered. "That's why Rasa stayed longer. They're fine, but...Rasa is concerned about one of the bodyguards my father has hired. I need to...I don't know. I need to know they're all right."

"All right." Mynygogg turned to Meristan. "Can we survive without the sunspire?"

"We might not have to," Allandria interrupted.

"Oh?" said Mynygogg. "Have we found...?"

"Found what?" Aranok asked.

Allandria turned to him and scrunched her lips together. "While you were sleeping, Mynygogg and I discussed finding another earth *draoidh*." Aranok opened his mouth to object, but Allandria stopped him with a hand. "Not a student. They're too young. An adult. Someone we can rely on. There are more *draoidhs* in Eidyn, Aranok."

"I know," the envoy answered. "All right. Who can we trust?"

"I had a note from Master Ipharia," said Allandria. "She's sent for someone she knows. Thinks they could be here in a few days."

"Who?" Aranok asked.

Allandria shrugged. "I don't know, but...if Ipharia trusts them, then...?"

"Yes. All right," said Aranok. "If the Thorns are staying here?"

"We can," said Meristan. "I'm afraid the army of Eidyn may come looking for us—for me. But here may be the best place to be, if we can reinforce the defences?"

Mynygogg turned to Samily. "Am I right in thinking your skill could work on the buildings, the *homes* of Traverlyn, as well as the people?"

"They could," she said. "But first, I am going back to the Auld Road. There are still people who need my help."

"Of course," Mynygogg agreed. "But when that is done? Perhaps you could return here? Help with the wounded and the repairs? I'm sure Master Dialla would work with you."

Samily nodded thoughtfully. "Yes, I can do that."

"If you're staying here..." Aranok turned to Allandria and opened a hand on the table. "Can I have it, please?"

Allandria raised her hands to the back of her neck and untied the leather strap there, then handed the charm she had been wearing to Aranok. He crossed to Samily and held it out. "You should have this. You're the only other one of us who can use it. There are still a lot of people here who need it."

"Are you...sure?" Samily asked.

"Certain," said Aranok. "If Anhel were able to find another memory *draoidh* and if he still has the Heart"—he turned to Nirea—"which I seriously doubt, but"—he returned to Samily—"if he did, and the spell was cast again, we'd be the only two unaffected. I think we're the best choices for that responsibility."

Samily took the charm from him and held it before her. "The word is *clìor*, yes?" Aranok nodded. "And it just has to touch their skin?"

"That's right."

Samily tied the strap around her neck and dropped the charm inside her armour. "I will protect it with my life."

"I know." Aranok smiled and returned to his seat.

"All right, then!" Mynygogg rubbed his hands together. "Nirea and Quellaria will go to Leet. The Thorns will stay here. Aranok, we'll go to Mournside. Allandria? You with us?"

She looked at Aranok and smiled. "Always."

"Right, then, we have a plan." Mynygogg stood. "Vastin? Where would you prefer to go? Stay here? Or...?"

Vastin honestly thought he'd been forgotten and had not expected to be asked any more questions. "Oh! Um..." What did he want to do? He wasn't much needed in Traverlyn. Nor in Mournside or Leet, really. He'd probably just get in the way. Especially if they needed to be sneaking around, which he assumed they would. Though Traverlyn was nice, and the Thorns would be there...

But actually, once he considered it, there was one thing he wanted to do. He wanted it done, anyway. Someone should do it.

"I think, if it's all right, maybe I'll go to Barrock? For Glorbad."

Nirea gasped next to him. She put her hand on his arm. "I would... That would mean a lot to me."

"Dangerous on your own," said Aranok. "I'd rather—"

"I'll go with him," said Meristan. "There are plenty of Thorns here to protect the town. They'll not miss me for a week. And I know where he is. We'll take a spare horse. Maybe a wagon. Bring him back here for a proper pyre."

That made it even better, because in all honesty, Vastin hadn't thought through going alone. There had been a demon there after all.

Suppose it made sense there might be another one. He'd much rather have Meristan there, that being the case.

"Good." Mynygogg crossed to the bar and lifted the bottle of whisky in salutation.

"So who else needs another shot of this? Because I fucking do."

# CHAPTER 18

Ismar had barely spoken a word on the walk back to the Sheep's Heid. Darginn and Isadona had both tried to comfort him, to support him, but he shied away from them at every attempt. Once, when they passed a cart stacked with bodies wrapped in sheets, the boy had almost fallen over himself trying to shift away from them, as if they might reach out and grab hold of him.

Darginn had asked him again and again to talk to them, to tell them what had happened to him, where he'd been—anything! But he'd lain in the hospital bed, pale arms wrapped around himself like he was trying to hold his ribs together. Saying nothing.

The miraculous joy of having him back, of Lady Samily arriving to save him, was so short-lived as to feel like a distant memory. Their boy was broken. He'd always been sullen, but this was... Darginn no longer felt the resentment he'd gleaned from Ismar's dismissive tones and offhand rejections. Now it was just... pain, seeping out of the boy like pus from a wound.

He balked at the door of the Sheep's Heid, from the noise inside. It was nowhere near back to where it had been before the siege, but the chatter of life had returned. People eating lunch and killing the afternoon hours with idle chatter—hiding from the carnage still lingering outside. The memories.

"It's all right, darling." Isadona took Ismar's hand and led him through the door. He followed, docile, like a lamb. Head down. Eyes on the floor. The chatter lowered a little as they crossed the bar and a few heads turned to see who had come in. Darginn tried to smile and nod to a couple of familiar faces, and while they returned the gesture, their smiles were sad. Sympathetic. They could see.

At the bottom of the stairs, Ismar caught sight of himself in the big silver mirror hung on the wall and flinched away.

"Oh, oh sweetheart. It's all right." Isadona cupped his face in her hands. "Just you look at me. Yes?" Ismar nodded piteously as Isadona bravely smiled back at him. "Good lad. That's my boy."

Ismar traipsed up the stairs after his mother, and Darginn trailed behind. He was dreading getting back to the room now. On the walk here they had a purpose—a focus. Something to take their minds off the great black cloud suffocating them. Once they were back in the room, there would be nothing else to do. Nothing else to think about. His boy was broken and he had no idea what to do about it. It was almost as bad as...No. No, nothing was *that* bad.

Darginn was relieved to find their room empty. Jena and Yavick must have taken Liana out for a walk. Maybe found a quiet spot to play with her ball. Somewhere away from the bodies. He'd been worrying over how Ismar's mood would affect his granddaughter. How to hide his damage from her, to keep a smile on his own face and assure her everything was all right. At least that was postponed now. A bit, anyway.

"Come, sit down." Isadona guided him toward a chair by the window, but Ismar ignored her. Instead he walked listlessly to the bed, perched on the edge and folded onto his side like a broken sail. He didn't even take off his boots.

Darginn knelt before him, taking the boy's cold hand in his own. "Ismar, please. I'm begging you, son. Tell me something. Anything. You know I went through some awful things too. Maybe I can help. Maybe I can...I dunno. Understand? Just...it's breaking my heart to see you like this. Is there nothing we can do?"

Ismar didn't answer, but a tear gathered in the hollow of his eye. It quivered there a moment, broke and ran off the bridge of his nose.

Darginn stood and turned away, lest the boy see his tears as well.

Isadona squeezed Darginn's arm gently, then kneeled in his place and untied Ismar's boots. When she was done, she gently lifted his feet onto the bed. He lay there, legs curled, arms wrapped around himself again like bandages. Isadona produced a handkerchief and wiped the tears from him. "You just lie there as long as you need to, darling. When you're ready, we'll be here. We love you." She kissed him gently on the forehead and stood.

As she took a step away, Ismar's weak voice finally returned. "You wouldn't."

"Pardon?" She turned back to face him.

"You wouldn't," Ismar repeated. "If you knew."

*Knew? Knew what?*

"What do you mean?" Darginn asked as both he and his wife crouched beside the bed again.

Ismar's eyes opened, ringed in red and pale as a winter sky. "What I am."

Darginn looked at Isadona. She had no more clue than him what their son was trying to say. "You're our son," he said.

Ismar's mouth crumpled and he lifted his trembling hands to cover his face. "I can't. I don't...I don't want to be here."

"All right, darling," said Isadona. "Let's get out. We'll go a wee daunder. See if we can find Jena."

"Not *here*!" Ismar sat bolt upright, spreading his hands to indicate the room. "Here!" He banged a hand against his chest. "I don't want to be *here*! You should've let me die." Grief burst from him in wracking sobs and he collapsed onto his mother's shoulder.

Isadona wrapped herself around him, stroking the back of his head. She looked at Darginn, wide-eyed. He could only stare back. What do you say to that? To a man who wishes himself dead? There ought to be words, something—how do you convince someone they should live, if they've no fire burning in them to do it? Worse, if they'd rather no?

"Ismar, son," he began, without really knowing where he was going. "Uh, what did...what did you mean? You said *what you are*. What are you?" A muffled answer into Isadona's shoulder. "I'm sorry, son. I couldn't understand—"

"A *draoidh*!" he suddenly screamed, lurching back upright. "I'm *draoidh*, all right? I'm an abomination!"

...

Darginn stepped back. He had no idea how to respond. Learning his son was a *draoidh* was...huge! But...

"Son, why would you...? I don't understand. Why would you think that a bad thing? We've never been anti-*draoidh*, have we?" he asked his wife.

"Of course not," Isadona said vehemently. "Never."

Ismar's face was defiant. Unmoving.

"And you've met Laird Aranok," Darginn carried on. "Great man. Incredible man! And Lady Samily. She saved your life. And she's a White Thorn! Why would you think...?"

"They're wrong," Ismar spat. "*You're* wrong. God doesn't tolerate *witchcraft*."

Whatever Darginn had imagined—awful things that had happened, Hells he'd dreamed of that his son might have been dragged through— he was totally unprepared for this. Words wouldn't come.

Thankfully, Isadona found some. "Ismar, where did you hear that word?"

"From Faither Victus."

"Victus?" Isadona turned to look quizzically at Darginn. He shrugged—he had no more idea who that was than she did. "Who's Faither Victus?"

"From the New Kirk."

"The *New* Kirk?" Darginn asked. "What's the New Kirk?"

"The real faith," said Ismar. "God's *original* words. Before they were changed to allow for witches."

"I..." Darginn was flailing. What on earth had his son gotten into? An anti-*draoidh* kirk?

"You listen to me." Isadona's tone had changed. "There is *nothing* wrong with being *draoidh*. You hear me? Nothing. And even if there *was*, you are my son. And I will love you with every ounce of my heart for as long as I live, and longer! You cannot..." Her voice broke then as her own tears came. "You cannot believe I could ever think badly of you, Ismar. You can't!"

"All right. You think that?" Ismar stood and crossed the room. He still looked so small. So pale. "I'm not just a *draoidh*." He straightened his shoulders and lifted his chin. "I'm a *necromancer*."

Isadona's face turned to ash. Darginn felt his heart stutter. God, of all the skills. And now. With everything that had…

No. This was his son. Ismar was his son. He was a good boy. It didn't matter what he could do. Darginn marched across the room and threw his arms tightly around his son. He squeezed with every drop of love in him. "I don't care. You're my son. You're my son and I love you. We will *always* love you."

Darginn felt Isadona come up beside them and wrap her arms around them both, and the three of them stood there a long time in silence. There were more tears. Lots more.

Finally, exhausted, they sat down again. Ismar on the bed with Isadona, and Darginn in the chair at the window.

It had taken that long for Darginn to figure out what he was going to say. And to accept it, if he was honest. Because it was a lot. He'd been held hostage by a necromancer. Thought he was going to die. But he needed to say these words. They felt wrong, but he had to say them. Because they were true.

"Ismar, Shayella was mad. The things she did, she did because she was mad. Not because she was a necromancer." Isadona sucked in a sharp breath but kept her calm, holding Ismar's hand between hers like a sandwich. "And do you know what drove her mad?"

The boy's eyes were on him now. Focused. He was really there, paying attention. "No."

"Her daughter was murdered. By folk who called her a witch. And she wasnae even *draoidh*. Just her mum was. Does that sound like good people to you?"

Ismar's eyebrows knit closer. "What people?"

"Kids," said Darginn. "Children whose folks told them *draoidhs* were evil. That they were *witches*. They drowned a wee girl. Cannae have been much more than seven." The image of the Dead girl, hovering around him, by the fireplace, came back, and his head went sideways. He blinked, long and slow, finding his balance again.

"I can feel them," Ismar said, rubbing his thigh with his free hand. "I can feel them all."

"Feel who?" Isadona asked.

"The dead," Ismar answered. "I can feel them, reaching for me. They want to be wakened. They want to rise. An itch in my brain. There's so many."

"All right. All right." Darginn stood and paced the room slowly. "We're going to get you to the university. Find Laird Aranok, maybe. Or a master. Someone you can talk to, right? Someone who'll know…how to help."

"Good." Isadona stroked Ismar's face, wiping away more wet tracks on his cheek. "That's good, isn't it?"

Ismar gave a half-hearted shrug. "Aye. All right."

"For now"—Isadona stood and guided Ismar back onto his side—"you rest. Sleep. Feel better. We'll deal with everything else when we've all had a chance to get some sleep, eh?"

Ismar allowed himself to be placed on the bed and closed his eyes. He was like an angel then. A wee boy again, who had dropped where he stood because he had not an ounce of energy left in him. And in that moment, Darginn's passion turned from love to fury. He pulled Isadona to the door, and they quietly slipped outside.

"What now?" she asked when the door was closed.

"You stay with the boy. I'm going to ask some questions. See what I can find out about the New Kirk."

He half expected Isadona to argue, but instead she placed a flat palm against his heart, nodded firmly, kissed him and slipped quietly back into the room.

---

The heat from the pyres warmed Aranok against the chill night. The low winter sky had been threatening snow all day, and the sharp air bit like needles. He'd even brought a warm sweetmilk out to brace him against the cold. For all the sunspire gave them light, it couldn't produce enough heat to counteract the weather. Having said that, he'd never looked into an *orach* that would store and reproduce heat the way a sunstone did light. In theory, it could work. He might ask Balaban about it. If he remembered.

For now, he looked on in reverential silence at the field full of burning corpses. The biggest pyre, in the middle, for Principal Keft. But the one that hurt, the one that mattered more to him, was a small one on the edge. One not many folk were interested in standing vigil for. But it was the one he, Allandria and Mynygogg had chosen.

"Tobin was a good kid." Allandria touched his back gently with the hand of her newly healed arm.

"Aye. He was." A good kid who'd got himself killed protecting his horses. And from what Vastin had said, messy. Like he'd pissed off the Thakhati. No chance they could have cocooned him. What was left of the boy had been wrapped tight in a shroud, but Aranok could see it had no shape to it. Not really. Burning him was the kind option—for everyone. A woman stood at the top end, near his head. His mother, Aranok assumed. Allandria moved across and put a hand on her shoulder. Said some comforting words he couldn't hear over the crack of the fire.

With the sheer number of dead needing dealt with, and the threat of disease—there had only been one way to handle it. Might have been easier to stack them in piles and light the lot, but there was no dignity in that. No respect. And when you've got nature *draoidhs* on hand, there's no shortage of wood. With Aranok, no lack of flame.

So there they stood, with the western fields of Traverlyn lit like a forest fire, full of folk milling around in hushed conversation, holding each other. Mourning their lost.

After the meeting that afternoon, they'd agreed everyone should get going as soon as possible. But Aranok couldn't leave until someone else could manage the sunspire. So the three of them were there, publicly representing the throne, for those who knew the truth. But more importantly, they were visible, so as to give Nirea and Quellaria the chance to get away through the eastern wall. Samily and Dialla would just leave through the main gate again—they'd managed to convince the Thorn to sleep three hours before going. Vastin and Meristan were going the same way, with a cart to retrieve Glorbad's body. But they'd decided it was best if the rest of them left in secret. Give any spy the least chance of knowing where they were—where they might be going. It'd help them if Anhel lost track of them for a while, at least.

Hell, there might be no spy here. But that illusionist assassin…
*Damn it.*
That just reminded him of the attempt on his family, and how he couldn't go to them. Samily had healed Rasa before she left, as well as a nature *draoidh* the metamorph had been especially insistent upon. Rasa had immediately offered to go back to Mournside, but they needed her here. Nirea had been right about her being their most vital means of communication. And whatever her reservations, the bodyguards his father had taken on had done their job. At least, one of them had.

So he had to be patient. Trust that they were safe until he could get to them. If he even could. The Guard would be watching them closely too. Waiting for Aranok to show up again. Or maybe they'd assume he wasn't stupid enough to do that.

Joke was on them. He was absolutely that stupid.

For now, though, he was stuck there, watching the ashes of Traverlyn's dead dance in the firelight. Reminding him of all they'd lost, and all they still might lose.

# CHAPTER 19

Samily's world had turned upside down. She was being pulled in so many different directions. Her main priority had been getting back on the road to help the Cured. When Dialla had been reluctant to leave Leondar quite so quickly, the kingsguard had insisted he would come with them. Nirea had easily given her blessing, and so they were three.

But on the road out, Leondar had spotted a cluster of cocoons high in the trees. They had a choice: stop and destroy them, risking more Cured lives lost; or leave them and accept the Thakati would likely kill or convert others into their ranks. Samily was tired of trading lives.

But Leondar had convinced her that the Thakhati were a greater threat, and likely to cause more deaths if they allowed them to survive.

It had taken them five hours to be sure—as sure as they could be—that they got them all. Dialla had used her energy skill to break the trees that held them, and Samily had dispatched them from within the tangled branches. It was necessary. But it was slow going. And she felt every minute.

Back on the road, her mind scattered like broken glass. To her mother. To discover now, as an adult, that her mother might still be alive? That she had given her away to Meristan for a better life? She didn't know what to do with that knowledge. Should she look for her? Did she want to? Would her mother want her to? Would she be proud of what her daughter had become? Would she...like her? She loved her. Meristan had assured her of that. She knew it, in her mind, but she wasn't sure she felt it. Not yet.

But maybe it didn't matter. The chances of finding her, even if she did go looking, must be tiny.

But still. A mother? *Her* mother? Did Samily have a responsibility to go looking?

What would God want of her in this? There was no clear answer. Though if her mother was still living a miserable life in Apardion, shouldn't she try to do something for her? She was, after all, a child of God. And Samily would make a better life for her. Somewhere.

She would speak to Meristan when they both got back.

"Hold!" Leondar raised a hand, pulling up Bear. It took Samily a moment to react, and she almost rode directly into the back of them. But her horse corrected to the right, avoiding a collision.

"What is it?" Dialla asked.

Dusk was falling and the road was becoming difficult to follow, but Samily could see something up ahead, coming around a bend. And now that they weren't riding, she could hear it too. The clatter of horses' hooves and the creak of wooden wheels. A merchant caravan?

Or no...Could it be? Samily kicked her horse into motion, galloping ahead. If it was, if it really was them, then maybe the delays hadn't cost them so much. Maybe all those choices had been for the best. Maybe she could still help everyone.

They ate up the ground and Samily soon saw who was driving the first cart. "Greste!" Joy swept through Samily. The wagons had come from Mournside!

"Samily!" Greste called back, waving her arm high.

Behind her, at least fifteen wagons rolled, each full of people. And behind them, more people, on horses or walking. It was—hundreds! Hundreds of people! Hundreds of the Cured!

Samily leapt off the horse and scrambled the last few yards. "Where should I begin? Who needs me most? Is Lady Ikara here?" She looked about frantically, searching for those who looked the most sickly, the most injured.

"Take a breath, girl." Greste gently grasped her shoulders. When had she dismounted? "You're like a moth caught between flames. Give yourself a moment." Her voice was reassuring. "We have gathered those most in need in the front wagons. Lady Ikara is not here; I understand her family needed her. But a gentleman named Corlas came in her place, with twenty wagons from Mournside."

*Twenty!* More even than Samily had hoped for. Ikara had done all she promised. Samily took the advice of her elder. She breathed deep, slowly and consciously. "All right. Can we begin?"

Greste smiled indulgently. "Come on."

The elder Thorn led her to the next cart, and s'grace, but it looked like a sea of corpses. Hideously frail men, women and children, their heads almost comically large, lolling on their stick-thin shoulders.

"I'm here, Samily!" Dialla called from behind her.

"Park up the wagons. Someone light us a fire," Samily ordered. People immediately busied themselves. Samily moved to the back of the wagon and dropped the gate open. There, looking back at her, a young girl. Her huge, hollow eyes stared blankly back at Samily. Her hair lank and filthy. No older than Samily must have been when…

She had all but assumed she was too late for the little soul, until the girl's throat bobbed in a pathetic swallow. "Heavens!" Samily placed a hand on the girl's cheek. *"Air ais."*

Colour flowed back into the girl's skin, and flesh returned to her cheeks. Her eyes brightened, her hair thickened. A black print appeared on her face, then faded as quick as it formed. The girl gulped in a breath of air as if bursting free from water, disentangled her arm from under herself and put her hand over Samily's. She smiled.

And Samily broke. All the emotion—the guilt, the responsibility, the confusion—it bled from her in that little girl's eyes. This was why she was here. This was what it was all for. Here was God. And God was glorious.

Samily felt tears stream down her cheeks. The girl pushed herself up to kneeling and looked at her sadly. Curiously. With a tiny thumb, she wiped at the tear tracks.

"Not sad. Happy." She smiled again, as if to demonstrate it for Samily. And then there was noise. A sound that was both familiar and unnerving. *Applause.* Again. Samily turned to see a crowd had gathered behind her. People stood on wagons, stretching to see her. And all of them, clapping. Grinning. Happy.

She turned back to the girl. "I am happy, child. I am *so* happy to see *you*."

---

"I'm looking for Faither Victus."

Darginn had spent a day asking around. Despite there being Thorns all over the town—or at least it felt like there were, which was a comfort—none of them had heard of the New Kirk. In fact, several had confidently told him it didn't exist. That there was only one kirk. But when he started asking around in pubs, he'd finally got answers. It was fairly new. Came up during the *draoidh* war. Or people first heard of it then. Might have been a thing outside Traverlyn. But with the university here and all the *draoidhs*—seemed to Darginn like the last place they'd set up camp. A place of learning and tolerance wouldn't be fertile ground for their ignorance. The masters wouldn't have it.

He'd not wanted to ask Ismar too much about it. Didn't really want him knowing his dad had gone looking for the bastards. Might have upset him even more. He'd hardly got out of bed since they brought him back. Jena was helping Isadona care for him, and wee Liana kept crawling onto the bed, just to sit near him. Yavick had been furious when he'd heard what had been done to his brother-in-law. So much so that Darginn had refused his offer to come with him. First thing Darginn needed was information, not blood. Not yet.

So there he was, standing on the doorstep of a cobbler's shop. The woman looking up at him must have been in her fifties. A bit younger than Darginn, but not so much as mattered. Her mop of curly grey hair was tied back in a loose bun with what looked like a leather strap, and she wore a light brown leather apron with pockets full of tools.

"Who's asking?" Her eyes defiantly scanned the street behind him.

"Darginn Argyll. King's messenger." The title wasn't necessary, but it lent him some official weight. He'd no idea what he was walking into here, but everyone in Eidyn knew that harming a king's messenger was treason. It was his armour, of sorts. It was why he was confident enough to come alone.

The woman looked him up and down sceptically with a frown. Darginn smiled and produced the royal seal that proved his claim from his inner jacket pocket. She leaned her head forward to examine it, turned and walked away from the open door.

Darginn took it as an invitation to enter. The cobbler walked slowly up a set of stairs at the back of her workshop to the upper floor, where her footsteps stopped in the middle and he heard a door open. Muffled words—pretty sure he heard "king's messenger" in there. Another voice, a pause, and then two sets of footsteps.

The woman reappeared first, followed by a man who aged with Darginn, with a round, kind face. He wore a simple shirt with a blue waistcoat and trousers. He didn't look like a priest.

The cobbler said nothing, sat back at her workbench and continued worrying at some leather, which would presumably be a boot by day's end. It was as if Darginn weren't even there.

"Victus," the man said, offering his hand. "What can I do for you?"

"*Faither* Victus?" Darginn grasped the hand half-heartedly. It was puffy and callused.

A moment, as Victus considered his answer, then a glint in his eyes. "Aye."

"Of the New Kirk?" Darginn asked.

Another pause. "Aye." Then a smile. "Always pleased to meet someone curious about the kirk."

He wouldn't be pleased long.

"I'm Ismar's father." He spoke the words like blades, intending them to cut. To see the shame in Victus's eyes. The guilt for what he'd done to Darginn's boy. The fear of what might come to him. Instead, the man's face lit with happy recognition.

"Ah, of course! Ismar said you were a messenger. I didn't make the connection, forgive me. Pleasure to meet you. I'm sorry I can't offer you something." He spread his hands to indicate the workshop. "As you can see, I'm reliant on the charity of the faithful since our house collapsed in the siege."

Their house? Was that where Ismar had been? Was that the basement he'd been pulled from?

"I'd like to know what exactly you've been saying to my son."

The cobbler, whose name he still didn't know, hammered on something. The impact jarred Darginn's teeth. She did it again.

"You become accustomed to it," said Victus. "Would you like to come upstairs?"

No, he would not. He was just about shaking with rage.

"What have you been saying to my boy?"

Victus cocked his head as if Darginn had said something confusing. "Only God's word, my friend." Again he spread his hands as if to demonstrate his innocence.

"God hates *draoidhs* now?" Darginn could feel the anger rising. He was in danger of flattening this "priest." "Because I know a few who'd beg to differ with that opinion."

"It's not my opinion. It's a simple reading of God's word. The oldest Recounts we have clearly state, 'Witches shall not be tolerated to live.' I find that harsh, so I have made it my mission to help those burdened with witchcraft to renounce its evil, and come to the kirk. It is my belief that God's love can save them, if they are open to it."

"Evil?" Darginn spat. "You telling me my son is evil?"

"Of course not!" Victus said, horrified. "But he is, sadly, burdened with it, and only through devotion to God can he remove that stain."

Darginn squeezed his fist tight, his nails digging into his palm. *"Stain?"*

"I am pleased he felt able to talk to you about it, at last," said Victus. "He has been afraid to tell you and your wife for a long time."

*A long time?* Darginn had thought this was a new thing. Something Ismar had just discovered. His face must have betrayed his surprise.

"Oh, don't feel bad." Victus put a consoling hand on Darginn's upper arm. "Many don't feel able to speak to their family about it. The feeling of shame, of self-loathing—it can be powerful. Nobody wants to be *draoidh* after all. It is a tragedy of birth."

Darginn's heart juddered between anger and sorrow. How long had Ismar been carrying this burden alone? How long had he hated himself? For nothing. "How... how long...?"

"He's been worshipping with Faither Cunnach in Haven. He only came to me when you arrived here in Traverlyn," said Victus.

Darginn took a step back and his legs went weak beneath him. Ismar had come to him? He'd come looking for this man? He'd been hiding this for…years, maybe? Oh God. His poor boy. Convinced there was something wrong with him by bloody charlatans. If only he'd spoken to them, if only…Ach, there was no good in that thought. He didn't. He'd chosen his path. A dark, lonely path, but he'd walked it. And now, finally, he'd come home. And damned if Darginn was going to allow him to be led astray again.

"Listen, you bastard." Darginn stabbed his finger at Victus. The cobbler stopped working. "You stay the fuck away from my son, you understand? You do not speak to him. You do not contact him. If I hear a hint that you've even tried to see him…"

Victus raised his hands defensively. "That is not what I do. I do not seek anyone out, my friend. I simply spread God's word and support anyone who comes to me. I am only here for comfort."

"Comfort?" The rage was ready to spill. "You made my son hate himself! Just for…existing! Just for being who he is. Who God made him!"

Victus clasped his hands together and gave Darginn another sympathetic look that was just more infuriating. He said nothing.

"Ah, *fuck you*!" Darginn turned on his heel and stormed out the still-open door.

No good would come of him belting the sanctimonious prick. Most important thing he could do now was keep Ismar away from him, and Cunnach, whoever the fuck that was. How had Darginn never heard of any of this? He was away a lot, certainly. Messengering was a hard ride, but it paid well. It had given them a good life. But maybe it had taken him too far from his son.

A sharp wind caught the back of Darginn's neck and he pulled up his collar against the cold. He needed to calm down. He was no use to Ismar like this. He needed a drink. He needed a drink and some time to settle down.

Out here on the north edge of town, not far from the fields that surrounded Traverlyn, there were mostly just houses. About as far from the university as you could get. About where you'd put a kirk that preached *draoidh* hate, Darginn reckoned.

But there had been a tavern, a few streets south. Dank-looking wee place on the corner, with a half-hung sign. The Fiddler's Arms? He'd stop back there. Get control of his emotions before he went home and figured out how to help his son understand there was nowt wrong with him.

Several hours and too many whiskies later, Darginn staggered back out of the pub. The sunspire had come on while he was in the tavern and he smiled up at it, lighting his way. He had a plan. Laird Aranok and Lady Samily were good people. Good *draoidhs*. He'd take Ismar to see them. They'd both sort of said he could ask for anything, and seemed quite genuine about it. If he was going to ask more favours of them, what better reason? And with the university right here...In some ways, maybe this was the best place for this to come out. Maybe Ismar could still study here? As an adult? Would they have him? Help him to learn how to use his magic safely? For good? If anyone could make that happen, he reckoned the Laird Envoy could.

If it could happen anywhere, Traverlyn was the place. But first, he was going to sleep. To be with his family. It had been a long, hard week, and Darginn's old bones were feeling winter like shards of glass. Rest for now, and tomorrow he'd begin again. Tomorrow, he'd get Ismar the help he needed.

# CHAPTER 20

Meristan felt a horrible sense of familiarity, staring down at the mouldering remnants of Barrock's gate. He'd stood here before, a different man in a different country. He and Vastin had left the cart at the base of the hill, unbuckling the horses and leading them up the sharp incline. It was late afternoon and they'd agreed that, all being well, they'd stay the night in Barrock and head back for Traverlyn in the morning. So they wanted the horses with them. They hadn't come across any Thakhati or demons on the journey, but there was no reason to think they were immune from their attacks here. Maybe especially here. Because there may not have been only one demon here waiting for them the last time. There could be another. More. But he hadn't said as much to Vastin. No point terrifying the boy. What they were here to do was already awful. Cathartic, hopefully, for both of them, but hard. It was going to be hard.

"Everything all right?" Vastin asked. He was putting on a brave face, but there was disquiet in his eyes. He was scared. Scared of what they were going to find. The boy had such a big heart. For him to be the one who insisted on coming here, to give Glorbad the respect he deserved—he was a good soul. He deserved better than he'd been dealt.

Meristan straightened up and found a smile for him. "Fine, lad. Let's get the horses settled and get inside." It would be nice to have a roof over their heads. Last night had been cold, camped in the wild. They'd found the same sheltered spot he, Nirea and Glorbad had camped in before, so they were protected from wind. That had helped keep the fire going, but he'd still had to hunt more wood during his watch when the chill was at its worst. He was glad to have a new set of White. Severianos had worked quickly, but the man was a genius with metal. It somehow fit like it had been tailored by Aranok's father, and was no heavier than the leathers he'd worn last he was here. Not many had that kind of skill.

And he had a new Green blade. One forged specifically for his size and reach. Pressed to say, Meristan doubted he could have discerned it from the one he'd lost, without his eyes. The old one had scuffs and scars he knew like his own reflection. This one had been pristine until he'd used it to kill Thakhati. Now it had its own scars. Best a sword tasted battle sooner rather than later. Once it had seen you through a real fight, you knew you could rely on it.

Meristan entered Barrock this time with more confidence than the last. This time, he knew he could handle anything that came for them. This time, it was Vastin relying on him to lead, to protect. Not him scuttling in behind the others.

The thought had occurred to him, more than once, that had he known himself that day, had he known what he could do, held his Green blade, then Glorbad might be alive. But would he have done differently than Glorbad? The demon's spike had cut right through the soldier's armour. Could Meristan be sure the White would have protected him? Maybe. But he would have had faith in God. And if it had been his time, then that was his time.

The fact that he'd killed the demon himself was some comfort now. He may not have been able to protect Glorbad, but he had certainly avenged him. And saved his best friend. He was confident the old goat would have taken comfort in both. Given the option, he'd have chosen her life over his own without hesitation.

It didn't take long to find their way back to the corridor. The smell led them. A demon corpse rotted like nothing living. Thorns burned the bodies to keep them from tainting the earth where they fell. Their blood was poison and their flesh a breeding ground for disease. And they stank to high Heaven.

"Oh God!" Vastin raised his hand to his face. The stone floor was thick with sticky black ooze and the walls had begun to wear away near the base. "Was he...in that?"

"No. Up there." Meristan pointed to the steps about twenty yards ahead, beyond the foul black slop. "But we're not going through that." He wasn't sure if their boots would stand up to the demon's remains, and he wasn't prepared to risk it. It was cold enough *with* a good pair of boots. "We'll find another way up and come down from above."

It took a wee while to work out, but a set of servants' stairs finally got them to the right floor. As they reached the top, Meristan raised a finger to quiet Vastin. He kept the boy a few steps down behind him, the stair walls providing him with some cover.

Nothing. No sign of movement. An open window creaked somewhere in protest against the wind. They'd need to find that and shut it, else the noise would keep him awake later. Otherwise, all was still. As they walked the corridor, Meristan's torch lit on relatively fresh gashes scratched into the wooden floor. This must have been where the thing waited for them. At the top of the stairs, he paused again. Was he ready to see this? Was the boy?

He had to be. Glorbad needed them. They crept down the steps, the stench rising again to catch in Meristan's throat.

And there he was. Just where they'd left him. Glorbad's body, a dark brown hole punched right through it. A huge stain of his blood, where it had poured down the steps like an obscene waterfall. And his face: drained, pale, and crawling with flies. Beside him, the shield Vastin had made for him, a matching hole through its heart.

"Aw, no," the boy whimpered. Meristan moved down, carefully manoeuvring himself over the soldier's legs, to allow Vastin to get to the body. "No. No!" Vastin swatted at the flies, which lifted, circled and went straight back to their places. "No!" He swiped again and again, until he accidentally made contact with the soldier's cheek and pulled back with a horrified gasp.

"It's all right," Meristan said quietly.

The boy's lips quivered, his hands trembled. "He's so...alone." Tears welled in his eyes. "He shouldn't be alone."

Meristan put a hand on the boy's shoulder. "He's with God.

Whatever he believed, I am certain he is with God now. He is not alone."

"I hope so," Vastin replied. He squatted down and ran his finger around the edge of the hole in Glorbad's armour, then did the same with the matching one in the shield, shaking his head mournfully. "Like it was cloth."

"Aye," Meristan agreed. "It was an awful thing. There was nothing stopping that spike."

Vastin nodded gently and turned his attention back to Glorbad. Carefully, he reached up and closed the soldier's pale, vacant eyes, disturbing the flies again. He took a deep breath and spoke. "We should move him. Wrap him in something. Find a room he can rest in until the morning. Aye?"

That was a sensible plan. There would be bedsheets somewhere. "Aye. Let's do that."

Meristan found a bracket to hold the torch, placed his sword on his back and got his hands under Glorbad's shoulders. Vastin put his axe and shield on the upper landing, came back and took hold of the soldier's legs.

"Right? On the count of three," said Meristan. "One, two…"

---

"Aranok, Allandria, this is Master Darragh." Ipharia gestured to the silver-haired, bearded man to her right, perched against the windowsill of her office. He gave an easy smile and a small bow of his head. His pale blue eyes sparkled with a humour that had Allandria warming to him immediately.

"Master?" Aranok asked suspiciously. "I've never heard of you."

"Before your time, son," Darragh answered. "I retired."

"Why?" Aranok leaned forward in the brown leather armchair before Ipharia's desk. In stark contrast to both Balaban's and Conifax's offices, this one was scrupulously neat and organised, with a forest of potted plants dotted around the room. A large fern drooped from the top of her bookcase and an exotic flower with white edges around a pink centre, which Allandria had never seen before, was behind glass on a lower shelf. The room smelled of *green* and something else earthy and sweet. It was pleasantly calming, and washed Allandria with a wave of emotions she hadn't felt since she walked the forest as a child.

"Love," Darragh answered, the wrinkles at his eyes deepening with his smile. "The only good reason to do anything."

Allandria liked the man even better.

"Darragh and Master Fioro chose to leave the university while both were still junior masters," Ipharia explained.

"Why?" Aranok asked again. "Why go to all the effort of becoming masters and then...leave?"

Darragh clasped his hands together and leaned back, looking at Aranok as if he were a child asking a question he did not understand himself. "Because we wanted to. Why does it matter?" As he shifted position, Darragh nudged a small plant and it toppled off the edge of the windowsill. With a lightning-quick gesture and the word *gluais*, he caught it just before it hit the ground, lifted it to his hands using his skill and carefully placed it back on the windowsill—in the corner, where he was unlikely to bump it again. Were Aranok's reactions that quick?

Ipharia smiled knowingly at the man and he gave her an apologetic bow.

Aranok carried on the conversation as if nothing had happened. "I just...You understand the weight of the responsibility you're offering to take on. Traverlyn relies on that sunspire. It has to stay lit, until we can deal with the Thakhati. I need to know that *you* are reliable, if I'm to trust you with that responsibility."

"Well, Laird Envoy," said Darragh, "s'pose there is a mutual trust to be had here, isn't there? Despite what I've heard to the contrary, Ipharia assures me that you're not guilty of regicide. I trust *her*, which is why I'm here. But I'm not sure I trust *you* yet."

So Darragh's memory was still compromised. They would have to deal with that. It meant a lot that he'd accepted Ipharia's word. It also meant news of Aranok's supposed crime was spreading, presuming the master hadn't come from Mournside—the only place they knew for certain it had been announced. No reason to assume it hadn't gone to all the major towns by now, though. Meaning it would also be spreading into the farmlands and wilds. Everywhere but Traverlyn.

"Fair." Aranok stood and slipped the memory charm from around his neck. "May I?" He asked the question of Darragh, but his eyes flicked between the two masters. Darragh looked to Ipharia quizzically, and she nodded solemnly.

"What do you need?" Darragh asked.

"Take my seat, then hold this," said Aranok.

Five minutes later, the older man opened his eyes with a sigh. "Huh."

"Trust me now?" Aranok asked.

"I suppose I do," he answered.

"Good. Ipharia will answer any more questions you have, I'm sure."

In response, Ipharia sat back in her chair, cradling her cup of tea, with a glint in her eye that seemed to be an almost permanent fixture. "Of course."

"So I'd appreciate it if you would answer my questions now." Aranok's tone was tetchy. But Allandria knew it was nothing to do with Darragh. He needed this to be real. He needed to trust this man, because he was absolutely desperate to get to Mournside and see his family. And he would know that himself, meaning that, if anything, he'd likely be even more scrupulous about confirming the man was reliable, to avoid any chance of later regretting a rushed decision.

"Fine." Darragh crossed his right leg over his left and leaned casually on his own knee. "Fioro, Ipharia and I were students together. Fioro was a few years below us two. We met in Quarters. She's a nature *draoidh*. You know how *draoidhs* cluster together here." He paused as if waiting for Aranok to agree, but the envoy remained stoically silent. Because Aranok did know, and that was a sore point right now. When he said nothing, Darragh carried on. "We fell in love. She became a master a few years after me. I was, what, thirty when we married? And then everything changed. We realised we wanted children. And a different life for them. A quiet life. So we bought a farm, northeast of Lochen. Turns out you can do quite well on a farm when you control the plants and the soil and can produce all the water you need." Darragh spread his hands. "And that's it."

"That sounds perfect," said Allandria. "Did you have children?"

"Four." Darragh grinned widely. "Three boys and a girl. All ended up here!"

"Wonderful," said Allandria. It was a lovely story. A beautiful vision of how life could be. She envied them, a little. Maybe more than a little.

"And you're willing to abandon your farm to come here for as long as you're needed?" Aranok asked. "I can't guarantee how long that will be. And you're going to have to be careful. The last person doing this job was murdered by an illusionist assassin."

Darragh's face turned serious. "I heard. Poor girl. Ipharia and I have discussed that. We're going to start laying revelation charms around the campus. There are no illusionist students here at the moment, so there's no good reason not to. We're going to make it as difficult as possible for them to be here, or the kirk. And Ipharia and I will travel there and back together every day. We'll be careful."

Aranok crossed his arms and stared into the middle distance for a moment before speaking. "All right. And the farm?"

"It's winter." He said it as if it explained everything, but Aranok gave no response. He was always a town boy. So Darragh continued. "Harvest came in a while ago. I did some work on the soil before I left, but our two eldest boys came back to work the farm with us, so between them and their mother, they can do the maintenance around the plots and keep the animals fed and breeding. Fioro can just about tend the animals herself, with her skills. But the boys will do the heavy lifting. They'll be fine."

"And if you're needed into spring?" Aranok asked. God, she hoped he wouldn't. The idea that they'd still be fighting this war through the winter and into next spring was a hideous thought.

Darragh sighed. "Well, since we heard about the Blackening ending, we've been talking anyway. Reckoned maybe after the snows we'd head down to the Meadows. See if we can't help get the farmers there back on their feet, y'know? Leave the land to our boys for the year. They'll inherit it one day anyway. And we can afford to hire a few extra hands if need be. So, you know, if it turns out I need to be here more than there...such is life, right?"

Allandria's instincts about this man were dead-on. And finally, *finally*, she could see it in Aranok's eyes too. The scepticism melting away. The appreciation for why Ipharia had chosen this man to stand in Aranok's place. He was selfless and wise. And prepared to sacrifice for others. Aranok turned to Ipharia, who sipped at her tea like a satisfied cat with a bellyful of fish. "All right. I see it," he said.

"I knew you would," Ipharia answered.

Aranok offered Darragh a hand, which he stood to take. "Darragh, I'd be honoured if you would take on the sunspire. Honoured and grateful."

"It would be my pleasure, young man," Darragh answered. "Considering what I've just learned, and what I suspect I'm going to hear, it seems like you have more important things to be doing."

"Tomorrow morning," Aranok said. "I'll come for you early. Before dawn. We'll introduce you to the priest and get you on the spire." He turned to Allandria. "And then we'll go. First thing."

There would be a lot of planning to do for that. Mynygogg would need to be ready, and he wanted the Reivers to come with them. Jazere would be able to let them out through the eastern wall, as she'd done for Nirea and Quellaria, but Mynygogg had reckoned it was also their best chance to get away and home. Travel south across the Black Meadows and head straight for the Malcanmore Wall. It'd be useful for them to report back as well—not only to let Burrox and the other chiefs know what was happening, but also just to demonstrate how they'd saved Teyjan. Well, how Samily had saved him. To demonstrate that Mynygogg's words before the council had meant something. She reckoned even Cuda would be an advocate for them now. And that was a comfort, knowing that Dacred was almost certainly agitating for war again in their absence. The poisonous little toad. So aye, work to do. But they could be ready.

"Right, let's get going," said Aranok. "We've got a lot to do and not a lot of time."

"Can I offer you a bit of advice, son?" Darragh asked.

"Aye?" said Aranok.

"You look like shit. Your skin's like poppy milk and you could use those sacks under your eyes as saddlebags. No offence." Darragh smiled. "Take it from someone who's made the same mistake. Look after yourself. Get a good night's sleep. Slow down when you can. Rest is as much a part of doing your job as everything else. You can't pour whisky from an empty bottle."

Aranok's initially defensive expression changed into a smile. "Conifax used to say that."

"He did indeed," said Darragh. "And *I* didn't listen to him either."

Aranok laughed gently, then turned to Ipharia. "Thank you. For arranging this."

"I didn't do anything, my boy," the master answered. "I just sent a couple of messages. You two are the ones who showed up."

"Still. Good choice," said Aranok.

"Oh, it was a stupidly easy choice, once I realised," said Ipharia.

"Realised what?" Aranok asked.

"How much *you*"—she nodded to Aranok, then to Darragh—"remind me of *him*."

And there it was, the reason Allandria had warmed to him so quickly. Ipharia was exactly right. She could see it plain as day. Darragh could be Aranok in twenty years. Not physically, necessarily, but there was something intangible about him. Something kind, and trustworthy. Something good. And he seemed so serene with it. So at peace with himself. She hoped that future waited for Aranok too.

It felt a long way off, though. Hard even to imagine. A little cottage, the two of them together, sitting by the fire? Maybe. Maybe one day.

But not today. Today, they had work to do.

# CHAPTER 21

A light dusting of snow was still falling when Aranok, Allandria and Mynygogg met up with the Reivers at Traverlyn's east wall in the early half-light. He'd been aware of their presence in the hospital, but what he hadn't realised until right then, when he'd watched her open the wall of trees without speaking an incantation, was that Jazere was mute.

"How the fuck did she do that?" he said, much louder than intended.

Cuda, the shaven-headed older woman, snapped her head round aggressively. "Pardon?"

Aranok nudged his horse toward the two women. "How did she do that?" Not all *draoidh* skills required incantations. Rasa's metamorph skill, for example, had neither gestures nor a need for spoken words. But nature *draoidhs* had incantations for everything. How could a mute nature *draoidh* even function?

"What d'you mean?" Cuda asked defensively. "You just watched her do it."

Jazere cocked her head curiously. She genuinely looked confused, and made a few unfamiliar gestures with her hands.

"She says, 'What's wrong?'" said Cuda.

"Aranok?" Mynygogg asked. "Is this urgent? We need to go."

It was urgent. He needed to know what he'd just seen. Aranok held up a hand, waving Mynygogg off. "How did she do it without the incantations? That shouldn't be possible."

Jazere made more gestures to Cuda. "Says she learned them that way. No need to speak them."

"So, she's *never* spoken them?" Aranok asked. "Has she always been mute?"

"No. And yes." Cuda's tone was definitely irritated now. She was defensive of her friend. Her clan.

Aranok sat dumbfounded. That shouldn't be possible. Nature spells required incantations. Simple ones, but still. They shouldn't work without them. At least, not under control. Not without them running amok the way they did for children newly discovering their abilities. "You *learned* them that way?"

Jazere shrugged and signed, "Yes."

"Do you know the words?" Aranok asked. "Were you taught them?"

Jazere nodded. "I do. I think them when I cast," she signed. "It works the same."

Aranok sat staring at the woman. That was...astonishing! Were incantations all like that? Would they work just as well thought as spoken aloud? Or was it different for Jazere, because she'd never been able to speak? If he could learn to cast without speaking, it could have huge advantages—maybe for times when stealth was important. Or surprise. This could change everything he knew about magic! She should stay there, at the university...

No. It was important these three made it back to the Reiver council. Told them the truth of what was happening in Eidyn. That was more urgent. For now. But he was going to get this woman back here, one day, to properly learn more about how she controlled her powers.

"Ari?" Allandria's voice nudged him from thought.

"I'm sorry; it's just...Al, do you know what this might mean?"

"No. But it's getting light outside." She nodded upwards. "And we do need to go. Right now."

Aranok looked up to the greying sky, tiny, soft snowflakes landing on his eyelashes.

"We right, then? Are we?" Teyjan asked.

Mynygogg raised his eyebrows at Aranok expectantly.

"Yes, sorry. Yes, let's go," he said. But he rode alongside Cuda and

Jazere as they made for the gap in the wall. "Would you mind if I asked you some more questions?"

Cuda looked to Jazere and then back to Aranok.

"As long as ye're no a prick about it."

---

"Hold the horses. Say nothing. Just let me speak." Meristan's voice was hushed and urgent, with a tone Vastin couldn't place, between irritation and fear. Both seemed bad. They were only a few hours out of Barrock. A light snow overnight had left the road rock hard and a little treacherous for the horses, so it had been slow going.

The low-hanging sun wasn't offering much warmth, and Vastin's riding cloak was pulled tight against the wind. They'd found sheets to wrap Glorbad last night and then blankets to cover him in the back of the cart.

When the battalion of soldiers appeared on the road ahead, Vastin's heart had jumped. They should be on his side. They probably *were* on his side, even now. He was just a boy, a poor blacksmith out on the road, collecting his friend's body for a decent funeral.

But Meristan had told him the story of what happened on the road to Baile Airneach. How he and the others had protected the Reivers they'd come across. How he had lied to a general, and ordered a runner kidnapped. How, chances were, these soldiers might well be their enemies now. And Vastin had no desire to fight Eidyn's army. A moot point, anyway, since there were at least fifty of them. Not a fight even Meristan could win, he reckoned. Though he did wonder if he might try. If anyone could...

"State your business!" the lead soldier called. The bright sun glinted off her polished armour.

"Just transporting a body for funeral rites," Meristan called back.

A pause as the soldier leaned to her left and spoke with the man beside her. "Where you coming from?" she asked. "This road comes direct from Barrock."

"Just near there, actually," Meristan answered. "Got himself killed by a demon."

"That right?" The woman's voice had an edge to it. The same edge Vastin had heard in his mum's voice when he'd lied about where he'd been and they both knew it. "Mind if we have a look?"

Meristan frowned, looked right into the trees, back to Vastin, sighed and answered. "Of course not."

This all felt very, very bad. Vastin's right hand was trembling, so he rubbed it together with his left and blew heat into them.

The lead soldier—a captain, Vastin guessed, or maybe a general—rode up to the cart with a grim-faced man on either side of her. She had a round face, sharp eyebrows and grey-brown hair, tied back in a bun. "White Thorn?" She nodded to Meristan's White armour, which was far too large to be hidden by his cloak.

"Aye," Meristan answered.

"Name?" the soldier demanded.

"Brontas." Meristan dropped the name as casually as if it really were his own.

"Mm-hmm," the soldier answered. The other two had flanked the cart, both sitting just behind Vastin and Meristan. He didn't like them there. Felt vulnerable. Both his axe and shield were in the cart, propped up alongside Glorbad. He had nothing to protect him but his armour. But Eidyn soldiers didn't just stab people in the back, did they? "And who's this?"

Vastin looked up from under his hood, trying to look as innocent as possible. He managed a nervous smile.

"Just an escort, sent to help me recover the body," said Meristan. "Blacksmith's apprentice."

"What's your name, boy?" the soldier asked.

*Shit.*

Should he lie? Meristan had lied. But did *he* need to lie too? What were the chances anyone knew his name? Surely not much. Why would Anhel Weyr care about a blacksmith? Then again, maybe he'd heard about Aranok rescuing his business for him. Maybe the name might have stuck. And maybe the fact that he'd been missing from Haven for weeks hadn't gone unnoticed. On balance, the risk of him being a terrible liar was maybe smaller than the risk of him blowing Meristan's story right then. So he lied.

"Curk. Son of Rorach, of Traverlyn." He'd been pretty sure Brontas was a real Thorn, so he took Meristan's lead and gave the first real name that came to mind. The actual blacksmith's apprentice. Course, he was a good five years older than Curk, but chances of one of these soldiers knowing that were small, surely. If any were from Traverlyn, maybe they'd heard the name...

"Open it." The lead soldier nodded to the man behind Vastin, who turned to watch him dismount and clamber into the back of the cart. Instinctively, he almost told him to leave Glorbad alone. Not to disturb his peace. But fear kept him quiet.

The man lifted the blankets and unwrapped the sheets around Glorbad's head. He recoiled and put a hand to his nose as the stench of death wafted free. The captain looked down impassively.

"And who's this?" she asked.

"Garrund," Meristan answered. "Old friend."

She looked at the Thorn for a long time, then back to Glorbad. Finally, she turned to the man mounted beside her. "Is it?"

He looked solemnly at Meristan, then nodded. As if it were a cue, all three drew their swords.

"Whoa!" Meristan raised his hands defensively.

"You'd have been better telling me the truth, Brother Meristan," said the leader. "This man here was one of those you attacked near Gardille. And I served with General Glorbad. That's not a face I'll forget. So do you want to tell me the truth, of why you're masquerading as a White Thorn to transport the dead body of an Eidyn soldier?"

Vastin felt his stomach drop. This was bad. Very, very bad.

Meristan sighed again and looked up the road at the mass of soldiers. He seemed to be calculating. If they had to fight, Vastin would. If they had to. But he trusted Meristan. He would know what to do. Finally, the Thorn turned to the soldier over his shoulder. "What's your name, son?"

The man sat up tall in his saddle. "Horgan."

"Horgan, I am a man of God. So tell me, in the sight of God, is that a fair recount of what happened? Did I attack your patrol? Was it that simple?"

"That Reiver *draoidh* tore a man in half," Horgan answered. "And you defended them."

"And why did she do that?" Meristan asked, his voice much calmer than Vastin's heart.

Horgan pressed his lips together, glowering just below Meristan's eyeline.

"Horgan?" the lead soldier asked. Still he said nothing. "Horgan, answer the question."

"Proviak accidentally shot a Reiver boy," he mumbled.

"*Accidentally?*" the leader asked. "What the Hell did he intend to do?"

"Just..." Horgan spluttered. "He was nervous. Just...scared. He never meant to fire the bolt."

The leader ran her hand over her head and muttered something Vastin couldn't make out, then turned back to Meristan. "What happened to the boy?"

Meristan touched two fingers to his throat. "Dead when he hit the ground."

"All right. All right," she said. "Still. You attacked a patrol of Eidyn soldiers. You're going to answer for that."

"I did not." Somehow Meristan's voice remained calm. "I stepped in to *prevent* further death. On either side. Right, Horgan?"

The soldier's face was hard. "S'not how I saw it."

"You're alive, aren't you?" Meristan asked. It was the closest he'd come to an aggravated tone.

"So?" Horgan spat back.

"So?" Meristan repeated back at him.

"For fuck's sake." The leader sheathed her sword and rode in front of their horses. "Either way, this isn't my decision. Brother Meristan, you are accused of treason against Eidyn. You will surrender to us and be taken to Greytoun for trial. King Anhel Weyr will decide what's to happen."

*Oh Hell. Oh no.*

Vastin jumped to his feet. "No! You can't do that! You don't understand what's happening! You're all—"

Meristan grabbed his forearm and yanked Vastin back to his seat. "Hush, boy. You know better."

Vastin was shaking with anger, frustration and fear. They couldn't take Meristan to Weyr. He would kill him. No question. Meristan would give him nothing, no information. Nothing. And Weyr would execute him. And Meristan would let it happen because he was far too good a man to do anything else!

"Please. No," Vastin begged.

"Fine," Meristan said to the soldier. "I'll come willingly. Just let the boy carry on; take the general for his rites."

The woman shook her head. "Glorbad was a soldier of Eidyn. He'll get the rites he deserves. A military funeral."

"No!" Vastin vaulted into the cart, lifted his shield protectively and knelt over Glorbad's body. "You can't have him. You can't!"

The soldier to his right tried to grapple Vastin off the cart, and he smashed him in the face with his shield, knocking him on his arse.

"Vastin!" Meristan bellowed. "This is not the way!"

"They can't have him," Vastin whimpered. He wasn't letting him go. He owed him that.

Horgan raised his sword and moved his horse to the back of the cart.

"Hold!" the leader commanded. He stopped but gripped his sword, ready. The other man got back to his feet, holding his bloody nose, eyes a black glower.

"Thought your name was Curk," the woman said.

*Shite.*

"It is, sorry, that's my fault," said Meristan. "Vastin is a Thorn initiate. Same age. Same attitude. *Curk*, please stand down. These soldiers are not our enemies."

"But..." Vastin's voice was all but gone.

"They will give Glorbad the military funeral he earned. He would have been proud to have it. We got him the dignity he deserves. That was our job, right?" Meristan stared hard at him, and the message was clear. Vastin needed to calm down and shut up before he made things worse.

"S'pose," Vastin answered.

Meristan turned back to the lead soldier. "I'll come with you willingly. You give the general his rites. Just let the boy go home, yes?"

Ah. There was the plan. Vastin had to get back to Traverlyn. To tell them what had happened. They needed to know. Which was why Meristan was talking him down. All right. All right. He could do that. Vastin bowed his head respectfully. "I'm sorry."

"Who was he to you, boy?" the woman asked.

Vastin swallowed hard. He would keep control of his feelings. He wouldn't cry. "He was my friend."

"Aye." She sighed. "Mine too. All right." She pointed to the man still holding his nose. "Lirix, you and Horgan on the cart. Get it turned around, back to Barrock and give the man a pyre worthy of him. Brother Meristan, you're going to take Horgan's horse, come with me and an escort to Greytoun. Boy, you take Lirix's horse and get yourself home. No more nonsense from you, or I'll change my mind. Right?"

Vastin looked sadly at Meristan, and the Thorn's face was as serene as ever. It was reassuring. This was what he'd planned, surely. Vastin just needed to get back to Traverlyn and then they could rescue him. All right. He could do this. He could do this. He nodded quietly.

"Right," the woman said. "Let's get on with it."

A short time later, Vastin was mounted on a strange horse adorned with Eidyn's military colours. Meristan, mounted beside him, put a hand on his shoulder. "It'll be fine. God is with us."

Vastin hoped so. As the battalion of mounted soldiers parted to let him pass, and Meristan was lost to sight behind him, Vastin had never felt the need for God's presence more keenly. As soon as he cleared the column of soldiers, he kicked the horse into a run.

He could make Traverlyn by tomorrow morning. King Mynygogg and Laird Aranok would know what to do.

# CHAPTER 22

Nirea breathed in deep. She could walk these streets with her eyes closed. The salt of the sea, the stink of the fish market and the rich, hoppy smell of the breweries. She was almost as at home here as on the ocean. It felt good.

They'd come into Leet quietly and carefully. The official reports said it was lost to pirates—it was no real surprise to find that was bollocks. The streets were full of half-cut sailors and women looking to fleece them of their coins for a quick fumble in a back alley.

Between Nirea's sea leathers and Quell's worse-for-wear fancy dress, they could pass for exactly that—a couple slipping into a dark street for a private transaction.

The King's Wark sat at the bottom corner of a store building, overlooking the Water of Leet, the river that split the town in half. The alley that led to its back door was littered with rubbish and stank even worse than the fish market. But it didn't go anywhere else, so their only concern might have been disturbing genuine streetwalkers in the course of their work. Nirea banged on the door, trying to find the balance between making sure she was heard and not alerting half the tavern to their presence. With no answer the first time, she went harder the second.

The man who threw the door open had a bit less dark hair and a bit more belly than the last time she'd seen him. "Away and rut against somebody else's— Oh…" Ailen's jaw dropped when the light fell on Nirea's face. "Well, this is…familiar."

A wave of relief washed over her, seeing her old friend's face again—that he was alive and well. That she hadn't got him killed by that old bitch Madu's assassin.

It had been a long time ago she'd first come here, bleeding, half conscious and desperate for help. Still a rebel then. Still a pirate. And he'd taken her in, dressed her wounds and kept her hidden for the days she needed to get back on her feet. It had cost him too. Hofnag's men had come looking for her. Demanded to search the building. If he hadn't kept her in his own chambers and been in good standing with the local porters, she wouldn't have survived. She owed Ailen her life, and maybe the kingdom. And here she was, repaying him by asking him to do it again.

"Is there another war on?" the innkeeper asked, his eyes glinting with mischief.

"Ailen, I'm so sorry to even ask…"

"I assume you'd have come to the front door if you weren't in trouble?"

Nirea nodded.

"Right. I've one room free. The rest are full. You'll have to make do."

Nirea looked back at Quell. "We can do that."

"You can wait in my chambers until the bar shuts. All right?"

Nirea threw an arm around the man's neck and kissed his unshaven cheek. "You're a hero."

"Seems that way, doesn't it? Come on." Ailen ushered them into the kitchen and through to his private chambers. A barmaid Nirea didn't recognise gave them a curious look as they passed through but was too busy serving up beers to come sniffing around. Hopefully she could keep her mouth shut too.

Nirea wasn't sure what she'd expected when she stepped through the door into Ailen's rooms—maybe a sense of familiarity and safety, maybe a wave of panic and fear. She did not expect to see a strong, dark-skinned man in a robe looking as surprised to see her as she was him.

"Hello?" His accent was pronounced, even in that one word. Not Eidyn. Not Reiver. Not one she could place at all.

Ailen drew Nirea across and presented her like a formal guest. "Nirea, this is my husband, Crinn."

"You're married? Wonderful!" Nirea threw her arms around Ailen again, but the surge of joy was short-lived, as the reality of what she was here to do crashed down upon her. She'd been coming to warn a man he was in danger. A dear friend. Now he was also someone's husband, and maybe she'd put both of their lives in danger. With a sharp breath she refused the tears and plastered on a smile to face Crinn. "Congratulations."

Nirea offered a hand and he took it, perplexed, looking to Ailen for some kind of answer as to why two strangers had just been ushered into his home. "Thank you?" He looked awkwardly at the woman behind Nirea. In response, she stepped forward, threw her arms around Crinn's shoulders and kissed him on the cheek.

"I'm Quell. Congratulations."

Ailen's eyebrows went up. Nirea smiled apologetically. He turned back to his husband. "Nirea is an old friend. I'll explain. Actually..." He turned to look pointedly at her. "...She'll explain. Won't you?"

"I will." And thankfully, she could. But best not to have Quell restore Ailen's memory now, when he had a pub full of customers and God knew how he'd react to having his mind unfucked. He may also not be totally comfortable with knowing Quell was a memory *draoidh* just yet. She'd need to broach that one carefully.

"Right. I've a pub to run. You make yourselves comfortable, and I'll be back in a few hours. All right?"

"Thank you," Nirea said. It was woefully inadequate. It always would be. But she meant it from the depths of her being.

Ailen smiled. Hopefully he saw that; how she recognised she could never repay him. And was asking for more anyway.

When he'd gone, Crinn looked at them both with exactly the surprise and confusion their arrival deserved. After a moment of consideration, he opened his hands. "Hungry?"

Samily stumbled up the steps to the hospital. The doors seemed too distant, like they moved farther back with every step she took toward them. Greste caught her elbow.

"Easy, girl."

They needed to find a medic. Egretta. Get some organisation. Get people help. Make sure they could keep them alive, fed, safe. Because, s'grace, Samily needed to sleep.

Hundreds of people came hobbling, limping, helping each other behind her. They'd got the wagons as far as the stables, but the streets were too narrow after that, so it had been a case of those who could support themselves helping those who couldn't.

A medic appeared at the door. An older man. Familiar. Maybe.

He caught Samily as she finally made it through the doorway.

"Lady Samily! What's happened?"

He did know her. She could barely think straight. His face swam, his eyes seeming to slide away toward his ears.

"She needs sleep, is all," said Greste. "And we need care for these too. Until Samily can recover."

Dialla had kept them both going, got them back here with the Cured. But Samily hadn't been able to heal them all. Just the worst. Just those on the verge of death. She'd been seeing things. People. Ghosts. Demons. Shapes in the shadows. Had she not known why, she'd have thought herself losing her mind. But her chest heaved with exhaustion now, and she knew, despite having the energy to walk, that her body was drained, her mind frayed and coming unspooled.

Greste helped her to a chair and she gratefully sat, as the walls of the hospital foyer spun around her. She closed her eyes for a moment, just to let them settle.

"Samily?" Egretta's familiar voice jolted her awake. Heavens, had she fallen asleep there in the hallway?

"Yes?" Her speech was slurred. Lazy. And the room still spun.

"Here, girl. Let's get you into this chair."

Samily felt hands under her armpits and allowed them to shift her from one seat into another. She wasn't sure what the point was, until it also seemed to move. She gripped the arms tight, hunting for balance. A hand on her shoulder.

"You're all right." Egretta again. "Just relax; we're going to get you to a room. You can go back to sleep, if you want."

A shiver ran through Samily. Really? Could she sleep now? "But..." she began. The chair stopped and Egretta knelt before her, taking her hands.

"You've done it, Samily. You brought them here. Now, please, let me take care of you. All right?"

She'd done it? Had she? It was hard to think, but...was this real? Was it a dream? She felt tears coming as her voice croaked out an answer. "Yes. All right. Thank you."

Her eyelids closed again, red became black and the fierce sting in her eyes turned cool and wet.

*Peace.*

---

Nirea scrunched her eyes closed against their stinging demand to stay shut. Exhaustion lay in her like a ghost of winter, whispering from the dark. Even with the fire roaring, her hands trembled. But she needed to stay up a little longer. She had to explain everything to Ailen. Then, maybe, she could sleep.

Her head dropped forward and bounced up as she shook herself awake. She needed to move. The rum she emptied down her throat might not help, but it made her feel better. The heat was what she needed, and her skin tingled as it hit her stomach.

Crossing to the fireplace, she stomped her feet, urging the blood to flow warmer and faster. The tavern was empty now. The inn residents had gone to bed and the drinkers had gone...away. To their own beds, or someone else's.

"What's all the noise?" Ailen appeared through the kitchen behind the bar, drying his hands. "People are trying to sleep, you know."

Even the mention of sleep drew a deep yawn from Nirea's chest. "Is everything locked up?"

Ailen looked around curiously. "Aye. Why?"

"Because it's important." She moved back to the table, poured another generous measure of rum and waited for Ailen to join her. When he did, it was with his own glass.

"What are we drinking to?"

"To better times." She tipped her glass against his and necked it.

"Bit maudlin." He smiled, joining her. "Here, you sure you're up for this tonight? Not to be a bastard, but you look like shite."

Nirea grinned weakly. "This is just what I look like now."

"Oh. Fuck. Bad luck."

She laughed despite the fatigue, despite the pain and the guilt and the fear—despite it all, she laughed, because she was drinking with an old friend. An old friend she knew absolutely she could trust with her life.

If only he could say the same.

"Ailen, there are things I need to tell you. They're not going to make sense, but it's best if you just keep quiet and let me speak, all right?"

The innkeeper tilted his head and raised his glass in consent.

"All right." Nirea lowered her voice to a whisper. "Janaeus is dead. The Laird Envoy has been framed for his murder. He is innocent. But the head messenger was involved. I can't explain why, but... as protection against the king's council, she claimed to have paid an assassin to murder certain people if anything happened to her."

Ailen's face drained of colour. Nirea felt the emotions overwhelm her, and her tired eyes became wet. "I'm sorry, Ailen. I didn't know about any of it. I don't know how she even knew."

"Are you telling me she's dead?" Now he looked over his shoulder, scanning the doors, assessing how secure they really were. Nirea could only nod. "You killed her?"

She shook her head. "No. It was... an accident. But I was there."

He was quiet for a long time, sipping at the rum, staring into the dancing flames. The weight of the silence hung like mist. "She mentioned me by name?"

"She knew what you did for me. What you've done for me. She knew, Ailen."

He was an intelligent man. He understood. An innkeeper could hardly avoid strangers.

"You're certain? It's real?"

How could she answer that? Could it have been a bluff? Of course. Did Madu have the money and the connections to make it happen?

Yes. If she told him the truth, he might choose to stay. And if it was true, and he died...could she live with that?

It wasn't her choice to make.

"No, I'm not certain. It could have been a bluff. But we had good reason to believe she could have been telling the truth. She was...prepared in ways we hadn't expected."

How else to say she was surprisingly in control of her own mind and behind a massive conspiracy to steal the throne? Hells, maybe she should have had Quell restore Ailen's memory first. She'd held it, because when she'd told him all this shit, she needed to be his friend, not his queen. He deserved to be angry and hurt and confused, and not be hampered by knowing who she really was. Well, there was the irony, really. He did know exactly who she was. Not the queen who entertained nobles and made decisions about fucking taxes; the pirate who drank into the wee hours, until she could barely keep her eyes open. The rebel, not the victor.

Ailen knocked back the rest of his rum and poured them both another one. "All right. All right. So you've told me. It's in my hands now. Your burden's lifted."

Fuck, that was a brutal way of looking at it. "Ailen, that's not why I came..."

He waved the glass dismissively. "I didn't mean it like that. I just... It's done. It is what it is."

That didn't make her feel any better. It was a smack in the face with a velvet glove. "It's not your fault; but it is." God, what had she expected? She owed the man her life and she was here to take his away, one way or another. Would it have been better if she hadn't come?

"So just me? That's it? I'm the only person you care about enough to be worth killing?"

*Ouch.*

"One's already dead." Ailen's eyes softened, his jaw loosened. Maybe it was harsh, but if it stopped him using her for sword practice, it'd be worth it.

"Fuck. I'm sorry, Nirea. I just...I know this isn't your fault, but... Fuck. Crinn came here for a new life and we're settled. He's settled. For the first time in his life. I can't tell him we have to abandon it all. I can't. It'll break him."

Nirea reached across the table and laid her hands over Ailen's. "What would your death do to him?"

The innkeeper pulled his hand away and stood abruptly, waving his arms at the walls. "He'd have this place! He'd have a home. That's *his*. He'd have a life."

"Without you?"

"Better than a life spent running from shadows." He knocked back the rum again and stood, contemplating the empty glass in the firelight.

He wasn't thinking clearly. She needed to get through to him. "Ailen, what if they come for you in your sleep?" He looked back at her blankly. "They won't leave a witness."

With her sluggish responses, Nirea barely ducked in time to avoid the glass that shattered against the wall behind her. "You fucking tell him, then! You tell him we have to leave! Go on, what are you waiting for?" Ailen stood like a signpost pointing to the bar.

Calm wasn't Nirea's natural response to threat, but it had to be, here. She stood slowly, palms open. "I will, if that's what you want."

"What the Hell is happening? You'll wake God with this racket." Crinn appeared behind the bar, wide eyes taking in the standoff, then the shattered glass on the bar floor. Neither answered. "Ailen?"

She could practically see the man's heart break in his eyes as he silently begged her to stay quiet. "It's nothing, my love." Ailen crossed to the bar and gently traced his hand down Crinn's cheek. "I'm just getting overexcited. I should know better. You're right, there are guests to think of."

Crinn placed a hand over Ailen's, lowered it onto the bar and looked at Nirea. It was a look of equal parts love and threat—only the latter for her. "You'll tell me later."

Without another word, Crinn turned and disappeared back into the darkness. Nirea sat again, but it was a long time before Ailen rejoined her. His face was hard. "If they come for me, for us, they'll regret it."

"Ailen, you don't..."

He cut her off as if she hadn't spoken. "Crinn was a soldier. A warrior. If they come for me, they'll have to go through him."

"Ailen, he can't follow you around all the time. He has to sleep. You're not being reasonable." Nirea regretted saying it immediately.

There was nothing reasonable about any of it, and she saw the word stab at her friend. "Sorry, no, that's... Ignore that. I shouldn't have said it. But the rest is true, Ailen. Assassins don't come straight at you—they'll come from the shadows, take you in the street with a subtle dagger or poison your beer while you piss. Don't live your life waiting for the blade. Please."

Ailen knocked his hand on the table and tapped his thumb almost idly as he stared thoughtfully at her. "I'll think about it. I'll talk to Crinn. And that's the end of it. All right?" Nirea opened her mouth to object, but Ailen held up a hand. "No. No more. I've heard you. We're done."

All right. She'd done what she could. And her head was pounding now, begging her to rest. She drained the rum and blinked away the wetness in her eyes.

"But really? I'm the only one?" Ailen asked.

"No. There are more. But only one other I need to warn. The rest... already know the dangers of their own lives."

"Hmm?" Ailen didn't need to ask the question aloud.

"Do you know a man called Joliander?"

The innkeeper sat back, looking thoughtfully to the ceiling. "Off the merchant boats? Scruffy bugger. Beard?" He stroked at his chin as if there was need to demonstrate.

"Sounds like him. Know where I can find him?"

Ailen frowned and shook his head. "At sea, most likely. Doesn't keep a house here, that I know of."

Nirea closed her eyes and felt the sting again as they begged to remain closed. The warmth of the fire washed over her and for a moment she wished she could just succumb to the dark. Forget everything and go back to sea. Life was simpler in Seafelde. You hid your gold and you watched your back. You were responsible for your crew and your ship. An entire country was bloody exhausting. But Mynygogg's vision was so compelling, so appealing. And after all she'd given up, after all the people she'd lost, who'd given their lives following her, how could she surrender now?

"What are you thinking about?"

Nirea opened her eyes and rubbed her face firmly. "Why?"

"You were smiling."

"Well, fuck. Can't have that, can we?"

A hammering at the door. Nirea was on her feet in a breath, knife in hand. She hushed Ailen and crept across the bar. Banging again. Insistent. Late.

Ailen followed her, trying to look relaxed, but there was a stiffness in his walk.

More banging.

"Shut for the night!" he called. "No rooms!"

A drunken grumble, cursing Ailen and his damned pub, followed by the stagger of feet back into the night.

Nirea breathed out. She hoped Ailen could see how sorry she was, how much she cared about him. She hoped he would listen.

"Come on, you need your sleep, lady."

"Wait." There was still another thing she needed to do. "Can we… can we just go to your rooms first? There's something Quell needs to… to show you."

# CHAPTER 23

The fire was as much necessary to thaw Aranok's fingers as to cook the hares they'd caught for breakfast. It was not the weather for camping. Especially not in the Black Meadows, where the wind had little to stop it whipping across the devastated farmlands. Being able to huddle with Allandria while they slept had helped. Their relationship was real now, and not a secret. It made life a damn sight easier. And a lot nicer. Jazere had also made some crops grow, creating something of a windbreak. Not as useful as trees or even bushes, but they were something. Not much out here to salvage.

Having six of them to take shifts on watch meant they all got a decent amount of time to sleep, and he was feeling a little less dull than he had for a while. The cold might have kept him awake if not for the bone-deep exhaustion he'd been carrying for days. The snow had stayed off overnight. That was something. They'd spend another night wild in the Black Hills before they made Mournside. And then they'd have a whole new problem. But that was for later. For now, he was itching to ask Jazere more about her skill. Having a conversation with her while they rode, needing Cuda to translate her hand gestures, would have slowed them down. The night before, they'd all been exhausted and cold. Conversation had been functional, focused on making the camp. Between Aranok and Jazere, a fire was no issue. Food and sleep had been everyone's priority, and Mynygogg had insisted on taking first watch for some reason. Nobody argued.

But tonight, when they reached the Black Hills, the Reivers would head on south, following the mountain range toward the Malcanmore Wall. So this was his last chance to find out how the woman's powers worked, between greasy mouthfuls of hare.

The three Reivers sat across the fire from him and Allandria, with Mynygogg sort of sitting at one end, as if he were part of both groups, and neither.

"Jazere, do you mind if I ask you some questions?" Aranok asked. The nature *draoidh* looked to Cuda on her left and shrugged her apparent agreement. "How old were you when your skill first manifested?"

Jazere frowned and held up both hands, extending all fingers except her left thumb. That she moved up and down with a considered frown.

"Nine or ten?" Aranok asked.

She nodded.

"And who taught you to control it?"

Jazere made a complex series of gestures and Cuda spoke. "There's a *draoidh* conclave each year in the Reiver Lands. Children are assigned a mentor and become their apprentice. I was sent to a Jethart man called Hol."

"Jethart?" Allandria's voice was sharp with surprise.

"Aye," Cuda answered flatly. She said nothing further, despite Allandria obviously having reason to find that unusual.

When the silence had gone long enough to be a little awkward, Teyjan spoke instead. "The *draoidh* conclave is independent of the clans. Children are assigned to those best placed to teach 'em, regardless. They dinnae change clan, but they do grow up in the other's town, for a bit. For their training. Then come home later."

Allandria wiped her mouth with the back of her hand. "How long?"

"Eight years," Jazere answered. "Nearly nine."

"How was that?" Allandria asked. She'd spoken of the Jethart chieftain. Said he was an awful, malignant man. Quick to anger and to violence, as long as it was others doing the violence. He knew the tales of Jethart justice: quick to hang, slow to regret. How a clan held together with such a volatile system of justice, he'd no idea. Look at the wrong man the right way and you could end up doing the hangman's jig.

"Fine," Jazere answered. "I kept to myself. Hol was a good man. Nobody else wanted to take on a mute girl. Couldn't see how I'd ever get control. Hol reckoned he could do it."

"He was a stubborn old fucker was what he was," said Cuda. "If somebody said it couldnae be done, he'd do it for bloody spite."

Jazere shrugged and smiled in apparent agreement. "That too."

"And *how* did he teach you?" Aranok asked. "How can you control your skill without words?"

"Hol reckoned intent was the important thing," she answered. "Taught me to 'say' the words in my mind. Think them, even though I couldnae speak them."

Fascinating. "And that worked?"

"Still does." Jazere reached her hand down to the dirt beside her, and after a moment, a handprint of tiny sprouts pushed free of the earth. They stopped at no more than an inch high, and Jazere brushed her hand gently across them.

"Incredible." It changed everything Aranok had been taught about magic. If the words did not have to be spoken to control a spell... maybe that explained what was happening with his own powers. If *intent* really mattered, maybe he wasn't losing control. Maybe... maybe he was *gaining* it.

Mynygogg slapped his hands together much louder than necessary and stood. "Right. Let's be getting at it! We've not got all morning to sit here chatting, pleasant as the company is." He looked up at the low-hanging grey clouds. "Could snow today. Let's try to get to the foothills and maybe find some better shelter against the wind before that, eh?"

As they each busied themselves packing up, Aranok turned to find Cuda at his elbow, a look even darker than usual across her brow. She gestured for Aranok to come closer, and he ducked an ear toward her.

"Hol saved her," she whispered. "Not for him taking Jazere in, they'd've executed her. Couldnae have a mute *draoidh* running about without control of her magic, ken? Ye'll no hear a bad word said about that man in ma hearing, for all he was a grumpy old fucker."

Cuda slapped Aranok's arm with the back of her hand, gave him a knowing nod and turned away, leaving Aranok in stunned silence. How many *draoidh* children might have suffered such a fate? How many had no Hol to stand for them? How many were lost because of ignorance and fear?

Aranok breathed in the sharp morning air, filling his chest with biting cold, and resolved to make sure it never happened again.

---

Darginn's head was thumping even more than it had been when he'd woken that morning. A beer too many last night. Maybe a few. But he'd needed them. Needed to burn off the anger at that sanctimonious old bastard Victus. Ismar had still barely spoken. But he was eating. And sleeping. He wasn't leaving the room at the Sheep's Heid, but that wasn't a problem. Darginn was a whole lot happier knowing where he was. And Isadona was fussing over him like he was a bairn again. Liana might even have got a smile out of him.

Darginn had got up and out early. Reckoned he might sneak a wee sup of poppy milk at the hospital to take the edge off his pounding head, but no such luck. They were running low and he'd got short shrift from the young medic he'd asked. Probably smelled the booze on his breath and knew exactly why he was asking. Fair enough. He'd earned his pain; he'd live with it.

But when he'd found his way to what he'd been told was the room Laird Aranok and Lady Allandria were staying in, and found it empty, the pounding had got worse. An hour or so asking around, and literally nobody had been able to tell him where they might be. Or King Mynygogg and Queen Nirea for that matter. In fact, the only person anyone had been able to point him to was Lady Samily, who had returned from the Auld Road and was apparently sparked out like the dead, sleeping off a week's work. She was such a good soul, no wonder she'd found her way to the Order. The girl would bleed for anyone who needed her.

Darginn sat on a chair opposite the door to her room, waiting for her to wake, so he could ask her for even more. But also, she should know.

She should know about the New Kirk, and Faither Victus and his ilk. Not one of the Thorns he'd spoken to had ever heard of them, and it seemed to Darginn like that was a worry. Why would a "kirk" keep itself quiet? Made no sense. Unless they had something to hide. And as far as he was concerned, their anti-*draoidh* hatred was just that. Something worth hiding. Well, he was going to shed some light on it. Set fire to it, if he could.

It was maybe a few hours before someone came to Samily's door. A cheery woman with a bob of dark hair and a steaming bowl in her hands. "Are you...waiting for something?"

"Oh, just hoping to have a wee word with Lady Samily when she's fit. Don't want to disturb her."

"I'm just bringing her some food." The woman raised the bowl as evidence. "Want me to ask if she's ready for visitors?"

"Only if it's no a bother." The last thing Darginn wanted was to be a burden.

"What's your name?" the woman asked.

"Darginn Argyll."

"Give me a minute." The medic smiled and entered the room. Not long passed before she came back out, empty-handed. "She's up and says to go right in. She lit up when I told her it was you."

That was a lovely thought, and kind of her to say, but he'd still not worked out why it was so. Maybe he reminded the knight of someone else she was fond of? Either way, he was taking the invitation.

The small room was as basic as any other in the hospital. The door opened onto the left-hand wall, which had a small fireplace embedded in it. Next to that, a Green blade. There was a window along the end of that wall, the shutters of which he reckoned had just been opened to let in some morning light, based on the stale funk of sleep that hung in the air. Under the window, a set of White armour was carefully placed. Along the right wall, a single bed and a plain bedside table. And one plain wooden chair, at the foot of the bed, with a pile of what must have been the rest of the knight's clothes.

Samily sat up in bed, the sheet pulled up over her chest, to which she held the bowl of porridge. "Darginn Argyll," she said, swallowing a mouthful. "How are you?"

"I'm well, Lady, thank you. Well, aye, I suppose. How are you?" Darginn looked about for somewhere to sit, not wanting to move the knight's clothes onto the floor.

Samily must have realised what he was thinking, because she pulled her feet up and pointed to the end of the bed with her spoon. "I am much better for a good sleep, thank you. What can I do for you?"

Darginn took the offer and perched on the end of the bed. "Well, it's a bit odd, actually, um…" *Actually*, he didn't know where to begin. He should have thought about this. Well, start with the basics. "We've just found out my son, Ismar, is a *draoidh*."

"I did not know you had a young child," said Samily.

"Aye, well, that's sort of part of it, y'see, he's not that young. Few years older than you, in fact."

Samily swallowed another mouthful of porridge. "Oh! I assumed; I am sorry. I had been told *draoidh* powers tend to develop in childhood." God, that was a thought. How old had Ismar been when this started? How long had he known? How long had he been hiding this? "Darginn? Did I…say something to upset you?"

His face must have registered his worry. "No, no, not at all, sorry, Lady. Just, well…Have you heard of the New Kirk?"

"The *New* Kirk?" Samily's face screwed up into confusion. "There is only one kirk."

That's exactly what every Thorn he'd already spoken to had said. "Aye, it's all a bit off, I think. Y'see, they're teaching that, well, that God doesnae abide *draoidhs*. In fact, *witches*, they call them."

Samily practically slammed the bowl down on her lap, her expression turning cold. "No. That is a lie. That is not the kirk. Who is teaching this? Where?"

Darginn was slightly taken aback by the change in her. He'd never seen her look so…hard. "Well, there's a priest called Victus in Traverlyn, but it seems like they're all about Eidyn. Ismar was seeing another priest in Haven, apparently, and—"

"Ismar is a member of the…?" Samily asked.

"Aye, well, no, but, he's been taking their teachings, see, and so, well"—Darginn caught his breath—"they've got him hating himself, Samily. Thinks he's *evil*." His voice failed on the last word. "I was hoping, maybe, if you wouldnae mind talking to him and, I dunno, maybe help him see..."

Samily leaned forward and grabbed his forearm gently. "Of course, Darginn. I have seen what people like this do. Their poison is the evil. And we will end it. Let me just..." She looked about the room a moment. "Um, you should wait outside, so I can dress."

"Oh, of course, aye, sorry." Darginn leapt up a little too quickly and his head spun, reminding him of its fragility. A second's pause, and he stepped into the hall, closing the door behind him.

He hadn't really known what response to expect, if he was honest, and he wasn't even sure he felt like he'd said all that needed saying. But if what he'd managed to say had lit the fire under Samily that it looked like, maybe that was all that was needed. He'd hoped to find someone as angry as he was, and it looked like he had.

---

"Ismar? Ismar?" Darginn gently shook his son's shoulder, and the man sluggishly opened his eyes. Samily was struck by him being asleep at that time of the afternoon, while the rest of the family were up and about. But she was reminded of Rasa's conversation about her mother's sickness, the one she suspected Aranok might share, and wondered if maybe it had also taken hold of Ismar. Aranok had spent a lot of time in bed after their fight, she understood. He did not seem a well man. And neither did the thin grey one lying before her. She had healed him only days ago. Barely really registered his face then. She'd been so frantic, in such a rush to heal those who needed it and be off again. But he had looked healthier then, in that hospital bed, than he did now, staring blearily up at her.

The room was a good size, but nowhere near big enough for the whole family. Isadona, Darginn's wife, smiled hopefully, wringing her hands in her skirt. His daughter, Jena, held her daughter, Liana, up to the window, pointing enthusiastically at something outside. Perhaps the birds nesting in the tree across the road. Yavick, her husband, sat on the floor, back against the wall, arms resting on his raised knees. He had the eyes of a man looking for something to break. She knew that anger. It was waiting in her too. But now was not the time. Compassion was needed now.

"Ismar, you've a visitor," Darginn said gently. "Ye remember Lady Samily?"

"Why?" Ismar asked, shading his eyes with his left hand.

"I, eh, I asked her to come and talk to you, son. Thought maybe you'd like that?" Darginn's voice was gentle, and Samily was reminded of how fragile he'd been, not so long ago. How brittle. When he'd first woken in Lestalric, she'd wondered if he'd ever be truly whole again. Quellaria seemed to have mended that. But here he was, just as tentative, just as troubled, but for his son now.

How much pain should one family have to suffer?

"All right." Ismar's voice was resigned. Flat. Samily could smell that he hadn't bathed in some time. He turned and pulled himself up to a sitting position, leaning against the bedstead. Samily struggled to understand how they all stayed in this one room. There were bedrolls tucked in the window bay, but with just the one large bed for five adults and a child... this was no way for them to be living. There must be a better answer. And for now, the room was too crowded. She could imagine that it would be challenging to have the conversation Darginn wanted her and Ismar to have with the whole family watching, however benign their intent. And truthfully, she was a little worried about saying something that accidentally triggered a memory in Darginn that caused him the kind of confusion she'd once seen in Nirea, while all their memories were compromised.

"Would it be possible for us to be left alone, perhaps?" she asked.

"Oh, em..." Darginn looked to his wife, nodding quickly but uncertainly. "Aye, we can... we can do that, eh? Go down the bar and maybe get Liana out for a bit?" He addressed the final question to Jena.

The woman held Liana before her. "Shall we go and see if the birds will sing for us?" The little girl grinned enthusiastically.

"Are ye sure?" Isadona asked. It made sense that his mother didn't want to leave him.

Samily took the woman's hands in her own. "I promise you I will do all I can to help your son. He is God's child."

Isadona's lips tightened, her eyes quivered and she grabbed Samily into a fierce hug. "Thank you."

It took them only a minute to clear the room, leaving Samily alone with Ismar. "May I?" She indicated the opposite side of the bed. He nodded half-heartedly and she sat, cross-legged, at the end. "I understand you have been seeing a man who claimed to be a priest of the kirk."

Ismar didn't turn his head to answer, just stared blankly at his own legs. "He is a priest. Of the New Kirk."

"There is no 'New Kirk.' There is the kirk, and there is God. Anyone who told you otherwise was dishonest."

"They split from the kirk because it's been corrupted. Moved away from God's truth." He recited the words as if they were written before him, in the manner of a schoolchild. Anger flared in her again, not just at the lies, but that they had been buried deep in Ismar.

"What truth is that?" she asked.

"Witches are evil."

That word. Again, Samily saw the girl in Caer Amon, her love's head raised in one hand, blood pouring down her arm. Aranok had been right about her being a victim, but so were the people who that charlatan had lied to. Had taught to hate. Everyone in that settlement had died because one man dripped poison in them every day until they thought it nectar.

And in that moment, clarity. Samily knew exactly what she had to do. Not now, but when she had finished here. When she had done what she could for Ismar.

"So, you think God detests you for being *draoidh*?" she asked.

"That is what the Recounts say," Ismar answered.

*The Recounts?* Samily had heard of those. Ancient scrolls, allegedly transcribing the word of God. But they were hideous. All Samily had ever been taught was that God loved all of God's children, and that only God would judge them in death. If the Recounts were what the "New Kirk" was based on...

"The Recounts were written by people, Ismar. People who corrupted faith in God for their own ends. For their own power. From what I have been told, it is clear in their writings that they were intended to benefit certain people, but not others. For example, is it true they teach that a certain amount of coin must be given to a priest each season?"

Ismar thought for a moment. "Aye."

"Who benefits from that? What need has God for gold?"

Again a pause. "You take charity. Same thing, isn't it?"

"Of course not!" Samily realised she'd raised her voice in horror at the suggestion. She took a breath and found a gentler tone. "We and the monks—and priests of the kirk too—we live a humble life. We serve God and protect God's children. We ask in return only as much as people can give in order for us to better serve them. We do not *tax* people in the name of God."

"Kirks need coin. Priests have to eat. Alms for the needy." Samily found herself wondering how this man could so easily, so casually defend a group who had taught him he was wrong just for being born. It was perverse.

"People willingly give their labour to the kirk. They donate food. Those who can give alms and it goes directly to those in need. Priests take no profit. Real priests. They have no need of it."

"Hmm." A grunt of concession? Was that a sliver of doubt? Maybe. If it was, she would use it as a wedge.

"May I tell you how I see the situation, as a child raised in God's light?" she asked.

The slightest tilt of Ismar's head. It was acknowledgement enough.

"If God hates *draoidhs*, why would we exist? Why would God create a person in order to hate them? Would that not be cruel? There is no love in that. I would not have faith in such a God. That would be a God of malice."

"God is unknowable," said Ismar. "You could as easily ask why evil exists at all."

"I am not sure that it does." Samily had seen that belief tested in recent times, but still, this was what she believed, in her heart. She'd called Shayella evil, but the woman had been mad. *Driven* mad. "I believe people are complex. Some do things we would call evil, but in truth, they are merely selfish. They lack care for others, or for the consequences of their actions. God allows us to choose, and judges our choices. To hate us for being born *draoidhs* would be as bizarre as damning me for being female or having blond hair—I am who God made me. And I have saved many lives with the gifts God gave me."

"I'm a necromancer," Ismar said quietly. "What lives can I save?"

Samily instinctively recoiled a little, and instantly regretted it. She hoped Ismar hadn't seen it. Not because she had a prejudice against necromancers—they were as much God's children as any other. She just hadn't been ready to meet another so soon after Shayella. She should have asked Darginn what his skill was. She could have been prepared. Did she have an answer? How could a necromancer do God's work?

She'd been silent too long. Ismar's breathing shuddered and she sensed he was on the verge of crying. Samily had been through so much with the Dead, seen them only as enemies. Blasphemies. Cut them down in Lestalric and Auldun. Ridden through their detritus on the Auld Road.

And there it was. A flash of inspiration, and she knew the answer.

"Ismar, Auldun was overrun with Dead. Now that Shayella is gone, the city will be littered with their bodies. You've seen the streets of Traverlyn after one night. Clearing out Auldun will take months, perhaps years, and many will die from disease. Unless a necromancer raises them and has them remove themselves. To make Auldun safe for the living. To undo what Shayella did. To give them peace. You could reclaim Eidyn's capital."

Ismar finally turned his head to look at her. "I . . . You think I could do that?"

"With training? I do. You will need help. To learn to control your skill. I could ask Master Ipharia." The master was keen to see more of Samily anyway, and she'd been considering asking her for help with her own skill. But she was sure she remembered her saying something about an interest in all unusual skills. Would necromancy come under that description? It was worth asking. "Who knows what other skills you may discover with training?" Shayella could do other things. Mad things with her own body. "I would wager there is a chance you survived your wounds because of your skill."

"Hmm." This time his voice was curious. That was good. He was thinking, hopefully.

"I promise you, Ismar, that God loves you as you are. I guarantee it. God gave you this skill. Your choice is what to do with it."

A smile. Weak, but there. Finally, maybe, he was hearing her. Thank God. Sharing God's light with others was one of the greatest joys of being a White Thorn. Allowing them to feel that same sense of calm and warmth... It was an honour, and one she never took lightly.

But the smile faded. Ismar turned onto his side and went to lie down again. "I'm tired."

"Oh. Of course." Samily climbed off the bed. Had something changed? Maybe not. Maybe he just needed time. She was sure she'd reached him. "I could come back later. If you like?"

"Maybe," he mumbled. She'd said enough. Hopefully. For now.

Samily left the room to find Isadona pacing the hallway, her eyes red and wet. She held the door open for the woman and gestured for her to go in. Isadona gave her a light touch on the arm and a smile as she passed.

*A mother's love.*

That brought Samily's mind back to her own mother. And a recognition. She was angry. Angry to have had that love denied her. Not by her mother—she understood that she had acted out of love. Denied by the bigots who had made her mother's life so hideous that she would give up her own daughter rather than have her suffer the same pain.

And she had one of those bigots to see. Now.

# CHAPTER 24

"Where the fuck *is* everyone?" Vastin turned frantically. He'd looked everywhere. Nobody in the hospital seemed to know anything. He knew Nirea and Samily had left when he and Meristan did, but he'd expected Aranok, Allandria and Mynygogg to still be there. They couldn't have sorted the sunspire already, surely? If they were all gone too, what the Hell did he do then?

"Keep your voice down, young man." An elderly medic scowled at him as she stalked toward him. "There are people resting."

"I know, but…" Vastin could barely stand still. His fingers rubbed frantically against his palms. "It's urgent!"

"For whom are you looking?" the medic asked.

"Laird Aranok. Lady Allandria. Mynygogg?" He wasn't sure whether to call the king by his title, though he was fairly sure most if not all of the hospital staff must have had their memories restored by now.

"Hmm." She frowned thoughtfully. "I don't believe I've seen any of them today. You've checked their rooms?"

"All of them." Vastin was starting to panic.

"Right. Well, one of my patients might have an idea. Follow me." The medic led Vastin up the stairs and along a corridor. She stopped and spoke quietly when she reached a door. "You must be quiet and calm. She is grieving a loss."

Grieving a loss? Had someone died that Vastin didn't know about?

Someone connected to their party? Vastin's chest tightened, but he breathed deep, stuffing the fear down. The medic knocked gently at the door and cracked it open with a quiet "May we come in?"

"Of course." A woman's voice. A little familiar?

The room was lit by a solitary candle, flickering on the bedside table. The voice had not come from the figure in the bed, but from the woman sitting in the chair beside it.

"Rasa, I'm sorry to interrupt," said the medic. "It's just that this young man is somewhat desperate to find the king or his envoy, and I thought perhaps you might know..."

"Vastin?" Rasa asked. The last time he'd seen her—the first time—Vastin had been helping get her and the nature *draoidh* in the door during the Thakhati siege. She'd had a hideous gouge out of her hip. And the other woman... Oh. The other woman was the one in the bed.

"Your friend—she didn't survive?" he asked.

"I'll leave you to it." The medic backed out quietly and closed the door behind her.

When it closed, Rasa answered. "No. They thought she would. Samily healed her jaw, the wound on her head, but... she didn't wake this morning. The medics think she may have had damage *inside* her brain. Or somewhere else unseen. They're unsure."

Vastin clenched his hands respectfully before him. "I'm so sorry."

"It's fine." Rasa wiped the back of her hand across her eyes. "Silly, really. I didn't know her. Just—we went through something, I suppose. And she was so brave. She opened the gate. Let the Thorns in. She deserved better."

*The Thorns!*

Vastin was shaken from his melancholy awkwardness. "I need your help. You know Meristan?"

"I do," Rasa answered.

"He's been taken by soldiers. Eidyn soldiers. They're taking him to Greytoun."

Rasa's face registered the same horror Vastin had lived with for almost two days. "You can't find the king? Or Laird Aranok?"

"No. And..." Should he tell her this? Should he be checking to be sure she wasn't the illusionist assassin they were worried about? How would he even do that? He didn't know the woman well enough to ask her a question.

*Shit!*

He had to risk it. He needed someone to help him save Meristan, and she was his only option. Besides, what benefit would it give an assassin to sit alone in the dark grieving a woman they didn't know?

"And they were planning to leave," he said. "All of them. Nirea and Samily left days ago and I thought that maybe the others would still be here, but I'm worried I've missed them, and now…"

Rasa raised her hand and Vastin stemmed the flood of words pouring from him. "I know. Aranok spoke to me a few days ago, but I didn't know they'd gone. I'm to visit Leet in a week to meet with the queen. But…"

Rasa looked at the floor and thought for a moment. Vastin was relieved to have finally, at least, shared the news with someone who might be able to help. To do something. To take the burden from his back, alone.

Rasa stood abruptly, opened the door and grasped Vastin's hand, pulling him after her. "Come on. Samily is here somewhere."

---

"You are Victus?" Samily's tone was barely contained fury. Darginn had agreed to bring her back to the cobbler's, to speak to the bastard who'd tortured his son, but he was beginning to worry what box he might have opened.

Victus stood in the doorway, arms crossed against the chill wind. "I am Faither Victus. What can I do for a knight of the Order of the White Thorns?"

"You are no priest," Samily answered flatly. "You are a charlatan and a liar. You take God's name in vain to spread hate. You will stop. Today."

Victus smiled, rubbed his hands together and blew into them. "Why don't you come inside, let us keep the heat in?"

"No, thank you," Samily answered. "I am here to order you to stop your lies. That is all. Do not give me reason to linger."

Victus gave a clearly false expression of confusion. "Young lady, you are in no position of authority over me. And to compound matters, you're also mistaken. As I already explained to Master Argyll here, I only preach love and the truth of God's word. For those willing to hear it. But if you will not come in, allow me a moment to put on a cloak and I will step out to preserve my host's good health."

Victus pushed the door to, fished a cloak from behind it, then stepped out with it wrapped around him and pulled the door closed. His breath smoked into the crisp air.

"Now, where should we begin?" he asked, as if preparing for a sermon.

"There is no need to begin anywhere," said Samily. "You preach that God hates *draoidhs*. Your lies make no sense. God does not make mistakes and God is not malicious. Therefore the only logical conclusion is that God made *draoidhs* just as any other person. God loves all of God's children. Your 'kirk' is a fraud."

Victus remained calm in a way that Darginn somehow found infuriating. His lack of ire or regret or even a hint of doubt was aggravating as Hell. Darginn remembered just how badly he'd wanted to beat the man to a bloody pulp the last time he'd been there.

"Well, that is your opinion, but—"

"It is fact." Samily cut him off. "You cannot dispute any of it."

"The Recounts say—"

"The Recounts are lies. Written by people who wished to use faith in God to their advantage. They convey power on the undeserving and hardship on the rest. They encourage people to suffer in life with a promise of reward in death. God does not wish suffering on God's children. It is clear to see who benefits from the Recounts. Do not quote them to me as God's word."

Mumbling from behind made Darginn turn. There was a crowd forming. People who had been walking past had stopped. It looked like some had come out of houses. They all kept their distance, but they made no pretence of doing anything other than watch the argument before them. Nosy buggers. Well, wouldnae harm any of them to hear this. Especially if they were thinking maybe the "New Kirk" was for them.

"You are, of course, entitled to your beliefs, young lady—"

"Lady *Thorn*, thank you."

Victus's smile wavered just a little, but he kept it in place. "Of course, Lady Thorn. But you are not entitled to force me to abandon mine. I see truth in the Recounts. I see God's guiding hand. And I see rules we must follow in life, if we are to be worthy of God's love in death."

"The only thing we must do to be worthy of God's love is to be kind," Samily replied. "To be decent. To care for God's children."

"That is what I do, child, I—"

"I am not your child," Samily interrupted. "Do not speak to me as if I were one of your victims."

Victus actually recoiled from the word. *"Victims?"*

"Victims," Samily repeated. "I have seen what men like you do. I have seen what it does to people. I have watched it destroy an entire settlement. Wipe out families. All were victims."

"Wipe out...?" There was genuine astonishment in Victus's eyes and Darginn shared some himself. He had no idea what Samily was talking about, but it sounded bloody awful. Explained why she'd been so quick to anger, maybe. Even before she'd seen Ismar. "I cannot begin to imagine what you think you've seen, but I can say with certainty it was nothing to do with the New Kirk."

"I did not say it was. But a man like you. A long time ago. And do you know why I am here to tell you about it?" Samily stepped right up to Victus. "Because *I* am *draoidh*."

There was defiance in the man's eyes still, but he was unnerved. "You...are?"

"I am," said Samily. "And I have saved many lives with my skill. Many more than I imagine you can claim. People who would have died. Here. Wounded by the Thakhati—and I healed them. So tell me, '*Faither*,' am I evil? Must I repent my sins? Should the lives I saved be ended, to purge the country of my darkness?"

Victus didn't speak for an age. Just looked down at Samily quietly, thinking. Trying to figure out what the Hell he could say that wasnae going to get him smacked in the face, likely. Darginn quite hoped he didn't manage it.

"You make a fine point, Lady Thorn," he finally said. "You are clearly a good person. You have been raised in God and perhaps that has overcome your nature. Perhaps God will see your dedication to God's work and forgive the stain of your birth. But, for certainty, the only way is to turn your back on that unnatural side of you. To deny it utterly and refuse to be seduced by it again. Magic is against God's teachings and can only, therefore, usurp God's plan."

Samily was quiet then. But with a completely different aura. Darginn genuinely worried what she might do next.

In the silence, a bird shrieked above them. Loud enough that it made Darginn look up and see the falcon swoop down toward them. All but Samily flinched away as it landed on the street and transformed into Rasa.

"Samily!" The metamorph's relief was clear. "I've found you!"

Victus stared, wide-eyed.

"Rasa? What...what do you need?" Samily asked.

"It's..." Rasa looked around at the crowd suspiciously, landing on Victus last. "Who's this?"

"No one important," Samily answered.

Rasa stepped toward her and leaned in urgently to her shoulder. Darginn was standing close enough to overhear her hushed words. "Vastin has returned. Meristan has been taken by soldiers. To Greytoun."

Samily's head snapped up. "No."

Rasa nodded urgently, half eyeing Darginn with some suspicion. Of course, he knew her—he'd ridden with her from Lestalric. But she'd been unconscious and they hadn't really met. Not properly. He smiled, hoping it was at least a little reassuring.

"Right." Samily turned back to Victus. "Will you stop poisoning people in God's name?"

Victus drew himself up to his full height. "I cannot stop doing something I have never done." His smile was so certain, so confident...

Samily stepped toward him, whipped her blade from its sheath and, in one movement, severed the man's head from his neck.

It toppled to the ground, landing moments before his body realised it was gone and collapsed like a puppet, its strings suddenly cut.

"Holy fuck!" Darginn shouted involuntarily, then clamped his hand over his mouth.

The crowd erupted. Screaming, shouting, running.

"Samily, what...who *was* that?" Rasa asked.

"An evil man." She turned to Darginn. "Yes?"

Darginn nodded, aware he was staring. The blood. God, the blood, pooling between the cobbles. He looked down and it was on his hands. On his sleeves. In a panic, he stepped back, swiping at his front to be rid of it. To wipe it off.

"Darginn?" Samily's voice was far away. "Darginn, are you all right?"

The blood. He was covered in it. How was he covered in it?

"Darginn?" Samily shook him, and he found focus again. There was no blood. Not on him. Why had he thought...? "Darginn, are you all right?"

"Aye, aye, just...just a shock, I suppose. I wasnae expecting..."

The crowd had gone. Scattered. Run. The cobbler hadn't come out to see what had happened. The street had gone silent as a kirkyard. Just Victus's corpse crumpled beside his head, staring in mute surprise. Did the man deserve that? Wasn't Darginn's place to say, he supposed. Ismar's life would certainly be better without him in it. But did he deserve to die? Darginn might have wrung his neck himself the other night.

"Darginn, I have to go," said Samily. "Will you be all right?"

Would he? Yes. Yes, he'd be fine. "Aye. On you go."

She looked at him a moment longer, placed a hand against his chest gently and turned to Rasa. "I'll meet you at the hospital?"

Rasa nodded and transformed back into the falcon. Samily took off running and was gone from sight within a minute. Darginn was left alone in the eerily silent street, standing over the corpse of the man he'd gotten killed.

He wasn't sure he regretted it, to be honest. Just...he needed some time to think on it. That pub wasnae far. A few drams in there—aye, that was a good idea. Clear his head. Before he went home. Before he had to tell Isadona what he'd done. And Ismar.

# CHAPTER 25

They had taken too long. Samily had gathered all those she could in the short time she'd allowed herself to collect her Thorn siblings to go after Meristan. She'd found Asha near the hospital, and Asha had known where to find Tull and Merrick. Greste had been by the stables but, after a brief conversation, had declined to come with them. Samily had been appalled, but the elder Thorn argued that Meristan had ordered the Thorns to defend Traverlyn, and that he would not have them abandon their posts for his sake. They had to serve the greater good. If the Order left Traverlyn and the Thakhati attacked again...

She may have been right, but Samily was going anyway. The remaining Thorns could fend off the Thakhati without her. And they had the sunstone. Greste allowed the others to make their own choices about coming. Asha and Merrick needed no thinking time. Only Tull took a moment to consider, before agreeing with Samily, and arguing that only overwhelming might had the potential to recover Meristan without unwanted violence.

Greste countered that Samily alone had the power needed, and perhaps that was true. But she had no idea how to control her powers for anything more than healing or short time jumps. If she could harness the stopping ability, without catching herself too, then maybe. For now, she needed the others.

The four of them had raced off after the soldiers. By Vastin's account, they shouldn't have been too far ahead, but if they reached the junction where the Auld Road met the Easter Road before them, the Thorns would have a problem. The soldiers might carry on west on the Auld Road, now that it was clear of Blackened, or they might turn north and head for the Nor Loch ferry.

They had to catch them before that.

Half a day of pushing the horses to their limits, and they saw a troop of mounted soldiers ahead. Even in the growing dark, Samily could see the shape of Meristan's White armour towering above the soldiers surrounding him. They seemed in no hurry. That was Samily's boon, and their error.

"Hold!" she called. "In the name of God, hold!"

The soldiers at the back of the column turned their heads and, seeing the Thorns riding toward them, turned their mounts to face them. "Arms!" one of them cried, drawing her sword. The others quickly turned to join them. Samily drew up her mount fifty yards from the soldiers, trusting the others would do the same. Her sword stayed in its sheath. She would only draw it when she intended to use it.

"You hold Meristan, head of the Order of the White Thorns. You have no authority over him and you will release him to us." Samily spoke plainly but loudly enough for all the soldiers to hear. "Now."

No answer, but a rumble of movement as the column parted to allow one rider to clear their ranks. A woman, bearing the mantle of leadership, rode out halfway across the distance between the two groups. She examined the four of them in silence, dropped her shoulders and sighed. "This is a bad idea."

What did that mean? Samily didn't care. "Release him."

"I can't do that," she answered. "He is accused of treason. Please don't open yourselves to the same charge."

"I do not wish to fight." Samily hoped the suggestion would be enough. She could see at most thirty soldiers. Four Thorns would win that battle, even without Samily's skill. She hoped she could see that in the leader's face. The woman looked over her shoulder a moment, turned back and crumpled her mouth.

"What is your name, Lady Thorn?"

"Samily."

"Samily, I'm Captain Cyrra. I need you to understand that there are no circumstances under which I can release Brother Meristan without the king's orders. He is credibly accused of treason against Eidyn. Were I to release him, that charge would fall on me."

*Brother* Meristan. It felt so long since she had believed that myth, the word rang like a cracked bell. But it also reminded her: Perhaps there was another way. She had a memory charm. If she could clear the captain's memory, reveal the truth to her—to all her soldiers—could they end this bloodlessly? Maybe. But was that the right thing to do here? It seemed a clear solution, but she had made so many clear decisions recently that others had called missteps. Her mind flitted back to Victus. She'd barely had time to consider that action. It had seemed obvious that his malignancy had to end, and Rasa's arrival had left her with no time to deliberate further. Sending him to God, protecting others from his misguided poison, was a clear solution. But the look on Darginn's face, the horror reflected back at her from the man who'd come to her for help... Had she acted hastily?

No point dwelling on it now. What was done was done and God would judge her. But it did give her pause, here and now. She looked over the captain's shoulder, just able to make out Meristan's shape in the dusk. Was there a bustle of conversation around him? Maybe. But whatever else she had to consider, Meristan was being led to his execution.

Of course she had to try. What else could she do?

"Captain, may I approach? I have something to show you that will change your mind."

Cyrra sat back on her horse, straightening her spine. "I have your word, on God's grace, that you will not attack?"

Samily gave an exaggerated nod. "You do."

Cyrra checked over her shoulder again. There *was* something happening. A murmur. A rumbling. "All right. Approach."

Samily raised a hand to her companions, indicating they stand down, and nudged her horse forward. When she drew level with the captain, Samily reached for the charm around her neck. Cyrra's hand clamped tighter on her sword's grip.

"May I ask you to...? Oh, wait." Samily hadn't allowed for the captain's gloves. The charm had to be in contact with her skin. How to do that without arousing her suspicion such that she refused? She'd thought to simply hand it to her and speak the word, but that wouldn't work. If she touched it to Cyrra's face, the only place her skin was exposed, it could seem an attack. She held the charm tight in her fist, desperately trying to find the right words to make this work.

"Samily, stop!" Her head snapped up at his voice. Meristan had emerged from the ruck of mounted soldiers. Relief washed through her. Meristan would know what to do. "Captain, may I approach? You continue to have my word that I will submit to your authority."

Cyrra looked back and forth between them, seemingly perplexed. She raised an open palm toward Samily as if to indicate that she was waiting for Samily to reveal her intent, then threw both hands up in exasperation. "Fine. Approach."

He did, despite some dark, suspicious looks from the soldiers he left behind. Meristan drew up between the two of them, his horse curiously sniffing at Samily's own mount. "Samily, what are you doing?" His tone was gentle but firm.

"I was..." How could she say it? "I was going to show Captain Cyrra the truth."

The captain's eyebrow went up.

"And what if she reacts badly, Samily? There is a troop of soldiers waiting on her orders," said Meristan. "Or perhaps she already knows the truth."

S'grace, Samily hadn't thought of that. What if the captain was a willing ally of Weyr? If she revealed the memory charm, and her *draoidh* nature...

"What truth?" Cyrra asked. "If there is some truth I should know, I'd like to hear it."

"There may be," said Meristan, turning to Samily. "But it could require revealing more than is safe. You understand, Captain, there are issues above one's level of authority."

Cyrra turned her mount to face directly at the two of them. "Listen. Unless you have a convincing reason otherwise, we're moving on."

Samily looked nervously to Meristan, praying he could give her the answer. She didn't know what to do. Risk everything to get the captain back on their side? He raised his eyebrows and tightened his lips. It was a warning. An acknowledgement, maybe, that there was no right choice? Just... a choice.

All right.

*Take it from basics, Samily.*

Her options were to let them go with Meristan—almost certainly leading to his execution; fight the soldiers here, on the Auld Road, and likely be forced to kill most of them; or try the charm. As the only option that might avoid someone's death, Samily decided it was the right choice after all. She pulled the charm from around her neck and moved her horse toward Cyrra's.

"Samily? Are you certain?" Meristan asked.

"I am." She held out the charm. "Captain, I am placing great trust in you by sharing this. I hope it is not misplaced."

"What is it?" she asked.

"A charm. A charm that will show you the truth of this matter, if you are willing to see it."

"Like, magic?" Cyrra asked.

Samily stifled the panic in her chest. "Yes. I am *draoidh*. And I can show you the truth of this situation, which will prove Meristan's innocence. May I?"

Cyrra looked to her soldiers, who bristled with nervous energy. The horses pawed at the ground impatiently. "What does it involve?"

"Would you be willing to remove your glove and hold this?" Samily asked as gently as she could.

Cyrra stared hard at her, and then at the charm. "You understand, if this harms me, my troops will charge before I hit the ground."

"I do, Captain. And mine will join them." She nodded to Asha, Merrick and Tull. "I would like to avoid that, by God's grace."

She seemed a sensible woman. Samily hoped she had read her correctly.

"Captain, you have my word on this as on everything else," said Meristan. "I hope you will allow that I have not broken that word in our short time together."

"Well, I find myself wondering about that," Cyrra answered. "Seems to me that the only way these Thorns came running, not least a *draoidh* Thorn, is if your trainee fetched them. In which case, he's certainly not gone back to Baile Airneach, has he?"

"In fairness, Captain, I said he was going *home*, not to Baile Airneach," said Meristan.

A brief laugh from the woman. "I suppose you did, at that. All right, Samily." Cyrra carefully removed her left glove. "I'll give you a little faith. Show me your truth."

*Thank God.*

Samily placed the charm in her hand, carefully keeping hold of the leather strap it hung from. "This may be unpleasant for a moment," she explained. "But it will pass. All right?"

"How unpleasant?"

"It varies from one to another. I cannot say." She hoped that it would be light on the soldier. They could do without her vomiting and falling from her horse.

Another sigh. "Fine." Cyrra gripped the reins tight in her right hand and set herself high in her saddle. "Now what?"

Samily had seen Aranok do this, but it was the first time she'd done it. She half worried nothing would happen when she spoke the word.

*"Clior."*

Cyrra jerked forward, closing her eyes and almost pulling the charm from Samily's grasp. Her hold on the strap was solid, though, and she tugged it quickly from the captain's hold. A murmur of discontent, a cry of distress from the soldiers, and hooves clipped against the road, preparing to move.

*Come on.*

Cyrra put up a hand toward her troops, one finger in the air, and they held. Grumbled, but held. Meristan moved to her other side. "Captain, are you...?"

Cyrra jerked the hand in front of Meristan's face, silencing him. They waited. A few moments, and the captain lifted her head, blinking as if the murky dark were morning light.

"God in Hell," she whispered. "This is...real?"

"It is, Captain," said Meristan. "All of it. You see, it is complicated."

"Complicated?" She looked up at him, eyes wide. "It's a damn sight more than that! Explains your actions, though, I suppose."

"King Mynygogg was with us that day," Meristan explained. "He was determined to avoid any harm, until..."

"Until one of our soldiers accidentally murdered a Reiver boy," said Cyrra.

"Indeed." Meristan spread his hands. "Then it became a matter of limiting the deaths between our allies."

Samily was afraid to say anything. It appeared their gamble had worked, but if she spoke, if she said the wrong thing...

The captain looked at the sky, closed her eyes and breathed out hard. "Cyrra, how on earth do you get yourself into these things?"

"If it helps, Captain, I reacted much worse myself." Meristan's smile was warm and genuine.

Cyrra snapped her head toward him. "Did you actually believe yourself a monk?"

"I did. And I passed out." Meristan gestured to the charm, and Samily was reminded to secure it back around her neck, tucked inside her armour. "Though I suppose I was also bleeding heavily at the time."

"That's a story I will hear another day, Laird Thorn. In the meantime, what do you propose I tell my soldiers?" She turned to Samily. "Can you give them all their memories back?"

Could she? Fifty men and women, without assistance from Master Dialla? She didn't know. The spell didn't seem to take a great deal of energy, but... "I could try?"

"Wait," said Meristan. "Captain, how well do you know each of these soldiers? Would you swear for them? Every one? Individually?"

Cyrra lifted her head as though Meristan had insulted her. "They will follow my orders."

"Yes, but..." Meristan leaned in and spoke even quieter. "Is it possible that any of them could be spies for Anhel Weyr? To whom we cannot risk tipping our hand?"

"Is that...likely?" the captain asked.

"We've come across a number, sadly," said Meristan. "Including the head messenger."

"Madu?" Cyrra almost shouted the name, then lowered her voice again. "That's why the envoy killed her?"

"Actually, he didn't. Nor Janaeus nor the lairds. All done by others. Weyr murdered the lairds so he could take the throne after Janaeus died. It suited him to hang those deaths on Aranok."

"I can see that," said Cyrra. "Damn. I'm relieved to hear it. I served with him, a little, during the war. I thought I'd misjudged him."

"Many have," said Meristan. "But not in this case."

Cyrra turned back to look at her column of soldiers, several of whom had now lit torches against the darkening sky. "So, we can't risk using your charm on all of them, but we can't take you back to ... Oh! Wait." The soldier turned to Samily. "Do you know?" She turned to Meristan. "About Baile Airneach?" Meristan's look was as blank with fear as Samily's own. What had happened to their home? "When soldiers went to arrest you, and you were gone, Bielsed was furious. In his anger, he arrested the only person he could. The only one who was not a monk or a child."

"Heavens, no." Meristan raised his hand to his mouth. "Severianos?"

The Green Laird had insisted on staying at Baile Airneach with the trainees. Meristan said he'd assumed Severianos's age and status would protect their mentor against repercussions for Meristan's deception. He'd been wrong.

"He was taken to Greytoun," Cyrra confirmed.

Samily's stomach flipped. If Weyr had executed the Green Laird, Hell itself would not stand between him and the Thorns. He was the father of the Order and its beating heart. Surely, Weyr could not justify murdering an old blacksmith for crimes he had not committed. And, in fact, would not yet even understand, as he would still be under Janaeus's spell.

Meristan rubbed his hands over his face. "All right. All right. Captain, you and I are still going to Greytoun."

"What? No!" Samily shouted instinctively.

"We have to get in somehow, Samily. This is how. Captain Cyrra can deliver me directly to the cells and we can find Severianos. We can get him out, yes?"

"I wouldn't be promising that. I mean, we can try, but the minute we come across anyone of higher rank..." Cyrra trailed off. Her meaning was obvious. As soon as she was outranked, they would be confounded. And they had precious few allies in Greytoun now. Not since Anhel falsely condemned Aranok.

"We will try," said Meristan. "And, Samily, you will go back to Traverlyn and—"

"No. I am coming with you. You need me."

Meristan gestured for Samily to calm, but she would not. She was not allowing him to go alone.

"Just, listen. Go back to Traverlyn. Get out of your armour and find some leathers. You can't travel as a Thorn. Darginn Argyll can get you into Haven—perhaps into Greytoun, if needed. Rasa will be able to help. The three of you, come to Haven, we'll find each other. Yes? In the kirk, if not before. We may need you to get out."

Samily's heart raced. She hated the idea of leaving Meristan to Anhel Weyr's clutches, but neither could they abandon the Green Laird if there was a chance to save him. "What about the others?"

Meristan looked to the other three, smiling. "They will return to their duty. This is a problem that does not need a Thorn, Samily. It needs your other skills. We must be subtle, quick and quiet. You understand?"

She did. Her time skill would be of greater use than her blade. Rasa's ability to disguise herself, and Darginn's knowledge of Haven... Yes. She saw it. It made sense. She hated it, but it made sense. Samily nodded, biting the inside of her lip against the fear.

"Good." Meristan grasped her shoulder. "Now, Captain Cyrra. It strikes me that if Weyr has not already executed Severianos, he may not be in a hurry to do so. So if he lives as we speak, then perhaps we should take our time in reaching our destination, do you think? Give Samily time to do what she must?"

S'grace, the calm with which he casually suggested the Green Laird may already be dead! But if that were so, it was so, and he would be with God. Few finer, more faithful men existed.

Cyrra held her hand out before her, as if she were having trouble seeing it in the gloom. "Perhaps it's time we made camp for the night."

Meristan grinned. "I concur. May I have a moment with my charge?"

Cyrra nodded and nudged her horse back toward her troops, turning back to give Samily a respectful nod. Thank God she'd been true. There were still some suspicious, disapproving looks from the soldiers as she reached them, but nobody would challenge her order to make camp.

"Samily, ride hard," Meristan said when they were alone. "Be quick, but be careful. Take the ferry. Cyrra and I will slow us as much as we can, but we should arrive in Haven in no more than four days. Try to get the Calladells, if you can. Yes?"

"Yes," Samily answered. "I will. All of it. We will be there. I swear it."

Meristan leaned over and kissed her gently on the head. "Go now. We have God's work to do."

# CHAPTER 26

"There's something out there. In the water."

Ailen had barely spoken to Nirea all day. He'd been furious with her for waiting to have Quell restore his memory the night before. For not immediately giving him the truth. The whole truth. She'd tried to explain why she'd waited, but he'd been livid. Said it wasn't her choice to make and that she should have known him well enough to know he always wanted the truth, however unpalatable. Her worry that he would have been restrained in his anger once he knew she was the queen couldn't have been more wrong. He was right too. She should have remembered. Ailen had been lied to before. The man who promised him forever and disappeared with half his money. He'd barely kept the King's Wark. Lived off one meal a day for a long time. But he could cook. And he cared well for his ale. So people kept coming, and he eventually got back on his feet.

Nirea knew all that. She just hadn't thought of it last night. Her friend deserved more respect. She'd been playing a lot close to her chest recently, and it had not always ended well. Maybe the complexities of the crown were meaningless in the street. And maybe she'd forgotten that.

Nirea had been keen to establish a plan for beginning to clear memories today, but Quell had insisted on a day's rest first, and a chance to get herself a new dress to replace the one that was now looking the worse for wear after the siege of Traverlyn and the ride to Leet. The dress that had saved her life. Had Tia not recognised it, Nirea would not have dragged Samily back to Traverlyn to heal her. She'd mentioned that to Quell, and the *draoidh*'s carefree mask had slipped more than a little. So Nirea had been unsurprised when the woman had returned in a new dress, but with news that she was having the other made into a smaller version.

There were few tailors in town. Most were cheap, offering affordable dresses and repairs to the town's streetwalkers. But there was at least one Ailen knew of that made better-class offerings for the wealthy sea merchant families whose larger houses sat on hills overlooking the port town.

It was unlikely Quell had actually paid the tailor. But to be honest, with all that was going on, and with her own history, Nirea wasn't about to object to some light larceny. Besides, she was running low on coin and had no prospect of seeing the inside of the royal treasury soon.

She'd at first worried about Quell going out alone in daylight, but the chances that anyone was looking for her were tiny. Nirea, maybe, and she was going to have to decide how to approach that soon. For the day, she'd stayed in the inn, mostly sleeping and bathing before spending a few hours after dinner sipping beer and watching people. If someone was looking for her, maybe it would be better to flush them out. With Quell around, they could always wipe their memories if need be. Ailen had avoided her, even so far as having Crinn bring her food.

He'd mooted the idea of staying closed for the day, but Nirea had argued it would just draw attention. Only when the last drinker had been shown back into the street and the doors locked up did he bring three beers to join her and Quell at the table. His first words had been the last Nirea was expecting.

"What do you mean, 'There's something in the water'? Where?"

Ailen pointed north, toward the sea. "Out there. No boats have left or landed in ages—the ones that tried were pulled under. Seems to me it started right about the time your man Janaeus cast his spell."

"Right. So...where are they going? Where are they docking?" Nirea asked.

Ailen's puzzled stare suggested that wasn't the response he'd been expecting. "Haven, I assume. Haven't had anyone in to say either way. But Haven's where they're meant to go if Leet's inaccessible, right?"

It was. Farther down the coast, the waters there tended to be more sedate than out here at Eidyn's northern tip. When Leet was storm tossed, Haven was often still safe.

"So we reckon Weyr's stuck a demon out there, do we?" Quell asked.

"We thought it was a leftover from Mynygogg, before. Assumed it would move on eventually. Seems less like that now, eh?" Ailen raised his cup briefly and drank from it before Nirea had a chance to match his salute. He was still angry.

Nirea was just going to have to ignore his ire until it faded. "Anyone who was far enough out when the spell was cast would be unaffected. They couldn't have boats full of folk landing in Leet, telling people how their memories were all to fuck, and that Mynygogg was the true king. But block off Leet, force them to land in Haven, arrest the crew and have Janaeus change their memories..."

"Doesn't work now he's dead, though, does it?" said Quell.

"It does not. Which makes me wonder what Weyr will do instead." He might arrest them just the same, but they'd never see the sky again.

"How's he even going to keep up trade by sea?" Ailen asked. "Anyone goes to another country's at risk of someone telling them their own kingdom's not as they think."

That was a good point. What would he do? "Best guess, right now, same as he's done to the Reivers. Make everyone our enemies, so nobody will trade with us. Then even if somebody does hear the truth, they'll never believe it. Our navy will become a blockade, 'protecting' us from attack."

"But... that'll kill the merchant sea trade!" said Ailen.

Yes, it would. But Weyr would see that as an acceptable sacrifice to keep himself on the throne. It could only possibly work in the short term, but by the time he'd consolidated his power, it wouldn't matter if people started learning the truth. With the backing of his demons, allies, other *draoidhs*... he'd still be king, and without having their memories properly cleared, most folk wouldn't be able to take the truth anyway.

The devious bastard.

"What about Seafelde?" Crinn had finished wiping down the counters and wandered over to stand behind Ailen, placing his hands on his husband's shoulders. "Is that not the same problem?"

Was it?

"Less so, I suppose," she said, working her own thoughts out loud. "Pirates stick to their own, and who's king makes little difference to them either way. Plus Seafelde's cut off by the Fire Crags. Not much mixing with the rest of the populace. I imagine he'd leave it alone."

But that wasn't all of it. If Weyr was as ruthless, as immoral as she believed, there was every chance he'd leave nothing to chance. If she were him, and she needed the truth kept down, she'd send a wave of demons to flatten Seafelde and make the Figgate Moors uninhabitable. Send the pirates offshore never to return. Kill as many as possible.

*If she were Weyr.*

"Well. Where does that leave us, then?" Quell asked. Crinn stopped rubbing Ailen's shoulders and pulled himself a chair.

"Makes little difference, for now," said Nirea. "We can't fight a sea demon. Not one big enough to pull a ship under." Could anyone? How many *draoidhs* would it take; how many Thorns? How would they even begin? Nirea had no idea. "So we focus on what we *can* do. We give folk their memories back."

"How you planning to do that?" Ailen asked.

Another good question. "Well, I've been thinking about that. Ideally, we'd start with people in positions of power—the Guard, the shore porters, navy captains—and use them to help us get to the rest. But after our experience with Madu..." Nirea trailed off, realising she was straying into dangerous territory, since she'd promised not to say anything to Crinn about the assassin contracts.

Ailen grunted. He looked at Crinn a moment, then back to Nirea. "I've told him. All of it. He knows."

"Oh!" Nirea wasn't sure what to make of that. She certainly hadn't expected such an abrupt change of mind. But, it now occurred to her, maybe his anger at her keeping the truth from him last night had changed his perspective on Crinn's right to know. And that being the case, maybe he should be cutting her a little more rope than she'd seen so far.

"Well, thank fuck for that," said Quell. "Because the chances of me opening my gob and saying the wrong thing after a few wines were pretty high."

Ailen pretended to smile, reached across the scarred wooden table and squeezed his husband's hand. Crinn gave him an affectionate look and Nirea's mind flitted to her own husband. Hopefully, he'd been able to get away to Mournside by now. Hopefully he was safe. Couldn't linger too long on that thought.

"So what have you decided to do?" Nirea asked instead.

It was Crinn who answered. "This is our home."

It took Nirea a moment to realise that was all he intended to say. Ailen gave her a tiny nod, as if to say, "I told you." Fair enough. She'd warned them. She couldn't live their lives for them.

"You did. All right. So, as I was saying, we have to be more careful about whose memories we choose to restore. We'll have to find people we can trust. Start there."

"Here, Red, you know I can tell if someone's memory's been changed, right?" Quell threw out the sentence as if it were the most casual piece of information she possessed.

"You... can?" Nirea, on the other hand, nearly fell off her chair. "But Aranok was having to..."

"Aranok's an earth *draoidh* with a charm, darling. *I'm* a *memory draoidh*. I can do a bit more than him." She supped her beer triumphantly, and now Nirea could see just how much she'd enjoyed dropping that spark. She could have told her that at any time on their ride to Leet, but she'd waited until this moment.

Nirea took a deep breath. "Well, all right. That certainly offers us more options. What do you need to do that?"

"Skin contact. Usually a hand."

"How long?" Could it be as simple as...?

"Longer than a handshake, if that's what you're thinking. But not much. A minute, maybe."

Hmm. That was a little more difficult. A minute of skin contact? Without it being odd?

"I'm not posing as a whore, before you ask," said Quell.

Well, that was one option. Risky, though. And reliant on everyone they wanted to clear being interested. Plenty would not be. "No, of course not," said Nirea. "But we do need something."

"In my country, there is a tradition," said Crinn. "Older women charge a coin to tell your fate. They take your hands and claim to see spirits."

Quell pursed her mouth dramatically. "Not enjoying *older* women, Muscles. But otherwise—how does that work?"

Crinn ignored both her mock offence and his new nickname. "We wrap you in some extravagant scarves. You pretend to tell their fortunes. Instead, you clear their minds. Simple, yes?"

It was, sort of. In that it was a pretence they could manage. And it offered another opportunity.

"If their memory *is* clear, can you poke around in their mind and see why?" Nirea asked.

Quell sat back and crossed her arms. "As long as you can hold them still long enough."

Nirea flipped a dagger out of her sleeve and banged it on the table with a smile, playing into Quell's dramatics. "I reckon I can do that."

---

In the sharp light of the low-rising sun, a light mist drifted over the frosted turf at the foot of the Black Hills. The fire's embers still smouldered, but there was no chance of anything catching from a stray spark once they left. The ground was like rock, a fact Allandria's hips would attest to after a night sleeping on it. She wasn't looking forward to the trek over the hills today, but getting moving might loosen her up. For now, they'd finished striking their camp and it was time to part with their Reiver companions.

Mynygogg grasped Teyjan's hand firmly and pulled the man into a brief embrace, thumping him on the back with his free hand. "It's been a genuine pleasure, my friend. For all that's happened, I'm glad to have met you. All of you."

"Pleasure's ours, Majesty," said Teyjan. "I mean, reckon I owe you ma life at least twice, so..."

"And we owe you peace," said the king. "If the three of you hadn't spoken for us in council, Eidyn and the Reivers might be at war even now. Whatever comes, I'm glad to call you friends."

"Let's no get carried away." Cuda's eyes sparkled with mischief as she finished strapping her pack back onto her horse. Her bald head and neck were wrapped in a grey woollen scarf-cum-hood that she'd apparently knit herself.

"Certainly not, Lady Cuda. Forgive my presumption." The king was equally merry with his words.

"*Lady*. Fuck off." Cuda laughed and the others joined in, except Aranok, who had been quiet all morning. He stood back from the rest of them, watching and rubbing his hands together. But even he cracked a smile. There was a lot on his mind, in fairness. Not least, his family. But he'd also been stewing over what he'd learned from Jazere, about her ability to control her skill without incantations. Everything Allandria knew about magic had come from him. It seemed as if what they "knew" was changing all the time. He'd not said much, but she'd caught him more than once staring at the nature *draoidh* across the campfire the night before, as if she were a miraculous curiosity he was struggling to understand.

Allandria stepped over to Jazere, who had already mounted her horse, and made the gesture she'd come to understand meant "thank you." The woman smiled and repeated it back to her, followed by another. "Good luck," Cuda translated.

"And you," said Allandria, before turning to the other woman. "I think I'll actually miss you, Cuda."

The Reiver gave an exaggerated grimace. "You'll get over it."

Had it been anyone else, she'd have offered the woman a hug, but as it was, she extended a hand instead. Even that felt overly familiar, but Cuda took it and, almost maternally, clasped her other hand over the pair. "You've got more sense than both of these. Try and keep them out each other's way."

"I will," Allandria answered. Teyjan, she had no hesitation in hugging. "Look after yourself. Mind your head."

"Aye, I will," he said, rubbing the spot where a Thakhati had split his scalp. Allandria had to think to recall a time when Samily's ability still seemed miraculous. She was becoming used to the idea that any wound could be healed. That was probably dangerous—especially when the girl was nowhere near.

Shortly, the three of them were mounted and ready to ride.

"Safe home," said Mynygogg.

Cuda gave him an odd look and seemed to be considering something. Finally, she spoke. "Can I give you some advice, King?"

Mynygogg clasped his hands before him. "Of course."

"Cuda..." Teyjan's tone was a warning. He seemed concerned by what might come out of the woman's mouth. Not without cause.

She waved him off with a "tut" before continuing. "I think you're genuinely a good man. And I think you actually want to make things better for folk. But for all your fancy words, you're naïve. You're clever, don't get me wrong, but you've got these ideals, and they're just no the way the world works. Most folk aren't as thoughtful as you. They're just thinking on their next meal and a warm bed. Ken what I mean?"

Mynygogg took a deep breath and released it in a sigh. Allandria knew he'd heard the sentiment before, because she had been there when Nirea said much the same thing.

"I take your point, Cuda. And I thank you for it. But I think when times are darkest, when people's lives are so difficult that they can only see what's right in front of them, maybe that's when ideals are most important. If nobody dreams of a better country, how will we ever make one?"

A snort of air and a smile from Cuda. "Aye. Pretty words. Be sure they don't get you killed, eh?"

"I'll do my best," the king answered.

After some cursory waves, the Reivers headed south, leaving the three of them to prepare for their own journey. They would have to lead the horses over the hills, meaning this would be the slowest part of their journey. But they didn't want to arrive in daylight anyway. Once they reached sight of Mournside's walls, they'd have to free the animals and use Aranok's skill to sneak over in the dark. It occurred to Allandria to wonder if there might be a similar path into the town to the one Aranok and the others had used to escape Haven, but she assumed that if either of the men knew about one, they'd have mentioned it by now.

"Right. We ready to go?" Mynygogg clapped his gloved hands together, the leather slap echoing off the frozen rocks.

"Aye." It was probably the first word Aranok had spoken since they ate. "Let's get on."

Allandria pulled her own gloves on and tucked her scarf into the front of her leathers. Moving would warm her up too. She wished she knew there was going to be a warm bed at the end of the day, but as things stood, God alone knew when she'd next sleep—or where.

# CHAPTER 27

"Samily!" As soon as Vastin had heard Samily was at the hospital, he'd gone running to find her. He'd hoped to see Meristan with her, but instead found her in urgent conversation with Rasa. Her head snapped to him with tight lips. "Oh. Sorry."

"It is fine." Samily turned back to Rasa. "Will you come?"

"How long do I have to pack?" the metamorph asked.

"I don't know. A few hours? Maybe more. I must find Darginn Argyll, and also"—Samily looked down at herself with a sigh—"find some leathers."

*What?* Why would Samily want leather armour? The White was known for being light as leathers, and stronger than steel. Glorbad had sworn no Thorn would ever surrender their White armour.

Oh.

Wait.

"Where's Meristan?"

"It is a long story, I am sorry," said Samily. "He needs us."

"All right. I'll pack." Vastin had wanted to go with the Thorns the day before, but Samily had insisted he'd only put himself in danger. He'd regretted not pushing the point all night, lying awake imagining Meristan's fate at the hands of Anhel Weyr.

"No, sorry, Vastin, I did not mean—"

Vastin interrupted, because if he let her finish the sentence he might not ever say what needed saying. "I have to come, Samily. Please. I *have* to."

Samily's face changed, as if she suddenly saw a different person before her. She looked to Rasa—who smiled and shrugged amiably. "All right. But we have to hurry." She pointed to his chest. "And *you* will also need leathers. No armour."

"Where will we meet?" Rasa asked. "The stables?"

"Yes, the stables. Three hours? I pray that will be enough," said Samily.

"I'll be there." With a nod, Rasa turned and stalked away.

Samily turned the other way and Vastin followed. "Why do we need leathers?"

"We must sneak into Haven. Weyr has the Green Laird in Greytoun. Meristan goes to rescue him. We are to follow and be ready to help with their escape. Weyr is likely watching for Thorns, so..."

"So we need leathers," Vastin finished. "I can help with that."

Samily stopped halfway down a set of steps. "You can?"

"I know a blacksmith—Rorach. He works in steel, but any armourer knows at least one tanner who deals in leathers. Business overlaps. Rorach'll know someone."

"Excellent," said Samily. "Please take me to him."

---

"Eh, now?" Darginn had not been prepared to find Samily at his door again. He'd not yet got over the shock of seeing her behead Faither Victus, or the thumping headache he'd earned from trying to drink away the image. Nor had he worked up the courage to tell Ismar. Might do the boy good or might drive him further into his black mist. He'd told Isadona quietly over breakfast. After a moment of shock, she'd just nodded firmly and said, "Good."

But she'd not been there. The man was rotten, aye, but...

And here Samily was again, asking him for help. To go back to Haven. To leave his family. He'd spent too much time away from them. He'd no desire to leave again. Especially not to go back into the bear's cave.

"I am afraid so," said the Thorn. "I am sorry to ask, but I understand you know how to get us into Haven quietly."

It only then occurred to Darginn that perhaps this wasn't a conversation to have in the hallway of an inn. "Come in, come in."

Samily glanced impatiently back at the stairs, before stepping inside. Once the door was closed, Isadona threw her arms round the girl and whispered a thank-you in her ear.

The knight looked for a moment like she'd no idea what for, only seeming to realise when she looked at Ismar, who had actually got out of bed and was sat in the window alcove looking out at the grey winter sky. "My pleasure. I am sorry to have to ask for your husband's help."

"Help? With what?" Isadona asked.

"Well, it's... going to Haven," said Darginn.

"Oh. What for?" Isadona was trying hard to keep a pleasant tone.

"It is complex, but my master, Meristan, has been taken by soldiers. He is travelling to Greytoun. But he goes to free Laird Severianos, the Green Laird. We must go to help."

"The Green Laird's the one makes the Thorns' armour and weapons," Darginn explained.

"Oh, he is more than that," said Samily. "He trains every Thorn from childhood. He is... everything to Baile Airneach. Without him..."

Ah, that was more than Darginn had known. Not just a blacksmith, but a teacher as well. Made sense why Samily was emotional about him.

"I just... wasnae sure if I should... You know." Darginn nodded toward Ismar, who'd made no sign of even noticing they were speaking.

Isadona straightened herself, the way she did when set on a notion. "No. You go. I insist."

"Really?" That hadn't been the response he'd expected.

"The Thorns have done more for Eidyn than anyone. And Lady Samily... How could we not do anything to help her?"

That seemed awfully adamant, even allowing for what Samily had done for Ismar. But it *was* adamant. "All right. Aye."

"I'll come."

The voice was so unexpected, Darginn actually flinched. "What?"

"I'll come," Ismar repeated.

"Oh, no, no, no." Isadona crossed to Ismar and met him as he stood to face the rest of them. "You need rest."

Ismar walked past his mother as if she'd said nothing, and stopped in front of Samily. "You said I could help, right?"

Samily's previous urgency melted a little and her face softened. "Not like this, Ismar. This is not your fight."

Ismar's voice trembled slightly, and Darginn had to resist taking his son's hand. "Please. Let me be useful."

Isadona shook her head in warning, but what was he meant to do? Their son was a man, and this was the most he'd said to anyone in days. And the first sign he'd given of wanting to leave the room.

"If... if you're sure...?" Samily seemed as reticent as Darginn.

"I am." Ismar's attention stayed fixed on the Thorn, but the answer was clearly meant for his father.

Well, at least it would mean Darginn wasn't leaving him again. He could keep an eye on him. And if it gave him a sense of purpose..."All right." Isadona started toward him, wide-eyed, but Darginn put up a placating hand behind Ismar's back. "It'll be good to spend time with you, son."

That finally drew Ismar's eyes from Samily to Darginn. They were still pale, insipid, but there was just a crack of light in them as he smiled weakly.

"How long do you need?" Samily asked.

"Ah, you're asking a king's messenger, Lady." Darginn looked to his pack in the corner, the one he'd kept ready to leave at a minute's notice for over thirty years. Ismar would need a change of clothes, though. And while he'd likely need a moment to mollify Isadona, it was probably wise that didn't go on too long, for everyone's sake. "Give us ten minutes."

---

"This is a game for young men." Mynygogg leaned against the interior of Mournside's wall, whispering the lament and rubbing at his back. Aranok smiled. If they couldn't laugh on the way to the rope, what was the point of it all? But the brief release of humour quickly subsided as

Aranok turned back to lift Allandria down with *gluais*. She landed the most elegantly of them all, of course, offering a little bow as if she'd just completed a dance on a tavern stage. The smile came back, along with a finger to his mouth.

She gave an exaggerated gesture to indicate she hadn't said anything, and Aranok grudgingly agreed, pointing to Gogg instead. "Traitor," the king mumbled.

They'd released the horses at the foot of the Black Hills. Any closer and they'd have raised suspicions. Either the animals would make their way home, back the way they'd come, or someone would find them wild and assume them the abandoned horses of Reiver victims. Too close and the city guard might start wondering if their riders were doing exactly what they were doing—sneaking in under cover of dark. Of course, most would have had to try it with ropes, lacking the *draoidh* ability to throw people about the way Aranok could, or blow himself up and over with *gaoth*. His way was quicker and quieter. In fact, he'd never really considered it before, but most *draoidhs* could find a way inside these walls. A metamorph could simply fly in, as Rasa regularly did. An illusionist or a memory *draoidh* could con their way past the guards. A physic could climb the wall at speed, if not leap it entirely. A nature *draoidh* could use a convenient tree. The rest—energy, necromancer and demon summoner—would likely have to break their way in, but they were all capable.

Maybe that was a small insight into the fears of unskilled humans. They relied on walls to feel safe, and those walls were meaningless to *draoidhs*. The terror that anyone who *could* hurt them *would* was the root. A fundamental assumption of malice. Vulnerability without solace. For too many, the solution was to eradicate all threats, real or imagined. Only then might they feel safe. Only then might they rest.

They'd discussed where to go tonight coming over the Black Hills. Aranok was desperate to check on his family, but that would be suicide. There was no chance the Guard were not watching them in case he turned up. They'd be delinquent in their duties if they weren't. Bak was smart enough to know they were probably wasting their time, but even so, he would have someone there.

Bak was another thought. Aranok was confident the captain was a decent man, but he didn't know him well. Getting him and the rest of the city guard on their side would make everything easier, but they had to do it right. Treat each of them the way he had Dialla—assume they were compromised and clear them without their knowledge. Now that they were out of Traverlyn, there was no way of knowing who might be taking Weyr's coin. Likely he'd have put some lackeys in place here, at the heart of Eidyn's economy. How many was the question. And where.

The Guard made sense, which was why they had to tread carefully there. Again, not a job for tonight.

Calador was another option, and Aranok was certain he could trust the innkeeper. It would be handy to have a man at the heart of the town's social life on their side. For all his discretion, Calador knew enough about the Canny Man's clients to bury many of them. He'd be an invaluable asset. But the inn was too exposed. They'd need to catch him away from it. Another for another day.

Not least amongst their considerations was shelter. It was too damn cold to be sleeping on the streets of Mournside. The snow might kill them before Weyr did. Aranok had suggested one of his father's warehouses, but Gogg had rightly pointed out that a competent captain would have someone watching those too.

So who could they trust? Who could they go to that would give Aranok time to even begin to explain himself without calling for the Guard? Who had the space to give them sanctuary and, maybe, a base to work from? And most importantly, where would the Guard not be looking for him?

When he'd realised the answer, a shiver had crashed through him. He'd almost kept the suggestion to himself, and when he'd said it out loud, both Allandria and Mynygogg had stared in silence. They knew what it meant.

"Are you sure?" Allandria had asked.

"We can find another option," Mynygogg had said.

But there wasn't one. Not a better one. Mynygogg knew it. Tactically, it was their best move. Their only move.

An hour, at least, creeping through the backstreets of Mournside, avoiding main roads, flinching at footsteps, and they arrived at the gate of one of the grandest homes in town. The ivy growing up the front of the building had expanded to cover the entire wall, and barely a line of stone was visible now by the light of the street torches. Aranok reached over the top of the fence and released the latch. It squeaked in complaint, and they all froze, listening for any response from the surrounding streets. When there was none, Aranok lifted and pushed the gate, keeping it quiet.

He'd walked this path so many times, careless. It meant nothing then, just a place he passed through. But now it was different. Now it was history and memory. Now it was innocence. Another life. A time before.

Up the steps to the door. A huge lump of oak with the brass knocker in the shape of some demonic face, ridiculing Aranok with a flick of its grotesque tongue. He stopped there a moment. It was late. Oddly late to be knocking unannounced. They'd be rightfully concerned. But Aranok didn't have the luxury of waiting for daylight, and they couldn't stand out there much longer without risking a passing guard.

A hand on his side, a gentle stroke. Allandria knew. She was there. And so was Gogg. If he had to come here, at least they were with him.

With a trembling hand, he lifted the knocker and rapped it gently, three times.

Silence, at first. Then footsteps upstairs. They were likely in bed—maybe already asleep. The creak of floorboards, then stairs. Slow feet descended, stopping behind the door. The hesitant turn of a key and the door creaked open, just wide enough for a blue eye to peer out.

"Yes?" The voice. Kind. Familiar.

He'd left a small chain, anchoring the door to the frame. He was wary. Rightly, this time of the evening. Servants would have gone for the night. Just the two of them at home, and both elderly.

This was it. Brave it now and hope to Hell that he'd calculated right. Aranok lowered his hood and smiled as solidly as he could manage. "Hello, Ferrod."

A moment of confusion, then the eyes widened. Silently, they stared at each other. Time slowed as Aranok's heart thumped a drumbeat. What would he do now?

The door slammed closed.

*Fuck.*

Aranok had been wrong. He wasn't welcome. His hands trembled more then, and he pressed them against his legs. Now what? The warehouse after all? Risk a guard? Try to get to Calador without waking the entire inn?

Aranok turned, expecting to see his disappointment mirrored in his friends' eyes, but instead, Allandria raised a finger, stopping him. He didn't understand. Why would they wait here, risking Ferrod calling for the Guard? Bad enough he might tell them tomorrow that the traitorous king killer was in town.

But then a clink, a rattle. A chain loosed.

Aranok turned to see the door open again, wider this time. Ferrod's head poked out from behind it.

"Come on, then."

*Oh, thank God.*

The three of them shuffled into the entrance hallway, past the old man in his nightcoat. Ferrod closed the door behind them, replacing the chain and turning the key. The lock clicked back into place.

Finally, he turned, examining them each in the candlelight. "Who have you brought?" Still the voice was gentle. Calm. Just as he remembered it.

Aranok struggled to find his voice. It was gone. Caught somewhere between gut and mouth.

"Hello, I'm Allandria." She stepped forward and offered a hand, which Ferrod took.

"Of course. I've heard of you."

"I've heard a lot about you too." Allandria smiled broadly. Indeed, Aranok had talked of him often, deep in his cups.

"Donal. Pleased to meet you. Thank you for seeing us at such a late hour." They'd agreed Mynygogg's real identity should wait until after Aranok had cleared their memories. For all the faith Aranok might be able to call on, bringing the dark *draoidh* into their home was likely pushing it too far. Again, Ferrod shook his hand. It was so odd, so formal, as if them being here in the middle of the night, after all this time, wasn't completely insane. Unhinged. How did they come to this?

But they had. And Aranok needed to get his head together. *Now.*

He swallowed deep and finally his voice returned. "Allandria, Donal, this is Ferrod."

Another swallow.

"Korvin's father."

# CHAPTER 28

Allandria had been deeply wary about coming here. Not just because of the emotional toll on Aranok, but because of the effect it might have on the rest of their mission. She'd just about got him functioning again after his complete breakdown in Traverlyn. He'd been fascinated by Jazere, and learning about her ability to use her skill without words seemed to have sparked another light in him. And Mynygogg had done an excellent job of lancing boils to bring them all back together. Nobody had left that meeting completely satisfied, but everyone had gained something. Which, as she had learned over the years, was the mark of a solid negotiation.

But Aranok's recovery was still in its infancy. He was a long way from the man who drove soldiers on during the Hellfire War, lifting morale by his very presence in the camp. That had always been something of an illusion, of course. They'd seen him as more than a man, but he was just as flawed and fragile as every one of them. He did a better job of hiding it then. And he could shoot fire from his hands.

That had been her major worry. For all she'd heard about Korvin's parents—their kindness, their acceptance of their *draoidh* son, and of Aranok—she'd never met them, and had no idea how they'd respond to him now, seven years since he'd last seen them. Aranok had been forced to go diving in the darkness of his past too often recently, and if this went badly, she worried he'd go under again. But the first steps were promising. They were in, which was already more than she'd feared might happen. And they were sitting in front of a newly stoked fire, which was a blessing she hadn't even thought to hope for, after shivering through the last few nights, feeling the bite of winter on her cheeks.

The logs burned on an iron grate below a triangular chimney hood, which was embossed with a crimson-on-cream pattern Allandria didn't recognise. A sort of diamond shape with a line through the middle. The rich crimson curtains displayed the same pattern embroidered in cream. A family crest of some sort, maybe? Allandria sat next to Aranok on a long cream sofa, and Mynygogg had taken a place in one of a pair of red leather armchairs on the opposite side of a simple but elegant low, wooden table. It was a tastefully decorated room without opulence, but she suspected it had still cost a lot more than she could ever have spent on it.

Ferrod finished tending the fire, placed the poker carefully back on its stand and took the remaining armchair. What she guessed had been fair hair and beard were faded to white, and pale blue eyes radiated with a glow of wisdom. "Well. Tell me everything."

Little had been said since introductions. Aranok seemed to be afraid to break the spell that had gained them entry, and neither Mynygogg nor she had felt the right to take control of the conversation. It needed to happen between these two. So they'd sat in awkward silence, waiting for Ferrod to settle. Now Aranok was going to have to say something.

"I... You must have questions, I suppose, so..."

Ferrod raised a hand and Aranok stopped dead.

"Let me help you a wee bit, son. I've heard what they said about you. Reckoned one of two things." Ferrod held up two fingers in demonstration, lowering each as he made the point. "One: You didn't kill the king. Or two: You did, but with good reason."

Aranok shifted uncomfortably. "It's... more complicated than that."

"All right. So did you kill him?" Ferrod asked. The man seemed so at ease, discussing the murder of the monarch. This was his house, she supposed, but even so, he exuded a reassuring calm.

"No. But I was there." Aranok glanced to Mynygogg. "You could argue it was done with good reason."

That was a big concession from him.

"I knew there would be a story," said Ferrod.

"There is, actually, a long story. And I was thinking maybe it was worth... Well, I don't know what I was thinking, I suppose. But there's something I'd like to show you, if I could? If you'll trust me?" Aranok fished the memory charm out and lifted the strap over his head.

"If I trust you?" Ferrod leaned forward, resting his elbows on his thighs. "Aranok, what would ever make you think I wouldn't trust you?"

God, even Allandria felt a tingle of relief in her chest. To see Aranok being treated with such kindness, such genuine affection, by this man he'd been terrified even to see for years was just... Ah! Aranok stood with a slight falter and walked round to offer the charm to Ferrod. His hand trembled as he held it out. "Would you hold this a moment, please?"

Ferrod took it with a look that suggested recognition, but confusion. Of course, it was Korvin's charm. He would have seen it often. But the memory of it was likely gone from him. Most of it, anyway.

"I need to cast a small spell. It will help you to understand, but it might make you feel sick for a moment. It'll pass, though. Is that all right?" Aranok asked.

Ferrod smiled warmly and nodded, sitting back in the chair. "Go ahead."

He barely moved when Aranok cleared his memory, only closing his eyes and taking a few minutes to compose himself. Aranok retook his seat and they waited in silence until Ferrod looked down and weighed the charm in his hand with a wry smile.

"As a parent, you can't really tell your children who to be friends with. Doesn't work out well for anybody. But I always had reservations about that Anhel Weyr. Korvin would tell me stories and it struck me that boy was always stirring trouble, you know? Like he couldn't just let people be." Ferrod shook his head. "Aye. He was a bad 'un."

*He is a bad 'un.*

"Is there anything you want to ask?" said Aranok.

"Not really," said Ferrod. "I assume Janaeus did this? Though how, I suppose, is a good question."

"He had a charm, sort of like that one, but bigger." Aranok pointed to the memory charm, and it occurred to Allandria that this was almost certainly the longest he'd let one out of his hands since Madu threw his into the sea. But it was Korvin's charm, and whether Ferrod knew that or not, Aranok did. "It amplified his skill. Enough to cover the whole country."

"Well. That's some charm." Ferrod leaned over and handed the yellow ball back to Aranok. "So, where's King Mynygogg now?"

Both Aranok and Allandria looked to the man in the chair beside him, and she actually saw the moment when realisation dawned on Ferrod.

"A pleasure to meet you properly, sir," said Mynygogg.

A short laugh and a broad smile from Ferrod. "Well. King of Eidyn in my living room. Taie would be fit to burst."

"That's a point," said Aranok. "Is she asleep? Might make sense to wake her, sort her memory too before the morning."

Ferrod's face fell into a sad smile. "It's just me now, son. Taie left us two years back, come spring."

"No." Aranok lifted his hands to cover half his face, eyes peering over the top. "How?"

"Age comes to us all," said Ferrod. "Just didn't wake up one morning. Best we can all hope for, I suppose."

"I'm sorry for your loss," said Mynygogg. "I'm sorry I never met her."

"And me," said Allandria. "I've heard such lovely things about her. About you both."

"Thank you." Ferrod smiled again.

Silence for a bit then, as the fire crackled and a gust of wind howled past the window, reminding Allandria how glad she was not to be out in it.

"I should have come sooner," said Aranok. "I'm so sorry. I just..."

"We understood," said Ferrod. "It was hard on all of us. Korvin loved you like family. You *were* family, Aranok. You are. But...I know, looking at you back then, all I would have seen was the space at your side. And it would have been the same for you. Taie and I talked about moving, for a while. But...in the end, we felt like we'd be leaving him behind, you know? Abandoning him. So we stayed. This was still home, so we stayed. And I'm glad of it now. I feel them both here with me."

Ferrod rubbed his hand across his chest, just over his heart, and Allandria felt hers break for him. He'd lost his son and his wife within five years of each other. She doubted she'd have his serenity. Her hand moved to Aranok's thigh almost on its own. She just needed to touch him.

"I...I got them," said Aranok.

"Who?" Ferrod asked.

"The ones who did it. I got them."

"You...*got* them? You mean you *killed* them?"

Aranok nodded fiercely. Ferrod stood and moved to the end of the table, looked down at Allandria and said, "Would you mind?"

It took her a moment to realise he wanted her seat. She jumped up with a mumbled "of course" and moved to stand in front of the fire. Ferrod took her place and sat down beside a visibly confused Aranok. The older man put his hand on Aranok's arm.

"That wasn't your responsibility, son. I'm sorry you felt you had to do that. I can't say I'm sad for them. But I'm sorry for you. Killing changes you, doesn't it?"

That threw her a moment. The idea that this gentle, quiet man had killed someone—well, hadn't they all? Sometimes life offered terrible choices. But he seemed haunted by it in a way that Allandria had been, once.

Aranok sat up, steel back in his eyes. "I'm not. Sorry. They deserved it."

"Aye, they did," Ferrod said. "But you didn't. Have you been torturing yourself all these years, Aranok? Blaming yourself?"

And like that, the steel collapsed again. Aranok's mouth crumpled and he couldn't speak. He didn't need to. Ferrod leaned in and hugged him, just as if it were his own son sitting there. Aranok lifted his hands to return the embrace. It was hard to see this, but by God he'd needed it. Ferrod had—maybe—finally offered Aranok the solace he'd craved. Finally absolved him of his guilt? Perhaps. But damn, if he'd come here before...If Allandria had known! Known what a kind, generous soul Ferrod was, and how he was a better father than the one Aranok had been born to... she might have dragged him here herself. God, he was his own worst enemy at times.

When Ferrod released Aranok, he held him at arm's length, hands on his shoulders. "Right. I'm an old man and I need sleep. Let's get you all beds and we can talk more over breakfast, yes?"

"Eh, Ferrod, there are things we—I—need to ask of you, if I may? It's a lot, but..." Mynygogg trailed off.

"You'll stay here as long as you need, sire. In the morning, we'll clear the minds of the staff when they arrive. I only keep a cook and a maid these days, and I trust them both with my life. Once they have their memories, they'll be grand. This house is yours for as long as you need it, as am I."

Aranok had undersold this man. He'd called him one of the kindest people he'd ever met. Ferrod was much more than that.

Mynygogg crossed his hands over his chest. "Thank you, sir. I am in your debt. As is Eidyn."

"Don't be daft." Ferrod stood and moved to the stairs. "Come on, let's get fires lit upstairs. The beds in the guest rooms will be cold, I'm afraid, but they'll warm up quickly."

They'd be a damn sight less cold than her bed the night before.

As they all moved to follow Ferrod, Allandria was suddenly aware of the fatigue in her bones. Nerves had kept her going. That and the cold. But now that she knew a bed was waiting for her, it was like her energy had leached directly into the ground. Suddenly her legs were heavy, her eyes stinging to close. She caught Aranok at the foot of the stairs and stroked a hand down his back. "You all right?"

He turned his head back to nod, and she saw, for the first time in a long time, peace in his eyes. Aranok had lived for so long on the precipice of despair that she'd stopped even noticing it. But now it was gone, it was like a flag waving at her.

And it made her wonder how much the man who lived before Korvin's death differed from the one she'd fallen in love with. How much lighter he might have been. And for the first time, she wondered whether she might meet him.

Aranok lay awake, staring at the ceiling, Allandria's sleeping head nestled on his shoulder. This was Korvin's room. He'd stayed here countless times as a child. The same red-and-gold carpet. The same four-poster bed with the cream curtains.

For the last seven years, he'd have sworn he had no right to be here. But now it felt more like home than maybe anywhere else. He'd never imagined Ferrod would be so welcoming. So happy to see him. So kind.

But in truth, he'd never been anything else. Him and Taie. And the sadness of her loss was compounded by his own stupidity. But Ferrod was right about that too. Korvin's shadow would have hung over them all. Maybe time was needed. Maybe he needed to be different before he could come back here.

When Ferrod had asked about the number of beds they'd need, and Aranok had explained Allandria and he were together, Ferrod had smiled and said, "Korvin would approve."

And of course, now that he was here, this was exactly what Ferrod would do. He'd always been so gentle, so clever, so wise when they were boys. Never the hard patriarch, he was their barrier against the storm. Ferrod and Taie had always, always been completely behind them. When they were caught fighting in school and Aranok's father was livid, they wanted to understand why the fight had happened. More often than not, some bigot had started it. Ferrod and Taie always had their backs when they needed them. And even now, with Korvin and Taie gone, Ferrod was at Aranok's back, after seven empty years, without a second thought.

This was going to work. They could build from here. For a man of Ferrod's standing in the town, the Guard would have absolute respect. Nobody was coming in here unwelcome. And considering Aranok had studiously avoided going anywhere near this house for so long, nobody would look here for him. As long as they really could trust the servants... Well, as in Traverlyn, they had to trust someone. Start with who they knew and work out from there.

Tomorrow, they'd figure out how to check in on his family. Maybe Mynygogg could go. Or maybe they could linger nearby and try to catch one of them outside. He needed to speak to them. Preferably to Ikara or his mother. Find out how things stood and ask about the assassin his father had hired. Find out if the man could really be trusted. But there was something else he was going to have to do too.

With all Ferrod had done, was going to do for them, he deserved the truth. He had a right to know that his family was not completely gone. Aranok had almost blurted it out that evening, sitting there sobbing in the living room, but something had kept his tongue. Because it wasn't entirely his secret to expose. Emelina had no idea Pol wasn't her real father. Hardly anyone did, outwith the family. Pol would be angry at that being revealed—about which, to be honest, Aranok gave not a single fuck. But it would affect both Ikara's and Emelina's lives if Pol knew. So he had to play it canny. He needed to speak to Ikara first. It would be wrong to tell Ferrod he had a granddaughter only to keep her from him. And Aranok couldn't promise that he would be able to see her without Ikara's permission. Though he was almost sure she'd want them to know each other, even if Emelina didn't know about their relationship—for now. Ikara had loved Korvin. And while she hadn't known Ferrod and Taie as well as Aranok did, she *had* known them, and they were fond of each other. In another life, they were her in-laws, and she may even have lived under this roof—in this room.

But aye, that was what he needed to do. Get hold of his sister. Make sure she was all right. And ask if he could introduce his niece to her grandfather.

"Ari?"

Aranok almost threw Allandria off him as he jumped at her voice. "I thought you were asleep," he whispered.

Allandria made a show of raising a hand to her neck and stretching it. "So I see. I was just thinking."

"Oh. Me too."

"What about?"

Aranok's first instinct was to consider what he should say, but he didn't need to do that. This relationship was real. Complete. He could tell Allandria anything. And that was new. "Ferrod. I want him to know about Em. To meet her. But I need to ask Ikara first."

Allandria didn't lift her head, and Aranok felt her "hmm" vibrate gently against his chest. "Yes, she needs to know first. But that's a nice idea."

"What were you thinking about?" Aranok asked.

This time she did move, raising herself onto her elbow so that she was looking down at him. "I need to say something to you. And more importantly, I think, you need to hear it. But please remember that I'm telling you this out of love. All right?"

That sounded ominous. "Should I sit up? Brace myself?" He smiled at her in the dark and was actually a little relieved when she smiled back.

"No, just... listen. And let me finish." Aranok nodded his agreement and Allandria took a deep breath. "Your father is an arsehole. And I don't just mean that in a flippant way. He's a terrible person. He's a vain prick who cares more about his reputation than his family. He's a bigot who treated you appallingly as a child and still does as an adult. He shows you no respect, and the way he speaks to you makes my blood boil. I have only ever tolerated him for you."

It came out like a waterfall lashing Aranok in the face. He barely knew how to respond but was aware he was blinking a lot. His father had always been difficult, yes, but...

"And you deserved so much better," Allandria continued. "You deserved a father like Ferrod. Or even Conifax, though I didn't like the way he spoke to you sometimes. But at least he cared. He loved you. And you deserved that. You *do* deserve that."

It was Aranok's turn for a deep breath. "I'm not sure what to say to that."

"Don't say anything. Just... don't let him talk to you the way he does. Don't be cowed by him. He might have fathered you, but I don't think he's ever been your father. And you don't have to give him respect he's never earned."

With that, Allandria put her head back on his chest and her left arm across him. Her touch still tingled with a mixed thrill of novelty and familiarity. Fuck, it was all complicated. But this was definitely good. This was his anchor. They lay for a time in silence then as Aranok considered what she'd said. Was she right? Probably. But she hadn't been there for his childhood. Had he made it sound worse than it was? Had he been unfair to his father? Made him a villain?

Maybe. But was it also possible he'd sugared the pill? Made less of the times he'd ground Aranok down? Understated his own pain? Aye, that could be true too. Allandria was a sound judge of character. And she'd seen enough of his father to form her own opinion. And seeing Ferrod... Remembering how he'd been when they were children... It was hard to not see him as a better man than his own father.

A better father.

Aye, maybe. But you only get one father. Usually, anyway. It was a tragedy Emelina would never know hers—was stuck with a man like Pol instead. And that made it even more important that she know her grandfather.

"You're clever. And very kind." Aranok stroked her hair gently. "If I end up king one day, you'd make a brilliant queen."

Allandria snorted. "Literally nobody wants me to be queen."

"I do."

"You don't count."

"I fucking do. I'm quite important, actually."

"Shut up."

Allandria poked him in the side, he yelped and slapped her hip, and they both giggled.

And then a comfortable silence, her body warm against his. She kissed his chest lightly.

"I assume we both think Pol's a cunt, right?" Aranok asked.

Allandria laughed again. "Oh, fuck yes."

# CHAPTER 29

"Homeless at eight." Quell knocked back the last rum in her glass and slapped it on the table like a challenge.

"Kidnapped by pirates at four." Nirea mimicked her and banged her own glass down.

"Oi! Mind my glasses," Ailen called across.

The two of them sat at one of the corner tables, farthest from the bar, while Ailen pottered behind it and Crinn mopped the floor. Despite the circumstances, it was nice being back in the King's Wark. And having this wee "lock-in" after the rest of the punters had been sent on their way was good. Its conspiratorial, dark wood tables with their intimate candles and the low ceiling always felt like they belonged more in Seafelde than in Leet. People could huddle in the half-light and have private conversations. Nirea liked a little darkness. It was liberating. And it had somehow led to a somewhat competitive sharing of tragic histories.

"Abandoned by my parents," said Quell.

"Don't even remember my family," Nirea countered.

"So they could be alive?"

Could they? It was unlikely. Kidnapped by pirates doesn't usually mean they did it quietly. Nirea had always thought it more likely that her family had been killed and she was the only survivor. The one they took pity on. Maybe didn't have the heart to slit a four-year-old's throat. Though that wasn't her experience of some of the bastards on that boat. For the moment, the gauntlet was at her feet, and she needed a response.

"You got into the university," she said. "Not homeless for long."

"And thrown out." Quell smiled smugly.

That wasn't what Nirea had heard. "Keft said you left."

The *draoidh* shrugged. "Memories differ."

She didn't know how to take that, given the woman's skill, and the uncertainty must have shown on her face, as Quell raised her eyebrows. Nirea needed something a little shocking.

"Killed a man at sixteen."

Quell's eyes widened. That had done it. "Wow, Red. That got dark."

"You started it." Nirea sat back and crossed her arms.

Quell sat forward in response. "Spat at, abused and beaten in the street."

Nirea leaned in slightly and mimicked Quell's tone: "Spat at, abused and beaten *on a boat*."

Quell's mouth crumpled in mock consternation. "Well, damn, if only things had worked out for you, Your Majesty."

Nirea made a show of looking around the bar. "Don't think much of my castle."

"Oi!" Ailen snapped. But there was humour in it.

"People are still taking your orders, aren't they?" Quell challenged.

"D'you want to see me try to order Ailen to bring us more drinks?"

Quell looked to the bar and finally her grin turned into a giggle. "All right, we've both had shit lives. Get us another drink, then, my queen."

Nirea was about to stand when she felt a presence over her shoulder. She turned to find Crinn had stopped mopping and stood watching them with an expression of consternation. "All right?" she asked.

"I just... I don't understand how you laugh about these awful things. Why?" the big man asked.

*Why?*

God, what else was there to do? Give up? Surrender to the dark and lock herself in a padded hospital room? But what was more interesting was why Crinn was asking. Ailen had said his husband had tragedy of his own. Maybe he had no way to let go of it himself. Nirea's first instinct had been to give a flippant answer, but maybe she needed to do better.

"I suppose it's like poison. You have all this shit inside you, eating you; it's only going to get worse. You let it out? Maybe laugh a little...I don't know. I think it helps."

"Hmm."

Was that a good answer? She couldn't really tell. The man didn't say much. He'd barely spoken all day. Nirea found it difficult to tell if he was just like that, or if he was angry about the assassin she'd inadvertently sent after his husband. Crinn gave a thoughtful frown, turned and splashed more water onto the floor. Nirea carefully walked around the area he scrubbed at on the way to the bar.

The first thing they had learned from a day of Quell posing as a fortune teller was to have a mop and bucket on hand, and to keep drinks off the table. Nirea had either forgotten or never really appreciated just how many people spewed their guts when their mind was cleared. She was no stranger to vomit—even the hardiest sea dogs could lose their lunch in stormy waters. And Ailen had to deal with it often enough that he kept a store of sawdust behind the bar. But when half a dozen people had spewed their guts in one afternoon, it was getting ridiculous. Nirea had a strong stomach, but the odour was pervasive.

Crinn had been happy to take on the mop, and once they'd started seeing the signs, Nirea had become adept at manoeuvring people toward a bucket, making the cleanup much easier. Quell had expressed no small amusement at the queen of Eidyn catching vomit in a pub's back room. Luckily, the smell of Aiden cooking fish was enough to keep the stench from seeping into the main bar. He'd chosen his menu deliberately.

They'd begun with the regulars—the ones Ailen knew well. He'd argued, rightly, that if they were going to be having people coming and going with their memories restored, the rest of the drinkers in the inn would get suspicious quickly unless they already knew what was happening. One man had been so irate at the revelation, Nirea had to talk him down from lifting the nearest sword and marching on Greytoun. He'd finally calmed enough to remember she was supposed to be his monarch and submit in that typically Leet way, adding a little touch of defiance to his deference. But he'd marched straight home and brought back his wife, presumably so he had someone else to vent his ire at.

Good. That was what they needed. People who'd been deceived being furious at the right people. The right person. It had gone surprisingly well for a first day, but they hadn't really gotten to anyone key, yet. They needed the likes of ships' captains and the town guard to really begin to make a difference. The key people who would help them to find the next people, and so on. There were a few captains Nirea knew well—if she could find them, and if they still remembered her. That was tomorrow's job. Ask around and see who she could track down. Preferably without getting herself arrested.

For tonight, though, there was drinking. Nirea put the empty glasses on the bar. "Can we have another two, please, barman?"

Ailen opened his mouth, closed it again and leaned closer. "Should we be drinking? I mean, seriously, Nirea. If someone might be hunting us...me...What if we're all stinking drunk and..."

It had been a while since Nirea had seen genuine fear up close, but there it was, staring back at her. And why wouldn't it be? Why shouldn't he be afraid? When Nirea had come here the first time, he'd hidden her at great risk. He could have been gaoled or even executed if Hofnag's men had found her there. But it had just been him then. Now, with Crinn, he had something to lose. Something he was afraid to lose. Not just an inn; a life.

Nirea had been in plenty of drunk fights, and she could still handle herself fine. Mostly. But Ailen had a point. Half the battle with an assassin was seeing them coming. One of the dangers was getting caught in her sleep. She needed to be more alert. It wasn't just her life that was at risk.

So she stifled her instinct to dismiss his fear and chose to respect it instead. "Fair point. You're right. Give me a rum for Quell and a water for me."

Ailen gave her a curious eyebrow. "It won't matter if *she's* drunk?"

"Can you see her throwing a punch in that dress?" Nirea turned back to the bar. "Quell, you any good in a fight?"

"Depends who I'm fighting!" she called back.

"Ailen's worried about you being ready if we need you." Nirea laughed, expecting the same from the other woman. But instead she cocked her head and walked to join them at the bar.

"Red, you understand I'm a *draoidh*, right? I can do actual magic."

"Of course, but, like, messing with people's memories, that's not really a *martial* skill, is it?" Nirea hoped she wasn't sounding insulting, because she wasn't intending to be, and she was a little worried this conversation was getting away from her.

Quell crossed her arms and straightened up. "Nirea, can I remind you that I took a Thakhati? Alone? You think all I can do is toy with your memory? You know I can do all the things that all *draoidhs* can do, right? *Orachs, mollachds...*"

Quell's tone was as serious as Nirea had heard it. And she'd actually used her name. It sounded odd coming from her. But she had a point. Quell hadn't just rescued Tia by running away with her. She'd stopped a Thakhati dead by wiping its mind. And somehow, Nirea had not taken that in—had not adapted how she saw Quellaria, and her potential. She'd underestimated her. Maybe not for the first time.

"*Mollachds?* You know how to curse?" Crinn's tone was hard now. Hells, why was this all suddenly going awry? The atmosphere had been so relaxed a moment ago.

Quell turned to him. "No, actually. But if I *did* know one, I could cast it. But I don't. Don't fret, Muscles. We're still friends."

Crinn frowned. "*Mollachds* are evil work."

Quell waved a dismissive hand. "Yeah, that's why they're banned. They're awful. It was just...I was just trying to make a point, big man. Don't worry."

With another "hmmph," Crinn returned to his work.

Quell turned to Ailen with an exaggerated grimace. "That was intense."

"Crinn was cursed into servitude," Ailen explained. "He only got free when the *draoidh* that cursed him died."

"Ah, shite," said Quell. "That's knowledge I could've done with a minute ago."

"Don't worry. He's just sensitive about it. Understandably," said Ailen. "But, you were saying...there's more you can do?"

"Well, yes," said Quell. "I mean, not anything they'll teach you in the university."

"Because you got thrown out," said Nirea.

"Exactly. But I've learned a few interesting things." Quell frowned and merriment danced in her eyes.

"All right, maybe we do need you sober, then," said Nirea.

"Wait. What?" Quell seemed genuinely horrified.

"That's what Ailen was saying. That we shouldn't be getting hammered in case..." Nirea lowered her voice. "...the assassin shows up."

Quell sighed dramatically.

"From now on, you two have to give me all the relevant information *before* I answer questions."

---

Weyr had apparently sent a messenger to Leet announcing his ascension, and still made no mention of Nirea. He'd placed all the blame for Janaeus's death on Aranok. Probably figured that since nobody knew who she was, thanks to Janaeus, there was little point in scapegoating her. Well, not scapegoating. She *had* been responsible for killing the usurper. But blaming Aranok stripped him of his reputation, and his fame would now work against him. On the other hand, her relative anonymity might be helpful. But if anyone was looking for her, it would be the Guard.

The simplest way to test that was for her and Quell to walk into the gaol and see if they arrested her.

So there they were, walking the early morning streets of Leet, finding out if Nirea was a wanted woman. They'd stopped in a bakery for a pair of fresh pastries on the way. It was a little disturbing how quickly she'd adjusted to letting Quell use her skill to get them what they needed. But they really were short on coin—and, as she was more aware here than anywhere, Nirea was hardly one with a solid soapbox to preach morality from. They also passed the wife who'd been dragged to the inn the day before. Her eyes near popped out of her head when she saw the two of them wandering along beside the river. She gave a panicked sort of nod, looked around like she'd stolen something herself and scurried back up the alley she'd appeared from.

"What's it like?" Quell asked. "Being queen?"

Gods, that was a question. *What is it like?* "A pain in the arse, a lot of the time. Bloody ceremonies and politics and fake, fawning lairds and ladies... I mean, the power's nice. The ability to do something you want done? That's good. But it comes with a price, you know? You sort of stop belonging to yourself. You have *responsibilities*. You're not free to walk the streets of Leet eating pastries with a mate."

It was refreshing just being herself with Quell now. Since she'd opened up, and that had been the thing that finally got Quell to agree to help... Well, before she'd run off and nearly got killed. But what Nirea had learned from it was that Quell was not a woman to manipulate. She was too sharp. Too guarded. Was it tactical that Nirea had chosen just to be straightforward with her now? Was she simply carrying on with what worked because it got her what she needed? Or was it just nice to let her mask go?

Didn't matter. Either way, it worked, and she enjoyed it.

"Comes with some benefits, though, right? Castle's not a bad place to live. Bet the food's decent. And you get to shag the king..."

Nirea's eyes widened with her laugh. "Well, yes, those *are* upsides!"

"Not a *very* hard life, then, eh?"

"I've had it worse."

"Oh, fuck, let's not start that again."

Five more minutes and they turned into the alley that led to the gaol. This was it. They were about to either start on the way to reclaiming Leet, or make a bit of a mess...

The gaol was a three-floor sandstone building tucked away amongst a square of housing just off the river. It was infamous for being where drunk sailors were taken to sleep off their excesses when they got a bit too "port giddy." The gaol was referred to as the "drunk bunk" amongst the locals. If you landed in there, you were likely to be stuck until your boat shipped out again. Some sailors on the last night of their leave would knowingly get themselves in bother just to get a free night's lodgings. Nirea and Quell pushed through the wrought-iron doors and into the foyer, where a grey-bearded man sat behind a barred window, picking his teeth. Heavy iron doors set into the thick stone walls on either side of his window were silent reminders that nobody got out of there easily.

"Sorry, give me a minute," the man said as Nirea approached. He continued picking at something in his teeth, then sucking and working at them with his tongue. He finally gave up with a grumble. "Bloody sausages. Sorry, what can I do for you?"

He didn't seem to recognise her, anyway. That was a start. "Um, hello. I'm Captain Nirea, and—"

"Say no more. Who you looking for?"

Nirea's red leathers marked her as part of Eidyn's navy, and if she wanted a sailor released back to duty, she'd get them. But that wasn't what she was here for. When she'd given her name, the guard hadn't even flinched. All he'd heard was *captain*.

But a thought occurred then. A fleeting one. While she was there anyway, might as well...

"Actually, it's not one of mine. I'm looking for a merchant. Man called Joliander?"

"Hmm." The man looked down at a ledger on his desk and flicked through the pages. "Don't think he's in just now. Name's familiar. Let me just be sure."

It was a long shot. If anything, Joliander not being ashore was a good sign. If he'd been at sea when Janaeus cast the spell, and no boats had been able to come in since, he was probably safer.

*Shit.* Unless his boat had been pulled under. Or he'd docked at Haven instead. If he had... Well, fuck, nothing she could do about that now. Haven was the last place she was going for a while. None of them were safe there.

"Nope, sorry. Not here. Have you tried the brothels?" The man looked up, clocked Quell behind Nirea and seemed to do a little mental arithmetic. "Oh, eh, sorry, miss, no offence, like."

"Miss?" Quell put an exaggerated hand up to her chest, only touching with her fingertips. "Don't worry, pal, you couldn't offend me if you tried."

"Oh." He didn't seem to know what to do with that response. "Well, anyway, your man's not here, Captain, sorry. Mind if I ask what you're after him for? Has he done something?"

"Wha... Oh, no, no. He's just... a friend. Got a message for him." *A warning.* Right, bugger it, they'd done what they came to do. If the

Guard were looking for her, this man knew nothing of it. And a royal warrant tended not to be missed, especially for an accessory to murdering the king. She was likely fine. "Thanks for your time." Nirea turned to leave, but Quell leaned in to block her path. "What?"

"You want me to...?" She nodded toward the guard.

Was that a good idea? Take advantage of the moment? Maybe the man could give them useful information. But then... if his memory was intact, he was behind bars, where they couldn't reach him. Then what? But if his memory was intact, he'd have known who she was—and feigned ignorance. The chances were probably tiny, but they'd already discussed the fact that the most useful place for Anhel to have allies in Leet would be in the Guard. No, they needed to do this in a controlled environment. She shook her head and stepped past Quell toward the door.

"Thank you," Quell lilted, following her out. She waited until they were back in the street to say anything more. "Joliander. That's the guy who..."

"Aye. The one Madu threatened." The two of them had spoken a lot on the journey to Leet, and at night. She was good company. The kind of person Nirea would have been drawn to in another life, where they hadn't been thrown together like this. It was a bit like having another pirate beside her—albeit one who'd never set foot on a boat.

"When did you last see him?" Quell asked.

"Oh God, years ago. Before we took the throne. Before I met Gogg."

"So you were still..." Quell ducked slightly and comically lowered her voice. "...a *pirate*?"

"Yes. I was still a pirate, Quell."

"So how does a pirate end up in a relationship with a merchant sailor? Aren't you meant to rob him?"

Nirea paused, grinned and strode ahead. "Who says I didn't?"

"Oh, oh, I *need* to hear this story." Quell hustled to catch up. "Wait. This isn't the way back to the inn. Where are we going?"

"Down to the dock. I want to see what ships are in. Once I know what captains might be in port, we can start thinking about who to approach first."

"Fair enough." They walked in silence for a few moments with Quell grinning at her.

"What?" Nirea asked innocently.

"So just to be clear," said Quell, "you robbed him and *then* you shagged him?"

# CHAPTER 30

It was the third day before Ikara left the house.

Aranok was just about climbing the walls, desperate to see either her or his mother. Dorann had left for some time each day, flanked by a pair of men. At least he was taking the threat seriously. Determined to keep up his public appearance, but not daft enough to put his life at risk for it. But there was no point in Aranok approaching his father. Aside from the fact that he had no idea what reception he'd receive, or even what he'd say, he wasn't sure that he could trust him. He might still be convinced Aranok had tampered with his mind, rather than freed it. But at least Aranok knew they were all right. Hovering in side alleys, keeping an eye on the house. Always careful not to be seen. Not to linger too long in one place.

Finally, that afternoon, the door opened, and it wasn't Dorann who stepped out. Ikara looked nervously up and down the street, pulled up the hood of her cloak and strode out, followed by a man large enough for Aranok to have mistaken him for a physic *draoidh*, if he didn't know his father better. Unless, perhaps, the man had kept it to himself. He must have been at least six foot seven, broad-shouldered with a clean-shaven head. Not the sort anyone would pick a fight with, given the choice.

Still—they could follow her now. Away from the house. Check if there were any guards watching and find a way to approach her. Where was she going? Market, maybe? Maybe just stretching her legs, sick of looking at the walls.

Aranok gave her time to be almost out of sight and lifted his foot to follow.

Then he felt the blade at his throat.

"Who are you?" A deep, slightly stilted voice in his ear. He'd heard nothing behind him. No warning of the man who now held his life at the flick of a wrist.

But he wasn't defenceless.

"You're good. Very good."

"Who are you? Last chance."

"Aye, well, problem for you is that the second I hit the floor, there'll be an arrow through your head." Aranok paused to let that sink in. "Look up." He felt the blade scrape gently up his neck as the man's hand rose with his eyes. He'd see Allandria perched above them. Who'd also missed his approach...

"You are Aranok? She is Allandria?"

No surprise he knew that. He was either there to kill them or to protect Ikara. "So, who are you?" Aranok had slowly performed the gestures for *gluais*. If he needed to, he could grab the knife with a word, but damn, it would be a test of speed to see if he could grab it before it cut his throat.

The man paused a moment himself, then released his grip, pushed Aranok away and threw his arms wide. "I guard Lady Ikara."

*Good.*

Aranok turned to see a dark-skinned man with long hair collected in a dozen thick braids bound up with strips of blue cloth. His lilac eyes flickered, but his soft, black clothes and boots devoured any other light. He looked every inch the assassin Rasa had described.

"What's your name?" Aranok asked.

"I am Kye Denassa."

Definitely not from Eidyn. The thick accent had given that away, if his name didn't.

"Tell her I want to see her. Please?" Aranok asked.

Kye looked briefly to the side, as if considering. "She expects you. One hour. Behind the butcher."

Ikara knew he would come. All right. "I'll be there."

The assassin nodded quietly, then launched himself off one foot toward the wall, bounced back off it to the one opposite, and continued back and forth four times until he reached the roof alongside Allandria. His lover watched with the same surprise and respect Aranok was feeling.

And then the man was gone, silently, over the rooftops.

How long had he been aware of Aranok? How had he gotten behind him? How was he so quiet? And how the Hell had he just gone up two stories in a few seconds? Aranok shielded his eyes as he looked up to where Allandria was still perched.

"Can you do that?" he asked.

She raised her eyebrows dramatically in return.

"Can *you*?"

---

The alley behind the butcher shop was a decent location for a secret meeting. It stank of discarded offal, meaning the only ones likely to be attracted there were stray dogs. It was long enough to stay out of sight, but only one door opened onto it—the back door from the butcher's. Aranok's family had used Kibbet for years—Cressida would usually place an order with him at the weekend and have the meat delivered fresh each day. But with all the oddity of their current existence, it wouldn't be surprising that Ikara had decided to get out and pick something up instead.

Allandria stayed on the roof above him as a lookout. She was good at keeping herself out of sight, but nothing like Kye Denassa. He'd been a ghost.

When Aranok had barely settled himself into a comfortable shadow, the door cracked open and a large, bald head poked out. When the man saw Aranok, he fixed him with a malevolent stare, silently threatening him. Aranok found himself glad the giant was looking after his little sister. The man stepped out from the doorway and stood to his full height before turning to see Ikara step out after him. When she found his eye, Aranok's smile was almost painful.

"Hey, kid."

She stepped as if to run to him, but the big man placed an arm across her path. "Wait." She stopped and watched as he stalked to the nearest end of the alley, scanned the street and took up guard there like a carved sentry. Curious, Aranok looked back to the other end, wondering what the plan was for that, only to see that Kye had put himself in position there, tucked against one wall, casually smoking a pipe.

Only then did Ikara close the door and hurry to him.

"Ari!" Despite her excitement, she kept her voice low. "Oh God, it's so good to see you. How have you been? How is everything? Did the carts arrive? How is the king? Where is Allandria?"

That was a lot of questions. He waved her to calm and pointed up to answer her final question. Allandria waved. Ikara returned the gesture enthusiastically.

"We don't have a lot of time," she said, before he'd had time to answer any of the other questions. "The Guard are watching me. Looking for you. They think we don't know, but Kye is very good."

"Yes, so I found out," said Aranok, touching his throat where the blade had been. "And what about him?"

"Loth?" Ikara asked. "He's the deterrent, right?"

Aranok widened his eyes in response. "Is he *draoidh*?"

"I haven't asked," said Ikara. "With Dad and all... But it did cross my mind. I mean, *look* at him. And he's very sweet, actually. Fascinating life. He paints."

"Kid, you said we don't have time..."

"Oh, of course, sorry. What do you need?"

"How is everyone? Rasa said there was an attack."

Ikara's face turned dark. "Yes. But honestly, Ari, we knew nothing about it. Slept through it. Kye caught him and... Well, first we knew was when we woke up to a body in the garden."

Right. That was what Rasa said. But she'd also said she was wary of the assassin. "What do you know about him? Kye?"

"Not a lot," his sister answered. "He's quiet. I think he's from Gaulle. Extremely good at the job."

Gaulle. Interesting. That explained the name and the accent. Most

Gaullic names ended in vowels. Half of them weren't even pronounced, but there they were anyway. "You trust him?"

Ikara looked at the man, then back to Aranok. "I have no reason not to."

Hmm. Was that good enough? It would have to be for now. "What about Dad? Is he still...?" Aranok waved his hands, searching for the words to describe the fucking mess of his father's situation.

Ikara's lips tightened. "Well. He accepts the truth now. But he's still angry about it. You know how he is. He'll get over it."

Well, that was something. He finally came round. Maybe that was hope. Maybe everyone would come round, eventually. Maybe they just needed to stop pussyfooting about and clear people's memories, with or without their permission. "And Mum? She's all right?"

"Worried about you, mostly."

"And Em?"

A huge smile this time. "She thinks she's on a big adventure, sleeping over at Grandma and Granda's house with a load of armed men lurking about."

"And how is it? I mean, having the guards? Is it...?"

Ikara chewed her lip as if considering how to answer. "It's...it's fine. People just... Well, they assume..." She trailed off. She was reluctant to say something.

"Kid, it's all right. What is it?"

"They assume we took protection because you killed the king. In case someone comes after us." Ikara's mouth curled down, but her eyes sparkled with sympathy. She hadn't wanted to tell him that.

"Has that...? Has anyone threatened you?" Aranok asked.

"No, no. Father's business is a little quiet, I think. Another reason for him to be sour. And Pol... Pol isn't with us."

"What? Where is he?" Not that Aranok was worried about the idiot.

"He stayed home. Our home. Said he needs to keep a distance. For the business." She shrugged as if it made no sense, but Aranok understood. He'd tainted the family name. His father's precious reputation, maintained despite his *draoidh* son, made better when Aranok had become the envoy, had suddenly turned to ash. For a crime Aranok hadn't even committed. Pol remaining separate, keeping his distance, was a signal to clients. He was not involved. He would not be painted with that brush. It might even have been Dorann's idea. The mind of a merchant. Keep the business away from the family scandal.

Pol would know fine well he was at no risk from someone who wanted to hurt Aranok. Likely had designs on getting his hands on the business too.

Ikara glanced over her shoulder at the door. "Ari, what do I need to know? Quickly." She was right. The guard watching her would get suspicious if she was too long inside. Might start wondering where she'd got to. Might come looking.

"Traverlyn was attacked. By Thakhati. A lot of people died."

A gasp. "Anyone... I know?"

"I don't think so. Anyway—the Thorns are there now. We have them on our side."

"Oh, wonderful!" Ikara lit up. That was actually good news, and maybe he hadn't appreciated it enough.

"We're here with Gogg. We're going to start clearing memories. Quick as we can without setting off suspicions too early. We'll likely start with the Guard."

Ikara nodded thoughtfully. "Makes sense. Where are you... staying?"

There was the thing. He lowered his voice and leaned in. "Ferrod's."

"Oh." Ikara leaned back and the next word was deeper, louder. "Oh." She was silent a long time, looking back at him. "How is he?"

"Did you know Taie died?"

"I heard. A few years ago." Genuine sadness in her voice. She must also long for the life she never had with the man she actually loved. "I wish..."

She didn't need to finish the sentence. "I know. Me too." And here was the question. "Kid, how would you feel about... Can I tell Ferrod? About Em? I'd like him to—"

"Oh, I'd love that!" Ikara cut him off. "I'd love them to spend time together."

That was a lot more enthusiastic than he'd expected. "What about Pol? And Father?"

The light in her flickered down again. "I think, maybe, when this is over, I think Em and I might *stay* at Mum and Dad's."

Well. That was unexpected. Their father had been so insistent that his unmarried pregnant daughter would not see her child fatherless. "Really?"

"Yes. Things change, you know? And I just...I won't have Em grow up like you did, Ari. I just won't. She deserves better."

"What you thinking?"

"I'm thinking maybe we'll move to Traverlyn, the two of us. She can go to the university and I'll...find something to do. I'm sure. Father may decide not to support us...but at least she'll get free tuition. And we know Rasa, so..."

"It's a brilliant idea, kid. Really. I'd have loved that at her age." He really would have. And maybe the Hellfire Club would never have existed. "So, you don't mind if I tell Ferrod?"

"No! And please...tell him...I'm sorry? And I wish...Just please let him know, if it had been my choice..." She'd have probably rather moved in with Ferrod and Taie than Pol, frankly. And they would have had her. Aranok had never really thought through that option for his sister. But maybe he should have. Back then, though, he was a mess. Not much use to anyone.

"I'll make sure he understands. Don't worry."

Ikara crossed her hands over her chest. "Thank you. Ah, I love the thought of Em getting to know him. He's such a lovely man."

"Right, listen, you better go. I'll leave a message here for you if I need to see you again, all right?"

"With Kibbet?" she asked. "You trust him?"

"I will do." Aranok fingered the charm at his neck. "As soon as he knows who I am."

Ikara smiled. "Of course. It's great to see you, Ari." She brushed his arm with her hand and waved to Loth. The giant came lumbering back up the alley toward them.

"Oh, wait, kid—one more thing. And your guards should know this too." He waited for Loth to come within hearing range, so that he could speak quietly. "It's possible an assassin could be an illusionist. Maybe not, but..."

"An illusionist? *Draoidh?*" Ikara asked.

"Yes. I mean, I hope the one Kye dealt with was...Well, maybe they were it. But Weyr has an illusionist and..."

"Weyr has an assassin?"

"He does. And listen..." This was the bit he'd been struggling with. Debating with himself whether to even say the words, because God knew what she'd do with it, or if it was even fair to put the idea in her head, but it might just save her life. And in the end, he'd decided it had to be her choice. "*Draoidhs* are immune to their own skills. An illusionist would see through an illusion. You understand?" He wasn't going to say it out loud, but he watched Ikara's eyes widen as she realised what he was telling her.

Emelina would know. And if she kept her daughter beside her... she'd be putting her in more danger, but... An impossible decision. One Aranok would never make. But it wasn't his choice.

Ikara took a breath and nodded. "I understand. Thank you for telling me. Loth, let's go. Quick." She turned just before disappearing through the door. "I'll see you again, soon, yes?"

"Absolutely."

She nodded again and the door closed. Aranok looked along the alley. Kye was gone.

Ikara would tell him of the risk. It was low. Weyr had no reason to kill Aranok's family—not like the assassins contracted to Madu. No *tactical* reason. But he was a spiteful cunt. And looking at what else he'd done, might he do it just to get at Aranok? To punish him? To wound him?

Yes, Anhel Weyr might do that.

# CHAPTER 31

It was pitch black by the time they arrived at the gates of Haven. But then, it was winter and dark by late afternoon. Captain Cyrra had held her word to Meristan, and the troop had travelled as slow as was reasonably excusable. It had been almost fully four days since they encountered Samily on the Auld Road. Four days for them to create a plan for getting Severianos out.

Like all plans, they'd decided that the simplest was the most likely to succeed. Cyrra would escort him directly to Greytoun herself, ordering her soldiers to busywork—tending to their mounts and the like—to prevent any of them from getting to Anhel Weyr quickly. That would make a spy's work a little harder, and maybe give them some time.

When they got to the castle, she'd take him directly down to the cells, where they were most likely to find the Green Laird. Once they had located him, Cyrra would leave for long enough to justify the pretence of coming back to fetch both of them to see the king. The three of them would then collect new cloaks and simply walk back out to head for Haven Kirk, where they could wait for Samily.

Speed was key. They needed to do it all before word reached Anhel that Meristan was there. As soon as he knew, Meristan suspected he'd scour the town to find him. The demon summoner was no lover of the Thorns, experts in killing his thralls. Trained by the man he already had in gaol.

Would his hatred for them have led him to execute Severianos immediately? Heaven, he hoped not. He had to believe that the need to keep up the appearance of the benevolent, faithful king would prevent Weyr from murdering the elderly patriarch of the most revered group in the country.

But he also couldn't put the idea beyond him.

No point speculating—they'd know the truth of it soon enough.

"All right?" Cyrra asked quietly as they dismounted.

"Aye," he answered, scanning the nearby soldiers for any signs of—what would he call it? Suspicious behaviour? Guilt? Anything odd, he supposed. Anyone in a hurry to get up to Greytoun. But they were all doing as commanded. Removing their packs from their mounts and leading them for stabling. Cyrra handed their two over to a stable girl who had been waiting patiently without a word. She was no more than thirteen and reminded Meristan of Samily at the same age—all limbs and elbows. The girl took the horses, and Cyrra led Meristan clear of the soldiers.

"You're going to have to give me the blade," she said quietly.

Of course. She'd allowed him to keep his Green blade on the ride as if it were a sign of respect for his position, in return for his own deference to her authority. But if she were to march him into Greytoun as a prisoner, it couldn't be with the most lethal weapon in the kingdom on his back.

"Aye, all right." Meristan unstrapped his scabbard and handed the whole thing over to the captain. It was nigh on heresy for a Thorn to surrender their Green blade without a fight, but under the circumstances, he was technically loaning it to an ally. And if any circumstances allowed for a bending of the rules, it was these.

The walk up the hill to Greytoun's gates was perilous. An icy wind whipped at their faces as soon as they were above the town's rooftops, and the ground underfoot was already forming a light coating of frost. Both moved ahead with one arm across their face and the other holding up their hood. By the time they reached the gate, Meristan's forehead and nose stung with sharp little needles. Cyrra had them waved through, and Meristan followed her dutifully along the tunnel from the external gate to the internal, with a glance up at the murder holes as he passed beneath. Just in case.

"Captain." The guard who opened the gate bowed his head slightly as Cyrra entered.

"Prisoner for the cells," she said, loudly enough for all of the soldiers milling about the courtyard to hear. A few puzzled looks, but Meristan assumed many of them would have heard of the altercation near Gardille and perhaps knew that a Thorn was wanted for it. Or a monk. He supposed the head of the Order being wanted for treason would be sufficiently interesting news to travel quickly. But nobody questioned, nobody commented.

"Right, move," Cyrra ordered, giving him a gentle nudge toward the castle door. Getting inside was pleasant. The heat of a torch hung inside the door bit back against the cold that had dug into his skin. It was nice to be out of the wind. But none of that mattered. Now it was all about haste.

"Right. Follow me." Cyrra marched ahead.

A convoluted journey taking them down three floors and right across the castle, Meristan reckoned, ended at a heavy oak door with a small, barred window. Cyrra knocked and a wooden panel on the other side slid back to reveal a pale young man with pockmarked skin.

"Captain? What can I do for you?" the guard asked.

"One for the cells." She nodded casually toward Meristan.

The guard looked him up and down. "You brought him down yourself?"

"You seen the size of him?" she asked. "Besides, he's important."

"Fair enough." The wooden panel slammed closed, keys jangled and three locks clunked open. No chances taken here, apparently.

The door swung open, and the guard moved as if to take Meristan's hand but stopped short.

"He's no in irons?" The tone was suspicious. Perhaps they should have put the irons on him for show, but the idea of him needing his hands free urgently... No, they'd decided that was more important.

"He's given me not a word of trouble in five days," Cyrra said. But there was a flicker in the back end of her voice. A quaver that did not belong to a captain addressing a guard. "I'll take responsibility for him."

Again the guard looked Meristan up and down. "You sure?"

Cyrra stared at the guard a moment, took a breath and set herself.

"Soldier, I have been travelling for a week. I cannot wait to get out of this sodding armour and into a warm bath. And the one thing in my way is, currently, *you*. *May I?*" The authority was back, and with it, the guard crumpled.

"Of course, Captain. Sorry." He backed through the door with a pronounced bow, pulling it wide and holding it for the two of them to pass. Once they were inside, the door slammed shut again, and three locks clicked back into place.

Buried deep in Grey Rock, the dungeon was as dank as Meristan would have expected, but surprisingly large. The open section behind the door was about fifty foot across and maybe thirty deep. To the left, three more guards stood at attention in front of a table where they looked to have been playing cards.

"At rest," Cyrra commanded, and all three relaxed back into their chairs, though their eyes lingered on Meristan. On his White armour. Word would reach Weyr before long.

At the back of the chamber, a small opening in the rock—a corridor. Cyrra nudged him toward it. "That way."

They were nearly at the opening when the guard's voice stopped them again. "Captain?"

Cyrra paused, turned and almost spat the reply back across the chamber. "What now?"

The guard stood with his left arm outstretched, a ring of keys dangling from his hand. Cyrra sighed and strode back to lift them from his grasp. "Thank you, soldier. It's been a long week."

This time they finally made it into the row of cells, and Meristan began scanning for Severianos. Each room was just an arch cut into the rock, with iron bars set at the front, a tatty mattress on a shelf to one side or the other, and a bench at the back, with a wooden lid covering the privy. The smell was a dense bludgeon of sweat and excrement.

They stalked down the aisle between prisoners, Meristan swinging his gaze left and right. In one cell, he almost mistook the inhabitant for a pile of rags left stacked on the bed until a skeletal arm moved. Heaven, he wondered what these wretches had done to find themselves down here. And had they been put here under Mynygogg's rule, where he would like to assume it was deserved, or put here by Weyr for some more devious cause? Aranok had said Janaeus was drafting prisoners into service. Perhaps a few of them had been replaced with those Weyr found inconvenient.

Twenty cells in, they met another corridor crossing their path. Right and left, more cells, extending beyond his view. It fleetingly occurred to him to wonder if earth *draoidhs* had created this place. It would have taken stonemasons an age. Or a lot of masons. "Which way?" he asked. The need to find the Green Laird was becoming an intolerable itch, and Meristan found himself flexing and closing his right fist anxiously.

Cyrra sighed in response. "I don't know. And there's another two floors." She looked back up the corridor. "Wait here."

Cyrra strode back to the entrance and Meristan heard her ask, "Soldier, was the Green Laird brought here?"

The response was muffled. But even so, Meristan made out a tone of surprise. Cyrra also lowered her voice, so that while he could hear that a conversation was happening, he could make out nothing more than the odd word, and nothing that helped provide any meaning. Meristan's nerves rose again. If he wasn't here—had Weyr done the unthinkable? Had he executed the old man?

*Damn it all!* If he had... *if he had*, no number of demons would keep Meristan from his throat.

After an age, Cyrra returned, her face showing more confusion than concern. Was that a good sign?

"What's happened?" Meristan asked.

Cyrra's eyes widened. "He's not down here..."

"Where is he?" Meristan cut across her.

Cyrra raised a calming hand. "Keep your voice down. Laird Severianos is in Greytoun at the king's pleasure and has been installed in guest quarters upstairs."

*What?*

Of all the things Meristan had suspected, feared, surmised... this had been nowhere on the list. Cyrra shrugged, mirroring his own befuddlement.

"All right, take me to him." Meristan went to walk back up the corridor, but Cyrra's hand on his chest halted him. "What? We can't wait—"

"*You* can't go anywhere," she said. "I can't walk you back out of here now without raising half of Greytoun's suspicions. And I'd rather you not have to kill those four guards for doing their jobs."

She was right. Damn it. "All right. What do we do?"

Cyrra grabbed his cloak and pulled him round the corner. There were no cells for the first thirty feet, so this was as far from prying ears as they were going to get. Still, she barely more than whispered. "There's no good option where I don't put you in a cell. Anything else and we're fighting our way out of here. Even with you, I'm not sure..."

They could make it, but not without killing a lot of innocent people in the process. And no way of knowing which might actually be enemies. "Could you not just say you're taking *me* to the king?"

"Why would I do that now, after bringing you down here? And asking about Severianos?" Meristan had no answer to that. She was right. It was the kind of behaviour that would have a guard sending for a senior officer. "As it stands, I can walk out of here without suspicion. As long as you don't."

A dark thought occurred to Meristan. Had he misjudged this woman? Had she just lured him directly into a trap? Coerced him to walk meekly into a cell with a cunning performance? Was he standing there, sharing secrets with a Weyr ally?

Damn it all, he had no way to know. He could do no more than trust that he was in God's hands, as always. "Fine. What do you propose?"

Cyrra pointed ahead. "Up here. The ones at the end are used less often. Should be a bit...cleaner."

Minutes later, Meristan sat on a cold stone bench, still adorned in his White armour and cloak, watching the door of his cell being closed behind the woman who now carried his fate with her. And maybe a good slice of Eidyn's too.

"I'll leave it unlocked," she whispered. "No reason for them to check it unless you give them one. And at least then..."

At least then if it all went to Hell, Meristan could get past the first obstacle.

"My blade?" he asked.

"They'll ask if I go back without it. Normally it would be surrendered to the armoury. But you'll never see it again if that happens. I'll keep it."

This felt all wrong, of course. He'd already lost one blade and here he was, giving up a second without a fight.

Cyrra pulled a dagger from her waist and slid it through the bars. "Here. Best I can do. Keep it hidden."

Meristan slipped it inside his cloak. It was better than nothing. If he had to fight his way out of there, it was a start.

"Listen, is there *anyone* here I can trust?" Cyrra asked. "Anyone who might help?"

Was there? He knew few people in Haven. Fewer in Greytoun.

"Just Severianos. Or another Thorn, maybe?" Chances of a Thorn being there were small, but if there were... "They won't have their minds cleared. You'll have to ask them to trust their faith. In me."

"Right." The word was flat. Resigned. She saw the problem as bleakly as he did. "And how do I get them to trust *me*?"

How could she do that? A good question. He gave her the best answer he could conjure in that moment. "Tell them to clear their mind, trust in God and stand their ground."

Cyrra nodded thoughtfully. "All right. If nothing else, I'll come back for you. We'll get out of here and..."

"We're not leaving without him," said Meristan.

"He's in less danger than you, at the moment." Cyrra cocked her head at him.

"At the moment," Meristan repeated.

"All right. I'll see what I can learn." The captain frowned and looked up the corridor, as if it might provide some inspiration. "Oh, wait. Here." Cyrra dug in a pocket and produced a small parcel. "Spare rations." She nodded toward the guards. "They won't give you much. And take this too—keep it all hidden." She passed her waterskin through the bars along with the food. If nothing else, this allayed his fear the captain might be an enemy. She could simply have locked him in, were that her aim.

As if she read his thoughts, Cyrra grasped one of the bars. "Keep faith, Laird. I will find an answer." A small nod. Meristan returned it. He had no words. But faith; faith he had in plenty.

# THE DAMNED KING

*Damn it.*

It was the slightest tug. The merest resistance at the side of his boot. But Darginn had felt it. He raised a hand in the dusty fug of the crypt. "Stop." If he lifted his foot, he had no idea what happened next. So he was going to stand very still. "Can someone please come and see what I've stood on?"

It was Rasa who came forward and crouched behind him. "Could you lower the torch, please?" Darginn did as she asked, careful to hold the flame away from her head. "Hmm. Let me take that." The metamorph reached up a hand and Darginn handed over their light source. Carefully, she crept between the sarcophagi, staring intently at the ground, following a straight line from Darginn's foot to the crypt wall, where shelves of Haven's dead lay stacked like bricks. The skull of one—second from the bottom—had fallen to face him. The hollow eyes seemed to scold Darginn for disturbing their peace.

"It's a length of twine," said Rasa. "Runs into a hole at the foot of the wall here. Who knows where it goes then."

Ismar huddled tight behind Darginn, one hand gently between his father's shoulder blades. It had been a way of them staying together, but now it was comfort.

"What does that mean?" Vastin asked.

"Would they have set a trap down here?" Samily asked in reply. "To catch an invading army?"

"Unlikely," said Darginn. "They'd be in danger of catching their own people. Can't have the king stumbling into his own trap while escaping the city."

"True." Rasa walked back toward them, more confidently. "It's more likely to be an alarm. A warning that there's someone down here. In case someone discovered the cave entrance."

That was unlikely, since it was extremely well hidden by overgrown flora, thanks, he understood, to a nature *draoidh*. You really had to know where it was. Be a terrible escape plan if it led an army under the walls instead.

"So, we should be fine?" Samily asked. "To carry on?"

"I *think* so?" Rasa's answer was very much more a question, and her uncertainty did nothing to bolster Darginn's wavering confidence in her theory. "But if it is an alarm... try to lift your foot slowly."

"Right." Darginn took a deep breath in. If it was a trap, and he hadn't triggered it by standing on it, he'd likely do it by releasing the pressure. "All the same, maybe you four should move ahead? And mind your feet."

Rasa stared at him a moment, took his meaning and nodded the others past her, as she held the torch down for them to see where the length of twine ran. Once they were all beyond it, they stopped and looked back at him. They were still too close. If something was going to happen... "Move on. Farther."

"But then... you won't be able to see," Ismar protested. He'd been hunched and anxious—more so than usual—since they entered the crypt. If he felt the pull of the Dead, this was probably the worst place to bring him. Darginn hadn't thought of that when he'd agreed to the idea. He wasn't even sure if Ismar knew *how* to raise the Dead. And he wasn't ready to ask. He wanted to get his boy out of this place as quickly as possible.

"It'll be fine, son. I'll walk toward the light. Just in case, aye?"

Ismar nodded tentatively. "Just in case."

When they were a good sixty feet ahead, the torch stopped moving. They'd be able to find their way from there, even without Darginn. But it was only an alarm. Nothing to worry about.

Darginn rested a hand on the sarcophagus to his right, letting it take the weight of his right foot. Gently, slowly, carefully, he lifted the boot, shoulders hunched, eyes tight against the coming impact.

There was none. He lifted his foot; felt the twine gently release its tension. Nothing happened. A deep sigh. Of course it was fine. It made no sense to trap their escape route.

But it did make sense to set an alarm.

Darginn carefully took a huge step where he knew the twine to be, and followed with his left foot, lifting it much higher than necessary—he wasn't taking chances.

Maybe someone upstairs knew they were coming now. Maybe they were calling for the Guard as he stood there in the gloom amidst some of Eidyn's most honoured dead.

Well, if they were, best get a damned move on. Darginn hurried to rejoin the group in the torchlight. Ismar's smile was one of relief. But the boy still looked strained. Darginn took the torch back from Rasa. "Come on. Let's get the Hell out of this place."

They hurried awkwardly forward, Darginn scanning the ground before him and nearly stumbling directly into a sarcophagus that had been unhelpfully placed out of sequence with all the others, right in his path.

Finally, they reached the door that led them out of the dark and into the back of Haven Kirk. This was the moment. If there was a squad of guards waiting for them, they were in trouble. Samily and Rasa could fight them off, but they were both currently stuck behind him and it was a small door. Darginn leaned in close, listening for any sound from the other side. For a whisper of boot on stone, of blade on scabbard. But there was nothing. Which was a little unnerving, despite being exactly what he hoped for. It almost seemed like there should be someone out there, because if there wasn't, then Haven was maybe vulnerable in a way Darginn had never considered.

*Bah! Stop your fretting, old man.*

His son needed out of that damned crypt. Darginn turned the handle, slowly, quietly, until he heard the latch click open. Gently he pushed against it. The bottom stuck momentarily against the stone floor on the other side, then opened with a jerk, pulling Darginn a little off balance. He recovered, stopped a moment and opened the door just far enough to step up and out of the crypt.

There, in the dark of the kirk, something that shouldn't be there. A light, maybe twenty yards away. Just a small one, though—not a torch. Just a candle. Someone *was* waiting for them. What was unsettling was not the flame, though.

It was the glint of light reflected against the dirk in their other hand.

# CHAPTER 32

"Best you know the Guard are on their way."

Darginn froze. Panic took him for a moment. If that were true... God, had he scuppered the whole plan with his damned clumsy feet?

*Come on, man. Think!*

A moment of calm and he realised. He recognised the voice.

"Maither Floreli. Apologies. It's Darginn Argyll. The king's messenger?"

He'd met the priest several times, but priests met a lot of folk, so he just had to hope she remembered him. Darginn reached back and pulled his son through the door. "Ye might remember my son, Ismar?"

The boy staggered blinking into the room. "Hello, Maither."

The priest softened, relaxing her stance. "You're Isadona's boy?"

"Aye." Ismar's lowered head had him practically looking through his hair at her.

"What in Heaven's name are the two of you doing creeping in through a secret tunnel that you are *not* supposed to know about?" asked Floreli.

"Eh, aye, well, I've known about it awhile, actually, Maither. Being a messenger and all, you know..." Darginn folded his hands in contrition, hoping his tone was equally respectful. If the Guard really were on their way, he needed to move this on quickly.

The priest stepped toward them and now Darginn could see her properly as she entered the glow of his torch. Her silver-grey hair hung loose to the shoulders of the thick grey housecoat she wore over a white nightdress buttoned up to the throat. Her look was stern, but her face was the same kind, benevolent one he knew. "Right. Still doesn't explain why a king's messenger is sneaking in past the town guard."

"It doesn't, I know. I'm sorry, Maither. But if you can indulge me a moment, I promise you I can explain." Darginn put his hand across his heart and prayed he looked as earnest as he was.

"Go on, then." Good. She was prepared to listen. But she didn't put down the dirk.

Darginn raised one finger, asking for her patience, turned and waved the others through the door. "This here's Lady Samily, of the Order of the White Thorns."

Samily stepped into the space and gave a respectful bow. "An honour to meet you, Maither."

Floreli raised an eyebrow. A Thorn out of her White was odd right enough, and the leathers Samily had got at short notice were a little ill-fitting. But Darginn hadn't time to explain all that now. "This is Lady Rasa, from the university. And this young man is Vastin. He has the forge on Grey Square?" Both made agreeable noises and smiled at the priest. Her look remained sceptical.

Now that they were all in, Darginn closed the door behind them, if only to signal that there was nobody else in there.

"Now, it's a bit complicated, but—"

"Darginn, if you will allow me..." Samily cut across him and stepped toward Floreli. "Maither, forgive me, but this is the quickest way to explain." Samily pressed her hands around the one in which Floreli held the blade. The priest didn't have time to react. *"Clior."*

"Oh!" Floreli almost stumbled backwards, but Samily caught her arm, holding her up.

"It will pass in a moment, Maither. You are all right, I swear." The knight manoeuvred her to a chair a few feet behind.

It was a bit brash, Darginn thought, giving her no warning of what was going to happen. But they might only have minutes, so needs must, he supposed.

Thankfully, Maither Floreli recovered her senses fairly quickly. "Well. That's... new. I... suppose I can guess why you're sneaking in now."

"Yes, Maither," said Samily. "But first, we need to deal with the guards. Can you turn them away?"

"Oh." Floreli waved a dismissive hand. "They're not coming. If I sent for the Guard every time a mouse set off that damn bell they'd be here every other night. But tonight... I just had a feeling."

Darginn breathed a deep sigh of relief. They were fine. It was all fine.

"Ah, good." Samily turned back to them. "We should move on."

The Thorn was already walking for the door when Rasa spoke. "Wait, Samily. We should explain..." She indicated the priest with an open hand.

"We do not have time," Samily answered.

"But... Samily, if... if we're meeting here, then doesn't it make sense to...?" Rasa seemed to be trying to say something without saying it: that having the priest of Greytoun Kirk on their side could be a bit of a boon.

"Maither Floreli would be a good friend to us," said Darginn. "Worth taking five minutes to explain to her. After all, if our friends get out quickly, they're coming here, are they no?"

Samily turned to the door and back toward them, flustered. She didn't seem to know whether she was coming or going. That was fair. They were all knackered. It had been a hard road getting there so quickly. Even Vastin's young eyes were hung with dark bags. And for all that Darginn was looking forward to a night in his own bed, this could be well worth their time.

"All right," the knight finally conceded. "Five minutes."

---

It had been too long. Meristan had been pacing his cell for hours, had put his hand on the cell door at least half a dozen times, only to stop short of opening it because it would mean an end to the hope of rescuing Severianos quietly. And without casualties. It must be daylight by now, and the only hope that Anhel Weyr was not yet aware of Meristan's captivity was that he was still asleep. Should he go now? Should he already have gone? Should he never have agreed to be left here?

*Gah!*

What to do? He had the knife in his hand when the noise came. A kerfuffle down the corridor. Clanging of metal and stiffened voices. Something was happening. Was Cyrra back? Had she found Severianos? Meristan sat anxiously back on the bed. He should be exhausted, but his hands trembled, aching to act.

Footsteps. Coming nearer.

Many footsteps.

*Too many.*

Maybe it was nothing to do with him. Just another prisoner being delivered to a cell. Maybe…

As the footsteps came incessantly closer, the notion that they weren't coming directly for his cell became an obvious fantasy. The voices had stopped.

Had Cyrra betrayed him after all?

Whatever was coming, Cyrra had been right about one thing. The best he could do was pretend to be captive. Couldn't let them know his door was not locked. If they realised, Cyrra was in trouble.

Closer and closer they came, and the fact that nobody was speaking became ominous. No casual conversation, no chatting at all. Guards were not known for being taciturn.

Finally, a clutter of despondent faces lit by the flicker of torches. Misery was writ deep in their hunched shoulders and lowered eyes. Not prisoners, but not guards either. What was this? They gathered silently before Meristan's cell, none of them addressing him or even looking directly at him.

They parted and a familiar figure stepped forward, smiling benevolently as if he'd found a lost lamb. His receding hair was tucked behind his ears, and he leaned gently on a gnarled cane topped with a morbid golden skull. Its hollow eyes stared blankly into the cell, quietly condemning Meristan for a fool.

"Brother Meristan. How sad I am to see you brought so low."

*Anhel Weyr.*

S'grace, he was done.

Meristan struggled for words. His mind raced with options. Could he make a dive for the door, get out of the cell and take the man before he could react? Should he? What would that mean for Severianos? What about the guards? And who were these lifeless souls with whom he'd surrounded himself? Not enough information, not enough to choose from. So he sat, silent, and waited, as the Green Laird taught him.

"You have no words for your king?" the usurper asked, voice sweeter than honey. "No explanation for your treason? No plea for clemency?"

Meristan breathed deep, sat upright, crossed his arms and stared directly into Weyr's eyes. And there he found the glint of joy, of malice and contentment. Of victory. But the two of them knew the truth, regardless of what these wretches surrounding him might think—were they even human. And he would not cede an inch of ground to the man's vainglorious satisfaction.

But what did give him pause, and caught a sharp breath in his chest, was that cane. Or rather, the skull that formed its top.

It may be just a skull. An appropriately grotesque statement of the demon summoner's self-aggrandised power. His *threat*. But it could also be something much, much worse.

"You admire my cane." Weyr lifted the ghastly thing as if examining it himself for the first time. "Isn't it magnificent? A little *cuimhnich am bàs* I like to keep close. It reminds me that we are all of us mortal, and must inevitably surrender to a greater power. Wouldn't you agree, Brother?"

It riled Meristan to see Weyr wearing the robes of faith like a carnival costume, but that blasphemy he also would not give satisfaction. He would give the man nothing further to fatten his ignoble glory. But of course, the words were a subtle blade—benevolently pious to the ignorant observer; a veiled threat to an informed man.

"You should ask the Green Laird for his wisdom on the nature of death," Meristan said lightly. "He is an inscrutable expert on the topic. And I flatter myself a capable pupil. The White Thorns have no need for a *cuimhnich am bàs*—death is ever present at the edge of our blades."

"Indeed." Weyr smiled disturbingly. "And yet here you sit, wretched, alone and without a blade to your name. I wonder, how was it so easy? To fall from God's high graces?"

"Ah, good king, you mistake yourself. A man of faith is never alone. God is always with us. Even those of us who may not have earned God's grace will find that God's eye remains upon them."

A raised eyebrow. "Indeed. As you say, *Brother*."

The sting of the final word was intended to rile him. But it meant nothing. Meristan's faith persisted, regardless of what might become of him now. It was only a matter of waiting for his opportunity. Patience would win the day. So again, he remained silent, smiling up at his captor. Waiting.

Weyr crossed his arms and stroked at his chin. He had the beginnings of a beard—almost completely grey but for a few spatters of light brown that persisted. An affectation, perhaps. One that made him feel more regal. "I imagine you find yourself wondering how you came to be here. What was the choice that might have made a difference?"

Meristan sighed as if actually considering the answer. This was an odd game the two were playing, but he had no intention of losing. "I don't suppose it matters, does it? I will still be here, either way. Sometimes, the path ahead is clearer than the one behind. And, in the end, we can all only move forward."

A flicker of ire crossed the demon king's eyes then. Fleeting, but unmissable. This wasn't the game he intended. He wanted his prey to behave like it. "Well, not for long, either way. Regardless of your actions—your treachery against your king—we can't have the former head of the Order of the White Thorns sitting here in the dungeons like some halfwit beggar. I have a special room reserved for you, Brother. One a little closer to me, where you can be more comfortable."

Closer to him? That would not be helpful. He might have to fight his way out after all. If Weyr wasn't going to leave him here, his options would dwindle with every manoeuvre. He gripped the dirk tight beneath the fold of his cloak.

"It occurs to me that you might have reservations about your safety." Weyr wandered as if idly to Meristan's right, taking him almost out of sight. A silent, reticent pair of men parted without comment to give him space. "Let me assure you, for example, that your friend the Green

Laird is even now surrounded by my personal guards. They will keep an unblinking eye on him and ensure that nobody can get close to him without my express permission."

Damn.

*Damn.*

"And you, Brother, will be escorted by my contingent here. You will be aware of the concept of indentured servitude, I assume?"

He didn't mean that. These were no indentured servants, forced to work until some unreasonable debt was paid. Meristan finally recognised what was before him. The haunted, mournful, piteous expressions he'd seen once before.

In Lestalric.

These people had been cursed. They were unwilling pawns in Weyr's awful game. In fact, now that he considered it, Weyr had most likely introduced the idea to Shayella. She was broken—mad—but he wasn't sure that even she would have dreamed up such a hideous notion— to make sure that not only did these wretches serve, but they suffered through it. At least the Blackened had no memory of their time as mindless ghouls.

"So," Weyr continued, "you're going to allow these servants to enter your cell, and you're going to allow them to bind your hands. And then you're going to allow them to escort us both, unmolested, to your new quarters." Weyr leaned slightly in toward the bars of the cell. "Aren't you?"

Blast it. Yes, he was. Because the truth of it was that while Meristan may have won their little war of wits, it was meaningless—as Weyr had just shown. He had Severianos surrounded by loyal guards, perhaps even demons, and he was going to use these innocent *damainte* as a protective shield for himself—and against Meristan trying to escape.

And that was that. How many innocent lives was Meristan willing to put at risk, to endanger by his own hand, to gain his freedom?

None.

There was no number low enough. He would not kill these people, whatever they might have done to deserve punishment. If anything.

And so he was going to be patient. It occurred to him to ask what happened to Captain Cyrra, but just in case her name had never reached Anhel's ear, Meristan chose to say nothing. One of the servants, a woman with mousy brown hair half fallen out of a bun at the back of her head, reached out toward the handle. She inserted a key and her eyes registered shock when it wouldn't turn in the lock. Still she said nothing—whether because of the curse or a desire to keep the information from Weyr, Meristan could not say. He quietly hoped it was the latter.

She opened the cell door and Weyr stepped back to allow three men to enter. One brought a handful of rope and bore an apologetic countenance. These were puppets. Meristan could no more harm them than children. He secreted the dirk in his sleeve, slowly stood and offered his hands to the man, wrists pressed together, all the while staring directly at the false king. Weyr maintained his pretence of benevolence, but as the rope wound gently about Meristan's wrists, he saw the malevolent glint behind the facade again. The smug contentment of undeserved victory.

Well, he was mistaken. The war was long from over. And even if Meristan didn't see it to the end, there were plenty of others who would.

---

"I...have a *granddaughter*?" Ferrod almost collapsed into the seat, his eyes alight, smile beaming. Aranok had been terrified to tell him, in the end. It felt like another betrayal, that he'd never told Korvin's parents the truth, and that Taie would never know. He'd made a point of waiting for the right moment. Got Ferrod in his own living room, in a moment where nothing was pressing. Asked Allandria and Mynygogg to give them space, just in case it was needed—and they'd both happily gone out for a few hours. But the smile on Ferrod's face was not bittersweet, it was pure joy. And with it, fear washed from Aranok like rain.

"And, if you want to, Ikara would love to spend some time with you, as soon as it can be arranged. It'll be a little difficult because, well..." Because his father and brother-in-law were arses. "Father was always worried about appearances, and, well, Emelina doesn't know. About Korvin. She thinks Pol is her father."

"Of course, of course, I understand." Ferrod ran his fingers up and down the arms of the chair. "I would probably like some time myself. Just to, you know..." Prepare himself. Of course. It was a lot. To discover your dead son had a daughter who's been living in the same city for six years. And maybe—maybe—you might see your dead wife reflected in her eyes. "I always liked Ikara, you know." Now the bittersweet tinge. "I would have loved..."

"I know. So would she."

Things could have been so different. But as Allandria kept telling him since they arrived here, there was little point mourning worlds that never existed. The only life he could live was right here in front of him, and he'd waste it by wishing it different. So he was grasping what happiness he could, what solace he could find. With Allandria. And here, with Ferrod, righting an old mistake. He'd never imagined he'd find forgiveness, in this of all places, and God, the absence of that weight—it was strange. As if he might float away in a strong breeze. That guilt had grounded him for so long, become who he was. He was still adjusting to life without it. Learning how *not* to be unhappy. Even with the godawful shite they found themselves in, there was joy. As Meristan said—"Seek light in the darkness."

And Ferrod was glowing with it. "I think—I think I need a drink. Will you join me?" He indicated the seat opposite his—the one Aranok assumed had been Taie's.

"Of course."

Ferrod rang a handheld bell and his maid, Vacha, appeared, took instructions and shuffled off to return a few minutes later with two glasses of whisky in elegant, sculpted glasses.

Ferrod held his glass up to the fire, turning it in his hand. "I love the way the light plays off the glass. Burns through the amber. As if you hold a glass of liquid flame."

"It certainly burns going down," said Aranok.

"Oh. Not this one." Ferrod brandished the glass like art. "This goes down smooth as a baby's cheek. Like warm silk, it is. Like drinking cake on a sunny day."

"Aye?" That did not describe any whisky Aranok had ever tasted.

"Oh, aye." Ferrod ran the glass beneath his nose and closed his eyes. "Bought this bottle the day Korvin was born. Wet his head with it.

Best bottle of whisky I've ever owned. Only comes out for special occasions." He opened his eyes again and raised the glass high. "To family."

"Family," Aranok repeated, sipping at the drink. It was exactly as Ferrod had described. Sweet, light, like honey, but not cloying, with a hint of peat and vanilla. More subtlety than he'd ever experienced from a whisky. And no burn, except a little across the roof of his mouth. "That's incredible."

Ferrod tilted his glass at Aranok with a wink and a smile.

"Better be. Cost me a bloody fortune."

# CHAPTER 33

"This is a terrible idea."

"It was your idea."

"How is that relevant?"

Allandria sat quietly in the dark, hands resting on her crossed legs. After learning that Bak lived alone, Aranok had suggested that the best way to catch him on his own would be to break into his house and wait. Aside from the stupidity of breaking into the home of the captain of the city guard, neither of them was an experienced burglar. Though they had become quite good at lurking in shadows and hiding in alleyways. Allandria's lock-picking skills were "key," as Aranok had put it—and then been unreasonably pleased with himself.

Now he paced circles around the kitchen table, as if he might somehow make the captain come home quicker if he walked the distance for him.

The house was modest but clean. A standard front room with a small fireplace backed onto a decent-size kitchen. Stairs led up to a bedroom, but Allandria had no desire to go looking up there—it already felt like they were invading the man's privacy.

It had been a deeply odd few days since they'd arrived. The journey had been largely quiet after they'd parted with the Reivers. Arriving at Ferrod's, her heart had been entirely lodged in her throat. She'd been exhausted, nerves shredded, joints aching.

And then it was wonderful. Allandria couldn't come up with a better word for it, despite how inappropriate it seemed. But here they were—skulking around Mournside, Aranok wanted for murder, Mynygogg framed as a monster—and Ferrod had somehow made it all right. Aranok had finally—*finally*—found some peace. And in finding it, ice she hadn't even known was there melted from him. He was more relaxed, more confident, but in an easy way. Less rigid. Less brittle. He was *at home* in a way she'd never seen him before. And with it, his humour returned. His smile. His light.

So she stopped worrying. Partly because his confidence was infectious; partly, perhaps, because his stress had been too. Even now, as he stalked about Bak's kitchen, his nerves were tempered with levity.

"You do have an extensive history of terrible plans."

"Exactly," he answered. "And *your* job is to talk me out of them."

"My job is to *get* you out of them. When they go wrong."

Aranok raised one finger. "*Was*. You're an envoy now."

"Damn right, I am." She uncrossed her legs and leaned on her thighs. "Kneel, peasant."

A wicked smile. A grin that said he was thinking the same thing. "Later."

A click of key in latch and they jumped to attention. Aranok gently waved both palms downwards. She wasn't the one who needed to calm down, her face told him.

The door creaked open, catching slightly on the stone floor. They'd tried to come in the back way, through the garden, but the rear door was bolted, meaning they had to risk going around the front.

Thankfully, there had only been one lock to spring, because every second she was crouched there she had been certain someone was going to start screaming at them.

No footsteps. That was odd. What was Bak waiting for? Aranok's crinkled eyebrows told Allandria he was just as curious.

She pointed to her eyes, then toward the front door. There was no line of sight from their position, but she could creep around and see what she could see.

"Whoever's in here, you've broken into the wrong house. I am the captain of the city guard and I am armed." Bak's voice boomed through the house with a tenor she had never noticed before. It was commanding. Impressive. A little intimidating.

"How?" Aranok mouthed at her.

She shrugged. Maybe some safeguard set up on the front door. Something that would only have moved when the door was opened. Something he would have noticed. Of course he was careful. The number of criminals who might want revenge against him? How could he not be?

Aranok breathed out heavily and clearly made a decision. A very risky decision. He stepped out of the kitchen and walked toward the front door, palms open wide before him.

"Captain. It's me. Aranok. I just want to speak to you."

That seemed to take Bak off guard, because he didn't respond for a long time. Allandria opted to stay quiet, just in case. If he turned on Aranok, it might be useful for him not to know she was here.

"Just you?" Bak finally replied.

"No. Allandria is here too."

*Or not.*

"Hello, Captain." She stepped out and walked forward until he could see her by the moonlight spilling through the open door.

"You're wanted," Bak said flatly.

"We are," Aranok replied. "And yet we're here."

"Which is an odd thing." Bak tapped the hilt of his sword. At the distance they had, he'd never reach them before Aranok could cast a spell, and Allandria would have her sword drawn the moment he did. There was little point in him attacking. And he knew it. If he wasn't going to listen, his best bet was to retreat and close the door behind him. He looked like he might. He was definitely considering it.

"Please? Just give us a minute?" Aranok asked. He sounded like the most reasonable man alive. Who could refuse him?

Bak made his decision. He pointed to Allandria. "All right. You, stay there. You"—now Aranok—"walk slowly toward me with your wrists together, fingers interlocked."

Aranok looked at her, gave a resigned eyebrow raise and did as he was asked. Bak fished something from his belt and fussed at Aranok's hands. When he turned back to face her, they were bound with rope.

## THE DAMNED KING

"Now, Allandria."

"Yes?" She wasn't enjoying the tone, but she was also a wanted criminal, so under the circumstances...

"Take off your sword belt and throw it over here." She did. "Now your bow and quiver." She did that too. "Now your knives. All of them." She paused, irritated at the thought of being completely without weapons. But Aranok gave her a tilt of the head that said *Do it*, so she did that too. "Aranok, step back into the room. Allandria, light that oil lamp on the sideboard."

They followed Bak's further instructions until they were both seated back in the kitchen, looking at him across the dining table, which was a little large for a man who lived alone, it occurred to her.

Bak stood its full length from them, sword now in hand. He was taking a huge risk. But he trusted them a little bit, or they wouldn't have got this far. "All right. Speak."

She still wasn't enjoying that tone.

"It's complicated," Aranok started.

"Make it simple," said Bak.

Aranok took a breath. "You've been lied to. Anhel Weyr is a fraud. I'm innocent. I can prove it."

That was simple. And true. And it did not test Bak's memory. Elegant. She'd have told him so in other circumstances.

"How?" was all Bak responded.

"Magic," Aranok answered.

"Well, that's a problem, isn't it?" said Bak. "Because the minute I untie your hands, I'm at risk again, aren't I?"

"If I'd wanted to hurt you, Captain, I could have burned you as soon as you opened the door. What purpose would that serve? Why would we have come here, just to kill you? With respect, are you that important?"

*Ooft*. That was a little barb. The tilt of Bak's chin said he felt it, but a subtle nod also suggested his agreement.

"All right. What magic? How can magic prove to me that the king is a fraud?"

*The king.* Hearing Weyr described that way made her fists itch. She rubbed her thumbs back and forth along her forefingers, soothing the irritation. But there was something in Bak's voice. A tinge of desire. Of need. He *wanted* to believe it.

"That's what's complicated," Aranok answered. "You should sit down."

"I prefer to stand, thank you." Bak was not putting himself in a vulnerable position. She wouldn't either, in his place. "Just tell me."

There was a risk here. If Bak was working for Weyr, if his memory was unaffected, they would be showing their hand. But if he was, surely he'd just have killed them both by now. Tried to, at least. The fact that neither of them had attacked the other *surely* told of their collective innocence? Their allyship? She hoped Bak saw that too. Her impression of him had always been that he was sharp. Insightful.

"It's...your memory. It's been altered. I can fix it." Aranok had made it simple, showing the man the respect he asked for.

"How?"

"With a charm."

"What charm?"

Aranok looked to her apprehensively. If they exposed the charm and Bak was a traitor, they could lose it, like with Madu. Which was why they'd come prepared.

"Around my neck, on a leather strap." Aranok nodded down. "Take it. Hold it."

Bak approached cautiously, one hand holding his blade to Aranok's chest—not that it would cut his leathers anyway—the other lifting the strap over his head to dangle the little yellow ball in front of him. "This thing?"

"That's it," said Aranok.

"And now what?"

"Hold that charm in your hand. I'll speak a *draoidh* word, and your memory will be returned."

Bak pondered the little orb. Dangling in the space between them. It felt as fragile as their peace in that moment. Easily broken.

"And if I take this?" Bak asked. "Have it examined by another *draoidh*? Have them tell me what it is?" Sensible. Cautious. He wanted surety. Facts.

"They won't know what it is," Aranok answered honestly. "Unless they are memory *draoidhs*."

"Memory *draoidhs*? I didn't know they existed."

"Neither did I," said Aranok. "Until I was reminded."

"Did you know about this the last time we met?"

"No. But I do know who killed Evenna. Or I know why she was killed. It *was* to stop her talking to me. This explains everything, Bak. It will all make sense, after this."

That tempted him. She could see the hunger in his eyes. This was a man who thrived on solving mysteries. He didn't like questions he couldn't answer. And here they were, offering him answers. Promising to make sense of the chaos. Literally, the truth in the palm of his hand. Sort of.

Bak flicked the charm up and caught it. "I must be fucking mad. But fine. Do it."

"*Clìor*," said Aranok.

Bak looked between them, blinking. Confused. He shrugged. "How long does it take?"

Aranok sighed with relief. "Thank you."

"For what?" Bak asked, a tinge of irritation in his voice.

"That's not the charm," Aranok explained. "Allandria's wearing the real one."

"What the Hell is this, then?"

"May I?" Allandria mimed taking out the charm. Bak nodded and she stood, lifting it from inside her leathers. This time, she would keep hold of the strap.

"We needed to know if we could trust you," Aranok said, "just like you needed to trust us."

He'd been confident of Bak. But he'd been confident of Madu, so he wasn't making the same mistake twice. Besides, having a decoy, that any assassin or other agent of Weyr would assume was real because Aranok was carrying it, just made sense. He'd had a glassblower make it in Traverlyn. Looked close enough for anyone who wasn't a *draoidh* not to know the difference.

They cleared Bak's memory for real—his reaction was as small as she'd seen. Aranok had a theory that the more open-minded a person was, the more willing to change their understanding when presented with new information, the easier it was on them to have their reality upended.

After a moment's pause, Bak sat forward excitedly. "Janaeus wouldn't have wanted you talking to Evenna because it might lead you back to him, asking questions."

"Or to Madu," Aranok added. "Same problem."

"She was in league with him?"

Aranok nodded.

"And you killed her?"

Aranok's face turned sharply at that. It was still a raw wound, even now, because the consequences hung over them like an axe.

"No. But I was there. And she deserved it."

That was definitely true.

"I need a drink." The captain released the straps on Aranok's hands and ushered them into the living room, where he poured three whiskies.

A half hour of further conversation, in much the same vein, with Bak offering his thoughts and Aranok filling in the details. Allandria sat, legs curled under her on a surprisingly comfortable armchair, sipping whisky. This was about as well as she'd hoped the evening might go. Everything had been going smoothly, in fact, since they arrived in Mournside.

It was weird. She was almost relaxed, but a small part of her brain was constantly waiting for the bad news to land. For the disaster that was always coming when she let down her guard.

"All right." Bak threw back the last of his drink and slapped the glass on the side table. "What can I do? Where do we start?"

"Well, it would help if I wasn't looking over my shoulder all the time, waiting to be arrested," said Aranok.

"You need to restore the guards' memories. Of course. Excellent plan. But you also need to be careful of tipping off any of Weyr's agents, yes?"

*Sharp as steel.*

Aranok nodded. "Exactly."

"Then we need another ruse?" Bak asked.

Aranok smiled broadly. "Actually, it's the exact same ruse."

"It has been too long!" Samily paced the floor of Darginn Argyll's home, barely able to keep her hands still. Two days. Two days they had waited! For any sign, for any contact from Meristan. Each day, they had taken shifts to visit the kirk, checked in with Maither Floreli. They had been careful. But trusting the priest was a difficult prospect for Samily. Too many people had turned out not to be who they seemed of late, and while her instinct was to have faith in the woman, her fear for Meristan and Severianos was almost crippling.

Meristan's plan had been to get in and out quickly. That could not have worked. He must be in trouble. They had to rescue him. Both of them.

Today. *Tonight.*

A light knock on the door. It was late. All five of them were in and accounted for. Rasa raised a finger to her mouth, stood by the window and nodded to Ismar, who sat quietly beside the fire. Darginn was tending food in the kitchen and Vastin was upstairs bathing. Ismar's eyes widened as he realised what Rasa meant for him to do, but he settled when Samily nodded at him encouragingly. The boy had seemed happier, stronger since they had arrived—perhaps the benefit of his childhood home. Darginn had chosen not to speak of her executing Victus yet, and Samily had respected his decision. She wondered why the boy would take badly the idea that his tormentor would not harm him again, nor anyone else. But it was not her choice to make.

With a considered nod, Ismar crossed to the door. He paused a moment, fingers just resting on the handle, then turned the lock and opened it about a foot—not enough to allow whoever was outside sight of Samily or Rasa.

"Oh! Hello. Um, what can I do for you?" S'grace, there was clear panic in Ismar's voice. Samily put a hand on her sword hilt, ready to strip it from its sheath. Whoever was at the door, it was not good.

"Eh, I was told that I would find a king's messenger here. Darginn Argyll? And his...friends?"

The voice was familiar. But not enough to place it. Samily looked enquiringly to Rasa, who shrugged in return.

"Um, yes, that's my father," Ismar answered, tucking his trembling right hand behind his back. "But we're about to eat, so..."

"It's urgent," the woman hissed. "The priest sent me."

The priest? If they had come from Maither Floreli, they may have word of Meristan. Samily swung the door fully open. "What do you...? Oh!" She instantly recognised the woman once she could see her face. The captain whose memory she had restored on the Auld Road. The one who held Meristan captive. Samily instinctively looked for her mentor, but there was nobody behind the woman in the gloom.

"Ah, Samily, right?" The captain looked over her shoulder. "Please... I should come in."

Ismar looked to Samily for guidance. Yes, she should come in. They shouldn't be holding this conversation in the street. Samily stepped back and made space for her to enter.

Rasa crossed the room toward the kitchen. "I'll get Darginn."

"We don't have a lot of time," the captain said, halting her. She looked at Samily questioningly. "I assume I can speak freely?"

"Ah yes," said Samily. "Ismar is Darginn's son. This is Rasa. Both allies. I am sorry, I have forgotten your name, Captain."

"Cyrra," she answered, as if it were an irrelevance. "Lady Samily, Meristan has been taken. Imprisoned. I had left him, I thought safely, in a cell, but he found out, somehow—Weyr. One of my soldiers, likely." Her eyes wavered at that. A pain at the perceived betrayal, Samily imagined, whether real or not. "And he has been moved. Quartered in a room, under guard, in the same tower where Weyr has taken residence. I'm told he refused the traditional king's chambers for a more 'austere' room in the tower. Farthest away from others. More defensible, I suppose. And more private."

"All right," said Rasa. "That's fine, actually. That's good."

*What?*

"Why is that good?" Samily asked.

"Because I can get into a window easier than I can get into a dungeon," she answered.

As a bird, of course. Perhaps Anhel Weyr had accidentally given them an advantage.

"But also..." Cyrra continued, "he has the Green Laird under guard. And I don't know any of the soldiers watching him."

"Likely demons," said Rasa.

A splash of water and feet hitting floorboards upstairs. Vastin may have been stirred by the sound of conversation.

Cyrra looked up and back at Samily nervously.

"Vastin," she replied. "Another ally."

"Good. We may need them all," said Cyrra. "The only way we're getting them both out of there is if we do it at the same time. If we just take Meristan, I believe he will have the Green Laird executed."

Even hearing the words cut into Samily's gullet. She had been against Meristan surrendering himself. And this was what she had feared. He had only ended up as hostage as their teacher.

"You have a plan?" Samily asked.

"I think I have an opportunity," said Cyrra. "I'm not sure about a plan."

"An opportunity is a beginning." Samily turned to Rasa. "Please fetch Darginn. Ismar, would you hurry Vastin into his clothing, please?" Both nodded and scurried away.

Samily gestured to a chair. "All right, Captain. Tell me about our opportunity."

# CHAPTER 34

Samily was deeply uncomfortable. Not just because the armour she was now wearing was ill-fitting and limited her movement; because she was entrusting herself once again to a woman she barely knew. But dressing in the uniform of Eidyn's army and following Captain Cyrra into Greytoun was her best chance of getting to Meristan. Worse was that her Green blade would not fit within a standard sheath due to its greater length. So it stayed at the kirk along with the leathers. She was without her White armour and her Green blade. It occurred to her that perhaps she had taken their merits for granted. The weight of this bog-standard armour was a hindrance, and the sword's balance was off—like carrying a bucket of water that sloshed from side to side. Still, she had her training and her *draoidh* skill. It would be enough.

They'd passed mostly unmolested, as Samily could once have done here wearing the White. Hopefully, she would again soon.

Given the chance, perhaps she might even end Anhel Weyr's tyranny, should they come across him. Send him to God. For justice.

They plodded up the tight round stairwell, designed for those at the top to have a substantial advantage over those trying to fight their way up. The castle was built as a fortress, of course. Made to be defensible at every stage. To withstand a siege. To fight off invaders.

Like her.

When they reached the landing, a pair of kingsguards stood on either side of a heavy oak door reinforced with iron bars. Samily imagined they would usually have had counterparts on the other side too, tasked to keep that door closed at all costs. This was not designed to be a prison, but a sanctuary. A *haven*.

The left soldier was a strongly built man with a bushy blond beard and dark circles beneath his eyes. The other was a woman with close-cropped grey hair and a fine scar down the side of her left eye. Both moved only their heads to look at Cyrra as she spoke.

"Soldiers. I've been asked to deliver these to the prisoner." She held out her arm, over which was draped a set of clothes they had collected from the kirk's stock of donations for the poor. They'd had very little that would fit him.

It was an excuse to get them in and maybe a disguise for Meristan. Hopefully. They may yet have to fight their way out.

The woman looked suspiciously at the bundle of clothes and up to Cyrra. The captain had no direct command over the kingsguards, but her rank should make her trustworthy. Still, the woman lingered a long time, looking her up and down. Finally, she gave a resigned nod toward the door. "Aye, all right."

The man lifted a ring of keys from his belt and turned each of the five locks, the bolts on the other side clunking out of place.

The woman swung the door open, stepping inside herself first and then, apparently satisfied, stepping back to make way for Cyrra and Samily.

The room was much larger than Samily had expected, and more lavish. A large four-poster bed to the left, a writing desk, a dark wood wardrobe and a leather sofa before a large fireplace, in which a healthy fire burned. Her master sat there, head bowed, examining something. Her first instinct was to run to him, but that would give them away. She had to restrain herself. Be patient.

"Give us a minute," Cyrra said to the guards. "I've to take away his old clothes too. Shut it, but don't lock it. He's not going anywhere." She put a hand on the pommel of her sword to emphasise the point.

The woman looked to Meristan, back to Cyrra, shrugged and closed the door. The moment it clicked back into place, Samily rushed to him.

"Meristan? Meristan?"

He sluggishly raised his head and turned toward her voice. His dull eyes wandered, searching for focus. His mouth fought to make words. "Sam... Samly?"

*Oh God.* She'd seen this many times. In the hospital.

"Help me," she ordered Cyrra. "He has been dosed with poppy."

---

Vastin was certain his face was plastered with guilt, screaming out to everyone they passed that he did not belong there. He kept his eyes low and found himself yawning each time they passed someone, as if doing something with his face freed him from meeting their eye.

Darginn's status as a king's messenger had got them into the castle, and his confident striding past guards had left them largely unbothered. He gave off such an air that he *belonged* there. Vastin and Ismar were meant to be apprentice messengers, shadowing their mentor as he went about his work. Nobody had actually asked about that, presumably taking it that Darginn had the authority to drag a couple of young men about the castle with him for whatever purpose he liked. Seemed to Vastin that he had almost as much authority as Captain Cyrra, who had left them at the gate to play out their own charade.

God, it was terrifying. But they had to do it this way. If one got free, Cyrra and Samily had been certain that the other would be in immediate danger. So this was it—get them both out together.

They'd expected to find the Green Laird secluded away in a tower somewhere, but when Darginn had asked directions of a scullery maid who'd come upon them stinking of gravy, with a bucket of grey-brown dishwater in each hand, she'd pointed them to a corridor of guest quarters.

"Odd," Darginn said quietly as they turned the corner onto the hallway. "These are meant for honoured guests. Foreign dignitaries and the like. Emissaries, no prisoners."

Along the left-hand wall were narrow stained-glass windows that looked like they would fold out of the way when needed as arrow slits. Their colourful panes lit the hallway with a scattered rainbow. Along with the pots of plants—most of them heather, from what Vastin could see—they made what would otherwise have been a fairly gloomy corridor into something welcoming and warm. Aye, seemed like the place they'd put guests.

As they approached the large double doors that stood out by virtue of the guards on either side of them, Vastin clocked the doors themselves. Instead of the usual wood with wrought-iron enforcements, these pair looked, if he was seeing them right, to be made of solid metal. Vastin nearly gasped out loud as he considered the very cost of that much metal and the size of the mould to make such things. Far beyond what he could have done, even if the mundane basics of household blacksmithing had been his trade. But he admired the artisanship that had gone into them. The lines of the decorative insets were crisp and balanced. It was nice work.

"Evening, gents." Darginn made a wee gesture like a sort of salute with half a bow. "Darginn Argyll, king's messenger. I have a note for Laird Severianos."

"All right," the larger of the two guards answered. "Give us it and we'll pass it on."

"Ah, well, no, I'm afraid," said Darginn, "it's to be put directly into his hands. May we enter?" He opened a hand toward the door, like the guard wouldn't know where he meant otherwise.

"I suppose, if you want," the guard replied. "You can leave it for him."

"Or wait," the second guard piped up in a voice that was more shrill than Vastin would have expected from his bushy black beard. "As long as you dinnae touch anything, eh?"

"*Leave* it for him?" The wee touch of panic in Darginn's voice echoed in Vastin's heart. "He's no here?"

"Had dinner with the king. Hasn't returned yet."

"Oh. Right." This time, the alarm in Darginn's voice was tangible, and Vastin's heart thumped hard. He glanced toward Ismar, to see if he was as panicked, but the man's head was still bowed between slumped shoulders, staring at his father's heels. "Eh, d'you know where? I'd like to get this done the night and get to bed, you know?"

"Couldn't tell you, friend, sorry," the bearded guard said. "We were told to stay here. Guard the room."

"Guard the room?" Darginn asked. "With nobody in it?"

The big guard shrugged. "Aye."

"That normal?" He was trying to sound like it was casual conversation, but Vastin reckoned these guards were going to get suspicious very soon if the king's messenger kept asking questions. He cleared his throat as inconspicuously as possible, hoping that Darginn would take his meaning.

*Let's just go.*

"Normal if the king says it is," said the bearded guard in a way that offered a clear exit from the conversation. He prayed Darginn would take it.

"We should find him, then, no?" Ismar said quietly.

Darginn turned as if he'd forgotten his son was there. "Aye! Aye, we should that, son." He turned back to the guards. "Sorry for bothering you."

The bearded guard gave a nod, but there was definitely a note of curiosity in his eye as they turned away.

They were round the corner again and well out of sight before Vastin dared speak. "Now what?"

"Kitchen," Darginn said plainly. "Find out where the king took dinner."

# CHAPTER 35

"Water! Is there water?" Samily's voice was shrill and urgent. "We need to...Ugh...Meristan, can you hear me?" Her master looked up at her with a blank, serene smile. His eyes flitted in and out of focus. S'grace, they couldn't move him out of there in that state. Now what?

"Here's water!" Cyrra crossed toward them with a clay jug and cup.

A thought stabbed at Samily. "No. Wait. We cannot eat or drink. Anything."

It took Cyrra a moment to follow her thinking. "Because we don't know where the opium came from."

Samily nodded.

What were they going to do? At the very least they had to change his clothes, or else the facade they'd entered under would be broken. Or did they? Would it make more sense to leave and try again later? Tell the guards he was not fit to change now, and hope the poppy had worn off by morning?

Would they manage an escape in the morning? Cyrra had been adamant it had to be tonight.

Meristan was far too heavy, too unwieldy for them to manoeuvre him out in his drugged state. But maybe Rasa would be able to help? If she could take a form big enough to...Actually, that was a point. Rasa. Samily moved to open the shutters and then the window. A blast of cold air nipped at her knuckles and bit her neck as a light dust of snow blew in. And with it, the owl she was expecting. She hopped down from the window and flitted across near the fire. And then...

Nothing.

The owl gave a confused turn of its head, agitatedly flapping about. What was happening?

"I assume that is your metamorph friend."

Samily's head snapped to the door. She hadn't even heard it open. But there, dressed in the regal purple robes of Eidyn, stood the man who'd murdered her the last time they met. He would not get another chance. Samily whipped her blade from its sheath and took a step toward Anhel Weyr.

And stopped.

From behind the false king, another figure stepped. This one more welcome, and yet wrong. Disturbing. Unsettling.

"Samily, stand down," the Green Laird commanded, hand on the pommel of his blade. "That is an order."

*S'grace.*

This was all wrong. He should not be here. Darginn and the others were sent to... Heavens, what would happen when they got to his chamber and... Everything was going wrong!

Samily was honour bound to obey the order from her superior, but he did not know the truth. Would it break her vow to God if she were to dismiss the order as coming from a corrupted source? Either way, she would not fight Laird Severianos. Without her White or Green blade, she would most likely lose anyway. Even with them, the old man's skill might best her speed and strength. He taught her how to fight.

But she had her other skill. And that, maybe, was how they could get out of this.

*"Air ais."*

...

Samily's breath stuttered in her chest.

Nothing happened.

She looked about, heart racing. Why hadn't it worked?

*"Air ais!"*

Guards poured into the room behind the two men, until there were six, eight, nine of them. Severianos stepped back, allowing Weyr to take the front. He smiled benevolently, as if she were a child caught awake after candlesnuff.

"I'm afraid your magic won't work in this room, my dear."

And suddenly, she was stripped of everything. Her armour, her weapon and her magic.

Still. She was a White Thorn. She would not surrender.

*Clear your mind, trust in God and stand your ground.*

"My laird Severianos, I need to explain..."

"No, Samily," the Green Laird cut her off. "I will hear no words in defence of your master. I have spent some days here with the king. There is no record nor any reason to believe Meristan's claim of a secret mission from King Janaeus or any of his other outlandish claims. In fact, there is evidence that he is in league with the former laird envoy, who murdered the king, head messenger and a roomful of lairds. I will not hear you speak more mad lies in his defence."

She had rarely heard the laird angry, but there was fury in his voice. He must believe everything Weyr had told him.

But perhaps Meristan had not shared enough truth with him. Perhaps if she did...

"This man is not who you think he is." Samily levelled her sword at Weyr and steel rattled as every guard in the room prepared to step forward. "He is an impostor. He is no king."

"Samily!" Severianos raged. "I have known Anhel Weyr for years. He has funded the White Thorns, paid for your bed, your food. And you would slander him? Here? In Greytoun?" Weyr raised a hand before him and her tutor calmed, visibly shrinking back. "I apologise, Your Majesty."

There was nothing she could do. Nothing she could say to convince the old man that Weyr was the villain here. Not without restoring his memory. And she couldn't do that.

What trap had she walked into? Aranok had told her nothing about *suppressing* magic. Had she known that was a possibility...

*Wait. Rasa!*

Without magic, she was stuck in the owl's form! She had to leave. *Now.*

Samily burst to the window, grateful it was opposite the door. "Rasa! Get out!"

The metamorph saw her meaning and spread her wings, arcing toward the open window. Samily was aware of movement toward her. She turned, braced to block their path, prevent anyone from closing that window before Rasa could escape.

Two guards came at her, one with an open hand, the second with sword drawn. Good. She could tangle up the first for enough time to…

A sharp twang. A hiss of air and a sickening thud as arrow hit flesh, and then stone. A shriek of agony.

"No!" Samily ducked away from the guards and scrambled to where Rasa lay crumpled against the wall. *"Air ais! Air ais!"*

Still nothing. *Heaven, no, please…*

The owl's head moved, turning its eyes toward her. The arrow had only pierced her wing, bringing her down.

"Oh, thank God, thank God."

Samily felt a sword at the back of her neck. She ignored it.

"Get up," the guard ordered. She ignored that too. A quick snap and the fletching was split from the shaft. She pushed the rest of it through and Rasa squirmed against the pain. When it was out, she gently scooped the bird into her arms and cradled her like a baby.

Only then did she stand and turn to face the usurper.

"You will regret that." She spoke the words to the king, but her eyes strayed also to the man whose crossbow now hung casually at his side.

"Samily!" Severianos snapped. "You will speak when the king addresses you. Do not disgrace the Order any further."

*Disgrace…!* Samily roiled with a mix of emotions. Anger, pain, pride and fear all stormed within her. What should she do? What *could* she do? Meristan was vulnerable, Rasa was wounded—again—and Laird Severianos was set against her by the king's lies!

"With respect, Laird, you really don't know the full truth here," said Cyrra. Samily had almost forgotten the woman was there. "Samily is no disgrace, I assure you."

"Captain Cyrra." Weyr took a few casual steps to her place at the back of the sofa, shaking his head mournfully. "It pained me deeply to learn that, of all people, the leader of the White Thorns, the very order to whom I have dedicated so much of my family's inheritance, had conspired against King Janaeus—against me! And yet, I feel that sting again now as I look at you. A soldier of Eidyn's army turning against your king, while the country still mourns for my more worthy predecessor."

"Liar." Cyrra spat at his feet. "You're no king. The country will not—" Whatever the captain planned to say next caught in her throat. With a click of a button and a swift thrust, Weyr's golden cane had produced a blade at the tip—a blade now held at the captain's throat.

"Wha's...? Who's...?" Meristan stirred, even his opium stupor pierced by the sudden change of atmosphere behind him. But his brain was too addled to finish his thought. His eyes roved aimlessly.

Were she alone, Samily would have taken the chance now to end the king and hang the consequences for herself. She would happily go to God content that her life was worth the ending of his.

But hers was not the only life at risk. Rasa would die here, trapped in her owl form. Cyrra and Meristan too, likely. If she had learned anything recently, it was that sometimes discretion is the only right approach. Patience to wait for better circumstances.

"The words of traitors are poison for righteous men," said Weyr. "And, Captain, I will not be poisoned further."

Cyrra lifted her head and turned slowly to look at Samily. A question? Was she asking for her guidance? Now was not the time. Samily looked down at the owl in her arms, then to her master, lolling on the sofa, and gave the woman a gentle shake of the head. They would have to bide their time.

Cyrra turned her head back to Weyr, puffed out her chest defiantly and said nothing.

"Better." Weyr lowered his cane and stepped back. "Take their weapons."

Samily stood completely still, her eyes never leaving Weyr as another pair of guards approached. One removed her sword belt while the other frisked her for knives. She wasn't carrying any. She'd only ever needed a good blade.

Heavens, how was she going to get out of this?

She couldn't look at the Green Laird. S'grace, if only she had known he would be here, she could have been prepared, she could have... It served no purpose to berate herself for past choices now. They had made a plan. It was a good plan. They had not allowed for Weyr expecting them. Not imagined he would have Severianos so close. So befuddled by his lies.

"Laird Severianos, if there is something you wish to say to your former charge, you may do so now." Weyr spoke with the charm of a benign regent. His smile only infuriated Samily further.

The Green Laird stood before her, sighing as he looked her up and down. "I never imagined a Thorn to fall so low. But to find *two* of you in league with a traitor... Samily, can you explain this to me? Can you make me understand why the leader of the Order of the White Thorns is actively rebelling against Eidyn's monarch? A godly man? And why you are working with him?"

"What has he told you?" Samily asked.

"Told me? Nothing. I have seen it with my own eyes! Meristan swore to me that he was on a secret mission for the king, but no such mission existed. Instead, I learn he has been conspiring with Laird Aranok to release Mynygogg, who murdered half the country, and overthrow the kingdom! Was I so blind, not to see two ungodly traitors under my nose? Explain it to me! How did this happen?"

Samily's hands trembled and tears of frustration welled. What could she say?

"You have been enchanted, Laird. You believe a lie. I could prove it, but..."

"But what?" he demanded.

Samily glanced to the king. And only then did her eyes fall on his cane's grip. A golden skull, upon which his hand rested. If that was the relic they had sought... S'grace, it was even worse than she imagined. Whatever Weyr had done to suppress her magic—and Rasa's—it may have been bolstered by the relic. And he may have drastically more power even than they feared. If he could find another memory *draoidh* to do his work, like Quellaria...

Her face must have changed, because Severianos turned to look back at the king too. "What? What is it, Samily? I want to understand. Tell me *something*."

# THE DAMNED KING

Rasa squirmed in her arms. What could she say? The truth would only cripple him. Better to keep that arrow in her quiver until the target was worth hitting. Instead, she looked her teacher in the eye, begging him to believe her. "Have faith, Laird. We serve God, still."

Did his face soften then? A little? Perhaps. But it was not enough. Severianos shook his head and turned back to Weyr with another sigh.

"I am sorry, Your Majesty. I wanted to believe there was some misunderstanding, some trick that I did not comprehend, but neither of them has been able to offer anything akin to reason. On behalf of the Order, I release them both into your custody to stand trial for their crimes."

"Thank you, Laird. I appreciate your candour, and your counsel, as always." Weyr turned to the guards. "Escort the laird back to his chambers. And give me a minute alone with the prisoners."

"Majesty?" the guard to his right asked. "Is that wise?"

"Oh, don't worry, son," Weyr answered. "I think young Samily fully understands who holds the power here."

A nod of respect, and the guards retreated from the room, four of them surrounding the Green Laird like walking bulwarks. There was his power. Severianos was an unwitting captive, holding Samily to ransom.

The door closed, leaving Samily and Cyrra facing the demon summoner, with Meristan and Rasa both helpless. She would not fail them. She stiffened, ready for whatever Anhel Weyr should do next.

His grin was no longer benevolent. It was sadistic. Triumphant. He raised his left hand, turned it slowly upwards and spoke. *"Nochdadh."*

In front of Cyrra, a hulking shape appeared from nowhere. A beast with skin of the deepest midnight blue, spikes protruding from its limbs like violent armour. Huge alabaster horns curled back over its head, and its blank white eyes somehow burned with malice. Its bulk was so great it had to crouch beneath the ceiling. Samily's blood turned cold. She could not defeat that thing unarmed.

"You didn't think I'd left the Great Bear unattended, did you?" Weyr sneered. "How else would I know when you'd arrived?"

Heaven, had it been there all along? An invisible sentry? She had no idea a demon could have such a power. Or was it Weyr? She looked again to the skull clutched in his fist. What greater powers had the relic granted him?

A tapping sound then. Cyrra's heel, clicking against the floor. Every inch of Samily's training told her the woman was about to strike. That was a mistake. "Captain. Stand down."

Cyrra turned her head, her eyes wide. S'grace, she was going to do it anyway.

"*Marbhadh i.*" Weyr nodded casually at Cyrra, and the demon lunged forward. She tried to dive from its reach, lurching toward Weyr, but the thing's huge hand caught her by the left leg. It yanked her from her feet, dangling her upside down.

"No!" Samily cried. "Stop!"

The demon grabbed Cyrra's head with its other hand and, with a gut-wrenching crack and a wet tear, ripped the woman in half.

It raised both arms, showing the severed halves of the woman's body like trophies to its master. She'd come apart at the waist, beneath her armour. Her upper body hung like a visceral ghost, trailing entrails. From its other hand, her legs dangled, intestines in a heap at its feet.

Samily prayed it had been a quick death.

"*Air ais*," she whispered. Just in case.

Weyr did not even turn to look at the macabre display. His eyes were on Samily. She would not scream. She would not cry. She would not give this man anything. A good woman had gone to God too soon. Another one, in Weyr's name. She would not become the next. Yet.

"Do we understand each other, young lady?" the false king asked, all pretence of benevolence now gone.

"Wha's, wha's...?" Meristan roused again from his stupor.

"It is all right, Master. You may rest." She hoped her voice would be enough. Having him settled, no threat to Weyr, may be the best way to keep him safe. He seemed comforted by her words and went to lie back down. Rasa wriggled in Samily's arms, forcing herself upright, her damaged wing sticking out at an unnatural angle.

"I believe I understand you, Anhel Weyr."

"Good." Weyr waved a hand at the demon and it dropped Cyrra's remains to the stone with a wet slop and a metal clatter. The demon summoner stepped slowly toward her, silently padding around her as he spoke. "It took me longer than it should have. To figure you out. It was the next morning. Dawn came too early. And I realised I had lost time. *Time.*"

S'grace, he had known about her since then? Since he tried to kill Allandria, Aranok and her at Wrychtishousis? Her time skill had been all that saved them. She'd hoped, maybe, that Weyr would not have understood. But as Aranok had said many times, Weyr was a cunning man. That was what made him so dangerous. Samily said nothing.

"That is some skill, girl. I mean, changing people's memories, that's one thing... Oh, I don't suppose you've got one of our charms, have you?"

Samily's skin crawled as she felt his finger at the back of her neck, sliding beneath her armour, then around her throat and down the front.

"No. Good. That's good." Weyr slid his clammy fingers from her neck and Samily shivered involuntarily. Rasa croaked an objection. "Memory magic is one thing, but actually turning back time? *Undoing* what's been done? That, my girl, is power." He stood facing her, not three feet away. "Power I can't have wielded against me."

Another jerk of the arm and the demon grabbed Meristan from the sofa, taking hold of him as he had Cyrra. "No!" Samily screamed, lurching toward them. "No! Stop! Stop!"

And it did. It stopped, frozen.

But just like before, so did she.

It was a moment before Weyr spoke. "Well! What is this?" He moved to stand in Samily's gaze, between her and the demon. "This is... wonderful! You should not have been able to... I am impressed!" With each final word, Weyr gave an exaggerated single clap. "I had intended to... But this... this might be better."

Weyr moved directly in front of her, tossing something back and forth between his hands below her line of sight. Rasa squawked and flapped fruitlessly in the nook of her right arm. Whatever he was holding, she didn't like it.

"This has the whiff of wild magic about it. The stuff of children! You're *new* to this, aren't you? Well!" Weyr paced slowly around her again, moving out of her line of sight. But she could feel Rasa shifting to follow him. "So, I think, maybe, you're not sure how to get out of this little rut, are you, Lady Samily? Maybe you're stuck like that. Is that right? Isn't that a conundrum? Because, of course, if you get yourself out of this mess, you'll release my demon too, right? And then Molloch might just snap God's Own Blade in half."

*Molloch?* This demon had a name?

Samily's mind raced, searching for a way out. Her skill wasn't supposed to work in here, Weyr had said. So why had this worked? Why *this*, of all things? *Why now?*

"So we're going to make a deal, you and I, Samily of the Order of the White Thorns. And here it is. You are going to stay just like this for a few minutes. Just until I can do what I need to. And then, when it's done, I will command my demon to release Meristan unharmed. And you will be free to release yourself from this—what shall we call it—frozen state? Regardless, that is my offer. A simple procedure, and I will be done. Deal?"

*Procedure?*

What on earth did he plan to do to her? Again, Rasa shifted and flapped agitatedly, and Samily was worried she'd fall from her perch, unable to protect herself from the fall with one broken wing. But what could she do? He was right. If she released herself, the demon would kill Meristan. She had no choice. Whatever Anhel Weyr intended, she would endure.

"I'm going to take your continued silence as agreement, Lady Samily." Weyr stepped toward her and she fought an instinct to flinch away from this vile man. If she moved, if she freed herself, Meristan would join Cyrra. She must stay calm. Calm and still.

"And look at that, you've even left your mouth open for me."

# CHAPTER 36

"Is that him?" Vastin breathed, terrified of speaking any louder for fear of alerting a guard to their presence. They'd been wandering the castle for at least an hour, and someone was going to get suspicious eventually. Darginn's credibility would only stretch so far, surely. They'd found the kitchen, been sent to the dining hall and found it empty bar servants clearing up. Even if they located the Green Laird, if he was in the king's company, there was no way they could approach him. The thought of facing Anhel Weyr left a cold pit in Vastin's guts. He hated the man, but he was also deeply afraid of him.

But maybe this was their chance. An older man in modest clothing was walking below them, surrounded by four huge guards. He carried a sizeable sword on his belt. Vastin, Darginn and Ismar leaned on the low wall, watching as he crossed the hallway below, toward the bottom of the stairs they'd just climbed.

"Could be," Darginn whispered back. "Looks like the man Samily described."

"How do we find out?" Ismar asked.

Darginn stood upright. "Like this." The messenger hurried back down the steps. "Laird Severianos? Is that you?"

The old man stopped and looked up, half in surprise, half in expectation. His face changed to confusion when he obviously didn't recognise Darginn. "Yes."

It was him! Now they just had to get him away from those guards. *Just.*

"Darginn Argyll, Laird. King's messenger." Darginn reached the bottom of the steps and stopped as the two guards facing him half drew their weapons. "No threat, my friends. Here, look."

He took something from his pocket and offered it in an open hand. One of the guards stepped forward, looked down at it and gave a dismissive nod. Darginn tucked it away again. The guard stepped back into place. None of them made space for Darginn to reach the Green Laird.

"What can I do for you, Darginn Argyll?" the laird asked.

"Well, eh, it's a delicate matter, actually, Laird. Would it be possible to have a word in private?"

Severianos looked at his guards and nodded. "Yes, fine." He went to step forward, but the other guard at his front raised a hand to block him and silently shook his head.

"Excuse me, son." Severianos pushed the guard's hand down.

"Sorry, Laird," the guard answered. "King's orders. You're not to be left alone with anyone. For your protection."

The Green Laird looked to Darginn with a smile and put his hand gently on his sword. "No offence, son, but this man is no more of a threat to me than you are." *Ouch.* "Now, may I please pass?"

Both forward guards turned to face him. "Sorry, Laird, but no," the same one said.

*Now what?*

Severianos opened his hands in defeat. "Seems we are held at the king's pleasure, Darginn Argyll."

"Well, eh, all right…" Darginn stumbled, looking up at Vastin and Ismar for help. Vastin had an idea. Probably a really bad idea. But maybe…?

"We've a package for you, Laird!" Vastin held out his right hand toward Ismar. When he felt nothing, he turned and nodded urgently at the man.

"You sure?" Ismar mouthed.

Vastin shrugged. He was not at all sure, but he didn't have a better idea.

A moment later, he was rushing down the steps with a bundle wrapped in cloth, which he held out to Darginn with what he hoped was a confident smile. Darginn's eyebrows met in the middle as he looked down, then up at Ismar. His son gave a barely noticeable shrug. It was a huge risk. But they might not get another opportunity, and they had to get Severianos out of there. Tonight.

"Aye. All right." Darginn took the package from Vastin and stepped toward the Green Laird. "It's just this, Laird. A wee gift."

"From whom?" Severianos asked.

"Eh, well, if you open it, Laird, you'll see." Darginn held it out. His hand was shaking.

*Come on, come on.*

Severianos went to take it, but one of the guards moved first, snatching the bundle from Darginn's hand.

*Shite!*

He opened the cloth and lifted the leather strap. The memory charm dangled in front of him. "What is it?"

"Well, as I say, it's a gift. For the laird." Darginn shifted on his feet. Vastin's heart threatened to burst from his chest. They just needed him to touch it. Just long enough for...

"No." The guard grasped the little yellow ball in his fist. "Not until I know what it is. Or the king says so."

*Shite!*

Wait.

The guard was holding it.

Vastin looked up to Ismar and mouthed, "Say it."

"What?" He looked befuddled with fear.

"Say it," Vastin urged him again.

Four swords slipped from their sheaths.

"Say it!" Vastin called out loud. "Now!"

"*Chor!*" Ismar blurted.

The guard holding the charm gave a low moan and slumped against the wall. The other three closed ranks around Severianos. "Sorcery!" one of them cried.

"Dracken. Dracken! Are you all right?" another asked urgently.

The stricken guard—presumably Dracken—looked as if he were

watching faeries flutter about his head. "I...Is this...? What is this?" He held up the charm, addressing the question to Ismar.

"Truth," the *draoidh* answered. "Just truth."

"Dracken!"

The guard looked up from where he now sat against the wall, as if he'd never seen the others before. "It's...No...He needs to see this." Dracken slid himself up the wall and made to offer the charm to Severianos.

"No!" The other guard batted it away, sending it skittering across the floor. Vastin was after it as soon as he heard it click on stone. He scrambled onto his knees, grasping the charm for dear life. Hells, this was getting messy!

"Right. You three. You're coming to the king." The first guard stepped toward Darginn, sword levelled at his gut.

The messenger raised his hands sheepishly. "All right, son. No need for violence, eh?"

"You! Down here!" the guard barked at Ismar. He looked fearfully at his father and slowly moved down the steps. Vastin got back to his feet. What now?

"Dracken!" he said. "Dracken, you need to tell him. Dracken? Please?"

Dracken seemed to be more in control of his senses now. He put a hand on the other guard's arm. "He's right. Hudlow. He's right. He's..." With a wet *hurk* Dracken stopped and slumped to the floor. One of the other guards, the quiet one, pulled his sword from Dracken's back. Hudlow turned, eyes wide. "What did you do? In the name of God, what have you done?"

The guard's entire body trembled, shimmered and transformed into a spindly grey thing with a nightmarish grin full of teeth.

"Dear God!" cried Hudlow, raising his weapon in defence. "Demon!"

Then it was chaos. The demon lunged at Hudlow and the guard slashed frantically, reeling backwards. Darginn retreated up the stairs, shooing Ismar back with him. Vastin was on the wrong side of the demon, though. He was cut off.

The remaining guard stood across Severianos, trying to pin him back against the wall. But the old man was having none of it, sidestepping him with graceful ease and drawing his own sword. "Please, son, get out of the way."

Now was Vastin's chance. While he had a clear shot. "Catch!" He tossed the charm at Severianos, and the old man clutched it out of the air with his left hand. "Ismar!" Vastin pointed furiously at the man. "Now!"

"Now?" he asked, gesturing to the demon. He had a point. Maybe they needed the Green Laird—and his blade. The demon was frantically clawing at Hudlow, backing him up against the bottom of the stairs. The guard might not last long. But it had to be now.

"Yes! Now!"

"*Clìor!*" Ismar's voice wavered with fear.

The demon snapped its head toward the *draoidh* and shrieked again. *Oh shite!*

Darginn and Ismar had nothing to defend themselves with. Vastin looked frantically for anything he could use as a weapon. His eyes settled on Dracken, still bleeding on the floor. He dived toward the stricken guard, grasped the hilt of his sword and turned to face the demon. "Hey! Bastard! Hey! Over here!"

The demon turned, growling. "Come on!" Vastin waved the sword provocatively. If it came at him, at least...

It leapt, so quickly, so fast, he didn't even have time to think.

A nudge at his hip sent him sideways and he stumbled, looking back to see the Green Laird step forward and skewer the demon through its chest. He drew the blade back, dripping with black ichor, and the thing stumbled, staring venomously. The Green blade cut the air again and the demon's head dropped to the stone with a dull thud, followed quickly by its body.

"Oh, thank God." Darginn relaxed the arm he held across his son.

Vastin was about to agree, but movement to his left startled him into silence. He barely managed a warning "No!" as the other guard lunged at Severianos. The old man spun away from the blow—God knows how he even knew it was coming—but grunted in pain as the blade still made contact with his side. He brought his own blade around in an arc and took his assailant's sword arm off at the shoulder.

Damn, it was sharp!

The man screamed in pain and collapsed to his knees, pawing at his lost limb as if he might put it back on with the other. Only for a moment, though, before his eyes rolled in his head and he dropped to the floor.

"S'grace," said Severianos, holding his right hand across his left side. "I suppose this is what armour is for." Blood seeped through his fingers and a red bloom grew on his moss-green shirt. The old man stumbled to the steps and sat.

"Let me see, let me see!" Darginn scrambled down the steps.

"What the Hell is going on?" Hudlow asked. Vastin had forgotten he was there. The guard was planted against the wall but seemed unharmed. His armour, covered in deep gouges, had taken the brunt of the demon's attack.

"Eh, Ismar, can you?" Darginn nodded toward the guard as he assessed the Green Laird's wound.

"Oh. Oh, aye, yeah." Ismar started back down the steps. "Where's the charm?"

"Laird?" Vastin asked.

"Oh, the ball? I dropped it, I'm afraid. Over there."

Vastin's heart skipped. The charm. Samily had entrusted it to them so that they could restore Laird Severianos's memory, but she had been extremely clear how important it was, and that it was vital they did not lose it. Under any circumstances.

And now he couldn't see it. Vastin rushed over to where Severianos had stood when he caught the charm—when Ismar had cast the spell that restored his memory—but there was no sign of it. He dropped to his hands and knees. Hells, how long would they have before some other guard, some servant came by—someone must have heard the noise, surely? They might only have minutes. Where was it?

And then he stopped breathing.

*Oh Hell. Oh God, no.*

A scattering of yellow shards lay beside the one-armed guard.

"Darginn...?" he managed.

"Aye, son?" He was distracted. Busy with the Green Laird's wound. But this was so much worse.

"It's...it's broken. Crushed."

"What?" Darginn was at his back in a moment. "Oh shite. All right, all right, it's all right. Listen, scoop it all up, aye? Get it in a pouch. Samily'll be able to...put it back. Right?"

Of course. Of course she would. It was fine. It was fine! Vastin frantically scooped up every fragment he could see and poured them into his empty coin purse. Samily would fix it.

"I'm afraid that's going to be a problem," said the Green Laird. "I've been a fool. Samily is in Weyr's custody, along with Meristan and the metamorph. And the soldier that was with her."

"No. How?" Darginn paused wrapping the rags he'd torn from one of the dead guards around the old man's waist.

"He knew they were coming. And somehow, he knew they'd arrived. We were taking tea in his antechamber and he just suddenly stood up and...he knew. And now he has them."

"What the Hell are you all talking about?" Hudlow asked.

Darginn ignored the guard. "Hells. We have to rescue them."

"No." Severianos shook his head gravely. "None of you are fighters—though you've got promise." The old man nodded to Vastin, and he felt a tingle of pride that seemed inappropriate. "I need a medic, and whatever your *draoidh* skill is..." He looked up at Ismar. "You're inexperienced. Correct?"

Ismar nodded silently.

"Indeed. And we would need that charm to show this one the truth, correct?" Severianos tilted his sword toward Hudlow, and Ismar nodded again. "Right. We are in no position to fight our way to the king's tower, where Samily and Meristan are held. For now, we're going to have to make an expeditious retreat."

It occurred to Vastin that the Green Laird was handling his memory restoration incredibly well. Maybe the best he'd seen. Certainly better than his own. And he must have had a lot changed. Samily had told them her teacher was wise, but this was...pretty incredible. And he hadn't even introduced himself yet.

"Sir? I'm Vastin. I'm...a blacksmith."

"Are you now?" The man's eyes raised with a touch of light in them. "Well, that's something else I like about you. I assume you are all allies of King Mynygogg?"

"Aye," said Darginn, finishing the makeshift bandage job. "This is my son, Ismar."

"Mynygogg?" Hudlow blurted. "That's it." He stood tall and raised his sword toward the Green Laird's head. "You're coming with me to the king…"

With barely a flick of his wrist, Severianos's blade disarmed Hudlow, his sword crashing to the stone. "Young man"—he stood slowly, with a groan as pain clearly bit him—"never raise your sword unless you are prepared to strike with it. Now, just listen. This is complicated, but you're going to need to trust me. You have been spun an elaborate lie. And while we can't currently unpick that for you, you are in danger. You were not meant to see this." Severianos gestured at the dead demon. "And now that you have, you will be a problem. If you report this to the king, you will be executed, or at best imprisoned. So you have two choices, as I see it: Help us escape or run for your life. Choose quickly."

That was a lot of information, simply put. The guard paused for a moment, then bent as if to pick up his sword. Severianos's blade came up again, just slightly, and the old man shook his head in warning. With that, Hudlow ran, disappearing back the way they'd come. Vastin had sympathy for the man, even more for Dracken, who'd got a sword through the back for his trouble. Bloody demons. Another death on Anhel Weyr's tally.

"Right. I hope you all have an escape plan," said Laird Severianos. His voice was strong, but his face was pale. He needed rest.

"Well, aye, we did," said Darginn. "But it's buggered." Aye, it definitely was. There was no way they were going to casually walk out of there under the Green Laird's authority now. Not after what had just happened. And if Hudlow did go to the king… "But there's another way. The sea escape. A tunnel that'll bring us out at the back of Grey Rock. There are rowboats, for transporting folk to ships. If we wait till dark, we could row to the harbour. But, wi' your wound, Laird…"

"Fine plan." Severianos clapped Darginn on the shoulder. "I have survived worse than this. Where are we going?"

"The escape's through the chapel, Laird," the messenger answered.

"Ah, that I am familiar with," said Severianos. "Let's get there quickly, before Weyr thinks to look for me."

# CHAPTER 37

"I thought this was a cult or something." The woman laughed nervously. Aranok understood her worry. Mynygogg had insisted he should be there when they were clearing the city guards' memories. He thought it was important they see him, know he was there, well, and more importantly, with them. The two of them and Allandria had set up in a back room in the Guard's headquarters, snuck in by Bak in the early morning. It must have been for interrogating suspected criminals, he reckoned, because it was sparsely furnished and not a little intimidating. Basically a stone arch with no window, a bench and a few hanging lamps. But it was perfect for their needs now. Nobody peeking in from outside.

Bak was bringing people in one at a time to go through the process. They gave them the fake charm first and waited for nothing to happen. Presumably if Anhel had agents here, they would pretend to have their memories restored by the false charm. If they didn't, it was a safe assumption they weren't working for him. Safe-ish. Especially when they then reacted to the real charm.

Aranok had thought to have a bucket brought in for those who lost their breakfast. Bak insisted on dealing with it each time it was needed. Which was fine, if it meant Aranok didn't have to.

In order to prevent the chaos of a guard recognising one of them and causing a riot before their memory was restored, they were all wearing their hoods up and scarves about their faces.

It did, indeed, have something of a cultish feel about it. Aranok might have assumed he was to be assassinated if he came into a room like this. So he tried to make his eyes as welcoming and friendly as possible when he greeted people. Which might have been making it worse.

The woman before them—*Annika? Something like that*—smiled awkwardly and, seeming to suddenly realise she was before the king and his envoy, snapped into a salute.

Mynygogg stepped forward and offered a hand to shake instead. "Please, that's not necessary, Akani."

*Akani!*

She took it hesitantly but stood a little taller as she did. "Your Majesty. I...I can't believe all this. How are you? Are you well?"

She was young to be in the guard. Maybe twenty. Her blond hair reminded him of Samily, and he wondered what she was doing now. Healing folk at the hospital, maybe? She should be back with the Blackened victims by now.

"Fine, thank you," Gogg answered. "It's kind of you to ask."

"What...what are we going to do? How are we going to...?" Akani sputtered.

"Captain Bak will explain everything. But I'm pleased to have you on our side, Akani. Thank you. I look forward to speaking to you again soon." Mynygogg's tone was warm but final. He wasn't inviting further conversation. They didn't have time for him to chat at length to everyone. The plan was for him to address the Guard in a group later. For now, they needed to get through as many people as possible.

Bak ushered Akani out of the room as she offered a walking, wide-eyed half bow to them all.

"She was sweet," Allandria said once the door was closed. She pulled her scarf back up in preparation for the next person. "Bless her for asking how you were."

"Yes." Mynygogg smiled brightly. "It's good to be reminded who we're doing this for."

It had been heartening to see the fondness people had for Mynygogg, once they remembered who he was. Not just the due deference his station required but honest, genuine warmth for a man who had tried to make their lives better. Aranok would usually have expected at least a few folk to be a bit more prickly toward "the *draoidh*," but even that hadn't really materialised. "The good *draoidh*," his father had called him. And that was still bitter. With everything Allandria had said to him the other night, about his father being an arsehole... she wasn't wrong. But what he'd said, about how people in Mournside saw him—one of their own, ascended to the royal court... Odd how people saw glory reflected back on them when a person who happened to be born near them had the audacity to succeed. As if somehow their own lives were vindicated. *"One of our own."*

Now wasn't the time to be surly about it. That odd parochial pride was doing them a favour right now.

The door opened again and Bak ushered in the next candidate. A man, maybe thirty at most. Tousled, dark brown hair, high cheekbones and mahogany eyes. A scar across his right ear. Lucky to take a blow that close to the head and get away with it.

"This is Feroul." Bak closed the door behind him and stood guard before it, as he'd been doing all morning.

Feroul scanned the three of them suspiciously. "What's happening here?"

For the umpteenth time that day, Bak repeated the script. "It has come to my attention that the Guard may have been infiltrated by an enemy spy. We have developed a way to test for that, and these people are here to administer the test on behalf of the king. It will only take a minute."

Their thinking was that this would alert any actual "spies" to be on guard—and give them the forewarning they might need to be ready to fake their own memory returning.

"How's that work?" Feroul asked, no less suspicious for the introduction.

"This man is a *draoidh*." Bak indicated Aranok. "He will ask you to hold a charm and then he will speak a *draoidh* word. If you are the spy, the charm will glow."

A nonsense. No magic could root out guilt. But most people didn't know that.

"I've never heard of magic like that."

Well, that was the first one today to query it.

"Few have." Aranok hoped he sounded suitably authoritative. "Rare, and well guarded. It will only take a moment. Please hold this." He offered the little glass bauble.

Feroul looked at it, then up to Aranok's eyes and back. Then he slowly closed his hand about it.

"*Clìor.*"

Nothing.

For a moment.

Then Feroul bucked his head backwards and yanked the charm away, slipping its leather cord out of Aranok's fingers.

*God damn it.*

He made an odd, nasal *nnnnnnn* sound, grabbing his forehead with his free hand. Aranok was torn between the ridiculousness of it and being livid that they'd found their first traitor. He glowered sideways at Allandria, saw the same mix of amusement and anger reflected back at him.

"What the fuck are you doing?" he asked as the man sunk to his knees, pressing his hands to his temples, still making that bloody stupid humming noise.

"I...I..." Feroul stuttered.

"Get up, man!" Bak snapped. "There's nothing wrong with you."

The captain was less than pleased to learn one of his people was working for the enemy.

Feroul looked up at him, confused and fearful. "But...my memories...I..."

"That's not a memory charm. This is." Aranok held up the real thing briefly, before tucking it back inside his leathers. He'd not have it vulnerable to this idiot. "But you shouldn't even know it exists."

Panic set on the guard's face as he tried to calculate his way out of the trap he'd sprung. Panic, and then desperation.

He lurched forward onto his feet, throwing himself at Aranok as he tried to draw his blade. Aranok placed one foot back to brace himself and watched as the idiot bounced off his charged armour, landing in a heap farther back than he'd started.

Allandria was straight at him with a knife in his face. "Don't do that again."

Well, this was the reason they'd created this whole farce in the first place. But far from pleased it had worked, Aranok was just disappointed. Finding yet another of Weyr's pawns only confirmed there would be more.

"Hand me your blade," Allandria growled. "Slowly."

Feroul picked up the sword and slowly offered it hilt first. Allandria drew it away and stepped back but kept both weapons ready.

"Get up!" Bak grabbed the guard's shoulder and yanked him onto his feet.

"Wait. Please." Mynygogg removed his hood and lowered his scarf. Bak held his man still. "Do you know who I am?"

"No," Feroul answered.

"My name is Mynygogg." Recognition lit fear in Feroul. But he said nothing. "Can you tell me why you're working for Anhel Weyr? I'd like to understand. Is it money?"

Of course it was money. It was always money.

Feroul swallowed hard. Bak jostled him like an unruly child. "Answer the king."

Feroul looked instead to Aranok. "You're the envoy, aye?"

Aranok lowered his own hood and scarf, awaiting the inevitable bigotry. "I am."

"Why aren't you with us, then? Why are you serving under a man who doesn't protect your own kind?"

Well. That was not what he was expecting.

"You're *draoidh*?" Mynygogg asked.

No, if he was, he'd have used his skill when he was discovered, not charged blindly at what was clearly enchanted armour. So, what...?

"My brother," said Feroul. "My little brother."

Mynygogg softened, almost sagged. "Aye."

"That's not an excuse," said Aranok, aware of the defensive tone. "Not for treason."

"You were supposed to be the difference." Feroul was throwing verbal daggers at Aranok. "You were supposed to make it better."

"No. That's not fair," said Mynygogg. "Don't blame him. Blame me. Aranok wanted to move faster. Do more. Make bigger changes. I was the one holding back. Going slowly. Those were my choices. At every stage, in every way, Aranok was an advocate for *draoidhs*. All *draoidhs*. And he was right. I should have listened."

That was even less like what Aranok had been expecting. They'd butted heads over this often. And in fairness, Mynygogg had conceded that maybe he'd been slow to act, but this...this was a full-throated acceptance of responsibility. And Aranok had no idea what to do with it. So he said nothing. But he looked at Allandria and saw the same gravity in her reaction.

"Well, good," said Feroul. "So we're better off with a *draoidh* on the throne, aye?" Again, he was answering Mynygogg but looking at Aranok.

Bak rattled him again. "Mind your tongue."

"Please, Captain, let him go. He has a right to speak," said Mynygogg. Unarmed, the man was no threat anyway. He'd barely been a threat while armed. With a brief hesitation, Bak did as asked and stepped back. Feroul dusted himself off and stood as proud as he could manage.

"Thank you."

Aranok wanted to scream at him, tell him what an arsehole Anhel was, how he'd murdered *draoidhs* to get what he wanted...But Mynygogg's record of getting through to people was a damn sight better than his. So he shut up and watched.

"What's your brother's name?" Gogg asked.

Feroul recoiled a little. "Rather not say."

"Of course. You're worried about retaliation. I understand. Wise. So, how old is he?"

"Nineteen," Feroul answered cautiously. "Twenty, in spring."

"What's his skill?" the king asked.

"Physic."

"Ah! Fairly rare, yes?" Gogg addressed the question to Aranok. He shrugged noncommittally. Rarer than some. About the same numbers as earth *draoidhs*. Both much rarer than nature. "At the university, is he?"

Again, Feroul turned defensive. Which meant yes.

Mynygogg raised a hand. "It's all right, you don't have to answer. Aranok—physic *draoidhs* at the university?"

What was he asking? If he knew them? Not by name, except for Opiassa. They'd been invaluable allies against...Oh, *of course*.

That's what he meant.

Aranok turned to Allandria. "Were any physic *draoidhs* killed in the attack on Traverlyn?"

She immediately understood where they were going. "I'm not sure. Maybe? Definitely several nature *draoidhs*. And Principal Keft, of course."

That still hurt. He hadn't particularly liked Keft, but he'd been an ally and he'd died fighting beside them. Saved the library too. But that wasn't a hole Aranok had time for.

"Of course." He nodded thoughtfully.

"Attack?" Feroul asked. "What attack?"

"Anhel Weyr attacked Traverlyn," said Aranok. "You know the Thakhati?" A tentative, nervous nod from Feroul. "Thousands of them. God knows how many dead. Many *draoidhs*. We barely survived. If not for the White Thorns the town would've been overrun."

"No. No." Feroul shook his head desperately. "Janaeus said Traverlyn would be left alone. He said he would *never* attack a *draoidh*."

*Except me.*

"Janaeus is dead," said Mynygogg. "Anhel Weyr is *not* Janaeus."

"And you killed him!" The guard turned on Aranok, spittle flecking his lips.

Aranok involuntarily took a step back, more from the accusation than the man.

"No. He did not. That was my decision too." Mynygogg put a hand on Aranok's back. "My envoy had nothing to do with it and argued that it was wrong. He may yet be proven correct, but I made that decision on the evidence before me."

Feroul turned on Mynygogg, less frantic, breath slowing. "So what I'm hearing is that *he* should be on the throne."

"Careful," Bak growled.

That was a whole garden full of weeds they could get lost in. Aranok looked at Allandria and she flashed a glint of recognition. Mynygogg took a deep breath.

"Perhaps. You're not the first to have that thought. But I'm afraid it is still a distinctly small opinion. Too many people still hate *draoidhs*, even with the man who was instrumental in liberating the country from Hofnag at the king's right hand." He was speaking to Feroul, but it felt like the words were for Aranok now. "Truthfully, it could have been either of us. Aranok on the throne; me his envoy. But the country is where it is, and rather than one of two men who want to make the country better for everyone, including—no, *especially draoidhs*—we have a self-centred, egotistical bastard who'll murder anyone that stands between him and power. Is that what you want?"

Feroul looked away, down at the ground. Anywhere but at the man before him. "No. But..."

"But you don't believe me," said Mynygogg. "Fine. What about this: We have a messenger coming here before long. Write a letter to your brother. She'll deliver it, if she can, and bring back a reply. Fair?"

Feroul was silent, still looking about the room as if for some magical answer to appear. He finally settled on Aranok with a pleading expression.

"Don't look at me," he said flatly. "I was going to throw you in gaol and try you for treason." And maybe beat some information out of him. Mynygogg obviously had his own ideas.

"So, what... what happens to me?" Feroul was much more civilised now. Cowed, maybe. Saw there might be a way out for him. Maybe Aranok had been wrong.

"That depends on you." Mynygogg gestured to Aranok. "Either you go to gaol. Or you work with us. Tell us what you know. Help us take the country back."

Was that a good idea? Could they trust him? Aranok was extremely sceptical, though he had to admit, a part of him liked that the fool's motivation was actually to improve things for his brother. His *draoidh* brother.

Assuming it was all true, of course.

"Ow!" Feroul yelped, and they all jumped. But there was nothing wrong that Aranok could see.

Then the man held out his right hand piteously. The fake charm. Shattered, the glass sparkling amidst the pooling blood in his palm. "I didn't... I didn't mean to..."

"God damn it." Aranok sighed. Now they needed another fake. Which meant wasted time.

"It's fine, it's fine." Mynygogg waved for calm. "We can replace it. Captain, you'll arrange medic care?"

"Aye, sire." Bak turned and left, closing the door sharply behind him.

"Feroul? What do you say? Are you with us?" Mynygogg asked.

"I don't know." The guard dropped the broken glass to the floor, deep red droplets trailing after it. "Maybe. I want to... Grancit. I want to speak to Grancit. Please."

"Grancit? That's your brother?" Mynygogg's tone was paternal now. Comforting.

"Aye," Feroul answered.

"Agreed." Mynygogg turned to Aranok. "Let's find him a room. A secure room, not a cell. But we'll keep it under guard, yes?"

He'd do well to find guards prepared to protect him. In Aranok's experience, guards did not take well to traitors in their ranks. Far from it. He'd heard tales. People dragged through town behind a horse. Hung from a windmill, naked, in winter. He might not last long once word of his treachery got out.

And maybe that would be a shame. For all he was a traitor, it was for a good reason. Jan had obviously convinced him he wanted to do good. That Mynygogg—and Aranok—had not done enough. Nirea shouldn't have killed him. It was hard to be angry at this man, despite the sense of betrayal. Some of this actually was their fault.

But not all of it. Not by a long way. And not with intent. There was no malice in their choices.

That was Anhel.

Bak returned with a roll of bandages. "I'm not particularly skilled with..."

"I'll do it." Allandria took the roll, moved to Feroul and waited for him to offer his hand. When he did, sheepishly, she looked it over gently and picked a few shards of glass from his wound. When that was done, she wrapped it carefully. "I think it needs stitching. Better get a proper medic to look at it."

Feroul nodded, almost shaking.

"So, may I ask, sire, what's been decided?" Bak asked.

"Lock him in a private room, guarded by people we've cleared," Mynygogg answered.

Bak nodded. "Aye. And then...?"

"And then—" said Aranok. "Do you know a good glassblower?"

# CHAPTER 38

Meristan rose slowly from slumber. A faint nausea stabbed at his gut, just beneath his ribs, and a matching pain sparked at the back of his head. He smacked his dry lips, but the lingering bite of whisky was absent. How had he earned this hangover?

"Give it a moment." A familiar voice. Not a welcome one. "Your head will clear."

Meristan rubbed his tongue against the roof of his mouth, searching for moisture. Used the tip to wet his lips. Slowly, the room formed about him. He saw his legs, the arms of a low-backed red leather chair. A rug, thick beneath his feet.

But he couldn't feel it. He couldn't feel his legs. Nothing below his waist. "What...?" he croaked, his mind swimming.

*Where am I?*

"Welcome back, Laird Meristan."

*Anhel Weyr.*

Meristan lifted his gaze to see the demon summoner sitting opposite him in an identical chair. He raised a glass as if in toast, his other hand resting on that golden cane. A fire crackled to their side. As Meristan's eyes cleared further, he took in the rest of the decadent surroundings. An intricately carved sideboard topped with fruit, bread and bottles of alcohol. Wood panelling; landscapes of Eidyn's wilds. A decorated bath on a dais in the corner. Double doors leading to a secondary chamber.

This was the king's quarters.

As his mind cleared, Meristan remembered more. He'd been in a room, alone. Confined by Weyr. He'd taken dinner. And then... it became hazy. Samily? Had he seen Samily? Or was that a wishful dream? And...a demon?

"I've given you a tincture." Weyr's voice was a drawl. Slow. But measured. Deliberate. "Clever bastard of a thing. Gives you back your tongue, but not your limbs. Gives us a chance to talk."

Meristan looked down and, right enough, he could see his arms resting on the chair, and his legs, neatly draped over its edge. Feet resting on the floor. But he could no more feel them than he could the table between them, or the open bottle of whisky that sat on it next to an empty glass. The realisation made his head swim.

"What are you doing, Weyr? What is this? Theatrics? Am I to be your audience?"

Weyr's smile was sly, his eyes glinting with delight. Delight in his power. In his leverage. Meristan was at his mercy and he liked it.

"Not at all. I just wanted to lay things out for you. So you understand your position. See where *God* has left you."

A snide dig. There were no witnesses here for his usual performative righteousness. The man had no more belief in God than in faeries. If he despised the Order for killing his demons, he hated Meristan especially. And now he had him.

"God has not *left* me. God is always here. *Waiting*."

That smile again. So certain. So self-satisfied. So aggravating. But Meristan would keep a cool head. Whatever happened now, he would give the demon summoner no further meat to chew.

Heaven, it was strange, not feeling his limbs. He was fleetingly transported to a memory of a nightmare where he was being chased by some unseen terror and desperate to run but his legs felt like they were encased in metal and he could barely lift his feet. His brain screamed at his hands to move, but there was a wall between the two that could not be breached.

"You truly don't see the ridiculousness of it, do you?" the usurper sneered. "The nonsense of a deity invented just to keep the depraved and desperate in line. Fools, the lot of you. Gullible idiots."

He'd already fallen to insults. Meristan wasn't giving him what he wanted, clearly. "And how does that work, in your theory?"

"How does it work? Oh, it's deliciously simple, isn't it? The poor would be in constant rebellion if they believed the meagre existences they scrape together were all they'd ever see. So we invent for them another life, where their suffering will be rewarded. We make suffering a *virtue*, with the promise of wealth ever after. Only then will they tolerate the wealthy and entitled living with golden privies and foreign wines while they struggle to put bread on their tables. An elegant trick, I concede. Easily spotted by anyone with an ounce of cunning."

"And the 'depraved'?" Facilitating the man's ego might give the "tincture" time to wear off, granting Meristan control of his body again. So why not let him wax lyrical with his ill-considered nonsense?

"If a man has no love for others, no care for their lives, and maybe he has a little lust within him? A desire for blood? A longing for viscera? You know the man. If he considers eternal damnation is at the end of his indulgence, perhaps he'll choose against it. Correct?"

"I would certainly hope so. But then, once a man recognises that he doesn't care for the lives of others, I'd argue he's as good as damned already," said Meristan. "What sort of a man murders without remorse?"

Weyr grinned again. "A man who knows there are no consequences. Because nothing matters but this." He spread his hands, indicating the lavish room. "This life and all he can take from it."

"No matter who suffers?"

"Some must lose, for others to win." Weyr toasted again and took a long, slow sip of whisky.

"Then why am I still alive?" Perhaps a dangerous question, but it was the obvious one. Why hadn't Weyr just executed him on sight?

"Because I am a politician now, my laird. Your life is useful to me."

*S'grace*, what fool purpose did this pompous dolt think Meristan might serve for him? "I won't be used by you, Anhel."

"Won't you? Let us see." Weyr lifted a carved wooden box from the low table beside him, placed it on the table between them and slowly slid it forward until it sat on the edge just in front of Meristan. It was about seven inches long and half that wide, and the lid was carved with a pastoral scene of a horse beneath a tree. It had rough edges, as if carved by an enthusiastic amateur.

"What is that?"

Weyr ignored the question as if it hadn't been asked. "Power is such a relative gift, isn't it? A soldier with a sword might dominate a larger enemy with a club, and yet be brought low by a boy with a crossbow. Power is circumstantial. Subjective. And here we are, alone, where a man of your skills, your stature, could easily best me." He gestured to his portly belly and made a show of his untrained muscles. "And yet, here I am with all the power." A tap of his cane on the rug. Either that skull was the relic, or Weyr wanted him to believe it so.

"If power is circumstantial, then it's also fleeting, *Your Majesty*. It comes and goes with the wind."

Weyr leaned in. "Then we must learn to command the wind."

He thought it a cutting barb of wit, based on the glitter in his eyes. Perhaps some of that was whisky. Meristan attempted to move his left arm, just a little, to see if it was any closer to returning. His shoulder came forward the tiniest bit, but nowhere near enough. He was going to need a lot more time. He needed to goad the preening idiot further. "So Aranok is your aspiration, is he? To become as powerful as your old friend?"

The first sign of irritation then. That arrow had cut flesh. "I've already bettered him. I have the crown. He was Mynygogg's lapdog."

"But you only have it because of Janaeus. It was his skill that took the crown, not yours."

"And whose idea do you imagine that was, Laird? Hmm? Skill without intent, without ambition, is just frippery. It takes a mind to apply a talent. A sharp mind to take a country."

"Then why burn it half to the ground first?" Meristan asked.

"There are few more grateful citizenries than those recently relieved of war. And few more pliable. You have to plough a field before you sow your seeds."

"Pfft." Meristan couldn't help the hiss of air that escaped him. The pomposity of the man was insufferable. From what Aranok had told him, Janaeus was the one behind the memory plan. Weyr was just trying to claim it for himself, now that there was nobody alive to refute him. History is written by those who survive. Then again, Janaeus had told Aranok that the heart of devastation was destroyed, and there was a good chance Meristan was looking at it. Maybe neither was a reliable source of the true tale.

"You scoff?" Weyr asked. "Then counter."

"Debating with you would be an entirely fruitless exercise," said Meristan. "Your mind is set. Were you someone I respected, the joust might be an amiable pastime, but as it is, I'm afraid I have no appetite to butt horns."

Weyr stared at him awhile then, and Meristan silently met his eyes, undaunted.

Weyr broke first and sat back. "Fine. Then let's move on to the meat of the conversation."

Meristan tilted his head and raised his eyebrows in acknowledgement.

"I don't need a martyr half as much as I need a disgrace," the *draoidh* continued. "And that is what you're going to be, Laird Meristan of the Order of the White Thorns. You're going to be my useful disgrace."

"Am I?"

"There's not many who could challenge the authority of the crown in Eidyn. Not many who could speak out against the king with any authority. Who would be taken seriously. One who could, thanks to your ubiquitous fantasies, is a White Thorn. And I won't have that, you see."

"You think I'll support you?" Meristan asked. "You're mad."

"Am I?" Weyr cocked his head. He was looking pleased with himself again. He knew something. "Do you know what a *draoidh* can do with a little bit of study? With a little boost to their powers? The possibilities are exciting." He licked his lips aggressively then, as if Meristan were a roast pig. "For example, would you have guessed it is possible to carve charms into the stones of a room that will actually *inhibit* the use of magic?"

"No," Meristan answered honestly. "But there's a very great deal I don't know about magic."

"Indeed, there is!" Weyr said gleefully. "There is *much* you do not know." He paused and sipped at his whisky again, contemplating the glass as if there were something to be learned from it. "And much that

I have learned, in *time*." His eyes flicked up to meet Meristan's on the last word.

*Oh Hell. Samily.*

Meristan took a deep breath, cooling the fire that had sparked in his chest. He looked blankly at the usurper.

"A time *draoidh*," said Weyr. "Very rare thing. Not been one of those in generations, as far as I know. And what a weapon that could be, eh?"

*Damn it.*

He knew. *All right, Meristan, keep the heid.*

"Samily will no more agree to be your weapon than I will, Anhel."

"Oh, she already is...you just don't understand it yet. It's chess. You have to think three moves ahead to win. When General Bielsed presented me with the Green Laird, I had the first move. You, attempting to rescue him, were the second. Then the prey became the trap, and now I have my weapon."

"What are you wittering about, man?" Meristan had let too much worry creep into his voice. But a dark fear was growing in him.

"I knew that even holding your old blacksmith hostage wouldn't be enough to make you disavow the entire Order. So here we are, Laird Meristan. Here's your offer of clemency. I will let you live. You will admit publicly to conspiring against the crown in league with Laird Aranok and the *draoidh* Mynygogg. You will confess that the entire Order was complicit in this conspiracy. In return, I will graciously accept your confession, outlaw the traitorous Order and banish you from Eidyn. Leaving the wise, merciful and godly King Anhel Weyr's reign to begin in earnest."

"Is that all?"

"Yes."

"No." Meristan tried to keep his voice firm, his rejection solid. But Anhel's confidence was unsettling.

Weyr smiled like a cat basking in catnip. He leaned forward and tipped the box. The lid swung open, and with a gentle, wet slap, a lump tumbled out. Weyr laid the box flat again. An odd piece of off-pink meat lay before him, dried blood encrusted around the severed end.

"Is...is that...?" Meristan stuttered.

"Lady Samily's tongue," said Weyr. "She won't be using her skill again."

Fury lit in Meristan then, and with every inch of himself he tried to leap forward, envisioning his hands about Weyr's throat, crushing the life from his eyes. "You bastard son of a goat! I will murder you!" But his limbs were still lost to him, and all he managed was to nearly tip over onto his own lap. "Damn you, Weyr. Face me like a man, you petulant coward! You arrogant shitebag!"

The demon summoner sat back with dramatic wonder. "Such language from a man of God. I can't see why you'd be shocked. This is the way we relieve *draoidhs* of their skills now, is it not?" The faux innocence of his question was a cold dagger. He knew about Shayella. He knew what Samily had done to her.

Weyr's face darkened and he demonstratively turned his glass in his raised hand, the firelight glinting off the amber liquid within. "I take it I have your attention now."

Meristan could find no words. His mind raced, desperately trying to force his damned limbs to respond to him.

"Samily and your metamorph friend, who is presently a quite charming owl, are currently ensconced in my heavily guarded tower, in a room devoid of magic. Well, *their* magic. They are guarded by a very special demon." He tapped the skull atop his cane, drawing Meristan's attention. "It has the rather wonderful ability to become completely *unseen*. Isn't that marvellous? That such a creature could exist?"

Heavens, he had Rasa too! Meristan shook with rage and frustration. But his limbs remained still as the grave.

"If only young Samily could heal her own tongue, she might have a chance against the demon. Ironic, isn't it?"

"Fuck you!" The words burst from Meristan as if from another man entirely.

"They will remain there, safe and well-fed, as long as you agree to my terms. You see? Lady Samily has become my weapon. Against you. And you will be my disgrace, Brother Meristan." He lifted the whisky bottle and poured a measure into the empty glass before Meristan. "Or I will proclaim an execution order on every Thorn and set the army after them. How many will die in that pursuit, do you imagine?"

Hundreds. At least. To kill the Thorns. Maybe thousands.

"I will send a legion of demons to Traverlyn. Beasts such as you have *never seen*, Great Bear. And *then* I will execute Lady Samily. Slowly. While you watch with lidless eyes." Weyr lifted his glass and relished a long, slow drink. "Do we understand each other?"

Meristan's breath came in bursts, an anger he'd never known burning furiously through him. "I will *fucking* murder you!"

"I'm sure you will." The *draoidh* clinked his all but empty glass against the newly filled one. *"Slàinte mhath."*

# CHAPTER 39

*E*ggs. How had Nirea forgotten how good eggs could be? She lifted another forkful into her mouth, savouring the light texture. Ailen was an artist. Too often, Nirea treated food like fuel. Even when she was queen, living in an honest-to-God castle, having her meals prepared by the best cooks in the land, sometimes she'd settled for cheese and bread because it was quick, easy and *there*.

But somehow, Ailen made these eggs fluffier and lighter and just *tastier* than they'd any right to be.

"I don't know what you're eating, Red, but you're smiling like your man's eating you." Quell sat down opposite her with a plate of the same sausage and eggs Nirea had. She lifted one of the sausages and nibbled suggestively on the end.

Nirea almost spat her eggs. "Stop it, you daft bitch. I'm eating breakfast!"

She'd never been a natural early riser, even less so in the deep winter dark, but she'd found herself waking early this last week or so. Maybe the urgency of their task, or the threat of an assassin's blade. Or maybe that she wasn't drinking as much.

After the initial load of lodgers had cleared out, Ailen stopped taking in new ones. It was a sore loss of income, but they'd agreed it was too much risk to have strangers in the building overnight. As it was, every door was bolted and barred, every window latched, every shutter locked tight. And more important, each of them bearing a charm, painted or carved by Quell. They'd made the King's Wark as impregnable as it could be. But they still opened by day, allowing Quell to carry on her facade of prognosticating while clearing minds when she could. Many of those whose minds were cleared came back with others, just like that furious man on the first day. He, himself, was often propping up the bar of an evening, and there was something comforting in that. Wayburn was his name. An old soak who'd made a fortune in the merchant navy and retired to drink it empty. Took nothing but rum and mint, a proper old sea dog's draft.

So far, they'd only come across one man whose memory was unaffected, and Quell had confirmed it was because he'd been offshore when the spell was cast. He hadn't realised there was anything wrong, though, because he simply hadn't had a conversation with anyone about the king. In fact, as a foreign sailor, he wasn't even certain of the king's name. He was only there to trade and get back on his way home—only he'd gotten stuck when the demon appeared in the harbour. Must have just squeezed in before Weyr got it in place. That meant there was a whole shipful of crew in the same situation, milling around Leet.

Sloppy. So Weyr wasn't quite the perfect tactician.

The more she thought on Weyr's plan, the more holes she found. He surely couldn't keep up the lie forever. Not now that Janaeus was dead, anyway.

But maybe that didn't matter. Maybe that was why he'd killed the lairds. And would likely kill more. Taking the throne by force hadn't worked, but holding it by force might, if he put the right buttresses in place. So they were likely racing a clock, to take him down before he could build those reinforcements.

They'd cleared a good few captains in the last week too. People Nirea trusted. And some of the upper echelons of the city guard. All of them had been charged with looking to their people—see who could be trusted and who might be suspect. Anyone in an elevated position compared with where they'd been. Anyone out of place. Anyone a lot better off than they should be.

"Good morning, ladies." Crinn reached his thick arms to a ceiling beam, placing his hands flat against it and stretching his back like a damned bear. The man was huge. Not quite Meristan's size, speaking of bears, but not far off it. He'd warmed to Nirea substantially over the time they'd spent together. Once Ailen got past being pissed off at her for the whole Quell thing, and they started sharing old stories, Crinn seemed to see the love between her and his husband, and decided it was good.

That's how Nirea saw it, anyway. And now that he was more relaxed, she could see what Ailen saw in him too. He was gentle and kind, and a wonderful singer. He may not have Ailen's talent with food, but he could pour a beer, worked hard to keep the place clean, and nobody wanted to pick a fight with him. One night, a drunken argument had almost got out of hand until the farmer who'd nearly swung a punch found Crinn holding his arm. He tried to shake him off, but once he turned to look up at the man, the fire burned out quick. He quietly finished his drink and scuttled off into the night. Crinn didn't even open his mouth. Just the kind of partner you want running a bar. But the way he sang when he thought nobody was listening—he had the voice of a troubadour. Nirea had seen highly paid minstrels in court whose voices were nowhere near Crinn's. He sang with the soul of a man who'd suffered, longed for solace and found it. Love. Nirea's skin rose to goosebumps every time she heard him.

"You ever been in love?" Nirea asked.

Quell sat back, eyes wide. "Holy fuck, Red, I just woke up. Where did that come from?"

Crinn huffed in amusement and seemed to decide this was the time for a graceful exit. He made an abrupt turn and headed for the kitchen.

"I was just thinking, you know, how nice that is." She nodded toward the bar that Crinn had just disappeared behind.

"Aye, well"—Quell lifted the sausage, took a large chunk out of it and spoke through the chewing—"s'not easy to convince anyone to get into a relationship when they're constantly wondering whether you've just tricked them into it."

Of course. She'd said it was a solitary life. It had been thoughtless of Nirea to ask. "I'm sorry. That was a stupid question."

"S'all right." Quell carried on eating through her words. "I get what I need. Had plenty of frolics. Some of them more than once. They just don't remember." A half smile.

God, what a life. No real emotional relationships, just a series of drunken fumbles in stolen beds. The more Nirea got to know Quell, the more she sympathised with her. No wonder she was reluctant to help them. Why should she help anyone when nobody ever helped her?

Nirea might be the closest friend the *draoidh* had had since childhood. And that made her heart break a wee bit.

"It can be better, you know. We can make it better. We *will* make it better."

Quell snorted air. "You can't make people unafraid, Red. You can't *make* them trust."

"No, but we can teach them respect. We can show them."

An exaggerated nod. "You do that, m'lady. I'm going to finish my breakfast."

Nirea laughed and flicked a lump of egg across the table.

"We're going down to the fish market." Ailen came out from behind the bar, slipping on a thick winter coat. It was getting worse every day. Dreich Eidyn damp had fully turned into sharp winter bite. They were getting through firewood at a rate of knots.

Nirea raised her laden fork in front of her mouth. "Get more eggs."

"That's not how a fish market works, m'dear," he said with a cheeky smile. "But I'll see what I can do."

Crinn appeared too, similarly wrapped against the weather. He lifted the bar and Ailen opened each of the three locks before turning to Quell. "Would you let us out please, madam?"

Quell pressed a hand against the sigil she'd carved into the back of the door and muttered some *draoidh* words, as she did every day—always too quiet to be heard. Probably out of habit, Nirea imagined. Her instinct was to hide her nature. Always.

She closed it again behind the men and repeated the action, then slipped the bar back across. She'd just got her arse back on her seat when someone rapped on the door. Quell rolled her eyes dramatically, stood with a huff and went back to open it again. "Pardon me." A deep, male voice. "I'm looking for Nirea? Captain Gert sent me."

Gert. One of the captains of the city guard that they'd cleared. Must be one of his men that he'd decided he trusted, if he'd been given her name and where to look for her.

"You are?" Quell asked.

"Name's Harp, ma'am."

"Harp? Like the instrument?" Quell strummed an imaginary one with her fingers.

"Aye. Thank my mother for that one. She just liked the sound of it."

"Well, don't we all?" Quell turned to face Nirea. "Visitor for you."

With her back to the door, Quell's face turned serious and her eyebrows raised. It was a warning. Nirea had already loosened a blade in her left sleeve. She crossed to the door and found a round, red-cheeked man smiling at her from behind a russet beard. He wore the uniform of the guard—a little tight here, a little shabby there. Kind, warm eyes shone as he asked: "Lady Nirea?"

"What can I do for you, Harp?"

"Captain asked me to deliver this." He produced a folded piece of parchment, sealed with wax in the symbol of Leet. "Said to only put it in your hands."

"All right." Nirea took the letter. "Is that all?"

"Well, em"—Harp looked nervously about him—"he also said you might have something to tell me? About my *future*?"

That was what she'd been waiting for. The sign she'd agreed with those she'd cleared. Send anyone they trusted to come and get their futures told by the *mad witch*. "Come in." She ushered him through the door and closed it behind him, waving a hand at Quell to finish the task of securing it again. "Harp, this is Quellaria. She'll sit with you while I read this."

"Step into my chambers." Quell made a typically dramatic bow with a flourishing wave of her arm, directing the guard to the room they were using for their charade. Harp looked at Nirea nervously, as if waiting for her to confirm Quellaria was serious.

Nirea nodded and smiled. "I'll be right there." Whatever was in the letter, she wanted privacy to read it. That seemed to be enough for him, and Harp took Quell's invitation.

Nirea sat back at the table, pushed her plate away and broke the seal. The letter was written in a surprisingly elegant hand.

> *Your Majesty,*
> *I have, as you asked, been assessing my people. I am confident Harp, who bears this missive, is worthy of our trust. There are a few whose loyalty I find questionable and I am undertaking investigations to ascertain whether they might be in service to the usurper.*

These were dangerous words to commit to paper. She'd be burning this as soon as she'd read it.

> *However, I am afraid I must also inform you of some potentially unhappy news. I have been keeping a watch for the man named Joliander, as you requested. I am sorry to say that the corpse of a man fitting his description was last night fished from the river.*

> *...*
> *Fuck.*
> *No.*
> *Fuck!*

Nirea dropped the letter, hands shaking. He was at sea. Surely he was at sea! She'd only asked Gert to look out for him on the off chance he found his way into the drunk cells. It wouldn't be him. It couldn't be him. It wouldn't be him. Lots of people fit his description. It would be some drunk who fell in after too many rums. She blinked back the tears forming in her eyes and picked up the letter again.

> *I have secured his body in a private room and prevented attempts to have him identified, for the moment, until such time as you might come to make your own assessment.*
>
> *Until then, I remain*
> *Your loyal servant*
> *Captain Gert*

It wouldn't be him. It wouldn't.

Nirea's chest felt like it was going to cave in on itself. Fear. Terror. Fucking fury at that traitorous bitch Madu!

It wouldn't be him. Joliander was off in some foreign port, knee deep in cheap rum and expensive women. He was fine. A man like him did not end up bloated and blue, floating in a river. He was too vital, too alive!

A shuffle of feet behind her. Nirea took a deep breath, composing herself. Wouldn't be right to have Harp's first sight of his queen after having his memory restored be of her quivering like a child.

*It will be fine.*

She turned, and her body stiffened.

Quell's mouth was bound with a gag, her wrists tied together, her eyes silently begging Nirea for help. Harp stood behind her, a knife at her neck.

"My lady," he sneered, his tone now sharp, his eyes hard. "Please don't move."

---

"See, everybody expects an assassin to be lean, shadowy—comes at you out of the dark. At night. Makes it easy to hide right in front of them. I've been watching you for a week." Harp stood behind the chair he'd forced Quell onto, one hand resting almost casually on her shoulder, the other still holding a knife to her throat. Only then did she notice the gloves. Preventing the skin contact Quell would have needed.

Nirea's instinct was to throw herself at the man. Blade against blade. See if he had enough to stop her. But he'd slit Quell's throat before she reached him. And he might already have murdered Joliander.

*Fuck!*

She'd been sloppy. The letter had distracted her, stopped her from following them into the back room. She'd left him alone with Quell. Exactly the thing she'd sworn not to do. And that's likely what the letter was for. To throw her off balance. So she'd make a mistake.

A tiny flare of hope, then, that the letter was a lie.

Maybe.

But that would wait.

The dirk lodged up her left sleeve was inches from her hand, but Harp—if that was his name—had explicitly told her to keep her palms on her thighs. He was a professional. Nirea needed to take control. To get him off balance the way he had done to her.

"So what are we doing here? Are you *boasting*?"

Quell's eyes widened again, and Nirea could practically hear her asking what the fuck she was doing. She had to needle the man. Make him move too far from Quell. Give Nirea time to get to him.

Instead, he smiled. Like an indulgent father at a precocious child.

"Stab yourself in the thigh."

Nirea stared back at him.

He pressed the knife tip into the hollow above Quell's rib cage. She was trembling like she was stood naked on the deck in a sleet storm. "What?" Nirea asked, mostly trying to buy herself more time.

"That dirk up your sleeve. The one you're trying to slip into your hand. Take it out and stab it in your thigh. Now."

"Are you...?" Harp lifted the blade to strike, knuckles white around the grip. "All right, all right, wait!" Nirea raised her hands, begging him to pause. He cocked his head, eyes like cold steel.

*Fuck.*

She scanned the room, looking for some salvation, some trick, some tool she could use to get them out of this.

Nothing.

She was going to have to do it.

Slowly, she pulled the knife from her sleeve with her right hand. Just as she considered throwing it, Harp lowered the blade back to Quell's throat.

He smiled as he saw the thought wither in her eyes. "Carefully. On the outside. Big vein on the inside. That'll kill you quick."

"Why?" Nirea asked.

"Because I told you to, *bitch*."

All right. She favoured her right side, so she'd do it on the left. Not too deep. She could live with that kind of wound. Just had to avoid any big veins, as he'd said. High up, as close to her arse as possible. More fat there. All of this raced through her head, as the bastard smiled back at her. *Waiting.*

"Now," he mouthed again.

Nirea took a deep breath, screamed and jammed the knife into her leg.

Fucking Hells and bastards, it hurt! Pain shot up into her back, down her leg, across her groin. Her left hand juddered and she let go of the handle, leaving it there, sticking out. But she gritted her teeth, clenched her fists and banged one on the table.

She would not scream.

"Good," Harp chimed in the singsong voice of a nanny. "Now, best leave it there. I know where it is and you won't bleed to death."

Nirea's heart raced, her stomach turning sour. Sweat beaded on her hairline. Her body was trying to compensate for the wound. She could feel the blood trickling down inside her clothes, running to pool where her leg met the chair and seeping under. She leaned forward, onto her right side, put her weight on the table to take it off the wound. "I like these trousers. I'm going to make you pay for new ones."

"We'll see." He smirked and pulled a chair alongside Quell's. "Now, I'm going to explain this once. We're all going to sit here patiently until your friends come back. Then I'm going to kill them, one at a time, and you're going to watch."

"Why?" Nirea spat through gritted teeth.

He answered matter-of-factly, as if she'd asked his opinion on the weather.

"Because Lady Madu paid me to make you *suffer*."

It was difficult to say how much time had passed when she heard Crinn's voice outside. No clock in the bar. Ailen didn't want his customers realising how long they'd been drinking.

Nirea was feeling drowsy. Struggling to stay awake. To concentrate.

Three knocks. Then one. The signal they'd agreed.

Now it got complicated.

Harp looked to the door and back at Nirea, questioning. Good. He didn't know everything.

"She needs to let them in." Nirea heard the slur in her voice. Her tongue was thick, her mouth dry.

"Why her?" Harp asked suspiciously.

"Magic. Needs to speak." Nirea mimed removing the gag from her mouth.

That hadn't settled the man's mind. "Why?"

"Look at the door." Nirea nodded toward it. Get him moving. Wondering. Unsure of himself.

Harp huffed and stood, dragging Quell to her feet. "Move."

She stumbled after him, eyes still pleading with Nirea.

The knock again. Louder. Insistent.

Harp traced his fingers over the sigil. Seemed to reluctantly recognise the truth of it. He lifted the bar with one hand, never taking the knife far from Quell's throat. It dropped to the ground with a thunk.

That should alert them. Surely. That something was wrong.

*Come on, Ailen. Be suspicious.*

"Now," Harp whispered. "I'm going to lower this gag, and you're going to quietly open this door. Right?"

Quell nodded piteously.

Harp snagged a finger under the edge of the cloth, pulled it from her lips and tugged it down.

As soon as it was free, Quell jerked her bound hands upwards and something small lurched into the air. Harp took a moment to respond. He'd underestimated her. He thought he'd cowed her.

But as she'd reminded Nirea several times, Quell was a *draoidh*.

"*Brag!*"

A burst of light and a resonant bang as the coin exploded in the air. Nirea instinctively shied away, closing her eyes against the flash, but her ears took in the full explosion and squealed in protest.

A moment of stillness. Of nothing, as sound was lost. When it began to return, she could hear struggling over the ringing. Quell needed help.

Nirea stood, and collapsed back onto the chair as the knife in her hip bit hard. She fumbled back to her feet, this time leaning heavily on her right leg. She felt the warm trickle of blood run down her wounded leg, tickling the crease at the back of her knee.

Limping forward, her eyesight returning, she saw the two of them rolling together on the ground. They'd both taken the explosion in the face, but Quell had been able to close her eyes against it. Her hands were still bound, though.

Banging against the door. Ailen and Crinn were trying to get in, alerted at last by the explosion. They wouldn't get past Quell's magic lock. But by the sounds of it, Crinn was going to try.

"Crinn! Help!" Nirea bellowed, stumbling across the room to where the two bodies rolled together.

Harp knelt above Quell, blade in his right hand. Quell was using her bound hands to hold it off, but his weight was winning. With a scream, Nirea wrenched the knife from her leg and jammed it into Harp's back. He roared and hit her with an elbow, sending her to the floor while he scrambled to reach the blade. Nirea tried to stand, but her legs were water, and now she could feel the flow of blood running freely down into her boot.

She staggered back, caught herself on the edge of a chair. Her hands shook uncontrollably.

Another bang at the door, wood cracking but not giving. If she could just get Quell near enough the door to release the lock…

She forced herself upright, demanding her legs hold. Harp was kneeling over Quell again, the knife gone from his back.

Nirea dropped to her knees and grabbed the assassin's shoulders, pulling him back. The man was a bull—surprisingly solid—much more muscle than she expected under that guard's uniform.

She buckled backwards as Harp's elbow came flying back again to smash her in the face. The world spun as her nose crunched and a tooth burst into her top lip. She reeled backwards, losing her grip on Harp. He lunged forward, bringing his arm down hard, with the sickening wet thud of steel in flesh.

Quell screamed.

Nirea fought to find her balance as Harp's hand came down again, and Quell was quiet.

Now Nirea screamed.

Harp made it to his feet, red blades in each hand—one dripping in their combined blood, one with Quell's. Nirea looked to her friend, and God, the blood. It was everywhere. Her chest was a bloom of burgundy wine.

Bastard!

But Nirea could barely stand. And he had the weapons.

With a final, resonant crack, the front door of the King's Wark splintered and burst. Crinn staggered through the gap with a roar. It took him only a moment to understand the situation and he lunged at Harp, long dagger in his hand.

Harp was taken by surprise, and though he stepped back to give himself some room, Crinn's speed was incredible, catching him once across the chest and again in the side before Harp could even set himself.

Staggering backwards, the assassin threw one of the knives. Crinn batted it away with his blade like a child's toy and kept coming, slashing, stabbing, hacking like a man possessed.

It was over in less than a minute. Harp was bloody carnage on the floor; Crinn stood over him, roaring like a wild beast.

Nirea crawled to Quell, the darkness threatening to overcome her. God, there was so much blood. Wounds in her shoulder and chest. Her face was pale as snow.

Nirea felt a hand on her shoulder. A distant voice.

"Are you all right?"

Ailen. Quell needed them. She needed help, she needed...

Nirea turned to look up, and black closed in around her like a tunnel.

"Medic..." she mumbled as her body surrendered to the dark.

# CHAPTER 40

Eight days since they'd slipped out of Greytoun, rowed to shore and escaped back to Haven Kirk. They couldn't go to Darginn's house. If that guard had reported back to the king—if he'd been paying enough attention to remember Darginn's name—there was a damn good chance his home was now being watched. They couldn't risk going there. That had been hard. The thought that his own home, bought and paid for with his years of service to the throne, might be sacked by the city guard—or even the kingsguard—damned if that wasn't a sore wound. But this mattered more.

And they couldn't risk Vastin's forge either. Too open, too on display, sitting right on Grey Square. No easy way in and out unseen, there—and too many people would notice a fire in that window, since Vastin had been away some time.

They'd been lucky too, in a way. Laird Severianos's wound hadn't healed so well. By the fifth day he was running a temperature, and the angry red wound along his side stank like an eggy fart. But Maither Floreli had some schooling in medicine. She was able to clean up the wound, at least, and pack it with a poultice to draw out the infection. She also had access to some opium for the pain. Severianos claimed it didn't hurt much, but the man had become almost frail in less than a week, and his balance seemed rightly suspect.

They were in no state to be mounting a rescue for their

comrades—assuming they were still alive. That was a topic that hadn't come up. And while Darginn was putting on a brave face for the sake of the boys, he couldn't ignore the dark, gnawing hole that was growing in his guts every day.

So when Maither Floreli had come in after morning service and told them there was to be a major announcement at the town square that afternoon—how could they not go along? Might be their only chance to find out something. Well, through the veil of Anhel Weyr's lies, certainly—but at least they'd have some information. Something to go on. Something.

Thoughts turned to who was best to go. Darginn could well be marked and Severianos was likely one of the most hunted men in the town. There was maybe half a chance Weyr would then go looking for his children, so Ismar was also at risk—which left Vastin. Except the boy had been famous in Traverlyn hospital, what with being Blackened and all. And if Weyr did have people there… Hells, they were all maybe at risk. Maither Floreli offered to go and see what she could learn, but to be honest, Severianos needed her about, and if anyone did come poking around, she would need to be there to fend them off before they looked too hard and found exactly what they hunted.

In the end, they decided Ismar was maybe the least likely to be under scrutiny. The boy offered to go alone, but Darginn couldn't have it. Not after all he'd been through. What if he ran into someone from the New Kirk? What would come of that? What if he *chose* to see them? Could that happen? Maybe. And that "maybe" was enough. So they agreed to something of a compromise.

Darginn and Ismar would go together. Vastin was to stay and help tend Severianos. The two of them had already spent many hours chatting about the intricacies of smithing—when the Green Laird was awake—and the boy was likely the best distraction the man could have from his aches.

Darginn had borrowed some holy vestments, including a hooded robe that was enough to put his face in shadow. He stooped like a much older man and allowed Ismar to "lead" him through the streets. They found a space at the edge of an alley, pressed between a bakery and a leathersmith. A sea of heads between them and the platform. An excited, dreadful murmur. Darginn had stood on many such stages, including that one, delivering news to towns. Plenty of times it had been bad news—and somehow that always drew the biggest crowds. As if the horror had drifted in on the wind, beckoning them all to bear witness.

And that meant he had a face folks might recognise here, which made him extra wary. Still, he couldn't have left Ismar to this alone. And if he was really honest, he had a mind to hear what was said himself. Every word. Sometimes the nuance was in the telling of it.

"What d'you think it'll be?" Ismar whispered, lowering his head.

"Dinnae ken, son. But I'd no be averse to hearing another king was dead."

Ismar's eyes widened and darted to the bodies just in front of them. But it was fine. Not only had he said it quietly, it was no worse than he'd heard whispered amongst expectant crowds like this himself. No matter how popular a monarch was, there was always someone wanted their taxes lower or their prices higher.

If, God forbid, their friends were dead or captured, if it had led to the end of the demon summoner, then at least maybe... No, he couldn't think on that. They were alive; he could feel it in his old bones.

An increase in the murmur until it became more of a hubbub, and a figure rose up the steps. Darginn craned to see if he knew the man—but it was odd. He seemed to be wearing monk's robes.

*Oh God.*

It was Laird Meristan, flanked by a pair of kingsguards. A flurry of emotions. Firstly, thank God, he was alive! But then... what did this mean? What could it mean?

One of the guards raised an arm for quiet and the voices hushed. After an age, when Darginn had begun to wonder if he was ever going to speak, Meristan's deep oak voice reverberated across the square as he looked down at a scroll of paper in his hands.

"Citizens of Haven, and of Eidyn. I am Brother Meristan, formerly head of the Order of the White Thorns."

*Brother?*

*Formerly?*

Ismar turned to Darginn with wide eyes. He recognised it too.

This was bad.

"I come before you to make a confession. I do so of my own free will. I and the Order, led by myself and Severianos, the Green Laird, have been involved in a conspiracy with the former laird envoy and his ally, Mynygogg, to overthrow the throne of Eidyn."

*Fucking Hells!*

Ismar grabbed Darginn's arm so tightly it was painful.

"We believed we were better placed to run the kingdom and sought to use our allies' *draoidh* abilities, combined with our holy training, to take that power, overthrowing King Janaeus and claiming his rightful place."

A long pause, and a muddle of chatter from the crowd. Darginn's stomach was flopping like a landed salmon.

"I was directly involved in devising the plan to assassinate King Janaeus, which was carried out by the former Laird Aranok, as well as the murder of the Lairds' Council—intended to hasten our claim on the throne."

Holy God. He was burying himself, and Aranok with him! The crowd was silent, confused. The White Thorns were legend in Eidyn—the holy arm of God. Would even this convince such reverent people to turn on them?

Again a long pause as Meristan stood with his head bowed.

"Thanks to the ministrations of the righteous and holy King Anhel Weyr, I have seen the error of my ways. And thus I come before you to lay bare my sins and ask for mercy."

It wasn't long. Barely a breath of silence before the first boo. Then another. And then a ragged chorus, tuneless and brittle. Something was thrown from the crowd and another few bits of detritus were lobbed until one of the kingsguards stepped forward and raised their hand. "He will be allowed to finish!" she bellowed, tapping her crossbow with her free hand. The crowd settled like surly children. There was fire in them yet.

When it had quieted enough, the guard stepped back and Meristan lifted the scroll again. It was difficult to tell from the distance, but he looked beaten. Just... surrendered. Darginn put an arm around Ismar's shoulders and pulled his son to him.

"In his benign and righteous wisdom, Good King Anhel Weyr has chosen not to execute me—the usual punishment for treason. Instead, in light of my confession and the admission of our plot, he has seen fit to commute my punishment to banishment. The Order of the White Thorns is hereby outlawed and disbanded, and any former members of the Order found to remain within Eidyn one month from today will be arrested or executed. I order them all to stand down, relinquish the symbols of their service and join me in exile."

Grumbles. Confusion. Everyone knew what the Thorns had done for Eidyn. The same was true of Aranok. Would they really believe this nonsense, when it made a lie of the world? Probably, aye. Tell a crowd to hate anything with enough conviction and half of them'll be foaming at the mouth before you're finished the speaking of it.

Meristan dropped the scroll to his side and looked out mournfully across the square. A deep breath, a long sigh and then his final words.

"I am sorry for what I have done."

That was the first line that sounded like it had a lick of truth, and it was nothing to do with the pack of nonsense he'd just confessed to. He was sorry for what he'd just done to King Mynygogg, to Laird Aranok and to the people of Eidyn. But there must be good reason for it. No chance he'd have said all that if it wasn't to save lives. If it wasn't for some other good. Weyr had something over him, absolutely no doubt. And it was then that the spark of hope lit in the shadows of Darginn's heart.

He pulled Ismar to face him. The boy's eyes were as fragile as he'd ever seen them.

"Samily's alive," Darginn said firmly. "Maybe Rasa too."

"What...? How...how do you...?" Ismar stuttered.

"Because there's no fucking chance Laird Meristan would have said a word of that if they weren't being held over him. D'you see? They're alive. And we're going to get them out, Ismar. If it's the last bloody thing I do, we're getting them out."

---

"Father."

Aranok dropped the word like a dull stone. Allandria had worried he'd revert to his usual deferential attitude when he was actually stood in front of Dorann, but there was no sign of it. They'd talked a lot about this moment. About what it would be like seeing him again.

And here it was.

Hopefully, Dorann would have the damned sense to be glad to see his son.

"What the Hell are you doing here? Are you mad?" Dorann stood from the dining table, where he was sitting with Pol, of all people, papers covered in numbers, drawings of frills and cuffs laid out before them. After what Ikara had said about moving to Traverlyn with Emelina, Allandria had hoped not to have seen the little weasel again. No such luck. She wasn't unhappy that he seemed to lean away from Aranok, though. And no barbed welcome either. Perhaps he'd realised his wife was no longer a shield from her brother.

"Dorann, be nice." Sumara had ecstatically greeted them at the door, vouching for them with the two bulky guards stationed there, and become surprisingly emotional when she'd seen Ferrod with them. Deep regrets passed between them with genuine warmth. They might have been family, once. They sort of still were. Sumara turned back to them now, smiling. "I'll fetch Ikara." Aranok's mother nipped up the stairs then with more dexterity than one would imagine for a woman of her age.

Dorann eyed the three of them suspiciously. "This is a mistake."

"No, it's not," said Aranok. "There are people who need to know the truth. Like him."

"Me?" Pol asked, somewhere between appalled and afraid.

"You," Aranok answered. "And Cressida. The guards. Everybody."

It had taken them more than a week to get through the Guard, not least thanks to having to get a new glass charm made. Aranok was also back to being limited in what he could do without an energy *draoidh* to support him. Rasa hadn't come yet, so they'd not been able to send Feroul's letter to his brother and convince him to help them. He remained locked up for now. But it did mean they could move around the city with much greater ease. No guards following Aranok's family, waiting for him to show up at the house. Instead, they were taking orders from Mynygogg now—reporting who went in and out of the city, and any news from Greytoun, which wasn't much. Bak met with the king daily, as they developed the next stage of their plan: the influential merchants, the richest, the most respected. Which included Dorann.

"Hello." Ikara's voice was gentle, as though she were speaking to a child. And indeed, Emelina trailed behind her, holding her mother's hand, with her grandmother at the back. Ikara's eyes were fixed on Ferrod, and his on Emelina. His mouth tightened to a pucker as his eyes welled with emotion.

Dorann gave a dark look between the two. "*This is* a mistake."

"No," Sumara said firmly. "Waiting was a mistake."

Pol's face also fell to black. There was fury in there, silenced by fear. Maybe he did know about Emelina's skill. Had he argued against Ferrod being allowed to meet her? Likely. Was it a coincidence that he was here now, scowling like a chastened child? Maybe not. If Ikara really was preparing to leave him, his position was tenuous. Linked to Aranok in a way that he likely considered a burden now—knowing that when they retook the throne, he'd find himself isolated. Would Dorann still allow him to inherit the business if Pol was no longer married to his daughter? All of that danced in the man's eyes as they burned toward Emelina's grandfather.

Ikara crouched down beside Em. "You can go say hello to Uncle Aranok and Auntie Allandria."

This time, that *Auntie* wasn't awkward at all. The world had changed so much since the girl had first used it that now it felt like a blessing. Allandria was part of the family.

Emelina glanced at Pol, and when he did not look back to her, she rushed across and threw herself into Aranok's arms.

"Hi, Princess!" He scooped her up. "How have you been?"

"Good," she said quietly, her lips drawn almost completely inside her mouth. And in her hand, her little wooden bird.

"Hi, gorgeous." Allandria stroked the girl's arm. "It's good to see you." A subdued smile. Em's world had become complicated since they last saw her. Living with her grandparents, surrounded by strangers. She wouldn't have seen her tutor for ages. And her parents on the verge of divorce. Her six-year-old world was in turmoil. And, perhaps, Ikara might have spoken to her about the illusionist—that she had to tell her mother if anyone was not who they said they were. What that might mean to a little girl... No wonder her carefree joy had been replaced with reticence.

"Em, this is our friend Ferrod. He's very keen to meet you."

With a pronounced "hmmph" Dorann flounced off into the kitchen, followed by Loth. The giant bodyguard had until that moment been sitting so silently in the corner that Allandria somehow hadn't even noticed him. Pol continued to stare intently at the work in front of him, despite clearly doing nothing. The tension in the room sat thick and cold.

"Hello, sweetheart." Ferrod's voice was cracked, but his face lit with delight. "It's lovely to meet you. You've got your mum's eyes."

Allandria wondered what else he saw in the girl. His son's smile? His wife's button nose? Allandria hadn't seen any images of either of them, if they existed, so couldn't say in which ways Em resembled her real father's family, but surely they would be screaming at Ferrod.

Em smiled at her mother before looking back to the grandfather she'd never known. "Hello."

Ferrod had stuffed his hands in his pockets, but he looked desperate to reach out to her, to touch her, to hold her. Allandria felt herself welling up just watching—she could hardly imagine what he was feeling.

"Would you take Ferrod upstairs for a bit, maybe?" Aranok asked. "Show him your room and play with him while we do some boring grown-up things?"

Again, she looked to Ikara, who smiled and nodded.

"All right," she said quietly.

"Brilliant." Aranok kissed her on the cheek. "We'll see you in a little while."

When he put her down, Em cautiously put her hand out to Ferrod, who took it with a stuttering breath and followed her and Ikara up the stairs.

Aranok waited until their footsteps told him they were in a bedroom before speaking again. "Right. Mum, can you maybe find us a bucket, please?"

An hour later, maybe less, Aranok had cleared Pol, Cressida and all six of the bodyguards in and around the house, including Kye Denassa, who had to be summoned from the roof.

"Incredible" was about all the assassin had said.

And at the end of it, somehow, almost inevitably, Allandria found herself alone in the kitchen with Dorann. She'd come in for a glass of water to address the tickle in her throat—hopefully nothing more than that—and found him standing there, staring emptily out the window.

"I suppose you think I'm a daft old bastard."

The bluntness stopped her in her tracks. "Pardon?"

"After what happened between my *son* and me. What he did. What I said."

Ah, she saw what this was, now. He was baiting her to criticise him. Putting his transgressions on display and challenging her to address them. Using his age, his home, his position as her lover's father, his *authority*, to dare her to insult him. If she did not, he'd consider her cowed. Run roughshod over her and know he could do as he pleased. It was a thing weak men did to appear strong. Browbeat others with a condescending tone. *You are just another fool if you challenge me.* Regardless of the facts. Regardless of reality. She'd stayed quiet in the past out of respect for Aranok. When she was just his bodyguard, it was not her place. Now she was more. She was his partner and his equal. And she was tired of this game.

"Yes. You are a bastard." She finished crossing to the pantry and found a jug of water.

"Charming," said Dorann, mocking her "rudeness." Trying to put her on the back foot.

"You asked the question, Laird," she replied. "If you didn't want the answer…"

Allandria found a cup and filled it, drank gratefully and cleared her throat.

Dorann had turned to face her when she looked again. "Well. I suppose we both know where we stand now."

"Do we?" The temptation to unleash on him was tantalising. But was it wise?

*Fuck it.*

This had been simmering for a long time and it was finally going to boil.

"I'm not sure we do. Because when I say you are a bastard, I don't mean because you were stupid and arrogant enough to dismiss your own son when he offered you the *truth*. And I don't mean because you threw a tantrum when he did it anyway and banished him because you didn't like what you learned—that you were *wrong*." The hint of smugness in Dorann's eyes was melting into anger. "When I say you are a bastard, I mean it is because you have spent his entire life raising him to believe he was *broken*. That he was *less* in your eyes. That he was a *disappointment*. You sowed doubt in him like wildflowers and they grew. So yes, you are a bastard, Dorann. You are a fool for not seeing all that your son is, and you are a bastard for making him doubt it. And that's before we discuss the oaf you forced your daughter to marry."

The old man stared indignantly for a long time before speaking, as if struggling to find words blunt enough for the insult he'd endured. Clearly, nobody spoke to him like this. Allandria leaned against the doorframe, heart racing, casually drinking her water and feeling the sweet catharsis of the moment, despite the minor tremor in her hands.

"Well," said Dorann. "I suspect that's been coming for a while."

"You have no idea."

"Looks like someone has found being the envoy's lover to her approval. Comes with benefits that a bodyguard doesn't, eh?"

*Oh, this will be fun.*

"Not as many as being the new queen's envoy."

That changed his face quick enough. Appalled; understanding; resentment. "Is that right? Well, congratulations, Lady Envoy. I am sure the realm will benefit from your wisdom. Once our queen is back on her throne."

He hadn't enjoyed that. A little barb at the end, of course.

But Allandria had revelled in it. She hadn't meant for it to happen and, once, she would have worried about how Aranok would feel. He would have been angry. Embarrassed. Felt he had to apologise to his father for her words. Chastised her for speaking up. But she was confident that was no longer true. He'd found balance. Dug himself out from under his father's neglect and abuse. He wasn't that boy anymore. And Dorann wouldn't tell him. Because if nothing else, he knew now, surely, that her relationship with his son was stronger, more vital than his own.

And if he didn't, he'd soon enough find out.

# CHAPTER 41

The pigsty stank much less than Vastin expected. The fenced-in section out the back was pretty honking, and seemed to be where the pigs went to do their business. But inside the stone structure, where they lounged on patchy straw, it was fairly clean. In fact, it had an odd smell of something syrupy. Not remotely what he'd expected.

The pigs had come grunting in excited anticipation when he'd snuck in earlier. Once they'd realised he wasn't their mistress come to bring them fodder, they'd poked and sniffed about him for a bit before deciding he was entirely unexciting and going back to huddling together away from the shuttered windows. There was a pregnant sow separated from the others. She lay on her side, breathing sharp, her turgid teats waiting for her bloated belly to produce the piglets that would relieve them. She looked knackered, bless her.

"Not long now," he whispered reassuringly.

He'd been huddled there for over an hour, he reckoned, occasionally nudged by a curious snout, before he finally heard the muddy footsteps he'd been expecting.

When Darginn and Ismar had come back to the kirk with the news of Meristan's speech, he'd been about ready to storm Greytoun single-handed. But Laird Severianos had tempered all their passions with reason. None of them were trained fighters. Darginn was, with respect, on the older side, and Ismar had little to no control over his necromancy skill. Vastin was the most experienced fighter of the three, and that was no real compliment.

And the memory charm was a bag of shards.

"Information is what we need," the Green Laird had said. "I'd assume, if they're still alive, that Samily and Rasa are being kept in that same tower room, where Weyr had done something to negate their *draoidh* abilities. We need to know for certain. And we need to know who's guarding them."

They couldn't exactly wander up to a guard and ask them for information. Where would they even start? Plus, there was a decent chance the Guard were looking for them! But Vastin had remembered there was one person he could trust, who spent a lot of time around guards when they were off duty and more inclined to say things they maybe shouldn't.

The door opened, and this time the pigs jumped excitedly for the right reason. Their mistress had come, as she always did, to bring them slops at the end of the night. She held a bucket in each hand and shushed them all back as she moved toward the troughs. "All right, all right. There's plenty, and you know that."

Vastin had hidden himself back in a corner, just in case it had been her pa who came instead. But luck was with him. Last thing he wanted to do was frighten her, though.

"Ama?" he said as gently as he could manage.

Amollari snapped her head round, nearly tipping one of her buckets. Vastin stepped out of the shadow, allowing the moonlight through the open door to hit his face. "It's all right. It's only me, Ama. It's Vastin."

"Oh!" Her startled face softened into a smile. "What are you doing in...here?" She moved as if to come to him, then seemed to realise she was still carrying two buckets of slops. "I have to..." She gestured with a shoulder to the two long troughs.

"Let me help." Vastin took the bucket from her left hand, weaving through the agitated pigs to empty its contents into the trough that was shared between the main pen and the sow's.

"When did you get back?" Amollari asked when they'd done pouring. "I didn't see the forge was open."

"Eh, aye, it's not. Yet." He wasn't sure how to begin to explain. But as much as he knew he trusted Ama, he was also sure she trusted him. Mostly sure. "Long story. But, em, how have you been?"

Standing this close to her, even surrounded by pigs and after she'd spent the day serving ale, Vastin caught that sweet whiff of heather and sunshine that always came with her. Even in the growing dark of winter, Amollari was a promise of spring. In fact, he was surprised at just how pleased he was to see her. They'd been friends as long as he could remember, with their parents' businesses sharing the same square. Maybe it was a fond remembrance of that time, before... everything. Or maybe it was because he'd been away. Or maybe it was just her there, then, that sent a rush of warring emotions washing through Vastin. Joy and sadness and regret and pain and relief and... all of it. He ached to just blurt out all that had happened to him. Travelling with Laird Aranok, turning Blackened, losing Glorbad, meeting the king, the Thakhati... all of it. But he'd hardly the time, and it would be gibberish to her unless she had her memory back. And yet, he needed to ask for her help. And hope her trust in him would be enough.

"Well, I suppose," she answered, clutching a handful of her overcoat's sleeve. "Business is still tight, Pa says. Just about keeping the wolves from the door, but, well, you know how it's been since..." Since the war. The war that took his parents, and his business. The war that was still happening, right under the noses of the people who had suffered for it. "Will you come into the bar?" Amollari brightened and smiled. "We've some stew left, if..." Again she trailed off. Because he knew the rest of that sentence too. *If you've not got the money for food.* So often Amollari had fed him when his pot simmered dry. Brought him in after closing and warmed him a bowl with a crust of bread. Even though it was a time when he barely had a copper to chew on, those evenings were happy memories. Amollari was as close to home as he had now. But that wasn't to be tonight. Tonight he needed information, not feeding.

"Thank you, but no, I can't. I wish I could, though. Really." He took her hand then without thinking and suddenly realised it was a bit odd. It felt different. Her skin was cold and Vastin's fingers tingled at the feel of it.

Amollari cocked her head and looked up at him curiously. "Did you get taller?"

Vastin dropped her hand and grabbed the back of his own neck, which was flushing with heat. "Eh, maybe, I suppose?" God, how long had he actually been away? It felt like years, but it had only been, what, a few months? And yet he was a completely different person. He felt... *older*. "Listen, Ama, I need a favour. Actually, I need a few favours."

One of the pigs grunted happily as it chomped down on something particularly wet, and Vastin made an exaggerated gesture of disgust. Amollari replied with a generous, silent laugh. "What do you need? Do you want to tell me inside? It's freezing..."

She wasn't wrong. Snow was in the air. Could well be laying by sunrise. That wouldn't help. "No, because, well, the first favour is... Could you not tell your pa I was here, please?"

Her eyebrows went up at that. "So I'm having a secret meeting with an older boy in the pigsty? What kind of favour are you after, Vastin? People will talk!" Her eyes lit with mirth and Vastin felt more heat rushing to his cheeks.

"Oh, eh, no, um, see I need you to..."

*God's sake, Vastin, just speak, you dolt.*

"Look, it's a long story, but..."

"Wait. Oh Hells, Vastin, I can't believe I didn't ask before! What happened? With the laird envoy? I mean... all we've heard. Did he hurt you? Are you all right?" Suddenly she grabbed at his shoulders and was scanning him for injuries like a medic.

"I'm fine." He gently pushed her away. "It's not what you think. Look. This is asking a lot, and I understand if you say no, but..." *Here goes.* "None of that stuff is true, Ama. None of it." He brought his voice down to a whisper. "Laird Aranok is innocent. I've been with him almost all the time and... he's a good man. A great man."

Amollari's brow crinkled. "Then why did Brother Meristan...?"

"Because he's being blackmailed, Ama. Because Anhel Weyr is the real villain. And he's holding two captives, forcing Meristan to say these awful things. That's why I need you to..."

"To what?"

"Be a spy? Sort of?"

She stood back then and crossed her arms, a bemused smile under mischievous eyes. "You're having me on."

God, he'd said it all badly. "Look, sorry, no, I just... A lot of the castle guards drink in the Chain Pier, right?"

She nodded warily, still unconvinced. "Aye. Sometimes."

"Well, could you just, maybe, like, listen to them? When they're talking? Especially when they're, you know..."

"Pished out their skulls?"

"Yeah." He smiled. "That. Please?"

They stood in quiet for a bit, her looking at him like he'd just told her he'd grown another leg, pigs snarfing down slop behind her. "You're serious."

"I really am." He took both hands this time and felt the same cool tingle run up his arms. "Please."

Another moment, and she released his hands. Stepped back. "You're mad."

*Bollocks*. He'd made an arse of it.

"No, Ama, I'm sorry. Listen, I...maybe...I shouldn't have asked, I just..." Vastin's voice cracked and whatever words he was hoping to find were lost to the night air.

But Amollari's face changed with it. "*Are* you all right?"

Where could he begin? What could he say? Enough truth to help her believe him?

"It's...complicated. I've..." *Come on, Vastin. Just tell her what you can.* "I almost died."

"What?" Amollari closed the distance she'd created between them and put a hand on his arm. Again, his skin responded with gooseflesh. "How? What happened?"

"Well, you know the Blackening?"

"Aye?" Her tone was curious but wary.

"I got Blackened."

Amollari's hand dropped from him and she stepped back as if Vastin were made of flame. He threw both hands up defensively. "It's all right. I don't remember it. And I'm cured. They all are."

"The Blackening is cured?" she asked, eyebrows raised. "How? When?"

Right. He could explain this. "Well, it turned out to be a curse, see, so magic, not sickness. Laird Aranok figured it out. And he, well, with help, and..." God, it was more complicated than he had considered. He had to keep it simple. "Laird Aranok lifted it, with help from a White Thorn called Samily." Not how either of them would describe it, but it would do.

"Well, first, I'm glad you're all right," she answered after a moment. "A curse? Seriously? Who set it?"

"A *draoidh*. A mad one." That was all true. "But the important thing is: She was working with Janaeus. And Anhel Weyr. They're all *draoidhs*."

Amollari cocked her head with wide eyes. "The king…is a *draoidh*?"

She'd said that a bit too loud and Vastin hushed her with urgent hands.

"And the people he's holding, they're friends of mine too. One is Samily. The Thorn? She's only a wee bit older than us, Ama. But she's brilliant. Saved my life at least twice."

"Twice?" Ama asked with genuine shock. "What else…?"

What the Hell, might as well give her that story too. "She killed a demon. When we met. In Mutton Hole. The one that was burning the farms."

"Oh. I heard about that. That was you?" She was curious now. Listening. Believing? It was good she'd heard of it.

"I was there. I didn't do much." He shrugged awkwardly. Felt mad to be telling this story, back here, with her. And a moment of sadness as he remembered the journey to Mutton Hole, trekking with Glorbad. Sharing his whisky. Sparring at the farm…

It must have shown in his face, because Amollari grabbed him into a hug. "Bloody Hell, Vastin. Bloody Hell." She felt tiny in his arms. Fragile. And yet again he feared for what he was asking her to do. To put herself in danger. Maybe he should walk away. Tell her to forget it. He'd never live with himself if she got hurt. God, she was a child still.

As much as he had been, not that long ago. Felt like another world, where the two of them played together. Laughed together. A world he missed. Well, the real world had come to them both now. And maybe knowing something of the truth would help protect her.

"Weyr is a demon summoner," he blurted, holding her at arm's length. "It was him behind the war. I can't explain how I know that or show you any proof, but I promise you, on my heart"—he put his hand on his chest—"it's the truth. He's dangerous, Ama. He's evil."

Her eyes were wide. Pale and fearful. Amollari knew something now that she couldn't forget. And she believed it. She moved back and sat on a hay bale against the far wall. One of the pigs, stuffed on scraps, nuzzled at her dangling hand and she stroked it absent-mindedly.

After a long silence, she looked across at him. "There's more, isn't there?"

"Aye," Vastin answered. "But not much I can tell you without just putting you in more danger."

Again, she stared at him for a while before speaking. "And you wouldn't ask me if you had another way."

It felt like it should have been a question, but her flat statement didn't seem like she needed an answer. Vastin nodded anyway. He hated himself for doing this. Now that she was in front of him. He'd broken her picture of the world and shown her how dark it really was. He was about to tell her to forget it when she leaned forward on her knees.

"All right. But listen, it's not like the guards sit around blethering about secrets and stuff, you know. Most of the time they're playing cards and talking tripe."

That wasn't going to help them. "Maybe you could...prompt them?"

"*Prompt* them?" She dropped both hands and stood up. "Like, *hello, by any chance have you got some people held captive in the castle you'd like to tell me about?*"

Vastin laughed nervously. "Well, maybe a bit more subtle than that."

Amollari sighed. "All right. What do I need to know?"

God, she was going to do it. Vastin's relief was tempered with a knot in his gut. If Weyr found out...

"There's the Thorn, Samily, and a *draoidh* called Rasa. We think they're in a room in one of the towers—maybe the same one where the king bides. We just sort of need to know—anything. Are they there? Who's guarding them? Do they ever leave the room? That sort of thing."

"Vastin, are you...are you thinking about..."—she looked around as if the walls might have grown ears—"...breaking into the castle?"

The look of absolute horror on her face told Vastin how mad the idea was. And yet, after everything he'd done since he last saw her, it hadn't seemed that odd at all. "Well, maybe. But not just me. I've got help."

Amollari's eyes went wide as moons. "Laird Aranok?" she whispered. "He's here?"

Hell, how Vastin wished that were true. If he were here, they'd have been in and got them by now. Not hung around for days waiting to hear something. Maybe they should have gone for the envoy. They'd discussed it. But it seemed too urgent to leave. To abandon the others to Anhel Weyr and go looking for help. Who knew what they'd miss in the days they were away? And Severianos was not fit to travel.

But maybe that was where this had to end. If not for the Green Laird's direction, Vastin's confidence in the idea might have drained well before now.

"No. Not him. But others. I can't say any more than that; I'm sorry."

His desperation must have shown on his face, because she softened again, her shoulders dropping. She paced in the straw, as if the walking was helping her think. "Right. I don't know how long it will take to get anything. And you can't be sneaking into the pigsty every night. Not least in case Pa comes down!" She raised an eyebrow at that and Vastin winced at the thought of her father finding him there and jumping directly to the wrong idea. But there was also a little thrill at that thought. *The wrong idea.* "So we'll need a signal. There's a hook out the front there. I'll hang a lamp on it after closing if I have news for you, all right? So you can stay away, and just come in if you see the lamp. Yes?"

"Yes. Yes, of course. That's brilliant. Thank you."

"What madness, eh? Who would've thought we'd be spies?" With a conspiratorial flash of her eyes, Amollari picked up the buckets. "I better bugger off before Pa wonders where I am. Wait a wee bit before you go. He's busy in the kitchen, but just in case..."

She made for the door and Vastin caught her arm. "Wait, Ama." She turned back to look and Vastin felt something melt inside him. He was scared. For her. More than he'd ever been for himself. "Be careful? Please? Don't... don't push too hard, aye?"

She smiled as if he'd asked her not to dance on her head. "I won't."

Amollari opened the door and paused against a sharp wind that billowed her coat and whipped her hair back.

And then she was gone, leaving Vastin both hopeful and terrified.

Nirea woke in the dark. Her body sunk like lead into the mattress, yet tingled and floated like air. She was shivering cold, but sweat pooled on her chest and ran from her fringe. Even in the pitch black, she felt the room spin about her like stars falling from the Heavens.

It was no better when she closed her eyes. She breathed heavily through her nose, fighting nausea and panic. Where was she?

She tried to speak, to call out for help, but all that came out was a guttural moan, a grunt. Another. She didn't have the energy, the focus for speech. She just wanted help, light, anything to give her an anchor.

Gogg.

She wanted Gogg.

*Please.*

A rustling, somewhere nearby. Movement.

She moaned again. Calling out to whoever that was, anyone, just someone to... She reached her right hand out from under the blankets. Cool air hit the sweat and she felt the chill course through her, pulling her arm defensively back across her stomach.

And then the pain. Fucking Hell, the pain. She remembered the knife. And her face... Hells, her nose throbbed with every beat of her heart like it would burst.

"I think she's awake."

A voice. Familiar. Comforting. More movement.

A flame.

Light.

Her eyes slowly focused.

"Hey. Be gentle. Take your time." Ailen. Thank God, Ailen.

"Wuuuuh..." Her mouth still wouldn't work, damn it.

"It's all right. You've been asleep. A long time. Nirea, do you remember? The attack? You were stabbed. You lost a lot of blood. You... you nearly didn't come back."

A tingling wave flushed down her body. She was hot. Too hot. She grabbed the edge of the blanket and flipped it down to her waist, feeling the blessed cold across her skin. The bite was a balm, and it sharpened her wits too.

The attack.

Yes.

Harp.

*Quell.*

"Quell!" She almost sat up, but as soon as she moved, her head spun and she dropped back to the pillow.

*Fuck, not this again!*

The candlelight was a dagger in her brain and she closed her eyes against it, swimming again in the liquid dark.

"Take time, my friend. Your body must heal." Crinn's voice. Calming. Gentle.

Crinn, who had saved them. Crashed through the Wark's door like a goddamned battering ram and cut that bastard assassin in half.

She'd been so fucking careless. So stupid. She should have been sharper. Should have been better.

Quell. She needed to know.

"Quell?" she whispered.

The long silence was enough. She already knew. A gentle, cool hand on her shoulder, and then Ailen's voice, soft and mournful.

"I'm sorry. We tried."

# CHAPTER 42

Meristan trudged up the gangway, weather-beaten boards creaking beneath his feet as jeers rang around Havenport. The low-hanging grey winter sky offered him no more solace than the chill wind snapping at his heels. The Guard had provided him with "traditional" monk's robes for this spectacle—a final little dagger from Anhel Weyr—parading him through the streets of Haven like a clown to board a ship out of the country. This was no more than a circus, demonstrating the king's strength and benevolence. A farce, throwing red meat to baying wolves, whose lives were so meagre, thanks to him, that having someone to blame, someone to hate, was a fine distraction from their grumbling bellies and cold hearths. Meristan was a puppet in a shadow play, making his scripted exit.

Something slapped hard against his back, jerking his head forward. A tomato, perhaps, by the feel of it. Long past ripe. He felt the wet of it seeping onto his shoulder blade and shivered. A small indignity, as it went. These people who'd come to ridicule and lambast him for his "treason" had no idea what they were really doing. No concept that they cheered their own servitude, howled against their own salvation.

Meristan reached over his shoulder and brushed off what was left of the vegetable, shaking pulpy lumps from his fingers. They hadn't even bothered to bind his hands, such was Weyr's absolute certainty that he had him.

And he did.

Even if it were just Severianos, Samily and Rasa held in the castle, he'd have struggled to do anything other than capitulate to the demon summoner's demands. Getting them out would mean fighting his way through the castle guards, likely killing many. And what right did he have to choose lives? The king's guards had family too. Folk who would grieve their losses—maybe suffer for the lack of their coin. How many lives would he put to ruin in order to save his friends? Especially when the alternative was just this.

Exile.

If the Order of the White Thorns was not built on sacrifice, it was nothing. His friends would live, at least for now, and the possibility of their emancipation remained. Just not by Meristan's hand. King Mynygogg, Aranok and their allies were still fighting. Still working to get the kingdom back. If they did that, then it was possible Samily and the others could have their lives back too.

In truth, Meristan had been a fool. So confident of his plan, so sure it was only himself he was risking. But he'd walked Samily and Rasa right into the same trap he'd unwittingly laid for Severianos. He should have insisted the old man come with them to Traverlyn.

No.

No point in walking that road. The Green Laird wouldn't have abandoned his charges, even had he known the consequences. He'd have been the first to tell Meristan to leave him, both then and now.

But it wasn't just them. It wasn't just three hostages. The whole country was hostage. And if that was the heart of devastation Weyr was carrying around, gaudily dripped in gold, then destroying Traverlyn and executing the White Thorns were likely the least of what he could achieve. With the relic to amplify his skill, he was the most powerful *draoidh* in history.

That was little solace as he stepped onto the deck of the boat and felt it rise beneath him on the sea's fractious ebb.

Once he was on board, the guards stopped and stood sentry at the end of the gangway, presumably to stop him breaking for freedom. Or perhaps to prevent the mob from rushing the boat and throwing him into the sea. Meristan turned to see the waves of fury directed at him. Faces contorted into demonic grimaces, red and ugly. Shrieks and wails.

"Traitor!"

"Scum!"

"Get out of our country!"

People who, a month ago, would have offered him a bed in their homes, now spitting venom at him from the safety of a mob. A sea of faces, filling the docks as far as he could see. A cacophony of ignorance and bile. And he couldn't blame one of them.

He'd told them, himself, of his crime. Read Weyr's letter as though the words were his own. Begged their forgiveness and praised their captor's virtue. They were only doing what he'd told them to: hating him and beatifying Weyr. And he'd done it to save them. Because living under Weyr's boot was a kinder fate than having it at their throats.

With a quiet sigh, Meristan turned his back on the sea of noise and faced a man who seemed to be waiting to greet him. He wore a dark grey cloak pulled tight over the red leathers of Eidyn's navy. The man's face was the salt-blasted leather of a life at sea, his story written in the deep creases around his eyes. A bright red headscarf hid what Meristan suspected was a retreating hairline, despite the long dark locks that hung at the back.

He was flanked by another pair in matching leathers: a woman with short grey/brown hair and sharp eyes, and a hefty man with the dull look of cattle under ginger locks. Each had a hand on the hilts of the sabres hung from their belts. The woman in particular watched him with suspicion.

They all had the look, like Nirea, of pirates, and there was a fine chance they were exactly that. She'd brought a good number with her to Eidyn's ranks when they defeated Hofnag. A life earning honest coin and an unqualified pardon had been an attractive proposition for many. And who better to counter piracy than those who'd perfected its art?

"Brother Meristan, I take it?" The man he assumed was in charge uncrossed his arms to offer a hand. "Captain Hylar. Welcome to the *Silver Kelpie*."

"Captain." Meristan accepted the handshake.

"You been at sea before?" the man asked, as if this were some merchant charter and Meristan the client.

"Not for some years." Not since he was doing missionary work for the Order. Since Samily. Once he'd brought her home, he stayed. And now he was leaving her.

"Well, I don't suppose the sea's changed much since then." Hylar smiled a rogue's grin. Definitely a pirate. Nirea would have been drinking rum with him before they left harbour. He hoped to see the queen again. In better times. "It's an honour to meet you, Brother. I'm sorry it's not under better circumstances." He waved as if to indicate the bitter winter wind and the dark, tumultuous sea. Right enough, it wasn't the best sailing weather.

As if he'd summoned it, a blast of icy sleet stung Meristan's cheek.

"Can I ask, Captain... I've not been told: To where do we sail?" With a few weeks to think on it, Meristan had come up with a plan. Wherever they landed, he'd find a way to make some coin. Manual labour, sellsword, whatever he could do to earn the cost of another boat. Or perhaps he'd be able to work his way onto a merchant ship.

The captain's face cracked into a grin. "We make for Londinjon."

*Damn it.*

Of course.

Of course Weyr wanted him as far away as possible. Londinjon was months away. As far south as land was found. A place Meristan had always wanted to see. Stories told of glittering towers and vast marketplaces straddling a glorious river. It was said to be the hub of the world, where every other country met to trade.

At least there should be plenty of work there. Maybe he could quickly find a place on a boat coming back north. He could do grunt work on a ship. His old body was still fit for it.

Hylar stepped back, that smile still lighting his pale eyes. "My first will show you where you can put your head down for a bit. If you like."

"That would be fine." Meristan kept his voice even. "Thank you."

Hylar opened a hand toward the woman and she gestured for Meristan to follow her.

With a final, mournful look back at Greytoun Castle, perched high above Haven, Meristan paced after the first officer, down into the ship's depths. For now, he would rest. There would be plenty of time to plan what came next.

---

Vastin huddled against the wall, pulling his cloak tight against the freezing rain. Winter had properly landed now, in that Eidyn way where the rain took its time deciding to become snow and battered you with stinging needles while it made up its mind.

But his half-numb cheeks and frozen fingers were not what lingered on Vastin's mind. Maither Floreli had heard an awful story from a parishioner after evening service: Meristan had been put on a boat out of Eidyn. They'd waited too long. If he'd only been exiled, though, that was better than... the alternative. He could look after himself.

But where did that leave them?

Laird Severianos's wound had started to improve after about a week of the priest's tending, the swelling going down and the stink receding. But he still wasn't fit to be fighting. And for all his skill, he was an old man. The last thing he should be doing was trying to infiltrate a castle. They should have run. They should have run for Mournside. They should have gone after Laird Aranok and the king and let them decide what to do. Maybe they could have made a difference. But he hadn't thought it would take this long. That it would be so hard to find out what was happening in the castle.

Maither Floreli had even offered to try to get in—to see if she could wheedle some information herself. But Severianos had cautioned that was too risky. If she brought herself to Weyr's attention, he might start looking a little harder at the kirk. At this point, they guessed that he probably assumed they were long gone—had the sense to run. If they'd known they'd be waiting, doing nothing for all this time, they might have. Except for Severianos, of course. He was in no state for travelling.

They were stuck in a rut where no decision was a good decision. So there he was, again, hunched against a wall, waiting for a light that never...

And then it did.

Through the stinging rain and the haze of night, Amollari's lantern was finally glowing from the door of the pigsty. A quick glance about confirmed there was nobody else mad enough to be out on such a dreich night, and he hurried across to the gate, almost as excited about getting out of the rain as he was to speak to Ama again.

When he carefully pried open the door and slunk inside, Amollari had already fed the pigs and was pacing back and forth, chewing on her thumb. She jerked her head round when she heard him, ushered him inside with a "Quickly" and shut the door behind him. The little rush of excitement at seeing her was instantly cooled when he saw her pale face and wide, fearful eyes.

"Vastin, you have to run," she whispered. "You have to run as quick and as far as you can."

"What? Why?" he asked, his own fear rising as he imagined what awful thing she had discovered.

"They *know your name*," she whispered. "They're looking for you. You and some king's messenger?"

*Shite*. That guard must have talked after all. Stupid bugger had probably lost his head as thanks for it too. "Right. Tell me everything."

Amollari shook her head and sighed. "You'll hardly believe me."

"Tell me. Please."

"So I got a guard in last night. Plied her with some 'oops' pours…" Vastin smiled at the reference. It was a phrase she'd used since she'd started serving with her pa after her mum died. An "oops" pour was a big one, reserved for friends and those she liked. Everybody else got a standard finger. "And when she was properly hammered, I got her chatting. Your knight and the other woman are in the tower, but nobody's allowed in the room. There's, like, two people allowed in with food, other than the king. She says there's always at least four guards on the door, as well as another half dozen at the base of the tower. And they've got a bell! A bell to pull if anyone tries to get in. She says they've got more protection than the king!"

Hells. That was bad. No way to sneak in, then. But they were alive! That news alone was a rush of relief. At least they were alive. That was somewhere to start. That was something.

"But none of that's…the bad bit," said Amollari. "There's…Listen,

I don't know, I'm just telling you what she said, and you can decide... because it makes no sense to me, but..." She was practically shaking with nerves now, and Vastin gently took hold of her shoulders just to keep her still.

"Ama, it's all right. Tell me."

She pulled her lips in and looked up into his eyes. "There's talk of *something* in the castle. Something big. Something..." Amollari took a breath. "Something folk can't see."

*What?*

"But if nobody has seen it, then... how do they... know?" Vastin asked.

"Well, that's the thing, I was thinking... She says folk have heard things. Like breathing in an empty corridor and... she said it was a ghost story, but after you said about the king and demons, I thought... maybe... Can they be... invisible?"

*Oh bollocks.*

*Invisible?* Had Vastin even known that was possible? He'd a vague notion Aranok might have mentioned it was a thing some folk thought *might* be possible. An invisible demon. Fuck.

Wind rattled the shutters just then and the pair of them near jumped out of their skins. They shared a relieved half laugh.

But she was right. They had to run.

"Ama, you need to stay away from this—from anything to do with it. In fact..." Was Vastin really going to suggest this? On the other hand, could he just leave her there? "Come with us. Come away. Haven's not a safe place to be. Seriously. Just... come. Please?"

A weak, watery smile. "Come where?"

That was a good point. Traverlyn? Mournside? Where would they even go? That wasn't his decision to make. For now, he would take all this back to the Green Laird. Severianos would decide what was best. "I don't know yet. But away. Somewhere safer."

Even as he said it, he knew there was no chance. And that was more distressing than he would have thought it.

"I can't. Pa'll never believe any of this. And he wouldnae leave the Chain without it being on fire. It's everything. We'll be fine. Nobody's looking for me. Who am I?"

Who was she? She was one of the only people who still felt like home. One of the last ties to a life that felt like somebody else had lived it. A childhood that was sunny and joyful. And long gone. "Ama, I…" What was he going to say? That now he'd seen her again, he was afraid to leave her? He'd only be putting her in danger. He'd already put her in danger. No, she had to stay with her pa. She'd be fine. "I understand. Of course."

Her face changed in an odd way then. Had he said something wrong? Had she wanted him to convince her to go? Had she offended her? He had no idea. So he smiled and gave her an awkward hug, hoping it didn't make things any worse.

"Vastin, you need to go," she said over his shoulder. *"Now."*

She was right. There was nothing more they could do there. No way they could break into that room. Not without killing more innocent guards or getting themselves killed in the trying. He had to go. They all did. "Thank you, Ama. Really. Just, stay out of it now, eh? Leave it alone."

She held his gaze for a moment, put a hand on one cheek and lightly kissed the other. Vastin's face flushed with heat.

"Fine. As long as you go," she said.

But the curious spark in her eyes gave him a horrible feeling she wasn't going to listen.

---

"Well, that is quite bad news." The Green Laird sat up in Maither Floreli's bed, leaning against a pile of pillows. His face was still pale, but there was a bit more colour in it than there had been, Darginn reckoned. The priest had insisted he take the room, not least because her bedchamber was the one place in the entire kirk she was certain she could prevent any curious guards from entering. The alternative was for them to bed down inside the crypt, so they could break for the escape tunnel in an emergency, but even the suggestion of that had Ismar trembling, and Darginn knew he couldn't put his son through that.

Floreli's room was basic but homely. There was a glass vase of flowers on the sill in front of the stained-glass window and a pleasant painting of a sunset behind Dun Eidyn on the wall opposite the bed. It had the look of being done by the priest herself. Otherwise it was relatively sparse, with a well-made wooden wardrobe and sideboard either side of the hearth. There was just about enough room on the floor for the three bedrolls the rest of them had been using.

Floreli was using one of the guest rooms, intended for visiting kirk dignitaries, and doing her best to keep up her regular duties while tending to the laird and gathering what information she could.

But the news they were getting went from bad to worse.

"There's no way we can get in there, is there?" Ismar asked quietly.

"None I can see," Darginn answered, looking to the laird. He hoped that maybe Severianos had some great plan. But he couldn't even imagine where it would start.

"No, lad, there is not." Severianos pulled back the bedsheet and every one of them took an instinctive step back before bustling toward him.

"Whoa, whoa," said Vastin, trying to shepherd the wounded man to stay in the bed.

Darginn went to offer a hand to support Severianos's arm, and Ismar did a hesitant wee dance back and forth as if he knew he should be doing something but didn't know what.

"Everybody, step back," said the Green Laird. "I am perfectly capable of removing myself from bed. I've been doing it my entire life."

"Aye, but..." Vastin stopped, cut off by a raised finger from Severianos.

"We are going to have to leave," said the old man. "And that being the case, the sooner the better, no? We can no longer hope to be of use to our friends here, so we must make haste to where we can be useful. And that place is Traverlyn."

"Not Mournside?" Vastin asked eagerly.

"No, son," he answered. "We've no idea what the situation is there, only that it's where you reckon King Mynygogg and the others were going. If it's true that the Guard are looking for all of us, then the only place it seems we can go where we will *not* be hunted is Traverlyn. And I must get to the White Thorns there, to warn them they have been disavowed by that godless cur sitting on the throne. Which makes our choice a simple one, no?"

"But, they need to know," Vastin protested. "They will want to know what happened here."

"I am sure they will. And we'll figure that out, once we're all safe. You never attack from a position of vulnerability, lad. And at the moment, I'm afraid to say we are all too vulnerable." The Green Laird touched his bandaged side then, as if any of them needed reminding.

Vastin sighed and frowned, but he didn't argue. He was right, though. The king needed to know.

Soon.

"Laird, are you fit to travel?" Darginn asked. "We've nae horses at the end of the tunnel, and it's a lot of walking for a man whose side's no long stitched back together. And with respect, we're neither of us as young as we were." Darginn rubbed his hand over his grey pate to illustrate the point.

Severianos swung his legs off the bed and stood proudly then, the hem of his borrowed nightshirt dropping just below his knees. Any stranger would have thought him a frail old man, barely able to look after himself, not the most skilled swordsman in Eidyn. And it was hard not to agree with that assessment, given the pale ghost stood before them.

"Darginn Argyll, are you not a king's messenger?" Severianos asked in an authoritative voice.

"I am, Laird."

"And is your first sworn duty to serve king and country?"

"It is, Laird."

"As mine is to serve God, and God's children. Neither of which we are doing by lounging here, overstaying our welcome at the pleasure of good Maither Floreli. So let's be off, shall we, before things get any worse than they already are."

"Are you sure, Laird?" Vastin asked. "Your side—"

"Is healing nicely thanks to Maither Floreli's ministrations," Severianos interrupted. "And God will see us well, young man. Fear not. Now, if someone could just arrange me some clothes. I recall that my previous shirt was somewhat blemished."

And with that, they moved. Ismar went to Maither Floreli to see about clothes, and it turned out she had cleaned and mended the laird's own shirt herself in preparation for his needing it again. Darginn set about collecting their bedrolls and Vastin picked up some rations from the kitchen. In fact, for all that Severianos had stood up, he ended up only sitting back down again and waiting. Which was probably for the best.

Maybe an hour later, they were ready to go and Maither Floreli was fussing over them like they were her own grandchildren. Darginn half expected her to take a kerchief to Vastin's face as she bade him farewell, but she just offered them all a blessing instead and promised to keep them in her prayers. She'd all but taken a fainting fit at the notion of Severianos travelling, even worse of him *walking* the distance, but she'd found an old cane in the kirk's storeroom and insisted he take it. It made an odd pair with the Green blade hanging from the opposite side of his belt.

As they trudged through the crypt later, the pale white remains of Haven's ancestors lit by the flame of Vastin's torch, it occurred to Darginn that they'd actually done what they came to do. Their task had been to free the Green Laird from Anhel Weyr, and here they were, escaping with him. They'd won their gambit, but at a higher cost than they'd ever have imagined. Laird Meristan exiled, Lady Samily and Rasa now captives in Severianos's stead. Had they played right into Anhel Weyr's hands, in the end? For him, sacrificing one piece to take three off his opponent was a fine play, Darginn reckoned. What would the king make of it? Would Mynygogg curse them for fools? Well, that wasnae for Darginn to decide. For now, they made for Traverlyn. And he'd be glad to get himself and Ismar back there. Back to Isadona and the kids. And Liana.

And maybe only then did it really sink in how lucky they were to be getting back at all. How lucky they were to still be together, through everything. Darginn looked to Ismar, trudging silently ahead of him, head down. The dead were calling him again. The boy had been all but crippled by those bastards in the New Kirk. And yet he'd come here with them and been a genuine help. If he'd not been able to use the charm to give the Green Laird his memory back, God alone knew what they would have done. Filled with an unexpected rush of love, Darginn reached forward and touched Ismar's shoulder. The boy turned with a questioning scowl, but his face softened as Darginn whispered, "I'm proud of you." The curious frown became a bemused half smile. But the light in his eyes sparked even more brightly than the torchlight, down there in the dark. Darginn hadn't seen that light in a long time. And it was worth everything.

# CHAPTER 43

It had taken Meristan a few hours to put it all together, lying in the relative quiet of the hold. There was a reason he was on *this* boat. A boat full of former pirates. The type who'd not balk at the morally dubious.

As he'd been considering how he'd get back to Eidyn, it had hit him. Why would Anhel Weyr risk having Meristan outside of Eidyn, able to tell anyone he met what had happened there? It was a hole in his plan. And he was not a man who overlooked such things.

It was dark when they came for him.

Careless feet on salt-soaked boards. Four of them.

They'd underestimated him.

Thought they were coming for a monk.

The hold was dank with shadows. Crates and barrels gathered like street hawkers, offering salt beef, cheese, ship's biscuits and rum. Strapped to each other or lashed to beams to keep them still. Enough to feed a crew of one hundred for a month, at least. The hatch creaked open and light spilled down the steps from the hammock deck. Footsteps, more gentle now, creeping down. They hoped to catch him asleep.

Meristan had positioned himself between two stacks of crates. A little corridor, too narrow to effectively swing a sabre. Too tight for more than one person. A bottleneck.

He didn't want to kill any of these people. But that didn't mean he'd go meekly to his own execution. He was needed. He still had a purpose.

The monk robe was not made for fighting, so he'd done the only sensible thing—remove it. He crouched now in the shadows, waiting for the first of the sailors to reach him. His left forearm wrapped in the robe, a length of rope coiled around his right fist.

"Where is he?" a voice hissed.

No reply. But a creak of leather suggested one of the others had waved him quiet. Meristan cleared his mind and prepared.

Footsteps stalked in different directions. They were hunting him.

Meristan concentrated on his breathing, keeping it slow, measured and silent. Patience was his weapon.

He listened to them stumbling about, their steps becoming more hurried, hushed expressions of exasperation mixing with more agitated leather creaks. And then, finally, steps approached. A silhouette at the end of his little mousetrap. The first officer, by the look of her shape. She paused a moment, surprised to actually see him crouched there. Meristan pounced forward, left arm blocking her reflexive prod with the sabre, rattling it against the crates, right hand coming up to punch her in the throat.

She dropped the blade, instinctively grabbing at her throat with both hands. Meristan whipped her second sabre from its scabbard and kicked her in the stomach, knocking her on her back.

One down.

And now he had a weapon. Lighter, flimsier than he would like. But it would do. He shook the rope off his hand and clutched the grip.

Movement from his right as another blade swung down toward him. Meristan stepped left, avoiding the swing, but there was another coming in from his left, toward his ribs. He parried that one, spinning in toward his attacker and elbowing him in the face. A knee to the crotch, an uppercut with the knuckle bow, and the assailant dropped to his knees, clutching his jaw with one hand and his balls with the other.

"What the fuck...?"

The other two had come together, standing in the beam of light from the hatch. He'd seen neither of them on the way in. Both of them unremarkable, with dishevelled hair and the unruly stubble of the sea. Nor had they seen him, he assumed by the wide-eyed stares.

They saw him clearly now.

A glance between them and they burst apart. One lunged for Meristan, the other for the steps. If he made it back up there, he'd bring more, and that could get difficult. Four was easy; forty would be challenging. People would die.

The man came flying at him like a drunken schoolboy—no form, all violence, blades flaring like a windmill. Meristan deflected his frantic blows left, stepped right, hooked the man's foot and sent him flying into Broken Jaw. The other stopped to look back, and Meristan saw terror then. He raced across and caught him by the leg just as he would have crested the hatch opening, and yanked him back down. He landed hard on his back, smacking his head against the wood. Meristan turned, ready to face him, but he didn't move. The head blow had taken him. Fine.

But the others weren't done. Two were at least quiet, as the first mate gasped for breath and the second man moaned, both hands supporting the damaged jaw. But the third man was back up, turned to face him, eyes wide.

"Who the fuck *are* you?"

Meristan grinned. "God's Own Blade."

Judging by the man's face, the name meant nothing, but it was enough to shake him from his stupor and make him consider reinforcements. He opened his mouth and took a breath, but Meristan crushed it from his lungs, shoulder charging him in the chest. The pair of them sprawled hard into a barrel, which burst underneath them, spilling fish across the deck. Meristan rolled away and retook his feet, as the sailor slipped and struggled on a bed of haddock. He made it to his knees before a blow to the temple sent him sideways again. This time he stayed down.

Broken Jaw was still moaning quietly, but the first mate had recovered the bulk of her senses and was crawling toward the sabre she'd left on the floor. Meristan moved across and grabbed the neck of her leathers, pulling the woman back from her weapon. He placed her other sword at her throat.

"I would strongly prefer not to kill you," he whispered, low and dark. "I will, if I must. And rest assured, it will be quick. But I would be happier if you allow me to subdue you quietly."

After a moment, the woman sighed and relaxed her broad shoulders, giving a subtle nod. A concession. Meristan lifted the rope he'd used earlier and bound the woman's wrists.

Broken Jaw had the sense to lie quietly, avoiding drawing attention to himself. Still, Meristan stole another length of rope and tied the man's wrists to his ankles. Safe enough now that they weren't going to alert anyone. A strip off the end of his robe formed a gag for the first mate, and Meristan crept up the steps onto the mid deck, pulling her behind him. When she stood up in the light, Meristan saw the fury and indignation in her eyes. The woman was livid she'd been taken by surprise by a half-naked monk. There was a small moment of amusement in that.

"Is there another way to the main deck?" Meristan asked. On the way down, they'd crossed through the hammocks, and he'd prefer to avoid that, for fear of waking half the crew in contained quarters. The woman nodded in the opposite direction, and indeed, there was another set of steps there, leading to a small landing and a door.

"Right," Meristan whispered. "This can go smoothly and end well for everyone, or it can go badly and a lot of people will go to God before their time. Can I trust you not to make a mess of this?"

There was dull hatred in her stare, but still the woman nodded.

"Good enough."

Meristan opened the door and forced the first mate through before him, sabre pointed at her back. He offered a quick thanks to God that it was a still evening, and the sleet had taken rest. He was cold enough as it was.

Once they were clear, he took hold of the first mate again, one hand gripping her arm, the other bringing the blade back to her throat. The dark gave him time to move out into the open, where he wanted to be. If this was to work, it would have to be a show. Finally, somebody spotted them and cried out.

"All hands on deck! All hands on deck!"

And suddenly the ship was alive, as if he'd shaken a beehive. Bodies dropped from nets and appeared from hatches. In the light of the moon they came swarming, hesitating when they arrived, confused as to why they'd been called. Meristan wordlessly moved his captive up to the quarterdeck, giving him a platform to preach from.

"Where is your captain?" he boomed.

"Right here, my friend." The voice came from behind him. Meristan turned to find the man calmly leaning on the poop deck rail, looking down at him. "What is all this?"

Meristan knew little about life at sea, and even less about the navy's customs. But of all the stories Nirea had told him while they were deep in their cups, there was really only one thing that seemed important right then. One fact that would matter for the rest of his life, one way or another.

*The only route to becoming a pirate captain is through the one before you.*

"I challenge you for the captaincy of this boat," Meristan roared, loud enough for the whole crew to hear. "Single combat."

A murmur of excitement and surprise ran across the main deck. It had likely been some time since they'd witnessed a mutiny. Maybe the first, for some.

Captain Hylar cocked his head, smiled and raised his arms wide. "My friend, this is no pirate vessel. This is a ship of the Eidyn navy. We do not *spar* for its captaincy. We *work* for it."

More murmurs. But the kind Meristan had hoped for. He was absolutely certain most of these men and women had converted when Mynygogg took the throne, his pirate fleet, led by Nirea herself, defeating Eidyn's navy. Mynygogg had promised them all a better way of life, but he knew well from the queen, a pirate is always a pirate, deep in their soul.

And pirates respected a challenge, not a coward.

"Are you sure, Captain?" Meristan asked. "You think your crew will still respect a man afraid of a naked monk?" Meristan opened his own arms then, mirroring Hylar's gesture. A ripple of laughter from the crew. A fleck of doubt in the captain's smile. He looked to his first mate, who stood docile in front of Meristan despite him releasing her from his grip. She knew how he could move. Hylar raised a questioning eyebrow and the woman slowly shook her head. She was warning him off. He needed to raise the stakes.

"Of course, if you are too *cowardly* to defend your position, *Hylar*"— Meristan deliberately left off his title as a mark of disrespect—"then I can simply behead your first mate and fetch you down here by force."

He kicked the back of the woman's knees and she dropped in front of him. Meristan held her shoulder with his free hand, raising the sabre high with his right.

Sucking breaths and hisses through clenched teeth. Sabres unsheathed. The crew would not see their second-in-command murdered without a challenge. But they expected their captain to lead. Nobody would come for Meristan without at least a nod from him. But the pirates amongst the crew had more expectation than that. And the captain knew it.

"Did your crew know you'd been ordered to murder me in my sleep, Hylar? That your king only pretended at grace? Only performed mercy?"

By the gasps, many had not. It made Meristan wonder whether Hylar might be one of those whose memories were uncorrupted. Whether he knew fine well who Anhel Weyr was, and served at the foot of whoever filled his coin pouch. His disinclination to fight Meristan certainly suggested he knew more than he might about what he was facing.

"You are mistaken, my friend. There was no such order." That smile again.

"So you didn't send your first mate with three men to kill me? There are not three men lying unconscious in the hold amongst a pile of salted fish?"

A woman perked up at that and made for the door they'd come through. A few others followed. Hylar's ground was becoming ever more unstable.

"Don't take that!" a gravelly voice called, and the smile was lost. "Fight him!"

The captain's eyes danced to his left, to the one who'd spoken—a brute of a man, as wide as he was high. Three parallel scars across his left cheek and tattoos from the neck down. No question he was pirate stock. And he'd just called out his captain.

Hylar paused a long time; Meristan left him to drown in his silence.

Murmurs became grumbles as the woman reappeared from below, supporting Broken Jaw limping his way onto the deck, one hand still cupping his wounded manhood.

"Come on!" Tattoo Neck barked. Whoever he was, he had the crew's respect, because his lead brought out supportive calls of "Do it!" and "Fuckin' murder 'im!"

Hylar took a deep breath and raised his arms for calm. Voices dipped, but the underlying grumble remained. "I accept your challenge, Brother."

The crew erupted in appreciation. Meristan released the first mate. Nobody would come for him now. And if they did, they'd quickly regret it.

"Form up!" Tattoo Neck called. Within minutes, there was a circle on the main deck with lanterns glowing all about it.

Meristan and Hylar made their way to the middle and stood facing each other, ten feet apart. Meristan tried to remember everything Nirea had told him about these challenges. There was some sort of code. But it didn't matter. The only thing that really counted was that the last one standing was in charge. But that was only for the pirates. Not everyone on board had come across. And so Meristan needed another concession.

"Captain. I assume you are a man of honour? A man of your word?" he asked.

Hylar grew an inch, indignant. "Of course."

"Then you will order your crew to accept me as their captain when I win?"

"*When* you win?" Feigned surprise. "Brother, you assume much."

Meristan met his eye silently and waited.

"Fine," Hylar conceded. "Should the brother best me, he is your new captain. Understood?"

A mixed chorus of "Aye, Captain!"

Meristan still hoped not to have to kill him. Though if, as he suspected, the man was a willing toady of Weyr, it would be less disagreeable. Either way, he wanted it done quickly. The lack of wind was likely the only reason he hadn't frozen already.

The captain spit in his hand and stepped forward, offering it to Meristan. "Good fortune."

Meristan placed the sabre in his left hand and took it with a smile. "And you."

Lightning quick, Hylar's free hand came up, bearing a glint of silver.

But all those late nights with Nirea, Meristan had listened.
*The one thing you must remember, above all else, is this: Pirates cheat.*
Meristan leaned left and pulled the pirate's right hand, jerking him forward, hooked Hylar's ankle with his right foot and sent the man flailing onto his face, his blade clattering across the deck and out of the circle.

Meristan turned and stepped back out of sword range. "You seem to have dropped your knife." A murmur of light mirth from the crew. Good. He needed not only to beat the man, but to humiliate him. Make sure nobody else would try to challenge him once he took command.

By the time Hylar was back on his feet, Meristan was set and waiting. A flicker of darkness from the captain faded as he plastered that smile back on. "You understand, I had to try."

"I'd have been surprised had you not," Meristan answered.

Hylar paced the edge of the circle, assessing Meristan. Did he know who he was facing? Was his mind clear? It didn't matter. He'd seen enough to know Meristan was formidable. But neither could Meristan take him lightly. A pirate captain did not come by the role through sound leadership.

Hylar swung his blade in a circle, then whipped it before him in a figure eight. Showing off. Wasteful. Winning a sword fight was about economy of movement. The one who tires first loses. Hylar was a peacock—but his crew liked it.

A sudden rush of wind and the ship lolled to the side. Meristan stumbled left, readjusting his balance, and Hylar struck. He lurched forward, swinging hard and fast for Meristan's head.

He would have expected Meristan to try to parry, off balance, and perhaps take first blood. Instead, Meristan leaned into his stagger, rolled over his left shoulder and back to his feet.

Hylar spun to face his new location and came again, swinging hard and fast.

Attack; parry; attack; parry; attack; parry.

On the next attack, Hylar came in too close. Meristan parried him away high, stepped forward and punched him in the jaw with his left hand.

Hylar staggered back, instinctively extending his blade out into longpoint, warning Meristan off advancing. He had some technique, then.

Meristan tested his mettle with a few slashes at the blade, but Hylar parried them all. He wasn't showing off anymore—his movements had become tight. Precise.

All right. A worthy opponent. That might be a bad thing. Harder for Meristan not to kill him.

Meristan pushed his advantage, dancing forward and slashing at Hylar. The pirate parried hard, and Meristan came on again, the force of his swing staggering Hylar back until he slipped to one knee. He held his blade high, still, and Meristan paused. The killing blow was open to him, but...

His hesitation was his undoing.

Hylar slashed low and Meristan only just danced back to avoid the full weight of the blade. Instead, it caught his right shin and Meristan staggered off that leg as the pain bit hard.

*Damn it!*

He put his right foot down gingerly, hoping it would take the weight...

It did. Just a flesh wound. The bone wasn't cracked, thank God. But he was bleeding. He couldn't let this drag on.

Hylar got back to his feet, wiping blood from his toothy grin.

Right. No more hesitation. He wasn't about to get himself killed either.

Meristan set his shoulders, moved to the centre of the circle and waited. Hylar came again, this time swinging up from the left. Meristan blocked him, but there was something odd about the shape of his attack.

A blade in Hylar's off hand. Of course. Nirea was always replete with knives.

Meristan reached across himself with his left arm and caught Hylar's wrist. In shock, the pirate froze, and Meristan did not. A deft flick of Meristan's sword disarmed the captain. He raised his own blade to the man's chest, and with a resigned shrug, Hylar opened his hand and let the second knife drop to the deck. The point stuck in the wood and it trembled there, upright, beside Meristan's bloody foot.

# THE DAMNED KING

He'd won, but he wasn't going to risk the man producing yet another blade.

Meristan turned the captain, pulling his arm up behind his back. A sudden wrench, and the shoulder popped free of its joint.

Hylar screamed.

A kick to his arse sent him reeling and he had to use his one good arm to catch himself as he fell to his knees.

Meristan stepped behind Hylar, tip of the sabre at the back of his neck. "Do you yield?"

"There's no yielding," growled Tattoo Neck. "Long as he lives and stands on this deck, he's captain."

*Blast.*

Fine.

Meristan dropped the blade and grabbed Hylar by his belt and collar. The man's feet scrabbled for purchase as Meristan dragged him across the deck, parting the ring of watching sailors. When they reached the edge, he stopped. "May God bless you, Captain."

With that, he tossed Hylar over the side. The resonant splash was all that broke the silence. Meristan turned to Tattoo Neck.

"Good enough?"

The man gave him a lazy salute. "Good enough."

"Right. You." He pointed to the first mate. "Get in the cockboat and fish him out before he drowns in the dark. I'd find yourself a foreign shore, if I were you. Anhel Weyr won't take kindly to hearing you lost your ship to a monk in his underwear. And you." Meristan indicated Broken Jaw. Neither of those two were going to serve under him. And the man needed a medic as well. A better one than what they were likely to have on board.

"Anyone else who is unhappy with me as captain, please feel free to join them."

Nobody moved.

Grand.

"You"—Meristan pointed to Tattoo Neck—"what's your name?"

"Clodenbach," he answered in that guttural growl.

"Clodenbach, you're first mate. Agreed?" The man clearly had the respect of the crew, and while it was maybe a risk having him next in line for command, Meristan also figured he'd earned the man's respect. And he didn't strike as the dirk-in-the-back type, anyway—pirate or not. If he came at Meristan, he reckoned he'd see him coming. Besides, Meristan had little or no notion how to run a boat, and he needed someone who did.

"Aye, Captain." Clodenbach stood up properly this time, giving a more respectful salute.

"Good man. Let's get this boat moving again. Who's the pilot?"

"Here, Captain." Meristan took a step back as he turned to find a young blond woman saluting him.

*Samily.*

No.

Not Samily.

"Pilot Luega, Captain." The resemblance was no more than superficial—the height, the hair—but it was enough. Too much. "Captain?"

"Yes, sorry, Luega. A pleasure. To where are we bound?"

"Londinjon, Captain."

Well, Hylar hadn't lied. Just omitted that Meristan wasn't going to make the whole trip. "Set a new course, please. Immediately."

"Aye, sir. Where to?"

The only place he could go, once he'd thought about it. Getting back to Eidyn alone now did them little good. If Weyr heard of his return, he might harm Samily out of sheer spite. He could order the Thorns executed. Send demons to Traverlyn. No, he was going to need to be sly. Quiet.

So he was going to the one place he might be able to find the help he needed to rescue Samily and, maybe, all of Eidyn with her.

"We make for Apardion."

# CHAPTER 44

"The first and most important thing you can all do is stop paying taxes."

A murmur of amused agreement spread around the room at Mynygogg's words. "How awful!" a man in a lime-green doublet called out, and the murmur became full-blooded laughter. Aranok smiled. Starting with the council members of the Merchants Guild had been his father's idea, and it was a good one. They'd helped to bring in the most successful and affluent members of the community, and now they sat before fifty of the wealthiest people in Mournside, all with their memories restored and all joyfully behind the idea of starving the false king of gold. What businessman would balk at an order from their king to keep their money?

"However," Mynygogg added with a grin, "I would appreciate it if you put that money aside. We will need it, and all of you, to repair the damage Weyr has done—and will continue to do as long as he holds the throne."

The levity became a sea of more serious nods.

The meeting room above the Merchant's Arms was functional, more than anything. Wooden floor, beams and walls, undecorated. A small, raised stage at one end, usually reserved for the committee, he understood, but tonight taken by the king and a pair of envoys. They were now largely free to come and go as they pleased, within reason, across

Mournside. Though Mynygogg had made the point they still needed to be discreet. Allandria had agreed, then regretted it when Aranok cut his hair short and started growing a beard out again. "It's scratchy. It's giving me a rash," she complained, half seriously. But she seemed to enjoy running her hand through his shorter hair.

It was nice to have her beside him, there on the stage, instead of guarding the door, where she'd usually be. But even now, as he looked at her, she was scanning the crowd, watching for suspicious behaviour—for anyone touching a blade or looking unhappy.

There was nobody, as far as Aranok could see. But he didn't have her trained eye.

Bak had assigned a few trusted guards to be there instead. Two on the door, another two on each side of the crowd scattered across benches.

Every single one of them who had been asked had come, as far as Aranok could see. Who would abstain from a meeting like this? To see their true king, in person. A rarefied treat for anyone, and often reserved for the hereditary lairds who expected a place at court. The merchant lairds usually found it more difficult to get such an audience, so they took it greedily when offered.

Mynygogg would likely address that imbalance when he retook the throne. Give these men and women more access to himself and Nirea. Thank them for their present support. An outcome the lairds most certainly looked for.

A hand raised in the audience. A woman with leathered skin and wrinkles that told of a life well lived.

Mynygogg opened a hand toward her. "Yes, please, speak up."

The woman rose to her feet. All five foot three of her, if she was lucky.

"Thank you, Majesty." She placed a hand on her chest and bowed. "Durla. Two questions, if I may. First, this isn't going to work quickly, is it? Starving the king of taxes, I mean. I take it we're looking at a long campaign? That being the case, how are we going to trade outside of the city? How will supplies get in? And second, all well and good, us withholding that money, but what are we going to do when the tax collectors show up at the gates demanding to be paid? Are the Guard going to protect us? Are you?"

"Fine questions, and fair," said Gogg. "You're right, this won't happen quickly. Not without bloodshed. And I'm not prepared to sacrifice our countrymen and women because they're in thrall to a charlatan. It is not their fault, and not their responsibility. So yes, it's going to take time. We have to accept that, unfortunately.

"The answer to your second question is also yes. Captain Bak understands that there may come a point where the city guard have to protect our citizens from not only the tax collectors, but the army itself. Anhel Weyr might well send them against us when he begins struggling to pay them. And yes, in that event, we will stand with you. We will protect Mournside. I hope that we will be able to do that by changing the minds of those who come against us."

"He'll just tax the rest of the country harder, won't he?" a male voice from somewhere in the crowd piped up as Durla sat down.

"He might," Mynygogg answered. "That is a possibility. He'll get no joy from Traverlyn, and we also have someone working in Leet." Wise not to mention it was the queen. Just in case. Best not to announce where she was and inadvertently put a target on her head. "So to answer your other question, Durla, Leet will hopefully become an accessible trade route. But yes, he may tax the rest of the country heavily. If it's the lairds, he'll undermine his own support amongst them, which will be difficult for him regardless of his power. If it's the rest of the country, he'll quickly make himself as unpopular as Hofnag, and we might find ourselves in a race to dethrone him before someone else does!"

Another murmur of laughter. It was odd, to be laughing about these things. These merchants lived such sheltered lives. They wouldn't experience the hardship of choosing between paying taxes and feeding their children. Most of them had barely been affected by the change in king, and many may not really have cared either way.

But having the rightful king here, sitting before them, that was currency. That was leverage. And that was important to all of them. A promise of jam tomorrow, but with the cook beholden to them.

The meeting carried on, with a number of salient questions and a few inane ones about things like future taxation levels—as if that were crucial at the moment. Mynygogg had always argued that what taxes were spent on was more important than their level, and he made convincing arguments for the betterment of the country providing more wealth for all. People with more money spent more money after all. And Gogg's velvet tongue had them all begging for the chance to eat from his hand by the end. There was just something about him when he got talking.

When it was all done, the meeting broke up into a dozen little negotiations. People stood raking over the coals of what had been said, discussing business opportunities, or just gossiping, which seemed a much greater element of these gatherings than Aranok had previously assumed.

As was the norm, they adjourned and took a quick drink downstairs, out of decorum more than desire, before drifting across the square to the Canny Man.

The snow was a foot deep, and Aranok missed his leathers as they trudged through it. They were warmer than the relatively staid outfits his father had offered as part of their "discretion." Well tailored enough to fit in; inexpensive enough to be ignored.

"Fuck, that's cold." Allandria brushed the dusting of snow off her cloak and stamped her feet against the frost. By the time they got to the bar, drinks were waiting for them.

Calador had been a useful ally since they cleared him, keeping an eye on comings and goings. If a messenger came, they'd come to the Canny Man, and he'd be able to send warning to them before they could spread more of Weyr's lies. If they could clear a messenger—and convince them to go back as if they were still under Janaeus's spell—that could be the beginning of getting agents inside Weyr's camp. Of getting *information*. But weeks had passed without sign of one. Which might be suspicious, or it might mean nothing.

Still, it was good that they would know first when it happened. Prevent Aranok from being framed for any more murders.

They'd also carefully selected regulars from the inn to clear, spreading the net out gradually such that most of those who drank and worked there now knew the truth. The place was always a little busier than usual, as patrons hoped to get a sighting of the insurgent king and his envoys.

And they were playing into that desire. Mynygogg felt it was a good way of keeping people invested. Let them see their king with them, drinking, planning, engaging. There was little that swung a person's allegiance more than being made to feel important. *Seen.*

This was as much a part of gathering their allies as spreading the truth, Mynygogg said.

Somehow, amongst the bustle and churn of the move across to the much nicer and noticeably warmer inn, Mynygogg had found himself engaged in conversation with Pol, who had come in lieu of Dorann. His father had said it was because he was technically still under threat, and guarded, but Aranok had a strong notion that it was also a little revolt against him. A small tantrum in an attempt to display some measure of power.

He'd said as much to Mynygogg, and his friend had smiled. "Aranok, the worst thing any child ever learns is that their parents are just people—the same flawed, scared, confused arseholes as the rest of us."

That was certainly true. He'd had little interaction with his father since they cleared the family. A few visits with Ferrod, who was completely besotted with Emelina. He swore she had her grandmother's smile, and that Taie winked back at him every time he saw it.

"This is nice, isn't it?" Allandria sidled up to him at the bar, slipping her leg between his and pressing against him. With the weather, she'd also opted for trousers and multiple layers under her cloak. "Us just out at the pub for a drink like normal people?" She sipped her wine and tipped the glass toward him. He met it with his own.

"It's almost as if we weren't planning a revolution."

"Another one? Didn't we just have one of those?"

Aranok laughed. "Feels like it, doesn't it? But...it's different this time. I mean, since we came here...Does it feel...I don't know, maybe I'm mad, but...I feel quite..." He looked around the crowded bar, at people talking, drinking, laughing. "Hopeful?"

Allandria smiled up at him as if at something more than what he'd said. He was about to ask what when she nodded behind him and said, "Shall we rescue our liege from the attention of that prick?"

Aranok turned and saw Pol was still prattling on at Gogg, who was doing a fine impression of being interested. They'd taken a pair of seats by the fire. Pol was gesticulating enthusiastically about something.

"Yes, I suppose we should," Aranok answered.

"Come on, then." She leaned in and brushed a gentle red-wine kiss across his lips, then stepped away.

"The thing is, facts don't actually matter!" Pol was excitedly preaching as they came into hearing. "Facts don't change people—feelings do. You have to woo their hearts if you want their minds. They have to want what you're offering because it will make them *feel* good about themselves." He cut off his invective and almost retreated into the back of his chair when he saw the two of them arrive.

"Ah, hello. Join us," said Mynygogg. "Pol was just telling me about the art of sales."

If Gogg was pretending to be interested in the little toad's nonsense, he was doing a good job. Aranok raised a questioning eyebrow, and Mynygogg gave a subtle nod in return. So they pulled up chairs.

"Please, go on," said Gogg.

Pol gave the two of them a shifty side-eye before leaning back in and lowering his voice. "The first key is to spot the opportunity. They're everywhere, if you're alert to them. When you respond to a need, rather than trying to create one yourself, you're not even selling, you're providing a service, you see? Give people what they *need*, *when* they need it—they'll throw gold at you and thank you for the opportunity. And then it's all in the delivery."

He held out his arm, turning his palm upwards flamboyantly. "If I tell you I have a shirt that would look wonderful on you, you might consider looking at it. If you were in want of a shirt. I might tell you that it is handsewn, double stitched or unique, and it is, but that is true of every shirt I sell. The trick, you see, is to sell them not the shirt, but a vision of themselves." His voice somehow found an even oilier octave as he performed the next: "Ah, sir, I have a shirt just in—handsewn in imported silk. I haven't shown it to anyone yet, but you, sir, I think might be the first person I've seen who has the shoulders to do it justice. Most men would be too small for this shirt; they couldn't fill it in the way that you will. But I am sure that you, sir, will make this unique shirt shine like the sun itself."

Pol sat back, clearly pleased with himself. "You see? You don't sell the shirt looking well on the man, you sell the man making the shirt look fabulous. You flatter their ego, make them feel special, and they will dance for you like a child."

Gogg rubbed his hand over his mouth, contemplating the man in front of him. "All right. You said this could help us. How?"

Again, Pol leaned in. "Well, Majesty, your plan relies on the truth, yes? On getting to everyone and giving them their minds back."

"Of course."

"But it's a long game—you said so yourself. There are quicker ways to do the job. As I said, the *truth* doesn't matter—how people *feel*, that's the key."

"All right. What are you suggesting, Pol?"

"I'm saying a good lie—the *right* lie—will spread quicker than the truth."

He let the idea hang in the silence, sitting back and crossing his legs as if he'd laid a bag of gems before them.

"I'll be honest, it's not an approach I like," Gogg said after a while. "But take me through it. What lie should we tell?"

"Well." Pol waved his arms dramatically as if plucking ideas from the ether. "You begin by accepting that Janaeus was the king. Don't argue it, since that only causes people distress. Yes?"

He addressed the question at Aranok, who he was suddenly acknowledging as he grew in confidence with each pronouncement. Aranok nodded once.

"So, don't contradict what they believe—build on it. Embrace the lie. Janaeus was a great man. A fine man. But he was betrayed: *not* by Laird Aranok, who has been unjustly accused, but by Anhel Weyr himself, who is secretly a *draoidh* and murdered Good King Janaeus and the Lairds' Council—and would have murdered Aranok too had he not bravely escaped."

The way he said *draoidh* came with such obvious derision that Aranok's hands curled involuntarily.

"*Draoidh?*" A voice from behind them, slow and slurred. "Did you say *draoidh*? What about *draoidhs*?"

Aranok turned to see a well-dressed man in his thirties who'd had at least three more than he could handle. His delicate complexion and finely coiffed hair spoke of money, and his attitude reeked of entitlement.

"Eh, no, sorry," said Pol. "You misheard."

"I didn't!" the twat insisted. "Bloody *draoidhs*. You're not one of them, are you?" He was practically leaning on Aranok's back now as he badgered Pol, who looked like he wanted to crawl under the chair. "Like bloody Aranok...used to swan around here, you know? Like he was special. Like *he* was the bloody king! No surprise he murdered Janaeus in the end. Fucker always had a swagger about him."

Allandria and Mynygogg both stood, a look of venom on the king that Aranok had never seen.

"All right, you, that's enough." Calador's tenor cut through the bar's chatter. He grabbed the man by the shoulders and turned him away. "Time for you to go home."

"Hang on!" he objected, holding up his cup for show. "I'm still drinking!"

"Not here, you're not." Calador marched him out the door, ignoring his continued protestations, and returned holding the now-empty cup.

Allandria sat back down, stroking Aranok's arm as she did. But Mynygogg didn't sit.

"Go after him. Clear him."

"Why?" Aranok asked. "He's hammered. And a prick. What use is he?"

He sat and looked Aranok in the eye. "Because I want him to know what he just did."

Calador appeared behind them, leaning between his and Allandria's chairs. "Very sorry, Majesty, Laird, Lady," he whispered. "He won't drink here again." The big man slapped a comradely hand on Aranok's shoulder.

Aranok patted it gratefully. "Thank you."

Once the innkeeper returned to the bar, Mynygogg picked up again. "He deserves to know what he did."

"It doesn't matter." Aranok shrugged. "He was a prick. He's not the first."

"It does matter," Gogg insisted. "It matters to *me*."

And then he saw it. The rage, the frustration, the pain all swirling in his friend's eyes. The guilt. It did matter to him. Not that Aranok had ever doubted it—not really. But he did care. And not just about

Aranok, though that was definitely making it worse. He reached a hand across to his friend's arm.

"I know. But we have bigger bears to hunt."

The king lifted his drink and emptied it. Pol's wide eyes flicked between the two of them. That was likely the first time he'd seen Gogg angry. And the first time he'd seen what might happen to someone who insulted *draoidhs* in his company. What might happen to someone with a history of insulting the king's envoy. Good. Might remind him of his place.

"All right." The king leaned back in his chair, composure returned. "Pol. You were saying."

Pol's eyes were still on Aranok, who sipped his drink and pretended his brother-in-law didn't appear to be shitting his breeks. And tried not to smile about it.

The sooner Ikara was done with him, the better.

---

Allandria breathed in the sharp winter air and pulled Aranok's arm tighter against her. There was something inherently peaceful about the fat flakes lazily drifting down about them. The crunch of their boots in the snow. The still night lent it an even softer tone, as if the world had been muffled. Lanterns glowed like captured stars, casting magical light on pristine white blankets.

Samily talked of times when she felt closer to God, and here, now, crossing Mourning Square with a cosy bellyful of wine as the Midwinter festival approached, she knew what that meant. There was solace in the air. Comfort.

Love.

She could see how, living there, it might be easy to forget about the problems outside these walls.

"What do you think?" Mynygogg's question broke the serenity.

Aranok paused and turned back to face him. "About what?"

"Pol's idea."

Aranok looked at him quizzically. "I think Pol's a fucking idiot."

"Well, he's an arsehole, but he's not thick," the king replied. "He's a talented salesman."

"Not sure I'd call that a talent." Aranok wiped his hand across his head, brushing away the flakes melting there. "Wait. You're not actually considering..."

Across the square, movement caught Allandria's eye. She turned to see a figure in a grey cloak, awkwardly coming toward them. Their stilted walk appeared like an attempt to hurry without drawing attention. It wasn't working.

"Aranok." She nudged him and nodded toward the figure.

Allandria looked around them. Several other groups wending their way home from the pubs after closing time. Drunken chatter. Was this a threat?

"What's happening?" Mynygogg asked.

"Someone coming at us," said Allandria. "Over there."

Mynygogg turned, clocked the figure and turned back. "Rasa?" he whispered.

The three of them had been wondering about her just that afternoon. They'd expected to see her by now, with an update from Nirea. That she hadn't come was making them all a little uncomfortable, but they agreed there were many reasons she might not be able to, and that there was no point worrying until they had a reason to—especially when things were going so well for them here.

They waited, smiling at folk who passed, pretending to be deep in conversation about nothing.

None of them were dressed for a fight. But Allandria had her knives. And Aranok was a weapon.

The grey-cloaked shape, head down beneath their hood, shoulders hunched, was almost on them when Aranok spoke.

"Hold." He raised his flaming hand. "Who are you?"

They pulled back their hood and a timid but relieved face grinned back at them.

"Thank God. I've been looking for you for days."

Allandria brushed past Aranok and grabbed the boy into a hug.

"Vastin!"

# CHAPTER 45

Vastin rubbed his hands together, still struggling to shake off the insistent cold, despite a roaring fire and the mug of tea Meja had brought him. It felt deeply odd, a cook bringing him a cup of tea, as if he was some sort of laird, but then Ferrod's house was like a wee palace, so it fit, he supposed. She sort of reminded him of Amollari, despite being twice her age, at least. But she had the same kindness about her, and also smelled sweet as a spring morning. Not heather, but floral. Maybe it was rose? Whatever, it was nice, and the warm tea felt like a significant kindness after all he'd been through to get there.

Laird Severianos had insisted that Vastin should stay in Traverlyn. That they should send a messenger—someone not being hunted by the Guard—to deliver the news about Samily, Rasa and Meristan. But Vastin couldn't stand the idea of not being sure they got the message. He would have worried himself sick that something had gone wrong, and that the king would have no idea what had happened until it was too late. He couldn't do nothing while Samily and Rasa were prisoners.

So he'd lied.

Promised he'd stay put, and taken a horse the next morning. Handy that the stable master remembered him. It had been strange, returning to the stable after all that had happened there. But nice to see Bear again. The big Calladell had maybe saved his life. The stable master wasn't for letting him have such a valuable horse, though, despite him claiming he'd an urgent mission to reach the king. He'd given him a fair bit of side-eye, in fact. But returning Bear to him after the Thakhati battle seemed to have bought him enough credit to get a horse. Made the journey a damned sight quicker and easier than the walk from Haven to Traverlyn had been—particularly with avoiding the ferry. That had been a hard road, especially with Darginn taking sick on the third day. But Ismar had looked after him, and Vastin had made sure the Green Laird's wound stayed well wrapped and clean, with the bandages Maither Floreli had sent with him.

He'd been bloody glad to finally see Traverlyn, though. They were all about done when they finally reached the Green Wall, as people had taken to calling it. There was talk of replacing it with stone too. No surprise, after what they'd been through.

But when he'd got to Mournside, he'd had to lie about his purpose. Said he was to be apprenticed to a blacksmith. A safe enough lie, if they asked questions about his trade. They'd been more interested in his name and where he'd come from. So he lied again. Once he'd started, it seemed to come naturally. But he hadn't known where to look once they let him in. So he took to hanging around busy places, listening to conversations and watching. He couldn't just go around asking if anyone had seen the envoy and the king—both of them wanted by the Guard, just like him.

Only it turned out they weren't, and if he'd just told the guard at the gates who he was and what he wanted, they'd have likely escorted him right here! That would have been good to know a few days previous! Sleeping in a warehouse he'd managed to break into had at least kept the snow off, but he'd been too concerned about attracting attention to build a fire.

Anyway, he was here now. And getting warmer. And he'd delivered the message, for all the chaos it had caused.

"Fucking Hell." Laird Aranok paced across the vast floor, wringing his hands. "An *invisible demon?*"

"It's...it's only a rumour." Vastin was keen not to set off alarms where none were needed. They had enough else to fret about. He'd feel a right fool if he brought such grave news to the king and it was just tavern talk after all.

"Is it even possible?" Mynygogg spread his hands wide on the chair opposite Vastin.

"Anything's *possible*," Aranok answered. "What we know of magic is probably only a tiny amount of what we have to learn, but...if it's true, it could be a form of illusion, but then...demons don't have magic, so..."

"Don't they?" Allandria leaned against a writing desk, arms folded. "I mean, aren't they, sort of, *made* of magic? They're not *natural*...are they?"

"Well, that's a debate in itself," said Aranok. "But it doesn't matter. If Weyr really has an invisible demon following him around..."

"Oh, and there's something else." Things kept coming to Vastin in waves. Every time he thought he'd told them everything, he remembered another detail. He should have written it down. "Laird Severianos said Weyr's got this gold cane that he takes everywhere. 'Unseemly and ostentatious,' he called it. But, well, he mentioned that it's got this grim skull at the top, coated in gold, and I thought...skull?"

If Aranok's face had dropped at the mention of the demon, he turned a sickening shade of pale then. "A skull?" He turned to Allandria. She looked as rattled as he did.

"Right." Mynygogg sighed and sat back in the chair.

Aranok turned to the king. "Gogg..."

Mynygogg raised a hand to cut him off. "It doesn't matter, Aranok. It may or may not be the heart. He might just want us to think he has it. We deal with what's in front of us. We have to assume it is, until we discover otherwise. So what do we do?"

"We have to rescue them," Allandria said. "We can't leave Samily and Rasa as Weyr's prisoners."

"Agreed. If nothing else, we need Samily to repair the second charm," said Aranok. "And Rasa for communication."

Vastin cringed a little at that. He didn't like them being spoken about as if they were assets. *Things* that were useful. They were their friends, and that was enough reason to free them. But he was sure Aranok hadn't meant it like that.

The king steepled his fingers in front of his mouth, eyes closed. He almost looked like he'd fallen asleep, until he spoke. "No. We can't risk it. This happened because Meristan went after Laird Severianos, and then Samily went after him. We're lucky that Vastin and the others made it out. And we've lost Meristan. Anhel Weyr has some magic-resistant prison. He knew they'd come for the Green Laird. He was waiting for them. Now he's waiting for us. We can't go. It's a trap."

Silence. Vastin's heart dropped into his belly.

Aranok and Allandria seemed as stunned as him. How could they *not* rescue their friends?

Vastin waited for someone to argue... but nobody did.

"You're right," Aranok finally said. "Fuck it all, but you're right."

Allandria sighed and looked at the floor. "God damn it."

And then nobody spoke for an age. Aranok slumped onto a sofa. Allandria crossed her arms and closed her eyes, lifting her face to the ceiling.

The crackle of the fire was the only sound to drown out Vastin's thumping heart. He should say something. He should convince them they were wrong! But what? How?

"Oh! Have I interrupted something terribly serious?" Ferrod's voice finally broke the awkward quiet. He'd appeared at the door in a gown and slippers.

"I'm afraid so," the king answered. "Bad news. We've lost some allies."

"Oh. Oh, I'm sorry."

"Not dead," Allandria said quickly. "Imprisoned. Banished."

"Oh!" Ferrod brightened at that. "Well, I suppose that's something, isn't it?"

"It's something," Aranok said wearily. "It is something." He crossed to stand in front of Allandria and took her hands. She looked up at him sadly.

Mynygogg stood, as if he was trying to bring up the mood. "Things are going well here. We have to keep up that momentum. We have the Guard. We have the Merchants Guild. We have key members of society and we're getting more every day. We already have Traverlyn, or at least enough that we can count on. Nirea is securing Leet, and with that, eventually, the navy. Now we know why Rasa hasn't come, and it's not because Nirea is in trouble. She never made it to Leet. Weyr will keep them alive because he knows he can use them against us. We will bide our time, and we will free them when we take back the kingdom."

"We assume Nirea is clearing Leet," said Aranok. "Without Rasa..."

Mynygogg's eyes wavered. A look of pain crossed him. "I know. We have to have faith. In her."

Aranok sighed deep and rubbed at his chin. "Aye." They both looked grey. Tired. Like the life had been drained out of them a bit. They looked like Vastin felt.

"What about Meristan?" Allandria asked.

Another sigh, from Mynygogg. "If anyone can look after themself, it's God's Own Blade."

God, Vastin felt sick. Everything the king said made sense, but he couldn't believe it meant abandoning Samily. After all she'd done, after she'd saved him... "But, Your Majesty..." Vastin cleared his throat to prevent his voice from breaking. "What if he kills them?"

Mynygogg put a hand on Vastin's knee.

"That is a risk, I won't lie. But let me ask you something. The only way we could hope to rescue them now would be an assault on Greytoun. People would die. We'd be risking ourselves and, if we lost..." He gestured to the others. "Any of us. It would be a risk to us retaking the kingdom, and maybe put Eidyn in Weyr's hands for good.

"If you were to ask Samily what we should do, if we should risk all of that to save her, what would she say?"

He was right. Of course, she'd tell them to leave her. "In God's hands." Because that's who she was.

A hero.

But that didn't make it right.

"I'm sorry there's not more I can do," Ferrod said sadly. "There are times when having an overabundance of gold feels as if one can do anything, but the world has a way of reminding you that there are problems beyond even wealth."

Aranok suddenly perked up. "Actually, Ferrod, that's...that's an idea."

"What is?" the old man asked.

"Gold," said Aranok. "I'd gotten used to being cut off from funds, but now, here...there might be a way that gold *can* help us."

"I am an assassin. You understand?" Kye Denassa leaned on the sideboard in Aranok's family kitchen. A pot of something that smelled like pork and apples simmered gently on the stove behind Aranok. He'd had to ask Cressida to leave them alone, and she'd scowled and warned him that if the dinner burned, she'd have words for him. He'd promised to give it a stir now and again, for the time they would be in there.

"Why did you take a contract as a bodyguard, then?" Aranok had been wondering about Kye for a while. Other things had taken precedence in his thoughts, of course, but a few things had just been niggling there in the background.

"Your father sought me," Kye answered. "It was the job."

"Yes, but being a guard and *evading* guards are very different things. And you seem to be an excellent guard, for an assassin."

Kye tipped his fingers against his head in a mock salute, a glint of recognition in his eye. "Thank you."

"And it occurred to me... Why would a Gaullic assassin be hanging around for work in Eidyn? Surely there's plenty of work in Gaulle, where he knows the country, and the language, much better. Unless there's a lack of business back home?"

Again, that look. Respect. Understanding. "There is not."

"So it made me wonder, what kind of person would be working in a foreign country, as an assassin, but who was also particularly skilled in being a bodyguard?"

"And what conclusion did you find, my friend?" Kye asked.

Aranok took a moment. This was a gamble, but he was fairly certain he was right. "You're a spy, aren't you?"

Kye crossed his arms and smiled. "I would not be a very good spy if you figured that out so easily, would I?"

"Well, I'm very clever," said Aranok. "Don't take it as an insult."

"And what would you want with a Gaullic spy, Laird Envoy?" Kye still looked as though he were casually leaning on the sideboard, but Aranok had watched Allandria work enough to know that he had a blade in one of his hands by now. Aranok had put his leathers on for a reason.

# THE DAMNED KING

"Well, by your skill, and your age, you've been a spy for some time. Which means you likely began under Taneitheia's rule. And maybe you came here with her when she was exiled, because maybe you didn't approve of King Delaure. And maybe, when she returned to Gaulle, she asked you to stay here and see how the war played out? And then your own memory was scrambled and..."

He'd sort of lost the thread of the theory there. But he hoped he'd got enough of it right to convince Kye to tell him the rest.

The assassin stroked his tight black beard for a moment, examining Aranok.

"Delaure is too much his father's son, and not enough his mother's. I was here with the queen. I left with her. She sent me back, as you say, to watch. But I found the country in madness, with a new king everyone thought was the old king. So I watched, and waited, until I could understand what had happened."

So he'd never had his memory changed. And he'd done an excellent job of convincing Aranok when he tried to clear it. That was a little worrying. Who else had conned him? That was a concern for later. For now, he'd been right about Denassa. And that was excellent news.

"And you ended up here...?"

"I hoped it an opportunity to get close to you, Laird Envoy. To understand what you were doing. How you might retake the throne. How, perhaps, Taneitheia could help, in return for..."

"For our help in taking her own throne back."

Kye nodded. "As you say."

Interesting. And useful. "It's not quite the same, but I suppose we both sit here with deposed monarchs we'd like to see back on the throne."

"Indeed."

"So...maybe we can help each other?"

Kye's eyebrows raised with a hint of surprise. "You want my help?"

"I do. And I offer ours in return." Ironic, that the fake mission Janaeus had given him so long ago, he was now volunteering for. "Help me get Mynygogg and Nirea back on the throne, and we'll do the same for Taneitheia." She *was* a better monarch than her son. And she'd be a useful ally.

Kye's face was difficult to read. But he'd now taken to openly playing with the knife in his hand, which felt like a gesture of peace—he was no longer worried about needing to use it. "Why do I trust you, Laird Envoy? Maybe I help you and then...?" He made a gesture with his left hand that looked like a small explosion. Aranok took it to mean that they might just abandon him.

"Well, there's this." Aranok dropped the pouch of coins on the table between them. "You'll need some of it for the work I'm going to ask of you, but the rest is yours. You could take that and disappear, if you wanted. I'm trusting you not to."

Kye didn't even glance down at the gold. Didn't ask how much it was. He just smiled again. "This was in case you were wrong? In case I was just an assassin, yes?"

It was. But it had turned into a useful gesture. "You'll need some for the job, as I said. Feel free to return the rest, if you have no need of it."

"A man who has no need of gold is already dead." Kye slipped the knife back into a hidden sheath up his sleeve. "All right, Envoy, I accept your offer. What of my contract with your father?"

There had been no sign of any threat to the family since Kye had killed the one assassin who'd come hunting before Aranok had even arrived. If there had been, Kye would have noticed. Chances were that Madu's contract on his family died with that assassin. But they would keep the other guards on for now. Just to be safe. "I'll handle that. I'll speak to him; don't worry. This is urgent."

Kye stood up tall and folded his hands behind him, like a soldier.

"All right, Laird Envoy. How am I to help you retake your throne?"

---

"You're not fit yet." Ailen's tone was resigned. He already knew Nirea wasn't going to listen. Which she wasn't.

"I know." Weeks she'd waited in this room, looking at the same four walls and a window. The same table and chair. And only once Ailen had decided she was ready to have her own room, instead of keeping her like a babe in arms on a cot in his and Crinn's chambers. A month of resting, letting the men look after her. Waiting for her damned wound to heal. For her strength to return. Every day thinking, *Maybe today; maybe Rasa will arrive.*

The metamorph was meant to come after a few weeks. Check in with Nirea—bring news from Traverlyn, maybe Mournside too.

But nothing. Nirea had been going crazy, with no idea what the Hell was happening outside of Leet—Hell, she barely knew what was happening outside the King's Wark, and that only because of the high-ranking people they had managed to clear before she got Quellaria killed.

Captain Gert had been incandescent about the attack—and apologetic. Turned out Harp really was his man, and a trusted ally. Whoever the assassin was, he'd murdered the real Harp en route to the Wark and taken the letter about Joliander. The body in the river wasn't his. A mercy she'd needed but hardly felt. But it wasn't Harp's uniform the assassin had worn. The real Harp was taller and slimmer than the killer. So he'd been planning it. Known enough that he could intercept Harp and use that letter. Meaning he probably had a contact inside the Guard. And without Quell, they had no way of knowing who. But Gert was bloody determined to find out. He'd been to visit at least weekly during her recovery, giving her any information he could, which wasn't a lot.

Until yesterday.

Yesterday, he'd arrived with the news that the Guard were to look for Severianos, the Green Laird, along with associates, Darginn Argyll and Vastin. Wanted by the king for treason. Conspiring with Aranok and Mynygogg. The entirety of the White Thorns disavowed and outlawed. And Meristan, banished after admitting his guilt. Baile Airneach claimed by the crown.

A total fucking disaster.

She had to find out what had happened. She'd been useless too long.

"You should be safe now," she said, tying up her pack and standing. Gert had promised her a horse, waiting at the southern stables. Still, as far as either of them knew, no warrant for *her* arrest. Nothing to suggest she was in danger. She should be able to travel unmolested.

"I know. But, Nirea..." Ailen's voice trailed off. "I'm worried about you."

She turned and put a gentle hand on his cheek. "Bless you."

Ailen took the hand and put it between his own. "No, that's not what I mean. I mean... Look, we haven't really talked. About Quell. About her death. You... I mean, after what you told me, about your friend Glorbad... Nirea, you need to *grieve*."

Grieve? Hell, it was all she was doing. Grief lived in her. It was a black shard in her throat; a phantom pain in her chest; a bitter weight in her gut. It was part of her. And she despised it. "I barely knew Quellaria."

"Nirea, that's not what I saw." Ailen squeezed her hand tight. "She was your friend."

"She was a tool. She was a weapon." Nirea pulled her hand away and picked up the pack. "Where's Crinn?" She should say goodbye.

"Nirea, for fuck's sake..." But she was already out the door and heading for the stairs. "Would you wait, please?"

Crinn sat at the table next to the door of the bar, eating breakfast. He smiled and nodded to the kitchen. "There is more."

"I don't have time, but thank you."

His face turned, as she expected.

"You're leaving?"

"I have to," she said, turning back to Ailen. "Can I take some rations? Some salt beef, bread..."

Ailen stood with his hands pressed together against his mouth, silently imploring her to stop and listen. "Is this what it's like?"

"What what's like?"

"Being queen. Never stopping. Never resting. Never... *healing*?"

Nirea took a deep breath and let the pack hang at her side. It brushed against her damaged hip and a spark of pain flashed across her pelvis. He wasn't going to stop until she gave him an answer.

So she did.

"No. This is the burn of seeing what needs to be done and having no power to do it. Of knowing the entire country has been lied to and not being able to give them the truth because they won't hear it. This is nothing like being a queen; this is being a revolutionary. This is demanding better and being prepared to sacrifice yourself for it. For that purpose. Being a queen is easy. Being a rebel is a bitch. And in either case, people die when you fuck up."

Ailen looked back at her—examining her. One arm across his chest, the other hand balled against his mouth. His eyes were pale. Sad. Mournful. Everything Nirea had no time to be.

"Please, Ailen. Can I take some rations?"

"Of course you can." Crinn crossed behind her. "Let me pack them for you." He stopped behind the bar and rested his hands on it, looking at his husband, who still hadn't spoken. "Ailen? Ailen, look at me."

Reluctantly, her friend turned his head toward his husband. "What?"

"Sometimes a warrior must be hard. Only later can they be human. It is how it is. You have to let her be."

Ailen nodded sadly, looked back to Nirea and forced a weak smile. "Come back. When it's done."

"I will," she promised, knowing fine well the odds of that happening. And ignoring those too.

# CHAPTER 46

Fucking snow. Nirea had absolutely had enough of snow. Days to get to Traverlyn. A few days there to learn what she could. That everything she feared was true. And worse. Quell dead, their second charm destroyed, Samily and Rasa captives and Meristan fuck alone knew where. Two days of Egretta fussing at her, demanding she rest, letting her tend to the wound on her hip.

She reckoned maybe Nirea had cut a nerve, and that was why she was getting the burning, stabbing pains. At least she had some poppy for it. And gave Nirea some to take with her.

Fucking Harp. The jolly little prick with his "kind eyes."

Then more days of travelling. The horizontal snow and Eidyn wind sanding the skin off her face, as if the broken nose didn't hurt enough.

"Not much we can do with that now," Egretta had said. "You need Lady Samily."

No shit, she did. And not just to fix these stupid bloody wounds.

Egretta had damn near refused to let her leave again, until she at least agreed to take a medic with her, in case she fell off her horse on the way. She'd not much fancied the idea of being lumbered with a stranger, but it had been a happy enough compromise when Egretta told her Morienne had returned from Lepertoun. She would do, the old medic had said, since her main job was to keep her upright and alive.

But Lepertoun had been hard on her. The light she'd been bursting with since her curse was lifted had been dimmed by the experience. And now here the two of them sat, cold, miserable and staring up at the end of a crossbow.

"Names!"

And that was the trick, wasn't it? If Gogg had done the same as her, and she reckoned he would've, then the city guard should know who she was. And they should welcome her with a fanfare. But without Rasa, she'd no idea if they were even fucking alive inside these walls. If they'd even got here. But she'd also no idea if anyone was looking for her. As far as she'd heard, no king's messenger had put out her name yet. Then again, no messenger had been to Traverlyn since the Thakhati attack. She doubted there would be another. Weyr had given up on taking the town and moved directly to levelling it.

Some fucking *draoidh* saviour.

Still. They needed to know.

"Name's Morienne! I'm a medic and I have a woman here in need of medical care!"

"Stay there!"

Hubbub behind the gates. Morienne gave her a nervous smile.

The gate swung open and a tall woman with short grey hair walked toward them. She came close and spoke quietly, so just the two of them would hear. "Lady Morienne, your name is on a list from the king. Please follow me."

*Oh, fuck.*

Nirea reared up her horse and yanked the reins, her hood falling as she barked a command to Morienne.

"Run!"

Any second a crossbow bolt might hit her in the back. She'd have to move quickly, to—

"Your Majesty?"

It was the guard's voice. Not Morienne's.

She paused, snapped her head round. "Pardon?"

"Queen Nirea. It's you?"

"You know me?"

"We met once. King Mynygogg will be glad to see you. May I take you to him?"

Ah. A list from *that* king. That was a good sign. And now her hood was down, she noticed the snow had let up.

Thank God, finally, something was going well.

---

"Fucking Hell, it's a disaster!" Mynygogg roared. "We're back to the start—one memory charm. One charm to do the whole bloody kingdom!"

He wasn't wrong. Allandria rubbed her hand across her chest, feeling the yellow orb beneath her palm. She was wearing the most valuable piece of jewellery in Eidyn. Again. And it was suddenly very heavy.

"You know the irony of it?" Nirea was slumped in the big chair by the fire in Ferrod's living room, a large glass of rum in hand. She bore the sickly, yellowing bruises of healing around her eyes, and her nose took a nasty bend in the middle. She looked like shit. Probably more like a pirate than she ever had. But she still held the regal air of command. "Quell wasn't even the target. Ailen was. I was. The fucker practically killed her by accident. And this was in his pocket." She pulled out an envelope and tossed it on the low table. "Read it. Read the last line."

Mynygogg lifted it, his cheeks flushed red. "It's a contract. On Ailen. Oh Hell."

"What is it?" Aranok asked.

Mynygogg read: "As far as is possible, carry out this contract so as to cause maximum suffering to Captain Nirea."

"Fucking Madu," Nirea spat. "Vindictive auld bitch. Wasn't enough to murder folk, she had to have it done vicious. And that's why Quell is dead."

"God damn it." Mynygogg threw down the paper, rubbing his eyes with his thumb and forefinger. "God *damn* it!"

"Maximum suffering?" Allandria felt sick at the thought. She still hadn't been able to confirm her parents were safe. She had to assume. They would have gone. They *did*. "Do you think all the contracts said that?"

"We don't know. And there's no point speculating," said Aranok. It was a worry when he was the one trying to lift the mood. "Nirea, I'm sorry."

She turned to him with an odd look, almost as if she wasn't sure how to take it. There was still distrust there. "Thank you."

"And also, there's something else," Aranok continued. "I want to be the one to tell you. It's possible Weyr has the heart of devastation. It's possible Jan— It's possible he lied to me."

Hells, that was a lot. A huge admission. Aranok hadn't even spoken to Allandria about that yet, though she'd been expecting it. She didn't want to push, but she knew he'd be questioning his judgement, fretting about it. But he'd taken the stand to face it, and admit the possibility to Nirea. Without venom or, by the look of it, shame. It was testament to how far he'd come—how much more stable he was.

This time, Nirea seemed to genuinely soften. "All right. Thank you for telling me." She turned back to Mynygogg. "So, what now?"

"That's the question, isn't it? One charm. And if Weyr does have the relic, and he finds himself another memory *draoidh*..."

That was the big fear. The race. One of the reasons Quellaria had been such an asset. If she'd chosen Weyr's side... God, what a mess.

"This is going to take too long, isn't it?" the king asked of the room.

They'd already been there a month and a half and still barely made a dent in the city's total population. Aranok could only use so much energy a day for clearing memories without an energy *draoidh*. They had safe havens, but the vast majority of the population still thought Mynygogg was a monster, Aranok a traitor and Anhel Weyr their reluctant saviour.

It was bleak.

"Yes, probably," Aranok answered morosely. "What else can we do?"

"I think, perhaps, we have to accept that this strategy might be a losing one," said the king. "It was a good one. An *honest* one. But in the heat of battle, few strategies survive engagement. Once the blood starts flowing, you adapt or you die."

"What are you thinking?" Nirea asked. "An assault? We've got the Guard here, the Thorns, the *draoidhs* in Traverlyn. If we go for Greytoun, we *could* take it. I might have cleared enough captains to have a small fleet at its back..."

"No." Mynygogg cut her off. "Greytoun and Haven were built to withstand a siege. Weyr might have the relic, making him the most powerful *draoidh* in history, and he was already holding us off during the war. With the new magics he seems to have developed—no. An assault could be suicide, even with the Thorns. And even if we won, if he didn't summon enough demons to make it impossible, we'd have to murder half our own army to do it. That's just not acceptable. We'd have no country left to rule."

The queen looked fairly exasperated at that but didn't argue. "Then what?"

Mynygogg looked at Aranok, and he quickly seemed to realise what the king was thinking. "No. Really? You're really considering that prick's idea?"

"What? Which prick?" Nirea asked.

"He's absolutely a prick," said the king. "But he might be right about this.

"Maybe we've reached the point where we have to give up on the *truth* and focus on winning."

---

"Oh. Hello." Of all the people Vastin had expected to bump into coming out of his room, Morienne was a surprise. A nice one, though. She trailed behind Ferrod, carrying a pack over one shoulder. "What are you...? When did you get here?"

"I just came in with the queen."

Nirea was there too? That was unexpected. And, likely, bad. She was meant to be in Leet. Morienne had the bedraggled look of having been out in the snow for days. And the commotion of their arrival was probably what had woken him. He'd not been feeling well, and Allandria had sent him to rest before dinner. Probably to do with how badly he'd been sleeping. Every time he closed his eyes, his dreams were hideous. In idle moments, his thoughts always turned to Samily. Or Amollari. Had he put her in trouble's sight? But here was someone he could do something for, no matter how small. "Are you warmed yet? I can make a pot of tea."

"Meja is already brewing a pot," said Ferrod.

"Tea would be lovely," said Morienne. "To be honest, I came up to escape the mood downstairs." She grimaced, confirming Vastin's suspicion that their arrival was bad news.

He was afraid to ask. If they'd lost anyone else... Better to know than to imagine the worst, though. Probably.

Ferrod showed Morienne to the room next to Vastin's. As far as he knew, that was the last empty one. Ferrod's home had become a boardinghouse by accident. Though he said it was a pleasure to have life back in it. He was kind, and warm, and reminded Vastin of his mother in some ways. Gentle but strong. A good man.

They went down to the kitchen, carefully avoiding the raised voices in the living room. Whatever they were discussing, they weren't agreeing about it.

"I'll leave you two to talk," Ferrod said once they were seated with the teapot between them. "It's a pleasure to meet you, Morienne."

"And you, sir. Thank you," she replied, smiling.

Vastin poured them both a cup. "So, how bad is it?"

It was bad.

Quellaria dead. Nirea wounded—but at least she'd survived. She'd made it here. Vastin told Morienne his story too, and how that had all gone wrong. She listened quietly until he was done.

"Aye, seems like a lot's gone to Hell recently, doesn't it?"

"What about you?" Vastin asked. "I heard you went to Lepertoun. How was that?"

Saying the name brought him an unexpected rush of anxiety and sadness. That was where he'd been Blackened. Where he lost so much time. But he couldn't remember that. Not really. The last thing he remembered clearly was washing his hands in the burn, chatting to Glorbad. And him being kind. Telling Vastin his folks would be proud of him. That was the last conversation they had.

Morienne didn't look up from her tea. "Bad. I hoped, maybe... Nobody survived. They were all there where I left them. Tied to the beds. Just... gone. I did what I could. Built pyres. Gave them the best rites I could. Took a few weeks to manage them all."

God, that sounded awful. What a miserable job to do. And all alone.

"Well, they won't have known anything, right?" Vastin hoped he sounded positive. "They'll have gone peacefully."

"I don't know," said Morienne. "I thought I was making them safe. Hoped I was...well, stopping it from spreading. But...what if...what if they woke up, tied to those beds and just couldn't move? What if they died there, alone and scared, because I didn't get to them soon enough?"

Oh Hell. That was a horrible thought. But Vastin wasn't going to let Morienne blame herself for it. She didn't deserve that guilt.

"But you saved my life. And Meristan's. And loads of others. And you're not even a medic. Didn't you just stay in Lepertoun because you were immune?"

Morienne nodded.

"What would have happened if you hadn't done that? I'd still be Blackened. And Meristan. Laird Aranok wouldn't have been able to work out the cure. Truth is, everybody who survived the Blackening has you to thank."

A tear dripped into Morienne's tea with a brittle little *plink*. "You're very wise, for your age."

Age? That was a point. God, how had he forgotten? So much of his world had changed. What mattered. What didn't. "This might seem an odd question, but do you know what the date is?"

Morienne wiped her eyes dry. "Twenty-third day of winter, I think. Why?"

"Huh," said Vastin. "There you are." Morienne looked at him curiously and he lifted his cup like he was giving a toast. "It's my sixteenth birth day."

---

"This is a mistake." Aranok was adamant. "You can't just lie to everyone without any evidence. Without any credibility. You're just going to... pretend to be someone else? And what then? What if it works? When you get the throne back, are you going to throw off your mask and say 'Surprise, I was Mynygogg all along!' How are people going to take that?"

He was verging on ranting, which wasn't helping anything. Allandria wanted to interject, just tell them all to calm down and take a breath, but that rarely helped. Letting them burn the fire out of their arguments was more useful before trying to pour water on the embers. And she wasn't sure where she stood on the issue yet.

"Once we have the throne back, we'll have all the leverage, all the power we need," said Nirea. "He's right. We can't keep relying on magic charms. They're too easily lost."

Aranok threw up his hands. "You're going to get yourself lynched! Why would anyone believe you? Most of them have no idea who you are!"

"We'll have the Guard. We'll have the Merchants Guild," Mynygogg argued. "We borrow their credibility."

"Aye, because the Guard have never been used to enforce a lie before." Aranok rolled his eyes. "D'you not remember Hofnag?"

"That's not the point." Mynygogg looked desperate, reaching for reasons to justify his plan. "I'm not Hofnag."

"They don't know that!" Aranok's frustration was bubbling over. "You're *a monster* to most of them!"

"Aranok, what else are we going to do?" Nirea asked curtly. "You think we can do this with just one charm? What happens if we lose that one? What are you going to do if Weyr gets another memory *draoidh* and he does have the heart? If he were to have that spell recast right now, Allandria would be the only one with her memory intact. Is she going to save the kingdom single-handed?"

Finally, the heat came down. Aranok had no answer to that, and Nirea was going to let him stew in it. Now was Allandria's moment.

"I could, actually."

All three looked at her.

"What?" Mynygogg asked.

"I could," she said flatly. "Save the kingdom on my own. Absolutely."

A pause, and Nirea laughed first, then the others. That did it.

"You fucking could." Aranok came to join her. The two of them stood in the middle of the living room, facing the fire, where Mynygogg and Nirea sat in the armchairs. It occurred to her that it was a bit like a makeshift throne room now. But she was also aware it was where

Ferrod and Taie would have sat together. Maybe, one day, she and Aranok would have chairs like that. That would be nice.

"All right. What's your plan?" Aranok asked. "How are you going to do this? How are you going to spread this cunning lie?"

"I've been considering that," Mynygogg answered. "We need a big announcement. One that will get people's attention and spread quickly. What's the best way to do that?"

"King's messenger," said Nirea.

"King's messenger," Mynygogg repeated. "We wait for a messenger, make sure Calador alerts us when they arrive. We go to meet them; you clear their memory, Aranok. Once we have them on our side, we let them make the initial announcement and introduce me. We have the Guard ready, Bak onstage with me, a few of the Merchants Guild's luminaries. All of them lending me their credibility, as you say."

That wasn't a terrible plan, now that she heard it laid out like that. If the town saw all of those people telling them Mynygogg's story was truth? Could that actually work? "Aranok, that's... not bad."

He frowned. "Go on."

"I'll take the Donal identity," the king continued, "and tell them that Weyr is a usurper. That he's a demon summoner—which is true—and that he framed you for the murders of Janaeus and the lairds—also true. We'll use the fact that he's turned against the White Thorns as further evidence—say he's trying to discredit those who would testify against him. The Thorns carry a huge amount of weight, especially amongst the farming folk, the ones who saw them take down demons during the war or heard about it from those who did."

"And what about Meristan's confession?" Aranok wasn't bending.

"The truth. He's holding hostages to force Meristan into a false confession."

So far, everything he'd said was true, right enough. Except for his name.

"And what if we don't get a messenger?" Aranok asked. "What if Weyr knows we're here and doesn't send one? What if he sends the army instead?"

Mynygogg raised his hands. "If we don't get a messenger, we use the Midwinter festival. Make the speech on Midwinter's Eve, when the bonfire's lit in Mourning Square. That'll have people out, and it'll get them talking. We lose the messenger's weight, but we can still make it work."

"That's, what, a month away?" Nirea asked.

"Just under," Allandria answered. "Not too long."

Sending everyone home to their Midwinter feast with talk of treason was a Hell of an idea. Families gathered together from far and wide, and then went back home—wherever home was. It might help spread the message even further. Or it might tip their hand to Weyr. A knife with two edges.

"And if it's the army..."

Nirea cut Mynygogg off. "The army's a threat anyway. Could happen any time."

"Indeed," Mynygogg agreed. "If that happens, we bargain with their general. You clear their mind, and they order the soldiers to stand down. If that doesn't work"—he turned to look directly at Nirea—"*then* we might have to fight."

It all sounded kind of reasonable, laid out like that. Like a plan. Like the king had been thinking about it ever since that night in the Canny Man.

"What do you think?" Allandria asked Aranok.

"What do *you* think?"

Good question. Her hand came up to her chest again. "To be honest, the fact that I'm wearing our only other option to free the country around my neck is bloody terrifying."

Aranok sighed. "I'm sorry." He turned back to Mynygogg. "It's still a fucking terrible idea. It muddies the water. Confuses people. Folk won't know what's happening. Some will know who you are; some won't. What happens when they start talking to each other?"

"That's already true," said Nirea. She was right. Their allies just needed to know what they were doing. Communication, as always, would be the key. Again, they would miss Rasa. But maybe if they could get the messengers...?

"Aranok..." Mynygogg looked like words danced in his mind as he grasped for the right ones. "Is it possible...? Might it be that you're against this because of where the idea came from?"

"Yes!" he roared. "And so it fucking should be. We're talking about *Pol*!"

"Pol?" Nirea asked.

"Ikara's husband," said Allandria.

"Oh, right." Nirea seemed to know why that mattered. "So what? Terrible people still make good plans. Some of the best plans, as it happens. Look what Janaeus came up with."

Aranok turned on her, glowering. "Janaeus was a better man than Pol will ever be."

*Shit.*

This was at risk of getting out of hand again. She needed to do something. "Aranok, wait. Listen." He turned to her and she saw the fire dim in the light of her smile. "You're right. Pol's a prick. A selfish, awful prick of a man. But I think you should talk to him again."

The word *What?* formed on his lips and she gently put two fingers to them, holding the moment.

"I think he's genuinely trying to help. Not for any good reason. Not because we can trust him. Because he thinks it's in his interest. That currying favour with the king will be good for him." She nodded to Mynygogg, who gave a slight nod of acknowledgement.

"I know the type," Nirea agreed. "We all do, Aranok."

"What would Pol not do in his own interest?" Allandria lowered her fingers and held Aranok's eyes with her own. It wasn't a perfect plan. And she wasn't even sure she believed in it. But it wasn't as bad an idea as she'd first thought it. Most of it was Mynygogg's, in fact, building on Pol's spark. Mad how a drunk conversation might be about to change the country's fate.

Aranok's shoulders slumped in resignation.

"Fine. I'll talk to Pol."

---

The door creaked open with a musty fug of whisky and sleep. Pol's pale, unshaven face appeared from the shadows. It was not long after breakfast and Allandria imagined Pol would normally have been up and dressed for the day hours ago. The burst of heat that escaped behind him suggested he'd at least lit fires.

A combination of slow business and an empty house, she assumed.

"Yes?" His face turned the moment he recognised Aranok. "Oh. Ikara's not here."

"I know." Aranok's voice was flat with a resentful tone. "I want to talk to you."

Pol stared at him as if he'd no idea how to react. "Why?" The question had more than a hint of fear about it.

"I'm not here to threaten you, Pol." Aranok turned to look at Allandria. "We want your advice."

"My...um...I'm not dressed for company." Pol looked down at his nightclothes and robe. "Could we...later?"

Aranok gestured to the foot of snow surrounding them. "Could we maybe wait in the kitchen?"

Again, a long pause. "All right. Fine. Come in."

Pol took a bit longer dressing than was probably necessary for a conversation in his own living room, but then, for a man who made his living in clothes, perhaps that was an important part of his day. "Never buy an outfit from a badly dressed tailor," as they said.

Aranok helped himself to a pot and brewed them some tea while they waited. It was good to feel the heat running up her arms when she cradled the warm cup in her hands.

When Pol finally appeared, he was as immaculately dressed as usual, and he'd even shaved, Allandria noticed. It occurred to her to wonder if this was Pol's armour—the uniform of his station.

"I made tea. If you want some." Aranok held up the pot.

A flicker of irritation crossed Pol's face, but he suppressed it quickly. "No. Thank you. How can I help?"

*How could he help?*

The world had become a very strange place. They say war makes odd alliances. This one was ridiculous.

Aranok rolled his shoulders, clearly feeling the same discomfort. So Allandria took the lead.

"Pol, we want to discuss your idea of...telling a different story." He looked puzzled. She was just going to have to put it plainly. "You suggested the king should lie."

"Oh!" Pol physically stepped back. "I mean, I didn't...It was just an idea."

"Pol, we're not here to fight." Aranok put his cup down on the counter. "I want to know how we can make it work. How do we convince the country our lie is...better than his?"

"All right." Pol was still wary. "Well, it's as I said to King Mynygogg, it's about belief. If you believe it, they will too. Facts are malleable."

"Truth is truth," said Aranok.

"But it doesn't matter as much as what people believe is true," Pol answered. "At the moment, everyone *believes* Anhel Weyr is king, so he is king. You see?"

"But he literally changed their memories," said Aranok. "We can't do that. Not quickly."

"You don't have to change their memories to change their beliefs," said Pol. "If you're going to tell a lie, tell a big one. Tell it with absolute conviction. And repeat it often. Make it a sign of intelligence that people believe your story. That they see through the charade that fools others. Dismiss anyone who questions you as unintelligent and gullible. Make it a mark of honour to believe your story. To be amongst the elite who see the *truth*. And most of all, give them someone to *hate*. If they can blame someone else for their life's ills, they'll dine at your table as long as you want them."

God. It was hideous. But it made sense, and Allandria hated it even more for that.

"I don't like it," said Aranok. "It's grubby. Messy."

Pol straightened his back and expanded his chest. "Aranok, for seven years, you've played your part in the story that I am Emelina's father. Why?"

That was a bold move. He knew Aranok wasn't happy about that, and he knew all the reasons why.

"Wasn't *my* idea," Aranok bristled.

"But why?" Pol pushed.

"Because Ikara asked me to," he answered.

"And why did she do that?" Pol was throwing questions like arrows.

"Because she thought it was best. For Emelina. For her." Aranok's back was up. Pol needed to tread lightly. He was on dangerous ground.

"So you conspired in that lie for a good purpose, yes? Why is this different? It's larger, but it's for a good purpose, isn't it?"

Damn. That was a sharp argument. Aranok looked to Allandria, questioning. Asking for her counsel. She raised her eyebrows and shrugged.

Pol was right, much as she disliked it. A lie for a good purpose. A benevolent lie? Such things were common, she supposed, in small measures. Between two people.

"What do you think?" Aranok asked her.

And the truth, the awful truth was that she could see it. And maybe it was a better plan. Maybe it gave them a chance.

"It makes sense to me."

"Hmm." Aranok fixed Pol with a hard stare. "Why are you helping us? What's in it for you?"

Pol's face softened almost into an indulgent smile. He opened his hands to indicate the room. "Look at me. My family is gone, my business; my entire fortune is failing. As long as people believe Weyr's lie, this is my future—tied to the most famous traitor in history. Like it or not, Laird Aranok, our needs are aligned."

Ikara had said the business was just a bit quiet. Either she'd lied to protect Aranok's feelings or she'd been lied to herself. So Pol had an even easier motive than getting into the king's favour—his livelihood was at stake.

Aranok crossed his arms and leaned back on the counter. "All right. I believe you. Come on." Aranok walked for the door.

"Where are we going?" Pol followed hesitantly.

"You're coming to help us plan this thing." Aranok turned and poked a finger at Pol. "But understand this: I don't like it. I think you actually know what you're talking about, and honestly, that does not endear you to me. But I believe you're selfish and this would be good for you. However, we are *not* allies. There is no role for you beyond this. You won't be a royal advisor, you won't be tailor to the king, if you have any ideas of it. But you might get your business back. Understood?"

Pol straightened and something tensed in his eyes. A flash of something steely and resolute Allandria hadn't seen in him before.

"Understood."

# CHAPTER 47

Three weeks.
Finally a message from Calador: Mournside had a messenger. Word would spread quickly through the town, but the innkeeper had sent word immediately, giving them a chance to get to him first.

Aranok was still deeply sceptical of the plan, but he saw the thinking behind it, at least. It was a massive gamble that went against all his instincts. But everyone else agreed it was the best way forward. Maybe the only way.

They'd made more progress on clearing key people in the town. They had mostly all of the community leaders, but vast swathes of the populace were still under Jan's spell. They had a long way to go, to do it the right way.

Calador gave him and Mynygogg a nod as they entered the Canny Man. Several heads turned to look. They might have clocked the messenger too and wondered if it would mean an appearance from the king. A few eyes widened; a few hushed discussions.

"Upstairs, room five." Calador said it quietly, handing over a pair of whiskies. To anyone else in the bar, it would have looked like he was just serving them.

"Thank you." Mynygogg raised his glass and knocked back the contents. Aranok did the same, enjoying the bite of heat that spread across his chest. Calador had given them the good bottle.

Mynygogg nodded toward the stairs and the pair of them went up as casually as they could. Still eyes watching, though. Of course.

They found room five and knocked. The messenger shouldn't recognise either of them—Mynygogg clean-shaven and Aranok hiding behind short hair and a beard—but they were braced for that anyway. Should he lunge at them or back into the room, Aranok had the charm in hand, ready. Press it against him and clear him before he could object.

What they did not expect was no answer.

An exchange of quizzical looks and Aranok banged harder on the door.

"Not tonight!" came a raspy voice from inside. "Wait for tomorrow!"

Interesting. Most messengers who stayed there came down in the evening and took advantage of the hospitality, some offering previews of their news to the clientele who plied them with drink. Not many locked themselves in their room for the night.

"Ah, it's important, friend. It'll just take a moment." Mynygogg sounded casual and convivial.

A grumpy huff from behind the door. "Unless the inn is on fire, it'll wait until morning!"

Movement then, and maybe another voice? A female voice. Ah. The messenger was partaking of different hospitality. Another thing some were known for.

"I'm afraid it won't wait," Mynygogg insisted. "Please."

He had the tone of a city guard now, and maybe they should have brought one. Allandria and Morienne had gone to let Bak know what was happening, and to prepare for them to take the stage in the morning. Hell, all they needed to do was get the man to open the door.

No response.

Well, he had said what it would take to get him out of the room.

"*Teine.*" Aranok slipped his lit fingers under the bottom of the door, letting the edge catch. It only took a moment.

"Fucking Hell! Fucking Hell!" Furious scrambling from inside and the door flew open, revealing the entirely naked messenger, whose previous excitement had not yet fully abated. "Do something!"

"Step back." Aranok pushed past the man and used *uisge* to put out the flames. Calador would be annoyed by the singed woodwork, but there was no structural damage, and they had access to the funds that would cover repairs now.

The woman sat up on the bed, sheet pulled around her. Aranok didn't recognise the face framed with dirty-blond hair. They'd have to clear her now too. Not ideal, as he was already knackered from a day of it. But he had about enough left, even allowing for the little magic he'd just used. Still, he'd be glad to get to bed sooner rather than later. Needed to be sharp for the morning.

The messenger moved to pull on a pair of trousers, grumbling all the while.

Rather than waste time with the fake charm, Aranok subtly touched the man's back with the real charm, once he had the trousers on, and whispered, "*Clior.*"

The messenger immediately tumbled over onto the bed, wailing as if he'd been smacked about the head. The woman jerked her legs up and pulled the cover tighter, staring wide-eyed at Aranok.

"He'll be fine," he said as Mynygogg closed the door. "Just give it a moment."

Once they cleared the woman too, both their moods improved significantly. Though the messenger, Kalik, was appalled to learn he had just stood buck naked at half-mast before royalty.

The woman, Melia, seemed quite amused by the whole situation, and the gold coin Kalik slipped her as she left confirmed Aranok's earlier suspicion. She'd probably been paid for a lot less than expected.

"I have to confess," said Kalik, once they were alone, "I'm relieved. I worried you were assassins."

Mynygogg laughed. "The opposite, son. We're giving you your life back."

"What can I do for you, then, sire?"

"First, we need to see the announcement you're supposed to make tomorrow."

"Of course." Kalik knelt down to his pack and pulled on the shirt that lay on the floor beside it. He dug out a scroll and handed it to Gogg, who unrolled it and studied it in silence.

"How bad is it?" Aranok asked.

"Bad," he answered. "Confirmation of what we knew: Meristan's confession, the White Thorns outlawed. You and I are working together to bring down the country—spreading lies about Janaeus and Weyr. Using magic to *confuse* people. Fuck's sake. And then this:

*"It has come to the attention of the crown that some taxes have become past due from Mournside. At such a time of war, the country needs funds to protect the people of Eidyn more than ever. Without that income, the king cannot guarantee the safety of the town."*

"Well. That's a threat," said Aranok.
"I think that part was for us," said Gogg. "Get out of Mournside, or I'll do what I did to Traverlyn."
"Mournside has proper walls, though."
"Aye, but not as many *draoidhs*. Or Thorns."
That was true. They'd have lost Traverlyn without the Thorns. How long would the Mournside city guard hold out against a real attack? The army was one thing, but if he sent demons...Hundreds could die. Thousands. Even with Aranok and the rest here. He'd be a damned sight better fighting one now than he had been at Mutton Hole, with his mind fogged by Jan. But if Anhel did have the relic, they could be facing a lot more than one—or an *invisible* one.
"And then the flourish," said Gogg.

*"Once the war against the traitorous draoidhs is ended, King Anhel Weyr intends to show his appreciation for the support of the merchant lairds by bringing taxes to a substantially lower level than those levied under Kings Janaeus and Hofnag."*

"A bribe," said Aranok. "A flat-out bribe to side with him."
"Good thing it'll never be read, eh?" Kalik laughed nervously.
Mynygogg tapped the scroll on his hand. "Aye, that it is. I'd bet my left eye he's stopped the stipend to the university as well. And the hospital. Starve them both of cash for supporting us."
That was exactly what he'd do. Anhel had always harboured a grudge against the university for refusing him admission. If he could bribe the

merchants with the gold he saved there, he absolutely would. And bugger the consequences for the young *draoidhs* who suffered. He wasn't in this for them. He never had been.

"Right. Well. Best we get on with it, then, eh?" said Aranok.

"Indeed. Kalik?" Gogg turned back to the messenger.

"Aye, sire?"

"Here's what we need from you tomorrow morning."

---

The low morning sun glared off the frosted windows of Aranok's childhood home. It should be a place of solace. Of comfort.

But that wasn't what he'd found this morning.

"Father, can I just come in, please?" He really didn't need an argument on the doorstep. Certainly not this morning of all days. He didn't have time. "I just need a minute."

"Your mother's out. And your sister," said Dorann, as if that were reason enough for him not to enter. But it explained why there was only one guard at the door. Presumably Loth was with them.

"Well, can I wait for them? It's important."

He needed them to stay home today. This speech... If it went badly, the town could fall into rioting. And chaos was an opportunity. Just in case there was still an assassin with a mind to harm them, Aranok wanted his family inside. Where he wouldn't have to worry about them. He had enough to worry about already.

And he'd rather not have to deal with his father right now. But that didn't seem to be up to him.

"Fine," Dorann grumbled, turned and walked back inside, leaving the door open for Aranok. He entered, and Dorann sat silently by the fire, lit a pipe and smoked it as if he were entirely alone.

*Fine.*

Aranok wasn't there to mend bridges with his father. There were more important things coming.

It was odd, the mix of excitement and trepidation. If today went well, it could change everything. But if it went wrong... Things had been good here, and yet, somehow, that increased Aranok's anxiety. As if having the little oasis they'd found here—with Ferrod; at the Canny Man—made the risk of losing it a terror. Maybe it was easier having nothing to lose than fearing the breaking of something precious.

Mynygogg had often said it was easier being a rebel than a king. Easier to complain than to rule. Was it the same thing? Was it the responsibility? Aranok hadn't been aware of it when they had the throne, but now... Now he felt it like a stone around his neck. This small peace was a fragile thing, too easy to break.

Instead of sitting in silence with his father, drowning in his own thoughts, Aranok went to the kitchen and found Cressida peeling potatoes for the day's lunch. They chatted for a while, exchanging well-intentioned jibes and laughing about nothing. She was a good soul, their cook. It was nice. After a bit, the guard from out front brought through a box the butcher's boy had dropped off, and Aranok offered to get out of her way, mostly as an excuse for leaving because the conversation had dried up, and he could do with a seat anyway. He helped himself to some tea from the pot and returned to the living room, where he might have thought his father had not moved an inch, but that he was now engaged in reading some papers rather than his pipe.

"Anything interesting?" he asked, sitting at the table.

"Designs, for the spring season," Dorann answered. "Got to keep the gold coming in somehow, with all I'm spending." He made a vague nod to the door, indicating the guard. A little dig, of course. A tiny barb. One of countless.

"When we take the crown back, I'll repay your costs, Father. I won't see you out of pocket for me."

"You'll have some bill due, then. I've been out of pocket for you your whole life, boy." But this time, it was said with humour. Genuine humour, it seemed, and Aranok smiled.

"Aye. Fair. I suppose kids are expensive to feed."

"And clothe and school, and..." He gestured to the house in general. It had been a decent childhood, from that perspective. He and Ikara had never wanted for anything. Except, maybe, some affection from their father. Some indication they were more than a burden on his purse. And later, a stain on his reputation. Both of them, in their ways: a *draoidh* and an unwed mother. Some ancient prejudices still lived in the old man. Remnants of his own childhood; fishhooks caught in his soul.

*Expectations.*

"*If* you take the crown back, though, eh?" Dorann said. "That's not happening tomorrow, is it?"

"We'll get there. One way or another, we'll beat Anhel. It's only a matter of time." He said the words, but even he could hear the lack of certainty. It was an uphill trek and Anhel had built some big walls around him. Still, he wanted to keep the conversation light. No need to get into anything deep. Just passing the time until Mum and Ikara got back.

"Where's Em? With Ikara?"

"Upstairs. Still sleeping, I think." Dorann didn't even look up to answer. "So today's the day, is it? The big lie?"

"How did you know?"

Aranok had discussed the plan with his family. It was important they knew what was coming. But he hadn't told them it was happening today. That's why he was here.

"Heard there was a messenger. Last night in the Canny Man. Heard he got caught with his pants down with a local strumpet. To hear her tell it, it was quite the sight."

Of course that story had spread. Bit of a worry, in fact. If she was telling that tale across town, it could augur badly for the speech. Might confuse folk. They should have thought of that the night before. Been clear with her about what was safe to say. But they'd been focused on Kalik and his message. Melia was a detail too many. But one they should have considered. Too late now.

"Aye, it was something to see." Aranok played into the humour.

"I don't know." Dorann gave a dramatic sigh. "Does it even matter who's on the throne? I mean, does it? Really? Would your life not be easier if you just... left it? No more war. Just let Weyr play king and get on with your life? How much worse can he make it?"

Fucking Hell. So much for keeping it light.

"I don't even know where to start," said Aranok. "He's tried to kill me multiple times. He killed hundreds of thousands in the war, hundreds more in Traverlyn. He'd likely kill you just for fathering me. What on earth makes you think he'd be a decent king?"

"Aye, but that's only because you're a threat!" said Dorann. "Give him peace. Tell him he can have the throne. Walk away. He's no reason to come for you, then."

Aranok's mouth wouldn't function. His tongue was suddenly rough as fish scales and dry as stone. What in the name of holy fuck was he hearing? That he should just walk away? Now? After everything? He took a mouthful of tea and swished it around his mouth. That helped.

"So just give up? That's what you're saying? Surrender?"

His father stood abruptly, dropping papers to the floor. "See, that's your problem. You're not seeing clearly. It's not 'surrendering' to recognise an opportunity. That's how business works. You encounter a problem, you find the opportunity. Can't get what you wanted? What can you do with what you have? That's how a man survives, Aranok. Provides for his family. Flexibility. Change."

"Change?" Aranok was floundering to find words. "You've never changed a day in your life! You're the most stubborn, obstinate..." No, that wasn't going to help. No point in him exploding at his father now. He needed to be clear-headed. Too much relied on him. If anything went wrong... "I'm sorry; I just—I didn't mean that. I just can't... You'd really just have me walk away? You honestly think that's a good idea?"

Dorann looked at him hard, took a breath and let it out slowly through his nose. "Look, son, you never wanted this in the first place, right? It was Mynygogg's idea. He's the one that talked you into this fool's campaign. You wanted a better country for *draoidhs*, right? Well, there's a *draoidh* on the throne now. Let him get on with it! What difference does it make *which draoidh* is in power?" His tone was coercive. As if Aranok were a child still.

"Mynygogg's not *draoidh*," he sputtered.

Suddenly, Dorann was waving his hands like a madman. "Well, he's a *draoidh* lover. You know what I mean!"

"A *draoidh* lover?" Aranok raised his hands to his head. "What the fuck are you saying? Do you... do you even realise what you're saying?"

"Ach, fuck, you're mixing me up!" his father countered. "I just mean... you know."

"No, I don't know, *Father*." Aranok was raging now. The heat of a hundred arguments; a thousand subtle cuts from his father; forty years of shame and pain, and a desperate little boy who just wanted his father to love him. "You tell me what you mean by referring to the king of Eidyn with a phrase used by absolute fucking *bigots*!"

A scream.

A shattering scream of absolute horror.

Aranok felt his stomach sink, watched his father's face turn from florid pink to pale grey.

It came from the kitchen.

Aranok bolted through to find Cressida backed up against the counter, hands over her mouth, eyes wide with terror. She was staring at the box. The butcher's box. With the cheesecloth lifted away, half dangling off the corner.

And suddenly, Aranok was aware of the thick, iron smell of blood. The rich, dark aroma of raw meat. And he felt the same horror he saw in the cook. Numbness took him, as he stepped forward, terrified of what he was going to find, but certain he had to know.

"What is it? What's wrong?" Dorann had come trailing behind him, breathless and agitated. "Cressida!"

The cook shook her head, tears streaming down her face. She couldn't speak. Could barely move. One trembling hand pointed at the box.

The damned box.

Aranok reached it.

Took a breath.

Looked down.

And the world ended.

Two pairs of lifeless eyes stared back up at him.

Mum and Ikara were home.

# CHAPTER 48

The pristine white blankets of Mourning Square had turned to muddy slush, churned beneath the bustling crowd of eager feet gathered to hear what news the king's messenger had finally brought.

Allandria huddled under her cloak against the chill wind. Her place on the roof across the square from the platform was an ideal tactical position, but it left her completely exposed to the swirling gusts buffeting the town. Her raised perch gave her a perfect view, though, and that was the important thing. She was to watch for anything suspicious. For signs of violence beginning. Be ready to protect Mynygogg. Just in case.

All being well, she'd crouch there and shiver, watch the speech and daydream about tea and a warm bath.

The buzz of the crowd below was getting louder all the time. More excited. As if they knew this was going to be something different. Something special. Life-changing. World-changing. From above, it was a sea of cloaks: grey, brown and black; boots stamping on slick cobbles and hands cupped to mouths. The chatter was incessant. Hundreds packed the square to bursting, spilling out into the edges of alleyways and back up main roads, everyone struggling to push closer and hear what was coming.

The thrill of the *impending*. The *potential*.

Allandria scanned the crowd, looking for one person. A moment, and she spotted her. One of the few with her hood down. Not watching the stage eagerly, but shifting through the massed bodies, examining faces. Assessing. Anticipating.

Nirea had insisted she come, despite Mynygogg's desire for her to stay at Ferrod's with Vastin and Morienne. For her safety. "Stupid to put both of us at risk," he'd argued. "I'll not see you lost because I wasn't there to defend you" was her answer. And it was a final one. The city guard were dotted about the square, out in force. Every one of them, she reckoned. The bulk of them were on the stage, lining the back like statues.

That in itself would have people intrigued. King's messengers didn't usually merit this show of force.

Something was about to happen.

Something *momentous*.

---

It was too tight. Too packed.

Nirea struggled to move through the crowd at all. If she had to draw her blades, she'd never get them in front of her without taking the hands off the folk beside her. Half the damn town had come out for this—and not just the folk they needed to reach either. She'd seen at least four or five people she knew were already cleared and with them. They didn't need to be there. They should have stayed home. But she could understand. The desire to be present. To see something happen.

Weyr had them thinking they were at war—which they were, just not how they thought.

Out of the corner of her eye, a flash of hair, flicked away. She turned instinctively.

*Quell.*

Not Quell. A woman near twice her age. A mistake she'd not have thanked Nirea for. Just a familiar hint of jawline, similar colour of hair. Nothing more than that. A ghost of her imagination, dreamed into being.

The hubbub rose, and Nirea looked up to see the messenger had appeared on the stage.

All right. *Here we go.*

She edged herself toward a wall. Better to have that at her back, seeing everything in front of her.

"Citizens of Mournside!" The messenger's voice boomed across the square and the chatter hushed. "I bring you incredible news." The man looked nervously behind him at the row of city guards. He was twitchy. Unconvincing. The sooner he got off the stage, the better. "It has come to light that there has been a great falsehood perpetrated against the people of Eidyn. A lie! A lie so comprehensive, it goes right to the top. To the crown itself!"

Gasps and a return to chatter. Speculation. Excitement.

"I now present to you, for further information, the leader of the city guard: Captain Bak!"

The messenger deferred and stepped away as Bak took the front of the stage. He stood, chest out with conviction. Much better. Much more trustworthy.

"Fellow citizens." He spoke slowly, deliberately. Loud enough to be heard but not shouting. Forcing the crowd to quiet again to hear him. "I have been presented with indisputable evidence that proves King Anhel Weyr is a fraud."

Chaos. The crowd erupted, howls of derision, cries of "Surely not!" and even "Heresy!" Expected, at least at first. They would need more.

"Please. Please!" Bak waved for quiet again. He was fighting against the tide. "You have to be silent!" It was a booming exhortation, and it did the trick.

Relative silence returned, conversations reduced to conspiratorial whispers.

"Anhel Weyr is not the devout man he would have us believe. He has lived a double life! While pretending to serve God, he has conspired to steal the throne. It was he who killed King Janaeus, and he who murdered the Lairds' Council in order to install himself on the throne!"

"Proof!" A cry from the crowd. "What proof?"

"A fine question!" Bak answered, pointing to the asker. "I have seen the proof, as have the loyal men and women of the Guard, as well as the Merchants Guild, who all agreed to this announcement today!"

An interested murmur then. Less scepticism, maybe? A little more interest? That's how it sounded to Nirea.

Perfect.

"Let me then introduce the man who can give you more: Laird Donal!"

This was it. This was their chance to turn the tide. To finally make major progress. Mynygogg emerged from behind the guards at the back of the stage, striding forward confidently. Every inch of him remained a king, regardless of the vestments of the role. Nirea felt a rush of pride, of love, of fear.

It was a good plan. It was going to work. Her husband could do this. He could do anything. Talking, speeches—this was his real talent. Reaching people. But even for him, this was a difficult task. And not a familiar one. Mynygogg had always been the one to see into the heart of things and explain them with an engrossing simplicity.

But this was going to be the hardest speech he'd ever given. The most Eidyn had ever asked of him. Needed from him.

His words better be damned pretty.

---

Mynygogg stepped forward. This was it.

Over the anticipation of the crowd below, though, something behind her. Rustling. Footsteps?

Allandria turned and looked back across the roof. There, coming toward her...

Aranok?

*What the fuck?*

"What are you doing?" she asked, just above a whisper. Just loud enough for him to hear. She waved her hands at him, encouraging him to crouch. They shouldn't be seen up here. Not yet.

But he didn't answer.

Just stepped toward her with an odd half smile. Something was wrong.

---

"My friends. Fellow citizens of Mournside and of Eidyn. I am honoured to have the opportunity to speak to you today. My name is Laird

Donal. Some of you know me already. The rest, I look forward to meeting." Mynygogg's generous smile bathed the throng in its warmth. Damn, he was good at this.

Maybe for the first time, Nirea felt confident.

It was going to work.

"I know the news we bring you today is upsetting. Confusing. But please understand, we can prove it. All of it. This is no hollow accusation. We have the proof and will present it to everyone who wishes to see it. As you can see"—he gestured to Bak and the messenger behind him, as well as a few of the senior merchants who had followed him onto the stage—"it has already convinced these good people behind me. They who represent the highest echelons of the town's offices. They are all with us."

Yes. Agreement, amazement from the crowd. Excited, hushed voices; heads turning. "Can it be true?" "There must be something in it." They were taking it in. In truth, there's little like a conspiracy to set hearts to racing.

"And I am most pleased, amongst this disturbing news, to be able to tell you that I have been working closely with your own Laird Aranok—falsely and maliciously accused of the very crimes committed by the usurper, Anhel Weyr!"

A mixed murmur then. There would certainly be a lot of people regretting some things they'd said of late, perhaps grateful they hadn't said them publicly.

But something was wrong. A long and awkward moment of quiet as the king looked behind him—scanned the crowd. Aranok was meant to join Gogg on the stage. And for the first time, her husband looked a little uncertain. A little unsure. He needed to keep going. Keep up the energy he'd created. Don't let the crowd stop to think too long. Maybe start to wonder if they could trust him.

Where the fuck was Aranok?

---

"You're supposed to be down there." Allandria pointed at the stage. "What's wrong?"

His face changed in an odd way. Like he was confused. Something was very wrong. He kept coming toward her, one hand raised as if asking her to wait. As if he would explain in a moment.

And then she saw it. The tilt of his head. The blankness in his eyes. The slump of his shoulders. She had known it as soon as she saw him. It had just taken her a moment to recognise.

She knew what was wrong.

Whisper quiet and rabbit quick, Allandria dropped her bow, slipped a knife free from her wrist, danced forward and stabbed it in Aranok's throat.

---

"Lies! All lies!" A deep, sonorous pronouncement from somewhere in the crowd.

Who was that?

Nirea clambered onto the bench in front of the candle shop, trying to see across the crowd.

"Everything you have heard here is a lie!"

A bearded, round-faced man, near the heart of the square. Shit. No way she could get across to him.

"Sir, I promise you, the evidence we have…!" Mynygogg was cut dead by the man's furious retort.

"Liar!" The crowd somehow parted around him, and he made his way forward. "I am General Bielsed of the army of Eidyn, and *this* man is a fraud."

*Oh, fuck.*

How the Hell had a general got in the walls without being noticed? Was he alone? Were there others? Soldiers, already in their midst? Was there a spy in the Guard that they'd missed? She knew of one they'd found early on—but he was in gaol, still, until they could bring him a letter from his *draoidh* brother. Was there another? More?

Chatter from the crowd. Excitement. Murmurs.

Damn it, they had them. *They had them!*

*Fuck!*

The big man pointed dramatically up at Gogg and turned to face the crowd. "This man is no laird of Eidyn. This is the demon Mynygogg!"

Chaos.

The assassin gagged on her own blood, eyes wide as her illusion faded. A woman. No more than thirty. Long dark hair, tied back in complicated braids. And now her illusion was pierced, a pair of blades—one in each hand. They'd been destined for Allandria's back.

She batted them both away and they clattered onto the roof.

The woman's eyes struggled to focus as she reached up, trying to plug the gushing wound in her throat. But she only had moments.

Allandria leaned in, grabbed her wrists and whispered.

"You think I wouldn't know him? That I don't know his every *movement*? His smile? The shift of his hips as he walks? His scent?"

She was drowning. Going fast.

"And if nothing else... If you *were* Aranok, *I wouldn't have heard you coming.*"

She drove the knife into the assassin's chest, just where it would pierce her heart. Giving her peace she didn't deserve.

"That was for Girette, bitch."

The woman's limp body slumped to the roof. Allandria's heart pounded in her ears.

But there was noise. More noise than there should be. From below.

Hell, what had she missed? There had been voices raised, but she hadn't... she'd not really heard. Too focused.

Darting back to the edge of the roof, she scanned the square. What the Hell had happened? People were falling over each other to move, one way or another. Some to get away, others to get closer to the stage. And what looked like a line of—oh Hells, were they... soldiers?

Yes.

Mynygogg stood surrounded by the city guard, facing a battalion of Eidyn's soldiers.

God, how had this gone so wrong so quickly? Where had the soldiers come from?

*And where the fuck was Aranok?*

Allandria knelt in place, drew her bow, took aim and prayed.

"Out of the way. Out of the way!" Nirea elbowed and damn near punched her way past the gawkers who'd stayed to see this play out. She needed to be closer. She couldn't help Gogg from where she was, damn it.

And fucking Aranok! Where was he? They needed him. Him and that memory charm were the way out of this. Clear the general, get back in control.

Gogg was debating with the general—too quietly to hear. Where the Hell had all these soldiers come from?

They must have been in the crowd from the start, cloaks disguising their uniforms. She'd not seen them. Not been able to properly move about and assess the crowd.

*Fuck, fuck, fuck!*

"Stand down!" she heard the general roar.

"Protect the king!" Bak's voice. Good. He was standing firm. Though that was only going to muddy matters in the minds of the uncleared. A stray shoulder caught Nirea in the face and she stumbled sideways, the pain of her broken nose sparking again.

*God damn it.*

A hand under her arm, pulling her back up. A kind face, smiling. "You all right?"

"Aye, thanks," she spat, shaking herself free and pushing forward again. More raised voices. She looked up. There, thank God, at least Allandria was where she was meant to be, up on the roof. On guard.

*Wait.*

If the army knew what was happening in advance...

Nirea whipped her head around the other rooftops, searching urgently, until...There. Opposite corner from her position. Couldn't be farther away. But with a perfect angle above the stage. Another archer.

"Allandria!" she screamed. "Allandria!" But her envoy couldn't hear her over the furore of the crowd. "Allandria!" She was gesticulating furiously, hoping that maybe she'd look down, see her and understand.

And then...Did she? Did she look right at her? Maybe. Maybe she did. And then a turn of her head. Recognition? Did she see it?

*She had to see it.*

# THE DAMNED KING

Nirea was frantic about something. Understandably, but it seemed like something specific. What was she pointing at? She seemed to just be indicating the stage, where Mynygogg stood surrounded by guards. The merchants had quickly taken themselves away. Ducked back inside the Canny Man. But the guards were standing firm. What did Nirea want her to know?

Was she supposed to kill the general? Was that wise? Would it help?

"Please!" she heard Mynygogg shout. "General, I ask you only for a moment of parlay. Allow me to show you the evidence..."

"I'll not fall for your tricks, *draoidh*!" the general bellowed back at him. "You'll surrender to me now or die here!"

The soldiers had all drawn weapons, and the guard had done the same. This was about to become Hell if she didn't... Wait. Movement? What was...?

*Fuck*. Of course.

That's what Nirea was trying to tell her.

---

The cobbles slipped beneath him like cold grey clouds. Aranok's feet stumbled forward, a slow march to a silent dirge. He saw them move, but they were not his. Some stranger's limbs propelled him on. Another man's eyes watched the ground as it wavered before him. He had somewhere to be. Somewhere he had to be.

Gogg.

Mynygogg needed him.

At the square.

But the numb, black void was screaming, beckoning him, begging him to slide into it and disappear. Disappear forever into the quiet nothingness.

But he couldn't. He had somewhere to be. People needed him.

A woman jostled him, going the other way. She looked... distressed? Did she pause to look harder at him? Question him? Maybe. It didn't matter.

Eyes.

Glassy, pale eyes, staring up at him. Eyes devoid of the life that had danced within them. Of the joy and love and, and… The ground swam beneath him and he staggered sideways, grabbed onto a wall. Felt the contours of the stone beneath his fingers. Ran them along its edges. Cold; hard. Solid.

His hand trembled. Had it been shaking before? He didn't know. It was cold. Cold and numb.

Aranok licked his dry lips, his tongue thick against the roof of his mouth. The taste of metal. He should drink. Hands fumbled fruitlessly at his belt for a waterskin. Must have left it at…

The black reared up, pounding in his ears until the chatter of the crowd was lost in a crashing roar of silence. A squeal of nothing.

*Hold on. Breathe. You have to hold on.*

His head hung forward, blank eyes wide, waiting for the screaming to pass, for the blackness to fade.

Slowly, the cacophony returned. A mumble at first, low and rumbling, then sharp, clear.

*Urgent.*

Something was happening.

Aranok's heart raced, pounding blood through him, forcing him to move. *Move!*

Head up. Chest out. Deep breaths. The cold air snapped into his lungs like a swarm of needles.

And then he was moving. Pushing through the crowd, into the square. Toward the raised voices and… Shouting. Some running away, others toward. Raised fists and screams of support, or attack. Who…? Why?

There. There on the stage. He saw him, just. Head almost lost between all the others. Guards and…

Soldiers?

*Shit.*

Soldiers should not be here.

He had to get to the stage. He was supposed to be on the stage.

"'Scuse me." He slid a shoulder between a grey-haired man and the younger woman next to him. She scowled and he grunted. Aranok kept pushing. Through another two, and another.

"Excuse me..."

"Fuck off," the big ginger spat over his shoulder. "Nowhere to go."

Aranok pushed back, but he was right. It was like shoving iron. The crowd had surged forward. Bodies were pressed hard against each other. Aranok couldn't even raise his left arm from his side without punching the boy in front of him.

He was stuck.

But he didn't have to be.

Aranok made the gestures for *clach*, but the word caught in his throat.

Through the morass of agitated heads, he saw Mynygogg again. He looked distressed. Desperate. Vulnerable.

Aranok was supposed to be there. Up on stage, with his friend.

He was late.

*Again.*

Pushing, jostling. Swords drawn from sheaths. A hand in the air.

Aranok had to get up there.

*Now.*

A distant thud, like a butcher's blade into a pig's rump.

A sudden hush. A vast sucking in of stunned breath.

Something wrong. Something impossible.

Gogg, frozen, as time stopped, just for a second. The briefest flash of absolute stillness that lasted an age.

An arrow through his head, like a grotesque weathervane, idling in the doldrums. Tilting.

Falling.

Gone.

The blackness roared, numbness reaching for Aranok, enveloping, consuming, clawing, rending. Screaming.

And the world turned red.

---

"Allandria!" Nirea screamed in vain. She couldn't see the archer. Fuck it.

"General! General Bielsed!" Nirea threw off her cloak, revealing her red sea leathers. "General, it's Captain Nirea, of the navy! Of the king's council. Please, listen!"

But he wasn't listening. He was completely focused on the throng before him. Single-minded.

Nirea couldn't hear what was said as she was bustled and battered back and forth, chattering and panic flowing all around her. The crowd finally thinned and she had a clear view at last.

Just in time to see Bielsed raise his hand. And drop it.

A hush of air, a thud of metal hitting meat. A scream. A body dropped from the roof opposite. Allandria had done her job.

But the stage had fallen into chaos.

And she knew.

She felt it like a knife in her own chest.

She knew.

Mynygogg was down.

A scream of rage tore itself from her chest.

She had to get up there. Get to the stage. Get to Gogg. He needed her. Nirea threw people aside, wrestled them to the ground, forcing herself forward, forward, toward the stage. Some dolt knocked into her, sent her sideways, almost to the ground, but she caught herself on a stranger's arm.

She had to get to the stage, had to—

A sharp, hot pain in her side. She stumbled, trying to catch her breath, but it wouldn't come. Heart pounding, legs turned to water beneath her, Nirea crumpled to her knees.

What was happening? Her head swam as someone a long way distant screamed, "No!"

A hand under her arm. A punch to her back. Another. Hot, and wet, and her eyes swam and her head dropped to her chest as strength bled from her.

Dark, wet cobbles danced before her. Spinning. Opening a cold, empty void.

A whisper in her ear.

Feather light.

"Madu sends her regards."

And then, finally, the cobbles faded to quiet darkness.

"Fuck!"

Allandria had missed the first shot. Bloody wind had kicked up just as she'd loosed, and thrown the arrow high. The second had got the archer, but too late. They'd got an arrow off. She hadn't seen where they'd hit, but by the carnage on the stage, it was bad. The guards were frantic. Bak was barking commands.

And she'd lost sight of Nirea in the crowd. Where had she gone?

A bellow of pain, like she'd never heard. A deep howl of agony. One distinct word. In a voice she knew.

"No!"

And suddenly, with a roaring wave of heat, Mourning Square was in flames.

Figures burning, dropping to the ground, running, trying to escape the fire on their own backs. A woman batted frantically at her own burning hair. Buildings going up—fuck, including the one she was on!

Where was he?

Where was Aranok?

She spotted him. Southwest corner, down to her left.

An empty circle had formed around him. Sheer terror. People stared at him, like a demon. Others ran—to help others or to get away.

She had to get to him. Whatever else, first, she had to get to him.

By the time she'd clambered down and fought her way to him, he was completely abandoned, standing alone, blankly watching the fire he'd set. The gawkers had run.

"Aranok! Aranok!" she pleaded. What the Hell had happened to him, that he'd lost control? Again?

"Aranok!" She came up in front of him, grabbed his hands and yanked his arms to shake him from his stupor. His blank eyes looked right through her. "Aranok!"

Nothing. He wasn't there.

The screams behind her were a roar. People burning alive there in the grey winter snow. God, she had to find a way to him.

Allandria grabbed his face between her hands, held him directly in front of her eyes. "Aranok! Look at me! It's Allandria. Look!"

God, the heat. The heat and the screams.

"Aranok!"

A blink of recognition. Of life. "Al?"

"Yes! Thank God, Aranok. You have to put out the fire! You see?" She opened her body to show him the blaze. The chaos of bodies, most of them now dropped to the ground, writhing, twitching. Some already still. "*Uisge!* You need to use *uisge*! Now!"

"They're dead," he muttered, broken and small.

"Not yet!" she answered. "You can save them! Come on! *Uisge!* Please! Aranok, I'm begging you. Please!"

A tiny spark of light and finally he saw her. A nod.

"*Uisge.*"

Water poured from his hands. Allandria pulled him across the square, directing his actions, sometimes just moving his arms herself. The water hissed and spat as it drowned the flames. Smoke poured upwards from charred buildings.

God, so many bodies. So many dead. So many in agony.

The awful tang of roasted flesh.

How had this happened? How had the army been there? How did they *know*?

She had no idea where Mynygogg and Nirea were. They would have to save themselves—she was going to be lucky to get the two of them out of there alive.

A child cowered against a wall, shivering, soaked, face a black char. She was alive, at least. Maybe...Maybe Samily would...one day...

She pulled him on. People staggered toward them, throwing themselves at the plume of water pouring from his hands. Collapsing at his feet. Groaning. Begging. Praying.

When the last of the flames was finally reduced to a smoulder, she let go of Aranok's hand.

"Enough. You can stop."

His hands flopped at his sides, and whatever life she'd seen in him was gone. His shoulders slumped, his face grey and hollow. He looked vacantly into the distance, lost in some private torture.

She was too terrified to ask, even to wonder...What happened to him? To make him like this? What horror had he seen?

The square was heavy with the unholy stench of burnt meat and wood, and the groans of survivors. At least they were alive. Cries of panic raised, as people scurried forward now from the edges. Looking for family. Hoping, praying they were alive.

The stage was empty, but for a few prone bodies scarred black with flames. Hopefully they made it back inside.

Hopefully Nirea was with them.

More people were gathering at the edges again. Coming back to see the aftermath. The moment someone thought to look for him, they were in trouble.

"Come on." She grabbed Aranok's wrist. "We have to go. Now."

———

Allandria dragged Aranok in Ferrod's door and all but dropped him on the floor. He slumped against the wall, eyes as vacant as they'd been in Mourning Square.

Vastin arrived first. His eyes shot wide when he saw the state of them. "What happened?"

"We were ambushed," Allandria answered, locking the door behind them. "Weyr had soldiers waiting. He knew."

"He knew? How?"

She'd been pondering that. And she had a good idea. One that sickened her.

Quick footsteps came pounding down the stairs. Morienne. Her face fell too. "Oh. Oh God. What can I do?"

"Help me get him up."

Between the three of them, they manoeuvred Aranok onto the sofa. He was like a giant, empty doll. He'd said nothing all the way there. Allowed her to lead him like docile cattle. For all the energy he'd used, she wasn't surprised he was exhausted, but what the fuck had happened before that? He'd been meant to be in the Canny Man with the others. On the stage. If he had been there, maybe...

No point playing games like that now. She had things to do.

"Can you get him some water?" she asked Vastin. The boy nodded and hastened off toward the kitchen. "Where's Ferrod?" she asked Morienne.

"Upstairs, I think," she answered. "Shall I get him?"

"Yes. And pack. Quickly. Both of you." She nodded after Vastin.

"Pack? We're moving?" Morienne asked.

"No," Allandria answered. "We're running."

# CHAPTER 49

"Oh God. Oh fucking God in Hell."

Allandria raised a trembling hand to her mouth. The Canny Man was a carnage of bodies, wounded, dead and dying. It had been a risk coming back here, but she needed to know. Needed to understand. To be able to...

She wasn't ready. Not for this.

Bak placed a hand on her shoulder. "I'm sorry, my lady. There was nothing we could do."

They'd brought the bodies into the back. Probably Calador's own quarters, she assumed. Placed them together on the bed. As if they were sleeping.

Mynygogg's right eye was collapsed, where the arrow had hit him. A professional shot. He was dead before he hit the ground. And Nirea. Nirea was a mess. Her red leathers, sticky with dark brown blood. Her hair burned to frazzles, the skin on her face bright red, bubbled and angry.

It wasn't real. It couldn't be real. They were so alive, so vital, so immortal! It made no sense.

"No. Surely...No..." Allandria stuttered. "It's...They..." Words would not form for her; her mind refused to accept the lie of her eyes.

The king and queen of Eidyn were not dead.

Her friends were not dead.

She stumbled forward, dropped to her knees beside the bed. Delicate fingers brushed Nirea's ravaged face as tears streamed down her cheeks.

"How? How?"

"We think... We believe someone must have informed them, my lady," said Bak, not understanding the real question she was asking. "It's possible they sent the messenger as bait. For the king."

A traitor in their ranks.

"I... I don't think it was one of mine," Bak continued. "I believe in them. All of them. I have to hope, to believe that..."

Allandria raised a feeble hand, asking him to stop. She couldn't hear it now. Not now. Not as she looked down at her friend, her sister, the woman who had believed in her so completely that she would have made her one of the most powerful people in Eidyn.

Whether she wanted the job or not, even if she disagreed with her more often than not, the queen of Eidyn had wanted her counsel. Had valued her counsel. Had relied on her.

And she was dead, because Allandria had failed. Because she'd been distracted.

Because she'd *missed*.

She could have killed that assassin quickly. One arrow. Dropped her. But her anger, her righteous fury, had drawn her to do it close. Violent. To make sure she suffered in the end. For Girette. For everyone else the bitch had murdered. For Weyr.

*Fucking Anhel Weyr.*

She turned again to look at the king's pallid grey face. Was this it? Was this what had driven Aranok mad?

Watching again as his best friend was murdered in Mourning Square? Was that enough...?

No.

No, because it didn't answer the question that had been nagging her since the fire. Since she'd found him.

She turned to the captain, her voice barely audible. "Why wasn't Aranok here? With you?"

Bak's eyes turned soft and downwards. God, what else could he be afraid to tell her? How bad could it be?

"I've only just heard, not ten minutes ago. Three bodies were found in a butcher's. Well, four, including the butcher. Two of them... Their heads were missing."

*No.*

"We think... we think them Lady Sumara and Lady Ikara. I've sent guards to the house. To confirm. But..." A kind grimace.

Allandria collapsed to the floor, weeping, sobbing, her heart pounding, fluttering like a wounded bird. How could they all be dead? How could they have lost... everything?

"I am so sorry," Bak said, crouching before her.

This was why. This was what broke Aranok. The fucking bastard had sent him the heads of his mother and sister.

Oh. Oh God. He'd said three bodies...

"Em... Emelina?"

"Pardon?" Bak asked.

"The third body. Was it...?"

"Oh. It was their guard, I believe. Tall man. Bald." He shrugged.

That was all he knew. Not Em. Emelina might be all right.

Maybe... maybe Ikara hadn't taken her. Even when Emelina's skill might have saved her life, she'd kept her safe first. Because chances were that illusionist Allandria had ended on the roof had been the one who killed them that morning. Murdered the butcher and taken his place.

And Emelina would have seen her. Would have known her. And maybe they'd all be alive.

Damn it all. Ifs, buts and maybes. Useless, all of them. Dead dreams and broken trees. Their branches went nowhere.

Weyr had won.

Sumara, Ikara, Nirea and Mynygogg all dead. Aranok broken. He'd outplayed them.

But someone had made it possible. And she had an idea who.

She reached out a hand to the captain. "Could you... please?"

Bak reached down and helped her stand. She had to move. God knew what time they had. The Guard weren't going to be hunting them and it looked like most if not all of the soldiers were wounded or dead from the fire. But people would eventually start looking for Aranok.

Someone would remember seeing him at Ferrod's. Eventually, they would come. Looking for justice, or vengeance.

Allandria gently patted Bak's chest and turned to take a last look at Eidyn's lost monarchs, cold and still in the back room of an inn.

"Give them good pyres," she said. "Please?"

"They will be honoured," Bak answered. "You have my word."

That was the best she could do for them now.

But it wasn't the only thing.

There was one more thing she could do for her friends. For her family.

---

She couldn't fall apart. Not yet.

It was all on her now.

Weyr had done this.

Because somehow, Weyr had known. And the more she learned, the more she thought about it, Allandria knew how. She knew exactly how.

Which was why she was here.

Aranok would want this done. He'd need to know this was done. It would help. Maybe. Later. If anything would ever help again.

The lock clicked open and she tucked her picks back in their pocket. Carefully, quietly, she pressed the door open and slunk inside.

The kitchen was instantly familiar, and sad. It smelled like home—a home, anyway. As much as anywhere was home, this had been.

Never again. Not now.

She crept into the living room—silence. Not a creaking floorboard. Nothing.

Carefully and quickly, she checked the whole house. All the bedrooms were empty. One hadn't been used for a long time. God, that was another thing entirely, threatening to crush her.

*Not yet, Allandria.*

*You have work to do.*

Once she was certain the house was empty, she had to choose. Wait or go? How long could she linger? They'd be safe at Ferrod's house. For now. He'd have the place locked tight. Bak had sent a pair of guards, who'd been well away from the flames, to watch the house.

The illusionist was dead.

Was she justifying this to herself? Was it her rage driving her? Her pain? Revenge?

Maybe.

But she was right about the other thing too. Aranok would never heal if she didn't do this. He'd need to know it was done.

So she waited.

Not long, it turned out.

Less than an hour, and the click of a key in the front lock. She'd had time there, simmering, numb, spinning out of control, to decide how to do it. She was sure. But she had to be *absolutely* sure. Because there was no coming back from this, once it was done.

She sat silently, hidden by closed curtains from the low winter sun. She let him get inside. Close the door. Lock and bar it.

Only then did she speak.

"The first key is to spot the opportunity."

Pol jumped like a startled cat.

"That was it, wasn't it?" Allandria asked calmly. "That was what you said?"

Only today did she realise. She'd seen it in his eyes that night. Dismissed it as her disdain for the man. But it was there—the moment Pol decided to betray them.

"I don't...I..." He moved for the door, and she loosed the arrow she had nocked, whistling it past his ear to thud into the thick oak.

"Don't."

Pol turned to face her. She watched options dance across his face. Lie. Run. Fight. Beg.

"I know it was you." She stood and replaced her bow with a dagger. "Admit it, and I'll let you live. For Emelina. Lie, and I'll gut you."

The girl was alive, thank God. Allandria had stopped by Dorann's house on the way. Emelina was there. Sitting at the kitchen table, legs swinging idly beneath her as she ignored a chunk of bread before her. She'd lost her mother. Her grandmother. The two people she trusted most in the world. And what was she left with? A half-wit bastard grandfather and a miserable snake pretending to be her father. At least Cressida was looking out for her. She'd been fussing about the two of them, feeding them—the kind of thing you did for broken people when nothing would help.

Pol's eyes trembled, darting about the room, looking for options. Allandria slowly crossed toward him. "You have five seconds."

"I had to!" he blurted. "He sent a man. Offered me a choice."

"Who did?" Allandria lifted the knife to his throat. "*Who* sent a man?"

"Weyr," Pol whimpered. "Anhel Weyr. Please..."

"What did he promise you?"

His lip quivered, his eyes piteous. Pleading. "Advisor."

"He would make you an advisor?"

Pol nodded frantically.

"*Or?*" she spat. "What was the 'or'?"

"Or he'd have Emelina killed."

Unexpectedly, involuntarily, a laugh burst from her. Vicious and cruel. "Bollocks."

"What?" Pol's voice was high-pitched now. Terrified. *Good*.

"I don't believe you, Pol. I don't believe he threatened Emelina. If he had, you would have told us. Tell Aranok that someone had threatened Emelina? What better way to get yourself in his good graces? He'd have trusted you. A little. Maybe. And that would have been your *opportunity*. Right?"

Pol swallowed hard. He was shaking like a wet dog.

"Tell me the truth." Allandria pressed the blade against his neck. "Now."

"Me," Pol whispered. "He was going to kill me."

"Exactly." She lowered the blade and stepped back. "And now your wife is dead. Your mother-in-law is dead. Your father-in-law knows what you did..." His face fell at that. "Of course I told him. There was a tiny part of me that even thought it might have been him, you know? Dorann? But as soon as I saw his grief, his anger, I knew. That wasn't a man wracked with guilt. This..." She pointed the blade at him. "This is what guilt looks like."

"I didn't know," he whimpered. "I didn't know he'd kill them."

"No. You thought he'd kill *us*."

She had no more time for this.

# THE DAMNED KING

"I was just going to kill you as you walked in the door, you know? But Emelina. She's lost her mother. Her grandmother. Maybe she needs her father?"

Pol nodded, hope flickering across his eyes. "Yes. Yes, she does."

Allandria jammed the knife in his chest, and watched as the hope turned to shock, disbelief... terror.

"But you're not her father, you fucking coward."

---

"I think we should come with you." Vastin's voice was as young as Allandria could remember it. The man he'd become sunk beneath the boy who'd lost everything, again.

They stood in Ferrod's kitchen, only because it felt wrong to stand and discuss these things in front of Aranok. He was still a ghost. Hadn't moved from the sofa since she put him there hours ago. Morienne was sitting with him, mostly to protect him from himself.

"No. We have to run, Vastin. After what Aranok did—nobody's going to listen. Nobody's going to understand. People saw him set fire to a crowd of people. Soldiers. It won't matter why. It's finished.

"We've lost."

"I know," he answered sadly. "But still. I'll come with you."

He would have too. He would have gone anywhere. "I need you to do something else. You and Morienne, get Ferrod and Emelina to Traverlyn. That's what Ikara wanted. Emelina at the university. It's the best place for her. The safest place. Maybe give her a different name. I've said to Ferrod. Let him decide. Once Aranok and I are gone, Weyr should have no need for her. Egretta and Balaban will look after you. And Darginn. You'll be safe there, with the *draoidhs* and the Thorns. Just keep your heads down." She smiled. Tried to. To give him some sort of hope. Truthfully, she had no idea how long Traverlyn would hold out against Weyr if he really came for it. If he had the relic. But it was safer than here. And safer than going with them. Allandria wasn't even confident she and Aranok would survive the day. That was step one.

"All right." Vastin stood tall again. All loyalty and duty. "We'll do that. I promise."

She put a hand on his shoulder. "I know you will."

Back in the living room, Ferrod pulled Allandria aside, away from the others. With his back to the room, he produced a leather pouch, jangling with coin, and pressed it into her hands. "Don't argue. Just take it."

She wasn't going to. Gold might just buy them another day. Maybe even a few—enough to get a safe distance from this godawful disaster. "Thank you."

"And listen," he added. "I've tried to tell him this, but..." Ferrod shook his head and she knew what it meant—Aranok wasn't in there. Not really. Not anymore. "But I need to say this to you—for both of you. What you did—what you tried to do for Eidyn—was a damned good thing. It was worth the trying, you understand?" He gripped her arm with an unexpected strength. "When he comes back, you tell him. It was worth the trying. Even..." His voice broke then, and Allandria's resolve almost went with it. The armour holding her together was fragile and full of holes. "You tell him it was worth trying."

"I will," she said, her own voice threatening to abandon her. "I will."

# CHAPTER 50

The sun dipped below the horizon, casting a pale yellow haze across the ice-blue winter sky before dipping finally into the dark sea. Samily watched it through the iron bars of the small window. It had become her custom, each day. One of the few things that still gave her that close sense of God. She spent a great deal of her time in prayer and meditation.

There was little else to do.

The room was furnished fit for a visiting dignitary. Lavish chairs; an elegant bed; a huge hearth. There was even a bookcase, with a collection of ancient histories and fantasy stories. They gave her some escape, at least, from the monotony.

She would speak to Rasa, if she could. The stump of her tongue had healed cleanly, but still she tasted her own singed flesh, ash-dark and bitter. Weyr had cauterised the wound immediately, to prevent her drowning in her own blood. That was all she tasted now. And yet, Anhel Weyr insisted on sending her lavish meals—scraps from his own table, she assumed—as if to remind her of what was lost. But Samily had never had a taste for fine food. She lived happily on what rations were to hand. So Weyr's attempted slights were mere water over steel.

Samily crossed to Rasa's cage, clamped to the wall, iron locks holding it closed. Her wing had healed from the crossbow bolt, but it hung crooked. She doubted it was capable of flight now. So even if she could break her friend from the cage and get her out of the window, beyond the reach of whatever spell Weyr had in place that stifled her skill, she might just fall to her death.

Samily stuck her fingers through the bars, and her friend leaned toward them, nuzzling them with her head. She was still Rasa. She may be trapped inside a different form, but as she'd said at that dinner a lifetime ago: At her core, whatever her outer form, she was always Rasa. In her soul. That was a comfort to Samily. Her own confinement may be silent, but it was not solitary. She was never alone.

And she had faith. Faith that this would not be the end, for either of them. God was not done with them yet. God would not tolerate Anhel Weyr to continue his tyranny in God's name. It could not stand.

She just had to be patient.

She'd kept track of the days as they passed, in the beginning. Counted them, as a way of marking their time. But after enough weeks, it had become meaningless. Day and night were the only measures that meant anything. She took to exercising her body in the morning, before meditation. Her strength would dwindle otherwise, her edge become dull. She used books as weight, resistance against her actions. She missed the feel of a blade in her hand. Samily hadn't gone this long without holding a weapon since she was a child. For all her communion with God, for her serenity in God's company, she was becoming restless.

Samily was not made to be caged.

Rasa became agitated, quavering for attention. Samily had learned what this meant. Her owl hearing had detected something sour. The false king was coming.

She settled herself onto an armchair facing the door, wearing the ridiculous silver-and-blue dress Weyr had forced on her. She could hardly sit down in the stupid thing but for ripping the seams at her hips, and her arms barely raised level with her shoulders. The bodice dug into her ribs and under her breasts, pushing them uncomfortably high. For his pretensions that the outfit was a gift, she was certain its main function was to limit her movement and prevent her acting against him.

Not that she could.

The door unlocked and three servants in grey hooded robes shuffled in, heads bowed. Innocents Weyr had cursed into servitude. They were a bulwark for him. When Samily refused to wear the dress, he'd beaten an elderly man unconscious with his golden cane. She hadn't seen him since.

Samily would have to go through these unwilling thralls to reach the man—sacrifice them for her own freedom. She would not do that. And Anhel Weyr knew it.

Then there was his impossible demon. The invisible one that also somehow changed shape to fit through doorways much smaller than its huge bulk. Even if she could see it, she couldn't fight it empty-handed. No dinner knife was going to pierce its dark blue hide. And the memory of what the unholy thing had done to Cyrra was still sharp as glass.

Anhel Weyr had made himself untouchable.

So Samily sat. And waited.

"Good evening, Lady Thorn." Why he insisted on using the honorific every time they spoke, she did not understand. There was no respect in anything he said after it. But his leering, greedy eyes looked even more pleased with himself than usual this evening.

She lifted the slate slab from the table before her and wrote on it with the stick of chalk. "What do you want?"

A wide-eyed show of offence and false humility. "Well, your manners are not improved. And here I have come to bring you good news. Your very own king's messenger, as it were." He smiled at his witticism. Three more thralls followed him in, eyes always to the ground. The last one closed the door. They circled the usurper like numbers on a clock. "You will be pleased to hear that peace has returned to Eidyn at last. The war is over."

His smile was more than just self-satisfied. There was triumph in it. And not a small amount of wine in his eyes, now that she saw him more clearly. "Is it?" she wrote. His games of wordplay and deception were tiresome, but she'd learned that allowing him to get on with them was the quickest way through.

"Indeed!" The demon summoner threw up his arms as if in celebration. "The king is dead; long live the king!"

What did that mean? He'd already taken Janaeus's crown, claimed the throne. What was this nonsense? She looked at him wordlessly, waiting for his explanation.

"I've just received word. The evil *draoidh* Mynygogg and his rebellious 'queen' Nirea are dead."

Samily's heart lurched.

*No.*

Anhel Weyr was a liar and a fraud. His words had no meaning.

Samily shook her head, her intention clear: She did not believe him.

But his look was triumphant. Delighted. There was no hint of weakness in it. It was the grim smile of a man who had won, and knew it. "Thankfully, Lady Thorn, your belief, as in everything, has no bearing whatsoever on reality. They remain, I assure you, entirely dead."

Rasa squawked and barked, rattling against the bars of her cage.

"Well," said Weyr. "*Someone* believes me."

Even if it were true, and she very much held her doubts, Samily would not give this vile, small man the satisfaction of her distress. "Then they are with God," she wrote. A glint of irritation. That had not been the response the usurper wanted. Good. Fine. She wiped the slate and added more. "Aranok? Allandria?" She was goading him. He'd have listed them too, if they were gone.

A darkening of his look. A slow nod. "He might yet live, yes. But not his family…"

*No.*

He had not murdered Aranok's family. *Surely.* There was no call. No reason. They were *innocent*. Samily leapt to her feet, appalled. The slate fell from her lap, cracking into three shards on the stone floor. Her hands found themselves in fists, her arms taut, jaw clenched.

"There she is," Weyr sneered.

Rasa's cage rattled harder as she threw herself against its bars.

The frustration that she could not speak threatened to overwhelm Samily—she could not tell the hideous monster before her what she thought of him, what she was going to *do* to him.

But Weyr saw it. Because he flinched. Took half a step back. For all his certainty, all his walls, he was still, at his core, a coward. And he knew she'd just seen it. His face flushed pink as he carved on a new smile. "I brought you dinner to celebrate. I *do* hope you enjoy it."

He turned and left then, a flurry of gold-laced purple, surrounded by solemn grey. One servant remained behind, carrying a silver tray. Once the door was closed, they brought it toward her, head bowed, as always. Samily waved them away and stalked back to the window. She was not hungry. She would not eat that man's scraps. If he had truly murdered Ikara... Emelina... Rage welled in her, threatening to burst from her stone walls.

If it was true—if the king and queen really were dead, if Aranok's family was murdered, would he still have the fight in him? So much of what he did was for them. He would be broken. She'd seen how fragile he could be.

And Meristan exiled...

Maybe it truly was finished. Maybe Anhel Weyr had bested them. And perhaps it would be her fate to live and die within the walls of this tower with only Rasa for company.

Perhaps God was all she had left.

"Lady Samily?"

She jumped at the voice. The servants Weyr sent never spoke. She had assumed they were incapable. And yet...

She turned to see the man stand upright, the tray he'd carried abandoned on the table before the fire.

He lowered his hood to reveal dark skin, long black hair bound in thick braids, and eyes that sparkled with an inappropriate mischief. He gave a small, deferential bow, both hands crossed on his chest.

"Forgive me. I had to be certain first that the demon was not with us.
"I am Kye Denassa. Laird Aranok sent me."

---

"Fuck me, look at the state of these two." Farin followed where Gille pointed up the road. Two horses hobbled slowly toward them. The front rider, a dark woman in filthy leathers, hair cropped almost to the bone on one side, braided on the other, and a bow hanging from the side of her horse. On the second animal, what appeared to be a bald-headed monk sat slumped in the saddle, staring vacantly into the distance. The woman led the second horse by a length of half-rotten rope that looked like she'd salvaged it from a fire. Two sorrier sacks of shit he'd rarely seen.

"Go down and see who they are," said Gille.

"What difference does it make?" Farin asked. "Our job's to stop people coming in, not stop them leaving."

Guarding the Eastern Gate of the Malcanmore Wall was about as piss boring a job as there was to be had in Eidyn's army these days. What traffic there was tended to come through the Western Gate—and there was precious little of that. Few folk came into Eidyn from the Reiver Lands with good intentions, and the Reivers didn't bother their arses with gates—just found the breaks in the wall and snuck in there. That was the job of the patrols to guard, not the gate watch.

So they played cards, drank and fucked. A battalion of sixty assigned to guard a gate nobody ever used. Officially, there should be twenty on guard at any time. Three shifts, in and out.

In reality, two folk drew short straws and spent the shift on the tower, keeping an eye out for anything unusual. This pair were the most unusual thing that had happened in weeks.

"Fucking get down there and do your job." Gille slapped him between the shoulder blades.

"How's it my job and not your job?" Farin complained. She gave him a withering look, daring him to argue. Technically, she outranked him. For all that mattered. They'd been friends since training and found themselves in plenty of drunken fumbles in the woods, full of cheap whisky and stale bread. "Fine."

He stalked dramatically down the steps and out before the gate. They were waiting for him by the time he got there.

Farin adjusted his armour and put his hand on his sword hilt. Just for appearances.

"Names?"

"Elana," the woman answered, without looking down.

"And you?" Farin asked the monk.

"He's Palomin," the woman answered for him. "Doesnae speak. Took a hit to the head." She mimed what looked like an axe with her hand. Hells. If he'd taken an axe to the head and survived... Farin walked toward him, curious to see the scar that had left. "Don't get too close!" the woman warned. "He can be violent if you spook him."

"Violent?" Farin put his hand back on his sword. "How violent?"

"The *horse*," said Elana. "The horse is twitchy."

Oh. That made more sense. "Where you coming from?"

"Gaulton."

No more information. Fair enough. Farin was only doing the minimum anyway. "Going to?"

"South," she answered. "We're nomads."

"Nomads?" Farin asked. "Where's your flock?"

Elana turned to look at him sadly. "Lost them."

"Fuck. Sorry to hear that. You've had your share of shite, eh?" He was actually starting to feel sorry for them now. The monk was pale as sin—looked as if he'd do well to see spring. Farin wondered whether maybe he was carrying some sickness Elana didn't want him knowing about. And if maybe that was why she'd told him to stay back. Time to get rid of them. "Gille! Open the gate!"

She waved an acknowledgement and after a minute the gears started squealing, wrenching open the massive, old wooden barriers. He was half surprised they moved. Gears could easily have been frozen solid—which reminded him he'd quite like to get back up to the fire pit on top of the tower.

When they were wide enough for the horses to pass through, Farin shouted, "Whoa!" and the grinding stopped.

"Know where you're heading?" Farin asked. Just making conversation, really. Felt like he should say something.

"Maybe Pebyl," Elana answered. "Maybe got some friends there."

Pebyl? All Farin knew of Pebyl was stories of stinking old witches and mad hairy priests worshipping trees. Actually, this pair would fit right in there. Once they were clear, Farin gave Gille the signal and the doors began to swing closed again. Elana sat on the horse, staring back through the closing gap. She looked right past Farin, as though there were something worth seeing behind him. Enough that he turned to look.

Nothing but trees and the winding road north. But when he turned back, her eyes glistened wet.

"See you again." He raised a hand in a half-hearted wave.

"You won't," she answered quietly. "We're not coming back."

# EPILOGUE

Tia's ball bounced off the floor with a thunk, onto the wall and back into her hand.

"Oi!"

She turned to see Payatta, one of the medics, with a finger to her lips. "Too late, Princess. People are sleeping."

Tia nodded and put her finger to her own lips. It was late, probably. But nobody really told her to go to bed anymore. She had a bed—maybe not a room, but a bed, at least—that she slept in when she wanted. But mostly, she was free to run around the hospital and do what she liked.

Everything was a mess.

Loads of people had been hurt by the monsters and needed help. A lot had died. Like Daddy.

But the monsters were gone. Burned. Not a bit of them left. And the white knights were guarding the town. Traverlyn was the safest place in all of Eidyn, Lady Greste had told her. She liked Greste. She reminded her of Granny. Before.

She told good stories. Sometimes, she would come and tuck Tia into bed and tell her about faeries, or magic crickets. Or princesses who lived far, far away.

But Tia wasn't tired yet. What she was, was hungry. She tucked her ball into the pocket of her apron—the one Mystolla had cut down for her. Said she was an "apprentice" medic. Gave her some bandages to carry.

Tia didn't want to be a medic. It looked hard. She didn't like blood. And hurt people were scary too. She didn't like seeing the hurt people.

Down in the kitchen, she begged some bread and ham from Durden, the cook. He ruffled her hair, gave her some warm milk and told her to behave. But she couldn't *mis*behave. She was the princess, and the hospital was her castle.

She took off her shoes, so as not to make too much noise, and skipped along the corridor, counting every step. *Thirty-eight, thirty-nine, forty…*

A few laps around the big hall and her eyes started to feel heavy. And it was getting chilly. She'd quite like to be in her bed now, actually. Cosy and warm under the blanket, with the pillow that smelled of her.

Like home.

She danced up the stairs, past Brode, fussing with something in her hands and muttering to herself, like she always was. She was odd.

Into the big hall, where all the beds were laid out in lines up the sides. It had always been busy when she'd started sleeping in here. She wanted to be around people then. Didn't want to be alone. The dark was scary on her own. There were always candles on here. Always someone about—a medic, looking after somebody.

It was quieter now. Less beds full. People got better and went home. But still too many for all the rooms in the hospital, even though it went on and on forever and ever. So there were still some people staying in here.

And that was why Tia liked it. For the company.

But as she walked toward her bed, she saw something odd. At first, she thought she was seeing it wrong, but no, once she got closer—there was somebody sitting on her bed. On *her* bed.

That was a bit rude. There were loads of other beds. Beds with nobody in them. Why were they sitting on *her* bed?

Was it one of the medics? Oh, maybe it was Greste, waiting for her!

As she got close, she saw it was none of them. Because the person was wearing all the wrong clothes to be a medic, or a white knight. She had on a pretty dress, with lacy edges and flowers sewn on. And when she saw Tia, she smiled. A really big, proper smile.

Then she stood and held out another dress that looked just like one Tia knew well, but smaller. Small enough to fit her. "Hi, Princess. I have a present for you."

Tia yelped with delight and threw her arms around the woman's waist.

"Quell!"

**The story continues in . . .**

Book Four of the Eidyn Saga

# ACKNOWLEDGEMENTS

OK, take a breath. Yeah, yeah, I know, you want to shout at me. It'll pass. First I have to thank some people.

It becomes more and more difficult to say thank you in new and interesting ways the more books you write, it turns out. Especially when you're largely thanking the same people. So I'll do my best to at least embrace some brevity, while also getting across no less gratitude than always.

Huge thanks, again, to Nathan, for giving me the chance to make this series happen, and to Sean, Kirsten, Craig, Neith and Jan for lending me their characters.

My eternal gratitude and admiration to my editor, Bradley, who always makes these books better; to all of the supportive team at Orbit US; and to Nadia, Nazia and all the guys at Orbit UK, not least for all the parties I got invited to this last year!

Thanks, as always, to my agent, Ian, for taking a chance on me.

Thank you to Jeremy Wilson and Lauren Panepinto for another evocative cover, and thanks again to Tim Paul for my beautiful map.

Big love to my beta readers and BFFs Kelvin and Kathryn, who were *not amused* with me when we met up in the pub to talk about this book. I believe the phrase was "*What* did you *do*?"

To my family—all of you—who are always so supportive and encouraging, and who show up en masse to every book launch: Thank you, I love you all.

## ACKNOWLEDGEMENTS

To all my friends in the SFF book world—authors, readers, reviewers, con goers and online buddies—thank you all. You make working in this genre delightful.

To my alpha reader, the person who has to talk me down off ledges every time I become absolutely certain that I have completely lost the ability to write anything even vaguely competent with a dry "Ah, we're at this stage again," my wonderful wife, Juliet: Thank you for keeping me sane. Mostly.

And finally, to you. Thanks for sticking with me through this story, and for bearing with me through plague and pestilence until we could get this book out. The last one won't be so long a wait. :)

Cheers!
J

# extras

orbit-books.co.uk

# about the author

**Justin Lee Anderson** was a professional writer and editor for fifteen years before his debut novel, *Carpet Diem*, was published and won the 2018 Audie Award for Humor. His second novel, *The Lost War*, won the 2020 SPFBO Award. Born in Scotland, he spent his childhood in the US thanks to his dad's football (soccer) career and also lived in the South of France for three years. He now lives with his family just outside his hometown of Edinburgh.

Find out more about Justin Lee Anderson and other Orbit authors by registering for the free monthly newsletter at orbit-books.co.uk.

**if you enjoyed**

# THE DAMNED KING

**look out for**

# BETWEEN DRAGONS AND THEIR WRATH

## The Shattered Kingdom: Book One

by

# Devin Madson

*Conquest built the Celes Basin. But when enemies once more threaten its borders, the Lord Reacher declares himself supreme ruler to enforce unity. Old angers erupt, threatening to tear the basin apart from within.*

*Tesha, a glassblower's apprentice, becomes a tribute bride as part of a desperate political plot. In the Reacher's court, she's perfectly placed to sabotage him, but her heart has other plans.*

*Naili is laundress to an eccentric alchemist, a job that has left her with strange new abilities that are slowly consuming her — and attracting the notice of the city's underground rulers. With time running out, she'll have to gain power by any means if she wants to survive, let alone change the world.*

*And in the desolate Shield Mountains, sharp-shooting dragon rider Ashadi protects the basin from the monsters of the Sands beyond, but when an impossible shot pierces his dragon's glass scales, he becomes the hunted one.*

*As chaos sweeps across the land, Tesha, Naili and Ashadi must fight to survive political enemies, long-buried secrets, and monsters both within and without.*

If you enjoyed

# THE DAMNED KING

of the

# BETWEEN DRAGONS
# AND THEIR WRATH

The Shattered Kingdom Book One

by

Devin Madson

# Tesha

**Afternoon Bulletin**

*To all criers for announcement throughout Learshapa*

*Grievous blow for the city as a second critical scale shipment fails to arrive from Therinfrou Mine. Attacks by Lummazzt soldiers to blame.*

*Emergency council meeting called to discuss rising border tensions with Lummazza, despite initial plans not to meet again until after next week's vote. "We would be stronger together," says Reacher Sormei.*

*Nine ritual carvings have gone missing from Lord Sactasque's public gallery. It is the second such incident this month. Information is sought regarding this assault on Celessi history.*

*200:49*

The shatter of warm glass hitting stone has a particular tenor, a sound that reaches deep, more feeling than noise. It touches every memory of broken glasswork and shattered dreams, of beauty lost and time torn away. Even when it's Assistant Jul's ugly carafe that looks better as a pile of shards.

"Sweep it up!" Master Hoye called over the roaring furnace. "Life is glass!"

"Life is glass," the boy mumbled back, the lesson still too sharp to fit into the ugly-carafe-shaped hole in his heart. Likely it would be a few more years before he realised what our master's favourite phrase really meant. Not that glasswork was all we lived for, but that life *was* glass. Like life, glass is infinitely malleable when warm and well-tended, yet fragile enough to shatter at a single wrong move. It can be moulded by any hands into any shape, but the more skilled and prepared the hands the better the outcome. Even the addition of scale for strength was akin to the way people gathered wealth and resources about themselves and called it resilience.

I'd been staring out the back window, lost in thought, but as broken glass tinkled into the scrap bucket I shoved the last bite of honey-crusted bread into my mouth. Outside, the slice of Learshapa that had been my lunch-break companion went on unchanged. Overhead, sunlight reflected off whitewashed walls beneath an endless blue sky, yet little light reached the courtyard of faded tiles on the other side of the window. Once it had been a fine atrium, but now it was full of dusty, cobwebbed pots owning lethargic plants more grey than green.

I licked my fingers and wiped the sticky residue down my apron as Master Hoye called, "The gather won't shape itself!"

To Master Hoye, everything was about glass. He likened his desire not to rush out of bed in the morning to glass being stronger when cooled slowly in vermiculite, and the suffering of stress to the drawing of thin canes. Even wrong words spoken at the wrong time earned a hiss from him, like hot glass being dunked in a quenching barrel.

Back at my workbench, I gathered materials for the next job. *Cobalt. A pinch of scale. Sand bed. Two moulds.* Even with the scale shortage, there was a lot to do. The upcoming vote to decide Learshapa's place in the Celes Basin seemed to have energised the city, sending everyone bustling about with renewed purpose and a determination to finish long-neglected projects. That afternoon, my list contained a dozen replacement armour scales, two matching brandy glasses, a trio of scaleglass blades to fit carved handles, and twenty unification badges I would rather have smashed on the floor. *Unification.* I sneered as I laid everything out ready. It was a fine word for conquest.

As I prepared to gather molten glass from the furnace, an arrival sent our bead curtain tinkling. "Good afternoon," a young man said, unclipping his veil and casting his gaze around the large, smoky space.

"Good afternoon." Assistant Borro hurried forward, wiping his hands on his apron as Master Hoye always did. "What can we do for you?"

"I'm hoping to leave a small pile of flyers on your counter in support of the vote." As he spoke, the man handed Borro a paper-wrapped sugar curl from a basket he carried. "Is there perhaps someone more senior I could speak to?"

A glance back found Master Hoye in the middle of shaping a vase and shouting at Assistant Jul, both dripping sweat, and poor Borro rolled his gaze my way.

I strode over, but before I could speak, the young man thrust one of his sugar curls into my hand—a traditional Memento curl of skulls and suns. "A Memento Festival token for next week's Memento Eve vote," he said, all bright cheerfulness. "Might I leave a small pile of flyers here for your customers?"

I glanced down at the flyers, able to make out only two words at the top of the page: *Stronger Together.* "I take it you're supporting the 'conquer us, please, we can't take care of ourselves' vote then," I said, utterly failing at what Master Hoye called civil indifference.

Likely the man had a ready response for most arguments, just not one so blunt. For a long moment he stared at me and I stared back, sugar curl growing sticky in my warm hand.

Behind him, the glass-bead curtain tinkled again, heralding the arrival of two women, arm-in-arm as they let down their veils. "Good afternoon," I said, grateful for the distraction. "Can I help you?"

"We're looking for scaleglass wedding bands," the younger said, a shy glance thrown at her companion. "I know scale is in short supply, but, well, we're asking around anyway."

"Wedding bands?" I scoffed, the disgusted words escaping before I could swallow them. The women froze—a startled tableau of horror.

With a hiss mimicking hot glass hitting water, Master Hoye stepped forward. "That's not Apprentice Tesha's field of expertise," he said, patting my arm with one hand while wiping his damp brow with the other. "Best to speak to me about that. I'm Master Hoye, and you're right, scale is..." His words trailed off as he guided them to the other side of the entry space, away from the ever-present roar of the furnaces. Neither young woman glanced back to see my heated cheeks.

"Oh, so you're that kind of Learshapan, are you?" the man said, finding his voice again. "Traditional. Against all change."

"You say that like change is a neutral term," I snapped back. "Like taking up a new fashion is the same as giving up our ability to decide our own future, because that's what this is. A vote for unification is a vote for assimilation into the Emoran empire."

"And a vote for separation is a vote to stay weak and risk further Lummazzt attacks!"

"Bullshit!"

Master Hoye and the two women broke off their low-voiced conversation, all three turning to stare at us. Cheeks reddening for the second time, I leaned over the counter, bringing my fury face-to-face with the flyer man's. "Lummazza has never attacked us and has no reason to now. But if you give Emora the power to make us in their image there will be no Learshapa. And certainly no Memento Festival." I crushed the softening sugar curl in my fist, snapping its artistry like tiny bones. "The answer is no, you can't leave your flyers here."

"And you think I'm the fear monger," the man scoffed, and in a flurry of skirts, he spun away, pushing through the glass-bead curtain and out into the bright heat before he'd even clipped his veil into place.

"That went well."

I turned to find Master Hoye watching, the two women having departed, leaving our entry empty.

"I'm sorry," I said, anger chilling to regret in a heartbeat. "I ought not to have lost my temper with him. It's not good for business."

"No, but neither is complete Emoran rule, so you're forgiven." There was nothing more to be said, yet he remained watching me.

"What is it?" I said, instantly breathless with worry.

"You need to be more respectful when people come in looking for wedding bands, but I think you know that already, don't you?"

I closed my eyes and gave a solemn nod. "It's just so ridiculous. Especially in a scale shortage."

"Times have been rough." His voice sank to a quiet murmur. "Who am I to judge what people choose to make them happy?"

"Marriage? Family?" I all but spat the words. "You know as well as I do how dangerous those customs are to our communes and care groups."

Master Hoye dropped his hand on my shoulder. "These are

concerns for the meeting house, not my workshop. And yes, I know you haven't been attending meetings, like I know you're a fool who can't find her place in the world, but I'd say it's been long enough, huh?"

I nodded slowly, shame at my outbursts weighing me down. "I'm sorry, Master. I will take more care."

"I know you will."

Again, he patted my shoulder, and would have turned back about his work had not a question burst from my lips. "What did you mean when you said I was 'a fool who can't find her place'?"

"I meant exactly what I said."

"I'm happy here. And in my care group."

"For now, yes. But happy has never been what you're looking for, has it?"

With a wink, he turned away, already calling for Assistant Borro to ready his punty. It was his way of ending conversations that had run out of usefulness, a sure sign that asking what he had meant a second time would earn no better answer.

As I returned to my work, hoping no one else would step through the door, a registered crier passed by in the street shouting the afternoon bulletin. "...scale shipment fails to arrive from Therinfrou Mine. Attacks by Lummazzt soldiers to blame," she called, her voice carrying well in the narrow street. "Emergency council meeting called to discuss rising border tensions with Lummazza, despite initial plans not to meet again until after next week's vote. 'We would be stronger together,' says Reacher Sormei..."

Her voice faded away on the reacher's name, leaving me with the bitter taste of it in my mouth. Reacher Sormei, leader of Emora and the rest of the Celes Basin. At that very moment he was somewhere in Learshapa campaigning for the unification vote so he could rule us too, and people like that idiot with his flyers wanted to help him do it.

A long time ago the Celes Basin had been home only to roaming Apaian tribes, who had done nothing more with the basin's vast scale deposits than carve death mementos into the stone. The discovery that it could be mixed into glass to create a substance stronger than any metal had changed everything. With scaleglass, the Apaians had built permanent settlements, water catchments, and roads that crossed the basin's empty stones, even made an early form of blasting powder that dug the pits of our great cities—Bakii, Orsu, and Learshapa. Perhaps it would have stayed that way had the Emorans not been forced from their own lands into the basin, or perhaps they would have attacked anyway, coveting the scale and all it could do. Either way, as the Lummazzt conquered Emora, Emorans had conquered the basin and built their own city—Emora—from which to govern. The war had been brutal, but so long ago now it hardly seemed real. Only Learshapa had kept any form of democracy when the Emorans finally took over, a concession earned through bloodshed that some were now ready to vote away.

Returning to my abandoned tasks, I couldn't extricate myself from the fear that grew daily. What if the unification vote won? What if my home was about to change forever no matter how tightly I clung? What would become of us then?

I might have relaxed had the day continued like any other, but in the middle of the afternoon it became even less like any other when Sorscha sauntered in, all at ease. His visits to the forge weren't rare enough to herald trouble, but I hadn't seen him for weeks. Not since I'd stopped volunteering at the west quarter meeting house. Not since I'd walked out on Uvao.

"Tesha. Master Hoye," he said, shaking out the dark hair he loosed from his veil. "A fine afternoon to you both."

He leaned on the counter, possessing none of the nervousness I felt at his arrival. As though I'd forgotten how to stand or smile or what to do with my arms. The urge to ask after Uvao was strong.

"Afternoon, yes. Fine, I'm not so sure," Master Hoye said, handing his work to the boys and striding over. "What can we do for you, Sorscha?"

"Always business with you, Master Hoye." Sorscha's smile held a mocking edge, and his single-slit brows hovered low and sleepy. "I'm well, thank you for asking. Though the heat out there is quite something. Almost as bad as the heat in here."

Despite his complaint, he looked cool and at ease, his dark hair ruffled in a careless style and his blackened leather tunic laced tight—as tight as the three brass bands constricting one arm. His glance flicked my way, his mocking smile unmoving, and I could only hope I looked untroubled lest he report my embarrassment to Uvao.

When Master Hoye didn't answer in kind, Sorscha sighed and pulled a folded paper square from his skirt pocket. "Here then," he said, unfolding it with painstaking diligence. "Something to keep you busy for the rest of the afternoon."

"This afternoon? I'm full up."

"Then give this one to Tesha."

"No."

Master Hoye's sharp refusal was entirely expected and yet utterly disappointing—a feeling for which I ought to have been ashamed. The jobs Sorscha sometimes brought in were not only illegal but flouted our customs. Learshapa had always sustained itself by being a collective political community in which decisions were made together, but with that on the verge of change there was much allure in being able to just... *do* something about it. Quickly. Quietly. Changing the world.

With a silky hush, Sorscha slid the paper across the counter.

Before Master Hoye snatched it up, I caught the words *identical wine glasses*, *fast-acting poison*, and *illness*. "And you need it tonight?"

"The client will accept tomorrow morning."

"Then tomorrow morning it is. Come at opening, not before."

"Naturally. Before would mean being up far too early."

Master Hoye grunted and walked away, leaving me facing Sorscha, who remained leaning against the front bench. "Long time, no see, Tesh," he said in his lazy way. "Arguments at the meeting house haven't been as fiery without you. Will you be attending tonight?"

A shrug was all I could manage. Mere weeks ago, I would have been there every night helping out, but accidentally uncovering Uvao's identity had changed everything. No matter how often I might wish, as I lay awake at night, that I'd never found out at all.

"This second scale shipment failing to arrive has everyone on edge," Sorscha went on, thankfully unaware of my thoughts. "Even more on edge than the coming vote and the presence of Reacher Sormei walking the streets shaking everyone's hand, that is."

For people who didn't know him, it was unnerving witnessing Sorscha's shift from charming insouciance to serious political discussion. I'd spent too long in his company to be shocked, but it sent a thrill up my spine every time. "I think we'd all be better off if someone killed Reacher Sormei and let us get on with our lives," he added. "And no, before you ask, that's not the job I just gave Master Hoye. Unfortunately. At least we get to vote, huh? Imagine living in Bakii and having no say over anything at all."

We both grimaced, momentarily in accord as he readied his veil to depart. "Catch you around, Tesh."

"Wait, before you go. Tell me...how do you think the vote will go?"

"Are you asking me as me, or asking me as someone whose friend turned out to be an Emoran lord who knows more of what's going on than we do?"

"Both."

A soft laugh brushed his veil as he drew it up, pinning it to his hair. "It's the same answer anyway. I don't know, so I find myself grateful that I'll be at least somewhat protected from the worst of the fallout by said friend turning out to be an Emoran lord. Same place you would be in if you hadn't made such a pointless moral stand when you found out who Uvao was."

"Pointless?"

"You asked," Sorscha said, and with a little wave, he headed for the door, skirt swishing. "Goodbye, Tesh."

He was gone on the words, leaving me stunned and flustered with an increasing urge to run after him and argue. An urge quashed only by Master Hoye dropping half a dozen jobs on my bench.

"No time for daydreaming, Tesha, we're swamped," he said, before retiring to the back of the workshop alone. There, the box he always used for Sorscha's special jobs already sat out. It was flat and rectangular, little bigger than a book, but with wooden panels so finely decorated it would have been worth a fortune even without the secretive contents. Master Hoye had never told me what was inside, but over the years I'd come to believe it was all poisons—poisons over which his hands danced with ease, each vial touched with the gentleness of old friends.

Having chosen vials from the box, he turned to make a fresh gather, and I spun away. Nothing was as sure to incite his ire as curiosity about his box of poisons and the glassware he sometimes put them in for money.

Despite my worries, there was so much work to do that for the rest of the day I lost myself in glass and heat and sweat. For a time, the mysterious box was forgotten, as was the vote, Uvao,

Sorscha, and the political plays of Reacher Sormei, each melting away beneath the singular focus of practising my craft and practising it well.

By the end of the day, I was worn out but satisfied and had started tidying the workshop when a registered crier passed, calling the evening news. As always, we all paused in our work to listen.

"—to the scale shortage, yet another shipment of sand has failed to arrive as scheduled due to ongoing blockades between Orsu and the northern mines. Learshapans advised to ration their glass needs," the crier shouted, slowly passing the open portico. "After this afternoon's emergency council meeting, Lord Councillor Angue is expected to address crowds in the chamber square at sundown, while Reacher Sormei..."

Her voice faded as she moved on, once more taking with her the Reacher's dreaded name and much of the air left in our stifling workshop.

"Sand too," Master Hoye grumbled. "I'll have to go through the orders and see what can be put off."

What more was there to say? With a huff of breath, he waved a hand at the assistants, both elbow-deep in the washing tub and looking miserable. "Go on, run along home, boys. I'll wash up tonight. You too, Tesha. I need to think."

Waved away with a preoccupied scowl, there was nothing to do but swap apron for veil and head out into the street, leaving him to his thoughts.

Although the sun was setting, the air outside still held the day's heat, drying everything it touched. Learshapa could get as hot as our forge, but the city never smelled of burning paper and coal and wax and scale; rather the street held tangs of life, of cooking food and warm earth and sweat, of water and flowers and spilled date brandy. It was all so very *Learshapa* that I breathed deep.

At the end of the street, the public house was already full of noise, all chatter and laughter and the squeak of worn sandals on the glass-tiled floor. A tangle of vines shaded the outdoor plaza, where cooler air gathered around the spill of a central fountain.

It took a few moments to find an empty table near the netting edge, but I soon had a tall glass of brandy laced with benki flowers and my very own sticky cake I utterly deserved. Overhead, the sky was turning pink with the setting sun, which meant Lord Councillor Angue would be speaking soon in the chamber square. I tried not to think about what he might have to say, tried not to think about the vote and its consequences, not to think about war with Lummazza or Reacher Sormei or scale and sand shortages, and ended up thinking about them all. Around me, people chattered and laughed and shared drinks, but not everyone was cheerful. Little knots of argument broke out here and there, each akin to the conversation I'd had with Flyer Man earlier that day. The sense that whatever the vote's outcome, Learshapa was fracturing couldn't but worry at me, and though I drank my brandy and ate my cake, I tasted neither.

Perhaps I ought to go to that evening's meeting after all.

While I weighed my desire for political debate against what I told myself was an aversion to seeing Uvao again, a scuffle broke out near the entrance of the public house. An argument over who was next in line for a table perhaps, fierce enough that someone was shoved against the netting, causing a wave to flow across the sheer roof—a sheer roof beyond which the sun had set. In the upper city, Lord Councillor Angue would already have spoken.

A knot of apprehension tightened in my gut as people at nearby tables rose to stare at the spreading disagreement in the entryway. Whispers hissed around me like a buzz of insects, abruptly cut off as someone cheered. Another screamed. Shouting broke out and patrons turned on one another, fingers jabbing into faces and spit flying, and for a moment all I could do was sit, frozen in place, holding tight to my terror.

At the next table, an old man who'd been drinking with a friend rose to his feet looking as confused as I felt. "What in dragon's breath is going on?" he demanded of no one in particular, but he needn't have.

Rising above the noise came the clear tone of a crier. "Due to the imminent war with Lummazza, the council have used their executive power to accept Reacher Sormei's treaty," she called. "There will be no vote. Learshapa is to unite with the rest of the Celes Basin."

The words rolled over me, along with a tide of shouts and cheers and cries I knew couldn't be real. The Learshapan people had a vote because we'd always had a vote; that was how the city worked. Yet someone threw a punch, others cried, and a group danced on their table while drinks were thrown at them. And amid the noise I found my gaze meeting that of the old man, his horror what made it all too real.

They'd sold us out.

Chest tight, I was up before I had a plan, pushing my way through the chaotic crowd. The crowd pushed back, all manic energy, but I needed to get out, needed answers, so I turned my shoulder and cut my way through, brandy splashing my skirt and fingers catching in my hair.

Outside was little better. Learshapa had erupted, equal parts joy and anguish and hissing with rage wherever the two met, but I had mind only for my destination, and for the question burning my tongue. A question only one person I knew could answer.

I hardly saw the city, hardly felt my own steps, time seeming to freeze and yet speed ahead like it had become untethered from the world, spooling away into nothing. One moment I was pushing through the crowd, the next I was at the back door of the meeting house—the door out which I'd walked when I'd cut

Uvao from my life. Now I dared not think what I would do if he wasn't inside.

The moment I pushed it open, a sweet-scented bundle crashed into me, slowing the world to its natural pace. "Tesh! You came back!"

"Jiiala!" I returned her tight embrace, grateful for the moment of comfort. We were alone in the narrow back room, a tiny air pocket in a world of noise that thrummed through the surrounding walls. "I heard the news. Is... is Uvao here?"

Still holding my arms, she looked up, lips parted upon words she couldn't utter—words lost as the door into the main meeting hall opened and closed upon a short burst of noise, spilling Sorscha free. He'd been bright and full of charm earlier, but this was a Sorscha buckling under unexpected weight.

"It's bad out there," he said, ruffling his hair and dropping onto the bench. "I guess it was always going to be if this happened, but not getting any warning..." He trailed off and blew out a heavy breath. "If you're here to shout at Uvao, Tesh, pick a better time."

"No, I—"

With another short burst of noise, the meeting hall door opened and closed again, wafting the scent of dusky panawood into the room. My chest constricted an instant before Uvao appeared in the corner of my vision—a memory at which I dared not stare. Seemingly as intent on ignoring me, he sighed. "What a fucking nightmare."

"Ought I go back out there?" Sorscha lacked all enthusiasm for his own suggestion.

"Maybe later, if the crowds stick around. I have to go, but I should be back in—"

"Go?" I blurted, forgetting the question that had brought me. "Something is more important than the council surrendering Learshapa?"

Uvao didn't turn, but his dark, tired eyes glanced my way in the barest acknowledgement. "Of course there is," he said. "You don't think my hair stays this nice without constant appointments with a pommadeur, do you?"

Jiiala gave a hearty sniff. "Don't listen to him, Tesh. He's just being silly."

"I would never dare be silly, Jii," Uvao said, grabbing his veil from its hook. "Such a thing is, of course, entirely beneath my exalted position."

Ignoring this jibe my way, I unlatched myself from Jiiala. "And what are you planning to do about all this, given that exalted position of yours?"

He turned then, anger simmering in his bright eyes. "Why, I'm going to wave a magic wand and fix it to my liking because that's what lords do. Strange I didn't think of that when you walked out on me. Now, if you'll excuse me, I really do need to go."

"Where?"

Uvao didn't look up from tying his veil. "To a meeting, if you must know. About *all this* that you want me to fix."

"A meeting of the council?"

Uvao barked a humourless laugh. "Hardly. Now I've let you throw your darts, Tesh, so goodbye."

"No!" I cried, desperation throwing me between him and the door. "No, please. I'm not trying to throw darts. I need to know what we can do. What... what *I* can do. This wasn't supposed to happen, not like this."

Caught there between him and his way out, it was all I could do to hold the fiery heat of his gaze as it raked my features, all anger but for a tiny hint of need that sent my thoughts wheeling back to a better time, when I'd been crushed to the wall by his passion, breathless and ecstatic. That heat boiled all air from the small room, silencing even Sorscha, and though I knew myself a fool for having come, I would have made the same choice given it again. Somehow in this moment he was the only one I trusted to give me answers.

At last, he gave a careless shrug. "Come then, if you must. Behind the old playhouse on Fourth. Twenty minutes. You make your own way."

"That's it?"

"That's it, Tesh, take it or leave it, just get out of my way."

I stepped aside, heart and mind racing with possibilities as he pulled open the door. A nod to Jiiala, a word to Sorscha, and he was gone, leaving me unsure if I still remembered how to breathe.

A clink startled me as Sorscha poured himself a drink. "Better you than me," he said, and raised the glass. "But I guess we all get what we deserve one way or another."

"Shush," Jiiala snapped at him. "Don't be more of a shit than comes naturally, Sorscha. And don't pour a drink without pouring one for me too." Two steps brought her to my side, and she squeezed my arm. "You'd better hurry if you're going, Tesh."

"Yes. Thank you, Jii. I'll..." I gestured to the door. "I guess I'll be going then. Yes."

Sorscha snorted. "Yes, do. Goodbye, Tesh."

Once again out in the warm evening air, the streets through which I hurried were packed with people and a breathless unease. Fear of imminent war sat on the tip of every tongue, and even those grateful for unification decried our lack of choice. The city itself hadn't changed, yet I couldn't shake the feeling I wouldn't recognise it come morning. Somewhere in the upper city, Reacher Sormei would be smiling at the chaos he had wrought—and at the expansion of his empire.

Behind the old playhouse, Uvao had said, and following his instructions I found a run-down, rambling house, built at a time when space hadn't been so tight. It looked empty, dead, but unpinning my veil, I knocked before fear could stop me. The dull sound of knuckles upon stained scaleglass faded quickly, but my thumping heartbeat continued the rhythm while I shifted foot to foot.

The door yanked open, letting free a whiff of stale korsh smoke and date brandy. "What do you want?" came a snap of high-born impatience, and I knew I was in the right place.

"Uvao invited me."

"Ah." The disembodied voice pulled the door open in somewhat reluctant welcome. "Hurry up, don't dawdle."

"I wasn't planning to," I muttered, stepping into the darkness. Inside, the heavy, musky scent had a physical presence, so strong I could taste it. "This place stinks."

"An infelicitous observation," the voice said as it strode deeper into the house.

"Only if it's infelicitous to be honest."

He stopped abruptly. "You know what *infelicitous* means?"

"You're surprised?"

"Only because Uvao's...friends have a tendency to be commoners, even the pretty ones."

"That doesn't mean uneducated" was all I managed before the man strode on, out into an atrium where moonlight sheared through the arches, lighting a garden filled alternately with dead plants and vigorous weeds, tumbling from their beds.

As my guide stepped into the light, I caught my first glimpse of his face—the face of a stranger who nevertheless looked vaguely familiar.

"Don't think you can take note of our identities and use this against us," he said, catching me staring. "It would end very poorly for you."

"That," I said, "would require you to be well-enough known for me to recognise you."

His loud laugh echoed around the atrium, a broad smile manifesting a completely different man. "Well struck, Miss...?"

"No *Miss*, just Tesha."

"Tesha. Like the Tesha who strode the brightstorm's fury in Creshen's Heart? How very fortuitous."

"Like what?"

A smirk teased about his lips. "I thought you said you were educated."

"Educated in important things, not in poetry."

His brows lifted—thin, shaped brows with the half a dozen slits of the upper nobility cut through them. "Are you telling me poetry is not important? To speak your heart in verse is to fly free, at least so Kamadan said, and he's considered quite knowledgeable about such things."

"Emoran men always are," I murmured, earning another grin. It didn't last, however. This Emoran seemed incapable of sustaining the appearance of humanity for more than a few moments at a time before his expression sank back in something I could only call punch-worthy.

"We're through here," he said, gesturing to a door on the far side of the atrium—a door that seemed to open into another house entirely. Lit with pink and gold glass lanterns, the room beyond owned a handful of men in padded chairs, each with a broad back like a petal shaped in twisted cane. Despite a lack of finery, the men were unmistakably Emoran, each layered linen skirt and tight, sleeveless tunic so finely sewn they had no need of the armbands and bracelets they would usually wear to mark their station.

At my arrival, their conversation stammered to a halt, every pair of eyes staring at me from beneath brows slit half a dozen times.

There was no sign of Uvao.

"This is Miss Tesha," my guide said. "One of Uvao's friends. She knows what the word *infelicitous* means, and I don't think she likes us very much."

The man in the chair nearest the door laughed bitterly at that.

"I often don't like us very much either, so she's welcome." He gestured to a chair as he spoke. "Get her a glass, Reve. Once Uvao arrives we can start."

Swallowing the urge to ask what exactly the meeting was about and who they were, I perched on the closest empty chair and tried not to exist. Conversation about the plans they'd dropped to be here murmured around me, cut off upon Uvao's arrival a few minutes later—he able to walk in without the mercurial escort. A perfunctory glance my way and he settled into the remaining chair like one well used to the shape of its cushion.

"I suppose we ought to begin since we're all here," my guide said. Reve, one of them had called him, though that didn't tell me which of our Emoran families he belonged to. "Unfortunately, the news isn't good. Firstly, nothing can be done about the executive order. It's been in the agreement between Learshapa and the ruling council since the beginning; they've just never openly used it because of the chaos it might cause."

"They were right about that," grumbled the man beside me. "We'll be lucky if the whole city isn't on fire come morning."

"Half of that noise is celebration, Jet," Uvao said. "There was always a chance the unification vote would win even without this."

"Then why pull this trick? That's what I don't understand. For weeks people have been talking about nothing but this damn vote, and now—"

"Because Sormei sweetened the pot, and they couldn't risk the city voting to remain independent." As all eyes turned back to Reve, my soul thrummed at being allowed to hear such secrets. "Father has been busy with Reacher Sormei here, so, you know me. I listened, I snuck around, and I found out things I wasn't supposed to know. Like that the council has been meeting frequently in secret, even before today, under pressure from Sormei to do away with the vote and accept the treaty offer."

A few jaded grumbles suggested this was no surprise, though one said, "Meeting in secret? Surely not. That's all right for us, Revennai, but not the council."

Revennai. Lord Revennai Angue? I didn't know many Emoran lords, but as the head of the council, his father Lord Councillor Angue was the most notable around Learshapa.

"You're right so far about the terrible news," said one of the older men present, owning a few greying hairs and a weary expression. "What's the rest?"

Lord Revennai sat back in his chair with a sigh. "That although it's just been announced, I think they agreed to the treaty at least a week ago. Plans for the treaty marriage are already underway. Sormei has put forward his candidate, but I haven't been able to find out who it is yet."

"It's Lord Kiren Sydelle."

Uvao spoke quietly, yet he might as well have shouted for the shock that rippled through the room.

"What?" Lord Revennai snapped. "His brother? Are you sure?"

"Quite sure. Highest possible bid on the table so the council will fight over him."

The man beside me—who I was starting to suspect must be a son of Lord Duzeunde by the symbols on his tunic—dropped his head into his hands. "No wonder they caved and accepted the deal."

I stared at the play of light on the brandy glasses as they threw the conversation back and forth like a ball going over my head. The political customs of our Emoran elite had always been a mystery to me, but as each man sagged with defeat, panic began to worm its way into my gut.

"Right, well, that's it then," said the one I was coming to think of as the Old. "Our hands are tied, because no matter what we suggest, the council will refuse. They've already made their decision. Right up to the point of having a marriage treaty with fucking Lord fucking Kiren fucking Sydelle on the table."

"Fucking is not really his forte," Lord Revennai murmured. "But yes. Something like that."

They lulled into silence, nursing their brandy glasses and glancing sadly at one another, because they had that luxury. Because this decision wouldn't turn their whole world upside down. "Are you telling me there's nothing you can do?" I said. "You're Emoran lords!"

The Old gave a derisive laugh and drank deeply, a few grumbled, and Uvao shot me a warning look. "And you," I added, pointing at Lord Revennai. "Your father is the head of the damn council!"

"We are sons and minor lords, and in Emora that makes you nothing," Lord Revennai said, tone subdued. "Not even trusted by our fathers most of the time. We aren't powerful."

I scoffed, too angry to stay silent. "Not powerful, but certainly protected. You won't have to worry about being conscripted into Reacher Sormei's wars or being forced out of a job when the need to compete with the other cities brings automation to every industry it can. You won't even have to worry about losing your way of life, your culture and communal care networks, because it's *your* way of life that will take over."

"We wouldn't be here if we didn't care about this city," snapped the man beside me. "We started meeting long before this damn vote, when Sormei began squeezing Learshapa with his excise taxes that—"

"*Sormei*," I repeated. "When you're on first-name terms with the tyrant, you'll do just fine."

The man swung his incredulous look toward Uvao. "Why is she here again?"

"Because as annoying as she is, she isn't wrong."

A collective outburst exploded from their puffed chests, but before I could discern individual words from the aggrieved roar, Uvao held up his hands. "Yes, thank you," he said in his best meeting-convenor voice. "But there is actually something we can do, it just isn't...nice. Not even safe. If you're in you have to be in all the way; if you can't do that, then you're welcome to leave. No hard feelings."

"Unsafe how?" the Old asked through his glare.

"Potentially reputation ruining. On the other hand, if we can make it work, anyone involved would be a power broker under a new reacher."

"Who?" came Lord Revennai's sharp question.

The Old scoffed. "Lord Romm, obviously, Reve. His father is making another bid for power. In which case, I'm out. No offence to you, Uvao, but you know how it is."

Two others rose from their chairs, followed by two more, each setting down their glasses and mumbling apologies. Uvao nodded to them, his expression blank, all the anger he ought to have been feeling roiling in my gut instead.

When the room settled once more into silence, only three of Uvao's companions remained—Lord Revennai, Definitely Lord Duzeunde's Son, and a man whose name I hadn't yet caught. The nameless one leaned forward, eyes bright. "So, what's the plan?"

"Father dearest wants to pull off an insult bride."

"A what?" the nameless one said.

"Yes, it's perfect." Lord Revennai's lips stretched into a grin with a predatory edge. "It hasn't been done for so long that no one will even think of it, especially since the council practically invited Sormei to take control."

"But what is it?" said Lord Duzeunde's Son.

"The substitution of a commoner in place of a high-born marriage candidate." Lord Revennai's eyes burned bright. "A last-ditch effort to force renegotiation when families were cornered into accepting deals they didn't like. Think of it like a fake relative."

Son of Lord Duzeunde and the Nameless One stared, their disbelief mirrored in the restless churning of my stomach. It sounded risky, a back-alley mugging in political clothes.

"The plan is that my father will deal with the rest of the council to ensure our candidate is most favoured for the match," Uvao said, the four remaining men all leaning forward in their chairs, heads close. "He'll also make the necessary arrangements to pass off our insult bride as a genuine member of the Romm family. My job—our job—is to find an insult bride and train her as fast as possible in everything she'll need to know to pull this off."

A few solemn, thoughtful nods met this, but I'd missed the part that made it all make sense. "But what will it achieve?" I asked. "It sounds like it will just make Reacher Sormei look bad."

"Looking bad is political death in Emora," Lord Revennai said, not looking around. "And even if he weathered it, if Lord Romm has everything in place he could trigger a conclave—that's the election of a new reacher. Likely Lord Romm, especially given how close he came to winning last time."

The Nameless One let out a bitter laugh. "At least he can't send you to the Shield if you fail, Uvao. He'd have no sons left!"

Ignoring this, I looked to Uvao. "And would your father reverse this decision?"

"It's unclear if that's still possible." He shook his head slowly. "But the treaty conditions would be renegotiated, and having a Learshapan reacher would be far better for ensuring the city is neither sucked dry nor used as a shield in a Lummazzt war."

"So we'd just be getting a better dictatorial leader?"

He sighed. "If you've got a better idea, do let us know."

I didn't, because all my ideas relied on the council having no secret executive power to do away with Learshapan democracy.

"Right, well, I'm in," said the young Lord Duzeunde. "I've

got nothing to lose, and if Lord Romm is going to put this on you for his own fucking deniability then we'll make damn sure it works."

Uvao gripped his lips tight and nodded, and it was all I could do not to reach out my own comfort like I'd done when he'd been just Uvao. When he would have taken my sympathy into his arms and held me close, whispering thanks into my hair.

"I'm in too," said the one whose name I didn't know. "So what do we need? I suppose she has to be pretty. And clever enough to learn what she needs to do."

"Has to speak well," Lord Revennai added. "We don't have time to train her out of a slum accent."

They went on talking, but I was no longer listening. I was thinking of a home I would no longer recognise, of a Learshapa lost to war, of Master Hoye's box of poisons and a deep yearning to do something just as powerful that could change the world. Because the woman they were describing was me. Foolish to volunteer for such a scheme, to throw myself into the world of Emoran politics, yet every possibility was an intoxicating whisper. I could do what they needed me to do, but once inside I could do so much more. Once inside, I could bring down Emora.

"Maybe if we—"

"I'll do it," I said, getting to my feet. "I'll be your insult bride."

Four shocked expressions turned my way. I met each with a defiant glare, except for Uvao, who pulled his gaze away to stare at the ceiling. "I could do it," I said into the silence, reassuring myself as much as them. "I am everything you're looking for with the bonus of not having to waste time looking elsewhere."

"She's not wrong," the Nameless One murmured. "Better the bee we have than the dragon we don't."

"That," I said, jabbing a finger at him, "is a very infelicitous remark."

A laugh burst from Lord Revennai, and though he shook his

head, he grinned. "But not infelicitous that you came. I think she'll do very well. Uvao? In fact I think she's perfect."

For a moment that stretched to eternity, Uvao didn't move. Didn't speak. His silence seemed to draw all breath from my body, tightening my chest until, at last, he nodded. "Perfect," he said, the word owning all the tenor of hot glass shattering on stone.

**Enter the monthly Orbit sweepstakes at www.orbitloot.com**

**With a different prize every month,** from advance copies of books by your favourite authors to exclusive merchandise packs, **we think you'll find something you love.**

facebook.com/OrbitBooksUK
@orbitbooks_uk
@OrbitBooks
orbit-books.co.uk